OUTSTANDING PRAISE FOR

THE PROMETHEUS DECEPTION

"Readers will remain in the dark right up until the explosive climax."
—*The San Francisco Chronicle*

"Reading a Ludlum novel is like watching a James Bond film ... slickly paced ... all-consuming." —*Entertainment Weekly*

"Ludlum's latest is a spy thriller that should keep even the most experienced readers guessing ... The pace is fast, the action plentiful ... a must read." —*Booklist*

"Ludlum delivers again another top-notch international thriller sure to please ... heart-pounding chase scenes, devastating double-crosses, gut-wrenching twists, fast-paced action, fierce confrontations, pressure that ratchets up to an explosive conclusion, and, as always, authentic international locales, high-tech gadgetry, and sophisticated spycraft."
—*Library Journal*

"If true mystery—mystery in the plot and mystery as to the true nature of principal characters—is the measure of a great mystery writer, then Ludlum just proved himself one of the best." —*Austin American-Statesman*

"A dead-on picture of contemporary corporate strategy."
—*The New Yorker*

"A *1984* for the new millennium ... a fast-paced cloak-and-dagger tale. By the end the reader will be left with the chilling feeling that just because you're paranoid doesn't mean they aren't out to get you." —*The Commercial Appeal* (TN)

"Robert Ludlum continues to jolt his readers with fresh juice ... a page-turner of nonstop action that should leave his fans begging for more." —*New York Post*

More . . .

THE PROMETHEUS DECEPTION

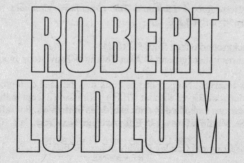

ROBERT LUDLUM

St. Martin's Paperbacks

THE PROMETHEUS DECEPTION

Copyright © 2000 by Myn Pyn LLC.
Excerpt from *Robert Ludlum's The Cassandra Compact* copyright © 2001 by Myn Pyn LLC.

Cover background image from Photodisc
Cover figures in background © Alan Thornton/Tony Stone Images.

Library of Congress Catalog Card Number: 00-062585

ISBN: 0-312-97836-7

Printed in the United States of America

St. Martin's Press hardcover edition / November 2000
St. Martin's Paperbacks edition / October 2001

St. Martin's Paperbacks are published by St. Martin's Press, 175 Fifth Avenue, New York, NY 10010.

10 9 8 7 6 5 4 3 2 1

Prometheus swept down from the heavens
bringing the gift of fire.

Wrong move.

PROLOGUE

The driving rain was unrelenting, whipped into a frenzy by howling winds, and the waves surged and crashed against the coast, a maelstrom in the black night. In the shallow waters just offshore, a dozen or so dark figures bobbed, clinging to their buoyant, waterproof haversacks like survivors of a shipwreck. The freak storm had caught the men unawares but was good; it provided better cover than they could have hoped for.

From the beach, a pinpoint of red light flashed on and off twice, a signal from the advance team that it was safe to land. *Safe!* What did that mean? That this particular stretch of Tunisian coastline was left undefended by the *Garde Nationale*? Nature's assault seemed far more punishing than anything the Tunisian coast guard could attempt.

Tossed and buffeted about by the heaving swells, the men made their way toward the beach, and in one coordinated movement clambered silently onto the sand by the ruins of the ancient Punic ports. Stripping off their black rubber dry suits to reveal dark clothing and blackened faces, they removed their weapons from their haversacks and began distributing their arsenal: Heckler & Koch MP-10 submachine guns, Kalashnikovs, and sniper rifles. Behind them, others now came ashore in waves.

Everything was precisely orchestrated by the man who had trained them so exhaustively, so tirelessly, for the last months. They were Al-Nahda freedom fighters, natives of Tunisia come to free their country from the oppressors. But their leaders were foreigners—skilled terrorists who also shared their faith in Allah, a small, elite cell of freedom fighters drawn from the most radical wing of Hezbollah.

The leader of this cell, and of the fifty or so Tunisians,

was the master terrorist known only as Abu. Occasionally his full nom de guerre was used: Abu Intiquab. The father of revenge.

Elusive, secretive, and ferocious, Abu had trained the Al-Nahda fighters at the Libyan camp outside of Zuwarah. He refined their strategy on a full-scale model of the presidential palace and instructed them in tactics both more violent and more devious than anything they were used to.

Barely thirty hours ago, at the port of Zuwarah, the men had boarded a five-thousand-ton, Russian-built break-bulk freighter, a cargo ship that normally hauled Tunisian textiles and Libyan manufactured goods between Tripoli and Bizerte in Tunisia. The powerful old freighter, now battered and decrepit, had traveled north-northwest along the Tunisian coast, past the port cities of Sfax and Sousse, then swung around Cap Bon and entered the Golfe de Tunis, just past the naval base at La Goulette. Alerted to the schedule of the coast guard patrol boats, the men had dropped anchor five miles from the Carthage coast and swiftly launched their rigid-hulled inflatables, equipped with powerful outboard motors. Within minutes, they had entered the turbulent waters of Carthage, the ancient Phoenician city so powerful in the fifth century B.C. that it was considered Rome's great rival. If anyone in the Tunisian coast guard happened to be monitoring the ship on radar, he would see only a freighter pausing momentarily, then heading on toward Bizerte.

On the shore, the man who had flashed the red signal was hissing orders and cursing in a low voice with unquestioned authority. He was a bearded man in a military-issue rain anorak worn over a keffiyeh. Abu.

"Quiet! Keep it down! What do you want, to bring out the whole godforsaken Tunisian *Garde?* Quickly, now. Let's move it, *move* it! Clumsy *fools!* Your leader rots in jail while you dawdle! The trucks are waiting!"

Next to him stood a man wearing night-vision goggles and silently scanning the terrain. The Tunisians knew him only as the Technician. One of Hezbollah's top munitions experts, he was a handsome, olive-skinned man with heavy brows and flashing brown eyes. As little as the men knew about Abu, they knew even less about the Technician, Abu's trusted adviser. According to rumor, he was born to wealthy Syrian parents and raised in Damascus and London, where he was schooled in the intricacies of arms and explosives.

Finally the Technician spoke, quietly and calmly. He pulled his black, hooded waterproof garment tight against the torrential rain.

"I hesitate to say it, my brother, but the operation is going smoothly. The trucks loaded with matériel were concealed just as we had arranged and the soldiers encountered no resistance on the short drive along the Avenue Habib Borguiga. Now we have just received the radio signal from the first men—they have reached the presidential palace. The coup d'etat has begun." As he spoke he consulted his wristwatch.

Abu nodded imperiously. He was a man who expected nothing less than success. A distant series of explosions told Abu and his adviser that the battle was under way. The presidential palace would be seized imminently, and in a matter of hours, the Islamic militants would control Tunis. "Let us not congratulate ourselves prematurely," Abu said in a low, tense voice. The rain was letting up now, and in a moment the storm passed just as suddenly as it had appeared.

Suddenly the silence on the beach was shattered by voices shouting at them in strident, high-pitched Arabic. Dark figures raced across the sand. Abu and the Technician tensed and reached for their weapons, but then saw it was their Hezbollah brethren.

"A zero-one!"

"An *ambush!*"

"My God! Mighty Allah, they're *surrounded!*"

Four Arab men approached, looking frightened and out of breath. "A zero-one distress signal," panted the one carrying a PRC-117 field radio on his back. "They were able to transmit only that they were surrounded by the security forces at the palace and taken captive. Then the transmission was killed! They say they were set up!"

Abu turned to his adviser in alarm. "How can this be?"

The youngest of the four young men who stood before them said, "The matériel left for the men—the antitank weapons, the ammunition, the C-4—all of it was defective! Nothing worked! And the government forces were lying in wait for them! Our men were set up from the *beginning!*"

Abu looked visibly pained, his customary serenity vanished. He beckoned his number-one adviser. "*Ya sahbee,* I need your wise counsel."

The Technician adjusted his wristwatch as he came close to the master terrorist. Abu put one arm around his adviser's shoulders. He spoke in a low, calm voice. "There must be a traitor in our ranks, an infiltrator. Our plans were leaked."

Abu made a subtle, almost undetectable gesture with a finger and thumb. It was a cue, and his followers immediately grabbed the Technician by the arms, legs, and shoulders. The Technician struggled mightily, but he was no match for the trained terrorists who held him. Swiftly, Abu's right hand shot out. There was a flash of metal and Abu plunged a serrated, hooked knife into the Technician's abdomen, yanking the blade down and then out to inflict the maximum damage. Abu's eyes were blazing. "The traitor is *you!*" he spat out.

The Technician gasped. The pain was obviously excruciating, but his face remained a stolid mask. "No, Abu!" he protested.

"*Pig!*" spat Abu, lunging at him again, his serrated knife aimed at the Technician's groin. "No one else knew the timing, the exact plans! *No one!* And you were the one who certified the matériel. It can be no one else."

Suddenly the beach was flooded with blindingly bright carbon-arc light. Abu turned and realized that they were surrounded and vastly outnumbered by dozens upon dozens of soldiers in khaki uniforms. The Groupement de Commando of the Tunisian *Garde Nationale*, machine guns pointed, had abruptly appeared from over the horizon; a thundering racket from above announced the arrival of several attack helicopters.

Bursts of automatic gunfire hit Abu's men, turning them

into jerking marionettes. Their bloodcurdling screams were abruptly silenced, and their bodies toppled to the ground in strange and awkward positions. Another burst of gunfire, and then it stopped. The unexpected silence that followed was eerie. Only the master terrorist and his munitions specialist had not been fired upon.

But Abu seemed to have only one focus of attention, and he spun back around to the man he had branded a traitor, positioning his scimitar-shaped blade for another attack. Badly wounded, the Technician tried to ward off his assailant, but instead began to sink to the ground. The loss of blood was too great. Just as Abu lunged forward to finish him off, powerful hands grabbed the bearded Hezbollah leader from behind, slamming him down and pinning him to the sand.

Abu's eyes burned with defiance as the two were taken into custody by the government soldiers. He did not fear any government. Governments were cowards, he had often said; governments would release him under some pretext of *international law* and *extradition* and *repatriation*. Deals would be struck behind the scenes, and Abu would be quietly released, his presence in the country a carefully kept secret. No government wanted to bring on itself the full fury of a Hezbollah terror campaign.

The terrorist master did not struggle, but instead caused his body to go slack, forcing the soldiers to drag him away. As he was dragged past the Technician, he spat full in his face and hissed, "You are not long for this world, *traitor! Pig!* You will *die* for your treachery!"

Once Abu was taken away, the several men who had grabbed the Technician gently released him, easing him down onto a waiting stretcher. Obeying the instructions of the battalion captain, they backed away as the captain approached. The Tunisian knelt beside the Technician and examined his wound. The Technician winced but uttered not a sound.

"My God, it's a wonder you're still conscious!" said the captain in heavily accented English. "You have been badly injured. You have lost a great deal of blood."

The man who had been known as the Technician replied, "If your men had responded to my signal a little more speedily, this wouldn't have happened." He instinctively touched his wristwatch, which was equipped with a miniaturized high-frequency transmitter.

The captain ignored the barb. "That SA-341 up there," he said, pointing up to the sky, where a helicopter hovered, "will take you to a high-security government medical facility in Morocco. I'm not permitted to know your real identity, nor who your real employers are, so I won't ask," the Tunisian began, "but I think I have a good idea—"

Just then the Technician whispered harshly, "Get *down!*" He quickly pulled a semiautomatic pistol from the holster concealed under his arm and fired off five quick shots. There was a cry from a copse of palm trees, and a dead man toppled to the ground, his sniper rifle clutched in his hand. Somehow an Al-Nahda soldier had escaped the massacre.

"Mighty Allah!" exclaimed the frightened captain of the battalion as he slowly raised his head and looked around. "I think we're even now, you and I."

"Listen," the Arab-who-was-not-an-Arab said weakly, "tell your president his minister of the interior is a secret Al-Nahda sympathizer and collaborator who conspires to take his place. He's in league with the deputy minister of defense. There are others . . ."

But the loss of blood had been too great. Before the Technician could finish his sentence, he passed out.

PART
ONE

CHAPTER ONE

The patient was conveyed by a chartered jet to a private landing strip twenty miles northwest of Washington, D.C. Although the patient was the only passenger on the entire aircraft, no one spoke to him except to ascertain his immediate needs. No one knew his name. All they knew was that this was clearly an extremely important passenger. The flight's arrival appeared on no aviation logs anywhere, military or civilian.

The nameless passenger was then taken by unmarked sedan to downtown Washington and dropped off, at his own request, near a parking garage in the middle of an unremarkable block near Dupont Circle. He wore an unimpressive gray suit with a pair of tasseled cordovan loafers that had been scuffed and shined a few too many times, and looked like one of a thousand midlevel lobbyists and bureaucrats, the faceless, colorless staffers of a permanent Washington.

Nobody gave him a second look as he emerged from the parking garage, then walked, stiffly and with a pronounced limp, to a dun-colored, four-story building at 1324 K Street, near Twenty-first. The building, all cement and gray-tinted glass, was scarcely distinguishable from all the other bland, boxy low-rises along this stretch of northwest Washington. These were the offices, invariably, of lobbying groups and trade organizations, travel bureaus and industry boards. Beside its front entrance a couple of brass plaques were mounted, announcing the offices of INNOVATION ENTERPRISES and AMERICAN TRADE INTERNATIONAL.

Only a trained engineer with highly rarefied expertise might have noticed a few anomalous details—the fact, for example, that every window frame was equipped with a piezoelectric oscillator, rendering futile any attempt at laser-acoustic surveillance from outside. Or the high-frequency white-noise "drench" that enveloped the building in a cone of radio waves, sufficient to defeat most forms of electronic eavesdropping.

Certainly nothing ever attracted the attention of its K Street neighbors—the balding lawyers at the grains board, the grim-faced accountants in their ties and short-sleeved shirts at the slowly failing business consulting firm. People arrived at 1324 K Street in the morning and left in the evening and trash was deposited in the alley Dumpster on the appropriate days. What else did anybody care to know? But that was how the Directorate liked to be: hidden in plain view.

The man almost smiled to himself when he thought about it. For who would ever suspect that the most secretive of the world's covert agencies would be headquartered in an ordinary-looking office building in the middle of K Street, right out in the open?

The Central Intelligence Agency in Langley, Virginia, and the National Security Agency in Fort Meade, Maryland, were housed in moated fortresses that proclaimed their existence! *Here I am*, they seemed to say, *right here, pay no attention to me!* They virtually dared their opponents to breach their security—as inevitably happened. The Directorate made those so-called clandestine bureaucracies look about as reclusive as the U.S. Postal Service.

The man stood inside the lobby of 1324 K Street and scanned the sleek brass panel, on which was mounted a perfectly conventional-looking telephone handset beneath a dial pad, from all appearances the sort of arrangement that appears in lobbies in office buildings around the world. The man picked up the handset and then pressed a series of numbers, a predetermined code. He kept his index finger pressed on the last button, the # sign, for a few seconds until he heard a faint ring, signifying that his fingerprint had been electronically scanned, analyzed, matched against a preexisting and precleared database of digitized fingerprints, and approved. Then he listened to the telephone handset as it rang precisely three times. A disembodied, mechanical female voice commanded him to state his business.

"I have an appointment with Mr. Mackenzie," said the man. In a matter of seconds his words were converted into bits of data and matched against another database of precleared voiceprints. Only then did a faint buzzing in the lobby indicate that the first inner set of glass doors could be opened. He hung up the telephone receiver and pushed open the heavy, bulletproof glass doors, entered a tiny antechamber, and stood there for a few seconds as his facial features were scanned by three separate high-resolution surveillance cameras and checked against stored, authorized patterns.

The second set of doors opened onto a small, featureless reception area of white walls and gray industrial carpeting, equipped with hidden monitoring devices that could detect all manner of concealed weapons. On a marble-topped console in one corner, there was a stack of pamphlets emblazoned with the logo of American Trade International, an organization that existed only as a set of legal documents and registrations. The rest of the pamphlets were given over to an unreadable mission statement, filled with platitudes about international trade. An unsmiling guard waved Bryson past, through another set of doors and into a handsomely appointed hall, paneled in dark, burled walnut, where about a dozen clerical types were at their desks. It might have been an upscale art gallery of the sort one might find on Fifty-seventh Street in Manhattan, or perhaps a prosperous law firm.

"Nick Bryson, my main man!" exclaimed Chris Edgecomb, bounding from his seat at a computer monitor. Born in Guyana, he was a lithe, tall man with mocha skin and green eyes. He'd been at the Directorate for four years, working on the communications-and-coordination team; he fielded distress calls, figured out ways to relay information to agents in the field when it was necessary. Edgecomb clasped Bryson's hand warmly.

Nicholas Bryson knew he was something of a hero to

people like Edgecomb, who yearned to be field operatives. "Join the Directorate and change the world," Edgecomb would joke in his lilting English, and it was Bryson he had in mind when he said it. It was a rare event, Bryson knew, that the office staff saw Bryson face-to-face; for Edgecomb, this was an occasion.

"Somebody hurt you?" Edgecomb's expression was sympathetic; he saw a strong man who had been hospitalized until recently. Then he continued hastily, knowing better than to ask questions: "I'll pray to Saint Christopher for you. You'll be a hundred percent in no time."

The Directorate's creed, above all, was segmentation and compartmentalization. No one agent or staffer should ever know enough to be in the position to jeopardize the security of the whole. The organizational chart was shrouded even to a veteran like Bryson. He knew a few of the desk jockeys, of course. But the field personnel all operated in isolation, through their own proprietary networks. If you had to work together, you knew each other only by a field legend, a temporary alias. The rule was more than procedure, it was Holy Writ.

"You're a good man, Chris," Bryson remarked.

Edgecomb smiled modestly, then pointed a finger upward. He knew Bryson had an appointment—or was it a summons?—with the big man himself, Ted Waller. Bryson smiled, gave Edgecomb a friendly clap on the shoulder, and made his way to the elevator.

"Don't get up," Bryson said heartily as he entered Ted Waller's third-floor office. Waller did anyway, all six feet, four inches and three hundred pounds of him.

"Good Lord, look at you," Waller said, his eyes appraising Bryson with alarm. "You look like you came out of a POW camp."

"Thirty-three days in a U.S. government clinic in Morocco will do that to you," Bryson said. "It's not exactly the Ritz."

"Perhaps *I* should try being gutted by a mad terrorist someday." Waller patted his ample girth. He was even larger than the last time Bryson had seen him, though his avoir-dupois was elegantly sheathed in a suit of navy cashmere, his bull neck flattered by the spread collar of one of his Turnbull & Asser shirts. "Nick, I've been tormenting myself since this happened. It was a serrated Verenski blade from Bulgaria, I'm told. Plunge and twist. Terribly low-tech, but it usually does the job. What a business we're in. Never forget, it's what you *don't* see that always gets you." Waller settled weightily back in the tufted-leather chair behind his oak desk. The early-afternoon sun filtered through the polarized glass behind him. Bryson took a seat in front of him, an unaccustomed formality. Waller, who was normally ruddy and seemingly robust, now looked pallid, the circles under his eyes deep. "They say you've made a remarkable recovery."

"In a few more weeks, I'll be as good as new. At least that's what the doctors tell me. They also say I'll never need an appendectomy, a side benefit I never thought of." As he spoke, he felt the dull ache in his lower-right abdomen.

Waller nodded distractedly. "You know why you're here?"

"A kid gets a note to see the principal, he expects a reprimand." Bryson feigned lightheartedness, but his mood was tense, somber.

"A reprimand," Waller said enigmatically. He was silent for a moment, his eyes settling on a row of leather-bound books on the shelves near the door. Then he turned back and said in a gentle, pained voice: "The Directorate doesn't exactly post an organizational chart, but I think you have some inkling of the command-and-control structure. Decisions, particularly ones concerning key personnel, do not always stop at my desk. And as important as loyalty is to you and to me—hell, to most of the people in this goddamned place—it's coldhearted pragmatism that rules the day. You know that."

Bryson had only had one serious job in his life, and this was it; still, he recognized the undertones of the pink-slip talk. He fought the urge to defend himself, for that was not

Directorate procedure; it was unseemly. He recalled one of Waller's mantras: *There's no such thing as bad luck,* then thought of another maxim. "All's well that ends well," Bryson said. "And it did end well."

"We almost lost you," Waller said. "*I* almost lost you," he added ruefully, a teacher speaking to a prize student who has disappointed him.

"That's not pertinent," Bryson said quietly. "Anyway, you can't read the rules on the side of the box when you're in the field; you know that. You *taught* me that. You improvise, you follow instinct—not just established protocol."

"Losing you could have meant losing Tunisia. There's a cascade effect: when we intervene, we do so early enough to make a difference. Actions are carefully titrated, reactions calibrated, variables accounted for. And so you nearly compromised quite a few other undercover operations, in Maghreb and other places around the sandbox. You put other lives in jeopardy, Nicky—other operations and other lives. The Technician's legend was intricately connected to other legends we'd manufactured; you know that. Yet you let your cover get blown. *Years* of undercover work compromised because of you!"

"Now, wait a second—"

"Giving them 'defective munitions'—how did you think they wouldn't suspect you?"

"Damn it, they weren't *supposed* to be defective!"

"But they were. Why?"

"I don't *know!*"

"Did you inspect them?"

"Yes! No! I don't know. It never crossed my mind that the goods weren't as they were represented."

"That was a serious lapse, Nicky. You endangered years of work, years of deep-cover planning, cultivation of valuable assets. The lives of some of our most valuable assets! Goddamn it, what were you thinking?"

Bryson was silent for a moment. "I was set up," he said at last.

"Set up how?"

"I can't say for sure."

"If you were 'set up,' that means you were already under suspicion, correct?"

"I—I don't know."

" 'I don't *know*'? Not exactly words that inspire confidence, are they? They're not words I like to hear. You used to be our top field operative. What happened to you, Nick?"

"Maybe—somehow—I screwed up. Don't you think I've gone over it and over it in my mind?"

"I'm not hearing answers, Nick."

"Maybe there *aren't* any answers—not now, not yet."

"We can't afford such screwups. We can't tolerate this kind of carelessness. None of us can. We allow for margins of error. But we cannot go beyond them. The Directorate doesn't tolerate mistakes. You've known that since day one."

"You think there was something I could have done differently? Or maybe you think somebody *else* could have done it *better?*"

"You were the best we ever had, you know that. But as I told you, these decisions are reached at consortium level, not at my desk."

A chill ran through Bryson upon hearing the bureaucratese that told him Waller had already distanced himself from the consequences of the decision to let him go. Ted Waller was Bryson's mentor, boss, and friend, and, fifteen years ago, his teacher. He had supervised his apprenticeship, briefed him personally before the operations he worked on early in his career. It was an immense honor, and Bryson felt it to this day. Waller was the most brilliant man he'd ever met. He could solve partial differential equations in his head; he possessed vast stores of arcane geopolitical knowledge. At the same time his lumbering frame belied his extraordinary physical dexterity. Bryson recalled him at a shooting range, absently hitting one bull's-eye after another from seventy feet while chatting about the sad decline of British bespoke tailoring. The .22 looked puny in his large, plump, soft hand; it was so under his control that it might have been another finger.

"You used the past tense, Ted," Bryson said. "The implication being that you believe I've lost it."

"I simply meant what I said," Waller replied quietly. "I've never worked with anyone better, and I doubt I ever will."

By temperament and by training, Nick knew how to remain impassive, but now his heart was thudding. *You were the best we ever had, Nick.* That sounded like an homage, and homage, he knew, was a key element of the ritual of separation. Bryson would never forget Waller's reaction when he pulled off his first operational hat trick—foiling the assassination of a moderate reform candidate in South America. It was a taciturn *Not bad:* Waller had pressed his lips together to keep from smiling, and to Nick, it was a greater accolade than any that followed. It's when they begin to acknowledge how valuable you are, Bryson had learned, that you know they're putting you out to pasture.

"Nick, nobody else could have accomplished what you did in the Comoros. The place would have been in the hands of that madman, Colonel Denard. In Sri Lanka, there are probably thousands of people who are alive, on both sides, because of the arms-trading routes you exposed. And what you did in Belarus? The GRU still doesn't have a clue, and they never will. Leave it to the politicians to color inside the lines, because those are the lines that we've drawn, that *you've* drawn. The historians will never know, and the truth is, it's better that way. But we know that, don't we?"

Bryson didn't reply; no reply was called for.

"And on a separate matter, Nick, noses are out of joint around here about the Banque du Nord business." He was referring to Bryson's penetration of a Tunis bank that channeled laundered funds to Abu and Hezbollah to fund the coup attempt. One night during the operation more than 1.5 billion dollars simply disappeared, vanished into cyberspace. Months of investigation had failed to account for the missing assets. It was a loose end, and the Directorate disliked loose ends.

"You're not suggesting that I had my hand in the cookie jar, are you?"

"Of course not. But you understand that there are always going to be suspicions. When there are no answers, the questions linger; you know that."

"I've had plenty of opportunities for 'personal enrichment' that would have been far more lucrative and considerably more discreet."

"You've been tested, yes, and you've passed with flying colors. But I question the method of diversion, the monies transferred through false flags to Abu's colleagues to purchase compromisable background data."

"That's called improvisation. It's what you pay me for—using my powers of discretion when and where necessary." Bryson stopped, realizing something. "But I was never debriefed about this!"

"You offered up the details yourself, Nick," said Waller.

"I sure as hell never—oh, *Christ,* it was *chemicals,* wasn't it?"

Waller hesitated a split-second, but just long enough that Bryson's question was answered. Ted Waller could lie, blithely and easily, when the need dictated, but Bryson knew his old friend and mentor found lying to him distasteful. "Where we obtain our information is compartmented, Nick. You know that."

Now he understood the need for such a protracted stay in an American-staffed clinic in Laayoune. Chemicals had to be administered without the subject's knowledge, preferably injected into the intravenous drip. "God*damn* it, Ted! What's the implication—that I couldn't be trusted to undergo a conventional debriefing, offer the goods up freely? That only a blind interrogation could tell you what you wanted to know? You had to put me under without my *knowledge?*"

"Sometimes the most reliable interrogation is that which is conducted without the subject's calculation of his own best interest."

"Meaning you guys thought that I'd lie to cover my ass?"

Waller's reply was quiet, chilling. "Once assessments are made that an individual is not one hundred percent trustworthy, contrary assumptions are made, at least provisionally. You detest it, and I detest it, but that's the brutal fact of an intelligence bureaucracy. Particularly one as reclusive—maybe *paranoid* is the more accurate word here—as we are."

Paranoid. In fact, Bryson had learned long ago that to Waller and his colleagues at the Directorate, it was an article of faith that the Central Intelligence Agency, the Defense Intelligence Agency, and even the National Security Agency were riddled with moles, hamstrung by regulation, and mired in an arms race of disinformation with their hostile counterparts abroad. Waller liked to call these, the agencies whose existence was emblazoned on Congressional appropriations bills and organization charts, the "woolly mammoths." In his earliest days with the Directorate, Bryson had innocently asked whether some measure of cooperation with the other agencies didn't make sense. Waller had laughed. "You mean, let the woolly mammoths know we exist? Why not just send a press release to *Pravda*?" But the crisis of American intelligence, in Waller's view, went far beyond the problems of penetration. Counterintelligence was the true wilderness of mirrors. "You lie to your enemy, and then you spy on them," Waller had once pointed out, "and what you learn is the lie. Only now, somehow, the lie has become true, because it's been recategorized as 'intelligence.' It's like an Easter-egg hunt. How many careers have been made—on either side—by people who have painstakingly unearthed eggs that their colleagues have just as painstakingly buried? Colorful, beautifully painted Easter eggs—but fakes nonetheless."

The two had sat talking through the night in the below-ground library underneath the K Street headquarters, a chamber furnished with seventeenth-century Kurdish rugs on the floor, old British oil paintings of the hunt, of loyal dogs grasping fowl in their pedigreed mouths.

"You see the genius of it?" Waller had gone on. "Every CIA adventure, botched or otherwise, will eventually come under public scrutiny. Not so for us, simply because we're on nobody's radar." Bryson still remembered the soft rattle of ice cubes in the heavy crystal glass as Waller took a sip of the barrel-proof bourbon he favored.

"But operating off the grid, practically like outlaws, can't exactly be the most practical way to do business," Bryson had protested. "For one thing, there's the matter of resources."

"Granted, we don't have the resources, but then we don't have the bureaucracy, either, the constraints. All in all, it's a positive advantage, given our particular purview. Our record is proof of it. When you work in ad hoc fashion with groups around the world, when you don't shy from extremely aggressive interventions, then all you need is a very small number of highly trained operatives. You take advantage of on-the-ground forces. You succeed by *directing* events, coordinating the desired outcomes. You don't need the vast overheads of the spy bureaucracies. All you really need is *brains*."

"And blood," said Bryson, who had already seen his share of it by then. "Blood."

Waller had shrugged. "That great monster Joseph Stalin once put it quite aptly: you can't make an omelet without breaking some eggs." He spoke about the American century, about the burdens of empire. About imperial Britain in the nineteenth century, when Parliament would debate for six months about whether to send an expeditionary force to rescue a general who had been under siege for two years. Waller and his colleagues at the Directorate believed in liberal democracy, fervently and unequivocally—but they also knew that to secure its future, you couldn't play, as Waller liked to say, by Queensberry rules. If your enemies operated by low cunning, you'd better summon up some good old low cunning of your own. "We're the necessary evil," Waller had told him. "But don't ever get cocky—the noun is evil. We're extra-legal. Unsupervised, unregulated. Sometimes *I* don't even feel safe knowing that we're around." There was another soft rattle of ice cubes as he drained the last drops of bourbon from the glass.

Nick Bryson had known fanatics—friendlies and hostiles both—and he found comfort in Waller's very ambivalence. Bryson had never felt he'd fully had the measure of Waller's mind: the brilliance, the cynicism, but mostly the intense, almost bashful idealism, like sunlight spilling through the edge of drawn blinds. "My friend," Waller said, "we exist to create a world in which we won't be necessary."

Now, in the ashy light of the early afternoon, Waller spread his hands on his desk, as if bracing himself for the unpleasant job he had to do. "We know you've been having a hard time since Elena left," he began.

"I don't want to talk about Elena," Bryson snapped. He could feel a vein throbbing in his forehead. For so many years she had been his wife, best friend, and lover. Six months ago, during a sterile telephone call Bryson had placed from Tripoli, she had told him she was leaving him. Arguing would do no good. She had clearly made up her mind; there was nothing to discuss. Her words had wounded him far worse than Abu's blade. A few days later, during a scheduled stateside debriefing—disguised as an arms-acquisition trip— Bryson arrived home to find her gone.

"Listen, Nick, you've probably done more good in the world than anybody in intelligence." Waller paused, and then spoke slowly, with great deliberateness. "If I let you continue, you'll start to subtract from what you've done."

"Maybe I screwed up," Bryson said dully. "Once. I'm willing to concede that much." There was no point in arguing, but he couldn't stop himself.

"And you'll screw up again," Waller replied evenly. "There are things we call 'sentinel events.' Early warning signs. You've been extraordinary for fifteen years. Extraordinary. But *fifteen years,* Nick. For a field agent, those are like dog years. Your focus is wavering. You're burned out, and the scary thing is, you don't even know it."

Was what happened to his marriage a 'sentinel event,' too? As Waller continued to speak in his calm, reasonable, logical way, Bryson felt a rush of different emotions, and one of them was rage. "My skills—"

"I'm not talking about your skill set. As far as fieldwork is concerned, there's nobody better, even now. What I'm talking about is restraint. The ability *not* to act. That's what goes first. And you don't get it back."

"Then maybe a leave of absence is in order." There was an undertone of desperation in his voice, and Bryson hated himself for it.

"The Directorate doesn't grant sabbaticals," Waller said dryly. "You know that. Nick, you've spent a decade and a half making history. Now you can study it. I'm going to give you your life back."

"My life," Bryson repeated colorlessly. "So you *are* talking about retirement."

Waller leaned back in his chair. "Do you know the story of John Wallis, one of the great British spymasters of the seventeenth century? He was a wizard at decrypting Royalist messages for the Parliamentarians in the 1640s. He helped establish the English Black Chamber, the NSA of its time. But when he retired from the business, he used his gifts as professor of geometry at Cambridge, and helped invent modern calculus—helped put modernity on its track. Who was more important—Wallis the spy, or Wallis the scholar? Retiring from the business doesn't have to mean being put out to pasture."

It was a vintage Waller rejoinder, an arcane parable; Bryson almost laughed at the absurdity of it all. "What did you have in mind for *me* to do? Work as a rent-a-cop at a warehouse, guarding T-beams with a six-shooter and a nightstick?"

" '*Integer vitae, scelerisque purus non eget Mauris jaculis, neque arcu, nec venenatis gravida saggittis pharetra.*' The man of integrity, free of sin, doesn't need the Moorish javelin, nor the bow, nor the heavy quiver of hunting arrows. Horace, as you know. In the event, it's all arranged. Woodbridge College needs a lecturer in near-eastern history, and they've just found a stellar candidate. Your graduate studies and linguistic mastery make you a perfect match."

Bryson felt eerily detached from himself, the way he sometimes did in the field—floating above the scene, observing everything with a cool and calculating eye. He often thought he might be killed in the field: that was an eventuality he could plan for, take into account. But he had never thought he would be fired. And that it was a beloved mentor who was firing him made it worse—made it *personal*.

"All part of the retirement plan," Waller continued. "Idle hands are the devil's workshop, as they say. Something we've learned from hard experience. Give a field agent a lump sum and nothing to do, and he'll get himself into trouble, as night follows day. You need a *project*. Something real. And you're a natural teacher—one of the reasons you were so good in the field."

Bryson said nothing, trying to dispel a wrenching memory of an operation in a small Latin American province, the memory of looking at a face in the crosshairs of a sniper-scope. *The face belonged to one of his "students"—a kid named Pablo, a nineteen-year-old Amerindian he'd trained in the art of defusing, and deploying, high explosives. A tough but decent kid. His parents were peasants in a hillside village that had just been overtaken by Maoist insurrectionists: if word got out that Pablo was working with their enemies, the guerrillas would kill his parents, and most likely in cruel and inventive ways— that was their signature. The kid wavered, struggled with his loyalties, and decided he had no choice but to cross over: to save his parents, he'd tell the guerrillas all he knew about their adversaries, the names of others who had cooperated with the forces of order. He was a tough kid, a decent kid, caught in a situation where there was no right answer. Bryson peered at Pablo's face through the scope—the face of a stricken, miserable, frightened young man—and only looked away after he squeezed the trigger.*

Waller's gaze was steady. "Your name is Jonas Barrett. An independent scholar, the author of half a dozen highly respected articles in peer-reviewed journals. Four of them in the *Journal of Byzantine Studies*. Team efforts—gave our near-eastern experts something to do in their down time. We do know a thing or two about how to build a civilian legend." Waller handed him a folder. It was canary yellow, which signified that the card stock was interlaced with magnetic strips and could not be removed from the premises. It contained a legend—a fictive biography. *His* biography.

He skimmed the densely printed pages: they detailed the life of a reclusive scholar whose linguistic capacities matched his, whose expertise could be quickly mastered. The lineaments of his biography were easily assimilated—most of them, that was. Jonas Barrett was unmarried. Jonas Barrett never knew Elena. Jonas Barrett was not in love with Elena. Jonas Barrett did not ache, even now, for Elena's return. Jonas Barrett was a fiction: for Nick to make him real meant accepting the loss of Elena.

"The appointment went through a few days ago. Woodbridge is expecting their new adjunct lecturer to arrive in September. And, if I may say so, they're lucky to have him."

"I have any choice in the matter?"

"Oh, we could have found you a position at any of a dozen multinational consulting firms. Or perhaps one of the behemoth petroleum or engineering companies. But this one is right for you. You've always had a mind that could handle abstractions as easily as facts. I used to worry it would be a handicap, but it turned out to be one of your greatest strengths."

"And if I don't *want* to retire? What if I don't *want* to go gently into that good night?" For some reason, he flashed back on the blur of steel, the sinewy arm plunging the blade toward him. . . .

"*Don't,* Nick," Waller said, his expression opaque.

"Jesus," Bryson said softly. There was pain in his voice, and Bryson regretted letting it show. Bryson knew how the game was played: what got to him wasn't the words he had been listening to so much as the man who was speaking them. Waller hadn't elaborated, hadn't needed to. Bryson knew he wasn't being offered a choice, and knew what lay in store for the recalcitrant. The taxicab that swerves suddenly, hits a pedestrian, and disappears. The pinprick a subject may not even feel as he makes his way through a crowded shopping mall, followed by the open-and-shut diagnosis of coronary failure. An ordinary mugging gone awry, in a city that still had one of the highest rates of street crime in the nation.

"This is the line of work that we have chosen," said Waller gently. "Our responsibility supersedes all bonds of kinship and affection. I wish it were otherwise. You don't know how much. In my time, I've had to . . . sanction three of my men. Good men gone bad. No, not even bad, just unprofessional. I live with that every day, Nick. But I'd do it again in a heartbeat. *Three men.* I'm begging you—don't make it four." Was it a threat? A plea? Both? Waller let his breath out slowly. "I'm offering you life, Nick. A very good life."

But what lay ahead for Bryson wasn't life, not just yet. It was a sort of fugue state, a shadowy half-death. For fifteen years, he had devoted his whole being—every brain cell, every muscle fiber—to a peculiarly hazardous and strenuous endeavor. Now his services would no longer be required. And Bryson felt nothing, just a profound emptiness. He made his way home, to the handsome colonial-style house in Falls Church that barely seemed familiar any longer. He cast his eyes over the house as if it were a stranger's, taking in the tasteful Aubussons that Elena had picked out, the hopeful pastel-painted room on the second floor for the child they never had. The place was both empty and full of ghosts. Then he poured himself a water tumbler full of vodka. It was the last time he would be fully sober in weeks.

The house was full of Elena, of her scent, her taste, her aura. He could not forget her.

They were sitting on the dock in front of their lakeside cabin in Maryland, watching the sailboat. . . . She poured him a glass of cold white wine, and as she handed it to him she kissed him. "I miss you," she said.

"But I'm right here, my darling."

"Now you are. Tomorrow you'll be gone. To Prague, to Sierra Leone, to Jakarta, to Hong Kong . . . who knows where? And who knows for how long?"

He took her hand, feeling her loneliness, unable to banish it. *"But I always come back. And you know the expression, Absence makes the heart grow fonder."*

"Mai rărut, mai drăgut," she said softly, musingly. *"But you know, in my country, they say something else.* Celor ce duc mai mult dorul, le pare mai dulce odorul. *Absence sharpens love, but presence strengthens it."*

"I like that."

She raised an index finger, wagged it in his face. *"They also say something else.* Prin depărtare dragostea se uită. *How do you say—long absent, soon forgotten?"*

"Out of sight, out of mind."

"How long before you forget me?"

"But you're always with me, my love." He tapped his chest. *"In here."*

He had no doubt the Directorate had him under electronic surveillance; he hardly cared. If they assessed him as a security risk, they would certainly sanction him. Perhaps with enough vodka, he thought grimly, he might even save them the trouble. Days passed, and he saw and heard from no one. Maybe Waller interceded at consortium level to cut him slack, because he knew it wasn't just the severance that caused him to fall apart. It was Elena's departure. Elena, the anchor of his existence. Acquaintances would sometimes say how *calm* Nick always seemed, but Nick seldom felt calm: calm was what Elena had provided. What was Waller's phrase for her? *A passionate serenity.*

Nick hadn't known he was capable of loving somebody as much as he loved her. In the vortex of lies where his career played out, she was his one true thing. At the same time, she too was a spook: she would have had to have been for them to build a life together. In fact, she was cleared almost all the way to the top, because she worked in the Directorate's cryptography division, and you never knew what sort of thing they'd come across. The typical hostile intercept often contained morsels of intelligence about the United States; decrypting them meant the possibility of being exposed to your own government's innermost secrets—information most of the agency's division heads weren't even cleared for. Analysts like her lived desk-bound lives, the computer keyboard their only weapon, and yet their intellects roamed the world as freely as any field agent.

God, how he loved her!

In a sense, Ted Waller had introduced them, though in fact they had met in the least promising of circumstances, a result of an assignment Waller had given him.

It was a routine package transport, which Directorate insiders sometimes called the "coyote run," referring to the smuggling of human beings. The Balkans were on fire in the late 1980s, and a brilliant Romanian mathematician was to be exfiltrated from Bucharest with his wife and daughter. Andrei Petrescu was a true Romanian patriot, an academician at the University of Bucharest specializing in the arcane mathematics of cryptography. He had been pressed into service by Romania's notorious secret service, the Securitate, to devise the codes used in the innermost circles of the Ceauşescu government. He wrote the cryptographic algorithms, but he refused their offer of employment: he wanted to remain in the academy, a teacher, and he was revolted by the Securitate's oppression of the Romanian people. As a result, Andrei and his family were kept under virtual house arrest, forbidden from traveling, their every movement watched. His daughter, Elena, said to be no less brilliant than her father, was a graduate student in mathematics at the university, hoping to follow in her father's footsteps.

As Romania reached a boiling point in December of 1989, and popular protests began to break out against the tyrant Nicolae Ceauşescu, the Securitate, the tyrant's Praetorian guard, retaliated with mass arrests and murders. In Timisoara, a huge crowd gathered on Bulevardul 30 Decembrie, and demonstrators broke into Communist Party headquarters and began throwing portraits of the tyrant out of the windows. The army and the Securitate fired on the unruly crowd throughout the day and night; the dead were piled up and buried in mass graves.

Disgusted, Andrei Petrescu decided to do his small part to fight the tyranny. He possessed the keys to Ceauşescu's most secret communications, and he would give them away to the tyrant's enemies. No longer could Ceauşescu communicate in secret with his henchmen; his decisions, his orders, would be known the moment he uttered them.

Andrei Petrescu wrestled with the decision. Would this imperil the lives of his beloved Simona, his adored Elena? Once they had discovered what he had done—and they would know, for no one else outside the government knew the source codes—Andrei and his family would be rounded up, arrested, and executed.

No, he would have to get out of Romania. But to do that he needed to enlist a powerful outsider, preferably an intelligence agency such as the CIA or the KGB, that had the resources to get the family out.

Terrified, he made cautious, veiled inquiries. He knew people; his colleagues knew people. He made his offer, and his demand. But both the British and the Americans refused to get involved. They had adopted a hands-off policy toward Romania. His offer was rebuffed.

And then very early one morning he was contacted by an American, a representative of another intelligence agency, not the CIA. They were interested; they would help. They had the courage the others lacked.

The operational details had been designed by the Directorate's logistical architects, refined by Bryson upon consultation with Ted Waller. Bryson was to smuggle out of Romania the mathematician and his family, along with five others, two men and three women, all of them intelligence assets. Getting into Romania was the easy part. From Nyírábrány, in the east of Hungary, Bryson crossed the border by rail into Romania at Valea Lui Mihai, carrying an authentic Hungarian passport of a long-haul freight driver; with his drab overalls and his callused hands, he was given barely a once-over. A few kilometers outside Valea Lui Mihai he found the truck that had been left for him by a Directorate contact. It was an old Romanian panel truck that belched diesel. It had been ingeniously modified in-country by Directorate assets: when the back of the truck was opened, the cargo bay seemed to be stacked with crates of Romanian wine and *tzuica,* plum brandy. But the crates were only one row deep; they concealed a large compartment, taking up most of the cargo area, in which all but one of the Romanians could be hidden.

The group had been instructed to meet him in the Baneasa forest, five kilometers north of Bucharest. Bryson found them at the designated rendezvous point, a picnic spread out before them, looking like an extended family on an outing. But Bryson could see the terror in their faces.

The leader of the eight was obviously the mathematician, Andrei Petrescu, a diminutive man in his sixties, accompanied by a meek, moon-faced woman, apparently his wife. But it was their daughter who arrested Bryson's attention, for he had never met a woman so beautiful. Twenty-year-old Elena Petrescu was raven-haired, petite, and lithe, with dark eyes that glittered and flashed. She wore a black skirt and dove-gray sweater, a colorful babushka tied around her head. She was silent and looked at him with profound suspicion.

Bryson greeted them in Romanian. *"Buna ziua,"* he said. *"Unde este cea mai apropiata statie Peco?"* Where is the nearest gas station?

"Sinteti pe un drum gresit," responded the mathematician. You are on the wrong road.

They followed him to the panel truck, which he'd parked in the shelter of a copse of trees. The beautiful young woman joined him in the cab, as was the preordained arrangement. The others took their seats in the hidden compartment, where Bryson had left sandwiches and bottled water to get them through the long journey to the Hungarian border.

Elena said nothing for the first several hours. Bryson attempted to make conversation, but she remained taciturn, though whether she was shy or just nervous he could not tell. They passed through the county of Bihor and neared the frontier crossing point at Bors, from where they would cross over to Biharkeresztes in Hungary. They had driven through the night and were making good time; everything seemed to be going smoothly—too smoothly, Bryson thought, for the Balkans, where a thousand little things could go wrong.

So it did not surprise him when he saw the flashing lights of a police car, a blue-uniformed policeman inspecting oncoming traffic, about eight kilometers from the border. Nor did it surprise him when the policeman waved them over to the side of the road.

"What the hell is this?" he said to Elena Petrescu, forcing a blasé tone as the jackbooted policeman approached.

"Just a routine traffic stop," she replied.

"I hope you're right," Bryson said, rolling down the window. His Romanian was fluent but the accent was not native; the Hungarian passport would explain that. He prepared himself to quarrel with the cop, as would any long-haul truck driver annoyed by some petty inconvenience.

The policeman asked him for his papers and the truck's registration. He inspected them; everything was in order.

Was something wrong? Bryson asked in Romanian.

Officiously, the policeman waved a hand toward the truck's headlights. One of them was burned out. But he would not let them go so easily. He wanted to know what was in the truck.

"Exports," replied Bryson.

"Open," said the policeman.

Sighing with annoyance, Bryson got out of the cab and went to unlock the tailgate. A semiautomatic pistol was holstered at his back, concealed inside his gray muslin work jacket; he would use it only if he had to, for killing the policeman was enormously risky. Not only was there the chance of being seen by a passing motorist, but if the officer had radioed in the truck's license plate numbers while he was pulling them over, his dispatcher would be waiting for a further communication. If none came, others would be called in, the truck's plates flagged at border control. Bryson did not want to have to kill the man, but he realized he might not have any choice.

As he pulled open the rear door, he could see the cop

eyeing the crates of wine and *tzuica* greedily. Bryson found that reassuring: perhaps a bribe of a case or two of spirits would be enough to satisfy the man and send him on his way. But the policeman began pawing through the crates as if inventorying them, and he quickly reached the false wall, a mere two feet or so in. Eyes narrowed in suspicion, the Romanian tapped at the wall, heard the hollowness.

"Hey, what the fuck is this?" he exclaimed.

Bryson slipped his right hand around to the holstered pistol, but just then he saw Elena Petrescu saunter around the back of the truck, one hand placed saucily on her left hip. She was chewing gum, and her face was heavily made up with too much lipstick, mascara, and rouge: she must have applied it while she sat waiting in the cab. She looked like a vamp, a prostitute. Working her jaw up and down, she leaned in very close to the policeman and said, *"Ce curu' meu vrei?"* What the fuck do you want?

"Fututi gura!" said the policeman. Fuck you! He reached behind the crates with both hands, running them along the false back, obviously feeling for a pull or knob or lever to open it. Bryson's stomach plummeted as the man gripped the indentation that opened the secret compartment. There was no explaining the seven concealed passengers; the policeman would have to be killed. And what the hell was Elena doing, antagonizing him further?

"Let me ask you something, comrade," she said in a quiet, insinuating voice. "How much is your life worth to you?"

The cop whirled around, glaring at her. "What the fuck are you talking about, whore?"

"I ask you, how much is your life worth? Because you're not just about to end a good career. You're about to buy yourself a one-way ticket to the psychiatric prison. Maybe to some pauper's grave."

Bryson was aghast: she was destroying everything, she had to be stopped!

The policeman opened the canvas pouch that hung around his neck and took out a bulky, old, military-style field telephone, which he began to dial.

"If you're making a call, I suggest you make it directly to the Securitate headquarters, and ask for Dragan himself." Bryson stared incredulously: Maj. Gen. Radu Dragan was the second-in-command at the secret police, notoriously corrupt and said to be sexually "dissolute."

The policeman stopped dialing, his eyes searching Elena's face. "You threaten me, bitch?"

She snapped her gum. "Hey, I don't care what you do. If you want to interfere with Securitate business of the highest and most confidential nature, be my guest. I just do my job. Dragan likes his Magyar virgins, and when he's done with them, I always drop my girls off across the border like I'm supposed to. You want to get in my way, fine. You wanna be the hero who makes Dragan's little weakness public, it's up to you. But I sure as hell wouldn't want to be you, or anyone who knows you." She rolled her eyes. "Come on, dial Dragan's office." She recited a number with a Bucharest area code and exchange.

Slowly, dazed, the policeman punched out the numbers, then put the handset to his ear. His eyes widened and he quickly disconnected the call: he had obviously connected with the Securitate.

He turned around quickly, striding away from the truck, muttering profuse apologies as he got into his cruiser and drove off.

Later, as the border guards waved them through, Bryson said to Elena, "Was that really the Securitate's phone number?"

"Of course," she said indignantly.

"How did you—?"

"I'm good with numbers," she said. "Didn't they tell you that?"

At the wedding, Ted Waller was Nick's best man. Elena's parents had been relocated, under new identities, to Rovinj, on the Istrian coast of the Adriatic, under Directorate protection; for reasons of security, she was not allowed to visit them, a proscription she accepted, with a heavy heart, as a terrible necessity.

She had been offered work as a cryptographer in Directorate headquarters doing code-breaking and signals-intercept analysis. She was immensely gifted, perhaps the finest cryptographer they'd ever had, and she loved the work. "I have you, and I have my work—and if only I had my parents near me, my life would be perfect!" she once said. When Nick first told Waller that things were getting serious between the two, he felt almost as if he were asking permission to get married. A father's permission? An *employer's* permission? He wasn't sure. A life in the Directorate meant that there were no sharp boundaries between matters private and professional. But he had met Elena on Directorate business, and it seemed appropriate to let Waller know. Waller had seemed genuinely overjoyed. "You've finally met your match," he said, grinning broadly, and he instantly produced an iced bottle of vintage Dom Perignon, like a magician extracting a nickel from a child's ear.

Bryson thought back to their honeymoon, spent in a tiny, verdant, nearly uninhabited island in the Caribbean. The beach was pink sand; a ways inland were almost magical groves of tamarisk beside a little brook. They went exploring there for the sole purpose of getting lost, or pretending to, and then losing themselves, losing themselves in each other. Time out of time, she'd called it. When he thought of Elena, he recalled their setting out to get lost—it was a minor ritual of theirs—and reminding themselves that so long as they had each other, they were never lost at all.

But now he had lost her for real, and felt lost himself, rootless, anchorless. The big empty house was silent, but he could hear her bruised voice over the sterile line as she said, quietly, that she was leaving him. It was a thunderbolt, yet it shouldn't have been. No, it wasn't the months of separation, she insisted; it was far deeper than that, far more fundamental. *I don't know you anymore,* she had told him. *I don't know you, and I don't trust you.*

He loved her, goddamn it, he *loved* her: wasn't that enough? His pleas were clamorous, impassioned. But the damage had been done. Falseness, hardness, coldness—they were traits that kept a field operative alive, but they were also traits that he'd started to bring home, and no marriage could survive that. He had kept things from her—one incident in particular—and for that he felt enormously guilty.

And so she was going to leave, to rebuild her life without him. Request transfer out of headquarters. Her voice on the sterile line sounded both as close as the next room and eerily distant. She said nothing heatedly, and yet her very lack of expression was what was so hard to bear. Seemingly, there was nothing to discuss or debate: it was the tone of someone pointing out a self-evident fact—that two plus two was four, that the sun rose in the east.

He remembered the stricken sensation that came over him. "Elena," he said, "do you know what you *mean* to me?"

Her response—leaden, beyond hurt—still echoed in his mind: "I don't even think you know who I am."

Once he returned from Tunisia and found her gone from their house, all her things gone, he'd tried to track her down, implored Ted Waller to help, with whatever resources were at his disposal. There were a thousand things he wanted to say to her. But it was as if she had vanished from the face of the earth. She did not intend to be found, and she would not be found, and Waller would not violate that. Waller was right about her; he'd met his match.

Alcohol, in sufficient quantities, is Novocain for the mind. The trouble is that when it wears off, the throbbing pain returns, and the only remedy is more alcohol. The days and weeks that followed his return from Tunisia became mere shards, fractured images. Images in sepia. He would take out the garbage and notice the sound, the bright clinking of glass liter bottles. The phone would ring; he never picked it up. Once the doorbell rang: Chris Edgecomb was at his door, in violation of every Directorate stricture. "I got worried, man," he'd said, and he looked it, too.

Bryson didn't want to think about what he himself might look like to a visitor—haunted, unkempt, unshaven. "They send you?"

"Are you kidding? They'd have my ass if they knew I was here."

Bryson supposed this was what was called an intervention. He couldn't remember the words he spoke to Edgecomb, only that he'd pronounced them with emphatic finality. The kid wouldn't come again.

Mostly, Bryson remembered waking up after a binge, twitching and blinking, his nerves feeling peeled raw; he had the vanilla stench of bourbon, the juniper acridity of gin. Staring at his morning face in the mirror, all inflamed capillaries and dark hollows. Trying to force down some scrambled eggs, and gagging at the smell.

A few isolated sounds, a few scattered images. Not a lost weekend; a lost three months.

His neighbors in Falls Church evinced little interest, perhaps out of politeness or indifference. He was, what, a corporate accounting exec for some industrial supplies firm, wasn't he? Guy must have got laid off. He'd either pull out of it, or he wouldn't. The professional-managerial casualties of the Beltway economy seldom invite compassion; besides, the neighbors knew better than to make inquiries. In suburbia you kept your distance.

Then one day in August, something shifted within him. He saw the purple asters start to bloom, flowers that Elena had planted the year before, pushing through with defiance, as if nurtured by neglect. He would do likewise. The trash bags no longer clinked as he toted them to the curb. He began to eat real food, three times a day, even. He still moved shakily at first, but a couple of weeks later he slicked his hair down, shaved carefully, got into a business suit, and made his way to 1324 K Street.

Waller tried to mask his relief with professional detachment, but Bryson could see it in his glittering eyes. "Who was it who said there are no second acts in American lives?" Waller said quietly.

Bryson returned the gaze steadily, calmly. Waiting, at peace with himself at last.

Waller smiled, just barely—one would have had to know him well to recognize it as a smile—and handed him the canary file folder. "Let's call this a third act."

CHAPTER TWO

Woodbridge College, in western Pennsylvania, was a small school, but it exuded a sense of quiet prosperity, of exclusivity beyond the norm. One saw it in the manicured *greenness* of the place: the emerald lawns and perfect flower borders of an institution that could pay lavishly for aesthetic incidentals. The architecture was the brick-and-ivy, collegiate-Gothic style typical of so much university construction from the twenties. From a distance, it might have passed for one of the ancient colleges of Cambridge or Oxford—if the college was taken out of those shabby, light-industrial towns and placed in the middle of Arcadia. It was a sheltered, secure, conservative establishment, a place to which America's richest and most powerful families had no anxieties about sending their impressionable scions. The campus convenience stores and eateries did a brisk business in latté and focaccia. Even during the late sixties, the college remained, as its then-president had once famously joked, a "hotbed of rest."

"Jonas Barrett," to his own surprise, turned out to be a gifted lecturer, his courses far more popular than the subjects he taught would normally have justified. Some of the students were bright, and almost all of them more studious and better behaved than he'd ever been in his own college days. One of his faculty colleagues, a wry, Brooklyn-bred physicist who used to teach at the City College of New York, had observed to him, shortly after he'd settled in, that the place made you feel like an eighteenth-century live-in tutor, responsible for educating the children of an English lord. You lived amid splendor, but it wasn't exactly yours.

Still, Waller had told the truth: this was a good life.

Now Jonas Barrett looked out over a packed auditorium, at a hundred expectant faces. He'd been amused when the

Campus Confidential had called him, after only his first year of teaching at Woodbridge, an "icily charismatic lecturer, more Professor Kingsfield than Mr. Chips," and remarked on his "stone-faced, slyly ironic visage." Whatever the reasons, his course on Byzantium was among the most popular classes in the history department.

He glanced at his watch: it was time to wrap up the lecture and gesture toward the next. "The Roman Empire had been the most astonishing political achievement in human history, and the question that has haunted so many thinkers is, of course, why it fell," he intoned in a high professorial manner laced with a tincture of irony. "You all know the sad tale. The light of civilization flickered and dimmed. The barbarians at the gate. The destruction of humanity's best hope, right?" There was murmured assent. *"Horseshit!"* he exclaimed suddenly, and a surprised titter was followed by a sudden hush. "Pardon my Macedonian." He looked around the lecture hall, his arched-brow expression challenging. "The Romans, so called, lost their claim to the moral high ground way before they lost their claim to empire. It was the Romans who avenged an early set-to with the Goths by taking Goth children they'd seized as hostages, marching them into the public squares of dozens of towns, then slaughtering them one by one. Slowly and painfully. As far as sheer calculated bloodthirstiness, nothing the Goths ever did could compare. The western Roman Empire was an arena of slavery and bloodsport. By contrast, the *eastern* Roman Empire was far more benign, and it survived the so-called fall of the Roman Empire. 'Byzantium' is only what the Westerners called it—the Byzantines always knew themselves as the true Roman Empire, and they safeguarded the scholarship and the humane values we cherish today. The west succumbed not to enemies from without, but rot from within—this much is true. And so civilization didn't flicker and dim. It just moved east." A pause. "You can come by and pick up your papers now. And enjoy your weekend, as much as you deem wise. Just remember Petronius: Moderation in all things. Including moderation."

"Professor Barrett?" The young woman was blond and fetching, one of those students who listens gravely and always sits in the front rows. He had stowed away his lecture notes and was fastening the straps of his battered leather satchel. He barely listened as she talked, complaining about a grade received, the tone urgent, the words banal, utterly familiar: *I worked so hard . . . I feel I did my very best . . . I really, really tried . . .* She followed as he walked toward the door, then to the parking lot outside the classroom building, until he reached his car. "Why don't we discuss this during office hours tomorrow?" he suggested gently.

"But Professor . . ."

Something's wrong.

"I guess I feel it's the grade that was wrong, Professor."

He hadn't realized he'd spoken aloud. But his antennae were buzzing. Why? Out of some sudden, baseless paranoia? Was he going to end up like one of those Vietnam posttraumatics who jump whenever they hear a car backfire?

A *sound,* something definitely out of place. He turned toward the student, but not to look at her. Instead, to look *past* her, beyond her, to whatever had flickered in his peripheral vision. Yes, there *was* something amiss in the general vicinity. Strolling too casually in his direction, as if enjoying the spring air, the verdant setting, was a broad-shouldered man in a charcoal flannel suit, white shirt, and perfectly knotted rep tie. That wasn't academic garb at Woodbridge, not even for administrators, and the weather was too warm for flannel. This was indeed an outsider, but one feigning—*attempting* to feign—that he belonged.

Bryson's field instincts were signaling wildly. His scalp tightened and his eyes began scanning from side to side, like a photographer testing different focal points in rapid succession: the old habits were returning, unbidden and somehow atavistic, rudely out of place.

But *why?* Surely there was no reason to be alarmed over a campus visitor—a parent, an official from Washington's educational bureaucracy, maybe even some high-level salesman. Bryson did a quick assessment. The man's jacket was unbuttoned, and he caught a glimpse of maroon braces holding the man's trousers up. Yet the man was also wearing a belt and the trousers were cut long, breaking deeply over the man's black, rubber-soled shoes. A surge of adrenaline: he'd worn similar attire himself, in a previous life. Sometimes you needed to wear a belt as well as suspenders because you were carrying a heavy object in one or both of your front pockets—a large-caliber revolver, say. And you needed the cuffs a little too long to ensure that your ankle holster was well concealed. *Dress for success,* Ted Waller used to advise, explaining how a man in evening dress could conceal a veritable arsenal if the fabric was tailored just right.

I'm out of the game! Leave me in peace!

But there was no peace; there never would be any peace. Once you were in you could never get out, even if the paychecks stopped and the health benefits expired.

Hostile parties around the world thirsted for revenge. No matter what precautions you took, no matter how elaborate the cover, how intricate the extraction. *If they really wanted to find me, they could.* To think otherwise was delusional. This was the unwritten certainty among the Directorate's operatives.

But who's to say they're not from the Directorate itself, doing a full sterilization, in that cynical phrase—removing the splinters, mopping up? Bryson had never met anyone who had retired from the Directorate, though surely such retirees did exist. But if someone at the consortium level in the Directorate came to doubt his loyalties, he, too, would be the victim of a full sterilization. It was a virtual certainty.

I'm out, I've put it behind!

Yet who would believe him?

Nick Bryson—for he *was* Nick Bryson now, Jonas Barrett gone by the wayside, discarded like a snake's shed skin— looked closely at the man in the suit. The man's salt-and-pepper hair was brush cut, the face broad and ruddy. Bryson tensed as the interloper approached, smiling as he did so and showing small white teeth. "Mr. Barrett?" the man called from halfway across the emerald lawn.

The man's face was a mask of reassurance, and that was the final giveaway, the mark of a professional. A civilian hailing a stranger always exhibited at least some tentativeness.

Directorate?

Directorate personnel were better than this, smoother and less obvious.

"Laura," he said quietly to the student, "I need you to leave me and go back into Severeid Hall. Wait at my office upstairs."

"But—"

"Now!" he snapped.

Speechless and scarlet, Laura turned and hurried back toward the building. A change had come over Professor Jonas Barrett—as she would explain it to her roommate that evening, he suddenly seemed different, *scary*—and she quickly decided she'd better do what he told her.

Soft footsteps were audible from the opposite direction. Bryson spun. Another man: redheaded, freckled, younger, wearing a navy blazer, tan chinos, and bucks. More plausible as a campus costume, except for the buttons on the blazer, which were too bright and brassy. Nor did the blazer lie quite flat over his chest: a bulge was visible where you'd expect to find the shoulder holster.

If not Directorate, then who? Foreign hostiles? Others from the more overt U.S. agencies?

Now Bryson identified the noise that had alerted him in the first place: the sound of a car that was idling, quietly and continuously. It was a Lincoln Continental with dark tinted windows, and it wasn't in a parking space but parked in the lane where he'd left his own car, blocking it.

"Mr. Barrett?" The larger, older man made eye contact with him, his loping stride swiftly decreasing the distance between them. "We really need you to come with us." The accent was bland, Midwestern. He stopped barely two feet away and gestured toward the Lincoln.

"Oh, is that right?" Bryson said, his delivery cold. "Do I know you?"

The stranger's reply was nonverbal: hands on hips, chest out to display the contours of his holstered handgun beneath his suit jacket. The subtle gesture of one professional to another, one armed, the other not. Then abruptly the man doubled over in agony, his hands grabbing at his stomach. With lightning speed, Bryson had driven the steel nib of his slim fountain pen into the man's muscled belly, and the professional responded with an unprofessional, if wholly natural, move indeed. *Reach for your weapon, never the wound:* one of Waller's many axioms, and though it meant countermanding a natural instinct, it had saved Nick's life more than a few times. This man was not top-rank.

As the stranger's hands flailed at the ruined flesh, Bryson plunged his hands into the man's jacket and retrieved the small but powerful blue-steel Beretta.

Beretta—not Directorate issue; then whose?

He slammed the butt against the man's temple—heard the sickening crunch of bone against metal, heard the senior agent slump to the ground—and with the weapon pointed, spun to face the redheaded man in the blue blazer.

"My safety's *off*," Nick shouted to him, urgent and demanding. "Yours?"

The play of confusion and panic on the young man's face gave away his inexperience. He had to have calculated that Nick would easily be able to squeeze off the first shot the instant he heard the click of the safety release. *Bad odds.* But the inexperienced could be the most dangerous, precisely because they didn't react in a rational and logical manner.

Amateur hour. His gun aimed steadily at the redheaded field man, Bryson backed up slowly in the direction of the idling vehicle. The doors would be unlocked for immediate access, of course. In one fluid motion, all the while keeping the Beretta leveled at the redheaded novice, he yanked open the car door and slid into the driver's seat. With a glance he knew the vehicle's windows and windscreen were bulletproof, as they had to be. Bryson had only to throw the gearshift out of park, and the car lurched forward. He heard a bullet strike the back of the car—the license plate, he judged from the clatter. And then another struck the rearview window, pitting it but doing no further damage. They were firing at the car's tires, hoping to stop his flight.

In a matter of seconds he was roaring through the tall, ornamental wrought-iron gates of the campus. Barreling down the tree-lined main drive, one assailant down and the other firing wildly yet ineffectually, his mind raced. He thought: *Time's up.* And: *Now what?*

If they'd really intended to kill me, I'd be dead.

Bryson sped down the Interstate, his eyes scanning the lanes ahead and behind for pursuers. *They caught me unarmed and unaware, deliberately so.* Which meant that they were up to something else. But what? And how did they find him in the first place? Could someone have gained access to a 5-1 classified Directorate database? There were too many variables, too many unknowns. But Bryson felt no fear now, only the icy calm of the seasoned field operative he had once been. He wouldn't drive to any of the airports, where they'd certainly be expecting him; instead, he'd drive directly back to his house on campus, the least expected place to go. If this was inviting another confrontation, so be it. Confrontation meant exposure of limited duration: flight could go on indefinitely. Bryson no longer had the patience for protracted flight: Waller had been right about that, at least.

Turning down the campus road to his residence on Villier Lane, he heard, then saw, a helicopter raking the sky, making its way toward the small campus helipad atop the science building tower donated by a software billionaire, the tallest building on campus by far. It was normally used only by major donors, but this chopper had federal markings. The helicopter was a follow-on; it had to be. Bryson pulled up in front of his house, a ramshackle Queen Anne–style dwelling with a mansard roof and plaster facade. The place was empty, and he knew from the alarm system, which he had installed himself, that no one had entered the house since he'd left it that morning.

Entering, he verified that the system hadn't been tampered with. The strong sun streamed through a parlor window onto the wide pine floorboards, giving rise to a resinous, evergreen smell. That was the chief reason why he'd bought the house: the scent reminded him of a happy year he'd spent in a half-timbered house outside Wiesbaden when he was seven and his father was stationed at the military base there. Bryson was no typical army brat—his father was, after all, a general, and the family was usually provided with comfortable living quarters and a household staff. Still, his childhood was all about learning how to pick up stakes and put them down again in some other part of the world. Transitions were helped by his natural facility with languages, which others always marveled at. Making new friends didn't come quite as easily, but in time he developed a skill at that, too. He'd seen too many army brats who styled themselves as surly outsiders to want to join their ranks.

He was home now. He would wait. And this time the meeting would be on his territory, on his terms.

It didn't take long.

Only a few minutes elapsed before a black government Cadillac sedan, complete with a small U.S. flag flying from the antenna, pulled into his driveway. Bryson, watching from the house, realized that the very overtness of the display was meant to provide reassurance. A uniformed government driver got out and opened the vehicle's rear door, and a short, wiry man stepped out. Bryson had seen him before—a fleeting face from C-SPAN. Some sort of intelligence official. Bryson stepped out onto his porch.

"Mr. Bryson," the man said in a husky voice, the accent New Jersey. He was in his mid-fifties, Bryson estimated, with a thatch of white hair, the face narrow and creased; he wore an unstylish brown suit. "You know who I am?"

"Somebody with a lot of explaining to do."

The government man nodded, his hands raised in a gesture of contrition. "We fucked up, Mr. Bryson, or Jonas Barrett if you prefer. I take full responsibility. Reason I've come up here is to apologize to you personally. And also to explain."

An image from a TV screen came to Bryson, white letters beneath a talking head. "You're Harry Dunne. Deputy chairman of the CIA." Bryson remembered watching him testify to a Congressional subcommittee once or twice.

"I need to talk to you," the man said.

"I've got nothing to say to you. I wish I could direct you toward your Mr. Breyer or whatever his name is, but I'm drawing a blank."

"I'm not asking you to *say* anything. I'm just asking you to *listen*."

"Those were your goons, I take it."

"Yes, they were," Dunne admitted. "They overstepped the bounds. They also underestimated you—they figured, wrongly, that after five years out of the field you'd gone soft. You've also taught them a couple of key tactical lessons that will no doubt come in handy for them down the road. Especially Eldridge, once he gets stitched up." There was a dry rattle in his throat when he laughed. "So now I'm asking you nice as I can. All aboveboard." Dunne walked slowly over to the porch where Bryson was leaning against a wooden column, his arms folded behind his back. Taped to his upper back was the Beretta, which he could mobilize in an instant if he had to. On television, on the Sunday-morning talking-head shows, Dunne possessed a somewhat commanding presence; in person, he seemed almost shrunken, a little too small for his clothes.

"I have no lessons to teach," Bryson protested. "All I did was defend myself against a couple of men who were in the wrong place and didn't seem to wish me well."

"The Directorate trained you well, I'll say that much."

"I wish I knew what you were talking about."

"You know full well. Your reticence is to be expected."

"I think you've got the wrong man," Bryson said quietly. "A case of mistaken identity. I don't know what you're referring to."

The CIA man exhaled noisily, followed by a rattling cough. "Unfortunately, not all of your former colleagues are as discreet, or maybe the correct word is *principled*, as you. Oaths of fealty and secrecy tend to loosen their holds when money changes hands, and I do mean serious money. None of your former colleagues came cheap."

"Now you've really lost me."

"Nicholas Loring Bryson, born Athens, Greece, the only son of General and Mrs. George Wynter Bryson," the CIA man recited, almost in a monotone. "Graduated from St. Alban's School in Washington, D.C., Stanford, and Georgetown's School of Foreign Service. Recruited while at Stanford into an all-but-invisible intelligence agency known to the very few who know about it as the Directorate. Trained in fieldwork, fifteen highly successful and secretly decorated years of service, with operations ranging from—"

"Nice bio," Bryson interrupted. "Wish it were mine. We academics sometimes like to imagine what it might be like to live an active life outside these cloistered, ivied walls." He spoke with some bravado. His legend was designed to evade suspicion, not withstand it.

"Neither one of us has any time to waste," Dunne said. "In any case, I do hope you realize that we intended no harm."

"I realize no such thing. You CIA boys, from everything I've read, have a long menu of ways to inflict harm. A bullet in the brain, for one. Twelve hours on a scopolamine drip, for another. Shall we talk about poor Nosenko, who made the mistake of defecting to our side? He got the red-carpet treatment from you gentlemen, didn't he? Twenty-eight months in a padded crypt. Whatever it took to break him, you were all too willing to do."

"You're talking ancient history, Bryson. But I understand and accept your suspicion. What can I do to allay it?"

"What's more suspicious than the need to allay suspicion?"

"If I really wanted to take you down," Dunne said, "we wouldn't be having this conversation, and you know that."

"It might not be quite as easy as you think," Bryson said, his tone blasé. He smiled coldly to let the CIA man pick up on the implied threat. He had given up the pretense; there seemed little point.

"We know what you can do with your hands and your feet. No demonstrations are required. All I'm asking you for is your ears."

"So you say." *How much did the Agency really know about him, about his Directorate career? How could the security firewall have been breached?*

"Listen, Bryson, kidnappers don't supplicate. I guess you know I'm not a man who makes house calls every day. I've got something to tell you, and it won't be easy to hear. You know our Blue Ridge facility?"

Bryson shrugged.

"I want to take you there. I need you to listen to what I've got to tell you, watch what I've got to show you. Then, if you want, you can go home, and we'll never bother you again." He gestured toward the car. "Come with me."

"What you're proposing is sheer madness. You do realize this, don't you? A couple of third-rate thugs show up outside my class and try to strong-arm me into a car. Then a man I've seen only on TV news shows—a high official in an intelligence agency with little credibility to speak of, frankly—shows up on my front lawn trying to entice me with a titillating combination of threats and lures. How do you expect me to respond?"

Dunne's gaze did not waver. "Frankly, I expect you'll come anyway."

"What makes you so sure?"

Dunne was silent for a moment. "It's the only way you'll ever satisfy your curiosity," he said at last. "It's the only way you'll ever know the truth."

Bryson snorted. "The truth about *what?*"

"For starters," the CIA man said very quietly, "the truth about yourself."

CHAPTER THREE

In the Blue Ridge mountains of western Virginia, near the borders with Tennessee and North Carolina, the CIA maintains a secluded area of hardwood forest interspersed with northern spruce, hemlock, and white pine, about two hundred acres in all. Part of the Little Wilson Creek wilderness, within the Jefferson National Forest, it is a rugged territory of a wide range of elevations, dotted with lakes, streams, creeks, and waterfalls, far removed from the main hiking trails. The nearest towns, Troutdale and Volney, are none too close. This wilderness preserve, enclosed by electric security fence and topped with concertina wire, is known within the Agency by the generic, colorless, and quite forgettable name of the Range.

There, certain exotic forms of instrumentation, such as miniaturized explosives, are tested amid the rocky outcroppings. Various transmitters and tracking devices are put through their paces there, too, their frequencies calibrated away from the surveillance range of hostile parties.

It is entirely possible to spend time on the Range and never notice the low-slung concrete-and-glass building that serves as combination administrative headquarters, training and conference facility, and barracks. This building is situated a hundred yards or so from a helipad clearing that, owing to peculiarities of elevation and vegetation, is nearly impossible to find.

Harry Dunne had said little during the trip there. In fact, the only opportunity for chat had been the brief limousine ride to the campus helipad; during the helicopter trip to Virginia, both men, accompanied by Dunne's silent aide-de-camp, wore protective noise-insulating headphones. Debarking from the dark green government helicopter, the three men were met by an anonymous-looking assistant.

Bryson and Dunne, the assistants in tow, passed through

the facility's unremarkable-looking main lobby and descended a set of stairs into a subterranean, spartan, low-ceilinged chamber. On the smooth, white-painted walls were mounted, like blank rectangular canvases, a pair of large, flat, gas-plasma display monitors. The two men took their seats at a gleaming table of brushed steel. One of the silent assistants disappeared; the other took a seat at a station just outside the closed door to the chamber.

As soon as Dunne and Bryson were seated, Dunne began to speak without ceremony or preface. "Let me tell you what I believe you believe," he began. "You believe you're a fucking unsung hero. This is in fact the central unshakable conviction that has enabled you to endure a decade and a half of tension so brutal, any lesser man would have cracked long ago. You believe you spent fifteen years in the service of your country, working for an ultraclandestine agency known as the Directorate. Virtually nobody else, even at the highest levels of the U.S. government, knows of its existence, with the possible exception of the chairman of the President's Foreign Intelligence Advisory Board and a couple of key players in the White House who've been cleared up the wazoo. A closed loop—or rather, as close as you can come to a closed loop in this fallen world."

Bryson took measured breaths, determined not to betray his emotions by any visible display of shock. Yet he was shocked: the CIA man knew of matters that had been cloaked with extraordinary thoroughness.

"Ten years ago, you even received a Presidential Medal of Honor for services rendered above and beyond," Dunne went on. "But, your operations being so hush-hush, there was no ceremony, no president, and I bet you didn't even get to keep the medal." Bryson flashed back to the moment: Waller opening the box and showing him the heavy brass object. Of course, it would have put operational secrecy unacceptably at risk if Bryson had been invited to the White House for the presentation; still, he'd swelled with pride all the same. Waller had asked him if it bothered him—the fact that he'd achieved the highest civilian honor in America and nobody would ever know. And Bryson, moved, told him honestly no—Waller knew, the president knew; his work had made the world just a little safer, and that was enough. He'd meant it, too. That, in a nutshell, was the ethos of the Directorate.

Now Dunne pressed a sequence of buttons on a control panel embedded in the steel-topped table, and the twin flat screens shimmered into vibrant display. There was a photograph of Bryson as an undergraduate at Stanford—not an official portrait, but a candid, taken without his knowledge. Another of him in a mountain region of Peru, clad in fatigues; this dissolved into an image of him with dyed skin and grizzled beard, impersonating one Jamil Al-Moualem, a Syrian munitions expert.

Astonishment is an emotion impossible to sustain for any length of time: Bryson felt his shock gradually ebbing into sharp annoyance, then anger. Obviously he'd been caught in the middle of some interagency squabble over the legality of Directorate methods.

"Fascinating," Bryson interjected dryly, finally breaking his silence, "but I suggest you take up these matters with others better placed to discuss them. Teaching is my only profession these days, as I assume you know."

Dunne reached over and gave Bryson a comradely pat on his shoulder, no doubt intended to reassure. "My friend, the question isn't what we know. It's what *you* know—and, more to the point, what you *don't*. You believe you've spent fifteen years in the service of your country." Dunne turned and gave Bryson a penetrating stare.

Quietly, steely, Bryson answered, "I know I did."

"And you see, that's where you're wrong. What if I told you that the Directorate in fact isn't part of the United States government? That it never was. Quite the fucking contrary." Dunne leaned back in his chair and ran a hand through his rumpled white mane. "Ah, shit, this isn't going to be easy for you to hear. It's not easy for me to say, I'll tell you that. Twenty years ago, I had to bring a guy in. He thought he'd been spying for Israel, and was a real zealot about it. I had to explain to him that he'd been false-flagged. It was Libya that was paying for his services. All the contacts, the controls, the hotel-room rendezvous in Tel Aviv—all part of the setup. Pretty flimsy one, at that. Fucker shouldn't have been double-dealing anyway. But even I had to feel sorry for him when he learned who his real employers were. I'll never forget his face."

Bryson's own face was burning hot. "What the hell does that have to do with anything?"

"We were supposed to arraign him in a sealed Justice Department courtroom the next day. Guy shot himself before we had the chance." One of the gas-plasma screens dissolved into another image. "Here's the guy who recruited you, right?"

It was a photograph of Herbert Woods, Bryson's adviser at Stanford and an eminent historian. Woods had always liked Bryson, admired the fact that he spoke a dozen languages fluently, had an unsurpassed gift for memorization. Probably liked the fact that he was no slouch as an athlete either. Sound mind, sound body—Woods was big on that.

The screen went blank, then flared with a grainy photo of a young Woods on a city street that Bryson immediately recognized as the old Gorky Street in Moscow, which after the end of the Cold War became Tverskaya once again, its pre-Revolutionary name.

Bryson laughed, bitterly, not bothering to hide his ridicule. "This is insanity. You're going to 'reveal' to me the 'damning' fact that Herb Woods was a commie when he was young. Well, sorry: everyone knows that. He never hid his past. That's why he was such a staunch anti-Communist: he knew firsthand how seductive all that foolish utopian rhetoric could be once upon a time."

Dunne shook his head, his facial expression cryptic. "Maybe I'm getting ahead of myself. I told you before that all I wanted you to do was listen. You're a historian now, right? Well, bear with me while I give you a quick history lesson. You know about the Trust, of course."

Bryson nodded. The Trust was widely regarded as the greatest espionage ploy of the twentieth century, bar none.

It was a seven-year sting operation, the brainchild of Lenin's spymaster, Feliks Dzerzhinksi. Shortly after the Russian Revolution, the CHEKA, the Soviet intelligence organization that grew into the KGB, secretly founded a fake dissident group involving a number of supposedly disaffected high-ranking members of the Soviet government who believed, or so the word was quietly put out, that the collapse of the USSR was imminent. In time, anti-Soviet groups in exile were drawn into working with the Trust; in fact, Western intelligence units grew dependent upon the information—entirely fraudulent, of course—it provided. Not only was the hoax brilliantly designed to mislead those governments around the world who sought the Soviet Union's demise, it was, further, a superbly effective way for Moscow to penetrate the networks of its chief enemies abroad. And it worked phenomenally well—so well, in fact, that the Trust became a case study of the perfect deception operation, taught within intelligence agencies the world over.

By the time the nature of the subterfuge was exposed, in the late twenties, it was too late. Exiled leaders had been kidnapped and murdered, networks of collaborators destroyed, would-be defectors within Russia executed. The in situ forces of opposition to Soviet rule never recovered. It was, in the words of one eminent American intelligence analyst, "the deception operation upon which the Soviet state was built."

"Now you're the one talking ancient history," Bryson said in disgust, shifting in his seat impatiently.

"Never discount the power of inspiration," Dunne said. "In the early sixties, you had a small circle of brainiacs at the GRU—Soviet military intelligence, if you don't consider that a contradiction in terms." He chuckled. "These guys concluded that their intelligence agencies were all neutered, ineffectual, feeding out of the same trough of disinformation each one had created—or, to put it another way, a whole lot of ink and not much squid. The way these guys figured it—and they were geniuses, understand, IQs off the charts, the real deal—the intelligence agencies were spending most of their time chasing their own tails. These guys, they called themselves the *Shakhmatisti*, the chess players, chess club. They despised their own clumsy Russky operatives, and they had utter contempt for the sort of Americans who cooperated with them: sad sacks and losers, in their book. So they took another look at the Trust and tried to see if there was a lesson to be learned. They wanted to recruit the best and the brightest within their enemy's camp, same as us, and they figured out a way to get them. Same as us. Recruit them for a life of adventure."

"I'm not following."

"Neither were we, until very recently. It was only in the last few years that the CIA learned of the Directorate's existence. And, far more crucial, what the Directorate meant."

"Try talking sense."

"We're talking about the greatest espionage gambit in the entire twentieth century. The whole thing was an elaborate ruse, do you see? Like the Trust. These GRU geniuses, their masterstroke was to establish a penetration operation right on enemy soil—our soil. A super-secret spy agency staffed by a lot of gifted people who had no idea as to the identities of their real bosses, known only as the consortium, and who were instructed to conceal their work from any and all U.S. government officials. Now, that's the beauty part. You can't tell anybody else, especially not the government you're ostensibly working for! I'm talking about good, red-blooded Americans who got up in the morning and drank their Maxwell House coffee and toasted their Wonder Bread and drove to work in their Buicks and Chevys, and went out into the world and risked their lives—yet never knew who their real employers were. It went like clockwork—like a classic 'big store' con of old."

Bryson couldn't endure this litany any longer. "Goddamn you, Dunne! Enough! This is all lies, a goddamn pack of lies. If you really think I'd fall for this crap, you're out of your goddamn mind." He stood up abruptly. "Get me the hell out of here. I'm tired of your little low-rent theatrical production."

"I hardly expected you to believe me—not at first," Dunne said calmly, barely even shifting in his seat. "Hell, I wouldn't believe it either. But bear with me for a sec." He gestured toward one of the screens. "Know this guy?"

"Ted—Edmund Waller," Bryson breathed. He was looking at a photograph of Waller as a much younger man, stocky but not yet obese, wearing a Russian Army dress uniform at what appeared to be some kind of ceremonial occasion in Red Square. Part of the Kremlin was visible in the background. Scrolling up to the side of the image were biographical details. Name: GENNADY ROSOVSKY. Born 1935 in VLADIVOSTOK. Childhood chess prodigy. Trained in American English, by a native speaker, since age seven. Certificates in ideology and in military science. A list of medals and other military honors followed.

"Chess prodigy," Bryson muttered to himself. "What the hell is this?"

"They say he could have beat Spassky and Fisher both, if he'd wanted to make a career of it," Dunne said, a harsh edge in his voice. "Too bad he decided to play for bigger game."

"Pictures can be doctored, pixels manipulated digitally—" Bryson began.

"Are you trying to convince me or yourself?" Dunne said, cutting him off. "Anyway, in a lot of cases we've got originals, and I'd be happy to have you inspect them. I can assure you we've been over everything with a microscope. We might never have known about the operation. Then our luck changes. *Mirabile* fucking *dictu,* Professor, we got access to the Kremlin archives. Money changed hands; buried archives were unearthed. There were one or two scraps of paper with pretty tantalizing stuff in them. Which would have told us nothing, to be honest, except for the lucky break of a couple of midlevel defectors, who gave us all they had. In isolation, their debriefings were meaningless. Taken together, with the Kremlin documents thrown in, patterns began to emerge. Which was how we learned about you, Nick. But it wasn't a whole lot, since apparently the inner circles kept the whole operation incredibly segmented, the way terror cells operate.

"So we started to wonder about what we didn't know. It's been a top-priority project for the past three years. We've got only the foggiest idea of who the real principals are. Except, of course, for your friend Gennady Rosovsky. He's got a sense of humor, got to hand him that. You know who he named himself after? Edmund Waller was the name of an obscure and extremely slippery seventeenth-century poet. He ever talk to you about the English civil war?"

Bryson swallowed hard and nodded.

"You'll get a laugh out of this, I know you will. During the interregnum, this Edmund Waller wrote praise poems for Cromwell, the Lord Protector. But, you see, he was also a secret conspirator in a Royalist plot. After the Restoration, he was honored at the Royal Court. That make any kind of sense to you? Guy calls himself after the great double-agent of English poetry. Like I said, I'm sure it's a laugh riot to you highbrows."

"So you're claiming that I was recruited at college into some . . . some kind of cat's-paw organization, that everything I did after that was a sham, is that what you're saying?" Bryson spoke bitterly, skeptically.

"Only the machinations didn't start then. They started earlier. A lot earlier."

He tapped a sequence on the control panel, and another digitized image came to life on the screen. On the left, he saw his father, Gen. George Bryson, robust, handsome, and square jawed, next to Nick's mother, Nina Loring Bryson, a soft-spoken, gentle woman who taught the piano, followed her husband to his postings around the world, and never breathed a word of complaint. On the right, another image— a grainy image from the police files—showed a crumpled vehicle on a snowy mountain road. The remembered pain slammed Bryson in the gut; after all these years, it was still almost unbearable.

"Let me ask you something, Bryson. Did you believe this was an accident? You were fifteen, already a brilliant student, terrific athlete, prime of American youth, all that. Now both your parents are suddenly killed. Your godparents take you in . . ."

"Uncle Pete," Bryson said tonelessly. He was in a world of his own, a world of shock and pain. "Peter Munroe."

"That was the name he took, sure, not the name he was born with. And he made sure you went to college where you did, and made a lot of other decisions for you besides. All of which pretty much guaranteed that you'd end up in their hands. The Directorate's, I mean."

"You're saying that when I was fifteen, my parents were murdered," Bryson said numbly. "You're saying my entire life has been some kind of . . . immense deception."

Dunne hesitated, wincing. "If it makes you feel any better, you weren't alone," he said gently. "There were dozens just like you. It's just that you were their most spectacular success."

Bryson wanted to press the point, argue with the CIA man, show the essential illogic of his reasoning, point out the flaws in his case. But instead he found himself overcome by an intense feeling of vertigo, a harrowing sense of guilt. If what Dunne said was correct, even anywhere near correct, then what in his life was real? What had ever been true? Did he even know who he was himself? "And Elena?" he asked stonily, not wanting to hear the answer.

"Yes, Elena Petrescu, too. Interesting case. We believe she was recruited out of the Romanian Securitate, assigned to you by the Directorate in order to keep tabs on you."

Elena . . . no, it was *inconceivable,* she wasn't Securitate! Her father was an enemy of the Securitate, a brave mathematician who turned against the government. And Elena . . . he had rescued her and her parents, they had built a life together . . .

They were horseback riding along an endless stretch of deserted sandy beach in the Caribbean. Coming off a full gallop, they slowed to a trot. The moonlight was silvery, the night cool.

"Is this island all ours, Nicholas?" she exulted. "I feel

like we're all alone here, that we own everything we see!"

"We do, my darling," Bryson said, *infected by her playful exuberance.* "Didn't I tell you? I've been diverting funds from discretionary accounts. I've bought the island."

Her laugh was musical, joyful. "Nicholas, you are terrible!"

" 'Nick-o-las'—I love the way you say my name. Where did you learn to ride so well? I didn't know they even had horses in Romania."

"Oh, but they do. I learned to ride on my grandmother Nicoleta's farm in the foothills of the Carpathian mountains, on a Hutsul pony. They're bred to work in the mountains, but they're so marvelous for riding, so lively and strong and sure footed."

"You could be describing yourself."

The waves crashed loudly behind them, and she laughed once more. "You never really saw my country, did you, my dear? The Communists made Bucharest so ugly, but the countryside, Transylvania and the Carpathians, is so beautiful and unspoiled. They still live in the old way, with the horse-drawn wagons. Whenever we tired of university life we would stay with Nicoleta in Dragoslavele, and every day she'd make us mamagliga, *fried cornmeal mush,* and ciorba, *my favorite soup."*

"You miss the homeland."

"A little. But mostly I miss my parents. I miss them so terribly. It's such agony for me not to be able to see them. The sterile phone calls maybe twice a year—it's not enough!"

"But at least they're safe. Your father has many enemies, people who would kill him if they knew his whereabouts. Securitate remnants, professional assassins who blame him for giving away the codes that led to the downfall of the Ceauşescu government that kept them in power. Now they're in hiding themselves, inside Romania and abroad, and they haven't forgotten. There are teams of them, called sweepers, who track down their old enemies and execute them. And *they desperately want revenge against the man they consider the worst turncoat of all.*"

"*He was a* hero!"

"*Of course he was. But to them he was a traitor. And they will stop at nothing to extract their vengeance.*"

"*You frighten me!*"

"*Only to remind you how important it is that your parents remain in hiding, protected.*"

"*Oh God, Nicholas, I pray nothing ever happens to them!*"

Bryson pulled on the reins, bringing his horse to a stop as he turned to face Elena. "I promise you, Elena. Anything I can humanly do to keep them safe, I will."

A minute of silence passed, and then another. Finally, Bryson, blinking hard, said, "But it doesn't make any sense. I did goddamned valuable work. Time and again I—"

"—fucked us up the ass but good," Dunne interrupted, toying with a cigarette but not lighting it. "Every one of your great successes was a devastating setback to American interests. And I say this with the greatest professional respect. Oh, let's see. That 'moderate reform candidate' you protected? He was in the pay of the Sendero Luminoso, the Shining Path terrorists. In Sri Lanka, you pretty much destroyed a secret coalition that had been on the verge of brokering a peace between the Tamils and the Sinhalese."

Another image was downloaded onto the high-resolution screen, as a spray of pixels scrambled into colors and contours. Bryson recognized the face while it was still half a blur.

It was Abu.

"Tunisia," Bryson said, breathing hard. "He—he was going to stage a coup, he and his followers—fanatics. I moved in, leveraged some opposition groups, figured out who in the palace was playing both sides . . ." It was not an episode he remembered altogether fondly: he would never forget the carnage along the Avenue Habib Borguiga. Nor the moment when Abu unmasked him and nearly took his life.

"Let's see now," Dunne said. "You burned him. Took him down, and handed him over to the government."

That was true. He'd turned Abu over to a trusted group of government security men, who jailed him along with dozens of his henchmen.

"Then what happened?" Dunne prompted, as if he was testing.

Bryson shrugged. "He died in captivity a few days later. I won't tell you I shed any tears."

"I wish I could say the same," Dunne said, his voice suddenly hard. "Abu was one of ours, Bryson. One of mine, I should say. I trained him. He was our chief asset in the whole region. I'm talking the entire goddamn sandbox."

"But the attempted coup . . ." Bryson put in feebly, his mind whirling. Nothing was making any sense!

"A bullshit cover story, to keep up his bona fides with the lunatics. He was leading the Al-Nahda, all right—right off the fucking cliff. Abu worked deep, deep cover. Needed to if he was going to survive the day. You think it's easy penetrating terrorist cells, especially Hezbollah, the big kahuna? They're all so goddamned suspicious. If they haven't known you and your family your entire goddamned life, they want to see you shed blood by the gallon, the blood of Israelis, otherwise they never trust you. Abu was a slick bastard who played rough, but he was *our* slick bastard. And he had to play rough. Thing is, he was getting close to Khadafy. Very close. Khadafy figured if Abu took Tunisia, he could make it a Libyan province, more or less. Abu was getting to be an asshole buddy of his. We were on the verge of having a direct feed to every Islamic terror group north of the Sahara. Then the Directorate sandbagged him, planted phony munitions—and by the time our people discovered we'd been stung, it was too late. Pretty much set back our whole network about twenty years. Brilliant work. Got to hand it to those *Shakhmatisti* whiz kids. Brilliant, really fucking brilliant, to have one American spy agency undoing the work of the other. You want me to go on? Tell you about Nepal and what you really accomplished? What about Romania,

where you guys probably thought you helped get rid of Ceauşescu? What a farce. Just about everyone from the old regime
changed clothes one day and became the new government,
you know that! Ceauşescu's underlings had been plotting the
bastard's downfall for years—they delivered their boss to the
wolves so they could stay in power. Which was just what
the Kremlin wanted. So what happens? There's a fake coup
d'etat, the dictator and his wife try to escape in a helicopter
that suddenly develops 'engine trouble' so they can't escape,
they get arrested and tried in a closed, kangaroo court, and
face a firing squad on Christmas Day. The whole thing was
a goddamned setup, and who benefited? One by one, all the
Eastern European satellites were falling like dominoes, kicking out the old Party apparatchiks, going democratic, breaking away from the Soviet bloc. But Moscow wasn't going
to lose Romania, too. Ceauşescu had to go, he was bad PR.
The guy was a goddamned pain in Moscow's ass anyway,
always was. Moscow wanted to keep Romania, maintain the
security apparatus, install a new puppet. And who's there to
do their dirty work? Who else but you and your good friends
in the Directorate? Jesus, man, how much do you really want
to know?"

"Damn it!" Bryson shouted. "This makes no sense! How
ignorant do you think I am? The goddamn GRU, the Russians—that's all the past. Maybe you Cold War cowboys at
Langley haven't yet heard the news—the war's over!"

"Yes," Dunne replied raspily, barely audible. "And for
some baffling reason the Directorate is alive and well."

Bryson stared at him mutely, unable to get any words out.
He felt his brain working, spinning in circles, circuits over-
heating, sparks flying.

"I'll level with you, Bryson. There was a time when I
wanted to kill you, kill you with my bare hands. That was
before we'd figured out the whole story, the way the Directorate worked. Nah, let's be straight with each other, I'd be
bullshitting you and me both if I said we have anything remotely approaching the whole story. We still hardly know
more than isolated segments. For decades there had been

rumors, no more substantial than dandelion wisps. Once the Cold War's over, the whole operation falls into quiescence, as best as we can figure. It's like the old parable of the blind men and the elephant. We can feel a trunk here, a tail there, but on the highest levels, we still don't know what kind of beast we're dealing with. What we do know—and we've had you under surveillance for the past few years—is that you were one deluded piece of shit. Which is why I'm talking to you real nice and not wrapping my hands around your throat." Dunne laughed bitterly, and the laugh turned into a cough—a smoker's hack. "See, here's what we speculate. Seems like after the Cold War, the organization broke off from its original masters. Control shifted into other hands."

Warily, sullenly, Bryson ventured: "Whose?"

Dunne shrugged. "Don't know. Five years ago, the organization apparently went into a period of relative dormancy: you weren't the only agent to be terminated—a whole lot of people were let go. Maybe the place was being shut down; it's impossible to say with any certainty. But now we've got reason to think it's being reactivated."

"What's that supposed to mean, 'reactivated'?"

"Not sure. That's why we decided to bring you in. We hear stuff. Your old masters appear to be accumulating arms, for some reason."

"For some reason," Bryson repeated dully.

"You could say they're poised to foment global instability—anyway, that's how our overeducated analysts might phrase it, in their Locust Valley lockjaw. But I ask myself, for what? What are they after? And I don't know. Like I say, what scares me is the stuff I don't know."

"Interesting," said Bryson sardonically. "You hear 'rumors,' you 'speculate,' you give me a goddamned digital slide show like some corporate consultant, yet you don't have the faintest clue what you're really saying."

"That's why we need you. The old Soviet system may be down, but the generals aren't down for the count. Look at General Bushalov—he's looking like a strong challenger on the political scene in Russia. Say something bad happened

that he could blame on the United States—my prediction is,
he'd be catapulted into power. Deliberative democracy?
Plenty of Russkies would say, Good riddance to that. In Beijing there's a powerful reactionary cabal within both the National People's Congress and the Central Committee. Not to
mention the Chinese Army, the PLA, the People's Liberation
Army, which is a force unto itself. No matter how you look
at it, a lot of yuan are at stake, and a lot of power is, too.
One school of thought has remnants of *Shakhmatisti* teaming
up with a handful of their Beijing brethren. But I'm just
blowing smoke out my ass. Because nobody really knows
but the bad guys, and they ain't saying."

"If you really believe all this, truly think that I was some
kind of chump in the biggest con game of the last century,
what the hell do you need me for?"

The two men locked eyes for a long while. "You appren-
ticed with one of their masterminds, one of their founders,
for Christ's sake. Gennady Rosovsky—back in Russia his
nickname was apparently *Volshebnik,* 'the Sorcerer.' Know
what that makes you?" Dunne's laugh turned into a hacking
cough again. "The sorcerer's apprentice."

"Damn you!" Bryson exploded again.

"You know how Waller's mind works. You were his best
student. You do realize what I'm asking you to do, don't
you?"

"Yeah," Bryson replied sardonically. "You want me to get
back inside."

Dunne nodded slowly. "You're our best bet. I could appeal to your patriotism, to the better angels of your being.
But goddamn if you don't owe us one."

Bryson's mind was reeling. He did not know what to
think, what to say to the CIA man.

"Don't take offense," Dunne told him, "but if we're trying
to scent them out, then at least we should send out the best
bloodhound we can find. I mean, how can I put this?" He'd
been toying with the unlit cigarette so long that tobacco
crumbs were beginning to spill from it. "You're the only one
who knows what they smell like."

CHAPTER FOUR

The strong midday sunlight bleached the buildings along this particular block of K Street, shimmered and glared against the plate-glass windows of the office buildings. Across the street, Nicholas Bryson intently watched 1324 K Street, a building at once deeply familiar and profoundly strange. Sweat rolled down his face, dampening his white dress shirt. He stood at the window of a deserted office space, tiny binoculars discreetly held to his face, curled in, and concealed by one hand. No doubt the commercial real-estate agent who had given him the keys to the vacant rental space thought it was strange that this international businessman wanted to spend a few minutes alone in what might be his office, in order to get a *feel* for it, the feng shui and all. The real-estate agent surely thought Bryson was another one of those touchy-feely New Age businessmen, but at least he'd left him alone for a while.

His pulse raced, his temples throbbed. There was nothing comforting or welcoming about the modern office building that served as the headquarters of his employer, that for so long had been home base, a place of sanctuary and renewal, an island of continuity and calm reassurance in his ever-shifting, violent world. He watched from the dark, empty office suite for a good quarter of an hour, until a knock at the door came; the real-estate agent was back and curious to know the verdict.

It was immediately apparent that 1324 K Street had changed, though the transformations were subtle. The plaques on the front of the building, announcing its occupants, had been replaced with others, though just as banal-sounding as the previous ones. Harry Dunne had told him the K Street headquarters had been abandoned, but Bryson refused to accept his assurance on face value. The Directorate was also great at hiding in plain sight. "Naked is the best disguise," Waller used to say.

So was it indeed gone? THE AMERICAN TEXTILE MANU-FACTURERS BOARD and THE UNITED STATES GRAINS PRO-DUCERS BOARD sounded just as plausible as the other notional organizations whose plaques had been put there by some creative camouflage artists within the Directorate, but what necessitated the change? Too, there were other altera-tions at 1324 K Street. In a quarter-hour of discreet surveil-lance, Bryson had seen an unusually high number of people pass through its front doors. Far too many, certainly, to be Directorate employees or blind contractors. So something different was going on here.

Maybe Dunne was right after all. But his early-warning system had been triggered. *Accept nothing at face value; question everything you're told.* Another of Ted Waller's lines. That went for Waller and Dunne and everyone else in the business for that matter.

The matter of how to get into the building without alerting its occupants was one he had been wrestling with for hours. He approached the issue as yet another fieldwork conundrum to be solved; in his mind, he had worked out dozens of in-genious methods of entry. Yet all of them carried risks with-out commensurate odds of success. Then he recalled one of Waller's—*damn it, Gennady Rosovsky's*—truisms: *When in doubt, go in the front door.* The best and most effective strat-agem would be to enter the building openly, brazenly.

Yet duplicity was a necessary part of the game plan; it would always be so. He thanked the real-estate agent, told him he was interested, and asked him to prepare a leasing agreement. He handed over one of his false business cards, and then told the man he had to rush off to another appoint-ment. He approached the building's front entrance, his senses hyperalert to any sudden movements, any shifts in crowd patterns or coloration, that might signal a threat.

So where was Ted Waller?

Where was the truth? Where was sanity?

The jarring traffic noises swelled all around him, the cacophony overwhelming. *"It's the only way you'll ever know the truth."*

"The truth about what?"

"For starters, the truth about yourself."

But where was the truth? Where were the lies?

"You believe you're a fucking unsung hero. . . . You believe you've spent fifteen years in the service of your country, working for an ultraclandestine agency known as the Directorate."

Stop it! This was madness!

Elena? You, too? Elena, the love of my life, now departed from my life as abruptly as you first appeared?

"You believe you've spent a decade and a half in the service of your country."

The blood I spilled, the gut-wrenching fear, the innumerable occasions I almost lost my life, extinguished the lives of others?

"We're talking about the greatest espionage gambit in the entire twentieth century. The whole thing was an elaborate ruse, do you see?"

"You're saying my entire life has been some kind of . . . immense deception!"

"If it makes you feel any better, you weren't alone. There were dozens just like you. It's just that you were their most spectacular success."

Insanity!

"You're the only one who knows what they smell like."

Someone crashed into him, and Bryson spun in a crouch, hands flat and stiff at his side, ready to attack. It was no professional, but instead a tall, athletic-looking executive carrying a gym bag and a squash racquet. The man fixed Bryson with a scowl contorted with fear. Bryson apologized; the executive glared and moved on, quickly, nervously.

Face it, face the past, face the truth!

Face Ted Waller, who was *not* Ted Waller! This much Bryson knew by now. He still had his own sources from the old KGB, the old GRU, men living in retirement or gone into new lines of work in a mercenary post–Cold War world.

Inquiries were made, records checked, data confirmed. Telephone calls placed, false names used, meaningless-sounding but in fact highly significant phrases employed. Men were contacted, men whom Bryson had known in a past life, a life he was sure he had left behind. A diamond dealer in Antwerp; an attorney-businessman in Copenhagen; a highly paid international trade "consultant" and "fixer" in Moscow. Once key sources all, former Soviet GRU officers who had since emigrated, left behind the spy world as Bryson thought he had. All of whom maintained records in safe-deposit boxes, stored on encrypted magnetic tape, or simply archived in their formidable brains. All of whom were surprised, some unnerved, frightened even, to be contacted by a man who had attained legend status in their former trade, who had once paid them generously for their information, their assistance. Separately, identifications were provided, checkable and confirmable several times over.

Gennady Rosovsky and Edmund Waller were one and the same. There was no doubt about it.

Ted Waller—Bryson's best man, boss, confidant, employer—was indeed a GRU sleeper agent. Once again the CIA man, Harry Dunne, was correct. *Madness!*

Arriving in the outer lobby, he noticed that the intercom panel where he had once entered a coded, constantly changing series of numbers had been removed; in its place was a glass-encased directory of law firms and lobbying organizations located within. Below each firm name was a list of its chief officers and their office numbers. He was surprised to find that the front door opened with no annunciation apparatus, no locks or barriers of any sort. Anyone could come in and out.

Beyond the glass doors, which now appeared to be of regular window glass, not bulletproof, the inner lobby looked little changed—a standard reception area with one security guard/receptionist seated behind a tall half-moon of curved marble counter. A young black man in a blue blazer and red tie looked up at him with little interest.

"I've got an appointment with—" He hesitated but a split-second as he called to mind a name from the directory in the outer lobby—"John Oakes of the American Textiles Manufacturers Board. I'm Bill Thatcher from Congressman Vaughan's office." Bryson affected a slight Texas twang; Congressman Rudy Vaughan was a powerful ranking member from Texas whose opinion, and committee chairmanships, no doubt meant quite a bit to the textile board.

The usual preliminaries were gone through. The director of the lobbying board was telephoned by security; his executive assistant had no record of any scheduled visit by Congressman Vaughan's chief legislative aide but was more than happy to accommodate such an important figure. A sprightly young woman with frosted blond hair came down and escorted Bryson into the elevator, apologizing all the while for the mix-up.

They got off on the third floor and were met right at the elevator by a blond man whose hair looked a little "refreshed," wearing an expensive suit, looking a little too polished. Mr. Oakes all but ran up to Bryson, arms outstretched. "We're grateful for Congressman Vaughan's support!" the lobbyist exclaimed, shaking Bryson's hand with both of his. In a confiding voice he added, "I know Congressman Vaughan understands the importance of keeping America strong, free of cheap, underpriced imports. I mean, *Mauritanian fabrics*—that is not what this country is about! I know the Congressman understands that."

"Congressman Vaughan is interested to learn more about the international labor standards bill that you're supporting," Bryson said, looking around as the two of them strode down the hallway that was once so familiar. Yet there were none of the old personnel, no Chris Edgecomb nor any of the others whom Bryson knew only by face. None of the communications workstations or modules, the global satellite monitors. Nothing was the same, including the office furniture. Even the floor plan had been altered, as if the entire floor had been gutted. The old small-arms storeroom was gone, replaced by a conference room with smoked-glass walls and expensive-looking mahogany table and chairs.

The too-well-dressed lobbyist led Bryson into his corner office and invited him to sit. "We understand the Congressman is up for reelection next year," the man said, "and we consider it *vital* to support those members of Congress who understand the importance of keeping America's economy strong."

Bryson nodded absently, looking around. This was the office that had once belonged to Ted Waller. If there had been even an inkling of doubt, that was now vanished. This was no notional organization, no cover.

The Directorate had vanished. There was no trace of Ted Waller, the only man who could confirm—or deny—the truth of CIA man Harry Dunne's account of the truth behind the Directorate.

Who's lying? Who's telling the truth?

How could he reach his old employers when they had vanished off the face of the earth as if they'd never existed?

Bryson had hit a wall.

Twenty minutes later, Bryson had returned to the parking garage, returned to his rented vehicle, and ran through all the checks that had once been second nature to him. The tiny pressure-sensitive filament he had pressed into place along the door handle on the driver's side was still in place, as was the filament on the passenger-side door handle; anyone who had attempted to pick the lock or otherwise gain entry to the car would have dislodged the indicators without knowing it. He knelt quickly and did a brief visual survey of the underside of the automobile, confirming that no devices had been placed there. He had not been aware of any attempts to follow him to K Street or into the parking garage, but he could no longer satisfy himself with such countersurveillance efforts. As he started the car he felt the old familiar knot in his stomach, the ganglion of tension that hadn't been there for several years. The moment of truth passed uneventfully; there was no ignition-triggered detonation.

He drove down through several levels to the garage exit,

where he inserted his magnetic-striped ticket into the card
reader that controlled the liftgate arm. The ticket popped
back out, rejected. *Damn it,* he muttered to himself. It was
almost amusing—almost, but not quite—that for all his precautions, he would be delayed by a simple mechanical glitch.
He inserted the card again; still, it failed to activate the arm.
The bored-looking parking attendant came out of his booth,
came up to Bryson's open window, and said, "Let me give
it a try, sir." The attendant inserted the ticket into the machine, but still it was rejected. He glanced at the blue paper
ticket, nodded with sudden understanding, and approached
the car window.

"Sir, is this the same ticket you were issued when you
entered?" the attendant asked, handing it back to Bryson.

"What's that supposed to mean?" Bryson said irritably.
Was the attendant questioning whether this was in fact Bryson's vehicle, whether Bryson might be trying to take someone else's? He turned to look at the attendant and was
immediately bothered by something, some aspect of the
man's hands.

"No, sir, you're misunderstanding me," the attendant said,
leaning in. Bryson suddenly felt the cold hard steel of a gun
barrel pressed against his left temple. The attendant held a
small-caliber, snub-nosed pistol to Bryson's temple! It was
insane! "I'm saying, *sir,* that I want you to keep both of your
hands on the steering wheel," said the attendant in a low,
steady voice. "I'd rather not have to use this thing."

Jesus Christ!

That was it! The hands, the manicured nails—they were
the soft, well tended hands of a man who took inordinate
care with his appearance, who likely traveled in exclusive,
moneyed circles and had to fit in—not the hands of a
parking-garage attendant. But the realization had come an
instant too late! The attendant abruptly opened the car's rear
door and leaped into the backseat, the gun once again to
Bryson's temple.

"Let's *go! Move* it!" shouted the fake attendant, just as
the barrier lifted. "*Don't* remove those hands from the wheel.

I'd hate to slip, pull the trigger by accident, you know? Let's go for a little drive, you and me. Get some fresh air."

Bryson, having stowed his weapon in his glove compartment, had no choice but to drive out of the garage and onto K Street, following the false attendant's directions. As the car entered traffic, Bryson felt the gun barrel cut into the flesh of his left temple, and he heard the low, steady, conversational banter of the man behind him.

"You knew this day was going to come, didn't you?" the professional said. "Odds are it'll happen to all of us at some point. You overstep, go a little too far. Push when you should have pulled. Stick your nose into something that's no longer your business."

"Care to fill me in on where we're going?" Bryson said, trying to keep his voice light. His heart hammered, his mind raced. He added, as an aside, "Mind if I put on the news . . . ?" He casually reached out his right hand for the radio knob, then felt the pistol's barrel slam into his head as the hit man roared, "*Goddamn* you, get those hands back on the *wheel!*"

"Jesus!" Bryson exclaimed as the pain spread. "Watch it!"

The killer had no idea that Bryson's Glock was nestled against the base of his spine, in his rear waist holster. But he was not going to take any chances.

Then how to retrieve it? The hit man—for he *was* a hit man, Bryson knew, a professional, whether on the Directorate payroll or a contract employee—insisted that Bryson keep his hands visible at all times. Now he had to follow instructions, waiting for a moment of distraction on the part of the hit man. The earmarks were in everything about the man: the confident plan of action; the quick, efficient moves; even the glib speech.

"Let's just say we're going someplace outside the Beltway, someplace where a couple of guys can talk freely." But *talking*, Bryson realized grimly, was the last thing on the hit man's agenda. "A couple of guys in the same business who just happen to be on different ends of a gun, that's all. It's nothing personal, I'm sure you realize that. Strictly business. One minute you're looking through the sights, next minute you're looking at the barrel. Happens. The wheel's always turning. I'm sure you were very good in your time, which is why I have no doubt you're going to take this like a man."

Bryson, considering his options, didn't reply. He'd been in roughly similar circumstances countless times before, though never, except during his early training days, on the other side of a pistol. He knew how the man in the seat behind him was thinking right now, the way the flow chart was patterned: *if A, then B* . . . How a sudden move on Bryson's part, a direction ignored, the steering wheel spun in the wrong direction, would initiate a countermeasure. The hit man would try to avoid pulling the trigger while they were in traffic, for fear the vehicle might careen out of control, imperiling both men. This familiarity with the options available to his enemy was one of the few cards Bryson had to play.

Yet at the same time Bryson was quite aware that the man would not hesitate to fire directly into Bryson's head if he had to, lunging forward to grab and steady the steering wheel. Bryson didn't like the odds.

Now they were crossing the Key Bridge. *"Left,"* the man barked, indicating the direction of Reagan National Airport. Bryson obeyed, careful to seem compliant, resigned, the better to put the other man off his guard.

"Now take this exit," the killer resumed. The exit would take them toward the area immediately outside the airport where most of the rental-car agencies had offices.

"You could have done me back there at the parking garage," Bryson muttered. "You *should* have, actually."

But the hit man was too skilled to be drawn into a discussion of tactics or to allow Bryson to challenge his competence. Obviously the expert had been fully briefed as to the nature of Bryson's mind, how Bryson would likely react in such a circumstance. "Oh, don't even try that," the professional said with a low chuckle. "You saw all the videocams back there, the potential witnesses. You know better than that. You wouldn't have done it there either, I'll bet. Not based on what *I* hear about your skills."

A slip there, Bryson reflected. The man was definitely a contract employee, an outsider, which meant any backup was unlikely. He would be operating on his own. A Directorate staffer would be protected by others. This was a valuable piece of data to store away.

Bryson steered the car into a deserted, vacant parking area, the far end of what was once a used-car lot. He parked as instructed. He turned his head to his right to address the other man, then felt the barrel of the gun grind painfully into his temple: the professional made no secret of his displeasure. "Don't *move,*" came the steely voice. Turning his head back around, staring straight ahead, Bryson said, "Why don't you at least make this quick?"

"So now you're feeling the way the other guys felt," said the professional, amused. "The fear, the sense of futility, of hopelessness. Of resignation."

"You're waxing entirely too philosophical for me. I'll bet you don't even know who's issuing your checks."

"Beyond the fact that they clear, I don't really care."

"No matter who they are, what they do," said Bryson quietly. "No matter whether they're working *against* the U.S. or not."

"Like I said, so long as the checks clear. I don't do politics."

"That's a pretty short-term way of thinking."

"We're in a short-term business."

"It doesn't have to be." Bryson let a moment of silence pass. "Not if we come to mutually agreeable terms. We all lock some away; it's *expected* of us. Discretionary accounts, reimbursed expenses, overstated of course—a percentage of our expense allowance salted away, laundered clean, invested in the market. Put your money to work for you. I'm willing to put some of it to work for me right now."

"To buy your own life," the professional said solemnly. "But you seem to forget that my livelihood goes beyond one transaction. You may be one account, but they're the entire goddamned bank. And you don't bet against the house."

"No, you don't bet against the house," Bryson agreed.

"You just report back that the mark was even better than you'd been led to believe, more skilled. Managed to escape, *Jesus,* the guy's good. They're not going to doubt you on that; it's what they *want* to believe anyway. You'll still keep your retainer, your deposit, and I'll double the contract amount. Sound business practice, my friend."

"Accounts are watched very carefully these days, Bryson. It's not like when you were in the game. Money is digital, and digital transactions leave tracks."

"Cash doesn't leave tracks, not if it's unsequenced."

"Everything leaves tracks these days, and you know it. Sorry, I've got a job to do. And in this case, it's facilitating suicide. You have a history of depression, you know. You had no personal life to speak of, and the groves of academe could never compare to the excitement of spy work. Your clinical depression was diagnosed by a top-rank psychiatrist and psychopharmacologist—"

"Sorry, the only shrinks I've ever seen were government-issue, years ago."

"A few *days* ago, according to your health-insurance records," replied the killer, a grim smile in his voice. "You've been seeing a shrink for over a year."

"That's *bullshit!*"

"Anything's possible in this day and age of the computerized database. Pharmacy records, too—antidepressants prescribed for you, purchased by you, along with antianxiety drugs, sleeping pills. It'll all be there. A suicide note left on your home computer, too, I'm told."

"Suicide notes are almost always handwritten, never typed or computer generated."

"Granted—we've both set up hits to look like suicides, I'm sure. But believe me, no one's ever going to dig into this that far. There'll be no postmortems for you. You have no family to request an autopsy."

The professional's words, though no doubt prescribed, still wounded, because they were the truth: he had no family, not since Elena had left. *Not since my parents were killed by the Directorate,* he added to himself bitterly.

"But let me say, I'm honored to be given this assignment," the hit man resumed. "They say you were one of the top field men, after all."

"Why do you think you were assigned?" Bryson said.

"I don't know, and I don't care. A job's a job."

"You think you're expected to survive it? You think they want you around telling tales? Who knows how much I might have told you? You think you're going to survive this last job?"

"I don't really give a shit," said the man unconvincingly.

"No, I don't think your employers ever planned to let you live," Bryson went on, grimly. "Who the hell knows *what* I spilled to you?"

"What are you trying to say?" asked the hit man after a moment of uncomfortable silence. He seemed to hesitate for an instant; Bryson could feel the grinding pressure of the pistol barrel momentarily let up. It was all the opportunity he needed, this second or two of genuine indecision on the part of his intended assassin. Quietly, he slipped his left hand off the steering wheel and slithered it down around to his back. He had the Glock! With lightning speed he pointed it toward the back of his seat and, firing blind, squeezed the trigger again and again in quick succession. Three rapid explosions filled the car's interior as the large-caliber bullets pierced the seat cushions, the noise ear-shattering. Had he hit the man? In an instant he got his answer as the barrel of the pistol fell away from the back of his head. Bryson spun around, whipping his pistol around, too, as he did so, and he realized that the man was dead, half of his forehead blown away.

They met at Langley this time, in Dunne's seventh-floor office in the Agency's new building. Standard security procedures were bypassed; Bryson was admitted to CIA headquarters with a minimum of ceremony.

"Why does it not surprise me the Directorate boys declared you beyond salvage?" Harry Dunne said with a hoarse laugh that became a sustained hacking cough. "I just think they must have forgotten who they were dealing with."

"Meaning what?"

"Meaning that you're better than anyone they can send after you, Bryson. For Christ's sake, you'd think those fucking cowboys would know that by now."

"They also know they don't want me in this office, in this *building,* spilling my guts."

"Wish you had anything to spill," replied Dunne. "But they knew how to keep all of you isolated, atomized. You don't know real names, just legends, and a fat lot of good that does us. Legends that are, or were, internal to the Directorate yield nothing in our own in-house data search. Like this 'Prospero' you keep mentioning."

"I told you, that's all I knew him as. Plus, it was over fifteen years ago. In the field, that's a geological era. Prospero was, I believe, Dutch, or at least of Dutch origins. Very resourceful operative."

"The best Agency sketch artists have produced a drawing based on your description, and we're trying to match the image against stored photographs, sketches, verbal descriptions. But the artificial-intelligence software still hasn't advanced enough yet. It's arduous, hit-or-miss work. So far we've had just one hit, as the digital hard-disk jockeys like to say. A fellow you said you worked with in Shanghai on a particularly sensitive exfiltration case."

"Sigma."

"Ogilvy. Frank Ogilvy, of Hilton Head, South Carolina. Or maybe I should say, *late* of Hilton Head."

"Moved? Transferred?"

"A crowded beach, a hot day. Seven years ago. Keeled over from a massive heart attack, apparently. Caused a minor commotion on the boardwalk that day, one witness told us, so crowded and all."

Bryson sat quietly for a moment, examining the windowless walls of Dunne's office, contemplating. Abruptly he said, "If you're looking for ants, go find yourself a picnic."

"Come again?" Dunne was once again absently shredding a cigarette.

"That was one of Waller's sayings. *If you're looking for ants, go find yourself a picnic.* Instead of looking for them where they *were,* we need to figure out where they *are.* Ask yourself: What do they need? What kind of spread are they in the *mood* for?"

Dunne put down the ruined cigarette and looked up, suddenly alert. "Weaponry, the word is. Seems they're trying to stockpile an arsenal. We think they're instigating some kind of turbulence in the southern Balkans, although their ultimate target is elsewhere."

"Weaponry." Something was turning in Nick's mind.

"Guns and ammo. But sophisticated stuff." Dunne shrugged. "Things that go boom in the night. When the bombs and bullets start flying, your own generals always start to look more appealing. Whatever they're hatching, we've got to put an end to it. By whatever means."

" 'Whatever means'?"

"You and I understand the definition. Though a straight-shooter like Richard Lanchester never could. A whole lot of good intentions, but where does all that idealism get you in the end? Notice all the saints are dead." The venerable and revered Richard Lanchester was chairman of the National Security Council in the White House. "Dick Lanchester believes in rules and regulations. But the world doesn't play by rules. Anyway, sometimes you gotta break 'em to save 'em."

"Can't play by Queensberry Rules, is that it?" Bryson said, recalling Ted Waller's words.

"Tell me how you used to get hold of weaponry. You sure weren't using U.S. government requisitions. You pick up stuff on the street, or what?"

"Actually, we were always particular about our 'instruments,' as we called them. The munitions. And you're right—given the restrictions, the deep secrecy, we had to round up the stuff ourselves. We couldn't exactly drive up to an army warehouse with a transfer order. Take a fairly typical ordnance-intensive operation—like the one in the Comoros, in 'eighty-two, where the idea was to stop a band of Executive Outcome mercenaries from overtaking the place."

"They were CIA," Dunne put in, almost wearily. "And all they were after was a dozen Brits and Americans that some loony-tunes named Colonel Patrick Denard had kidnapped and was holding for ransom."

Bryson flinched, but pressed on. "First, a few hundred Kalashnikov assault rifles. They're cheap, reliable, lightweight, and they're made in about ten different countries, so they're hard to trace. You'd want a smaller number of sniper rifles with night-vision scopes—preferably a BENS 9304 or Jaguar Night Scope. Rocket launchers, and rocket grenades, preferably CPAD Tech. Stinger missiles can come in handy—the Greeks make a lot of them under license, and they're easy to come by. You've got your Kurdish guerrillas, the PKK, raising cash by selling them to the Tamil Tigers, the LTTE."

"You're losing me."

Bryson sighed impatiently. "Where you're routing arms illegally, there's always substantial quantities that go astray. Somehow they lose a few with every truckload."

"Fall off the back of the truck."

"In a manner of speaking, yes. Then, of course, you want to stockpile ammunition rounds. That's where the amateurs would always go wrong—they end up with more guns than ammo."

Dunne looked at him strangely. "You *were* good, weren't you." It wasn't a question, and it wasn't a compliment either.

Bryson stood up suddenly, his eyes wide. "I know where to find them. Where to start, anyway. Right around this time of year"—he looked at the date on the face of his digital watch—"hell, in about ten days' time or so, there's going to be an annual floating arms bazaar off the Costa da Morte—in international waters off Spain. It's something like a twenty-year institution, as regular an event as the Macy's Thanksgiving Day parade. An immense container ship filled with major-league munitions, and a lot of major-league gunrunners to keep them company." Bryson paused. "The ship's registered name is the *Spanish Armada*."

"The picnic," Dunne said with a sly smile. "Where the ants gather. Sure. Not a bad idea."

Bryson nodded, his thoughts far away. The thought of returning to his old line of work—especially now that he realized how he was deceived into it—filled him with repugnance. Yet there was something else, too, another emotion: rage. The desire for revenge. And one more emotion as well, a quieter one: a need to *understand*, to delve into his own past. To force his way through all the secrets and lies to something like truth. A truth he could live with. "That's right," Bryson added wearily. "For any group, whether outlaw or deep-undercover governmental, that's interested in acquiring arms without official scrutiny, the *Spanish Armada* is always a picnic."

CHAPTER FIVE

The immense ship seemed to materialize out of the fog, looming vast and unlovely, as long as a city block, maybe several city blocks. It was a thousand feet long, its black hull sunk deep in the water. The supercarrier was loaded with cargo, multicolored, corrugated metal containers stacked three high and eight across, maybe ten rows from bridge to bow, each box twenty feet long and nine feet high. As the Bell 407 helicopter circled the ship and then hovered directly above the forecastle, Bryson did a quick calculation. Two hundred and forty giant boxes, and that was just on deck; belowdecks, in the hold, he knew, the ship could carry three times the number of containers above. It was an immense load of cargo, made all the more ominous by the bland sameness of the metal boxes, the contents of each a mystery.

The helicopter's lights garishly illuminated the flat, cleared deck; all the way at the stern end of the ship, the tall superstructure towered above the rows of containers, white with dark windows, its bridge bustling with modernistic-looking radar and satellite antennae. The deckhouse looked as if it belonged to another type of vessel entirely, a luxury yacht, not a freighter. For this was no mere container ship, Bryson reflected as the helicopter gently landed atop the giant H in a circle that was painted on the forecastle deck.

No, this was the *Spanish Armada,* a legend in the shadowed world of terrorists and covert operatives and other illegal, or semilegal, operators. The *Spanish Armada,* though, was no armada, no fleet: it was just the moniker of one immense ship packed with weaponry both exotic and mundane. No one knew where Calacanis, the mysterious lord of this floating arms bazaar, obtained his wares, but it was whispered that he purchased many of them quite legally from the stores of nations with too many arms and not enough cash, countries like Bulgaria and Albania and other Eastern European states; from Russia, from Korea and China. Calacanis's customers came from all over the world, or really the underworld: from Afghanistan to Congo, where dozens of civil wars raged, conflagrations stoked by illegal arms purchased by representatives of legally elected governments who came to pay their calls on this very ship, anchored thirteen nautical miles off the Spanish coast, above the relatively shallow continental shelf yet outside Spanish territorial waters, and thus free to do business, constrained by no country's laws.

Bryson removed his headset when the other three passengers did the same. He had flown to Madrid, then took a connecting flight on Iberian Airlines to La Coruña, in Galicia. He and another had boarded the helicopter at La Coruña, then made a quick stop at the harbor town of Muros, forty-seven miles southwest, and from there flew the thirteen miles to the ship. They had said little to one another beyond polite, meaningless banter. Each assumed the others were coming to shop, to strike deals with Calacanis; nothing needed to be said. One of them was Irish, probably Provo; another appeared Middle Eastern; the third Eastern European. The pilot was a sullen, equally taciturn Basque. The interior of the helicopter was luxurious, with leather seats and bubble door windows: Calacanis seemed to spare no expense anywhere.

Bryson wore a stylish Italian suit, far flashier than the conservative clothes he normally wore, purchased and tailored just for the occasion at Agency expense. He was traveling under an old Directorate legend that he had himself created some years ago.

John T. Coleridge was a shady Canadian businessman known to be deeply involved in some dirty business deals, acting as a middleman for several crime syndicates in Asia and a few outlaw states in the Persian Gulf, occasionally even a procurer for assassinations. Although Coleridge was an elusive figure, his name was known in certain circles, and that was the important thing. True, Coleridge hadn't been seen for seven years, but that wasn't so rare in this strange business.

Harry Dunne had insisted that Bryson use a new legend specially created for him by the wizards of the CIA's technical services division, graphic arts reproduction branch—master forgers who specialized in what was euphemistically called "authentication and validation." But Bryson refused. He wanted no leaks, no bureaucratic paper trails of any kind. Whether he could trust Harry Dunne was an open question; he *knew* he didn't trust Dunne's organization. Bryson had spent too many years watching and hearing tales about CIA leaks and gaffes and indiscretions to trust them. He'd provide his own cover, thank you very much.

But Bryson had never met Calacanis before, never once set foot on the *Spanish Armada,* and Basil Calacanis was famously careful about who he was willing to meet with. In his business it was too easy to get burned. So Bryson had prepared the way to ensure his acceptance here.

He had brokered an arms deal. Money hadn't changed hands—it hadn't gone that far, the deal hadn't been consummated—but he established contact with a German arms broker he had met a few times as Coleridge, who lived in a luxury hotel in Toronto and who had recently been ensnared in a web of bribes he had paid to leaders of Germany's Christian Democratic Party. Now the German was living in Canada, in fear of being extradited to Germany, where he would surely stand trial. He was also known to be badly in need of funds. So Bryson was not surprised that the German had been extremely interested in John Coleridge's proposal that they do a little business together.

Bryson made it known that, in the guise of Coleridge, he represented a consortium of generals in Zimbabwe, Rwanda, and Congo who desired to purchase some high-powered, hard-to-procure, and very expensive weaponry—which only Calacanis could provide. But Coleridge was realistic enough to know that he could hardly broker the deal without entrée to Calacanis's arms bazaar. If the German, who had done quite a bit of business with Calacanis, would make that introduction, he would get a piece of the action, a decent chunk of the commission for doing little more than sending a fax of introduction to Calacanis's ship.

As Bryson and the other passengers got out of the helicopter, they were met by a young, powerfully built, balding redheaded man who shook their hands and smiled obsequiously. He did not say their names aloud, but introduced himself as Ian.

"Thank you *so* much for coming across," Ian said in an upper-class British accent, as if they were old companions come to help a sick friend. "You've picked a fine night to pay us a visit—calm seas, full moon, couldn't ask for a more glorious evening. And you're all just in time for dinner. Please, step over this way." He indicated a spot just off the landing pad where three bulky guards toting submachine guns stood waiting. "I'm dreadfully sorry to make you go through this, but you know Sir Basil." He smiled apologetically, shrugged. "Terribly security-conscious, you know. Sir Basil can't be too careful these days."

The three swarthy guards expertly frisked the four new arrivals, glowering at them suspiciously. The Irishman was outraged and snapped at the man frisking him but made no move to stop him. Bryson had expected this ritual, and so he had brought no weapon. The guard who patted him down checked all the usual places and some of the unusual ones besides, but of course found nothing. He then asked Bryson to pop open his briefcase. "Papers," the guard said in an accent he determined was Sicilian.

The guard grunted, mollified.

Bryson looked around, noticed the Panamanian flag at the bow, saw the Class One/Explosives labels plastered over many of the containers. Certain privileged buyers were permitted to inspect the goods they were buying, actually look into the containers. But nothing was offloaded here. The *Spanish Armada* would later call at selected safe harbors, such as the port of Guayaquil, in Ecuador, which was believed to be Calacanis's home base; or Santos, in Brazil—

the two ports were the most corrupt pirates' dens in the entire hemisphere. In the Mediterranean the ship would call on the Albanian port of Vlorë, one of the world's greatest smuggling centers. In Africa, there were the ports of Lagos in Nigeria, and Monrovia in Liberia.

Bryson had passed.

He was in.

"This way, please," Ian said, gesturing toward the deckhouse, where the crew's quarters, the bridge, and Calacanis's staterooms and offices surely were. As the four passengers walked, they were shadowed at a discreet distance by the armed guards. The helicopter lifted off, and as they reached the superstructure, the racket subsided. Now Bryson could hear the familiar sounds of the sea, the gulls, the lapping waves, and he could smell the saline odor of the sea mixed with the powerful, acrid smell of the ship's diesel fuel. The moon shone brightly over the Atlantic waters.

The five men just barely fit in the small elevator that lifted them from the main deck level to the 06 deck.

When the elevator opened, Bryson was astonished. He had not seen such luxury in the yachts of the most extravagant billionaires. No expense had been spared. The floors were marble-tiled; the walls, dark mahogany paneling; the fittings, gleaming brass. He passed an entertainment center and screening room, a fitness center equipped with the most elaborate machinery, a sauna, a library. Finally they came to an enormous saloon, the owner's stateroom, which faced aft and to port. It was two levels high, and it was outfitted with an opulence rarely seen in the grandest of grand hotels.

There were four or five other men standing by a bar, which was tended by a bartender in black tie. A white-uniformed stewardess, a dazzlingly beautiful blonde with stunning green eyes, offered him a flute of Cristal champagne and smiled shyly. Bryson took the champagne, thanked her, and looked around, trying not to be too obvious about it. The marble floors were mostly covered with oriental rugs; plush sofas were arranged in seating areas; several walls were lined with books that, upon closer inspection, proved to be fake.

There were crystal chandeliers. The only peculiar touches were large fish, stuffed and mounted on the walls, evidently trophies from game fishing.

Looking at the other guests, some of whom were chatting with one another, he realized that he recognized a few of them. But who were they? His head spun; his prodigious memory was being taxed to its limit. Gradually, dossiers attached themselves to vaguely familiar faces. A Pakistani middleman, a highly placed officer in the Irish Provisional Army, a businessman and arms trader who had done more than perhaps anyone to stoke the Iran-Iraq war. These and others were middlemen, retailers, here to acquire their goods wholesale. He went cold with tension, wondering whether any of these men had met him in his previous life. Did anyone here know him, whether as Coleridge or by another one of his many identities? There was always the risk of being unmasked, being hailed by one name when he had identified himself by another. The risk went with the job; it was one of the many occupational hazards; he always had to be on the alert for such a possibility.

Still, no one gave him more than a curious glance, the sort of look cast by fellow predators who want to know their competition. None seemed to recognize him. Neither did he get that prickly feeling at the back of his head that told him he was supposed to have known any one of the men here. Slowly he felt the tension subside.

He overheard one of them muttering something about a "multimode Doppler radar," someone else mentioning Scorpions, Czech-made Striela antiair missiles.

Bryson caught the blond waitress stealing a glance at him, and he smiled pleasantly. "Where's your boss?" he asked.

She looked embarrassed. "Oh," she said. "Mr. Calacanis?"

"Who else could I mean?"

"He will be joining his guests for dinner, sir. May I offer you caviar, Mr. Coleridge?"

"Never liked the stuff. Al-Biqa?"

"Pardon me?"

"Your accent. It's a Levantine dialect of Arab, from the Bekaa Valley, am I right?"

The waitress blushed. "Nice party trick."

"I see Mr. Calacanis draws from all over. Sort of an equal-opportunity employer."

"Well, the captain is Italian, the officers are Croatian, the crew Filipino."

"It's like a model U.N. here."

She smiled bashfully.

"And the clients?" Bryson persisted. "Where do they come from?"

Her smile faded at once, her manner suddenly cold. "I never ask, sir. Please excuse me."

Bryson knew he had pushed too far. Calacanis's staff would be friendly but above all discreet. It would not do to ask about the man himself, of course, but between Dunne's briefing and his own time with the Directorate, he had managed to put together a profile. Vasiliou Calacanis was a Greek born in Turkey to a good family, was sent to Eton with a son of one of England's most powerful arms-manufacturing families, and somehow thereafter—no one knew for sure how—established an alliance with the classmate's family, then went into business selling arms on behalf of the British family to the Greeks fighting the Cypriots. Somewhere along the way, powerful British politicians were paid off, potent connections established, and Vasiliou became Basil and then Sir Basil. He belonged to the best London clubs. His ties to the French were even stronger; one of his main residences was an enormous château on the Avenue Foch in Paris where he entertained regularly the powers from the Quai d'Orsay.

After the collapse of the Berlin Wall, he did a major trade in surplus Eastern European weaponry, particularly dealing with Bulgaria. He profited immensely from selling to both sides of the Iran-Iraq war, shipping scores of helicopters to both. He struck major deals with the Libyans, the Ugandans. From Afghanistan to Congo, several dozen civil wars raged, ethnic and nationalist conflagrations, which Calacanis had fueled by providing easy access to assault rifles, mortars, pistols, land mines, and rockets. He had furnished his yacht-cum-freighter with the blood of hundreds of thousands of innocents.

One of the stewards began to speak discreetly to each of the guests one by one. "Dinner is served, Mr. Coleridge," he said.

The dining room was even more opulent, more outlandishly extravagant, than the stateroom from which they came. On each wall was painted a fantasy mural of the sea, so that it appeared as if they were dining alfresco, on a calm ocean during a bright afternoon, surrounded by graceful sailboats. The long table was covered in a white linen cloth, set with crystal and candles, beneath a great crystal chandelier.

One of the stewards escorted Bryson to a seat near the head of the table, next to a very large barrel-chested man with a close-cropped gray beard and olive complexion. The steward inclined his head toward the great bearded man, whispering something.

"Mr. Coleridge," said Basil Calacanis in the deep rumble of a Russian basso profundo. He extended his hand to Bryson. "Pardon me if I don't get up."

Bryson shook Calacanis's hand firmly as he took his seat. "Not at all. It's a pleasure to meet you. I've heard so much about you."

"Likewise, and likewise. I'm surprised it's taken us so long to meet."

"It's taken me altogether too long to eliminate the middleman," Bryson said wryly. "I got tired of paying retail." Calacanis responded with a booming laugh. As the others were seated around the table, they pretended not to be eavesdropping upon the exchange between their host and his mysterious, favored guest. Bryson noticed one of the dinner guests who seemed to be listening intently, a guest he had not seen at the bar. This was a stylishly dressed man in a pinstriped double-breasted suit with a shoulder-length mane of silver hair. Bryson felt himself go cold with foreboding; the man was familiar to him. Though they had never met each other, Bryson knew the face from surveillance videos and photographs in dossiers. He was a Frenchman who moved nimbly in these circles, a renowned contact for extremist terrorist groups. Bryson could not recall the name, but he knew the longhaired man was an emissary from a powerful, far-right French arms dealer named Jacques Arnaud. Did that mean that Arnaud was supplying Calacanis, or the other way around?

"Had I but known how pleasant it is to shop here, I'd have come long ago," Bryson continued. "This is an extraordinary ship."

"You flatter me," the arms dealer said dismissively. " 'Extraordinary' is hardly the word I would use for this old rust bucket. She's just barely seaworthy. Though you should have seen her when I bought it a good ten years ago from the Maersk shipping line. They were retiring the old tub, and I'm never one to pass up a bargain. But I'm afraid Maersk got the best of me there. The damned boat was badly in need of repair and repainting. Plus about a ton of rust had to be scraped off." He snapped his fingers in the air, and the beautiful blond stewardess appeared with a bottle of Chassagne-Montrachet, pouring a glass for Calacanis and then for Bryson. She barely acknowledged Bryson's presence. Calacanis lifted his glass in Bryson's direction and said with a wink, "To the spoils of war." Bryson toasted as well. "Anyway, the *Spanish Armada* sails at a decent clip—twenty-five, thirty knots—but she gulps two hundred and fifty tons of fuel a day. This is what you Americans call overhead, hmm?"

"I'm Canadian, actually," Bryson said, suddenly alert. Calacanis did not seem the sort of man who made such slips. He casually added, "I doubt she came furnished like this."

"The damned living quarters looked like an old city hospital." Calacanis was looking around the table. "They never come with the amenities one requires. So, Mr. Coleridge, I understand your clients are Africans, is that right?"

"My clients," Bryson said with a polite smile, the avatar of discretion, "are highly motivated buyers."

Calacanis gave another wink. "The Africans have always been some of my best customers—the Congo, Angola, Eritrea. You've always got one faction battling another one down there, and somehow there always seems to be plenty of money on both sides. Let me guess: they're interested in plain-vanilla AK-47s, crates of ammo, landmines, grenades. Maybe rocket-propelled grenades. Sniper rifles with night-vision sights. Antitank weapons. Am I barking up the right tree?"

Bryson shrugged. "Your Kalashnikovs—they're genuine Russian?"

"Forget Russian. That stuff's crap. I've got boxes of Bulgarian Kalashnikovs."

"Ah, nothing but the best for *you*."

Calacanis smiled in appreciation. "Quite so. The Kalashnikovs made by Arsenal, in Bulgaria, are still the finest ones around. Dr. Kalashnikov himself prefers the Bulgarian make. How do you know Hans-Friedrich again?"

"I helped him broker a number of big sales of Thyssen A. G. Fuchs tanks to Saudi Arabia. I introduced him to some oil-soaked friends in the Gulf. Anyway, as for the Kalashnikovs, I'll certainly defer to your expertise," Bryson said graciously. "And assault rifles—"

"For those you simply can't do better than the South African Vektor 5.56mm CR21. Terribly sleek. Once they've tried it, they'll never use anything else. Its integral Vektor reflex optical sight can enhance the probability of a first-time hit by sixty percent. Even if you don't know what the hell you're doing."

"Depleted uranium shells?"

Calacanis arched an eyebrow. "I may be able to dig some up for you. Interesting choice. Twice as heavy as lead, the best antitank weapon you can find. Slices through tanks like a hot knife through butter. And radioactive besides. You say your clients are from Rwanda and Congo?"

"I don't believe I said." The back-and-forth was stretching Bryson's nerves to the breaking point. It was not a negotiation, it was a gavotte, a highly orchestrated dance, each partner watching the other closely, waiting for a misstep. There was something about Calacanis's manner that seemed to indicate he knew more than he was letting on. Did the wily arms merchant accept John T. Coleridge at face value? What if his web of contacts extended deeply, *too* deeply, into the intelligence world? What if somehow, in the years since Bryson had left the Directorate, the Coleridge legend had been rolled up, exposed as fiction by a hypercautious—or vengeful—Ted Waller?

A tiny cellular phone on the table next to Calacanis's dinner plate suddenly rang. Calacanis picked it up and said harshly, "What is it? . . . Yes, Chicky, but he has no credit line with us, I'm afraid." He disconnected the call and placed the phone back on the table.

"My clients are interested in Stinger missiles as well."

"Ah, yes, these are very much in demand. Every terrorist and guerrilla group seems to want a crate of them these days. Thanks to the U.S. government, there's quite a decent inventory of them floating around. The Americans used to pass them out to their friends like candy. Then in the late 1980s some of them found their way onto Iranian gunboats and shot down U.S. Navy helicopters in the Gulf, and suddenly the U.S. was in the embarrassing position of having to buy them back. Washington's offering a hundred thousand dollars for the return of each Stinger, which is four *times* their original cost. Of course, I pay better." Calacanis fell silent, and Bryson realized that the blond stewardess was standing to the Greek's right, bearing a covered serving tray. When Calacanis nodded, she began to serve him a breathtakingly elaborate timbale of salmon tartare with pearly black caviar.

"I take it Washington's a good customer of yours as well," Bryson suggested quietly.

"They have, how do you say, deep pockets," Calacanis murmured vaguely.

"But in certain circles one hears that the *pattern* of buying is being stepped up recently," he went on in a low tone of voice. "That certain organizations in Washington, certain covert agencies that have the latitude to operate without over-

sight, have been acquiring rather . . . *heavily* from you."
Bryson tried to affect a casual tone, but Calacanis saw right
through it and gave Bryson a sidelong glance. "Are you interested in my wares, or in my clients?" the arms dealer said
coldly.

Bryson felt himself go numb, realizing how badly he'd
miscalculated.

Calacanis started to get up. "Will you excuse me, please?
I believe I'm neglecting my other . . . guests."

Quickly, in a low, confiding voice, Bryson said, "I ask
for a reason. A *business* reason."

Calacanis turned to him warily. "What sort of business
can you possibly have with government agencies?"

"I have something to offer," Bryson said. "Something that
might be of interest to a major player not officially connected
with a government but who has, as you put it, deep pockets."

"*You* have something to offer *me?* I'm afraid I don't understand. If you wish to transact your own business, you
certainly don't need me."

"In this case," Bryson said, lowering his voice yet further,
"there's no other acceptable conduit."

"*Conduit?*" Calacanis seemed exasperated. "What on
earth are you *talking* about?"

Bryson was almost whispering now. Calacanis bent his
head to listen. "Plans," Bryson muttered. "Blueprints, specifications that may be worth a great deal of money to certain
parties with, shall we say, unlimited budgets. But in no way
can my fingerprints be on this. I can't be connected in any
way. Your services as conduit, as middleman, for want of a
better word, will be remunerated quite handsomely."

"You intrigue me," Calacanis said. "I think we should
continue this discussion in private."

Calacanis's library was furnished in delicate French antiques
that were invisibly bolted to the floor. Roman blinds and
curtains covered two glass walls; the other walls were decorated with framed antique nautical charts and maps. In the

middle of one wall was a paneled oak door; where it led, Bryson had no idea.

That the Greek had been so quick to leave his own dinner party was testament to the allure of the blueprints and specification sheets Calacanis now held in his hand. They had been prepared by the graphic artists of the Agency's technical services division, designed to pass close inspection by an arms dealer with long experience in reading such plans.

Calacanis made no attempt to hide his excitement. He looked up from the blueprint, his dark eyes gleaming with avarice. "This is a new generation of the JAVELIN antitank weapon system," he said in hushed awe. "Where the *hell* did you get this?"

Bryson smiled modestly. "You don't divulge trade secrets, and neither do I."

"Lightweight, man-portable, fire-and-forget. The round's the same—the 127-millimeter-diameter missile, of course— but the command launch unit appears to have gotten far more sophisticated, highly resistant to countermeasures. If I'm reading this right, the hit rate's now almost one hundred percent!"

Bryson nodded. "So I'm given to understand."

"Do you have the source codes?"

Bryson knew he meant the software that would allow the weapon to be reverse-engineered. "Indeed."

"There will be no shortage of interested parties; the only question will be who has the resources. This will fetch quite a price."

"I take it you have a customer in mind."

"He's on board the ship at this very moment."

"At dinner?"

"He very politely turned down my invitation. He prefers not to mingle. At the moment he's inspecting the goods." Calacanis picked up his cellular phone and punched out a number. As he waited for it to ring, he remarked, "This gentleman's organization has been on quite the buying spree of late. Massive quantities of mobile armaments. A weapon such as this will interest him, I have no doubt of it, and money seems to be no object for his employers." He paused and said into the phone, "Can you ask Mr. Jenrette to stop by the library, please?"

The interested party, as Calacanis had identified him, appeared at the door of the library barely five minutes later, escorted by the balding redheaded man named Ian who had first greeted Bryson at the helicopter.

His name was Jenrette, but Bryson knew at once that "Jenrette" was only the latest in a series of cover identities. As the middle-aged, tired-looking man with the scraggly gray hair crossed the study to Calacanis's desk, his eyes met Bryson's.

Kowloon.

The rooftop bar at the Miramar Hotel.

Jenrette was a Directorate operative he knew as Vance Gifford.

"This gentleman's organization has been on quite the buying spree of late. Massive quantities of mobile armaments. A weapon such as this will interest him, I have no doubt of it, and money seems to be no object for his employers."

Money no object . . . this gentleman's organization . . . quite the buying spree.

Vance Gifford was still attached to the Directorate, which meant that Harry Dunne was right: the Directorate still lived.

"Mr. Jenrette," said Calacanis, "I'd like you to meet a gentleman who has an interesting new toy I think you and your friends might like to purchase." Ian the bodyguard and aide-de-camp stood with his back erect against the doorjamb, watching in silence.

Vance Gifford stared in shock for the briefest instant before his expression softened, and he gave a smile that Bryson immediately recognized as false. "Mr.—Mr. Coleridge, is it?"

"Please call me John," Bryson said casually. His body was paralyzed; his mind raced.

"Why do I have a feeling we've met somewhere before?" said the Directorate man, feigning joviality.

Bryson chuckled, causing his body to relax. But it was a feint, a ruse, for he was studying the man's eyes, the minute changes in facial musculature that signaled the truth beneath the lie. *Vance Gifford is an active, present Directorate operative.* Bryson was sure of it.

He was active when they met eight or nine years ago in East Sector, a strictly scheduled rendezvous in the Miramar bar in Kowloon. *We barely knew each other, spent maybe an hour talking business, covert funding and dead drops and the like. Given the compartmentalization, neither one of us had any idea what the other really did in the organization.*

And Gifford had to be active still, otherwise Calacanis wouldn't have summoned him here to inspect the prototype— the lure.

"Was it Hong Kong?" Bryson asked. "Taipei? You look familiar as well." Bryson acted blasé, even amused by the unspecified, unexplained mix-up in identities. But his heart was racing. He felt perspiration break out on his brow. His field instincts were still there, still finely honed; but his psychology, his emotions, were no longer in the proper, hardened condition. *Gifford's playing it straight,* Bryson realized. *He knows who I am, but he doesn't know why I'm here. Like a seasoned field man, he's rolling with it, thank God.* "Anyway, wherever and whenever it was, it's good to see you again."

"I'm always in the market for a new toy," the Directorate man said offhandedly. Gifford/Jenrette's eyes were keen; they regarded Bryson furtively. *Surely he knows I'm out.* When a Directorate agent was burned, the word was circulated at lightning speed, to prevent infiltration attempts on the part of the disenfranchised one. *But how much does he know of the circumstances of my termination? Does he regard me as a hostile? Or as a neutral? Will he assume that I've gone private, like so many covert operatives did after the end of the Cold War, gone into military procurement? Yet Gifford's smart: he knows he's being offered stolen top-*

secret technology, and he knows that's hardly an ordinary business deal, even in this strange world of black-market arms dealing.

One of several things can happen now. He may assume he's being set up, offered bait with a hook in it. If he does, then he'll conclude I've gone over—to another government agency, even another side! Baited hooks were a classic recruitment technique employed by the main foreign intelligence services. Bryson's mind whirled. *Maybe he'll assume I'm part of some interagency, internecine bureaucratic battle, a sting of some sort.*

Or worse—what if Gifford suspects me of being an impostor, of running an operation against Calacanis, maybe even against Calacanis's clients?

This was madness! There was no way to anticipate Gifford's response, no way to be sure. The only thing was to be prepared for anything.

Calacanis's face betrayed nothing. The Greek beckoned the Directorate man to his desk, across which he had spread out the blueprints and specs and source codes for the sophisticated weapon design. Gifford walked over and bent down to inspect the plans with great intensity.

Gifford's lips barely moved while he whispered something to the arms merchant without looking at him.

Calacanis nodded, looked up, and said blandly, "Will you please excuse us, Mr. Coleridge? Mr. Jenrette and I should like to confer privately."

Calacanis rose and opened the oak paneled door, which Bryson now saw led to a private study. Jenrette followed, and the door closed behind them. Bryson sat on one of Calacanis's antique French side chairs, frozen like an insect trapped in amber. Outwardly he was waiting patiently, a middleman greedily contemplating great riches from a deal about to be consummated. Inwardly his mind was spinning, desperately trying to anticipate the next move. It all came down to how Jenrette decided to play it. What had the man whispered? How could Jenrette reveal how he knew Bryson without telling Calacanis about his work with the Directorate?

Was Jenrette prepared to do that? How much could be divulged? How deep was Jenrette's cover? These were unknowable things, fundamentally. Too, the man who called himself Jenrette had no idea what Bryson was doing here. For all he knew, Bryson had indeed gone private and was selling weapons designs; how could Jenrette/Gifford know otherwise?

The study door opened, and Bryson looked up. It was the blond stewardess, holding aloft a tray of empty glasses and a bottle of what looked like port. Obviously she had been summoned by the Greek and had entered Calacanis's private study by means of another passage. She seemed not to notice Bryson as she retrieved used champagne flutes and wineglasses from the desk Calacanis had been using, then approached Bryson. Briefly stooping to pick up a large glass ashtray, laden with the remains of Cuban cigars, from the small end table next to Bryson, she suddenly spoke, her words low and almost inaudible.

"You're a popular man, Mr. Coleridge," she murmured without even giving him so much as a glance. She placed the ashtray on her serving platter. "Four friends of yours await you in the next room." Bryson looked up at her, saw her eyes dart to the oak paneled door on the other side of the library. "Try not to bleed on the Heriz runner. It's quite rare, and one of Mr. Calacanis's favorites." Then she was gone.

Bryson stiffened, his body surging with adrenaline. Yet he knew enough to keep still, betray nothing.

What did this mean?

Was an ambush being set up in the adjacent study? Was she part of the setup? If not—why had she just warned him?

The door to Calacanis's study suddenly opened again. It was Calacanis himself, with Ian, his bodyguard, looming just behind him in the doorway. Gifford/Jenrette stood farther in the background.

"Mr. Coleridge," Calacanis called out, "won't you join us, please?"

For a split-second Bryson stared, trying to assess the

Greek's intentions. "Certainly," he replied, "in a moment. I think I left something important in the bar."

"Mr. Coleridge, I'm afraid we really have no time to waste," Calacanis said in a loud, harsh voice.

"This won't take a minute," Bryson said, turning toward the exit door that led to the dining room. It was blocked, he now saw, by another armed guard. But instead of staying put, Bryson continued his stride toward the exit as if nothing were wrong. Now he was but a few feet away from the stocky bodyguard who had just arrived.

"I'm sorry, Mr. Coleridge, we really must have a word, you and I," Calacanis said with a slight nod that was clearly a signal to the guard at the door. Bryson's body surged with adrenaline as the stocky bodyguard turned to secure the door.

Now!

He lunged forward, slamming the bodyguard against the hard wooden doorframe of the open door, the sudden movement catching the bodyguard unprepared. The guard struggled, reaching for his weapon, but Bryson hammered his right foot into the man's abdomen.

An alarm suddenly went off, ear-piercingly loud, clearly triggered by Calacanis, who was shouting. As the bodyguard momentarily lost his balance, Bryson took advantage of the brief moment of vulnerability to sink his right knee into the man's midsection, at the same time gripping the face with his right hand and forcing him to the floor.

"Stop right there!" thundered Calacanis.

Bryson turned quickly and saw that Ian, the other bodyguard, had assumed a marksman's stance, leveling a gun, a .38 caliber pistol, with both hands.

In that instant, the stocky bodyguard beneath him managed to rear up, screaming, exerting all of his strength, but Bryson leveraged that motion against his adversary, pushing the man up and over, his right hand clawing the bodyguard's eyes, so that the man's head was a shield of sorts, right in front of his own face. Ian would never fire with such a high probability of striking another guard.

Suddenly there was an explosion, and Bryson felt the

spray of blood. A dark red hole appeared in the middle of the bodyguard's forehead; the man slumped, dead weight. Ian had, surely by accident, killed his own colleague.

Now Bryson pivoted, arced his body suddenly to one side, just missing the explosion of another bullet, and spun through the open door and into the hallway. Bullets exploded behind him, splintering wood and pock-marking the metal bulkheads. With alarms shrieking all around him at deafening volume, he broke into a run down the corridor.

WASHINGTON, D.C.

"Let's face it. You're not going to be deterred whatever I say, isn't that right?" Roger Fry looked at Senator James Cassidy expectantly. In the four years that Fry had been his chief of staff, he had helped draft policy statements for the Hill and speeches for the hustings. The Senator had turned to him whenever a thorny issue arose. Fry, a slight, red-haired man in his early forties, was someone he could always depend upon for an instant electoral read. Price supports for dairy farmers? City advocates could cry bloody murder if you took one position, while the agribusiness lobby would come after you if you took the other. Often enough, Fry would say, "Jim, it's a wash—vote your conscience," knowing that Cassidy had made a career of doing so anyway.

The late-afternoon sun streamed through the venetian blinds, casting slats of shadows on the floor of his Senate office and bringing out the glow from Cassidy's burnished mahogany desk. The senator from Massachusetts looked up from his briefing papers and met Fry's gaze. "I hope you realize how valuable you are to me, Rog," he said, a smile playing at his lips. "It's because you're so good at looking after the pragmatic, temporizing, horse-trading side of this business that, every once in a while, I can actually get on my hind legs and say what I believe."

Fry was always struck by how distinguished, how damned *senatorial* Cassidy looked: the coifed mane of wavy silver hair, the chiseled features. A little over six feet, the senator was photogenic with his broad face and high cheekbones, but up close, the eyes were what made him: they could grow warm and intimate, making constituents feel as if they'd found a soul mate, or turn cool and unsparing, drilling through a squirrelly witness who'd come before his committee.

"Every once in a while?" Fry shook his head. "Too damn often, if you ask me. Too damned often for your own political health. And one of these days, it's going to catch up with you. The last election wasn't a walk in the park, if I may remind you."

"You worry too much, Rog."

"Somebody has to, around here."

"Listen, the constituents care about these things. Did I show you this letter?" It was from a woman who lived on Massachusetts's north shore. She had sued a marketing company and discovered they had thirty single-spaced pages of information on her, going back fifteen years. The company knew, and was in the business of selling, more than nine hundred separate items of information about her—including her choice of sleeping aids and antacids and hemorrhoid ointments and the soap she used when she showered; it itemized her divorce, medical procedures, credit ratings, her every traffic infraction. But there was nothing unusual about this; the company had similar dossiers on millions of Americans. The only thing unusual was that she found out about it. That letter, and a few dozen like it, was what first aroused Cassidy's concern.

"You forget, Jim, I answered that letter personally," replied Fry. "I'm just saying you don't know what you're stirring up this time around. This goes to the heart of the way business works today."

"That's why it's worth talking about," said the senator quietly.

"Sometimes it's more important to live and fight another day." But Fry knew what Cassidy was like when he had a bee in his bonnet: moral outrage would trump the cool calculation of political interest. The senator wasn't a saint: he sometimes drank too much and, especially in his early years when his hair was a glossy black, slept around too freely. At the same time, Cassidy had always maintained a core of political integrity: all things being equal, he did try to do the right thing, at least where the rightness of the thing was as clear as the political cost of doing so. It was a strain of idealism that Fry railed against and, almost despite himself, respected.

"You remember how Ambrose Bierce defined a statesman?" The senator winked at him. "A politician who, as a result of equal pressure from all sides, remains upright."

"I was in the cloakroom yesterday and found out you've got a new nickname," Fry said, smiling thinly. "You'll like this one, Jim: 'Senator Cassandra.' "

Cassidy frowned. "Nobody listened to Cassandra—but they should have," he grunted. "At least she could say she told 'em so. . . ." He broke off. They'd been through it; they'd had this conversation. Fry was being protective of him, and Cassidy had heard him out. But on this subject, there wasn't anything left to talk about.

Senator Cassidy was going to do what he was going to do, and there was no stopping him.

No matter what it cost.

CHAPTER SIX

Footsteps thundered behind him on the steel deck as Bryson raced toward the center stairwell. Spying the elevator, he paused but a split-second before he rejected that option; the elevator moved slowly, and once inside it, he would be in a vertical coffin, easy prey for anyone able to shut off the elevator mechanism. No, he would take the stairs, noisy as they were. There was no other way out of the superstructure. He had no choice. *Up or down?* Up toward the wheelhouse, the bridge, would be an unexpected move, yet it risked his getting trapped on an upper deck with few egresses. No, that was a bad idea; down was the only way that made sense, down to the main deck and escape.

Escape? How? There was only one way off the ship, and that was off the main deck and into the water—whether by jumping, which was suicide in these cold Atlantic waters, or down the gangplank, which was too slow and too exposed a descent.

Jesus! There was no way out!

No, he mustn't think that way; there had to be a way out, and he would find it.

He was like a rat in a maze; that he didn't know the layout of this immense ship put him at a distinct disadvantage to his pursuers. Yet the very size of the vessel guaranteed endless passages in which to lose the chasers, hide if needed.

He vaulted to the stairs and began taking them two and three at a time, while above him came shouts. One of the bodyguards was dead, but there were no doubt quite a few others, alerted and summoned by the various alarms and by two-way radios. The footsteps and shouts grew increasingly loud and frantic from the stairwell. His pursuers had increased in number, and it was likely a matter of just seconds before others emerged from other parts of the ship.

The ship's whistles and alarms sounded in a cacophony

of raucous whoops and metallic grunts. A landing led to a short passageway that seemed to open onto an outside section of a deck. Quietly he opened the door, closed it behind him silently, ran straight ahead, and found himself on the aft deck, open to the elements. The sky was black, the waves lapped gently at the stern. He ran to the railing, looking for the welded steel grips and steps one sometimes found on the side of ships that were used for emergency escape. He could climb down to another level of the ship, he quickly thought, and lose them that way.

But there were no steel grips on the hull. The only way out of here was down.

Suddenly there came the explosion of gunfire. A bullet ricocheted off a metal capstan with a high-pitched pinging sound. He spun away from the railing and into the shadow behind a steel mooring winch on which the steel hawse cable was wound around capstan drums, like some giant spool of thread, then dove behind it for cover. Another round of bullets pitted the metal just a few feet from his head.

They were firing without restraint here, and he realized that with the open sea behind him they could fire heedlessly without fear of damaging any of the ship's delicate navigational equipment.

Inside the ship they would have to be more careful when firing rounds. And that was his protection! They would not hesitate to kill him, but they would not want to damage their ship—or its precious cargo.

He would have to get out of the open areas and back into the belly of the ship. Not only would hiding places be numerous there, but he could take advantage of their hesitance to fire freely.

But now what? Here he was, trapped out in the open, with only a great steel capstan as protection. This was the most hazardous place for him on the entire ship.

There seemed to be two or three gunmen here, no more and no less. Clearly he was outnumbered. He needed to divert them, misdirect them, but how? Looking around wildly, he spotted something. Behind an iron bollard, a tall cylinder rising several feet from the deck, he noticed a paint can, left there no doubt by a deckhand. He crawled forward along the deck and grabbed the can. It was almost empty.

There was a sudden burst of gunfire as he was spotted.

He drew back quickly, grasping the handle of the can, then immediately hurling it forward toward the railing, where it struck the hawse pipe. He peered around the barricade, saw both men turn toward the source of the clatter. One of them ran toward it, away from where Bryson had concealed himself. The other spun around in a classic marksman's position, looking from one side to another. As the first man raced toward the starboard side of the ship, the second circled around toward the port side, his weapon pointed toward the mooring winch the whole time. This man saw through the ruse, suspected Bryson of having caused the diversion, believed Bryson was still huddled behind the winch.

But he did not expect Bryson to come around the winch toward him. Now Bryson was just a few feet away from the second security guard. A sudden shout came from the first man, a declaration that Bryson was not there, an unprofessional move. The second man, just inches away from Bryson, turned, distracted.

Move!

Now!

Bryson lunged and tackled the man to the deck, slamming his knee into the man's stomach. The man gasped as the air left his lungs, and as he reared up, Bryson slammed his elbow into the man's throat. He could hear the crunch of cartilage as he vised the man's throat in a hammerlock. The man roared in pain, which gave Bryson the opportunity he needed to grab the security man's gun, try to wrench it out of his hand. But the security guard was a professional, and he would not give his weapon up so easily; despite the great pain Bryson was inflicting, Calacanis's soldier struggled, refusing to yield the pistol. Gunfire came from the other side of the deck, fired by the first gunman as he ran toward his colleague, which was jarring his aim. Bryson twisted the weapon around until the man's wrist cracked; the ligaments tore audibly, and the gun now turned back toward the man's own chest. His index finger jabbed at the trigger, finally grabbed it, and Bryson bent his wrist and fired.

The soldier arched backward, his chest punctured. Bryson's aim was perfect, even in the confusion of the struggle; he had hit the man's heart.

Grabbing the weapon from the limp fingers, he sprung to his feet and began firing wildly in the general direction of the running man, who stopped to fire back, knowing that firing while running made for terrible aim. That instant's pause was the window Bryson needed. He let loose a volley of semiautomatic fire, one round piercing his attacker's forehead. The man toppled to one side, crumpled against the railing, dead.

For a few seconds he was safe, Bryson calculated. But he could hear footsteps on the deck, growing louder and coming closer, and he heard the accompanying shouts, and that told him he was hardly safe at all.

Now where?

Immediately up ahead he saw a door marked DIESEL GENERATOR ROOM. This had to lead to the engine room, which at the moment seemed the best place to escape. He raced across the deck, yanked open the door, and ran down a steep, narrow set of metal stairs painted green. He was in a large, open area that was deafeningly loud. The auxiliary diesel generators here were in operation, providing power for the ship, since its engine was off. With several large strides he ran across a railing that circled the room above the mammoth generators.

Through the rumble he could hear that his pursuers had followed him down here, and in a moment he saw several silhouetted figures racing down the metal steps, visible only as shadows in the dim light with its sickly green cast.

There were four of them, running down the steep stairways with a stiffness, an awkwardness, that puzzled him for a moment, until he saw that two of them were wearing night-vision goggles, the others carrying sniper rifles outfitted with night-vision scopes. The outlines were unmistakable.

He raised the stolen pistol, quickly aimed at the first man down the stairs, and—

Suddenly all was darkness!

The lights in the room had been extinguished, probably from some central control room. No wonder they carried such equipment! By eliminating all light they hoped to gain the advantage provided by their sophisticated weaponry. On a ship such as this, a floating arsenal, there would be no shortage of such matériel.

But he fired anyway, into the darkness, in the direction toward which he had been aiming just a second or two ago. He heard a cry, then a crash. One man was down. But it was insanity to just keep firing into the darkness, using up precious ammunition when he had no idea how many rounds remained in the weapon and had no way to obtain any more.

It was what they wanted him to do.

They expected him to respond like a cornered animal, a drowning rat. To flail away desperately. To fire into the darkness with abandon. Use up the ammunition pointlessly, foolishly. And then, aided by their night vision, they would easily hunt him down.

Blinded in the darkness, he extended his arms, felt around for obstacles, both to avoid and to hide behind. The men wearing infrared monocular night-vision units, the lenses strapped against their eyes by means of a head harness and helmet mount, were doubtless also carrying handguns. The others had rifles fitted with advanced infrared weapon sights. Both allowed the user to see in total darkness by detecting the differentials in thermal patterns given off by animate and inanimate objects. Short-range thermal-imaging scopes had been used with great success during the Falklands war in 1982, in the Gulf in 1991. But these, Bryson recognized, were state-of-the-art RAPTOR night-vision weapon sights, lightweight, super accurate, with extreme long-range accuracy. They were often used by combat snipers, mounted on their .50 caliber sniper rifles.

Oh, dear God. The playing field was hardly level, as if it ever was. The noise of the generator seemed, in the darkness, even louder.

In the pitch blackness he saw a tiny, dancing red dot flit across his field of vision.

Someone had located him and was aiming directly at his face, his eyes!

Triangulate! Estimate the sniper's location based on the direction from which the infrared reticule was aiming at him. This wasn't his first time as the target of a sniper with a night-vision scope, and he had learned to estimate the distance of the shooter.

But every second he paused to aim gave his enemy, who saw him as a green object against a darker green or black background, time to aim as well. And his enemy knew for certain where he was located, whereas Bryson was relying on luck and rusty experience. And how could he possibly aim at blackness? What was there to aim at?

He squinted to bring up available light, but there really was none to be summoned into his eyes. Instead, he raised his pistol and fired.

A scream!

He had hit someone, though how well he couldn't yet tell.

But a second or two afterward, a bullet spat against the machinery to his left, pinging loudly. Night vision or no, his enemies had missed. They did not seem to care whether their rounds struck the generator or not. The machinery was encased in steel, heavy-gauge and durable.

That meant they did not care what they hit, or whether they missed.

So how many more were there? If the second man was indeed down, that meant two remained. The problem was that the generator was so loud he could not hear footsteps approaching, nor the ragged breathing of a wounded man. He was in effect both blind *and* deaf.

As he raced down the catwalk, one hand outstretched before him to protect him from striking unseen objects, the other grasping his weapon, he heard gunfire again. One round whizzed so close to his head he could feel the gust of wind against his scalp.

Then his searching hand struck something hard—a bulkhead. He had come to a wall at one end of the cavernous room. He swung his weapon first to one side, then to the other, each time striking steel railing.

He was trapped.

Then he became aware of the dancing red bead in the darkness, as one of the snipers aimed at the green oval that was, in the night-vision scope, his head.

He thrust the pistol into the air in front of himself, prepared to aim at nothing again. Then he shouted: "Go ahead! If you miss me, you risk damaging the generator. That's a lot of delicate electronic equipment there, microchips easily shattered. Kill the generator, and you kill all the power in the ship—and see what Calacanis thinks about that."

A split-second of silence. He even thought he saw the red dot waver, though he knew he might be imagining things.

There was a low chuckle, and the infrared reticule passed across his field of vision again, steadied, and then—

The spit of a silenced weapon, and then three more spits, and then came a scream and the sound of another body crashing to the steel floor of the catwalk.

What?

Who had fired at his enemy? Someone had done it—Bryson knew it hadn't been him! Someone had fired a round of shots using a silenced pistol.

Someone had fired at his pursuers—and perhaps even eliminated them!

"Don't move!" Bryson shouted into the darkness at the one remaining gunman he calculated had to be out there. His cry made no sense, he knew—why should any of his adversaries, equipped as they were with night-vision goggles or sights, pay any attention?—but such a shout, unexpected and even illogical, could buy him a few seconds of confusion.

"Don't shoot!" came another voice, faint against the deafening noise of the generators.

A woman's.

It was the voice of a woman.

Bryson froze. He thought he had seen only men descend the metal stairs into the room, but the bulky equipment could easily disguise a female silhouette.

But what did she mean, *don't shoot?*

Bryson shouted, "Put down your weapon!"

Suddenly he was blinded by a flash of light, and he realized that the lights in this room had suddenly gone on! Brighter than they'd been before.

What was going on?

In a second or two his eyes readjusted to the light, and there, standing on a catwalk high above, he could make out the shape of the woman who had been speaking to him. The woman wore a white uniform—the uniform of Calacanis's steward from the dinner that seemed so much a part of the distant past.

On her head she wore a helmet and head-harness, the lens of an infrared monocular night-vision unit obscuring half her face. Yet Bryson recognized her as the beautiful blonde he had exchanged a few words with before dinner, and who had spoken a few hasty words to him just before the violence had begun—words he now recognized as indeed a genuine warning.

And here she was, crouched in a marksman's stance, gripping the butt of a Ruger with a long silencer attached, moving it from one side to another, steadily back and forth. He realized, too, that there were four bodies sprawled at different points around the generator room—two from the deck close to the generator, one at the beginning of the catwalk on which he was standing, and a fourth lying a mere six feet away, alarmingly close.

And he saw that the woman was not aiming at him. She was covering him, aiming everywhere else, protecting him against others! The stewardess was standing by a small bank of controls and switches; that was where she had turned the lights on. "Come on!" she shouted over a dull roar. "This way!"

What the hell was going on?

Bryson stared in bafflement.

"Come on, let's go!" the woman shouted angrily. Her accent was definitely Levantine.

"What do you want?" Bryson shouted back, more to stall for time than to elicit any response. For what could this be but a trap—a clever one but a trap nonetheless?

"What the hell do you think?" she shouted, turning her gun toward him, returning to the marksman's stance. He aimed his gun directly at her, and just as he was about to pull the trigger, he saw her shift the barrel a few inches to her right, heard the cough of another silenced round.

And at the same instant he both heard a crash and saw a body topple from the catwalk just above him.

Another sniper with a night-vision-equipped rifle. Dead.

She had just killed him.

The sniper had stolen silently up to him, about to kill him, and she had dropped him first.

"Move it!" the woman shouted to him. "Before any others come here. If you want to save your own life, move your ass!"

"Who are you?" Bryson shouted back, stunned.

"What does it matter right now?" She pushed the night-vision monocular up and off her face, so that it rested on the top of her head. "Please, there's no time! For God's sake, look at your situation, calculate your odds. What the hell *choice* do you have?"

CHAPTER SEVEN

Bryson stared at the woman.

"Come *on!*" she called, her voice rising in desperation. "If I wanted to kill you, I would have done so already. I've got the advantage, I've got the infrared—not you."

"You don't have the advantage now," Bryson called back, his grip steady on his stolen weapon, lowered at his side.

"I know this ship inside and out. Now, if you want to stay here and play games, be my guest. I have no choice now but to get off the ship. Calacanis's security force is large—there are plenty of others, probably on the way right now." With her free hand she pointed toward an object mounted high on one of the bulkheads near the ceiling of the generator room. Bryson recognized it as a surveillance camera. "He has much of the ship on camera, but not all. So you can follow me and save your life, or you can stay here and be killed. The choice is yours!" She turned quickly and raced down the catwalk and up a short set of metal stairs to a hatch cover. Unlatching it, she glanced back and jerked her head toward the opening, signaling him to follow.

Bryson hesitated no more than a few more seconds before he did so. His mind spun; he tried to make sense of the woman. *Questions!* Who *was* she? What was she doing, what did she want, why was she here?

The woman was obviously no mere ship's steward.

So who *was* she?

She beckoned; he came through the hatchway behind her, all the while gripping his weapon.

"What are you—?" he began.

"Quiet!" she hissed. "Sound carries far here." She shut the hatch door behind him and slid home a large deadbolt. The painfully loud noise of the generator room was gone. "This is an antipirate ship, fortunately for us. Specially constructed so passages can be closed, locked."

He caught her eyes, momentarily distracted by her remarkable beauty. "You're right," he said quietly yet forcefully, "I don't have much choice right now, but you'd better tell me what's going on here."

She gave him a stare that was at once forthright and defiant and whispered, "No *time* for explanations right now. I'm undercover here, too. Following arms transfers to certain parties that want to blast Israel back to the Stone Age."

Mossad, he told himself. But her accent told him she was Lebanese, from the Bekaa Valley; something wasn't quite right. Would a Mossad field operative be Lebanese, not Israeli?

She cocked her head as if hearing some distant noise he could not perceive.

"This way," she said abruptly, vaulting up the steel stairs. He followed her to a landing, then out a hatch that opened into a long, empty, dark corridor. She paused for a moment, looked both ways. As his eyes adjusted to the dim light, he saw that the tunnel went on and on, as far as he could see. It seemed to run the entire length of the ship, from bow to stern; it appeared to be a little-used service alley. "Come!" she hissed, suddenly breaking into a run.

Bryson followed, lengthening his strides to adjust to the woman's lightning-fast pace. He observed that her tread was odd: springy and light, virtually silent. He emulated her, realizing that she was attempting to minimize the reverberation against the steel surface—both to keep from being heard and to be able to listen to any followers, he guessed.

Within a minute, when they had run a few hundred feet down the dark tunnel, he thought he heard a muffled noise coming from the aft end, behind them. He turned his head, noticed a shift in the pattern of the shadows at the far end. But before he could say anything to her, he saw her swerve to the right and flatten herself against the steel bulkhead, behind a vertical steel girder. He did the same, though not a second too soon.

There was an explosion, a burst of automatic gunfire. Bullets spat into the bulkhead, ringing, clattering against the deck.

Whipping his head to his left, he saw a plume of flame shooting from a machine gun at the far end of the tunnel, the shooter shadowy and indistinct. There came another burst of gunfire, and then the killer was running down the corridor toward them.

The woman was struggling with a hatch cover. "Shit! It's painted shut!" she whispered. With a quick glance back down the long, dark passage at the approaching assassin, she said, "This way!" Suddenly leaping forward, away from the protective shelter of the bulkhead and its steel girders, she raced ahead. She was right to move; otherwise, they would be trapped here, obvious targets. He peered quickly around the girder, looked back, and saw the shooter slow his pace, raise his Uzi submachine gun, and aim it directly at the woman.

Bryson did not hesitate. He pointed his pistol toward the killer, squeezed the trigger twice in succession. One round exploded; the second squeeze of the trigger produced nothing more than a small click. The chamber was empty, as was the magazine.

But the shooter was down. The pursuer's Uzi crashed to the deck as he tumbled awkwardly to one side. Even from this distance Bryson could see the man was dead.

The steward turned back with a grim, fearful expression and saw what had happened. She gave Bryson a quick look of what might have been appreciation, but said nothing. He raced to catch up with the woman.

For the moment they were safe. Now, suddenly, she veered off to the right and stopped abruptly at another section of bulkhead, also divided by vertical girders. She leaned over, grabbed a bar that was mounted over an oval opening in the bulkhead the size of a manhole, and agilely swung her feet into the hole like a child playing on monkey bars. In an instant she had disappeared. He did the same, though somewhat more awkwardly: as physically agile as he was, he lacked her apparent familiarity with the ship.

They were in a box-shaped, low-ceilinged compartment that was almost totally dark, the only light coming from the dim service alley. When his vision adapted to the dark, he realized they were in a square space that connected to another one, by means of another manhole, and then another, and another. He could see clear across to the other side of the ship. This was a thwartships passage, he realized, the sections separated by heavy steel girders. She was peering into the next compartment, then without warning she grabbed on to the bar and swung her body inward, feet first.

He followed suit, but the moment he got to his feet, he heard her whisper, "Shh! *Listen!*"

He could hear the distant hammering of footsteps on steel. The sound seemed to be emanating from the service alley from which they had come, and also from a level above. It sounded like at least half a dozen men.

She spoke quickly, in a low voice. "I'm sure they've found the one you killed. Which tells them you're armed, probably a professional." Her English was heavily accented but remarkably fluent. Her intonation seemed to be questioning, though he couldn't see her facial expression. "Although it's obvious you are, if you've survived this far. They also know you—we—can't have gotten too far yet."

"I don't know who you are, yet you're risking your life for me. You don't owe me anything, but an explanation would be appreciated."

"Look, if we get out of here, we'll have time to talk. Right now we don't. Now, do you have any other weapon on you?"

He shook his head. "Just this damn thing, and it's empty."

"Not good. We're way outnumbered. There are enough of them to fan out, search every passage, every hold. And as we've just seen, they're equipped with some serious weaponry."

"There's no shortage of it on this ship," Bryson remarked. "How far are we from the containers?"

"Containers?"

"The boxes. The cargo."

Even in the semidarkness he could see a white flash of

smile as she realized what he was saying. "Ah, yes. Not far at all. But I don't know what's in them."

"Then we'll just have to look. Do we have to go back out to the service alley?"

"No. There's a passageway cut into the floor of one of these box girders. But I don't know which one, and without lights, we run the risk of just stepping down into it."

Bryson reached into a pocket, retrieved a book of matches, lit one. The compartment instantly lit up with a feeble amber light. He walked over to the next opening, the rush of air extinguishing the flame, and he lit another. She ran alongside and looked into the adjoining space. "There it is," she said. Bryson waved the match out just before it burned down to his finger. She reached out her hand to take the matchbook; he handed it over, understanding that, since she was in the lead, she had the more immediate need.

As soon as the darkness returned, she grabbed the steel bar, lifted her feet, and thrust them through. As she pulled herself erect by means of another handhold mounted inside the next compartment, she tapped her feet against the deck, searching out solid steel. "Okay. Careful."

He swung himself through the manhole, alighting carefully, keeping to the edges of the compartment floor. She was already descending into the vertical passage by means of a steel ladder that was welded in place. As Bryson waited to follow her down, he heard loud footsteps approaching, accompanied by shouts; then he could see a beam of light from a powerful flashlight illuminate the service alley they'd come from. He ducked down to the steel floor just as a flashlight beam shone directly at them. The light moved from side to side slowly.

He froze, his face pressed against the cold steel. He was aware of the loud ship's Klaxons, still blaring ceaselessly, but strangely, they had become almost background noise against which he could now hear other, more subtle, sounds.

He held his breath. The light moved to the center of the passage, then stopped, as if they had located him. He felt his heart hammer so loudly he swore it was audible. Then the beam moved off to one side and was gone.

The loud footsteps seemed to be passing by. "Nothing here!" a voice called out.

He waited a full minute before allowing himself to move. It seemed an eternity. Then he gingerly felt around for the smooth round edges of the opening in the floor until his fingers encountered the jutting steel of the ladder.

In a few seconds he, too, was climbing down the ladder.

They seemed to be descending for hundreds of feet, though he knew it had to be less than that. Finally the ladder came to an end, and the two of them were crawling through a long, dark horizontal tunnel whose floor was damp and smelled of bilge water. The tunnel was so low that they could not stand erect. The footfalls of the pursuers were now so distant and muffled they were all but inaudible. The woman moved rapidly through the tunnel, bent over, almost crab-walking, and Bryson found himself doing the same. Then the tunnel branched to the right, and she grabbed hold of another vertical metal ladder and began climbing nimbly upward. Bryson followed, but this ascent was a brief one; it led to what looked like another alley. The woman lit a match, whose flame revealed that on either side of the alley were steep, high corrugated-steel walls; in a moment, he realized that the walls were in fact the ends of steel shipping containers packed closely together. The walkway ran between two long rows of containers.

She stopped, knelt, lighted another match, and inspected a label plastered at the end panel of one container. "Steel Eagle 105, 107, 111 . . ." she read quietly.

"Knives. Field-grade, tactical-ops. Keep looking."

She moved on to the next container. "Omega Technologies—"

"Electronic warfare components. Jesus, they've got everything here. But that's not going to do us any good."

"Mark-Twelve IFF Crypto—"

"Crypto systems for transponders or interrogators. Try the next bay. Hurry!"

Meanwhile, Bryson was squatting in front of a container in the row opposite, trying to make out the label by the dim light emitting from the woman's match a few feet away. "I think we got something here," he said. "XM84 stun grenades, nonlethal, nonfragmentation. Flash-and-bang." He muttered to himself, "I'd prefer something lethal, but beggars can't be choosers."

Quietly, she continued to read aloud: "AN/PSC-11 SCAMP."

"Several-Channel Anti-jam Man-Portable. Keep going."

She waved out one match and lit another. "ANFATDS?"

"Army Field Artillery Tactical Data System. Not going to help us much either."

"AN/PRC-132 SOHFRAD?"

"Special Operations High Frequency Radio. Nope."

"Tadiran—"

He cut her off. "Israeli telecommunications and electronics maker. From your homeland. Nothing we can use."

Then he noticed the label on the adjoining container: M-76 grenades, and M-25 CS riot grenades, used by the military and police for crowd control. "Here we go," he said excitedly, though restraining the volume. "This is exactly what we need. Now, do you know how to open these things?"

She turned back toward him. "All we need is a bolt-cutter. These containers are high-security-sealed to prevent pilferage—they're not really locked in any serious way."

The first container came open easily once the high-security seal was snapped off. The metal lashing gear crisscrossing the front end of the nine-foot-high container slid out quickly, and then a door opened. Inside were stacked wooden crates of grenades and other armaments: a veritable Aladdin's cave of weaponry.

Ten minutes later they had assembled a pile of assorted arms. Once they had familiarized themselves with how to use them and how to keep them from going off accidentally, Bryson and the woman began stuffing the smaller objects, the grenades and ammunition and the like, into the pockets of their Kevlar body armor plates. The larger objects, they secured to their shoulders and backs by means of makeshift holsters, rucksacks, and slings of rope; the largest ones they would simply carry. Each wore Kevlar helmets with attached face shields.

Suddenly there came an enormous crash from directly overhead, then another. The screech of metal scraping against metal. Bryson slipped into the narrow gap between two containers and wordlessly signaled to the woman to do the same.

A sliver of bright light appeared above as a trapdoor in the ceiling appeared to open, actually an opening in the hatchway covering this bay of the cargo hold. The light came from high-intensity flashlights, several of them, in the hands of three or four of Calacanis's soldiers. Behind them, beside them, there were others, many others, and even from this angle, diagonally below, Bryson could see they were heavily armed.

No! He was expecting a confrontation, but not here, not so soon! There had been no opportunity to formulate a strategy, to coordinate with the nameless blond woman who had for some reason become his accomplice.

He seized the grip of the Bulgarian-made Kalashnikov AK-47 assault rifle and slowly angled it upward, mentally running through his options. To fire at the men from here would be the equivalent of sending up a flare confirming his location. Calacanis's men couldn't be certain that Bryson and the woman were here.

Then Bryson caught a glimpse of the array of large weapons that lay abandoned on the steel walkway floor. That told his enemies that they had guessed right, or rather, that they had accurately pinpointed the sounds from below—that their quarry was either here or had just been here.

But why weren't they firing?

When you're outnumbered, go on the offensive. His instincts told him to fire first, to pick off as many of his pursuers as he could, whether it gave away their positions or not.

He raised the Kalashnikov, peered through the low-light,

variable-intensity illuminated sight to zero the reticle, and squeezed the trigger.

An explosion, followed instantly by an agonized scream, and one of Calacanis's soldiers toppled from the ramparts above all the way down to the steel ramp a few feet away. Bryson's aim was precise; the man, struck in the forehead, was dead.

Bryson pulled into the shadows of the recess between containers, bracing for the full-automatic explosion of gunfire that he knew would be the response.

But nothing came!

There was a shout from above, a barked command. The men drew back and assumed firing stances, but did not fire!

Why the hell not?

Baffled, Bryson raised his weapon again and squeezed off two more carefully aimed shots. One of the men went down right away, dead; another sagged to his feet, screaming in pain.

Suddenly Bryson realized: they had been ordered to hold their fire!

They could not risk firing their weapons so near the containers! The corrugated-steel shipping crates were filled with the most explosive, highly flammable arms—not all of them, of course, but enough to make it dangerous. One misplaced round that penetrated the thin steel skin of a container might detonate a cache of bombs, of C-4 plastic explosives, or who knows what else, setting off a conflagration so immense that it might sink the vast ship.

As long as he sought cover between containers, then they would not fire. Yet the instant he or the woman emerged and were safely away from the containers, a sharpshooter would attempt to take them out. This meant that Bryson was safe as long as he remained in position here—but there was no escape, no way out, and his enemies surely knew that. They could wait him out, wait for him to blunder.

He released his hold on the Kalashnikov, let it dangle by its strap at his side. From here he could see that the blonde was crouched between two containers twenty feet away or so, watching him, waiting to see what he would do. Bryson jabbed his thumb first to the left, then to the right, an un-spoken question: *Which way out?*

Her reply was immediate, also signaled by means of hand gestures: the only way out was to emerge from the shelter of the containers, and take the ramp back in the direction from which they had come. Shit! They had no choice but to expose themselves! Bryson pointed to himself, telling her that he would go first. Then he raised his other major tactical weapon, a South African–made Uzi submachine gun. At the same time he began to sidle out from the protective alley, keeping his back against one of the containers, until he was out in the open, the Uzi pointed toward the guards above. As swiftly as they could, given the burden of the load of weaponry they were saddled down with, they moved toward their only escape.

Slowly the woman emerged, too, and now both of them sidled down the ramp, their backs against the enormous steel boxes. Several powerful, crisscrossing beams of light shone directly at them, in their eyes, illuminating their every move. In his peripheral vision Bryson could see several of the shooters shifting positions, aiming at them from oblique an-gles so they could fire at them without fear of striking the containers. But it would take precise marksmanship.

And Bryson did not intend to allow them the opportunity.

He shifted the Kalashnikov toward the shooters, and as he released the safety, he heard a loud clattering from behind. He turned quickly to look and saw men clambering out of the hatch that had been their escape route! These men, at much closer range, their aim therefore more reliable, might not be so hesitant to fire. Now they were surrounded, their sole means of escape gone!

A sudden hailstorm of machine-gun fire. It was coming from the woman, who then ducked back between the shelter of two containers. There were shouts, screams, and several of the advancing men collapsed to the ground, wounded or dead. Taking advantage of the gunfire, Bryson reached into the pocket of his flak jacket, retrieved a burst-fragmentation grenade, pulled out the pin, and hurled it up toward one group of Calacanis's men above. A chorus of shouts arose and the men scattered just as the grenade exploded, sending an immense shower of shrapnel everywhere, knocking several of the men out. Metal fragments clattered against Bryson's own face shield.

Another round of machine-gun fire from the woman, just as several of the men who had just emerged from the hatch advanced toward them, fanning out, pistols drawn. Bryson pulled out another grenade and hurled it upward; this one exploded much more quickly, with equally devastating results. He then fired a burst from the Uzi at the approaching soldiers. Several were hit; two of them, equipped with bulletproof vests, kept moving. Bryson fired at them again. The impact of the rounds even against the Kevlar vests was sufficiently powerful to knock one of them over. Bryson fired one long sustained burst and hit the other man in an exposed portion of the throat, killing him instantly.

"Come!" the woman shouted. He saw that she was backing up farther into the narrow passage between containers, deeper into the darkness. She seemed to have another route in mind; he would have to trust her, take on faith that she knew what she was doing, where she was going. Wildly firing off another long burst of artillery as cover, Bryson dove out from his protective cover to the open ramp. As he ran he was firing all around him, seemingly crazily. But it worked: he made it to the passage across the way, just in time to see her disappear to the left in a crawlspace between the ends of several containers, dragging a long heavy object behind her.

He recognized the weapon. Just before he turned, he pulled out another grenade and hurled it back toward Calacanis's men—at least, those who remained standing.

It was insanity! The woman was lugging this oversized, rifle-shaped weapon that was slowing down their escape!

"Go on," he whispered to her. "I can get it."

"Thank you."

He grabbed the weapon, swung it over his shoulder, pulling the canvas strap around his chest. Now she was climbing down a railing that led to the next row of containers below. He climbed down as well, then followed close behind as she shimmied between another set of containers. Now he could hear footsteps all around, though chiefly above and behind, and he deduced that their pursuers were splitting up into small teams. Where was she going? Why did she insist on their carrying this goddamned weapon?

She was weaving a strange, jagged path—between containers, then climbing down the railing to the next level down. There were eight or so levels of containers below-decks, below the hatch covers, and who knew how many rows, which provided a great maze. That's what she was doing: she was trying to lose them in the maze! He was disoriented; he had no idea which way she was going, but she was moving quickly and seemingly with purpose, so he continued to follow her, his agility somewhat impaired by having to carry the weapon.

At last they came to another vertical tunnel with a steel ladder mounted within. She vaulted up it almost as if running. Bryson was starting to feel winded. The additional thirty or forty pounds he was carrying didn't help. The woman was in peak physical condition, he observed. This tunnel rose fifty feet or so and stopped at a dark, horizontal tunnel that was tall enough to stand up in. As soon as he had come through, she shut the hatch door behind him and bolted it shut.

"This is a long tunnel," she said. "But if we can make it to near the end, to the oh-two deck, we're out of here."

She broke into a run, her stride long, hurried; Bryson followed close behind.

A sudden loud, echoing, clicking sound, and they were instantly plunged into absolute darkness.

Bryson threw himself onto the steel deck by force of habit, learned from long years of field ops, and he heard the woman do the same.

The explosion of a gunshot was followed immediately by the sound of steel hitting steel as a round hit the bulkhead just inches away. The aim was too good, too close, to be anything but enhanced by a thermal night-vision scope. Another explosion, and Bryson was immediately struck in the chest!

The bullet tore into his Kevlar vest with the impact of a powerful fist slamming him in the chest. Bryson had no night-vision; that had not been among the Aladdin's cave of armaments they had managed to turn up in their quick forage through the shipping containers. But the Lebanese woman did.

Didn't she?

"I don't have it!" she whispered harshly, as if reading his thoughts. "I dropped it somewhere back there!"

Now they could hear footsteps coming closer and closer in the blackness—not running but briskly walking, with great determination. The determination of someone who can see in the dark, can see his target as clearly as if it were high noon. The confident stride of a killer approaching in order to improve his sight lines.

"Stay down!" Bryson hissed as he took out the Uzi and fired off a burst in the general direction of the killer. But it did nothing; the killer was advancing toward them steadily, Bryson could sense.

In the left pocket of his flak jacket was a jumble of hand grenades. M651 CS teargas grenades, which would be a mistake, because in this contained space it would get them, too: they had no protection. M90 pyrotechnic smoke grenade dischargers, which generate thick smoke screens, would do no good either, since thermal scopes could see through it.

But there was another one, he knew: a high-tech species of hand grenade that might do the trick.

There had been no time to explain to the woman what he was about to do. He had simply grabbed a few of the weapons from Calacanis's store. Now what? He needed to tell her without the killer, or killers, understanding.

Just move!

He found the grenade, identifying it by its unusual contours, its smooth body. Swiftly he pulled out its pin, waited the requisite few seconds, and lobbed it a few feet short of where he estimated Calacanis's soldier had reached.

The explosion was brief but blindingly bright, phosphorus-white, and it illuminated the killer in freeze-frame like a trick of the camera. Bryson could see the man, submachine gun hoisted in firing position, jerk his head up in astonishment. But the light disappeared just as quickly as it had appeared, and Bryson could feel the air fill at once with burning-hot smoke. The killer was caught off guard, taken by surprise, and Bryson seized the moment to scoop up the long steel projectile and then propel himself forward, coming at the woman with great velocity. As he did so, he called to her in Arabic, "Run! Straight ahead! He can't see us now!"

Indeed, the American-made M76 smoke grenade, once detonated, had released a thick smoke screen laced with hot brass flakes that floated in the air and descended to the ground very slowly. It was a high-tech obscurant, specifically designed to block detection of infrared waves by thermal imaging systems. The hot metal fragments confounded the killer's scope, so it could no longer distinguish the heat of the human body from the cooler background. Now the air was filled with a hot metallic haze; the assassin's field of vision was now nothing more than a densely speckled cloud.

Bryson rushed onward, the woman racing just ahead of him. By the time their enemy recovered a few seconds later and began firing madly, indiscriminately, Bryson and the woman were well beyond him down the corridor. Artillery exploded everywhere, clattering against the steel bulkheads aimlessly.

He felt a hand reach out to make contact with him: the blond woman was guiding him through a hatchway, pulling him up onto a steel ladder until he had his bearings and was able to make his way up the rungs in the utter darkness. From behind he could hear another hailstorm of bullets as the soldier fired away blindly, and then the barrage abruptly stopped. *He's out of ammunition,* Bryson thought. *He'll have to reload.*

But he won't have time.

The woman opened a hatch cover, and suddenly he could see. In the same instant as he felt the welcome, cold night air hit his lungs, he saw that they were outside, in the open, on a small, starboard section of deck. She closed the hatch behind them and slid home the deadbolt. The sky was dark and starless, cloudy, but it seemed almost bright by contrast.

They were on the 02 deck, one level above the main deck. Bryson noticed that the Klaxons had ceased; the alarms had stopped ringing. Nimbly making her way around several large piles of greasy cables, like tangles of snakes, the woman took several quick strides toward the bulwark.

She knelt and untied a cable from a pelican hook, which released a boom, a davit arm, which now swung outward. Secured to the davit cradle was a twenty-seven-foot-long rescue boat, a Magna Marine patrol craft, one of the fastest speedboats made.

Then the two of them climbed into the boat, which swayed unsteadily on its bridle rig. She yanked at a line, releasing the brake, and abruptly they plummeted downward, the boat crashing into the water, free of all restraints.

She powered it up and the motor came on with a throaty roar, and then the boat lurched forward, almost flying over the surface of the water. The woman took the steering wheel while Bryson maneuvered the long steel tube, the immense missile he had lugged throughout the ship. They barreled full-throttle ahead at a speed of around sixty miles per hour. Calacanis's immense ship loomed as large as a skyscraper, its tall black hull ominous.

The loud noise emitted by the Magna patrol boat seemed to have alerted Calacanis's security forces, for suddenly the black sky was lit up with blindingly bright beams of light, thunderously loud explosions. Security men now ringed the bulwarks, standing on the railings and various other perches, their submachine guns and sniper rifles blazing. They were ineffective; Bryson and the woman were out of range.

They had escaped, and they were safe!

But then Bryson noticed the rocket launchers being

hoisted onto the deck, targeted directly at them.

They're going to blow us out of the water.

He became aware of the whine of an outboard motor, which crescendoed into a powerful roar. Directly ahead, coming around the ship's stern, was a Boston Whaler patrol boat, twenty-seven-foot Vigilant class, with mounted machine guns. This was no Spanish coast guard vehicle; it was clearly private.

And as it raced toward them, growing closer and closer, its machine guns were firing nonstop.

The woman heard, then saw, and she didn't need to be prompted. She opened the throttle even further, accelerating to maximum speed. The boat they were on had no doubt been chosen by Calacanis for maximum speed, but so had the approaching patrol boat.

They were speeding toward the shore, but there was no certainty that they would win any contest. Now the pursuing patrol boat was almost within firing range, its guns blazing all the while. It was a matter of seconds before it overtook them. The sea was flecked, churned, by the hailstorm of bullets from the machine guns.

And the huge rocket launchers on board the *Spanish Armada* were clearly about to fire; the missiles were within range.

"Fire it!" the woman shouted. "Before they blow *us* up!"

But Bryson had already raised the Stinger to his shoulder, the gripstock in his right hand, launch tube in his left, canvas strap around his chest. He peered through the sight, squinting his other eye. The Stinger's super-advanced software made for extreme accuracy, using a passive infrared seeker. They were well beyond the recommended minimum distance of two hundred meters.

Bryson aligned the target in the optical sight, hit the override on the Identification Friend or Foe interrogation function, then actuated the missile function.

The audible tone signaled that the missile had locked on the target.

He fired.

There was an explosion of astonishing force, a recoil that knocked him backward as the dual-thrust rocket motor ignited, propelling the missile forward. The disposable missile launch tube dropped into the water.

And the heat-guided missile soared into the air, tracing a long arc toward the patrol boat, trailing a long plume of smoke like a hasty scrawl in the night sky.

A second later the patrol boat exploded into a fireball, a sulphurous cloud of smoke spewing upward. The ocean was roiled, huge waves rushing toward them even as they raced on ahead.

The air was pierced by a long, loud blast of the *Spanish Armada*'s emergency whistle, followed by a series of short blasts and then one long one.

The woman had turned around, staring in horrified fascination. Bryson could feel a wave of intense heat on his face. He lifted the second missile—the only remaining one, which had been bundled with the first—and shoved it into the firing apparatus. Then he turned the missile-launcher to his left and fixed in the infrared sights the superstructure of the *Spanish Armada* itself. It began to beep, indicating that it had locked onto the target.

Heart pounding, holding his breath, he fired.

The missile streaked toward the enormous container ship, swerving as it corrected its own path, headed right for the very heart of the ship.

An instant later came the explosion, which seemed to begin within the bowels of the ship and expand outward. Pieces of the ship flew upward amid the black smoke and thrusting flame, and then, in some sort of peculiar sequence, there came another blast, even louder.

And then another. And another.

One by one the containers had superheated, detonating their highly flammable contents.

The sky was filled with fire, an immense rippling sphere of flame and smoke and detritus. The noise hurt their ears. A black oil slick spread into the water, and that, too, immediately burst into flames, and everything was smoke and fire and crashing waves.

Calacanis's huge vessel, now a ruined hulk, listed to one side, the wreckage all but hidden in an acrid black cloud, and it began to sink deep into the ocean.

The *Spanish Armada* was no more.

PART TWO

CHAPTER EIGHT

They came ashore at a narrow, rocky spit of land, buffeted by violent waves crashing against the steep cliffs. This was the *Costa da Morte*, the Coast of Death, so named for the uncounted legions of ships wrecked upon the perilous, harsh coastline.

Wordlessly, they pulled the rescue boat as far up the sandbar as they could, stashing it in a hidden cove, away from the searchlights of the coast guard and the avaricious eyes of smugglers; at least the boat would not be washed away by the next big wave. He unstrapped the two large weapons from around his chest, the AK-47 and the Uzi, and hid them beside the boat, concealing them with sand, rocks, pebbles, and an arrangement of smaller boulders so that they could not be seen even from close up. It would not do to be observed walking around like a couple of mercenaries, and besides, they had plenty of other, smaller weapons stuffed in their vests.

The two maneuvered awkwardly among the rocks, weighed down by the artillery that filled every pocket, was slung around their shoulders and their backs. Their clothes were drenched, of course—her white uniform, his Italian suit—and they shivered from the cold of the icy water.

Bryson had some idea of where they had landed, having studied detailed Agency maps of the Galician coast of Spain, the stretch of land nearest the point at which the *Spanish Armada,* according to surveillance satellite reports, had dropped anchor. He believed they had come ashore at, or near, the village of Finisterre, or Fisterra, as the Galegos call it. Finisterre: the end of the world, just about Spain's most westerly point. Once the westernmost limit of the known world to the Spaniards, the place where untold numbers of smugglers met their gruesome, but mercifully sudden, end on the barnacle-encrusted rocks.

The woman was the first to speak. Sinking down on the edge of a boulder, visibly shivering, she placed her hands on her head, inserted her fingers into her hair, and tugged off a blond wig, revealing short auburn hair. She took out a sealed plastic pouch and removed from it a small, white plastic case, a holder for contact lenses. Swiftly, she touched her fingers against her eyes and removed the colored contact lenses, placing first the right, then the left, into the case. Her dazzling green eyes had become a deep brown. Bryson watched in fascination but said nothing. Then she took from the plastic pouch a compass, a waterproof map, and a tiny pinpoint flashlight. "We can't stay here, of course. The coast guard will be combing every inch of shoreline. My *God,* what a *nightmare!*" She switched on the penlight, cupping a hand around it as she examined the map.

"Why do I have the feeling you've been through nightmares like this before?"

She looked up from the map, regarded him sharply. "Do I really owe you an explanation?"

"You owe me nothing. But you risked your life to save me, and I'd like to understand. Also, I think I like you better as a brunette than as a blonde. Earlier you said you were 'following arms transfers,' presumably for Israel. Mossad?"

"In a sense," she said cryptically. "And you—CIA?"

"In a sense." He had always adhered to the principle of need-to-know and saw no need to divulge more.

"Your target—your area of interest?" she persisted.

He hesitated for a moment before he spoke. "Let's just say that I'm up against an organization that's vastly more far-reaching than anything you might have in your sights. But let me ask you this: Why? Why did you do it? Scrap the entire infiltration, then put your own life on the line?"

"Believe me, it wasn't my choice."

"Then whose choice was it?"

"It was the circumstances. The way things worked out. I made the foolish mistake of warning you, failing to take into account the surveillance cameras Calacanis has everywhere."

"How do you know you were observed?"

"Because after the madness began I was pulled away from my duties and told that a Mr. Boghosian wanted to see me. Boghosian is—*was*—Calacanis's head thug. When he asks to see you, well, I knew what that meant. They had checked the surveillance tape. At that point I knew I had to escape."

"But that begs the question of why you warned me in the first place."

She shook her head. "I saw no reason to let them claim more victims. Especially since my ultimate purpose was to prevent the spilling of innocent blood by the terrorists and fanatics. And I didn't think it would place my own operational security at stake. Obviously I miscalculated." She resumed studying the map, all the while shielding the penlight with a cupped hand.

Touched by the woman's candor, Bryson said gently, "Do you have a name?"

She looked up again, gave a half-smile. "I'm Layla. And I know you're not Coleridge."

"Jonas Barrett," he said. He let the question of what he was doing here hang in the air. Let her probe, he thought. Information will be exchanged when, *if,* the time was right. Lies, legends, cover names all came so easily to his tongue now, as they once had. *Who am I really?* he wondered mutely: the melodramatic question of the adolescent, strangely transposed to the maddened consciousness of an ex–field operative who'd found himself very lost. Waves crashed noisily around them. There was the mournful sounding of a foghorn from a lighthouse perched high above the sea. The famous lighthouse at Cabo Finisterre, Bryson knew. "It's not clear you miscalculated," he said, appreciatively, almost under his breath.

She gave him a quick, sad smile as she switched off her penlight. "I need to charter a helicopter or private plane, something that will get me—us—out of here, and quickly."

"The most likely place to do that is Santiago de Compostela. About sixty kilometers east-southeast of here. It's a major tourist destination—a pilgrimage town, a holy city. I believe there's a small airport outside the city that has some direct international flights. We may be able to charter a plane or a helicopter there. Certainly worth a try."

She gave him a hard stare. "You know this area."

"Barely. I've studied the map."

A sudden, powerful beam of light lit up the beach just yards away, propelling them both to the ground, their instincts honed by field experience. Bryson threw himself behind a large boulder and froze; the woman who called herself Layla flattened herself beneath a ledge. Bryson felt the sand on his face, cold and wet; he could hear her steady breathing a few feet away. Bryson had not worked with many female operatives in the course of his career, and it was his belief, rarely vocalized, that the few women who actually made it over the obstacles placed there by the spymasters, almost all of whom were men, had to be exceptional. About this mysterious Layla he knew virtually nothing except that she was one of the exceptional ones, highly skilled and calm under pressure.

He could see the searchlight sweep down the beach, its beam pausing for a moment at just about the point where he had concealed the boat in the hidden cove, providing additional cover with rocks gathered from the sand. Perhaps experienced eyes could discern the disruption he had caused in the natural pattern of the rocks, seaweed, and other jetsam and flotsam. From behind the boulder that shielded him from the searchers, Bryson was able to peer around. The search craft was moving parallel to the coastline, a pair of high-powered beams moving back and forth along the jagged cliffs. No doubt powerful magnifying binoculars were being employed by the searchers as well. At such a distance, night-vision scopes were useless, but he did not want to take a chance by getting up prematurely, simply because the searchlights had moved on. Often the extinguishing of the search beams was merely the prelude to the *real* search: only when the lights went out did the creatures scuttle forth from under their rocks. So he remained in place for five minutes after the beach had gone dark again; he was impressed that he did not have to urge Layla to do the same.

When they finally emerged from their hiding places, shaking the cramps from their limbs, they began scrambling up the rock-strewn hillside, dense with scraggly pines, until they came to a narrow gravel road on the ridge of the cliff. Along the road was a succession of high, massive granite walls enclosing tiny plots of land and dominated by ancient stone houses covered with moss. Each had the same granary built high on pillars, the same conical hayrack, the same trellis overgrown with green grapes, the same collection of gnarled trees heavy with fruit. This was a territory, Bryson realized, whose denizens lived and worked the land as they had always done, for generations upon generations. It was a place where the intruder was not welcome. A man on the run would be regarded with the utmost suspicion, strangers sighted and reported.

There was a sudden scuff of feet on the gravel not more than a hundred feet behind them. He spun around, a pistol in his right hand, but saw nothing in the darkness and fog. Visibility was extremely limited, and the road bent around so that whoever was approaching could not be seen. He noticed that Layla, too, was aiming a weapon, a pistol with a long perforated silencer screwed onto the barrel. Her two-handed marksman's stance was perfect, almost stylized. The two of them froze in place, listening.

Then there was a shout from the sandbar below. There were at least two of them; there had to be more. But where had they come from? What were their precise intentions?

Another sudden noise: a gruff voice nearby, speaking a language Bryson did not immediately understand, then another scuff of feet on gravel. The language, he quickly realized, was Galego, the ancient language of Galicia that combined elements of Portuguese and Castilian Spanish. He could make out only isolated phrases.

"Veña! Axiña! Que carallo fas aí? Que é o que che leva tanto tempo? Móvete!"

With a quick glance at each other, they each silently advanced along a stone wall toward the source of the noise. Low voices, thuds, a metallic clatter. When they rounded a bend in the wall, Bryson could see two silhouetted figures loading crates into an ancient panel truck. One was in the cargo bay of the truck, the other lifting crates from a stack and handing them to him. Bryson glanced at his watch: a little after three o'clock in the morning. What were these men doing here? They had to be fishermen, that was it. Peasant fishermen gathering the local crop, *percebes,* barnacles scooped from the waterline, or perhaps harvesting mussels from the *mejillonieras,* the rafts floating in the water just offshore.

Whoever they were, the men were locals hard at work and no direct threat. He put away his weapon and pantomimed to Layla to do the same. Pointed guns would be a mistake; confrontation would be unnecessary.

Upon closer examination, Bryson could see that one of the men looked middle-aged, the other not long out of his teenage years. Both looked rough, peasant laborers; they also looked like father and son. The younger was the one inside the truck's cargo bay; the older one was handing him cartons to stack.

The elder one spoke to the younger: *"Veña, móvete, non podemos perde-lo tempo!"*

Bryson knew enough Portuguese from countless operations in Lisbon, and a few in São Paulo, to understand what the men were saying. "Come on, move it!" said the elder. "We're on a tight schedule. No time to waste!"

He gave Layla a quick glance and then shouted in Portuguese, *"Por favor, nos poderían axudar? Metímo-lo coche na cuneta, e a miña muller e máis eu temos que chegar a Vigo canto antes."* Can you please help us? Our car ran off the side of the road, and my wife and I are trying to get to Vigo as soon as possible.

Both men looked up suspiciously. Now Bryson could see what they were loading, and it was not crates of barnacles or mussels. It was sealed cartons of foreign cigarettes, mostly English and American. These were not fishermen. They were smugglers, bringing in contraband tobacco to sell at grossly inflated prices.

The older man set down a carton on the gravel road. "Foreigners? Where do you come from?"

"We drove down from Bilbao. We're on holiday, seeing the sights, but the damned rental car turned out to be a piece of crap. The transmission gave out and we went into a ditch. If you could give us a lift, we'd make it worth your while."

"I'm sure we can help," said the older man, signaling to the younger, who then jumped out of the back of the truck and began approaching them from at an angle, moving noticeably closer to Layla. "Jorge?"

Suddenly the younger one had a revolver out, an ancient Astra Cadix .38 Special, which he leveled at Layla. Taking a few steps closer to her, he screamed, "*Vaciade os petos! Agora mesmo!* Empty your pockets. *All* of them! Quick, everything, and don't try anything fancy! *Now!*"

Now the older one had a revolver out, too, this one pointed at Bryson. "You, too, my friend. Drop your wallet, and kick it toward me," he barked. "That expensive-looking watch, too. *Move* it! Or your lovely wife gets it, and then you!"

The young man lurched forward, grabbing Layla by the shoulder with his left hand, jerking her toward him, his revolver at her temple. He did not seem to notice that Layla's facial expression had not changed, that she did not cry out or seem moved in any way. Had he noticed the calmness of her demeanor, he would have had cause for alarm.

She caught Bryson's eye; he nodded all but imperceptibly.

With a sudden jerking motion, she produced two handguns at once, one in either hand. In her left was a .45, a Heckler & Koch USP compact; in her right was a massive, extremely powerful .50 caliber Israeli Desert Eagle. At the same time, Bryson whipped out a Beretta 92 and leveled it at the older smuggler.

"Back!" Layla suddenly shouted in Portuguese at the teenager, who stumbled backward in sudden fright. "Drop the gun right now or I'll blow your head off!" The teenager regained his footing momentarily, hesitated as if considering how to respond, and she immediately squeezed the trigger on the enormous Desert Eagle. The explosion was astonishingly loud, all the more terrifying because it went off so near the young man's ear. He dropped his ancient Astra Cadix, flung his hands into the air, and said, *"Non! Non dispare!"* The revolver clattered to the ground but did not go off.

Bryson smiled, advancing toward the older man. "Put the gun down, *meu amigo,* or my wife will kill your son or nephew or whoever he is, and as you've just seen, she's a woman who's not able to control her impulses very well."

"Por Cristo bendito, esa muller está tola!" the middle-aged smuggler spat out as he knelt down and gently dropped his gun to the gravel. Christ almighty, she's a crazy woman! He put his hands in the air, too. *"Se pensan que nos van toma-lo pelo, están listos! Temos amigos esperando por nós ó final da estrada."* If you're planning to rip us off, you're an idiot. We have friends waiting for us down the road—

"Yeah, yeah," Bryson said impatiently. "We have no interest in your cigarettes. We just want your truck."

"O meu camión? Por Deus, eu necesito este camión!" Good Christ, I *need* this truck!

"Well, you just ran into a patch of bad luck," Bryson said.

"Kneel!" Layla ordered the teenager, who did so at once. The boy was red-faced and shivering like a frightened child, wincing each time she waved her Desert Eagle.

"Polo menos nos deixarán descarga-lo camión? Vostedes non necesitan a mercancía!" pleaded the old man. At least will you let us unload the truck? You don't need the merchandise!

"Go ahead," Layla said.

"No!" Bryson interrupted. "There's always another weapon concealed inside, in case of hijacking. I want both of you to turn around and start walking back down the road. And don't stop until you can't hear the truck anymore. Any attempts to run after us, to fire a weapon, to place a phone call, and we'll turn right around and come at you with weapons you've never even seen before. Believe me—you don't want to test us."

He ran toward the truck's cab, indicating with a jerk of

his head that Layla should get in on the other side. With the Beretta trained on the two Galegos, he ordered, *"Move* it!"

The two smugglers, young and old, rose unsteadily, their hands still raised, and began walking away down the gravel road.

"No, wait," she said suddenly. "I don't want to take any chances."

"What?"

She jammed the smaller-caliber pistol into a pocket of her flak jacket and pulled out another gun, this one strange-looking, which Bryson recognized at once. He nodded and smiled.

"Non!" the young smuggler screamed, turning back.

The older one, presumably the father, shouted, *"Non dispare! Estamos facendo o que nos dicen! Virxen Santa, non imos falar, por que íamos?"* Don't shoot! We're doing what you say! Mother of God, we're not going to talk, why should we?

The two men each broke into a run, but before they got more than a few yards, there were two loud pops as Layla fired a shot at each one. With each shot, a powerful carbon dioxide charge propelled a syringe of a potent tranquilizer into each man's body. This short-range projector was designed for overpowering wild animals without killing them; the tranquilizer would last, in a human being, perhaps thirty minutes. The two men toppled to the ground, their bodies writhing briefly before they passed into unconsciousness.

The old truck rattled and clattered as its arthritic engine strained against the steep grade of the winding mountain road. The sun was coming up the jagged cliffs, painting the horizon with pastel brushstrokes and casting a strange pale glow on the slate roofs of the fishing villages they passed.

He thought about the beautiful, remarkable woman sleeping in the front seat next to him, her head leaning against the vibrating window.

There was something tough and flinty about her, yet at the same time vulnerable, even melancholy. It was in fact an appealing combination, but his instincts warned him away for a multitude of reasons. She was too much like himself, a survivor whose tough exterior shielded a supremely complicated interior that at times seemed at war with itself.

And there was Elena, always Elena—a spectral presence, a mystery in her own way. The woman he never really knew. The promise of searching her out had become for him a beckoning siren, elusive and treacherous.

Layla meant at most a strategic partnership, an alliance of simple convenience. She and Bryson were using each other, assisting each other; there was something almost clinical, tactical about their relationship. It was nothing more than that. She was a mere means to an end.

Exhaustion was now overcoming him, and he pulled the truck over into a copse and dozed for what he thought was twenty minutes or so; he awoke with a jolt several hours later. Layla was still sleeping soundly. He cursed silently to himself; it was not good to lose this much time. On the other hand, bone-tiredness usually caused miscalculations and misjudgments, so maybe the sacrifice had been worth the cost.

Pulling back onto the highway, he noticed the road was becoming crowded with people walking in the direction of Santiago de Compostela. What had been an isolated few pedestrians had become a line of them, even a throng of them. Most were walking, though a few were on old bicycles, even a few on horseback. Their faces were sunburned; many of them walked with crook-necked sticks, wore simple, rough clothing, and had backpacks with scallop shells tied to them. The scallop shell, Bryson recalled, was the symbol of the pilgrim along the *Camino de Santiago*, the pilgrim's road of some one hundred kilometers from the pass at Roncesvalles in the Pyrenees to the ancient shrine of Saint James in Santiago. It usually took a month to make the journey on foot. Here and there along the roadside were pushcarts, gypsy vendors selling souvenirs—postcards, plastic birds with flapping wings, scallop shells, brightly colored cloths.

But soon he noticed something else, something for which he had no easy explanation. A few kilometers before Santiago, the traffic was becoming increasingly congested. Cars and trucks moved more slowly, almost bumper to bumper. Somewhere up ahead was an obstruction, perhaps a traffic jam. Road work?

No.

The wooden barricades and flashing lights from the cluster of official vehicles, which became visible as he rounded a turn, supplied the answer. It was a police roadblock. Spanish police were inspecting vehicles, surveying drivers and passengers. Cars seemed to be waved through quickly, but trucks were being detained, pulled over to one side as licenses and registrations were checked. The throngs of pilgrims passed by with curious looks, unhindered by the police.

"Layla," he said. "Quick, wake up!"

She jerked awake, startled, immediately alert. "What—what is it?"

"They're looking for our truck."

She saw at once what was going on. "Oh, God. Those bastards must have come to, filed a report with the police . . ."

"No. Not them, not directly. People like that tend to avoid the authorities whenever possible. Someone must have got to them, offered them a handsome bribe. Someone with direct lines to the Spanish police."

"Guardacostas? Unlikely to be any of Calacanis's people, even if any of them survived."

He shook his head. "My guess is that it's another entity entirely. An organization that knew I was on board the ship."

"A hostile intelligence organization."

"Yes, but not in the way you may think." *Hostile isn't the word,* he thought. *Diabolical, maybe. An organization with tentacles reaching high into the governments of several world powers. The Directorate.* He suddenly swerved the truck over to the side of the road, locating a gap in the stream of pilgrims. There were shouted protests from pushcart vendors, the honking of car horns.

Hopping out, he quickly unscrewed the license plates with

the screwdriver blade of a pocket knife, then returned with them to the front seat. "Just in case any of the search party is stupid enough to look only for the license plate. The trick is going to be us: they'll be looking for a couple, a man and a woman together matching our description, perhaps wearing disguises quickly thrown together. So obviously we'll have to split up, and go on foot, but we'll have to do more . . ." Bryson's voice faded as he caught sight of one of the push-carts nearby. "Hold on."

A few minutes later he was conversing, in Spanish, with a rotund gypsy woman selling shawls and other native costumes. She expected this customer—a native Castilian, from the fluency of his Spanish and the lack of accent—to drive a hard bargain and was surprised when the man all but threw down a wad of peseta notes. Moving quickly from cart to cart, he assembled a pile of clothing and returned with it to the truck. Layla's eyes widened; she nodded, then said solemnly, "So now I'm a pilgrim."

Chaos, utter chaos!

Car horns blared, angry drivers yelled and cursed. The stream of pilgrims grew into a throng, a crowd of strikingly diverse people whose only commonality was their devout faith. There were old men with walking sticks who looked as if they could barely take another step, old women garbed entirely in black, black headscarves revealing only the upper part of their faces. Many wore shorts and T-shirts. Some walked with bicycles. There were weary-looking parents carrying squalling infants, their older children squealing with delight and weaving in and out of the crowds. There was the odor of sweat, onions, incense, a whole range of human smells. Bryson was dressed in a medieval cassock with a crook-handled walking stick, monk's garb from a distant past that was still worn in certain isolated orders. Here, it was being peddled as a souvenir. It had the advantage of having a hood that Bryson put up, concealing some of his features, the rest obscured by shadow. Layla, fifty yards or so behind him, wore a peculiar shift fashioned of a coarse fabric that

looked like muslin, with a gaudy sweater covered with se-
quins, and on her head, a bright red kerchief. As strange as
she looked, she blended in with the rest of the crowd perfectly.

The wooden barricades just ahead had been arranged to
allow a broad passage for pedestrians to move through; two
uniformed police officers stood on either side of the barricades perfunctorily examining faces as they passed. On the
other half of the road, cars and trucks were being admitted
one at a time. Those on foot were moving at a normal pace,
hardly slowed at all, Bryson was relieved to observe. As he
passed the policemen, Bryson walked unsteadily, leaning
hard on the stick, the gait of a man nearing the end of a
brutally long journey. He neither glanced at the faces of the
policemen nor pointedly ignored them. They seemed to pay
him no attention. In a few seconds, he was safely through
the barricades, buffeted along by the stream of people.

A flash of light. It was the strong morning sunlight glinting off something reflective nearby; he turned his head to
see a pair of high-powered binoculars being held up to the
face of another uniformed policeman, who was standing atop
a bench. Like his colleagues manning the barricades, he was
also scrutinizing the faces of those entering the city along
Avenida Juan Carlos I. He was a backup, or perhaps a second
filter, and he was scanning the crowd with a methodical reg-
ularity. The sun was already beating down, though it was
early morning, and the man's pale complexion was flushed.

Bryson did a double-take, puzzled by the paleness of the
man's skin, the blond hair beneath the visored cap. Blonds
were not common in this part of Spain, but they were not
unheard of. Yet that wasn't what drew his attention. It was
the pale skin, almost white. No policeman or border guard
could last for long in this climate without his face tanning,
or at least turning ruddy, from the powerful sun. Even a desk-
bound official couldn't avoid being out in the sun on his way
to work or at lunchtime.

No, this was not a local, not a native. Bryson doubted the
man was even a Spaniard.

The blond policeman was sweating profusely, and he briefly lowered his binoculars to mop his face with a crooked elbow, and that was when Bryson first saw the man's facial features.

The sleepy-looking gray eyes that belied the ferocious concentration, the thin lips, the chalky skin, the ash-blond hair. The man was familiar.

Khartoum.

The blond man had been posted as a technical expert from Rotterdam, visiting the Sudanese capital with a group of European specialists advising Iraqi officials on the construction of a ballistic-missile plant and taking orders for turnkey equipment that could be used to assemble Scud missiles. The blond man was in fact an interloper, an infiltrator, a penetration agent. He was Directorate. He was also a dispatch agent, an expert in the quick-kill. Bryson had been in Khartoum to install surveillance, obtain hard evidence that could later be used against the Iraqis. He had done a brush-pass exchange with the blond killer, providing him with microdot dossiers of the desired targets, including information on where they were staying, their schedules, the presumptive holes in their security. Bryson didn't know the blond man's name; he knew only that the man was a stone killer, one of the best in the trade: supremely skilled, probably a sociopath, the perfect dispatch agent.

The Directorate had sent one of their best here to kill him. Now there could be no doubt his former employers had marked him "beyond salvage."

Yet how had they found him? The smugglers must have talked, angry about their stolen truck, eager to earn a no-doubt generous bribe. There were not many roads in this part of the country, very few routes from Finisterre, therefore easily scrutinized by air if they had quick access to a helicopter. Bryson had not heard or seen a helicopter, but there had been that stretch of time when he had been asleep. Also, the old farm truck had been so loud that a helicopter could have passed directly overhead and he would not have heard it.

It had to be the hastily abandoned truck, which served as a veritable beacon to their pursuers, evidence that he and Layla were in the immediate vicinity. And there were only two ways to go on that road: into Santiago de Compostela, or away from it. No doubt both possibilities had been covered, roadblocks placed at points of convergence.

He wanted to turn back, confirm that Layla was still behind him, still safe, but he could not risk doing so.

Bryson's pulse quickened. He looked away, but it was too late. He had seen the instant of recognition in the killer's eyes. *He saw me; he knows me.*

Yet to run, to make any sudden moves that made him stand out from the crowd, was to throw up a flag, confirm the killer's suspicions. For the dispatch agent could not be sure at that distance. Not only had it been years since Khartoum, but the hooded cassock Bryson was wearing obscured his face, and the killer would not fire indiscriminately.

Time had slowed almost to a stop as Bryson's mind raced. His body surged with adrenaline, his heart pounded, yet he restrained himself from accelerating his pace. He could not stand out from the crowd.

In his peripheral field of vision Bryson saw the killer turn toward him, his right hand moving toward the holstered weapon at his waist. The crowd of pilgrims was so thick that it almost carried Bryson along, but at a rate that was excruciatingly slow. How can the killer be sure I'm the man he wants? With this hood . . . and then Bryson had the sickening realization that it was the very fact that he was wearing a hood that made him stand out from the crowd; in the brutally hot sun, some of the men wore caps to shield their heads from the rays of the sun, but a hood trapped in the heat and was unbearably hot; none of those who had hoods on their old-fashioned monastic garb wore them up. He stood out.

Though he did not dare turn to look, he became aware of the sudden, jerking motion in his peripheral vision, the glint of light on a metal object that was surely a gun. The killer had his weapon out; Bryson sensed this almost instinctually.

Suddenly he sagged to his feet, feigning heat stroke, causing those immediately around him to stumble. Shouts of annoyance; a woman's cry of concern.

And then a split second later came the deadly cough of a silenced weapon. Screams, shrill and terrified. A young woman just a few feet to his left crumpled, the top of her head blown off. Blood sprayed in a radius of six feet or so. The crowd began to stampede; cries of fear, shouts of anguish went up. Dirt exploded nearby as bullets sprayed the ground. The killer was firing rapidly, in semiautomatic mode. Having spotted his target, he no longer cared whether he struck the innocent.

Amid the pandemonium, Bryson found himself nearly trampled by the frenzied, stampeding crowd; he struggled to his feet, his hood down, only to be knocked to the earth again. All around him were the screams and cries of the wounded and the dying, and those surrounding them. Managing to gain a foothold, he lurched forward, enduring repeated impact from those trying to flee the madness.

He had guns, but to take one out, to return fire, would be suicide. He was certainly far outnumbered; the moment he squeezed the trigger, he was in effect sending up a flare, advertising his location to the single-minded killers sent here by the Directorate. Instead, he rushed forward, keeping his head down, low to the ground, camouflaged by the tangle of bodies.

A fusillade of bullets ricocheted off the steel of a street sign ten feet away, indicating that the blond killer had lost sight of him, disoriented by the surging crowd. Twenty feet ahead, there was another scream, and the body of a man on a bicycle arched as he was struck in the back. The blond was firing at phantoms now; this only served Bryson's purpose, creating a maximum disturbance into which he could disappear. He risked a glance around, as so many others were straining to see the source of the gunfire, and was astonished to see the blond killer suddenly propelled forward as if shoved from behind. He had been hit by a bullet! The marksman twisted his torso, then toppled off the fence, either dead or seriously wounded. But who had gotten off the shot? A flash of scarlet: a bright red kerchief, which then disappeared into the crowd.

Layla.

Relieved, he turned back around and kept moving with the crowd, like a piece of driftwood borne on a powerful current. He could not move toward her, against the stream, if he wanted to; he certainly dared not flash her a signal. He knew how the Directorate staged high-priority hits, of which this was certainly one. They did not stint on manpower. A dispatch agent was like a cockroach: where you found one, there were certain to be others. But where? The blond marksman from Khartoum seemed to be operating like a lone asset, which meant that the others were backup. Yet no backup was visible. Bryson knew the Directorate's methodology too well to believe that the blond was acting alone.

The crowd of pilgrims was now out of control, a riot, a seething, teeming mass of frightened people, some trying to run down the *avenida,* others running in the opposite direction. What had been ideal cover but a few moments ago had become dangerous, violent. He and Layla would have to detach themselves from the panicked throng, disappear into Santiago, and find a way to the airport at Labacolla, eleven kilometers to the east.

He pulled out of the stream of pedestrians and cycles, nearly sideswiped by an unsteady bicyclist, and grabbed hold of a street lamp to steady himself against the onrush while he waited for Layla to emerge. He searched the passing crowd for her face, but mostly for her scarlet kerchief. Alert, too, for other anomalies: flashes of steel, police uniforms, the unmistakable look of a hired killer. Bryson knew he must have been a strange sight: he was attracting stares. One pilgrim in particular, clutching what seemed to be a Bible beneath the folds of his brown monk's outfit, seemed to be peering at him with undisguised curiosity from across the swarming Avenida Juan Carlos I. Bryson caught the monk's eye just as the man pulled out his Bible, but the object was long, blue steel.

A gun.

In the split second that his brain processed what his eyes were seeing, Bryson lurched to his right, crashing into a bicycle and causing it to topple, its middle-aged male rider frantically trying to steady himself while shouting angrily.

A spit; an explosion of blood that spattered Bryson's face. The bicyclist's temple had been blown off, leaving only a gaping wound, a sickening mass of crimson. Screams erupted anew from all around. The man was dead, the shooter a man in a monk's cassock fifty feet away, his gun still pointed, still firing.

It was insanity!

Bryson rolled over, enduring kicks to his head and back inflicted by the panicked, stampeding crowd. He grabbed a holstered weapon, the Beretta, yanked it out.

A man screamed: *"Unha pistola! Ten unha pistola!"* He's got a gun!

Bullets struck the iron street lamp, ringing loudly, and spit into the ground a few yards away. Bryson scrambled to his feet, steadied himself, located the monk-killer, squeezed the trigger.

The first shot hit the assassin in the chest, causing his gun to drop; the second shot, squarely to the center of his chest, knocked the man over entirely.

Off to his left, glinting in his peripheral vision, was an object that Bryson's instincts told him was another weapon. He turned just in time to see another man, also in the guise of a pilgrim, leveling a small black pistol at him from less than twenty feet away. Bryson spun to the right, out of the line of fire, but the sudden explosion of pain in his left shoulder, shooting lines of fire down his chest, told him he had been hit.

He lost his footing, his legs collapsing beneath him. He crumpled to the pavement. The pain was excruciating; he felt blood hotly soaking his shirt, his left arm going numb.

Hands grabbed at him. Disoriented, seeing through a scrim of haze, Bryson reflexively pummeled his attacker just as he heard Layla's voice. "No, it's me. *This* way. This way!"

She was clutching his good shoulder, his elbow, helping him to stand erect, supporting him.

"You're all right!" Bryson shouted with relief, amid the chaos—illogically, for it was *he* who had been shot.

"I'm fine. Come *on!*" She pulled him toward one side, across the stampede of frenzied pilgrims whose panic had now reached fever pitch. Bryson forced himself to move, quickening his stride, moving through the pain. He caught sight of another monk watching him from a few feet away, also clutching something. Jolted into action, Bryson raised his pistol, pointing it, just in time to see the monk lift the oblong object—a Bible—to his lips, kissing it, praying aloud amid the violence, the madness.

They were entering a large park, broad and spacious, with manicured gardens and rows of eucalyptus trees. "We must find a place to let you rest," Layla said.

"No. The wound is superficial—"

"The *blood!*"

"I think it's more of a graze. Obviously it nicked blood vessels, but it's nowhere near as serious as it may look. We can't afford to rest here; we have to keep moving!"

"But where?"

"Look. Straight ahead—across the road—a cathedral, a square. The Praza do Obradoiro—it's jammed with people. We have to stay with the crowds, disappear into them whenever we can. Whatever we do, we can't stand out." He sensed her momentary hesitation and added, "We'll take care of my wound later. Right now it's the least of our problems."

"I don't think you know how much blood you're losing." With an almost clinical detachment, she unbuttoned the top few buttons of his shirt and delicately pulled the blood-matted cloth away from the skin of his shoulder; he felt a twinge of pain. She gently palpitated the wound; the pain intensified, a jagged bolt of lightning. "All right," she pronounced, "we can tend to it later, but we have to stanch the blood flow." Whipping the red scarf from her head, she tied it firmly around his shoulder, anchoring it at the underarm, fashioning a sort of tourniquet that would do for the time being. "Can you move your arm?"

He lifted it, winced. "Yeah."

"It hurts? Don't be a hero."

"I'm not. I never ignore pain; it's one of the most valuable signals the body gives us. And yes, it does hurt. But I've suffered a lot worse, believe me."

"I believe you. Now, there's a cathedral up the hill—"

"The main Cathedral of Santiago. The square surrounding it, the Praza do Obradoiro, sometimes called Praza de Espana, is the endpoint of the pilgrim's journey, always crowded. A good place to lose our pursuers, find a vehicle. We have to get out of this open area immediately."

They started up the eucalyptus-lined path. Suddenly a pair of bicyclists zoomed by, veering around them just a few inches away, then continued up the path. Entirely innocent, presumably a couple of pilgrims heading for the center of town, but it startled Bryson. Perhaps the loss of some blood had dulled his reactions. The assassins sent by the Directorate were disguised, with diabolical cleverness, as religious pilgrims. Anyone they passed, anyone in a crowd, could be a killer sent to terminate him. At least in a minefield the trained eye could distinguish the mine from the field. Here, there was no such distinction.

Except the familiarity of the faces.

Some—not all, but some of the dispatch agents, the leaders—were men Bryson knew, had had dealings with in the past, however casual or distant. They had been sent because they could more easily find him in a crowd. But the sword was double-edged: if they recognized him, he would recognize them. If he remained alert, watchful, he would see them before they saw him. It was not much of an advantage, but it was all he had, and he would have to exploit it to its maximum extent.

"Wait," he said abruptly. "I've been spotted, and so have you. They may not know who you are, not yet. But me, they know. And there's the bloodstained shirt, the red tourniquet. No, we can't give them that."

She nodded. "Let me get us another change of clothes."

They were thinking along the same lines. "I'll wait here—no, strike that." He pointed to a small, moss-covered ancient cathedral surrounded by gardens planted with exotic species of flora. "I'll wait inside *there*."

"Good." She hurried up the path toward the main square while he turned back toward the church.

He waited anxiously in the dim, cool, deserted cathedral. A few times the heavy wooden doors to the church opened; each time it was a genuine pilgrim or tourist, or so they appeared. Women with children, young couples. Watching from a concealed alcove off the narthex, he studied each one. One could never be sure, but none of the signs were present, nothing that alerted his internal alarms. Twenty minutes later the doors opened again; it was Layla, holding a paper-wrapped bundle.

They changed, separately, in the cathedral's restrooms. She had accurately estimated his size. Now they were dressed in the plain garb of middle-class tourists: a simple skirt and blouse for her with a broad-brimmed, gaily decorated sun hat; khaki pants, a white short-sleeved knit shirt, and a base-ball cap for him. She had managed to locate a couple of large bandages and an iodine-based disinfectant to tempo-rarily cleanse the wound. She had even provided them with cameras—a cheap video camera, sans film, for him; an even cheaper 35mm camera on a neck strap for her.

Ten minutes later, each of them wearing modish sun-glasses, walking hand in hand like honeymooners, they en-tered the immense, bustling Praza do Obradoiro. The square was filled with pilgrims, tourists, students; vendors hawked postcards and souvenirs. Bryson stopped before the cathe-dral, pretending to take some video footage of the baroque eighteenth-century facade, the centerpiece of which was the Pórtico de la Gloria, the astonishing Spanish Romanesque twelfth-century sculpture crowded with the likenesses of an-gels and demons, monsters and prophets. As he looked through the telephoto lens of the viewfinder, he moved the camera from the portico, sweeping across the facade of the cathedral, then panning across the crowd of tourists and pilgrims, as if capturing the entire scene on video, an amateur cinematographer.

Putting down the video camera, he turned to Layla, smiling and nodding like a proud tourist. She touched his arm, the two of them engaged in an exaggerated pantomime of honeymooner affection in order to deflect the suspicions of any who might be watching. His disguise was minimal, but at least the peak of the baseball cap cast a shadow across his face. Perhaps it would be enough to induce uncertainty, raise doubts in any watchers.

Then Bryson became aware of a movement, a synchronized shifting, on several points in the distance. Everywhere around him was filled with motion, but against that background was a coordinated, symmetrical movement. The perception would not have registered with anyone who had not had his extensive field experience. But it was there, he was sure of it!

"Layla," he said quietly, "I want you to laugh at something I just said."

"Laugh . . . ?"

"Right now. I've just told you something hysterically funny."

Abruptly she laughed, throwing her head back in abandon. It was an utterly convincing act that Bryson, even though he had requested it, expected it, found unnerving. She was a skilled performer. She had instantly become the entranced lover who found her new husband's every witticism hugely entertaining. Bryson smiled in modest, yet gratified, acknowledgment of his own cleverness. As he smiled, he picked up the video camera and looked through the viewfinder, panning it over the crowd around them as he had done a moment ago. But this time he was looking for something specific.

Through her smile, Layla's voice was tense. "You see something?"

He found it.

A classic triad formation. At three points around the

square, three persons stood very still, peering through binoculars in Bryson's direction. Individually, none of them was remarkable or worthy of attention; each might have been a tourist taking in the sights. But together, they represented an ominous pattern. On one side of the *praza* was a young woman, with flaxen hair worn up, wearing a blazer that was too warm for such a hot day, though it would serve to conceal a shoulder holster. On another side, representing the second point of an isosceles triangle, was a fleshy-faced, bearded man of chunky build, garbed in black clerical vestments; his high-powered binoculars seemed jarring, not the sort of optical equipment likely to be used by a man of the cloth. At the third leg of the triangle was another man, of sinewy build and swarthy complexion, in his early forties; it was this man who tugged at Bryson's memory, demanded closer inspection. Bryson touched the button for the zoom lens, tightening the shot, moving in for a close-up of the swarthy man.

He felt his insides go cold.

He knew the man, had dealt with him several times on some high-priority assignments. He had in fact hired the man on behalf of the Directorate. He was a peasant named Paolo from a village outside of Cividale. Paolo always operated in tandem with his brother, Niccolo. The two of them had been legendary game hunters in the remote hill country of northwestern Italy where they had grown up, and so they had easily become highly skilled hunters of human beings, assassins of rare talent. The brothers were much-sought-after bounty hunters, mercenaries, killers for hire, jobbers. In his past life, Bryson had hired them for the occasional odd job, including a dangerous infiltration of a Russian firm called Vector, which had been rumored to be involved in bioweapons research and manufacture.

Where Paolo went, so did Niccolo. That meant there was at least one other, positioned somewhere outside the legs of the triad.

Bryson's heart thudded; his scalp went prickly.

But *how* had they located him and Layla so easily? They

had lost the pursuers, he had been sure; how had they been found once again, in a crowd of this size, particularly having changed outfits, altered the configuration?

Was it something about the clothes—too new, too bright, somehow not quite right? But Bryson had taken pains to scuff up his brand-new leather loafers on the pavement outside the church where they had stopped, and had seen to it that Layla did the same. He had even soiled their clothes with a light sprinkling of dust.

How had they been found?

The answer came to him in a slow, sickening realization, a terrible certainty. He felt the warmth of blood on his left shoulder, which had oozed out from the bandage; he did not have to look at it, or touch it, to be sure. The gunshot wound had continued to bleed steadily, profusely, seeping into the fabric of his knit shirt, turning a large area of his yellow shirt crimson. The blood had been the giveaway, the beacon, negating all the precautions they had taken, penetrating their disguise.

His pursuers had finally located him, and now they were moving in for the kill.

WASHINGTON, D.C.

Senator James Cassidy could feel the eyes of his colleagues on him—some bored, some wary—as he stood up heavily, spread his thick, spotted hands on the well-rubbed wooden rail, and began to speak in a rich, dulcet baritone. "In our chambers and committee rooms, we go on a great deal, all of us, about scarce resources and endangered species. We talk about how best to manage our diminishing natural resources in an era when everything seems to be for sale, when everything has a price tag and a bar code. Well, I'm here to say something about another kind of endangered species, a vanishing commodity: the very notion of privacy. In the papers, I read an Internet maven who says, 'You already have zero privacy. Get over it.' Well, those of you who know me know I'm sure as hell *not* one to get over it. Stop and look around you, I say. What do you see? Cameras and scanners and mammoth databases of a reach that defies human comprehension. Marketers can follow every aspect of our lives, from the first phone call we make in the morning to the time our security systems say we have left our houses, to the video camera at the toll booth and the charge slip we get at lunch. Go on-line, and every transaction, every 'hit,' is tracked and recorded by so-called infomediaries. Private companies have been approaching the Federal Bureau of Investigation with the proposal that the Bureau sell them their records, their information, as if *information* were just another government asset to be privatized. This is the beginning of something troubling: the naked republic. The surveillance society."

The senator looked around and realized that he was experiencing a rare moment: he actually had his colleagues' attention. Some of them appeared transfixed, others skeptical. But he had their attention.

"And I ask you one question: Is this a place you want to live in? I see no reason to hope that the cherished notion of privacy has a ghost of a chance against the forces arrayed against it—overzealous national and international law-enforcement bodies, marketers and corporations and insurance companies and the new managed-care conglomerates and the million tentacles of every enmeshed corporate and governmental concern. The people who want to maintain order, the people who want to squeeze every penny they can out of you—the forces of order and the forces of commerce: that's a formidable alliance, my friends! That's what privacy, *our* privacy, is up against. It is a pitched, yet terribly one-sided, battle. And so my question, my question for my distinguished colleagues on either side of the aisle, is simple: *What side are you on?*"

CHAPTER NINE

"Don't look," Bryson commanded softly, still panning the crowd and peering through the magnifying viewfinder. "Don't turn your head. It's a triad, as far as I can tell."

"What distance?" She spoke quietly, intensely, while at the same time grinning, the effect bizarre.

"Seventy, eighty feet. An isosceles triangle. At your three o'clock, a blond woman in a blazer, hair up, oversized round sunglasses. At six o'clock, a big bearded man in a black priest's getup. At nine o'clock, a slender man, late thirties, swarthy complexion, dark short-sleeved shirt, dark pants. All of them have small binoculars, and I'm sure each has a gun. Okay?"

"Got it," she said almost inaudibly.

"One of them's the team leader; they're waiting for his signal. Now, I'm going to point something out and ask you to look through the video camera. Tell me when you've located them."

He abruptly gestured at the cathedral's portico with an open, flat hand, like some amateur cinematographer, holding the video camera out for her. "Jonas," she said, alarmed. It was the first time she had called him by name, though it was a cover name. "Oh, my God, the *blood!* Your shirt!"

"I'm fine," he said shortly. "Unfortunately, it's what drew their attention."

She instantly turned her look of alarm into a bizarre, inappropriate grin, followed by a giggle, play-acting for an audience of three, the effect bizarre. She leaned in, peering through the viewfinder as he rotated it in a slow arc around the square. "The blond woman, check," she said. A few seconds later, she added, "The bearded priest in black, check. The younger guy in the dark shirt, check."

"All right." He smiled, nodded, continuing the performance. "I suspect they're trying to avoid a repeat of what happened by the barricades. Obviously they're not averse to killing innocent bystanders if need be, but they'd rather avoid it if possible, if only because of the political fallout. Otherwise, they'd have already taken a shot at me."

"Or they may not be certain it's you," she pointed out.

"Their positioning indicates that if they were uncertain a few minutes ago, they no longer are," Bryson said in a hushed tone. "They've moved into place."

"But I don't understand: Who are they? You seem to know something about them. These are not just faceless pursuers to you."

"I know them," Bryson said. "I know their methods; I know they work."

"How?"

"I've read their field manual," he said cryptically, deliberately so, unwilling to elaborate.

"If you know them, then you must have an idea of what kind of risks they'll take. You say 'political fallout'—are you saying these are government operatives? Americans? Russians?"

"I think transnational is the best description. None of the above, or maybe all of the above—neither Russian nor American nor French nor Spanish, but an organization that operates between the cracks, operating on a subterranean level where borders aren't delineated. They work with governments but not for them. It appears as if they're watching, waiting for a clearing to form around me. Given their distance, they want a space large enough to allow for a standard margin of error. But if I make any sudden movements, appearing as if I'm about to bolt, they'll simply fire away, bystanders be damned."

They were surrounded by tourists and pilgrims, jammed up against them so closely it was hard to move. He continued: "Now, I want you to cover the woman, but be very subtle about taking out your gun, because they can observe your every move. They may not know who you are, but they know you're with me, and that's all they need to know."

"What does that mean?"

"It means they consider you at the very least an accessory, if not an outright accomplice."

"Great," Layla moaned, then flashed a discordant smile.

"I'm sorry—I didn't ask you to get involved."

"I know, I know. I made the choice."

"As long as we're hemmed in like this by all these people, you're free to move your hands below waist level. But you should assume they can see all movements from mid-torso up."

She nodded.

"Tell me when you have your gun out."

She nodded again. He could see her reach into her large woven handbag.

"Got it," she said.

"Now, with your left hand, lift the camera from around your neck and take a picture of me with the cathedral behind me. Go for a wide-angle shot; that'll allow you to see the blond woman at the same time. Take your time doing it: you're an amateur photographer, and you're not good with cameras. No hurried motions, nothing smooth or professional."

She put the camera up to her face, squinted her right eye.

"All right, now I'm going to seem to be joking around with you, pretending to take a video of you taking a picture of me. As soon as I hold the video camera to my face, you will react with annoyance; I'm ruining your perfect frame. You whip the camera away from your face with unexpected force, a sudden movement that will distract and confuse the watchers. Then, aim right and squeeze off a shot. Take down the blond woman."

"At *this* distance?" she said incredulously.

"I've seen your accuracy. You're one of the best I've seen; I have confidence. But don't wait for a second go; dive right for the ground."

"And you? What will you be doing?"

"Aiming at the bearded guy."

"But there's a *third*—"

"We *can't* cover all three, that's the maddening thing about this damned arrangement."

She gave another disconcerting false smile, then put the 35mm camera up to her face, clutching her Heckler & Koch .45 in her right hand at about waist level.

He smiled impishly as he drew the video camera to his face. At the same instant, with a small, barely detectable movement, he reached his free hand around to the small of his back and pulled the Beretta from his waistband. His hands were trembling; he could hardly breathe.

Directly behind her, visible through the video camera lens and some fifty to eighty feet distant, the bearded false priest lowered his binoculars. What did that mean: that they had decided to hold their fire, confused by Bryson's ruse? That they did not want to fire indiscriminately with innocent bystanders just inches away? If so, they had just bought themselves a little time.

If not . . .

Suddenly the bearded man shook his wrist, ostensibly an innocent gesture designed to restore circulation in a tired hand, but clearly a sign to the others. A signal, delivered moments before Bryson had anticipated it would come. *No!*

They had *no* time.

Now!

He dropped the video camera just as he swooped the gun upward, squeezing off three rapid shots just over Layla's shoulder.

At the exact same moment, she let her camera drop from its neck strap, whirled her .45 magnum up and over, and fired over the heads of the crowd.

What followed was a bewildering sequence of explosions, shot answering shot in rapid-fire fashion, provoking terrified screams from all around. As Bryson dove to the ground, he was able to catch a glimpse of the bearded man staggering, sinking, obviously hit. Layla threw herself downward, tumbling against Bryson, slamming against the limbs of those surrounding them, knocking a young woman over. Someone very near had been struck by a stray round, wounded but not fatally so, a collateral injury.

"She's down!" Layla gasped as she rolled to her side. "The blonde—I saw her go down."

The gunfire ceased as abruptly as it had begun, but the shouts, the horrified clamor, continued to rise.

Two of Bryson's would-be assassins were down, perhaps permanently so; but at least one certainly remained standing: Paolo, the assassin from Cividale. And surely there were others as well; Paolo's brother was almost certainly in the vicinity.

Running feet kicked at them, others tripped over them, stumbled. Once again a crowd had become a stampede, and as they plunged into the middle of the chaos, Bryson and Layla managed to get to their feet, rushing headlong with the others, disappearing into the maddened crowd.

Weaving in and out of the onrushers, Bryson saw a narrow cobblestone street, almost a lane, coming off the *praza*. It was little more than a lane, barely big enough for one car to pass through it. He ran toward it, weaving around human obstacles, determined to follow it as far as he could until they lost the Italian brothers or whoever else was chasing him. It appeared likely that there would be small, ancient houses on this street, perhaps small courtyards, alleys leading to other alleys. Mazes in which to lose themselves.

His shoulder wound was once again throbbing, blood oozing thick and hot; what had begun to heal had been wrenched open. The pain had become incredible. Yet he forced himself to run faster. Layla kept up easily. Their footsteps echoed in the empty street. As he ran, he was searching the narrow, shadowed street, searching for a courtyard, a shop, any place into which they could duck. There was a small, Romanesque church tucked between a couple of even older stone buildings, but it was locked; a handwritten sign pasted on one heavy wooden door declared that it was closed for repairs. In this town of churches and cathedrals, the smaller houses of worship, which did not attract tourists, probably got little attention and less funding.

Approaching the church, he stopped short, grabbing a massive iron door handle and rattling it.

"What are you *doing?*" Layla asked, alarmed. "The *noise*—come on, let's keep going!" She was breathing hard, her chest heaving, her face flushed. Footsteps echoed in the street, approaching.

Bryson did not reply. He gave the door handle one last, mighty tug. The padlock was small and rusted, and it looped through an even rustier hasp, which easily came off the door with a splintering sound. People did not break into churches as a rule; the lock was mostly symbolic, all that was required in this town of the devout.

He yanked the door open and entered the dark central portal. Layla, giving a small grunt of frustration, followed, shutting the door behind them. Now the only light in the dim narthex came from small, dusty quatrefoil windows high above. There was a dank, mildewy smell here, and the air was chilly. Bryson looked around briefly, then leaned back against a cold stone wall. His heart was pounding from the exertion, and he felt weak from the searing pain of his wounded shoulder, and from loss of blood. Layla was pacing the length of the nave, presumably looking for exits or hiding places.

After a few minutes he had caught his breath, and he returned to the entrance doors. The broken lock would draw the attention of anyone who knew the town; either it should be reassembled so that it looked intact, or it should simply be removed entirely. As he reached for the handle to pull the door open, he listened for any approaching footsteps.

There *was* the sound of running feet, and then a voice, a shout in a strange language that was neither Spanish nor Gallego. He froze, glancing at the floor, at the narrow bands of light that came in through a small louver at the bottom of the door. Kneeling, he put his ear against the slats and listened.

The language was oddly familiar.

"*Niccolò, o crodevi di velu viodût! Jù par che strade cà. Cumò o controli, tu continue a cjalà la 'plaza'!*"

He recognized it, understood the words. *I thought I saw him, Niccolo!* the voice was saying. *Down the street. You watch the plaza!*

It was an obscure, dying language called Friuliano, a tongue he had not heard in years. Some said it was an ancient dialect of Italian; others believed it was a language in its own right. It was spoken only in the northeast corner of Italy near the Slovenian border, by a dwindling number of peasants.

Bryson, whose facility with languages had often proved as useful a survival mechanism as his ability with firearms, had taught himself Friuliano a decade or so ago, when he had hired two young peasants from the remote mountains above Cividale, remarkable hunters, assassins. Brothers. When he had hired Paolo and Niccolo Sangiovanni, he had made it a point to learn their strange tongue, largely so that he could keep close tabs on the brothers, listen to what they said to one another, though he never let on that he understood what they were saying.

Yes. It was Paolo, who had indeed survived the shootout in the Praza do Obradoiro, shouting to his brother, Niccolo. The two Italians were superb hunters and had never failed him in any assignment he had given them. They would not be easy to evade, but Bryson did not intend to evade them.

He heard Layla approach, and he looked up. "I need you to find us some rope or cable," he whispered.

"*Rope?*"

"Quickly! There must be a door off the chancel, maybe leading to a rectory, a supply closet, something. Please, *right away!*"

She nodded and ran back down the nave toward the sanctuary.

He stood quickly, opened the door a crack, and called out a few words in Friuliano. Since Bryson's ear for languages was almost pitch-perfect, he knew the accent would closely approximate that of a native. But more than that, he pitched his voice higher, tightening his throat to match Paolo's timbre. His mimicry was uncanny, he knew; it was one of his most useful talents. A few snatches of muffled, shouted phrases, heard at a distance and distorted by echoes, would sound to Paolo like his own brother. *"Ou! Paulo, pessèe! Lu ai, al è jù!"* Hey! Paolo, come quick! I've got him—he's down!

The response came rapidly. *"La setu?"* Where are you?

"Ca! Lì da vecje glesie—cu le sieradure rote!" This old church—the broken lock!

Bryson got to his feet quickly, spun to one side of the portico, flattening himself against the doorframe, the Beretta gripped in his left hand.

The footsteps accelerated, slowed, then approached. Paolo's voice now came from just outside the church door. "Niccolo?"

"Ca!" Bryson shouted, muffling his voice in the cloth of his shirt. *"Moviti!"*

A brief hesitation, then the door was flung open. In the sudden flood of light, Bryson saw the swarthy skin, the lean, sinewy build, the tight black curls of the close-cropped hair. Paolo squinted his eyes, his expression fierce. He entered warily, looking from side to side, his weapon down at his side.

Bryson sprung forward, slamming into Paolo with the full force of his body. His right hand was a rigid claw, smashing against the cartilage of the Italian's throat, twisting the larynx enough to disable, not to kill. Paolo let out a loud scream of pain and surprise. Simultaneously, with his left hand, Bryson cracked the Beretta against the back of Paolo's head, aiming with precision.

Paolo slumped to the floor, unconscious. Bryson knew the concussion was minor, that Paolo would be out no more than a few minutes. He grabbed the Italian's weapon, a Lugo, and quickly searched his body for any concealed weapons. Since Bryson had trained the Sangiovannis in field tactics, he knew there would be another weapon, and he knew where to find it: strapped to the left calf, under loose-fitting slacks. Bryson took that, too, and then removed a jagged fishing knife from a scabbard on the Italian's belt.

Layla was watching, stunned, but now she understood. She threw Bryson a large spindle of insulated electrical wire. Not ideal, but it was strong, and in any case it would have to do. Working quickly, the two of them bound the Italian's hands and feet so that the more he struggled, the tighter the knots would become. The design was of Layla's invention, and it was a clever one. Bryson tugged at the knots, satisfied that they would hold, and then he and Layla carried the assassin into a sacristy off the north transept. Here it was even dimmer, but their eyes had by now become accustomed to the low light.

"He's an impressive specimen," Layla said dispassionately. "Powerful—almost like a coiled spring."

"Both he and his brother were supremely gifted natural athletes. Hunters, both of them, with the innate skills, the instincts, of mountain lions. And just as ruthless."

"He once worked for you?"

"In a past life. He and his brother. A few brief assignments and one major one, in Russia." She looked at him questioningly; he saw no reason to hold out. Not now, not after everything she had put herself through for him. "There's a Russian institute known as Vector, in Koltsovo, Novosibirsk. In the mid- to late 1980s, rumors circulated in American intelligence circles that Vector was no mere research institute, but was involved in the research and production of agents of biological warfare."

She nodded. "Weaponized anthrax, smallpox, even plague. There were rumors . . ."

"According to a defector who came over in the late eighties—the former deputy chief of the Soviet biological warfare program—the Russians were targeting major U.S. cities for a biological first strike. Technical intelligence told us very little. A compound of low-rise buildings surrounded by high electrified fences and patrolled by armed guards. That was all the conventional U.S. intelligence agencies had, CIA or NSA. Without concrete evidence, neither the U.S. nor any other NATO government was willing to act." He shook his head. "Typically passive response on the part of the intelligence bureaucrats. So I was sent in to do a high-risk, dangerous penetration no other intelligence agency would ever dare. I assembled my own team of black-bag specialists and muscle, which included these boys. My employers had a shopping list—high-res photographs of containment facilities, air locks, fermentation vats for growing viruses and vaccines. And most of all, they wanted actual samples of the bugs—Petri dishes."

"My God . . . Your employers—but you said 'no other intelligence agency' would ever attempt such a thing. . . . Did CIA . . ."

He shrugged. "Leave it at that." He thought, *But what's the point of withholding anything, anymore?* "These fellows, the Sangiovanni brothers, were there to overpower night sentries, take out armed guards swiftly and silently. So they were muscle, of a rarefied sort." He smiled grimly.

"How'd they do?"

"We got the goods."

While they waited for Paolo to come to, Layla went to the church's front door and reassembled the broken hasp and padlock so that it appeared unbroken. Meanwhile, Bryson stood watch over the Italian assassin. In about twenty minutes, Paolo began to stir, his eyes shifting beneath his closed lids. He groaned slightly, and then his eyes came open, unfocused.

"Al è pasât tant timp di quand che jerin insieme a Novosibirsk," Bryson said. It's been a long time since Novosibirsk. "I always knew you were devoid of any allegiances. Where's your brother?"

Paolo's eyes widened. "Coleridge, you bastard." He tried to pull his hands up, grimaced as the thin wires cut into his wrists. He snarled through bloody teeth, *"Bastard, tu mi fasis pensà a che vecje storie dal purcìt, lo tratin come un siôr, a viodin di lui, i dan dut chel che a voe di vè, e dopo lu copin."* Bryson smiled and translated for Layla's benefit. "He says there's an old Friulian peasant proverb about the hog. They treat it like a prince, cater to it, serve its every need— until the day they slaughter it for meat."

"Who's the hog supposed to be?" asked Layla. "You or him?"

Bryson turned back to Paolo, speaking in Friuliano. "We're going to play a little game here called truth or consequences. You tell me the truth, or you face the consequences. Let's start with a simple question: Where's your brother?"

"Never!"

"Well, you've just answered one of my questions—that Niccolo came here with you. You almost killed me back in the square. What kind of gratitude is that to show your old boss?"

"No soi ancjmò freât dal dut!" Paolo bellowed. I'm not done yet! He struggled against the restraints, wincing.

"No," Bryson said with a smile. "Neither am I. Who hired you?"

The Italian spit a gobbet of saliva, which hit Bryson's face. *"Fuck you!"* he shouted in English, one of the few phrases he knew.

Bryson wiped at the spittle with his sleeve. "I'll ask you one more time, and if I don't get a truthful answer—the operative word being *truthful*—I'll be forced to use this." He held up the Beretta for display.

Layla approached, spoke quickly in a low voice. "I'm going to keep watch at the door. All this shouting may attract some unwanted attention."

Bryson nodded. "Good idea."

"Go ahead and kill me," the assassin taunted in his native language. "It makes no difference to me. There are others, *many* others. My brother may have the pleasure of killing you himself—it would be my dying gift to him."

"Oh, I have no intention of killing you," said Bryson coolly. "You're a brave fellow; I've seen you face down death fearlessly. Death doesn't frighten you, which is one of the things that make you so good at what you do."

The Italian's eyes narrowed in suspicion as he attempted to puzzle out the meaning. Bryson could see him shifting his ankles, his wrists, testing the restraints for weaknesses. But there were none.

"No," Bryson continued, "instead, I would rather take away the only thing that means anything to you: your ability to hunt, whether it's *cinghiale,* your beloved wild boar, or human beings placed 'beyond salvage' by the liars who control the secret arms of government." He paused, aimed the Beretta at the assassin's kneecap. "The loss of one knee, of course, won't keep you from walking—not with all the advanced prosthetic joints that are available these days—but you certainly won't be able to run very well. The loss of both of your knees—well, that will certainly deprive you of your livelihood, don't you think?"

The assassin's face went ashen. "You goddamned sell-out," he hissed.

"Is that what they tell you? And who do they say I sold out *to?*"

Paolo stared defiantly, but his lower lip quivered.

"So I ask you one more time, and consider very carefully before you either refuse to answer or attempt to lie to me: *Who hired you?*"

"Fuck you!"

Bryson fired the Beretta. The Italian screamed, and blood drenched his pants at the knee. Most if not all of the kneecap was probably gone. He would not likely hunt prey, human or animal, again. Paolo writhed in pain. At the top of his lungs he shouted a string of curses in Friuliano.

Suddenly there came a crash at the church door, followed by a male voice shouting and a throaty cry in Layla's voice. Bryson whirled around to see what had happened—had she been struck? He rushed to the entrance just in time to see two silhouetted figures struggling in the darkness. One of them had to be Layla; who was the other? He leveled his gun and shouted, "Stop or you're dead!"

"It's all right," came Layla's voice. He felt a surge of relief. "Bastard put up a nasty fight."

It was Paolo's brother, Niccolo, his arms trussed behind his back. A wire that hung loosely around his neck was all that remained of a garrote she had evidently used to pull tight around his throat the second he burst in. A thin, crimson line at the base of his neck was the telltale evidence of his near-strangulation. She had had the advantage of surprise, and had utilized it well; she had fashioned the restraint ingeniously so that the harder Niccolo pulled his arms, the harder the wire cut into his throat. His legs, however, were unbound, and though he sprawled on the floor, he kept kicking, wheeling around to try to gain his footing.

Bryson leaped atop Niccolo's chest, slamming his feet down to knock the wind out of him, and at the same time holding him down, enabling Layla to toss a loop of wire around his knees and ankles and bind them tightly. Niccolo bellowed like a gored ox, joining the bloodcurdling screams of his brother from the sacristy fifty feet away.

"Enough," Bryson said disgustedly. He ripped a length of cloth from Niccolo's khaki shirt, and, bunching it up, jammed it into Niccolo's mouth to muffle the bellowing. Layla produced a roll of strong packing tape she had located somewhere, probably in the supply closet where she had found the electrical wire, and she used it to secure the gag over Niccolo's mouth. Bryson ripped off another piece of Niccolo's shirt, handed it to Layla, and asked her to gag the brother as well.

While she did that, he dragged Niccolo down the nave to another alcove, shoving him into a confessional booth. "Your brother's just been shot, badly," Bryson told him, waving the Beretta. "But as you can hear, he's still alive. He won't be walking again."

Niccolo whipped his head back and forth, roaring through the gag. He bucked his legs up and down against the stone floor in a mute, animal-like display of defiance and anger.

"Now, I'm going to make this as simple for you as I can, my old friend. I want you to tell me who hired you. I want the complete verbal dossier, the codes, the contact names and procedures. Everything. As soon as I remove your gag, I expect you to begin talking. And don't even *contemplate* fabricating anything, because your brother has already told me a good deal, and if anything you say doesn't jibe with what he said, I'm going to assume that *he's* the one who's lying. And I will kill him. Because I really don't like liars. Are we clear?"

Niccolo, who had stopped bucking his legs, nodded frantically, his eyes wide, searching Bryson's face. The threat was obviously effective; Bryson had located the killer's single area of vulnerability.

From the other side of the church, Bryson could hear Paolo whimpering and groaning, muffled by the gag Layla had put in his mouth.

"My partner is across the aisle with Paolo. All I have to do is give her the signal, and she'll fire one single round into his forehead. Are we clear?"

Niccolo's nodding became even more frenzied.

"All right, then." He ripped the wide plastic tape off Niccolo's mouth, leaving a red stripe on the skin that had to have been extremely painful. Then he grabbed the bunched-up wet rag and yanked it out.

Niccolo took several deep, ragged breaths.

"Now, if you make the serious mistake of lying to me, you'd better hope your brother has already told me the exact same lie. Or you'll have killed him, just as if you yourself squeezed the trigger against his temple, understand?"

Niccolo gasped, "Yes!"

"But if I were you, I'd stick to the truth. The odds are much better. And bear in mind, I know where your families live. How's *nonna* Maria? And your mother, Alma—does she still have her boarding house?"

Niccolo's eyes were at once fierce and wounded. *"I am telling you the truth!"* he screamed in Friuliano.

"As long as we're clear about that," Bryson replied blandly.

"But we don't *know* who hired us! The procedures are the same as when we worked for you! We are the *mus*, the beasts of burden! They tell us *nothing!*"

Bryson shook his head ruminatively. "Nothing is ever sealed in a vacuum, my friend. You know that as well as I.

Even when you deal with a cutout, you know your contact's cover name. You can't help but pick up bits and pieces of information. And they may not tell you *why* you're doing a particular operation, but they always tell you *how* to do it, and that can be quite revealing as well."

"I told you, we don't *know* who our employers are!"

Bryson raised his voice, speaking with controlled fury. "You worked with a team, under a team leader; you were issued instructions; and people *always* talk. You damned well know who hired you!" He turned toward the aisle as if preparing to call out a signal.

"No!" cried Niccolo.

"Your brother—"

"My brother doesn't know either. I don't know what he said to you, but *he doesn't know!* You know how the lines, the—compartments—how this works! We're only the hired help, and they pay us in cash!"

"Language!" Bryson demanded.

"Che . . . language?"

"The team you're working with here. What *language* do they speak to one another?"

Niccolo's eyes were wild. "Different languages!"

"The team *leader!*"

"Russian!" he shouted desperately. "He's a *Russian!*"

"KGB, GRU?"

"What do we know of these things?"

"You know faces!" Bryson spat out. Louder, he called: "Layla?"

Layla approached, understood Bryson's gambit. "Would you like me to use a silencer?" she inquired in a matter-of-fact way.

"No!" Niccolo thundered. "I tell you what you want to know!"

"I'll give him another sixty seconds," Bryson said. "Then, if I don't hear what I want to hear, fire away—and yes, actually, a silencer might be a good idea." To Niccolo, he said, "They hired you to kill me because you know me, know my face."

Niccolo nodded, his eyes closed.

"But they knew you once worked for me, and they wouldn't just hire you to kill your old employer without a plausible cover story. No matter how little loyalty you two have. So they told you I was a sellout, a traitor, is that right?"

"Yes."

"A traitor to what, to whom?"

"They only said you were selling names of agents, that we and everyone else you'd ever worked with would be identified, flushed out, executed."

"Executed by *whom?*"

"Hostile parties . . . I don't know, they didn't say!"

"Yet you believed them."

"Why would I not believe them?"

"Was a bounty placed on my head, or was this a straight job price?"

"Yes, a bounty."

"How much?"

"Two million."

"Lire or dollars?"

"Dollars! Two million *dollars*."

"I'm flattered. You and your brother could have retired to the hills and hunted *cinghiale* to your hearts' content. But the problem with offering a bounty to a team is that it diminishes the incentive for the team to coordinate; everyone wants to make the hit separately. Bad strategy, self-defeating. The bearded one was the team leader?"

"Yes."

"Was he the Russian-speaker?"

"Yes."

"You know his name?"

"Not directly. I hear someone call him Milyukov. But I know the face. He's like me, like us—he does assignments."

"Freelance?"

"They say he works for a—a plutocrat, a Russian baron. One of the secret powers behind the Kremlin. A very rich man who owns a conglomerate. Through it, they say he secretly runs Russia."

"Prishnikov."

There was a glint of recognition in the Italian's eyes. He had heard the name before. "Maybe, yes."

Prishnikov. Anatoly Prishnikov. Founder and chairman of the mammoth, shadowy Russian consortium Nortek. Immensely rich and powerful and, indeed, the power behind the throne. Bryson's heart began beating rapidly. Why would Anatoly Prishnikov have sent someone to eliminate Bryson? Why?

The only logical explanation seemed to be that Prishnikov was controlling the Directorate, or was among those controlling it. Harry Dunne of the CIA had said that the Directorate had been founded and, from its beginning, been controlled by a small cabal of Soviet GRU 'geniuses,' as he put it.

"What if I told you that the Directorate in fact isn't part of the United States government?" Dunne had said. *"That it never was . . . The whole thing was an elaborate ruse, do you see? . . . A penetration operation right on enemy soil—our soil."*

And then, after the Cold War ended, as the Soviet intelligence services fell into collapse, control of the Directorate *shifted into other hands,* he had said. Agents were terminated.

I was set up, then pushed out.

And Elena? She had disappeared—meaning what? That she was deliberately separated from him? Could that explain it? That the masters had to keep the two of them apart from each other for some reason? Because they knew things, could put things together?

". . . Now we've got reason to think it's being reactivated," Dunne had said. *"Your old masters appear to be accumulating arms, for some reason. . . . You could say they're poised to foment global instability. . . . Seems they're trying to stockpile an arsenal. We think they're instigating some kind of turbulence in the southern Balkans, although their target is elsewhere."*

Their ultimate target is elsewhere.

Generalities, blanket statements, vague assertions. The outlines remained murky and uncertain. Facts were all he had to work with, and there were altogether too few of them.

Fact: A team of assassins made up of Directorate operatives—past or present ones, he had no idea—had been trying to kill him.

But *why?* Calacanis's security forces may simply have considered him an interloper, a penetration agent to be eliminated. But the assassin-squads here in Santiago de Compostela seemed too well organized, too orchestrated, to be simply a reaction to his appearance on Calacanis's ship.

Fact: The Sangiovanni brothers had been hired to kill him even before his appearance on the *Spanish Armada*. The controllers of the Directorate had decided he was a threat prior to that. But how, and why?

Fact: The leader of the assassin squad was also in the employ of Anatoly Prishnikov, an immensely wealthy private citizen. Thus, Prishnikov had to be one of the controllers of the Directorate—but why would an ostensibly private citizen be running a rogue intelligence outfit?

Did this indicate that the Directorate had gone private— had been the object of a hostile takeover, co-opted by Anatoly Prishnikov? Had it become a private army of Russia's most powerful, most secretive mogul?

But something else occurred to him. "You said the team spoke other languages," he said to Niccolo. "You mentioned French."

"Yes, but—"

"But nothing! Which member of the squad spoke French?"

"It was the blonde."

"The blond woman in the plaza—her hair was up."

"Yes."

"And what are you holding back about her?"

"Holding *back?* Nothing!"

"I find this very interesting, because your brother was much more talkative on the subject." The bluff was audacious, but made with enormous certitude and therefore quite convincing. "*Much* more talkative. Perhaps he *invented* things, made up a story—is *that* what you're telling me?"

"*No!* I don't know what he told you—we just overheard things, little scraps. Maybe names."

"Maybe names?"

"I heard her speaking in French to another agent who was aboard the arms ship that blew up. The *Spanish Armada.* The agent was a Frenchman who was there to make some kind of arms deal with the Greek."

"A deal?"

"This Frenchman is—*was*—a double, I heard them say."

Bryson recalled the longhaired, elegantly dressed Frenchman from Calacanis's dining room. The Frenchman was known to be an emissary from Jacques Arnaud, France's wealthiest and most powerful arms dealer. Was he with the Directorate as well, or at least working with or for them? What did it mean that Jacques Arnaud, the extreme-right-wing French arms merchant, was somehow in league with the Directorate—and therefore in league, too, with the richest private citizen in Russia?

And if it was true that two powerful businessmen, one in Russia and one in France, were controlling the Directorate, using it to foment terrorism around the world—what was their objective?

They left the two Italian brothers bound and gagged in the old cathedral. Bryson asked Layla, who had had paramedic training, to attempt to stanch the blood flow from Paolo's ruined knee, using a tightly fastened rag to compress the wound.

"But how can you be so considerate to a man who tried to murder you?" she asked later, genuinely puzzled.

Bryson had shrugged. "He was just doing his job."

"This is not how we work in the Mossad," she protested. "If a man has tried to kill you and failed, you must never let him get away. It is an inviolable rule."

"I have a different set of rules."

They spent the night in an anonymous, small *hospedaje*

outside Santiago de Compostela, where she immediately set to work dressing his shoulder wound, cleansing it with peroxide she had purchased at a *farmacía,* suturing it and applying an antibacterial ointment. She worked quickly, with the practiced skill of a medical professional.

Appraising his shirtless torso, she ran her finger along a long, smooth welt. The wound inflicted by Abu in Tunisia, on Bryson's last assignment, had been repaired by a top-flight surgeon on contract with the Directorate. No longer did it throb painfully, though the memory remained, as traumatic as ever.

"A memento," he said grimly, "from an old friend." Outside the small window, the rain was coming down in sheets over the moss-stained cobblestone.

"You nearly died."

"I had some good medical care."

"You have been attacked often." She fingered a much smaller wound, a dime-size area of puckered flesh on his right biceps. "This?" she inquired.

"Another memento."

The memory of Nepal came flooding back, overpoweringly so, of a fearsome adversary named Ang Wu, a renegade officer in the Chinese Army. Now Bryson wondered what had *really* happened in that exchange of gunfire. What had he really been sent to do, and on whose behalf? Had he really been only a pawn of a malevolent conspiracy he still didn't understand?

So much blood spilled; so many lives wasted. And for what? What had his life meant? The more he learned, the less he understood. He thought of his parents, of the last time he saw them alive. Was it truly possible they had been killed by the masterminds behind the Directorate? He thought about Ted Waller, the man he had once admired more than anyone in the world, and he felt a surge of rage.

What was it that Niccolo, the Friulian assassin, had called himself and his brother—beasts of burden? They were hired muscle, pawns in the service of an odious game whose rules were never explained to them. Now it occurred to Bryson that there was no difference between him and the Italian brothers. They were all no more than instruments used by shadowy forces. Nothing better than pawns.

She had been sitting on the edge of the bed; now she got up and went to the tiny bathroom, returning a moment later with a glass of water. "The pharmacist gave me a few antibiotic pills. I told him I'd be getting a prescription in the morning, so he was willing to give me enough to tide you over." She handed him a few capsules and the glass. A flash of the old suspicion spoke to him silently, warningly: What were these unmarked pills she was giving him? Until the more rational voice in his head: *If she wanted to kill you, she's had plenty of opportunities to do it, more directly, in the last twenty-four hours. More than that, she simply didn't have to risk her own life to save yours.* He took the capsules from her and washed them down with a swallow of tap water.

"You seem distant," Layla said as she packed up the medical supplies. "Far away. You're thinking of something troubling."

Bryson looked up, nodded slowly. Sharing a room with a beautiful woman—even though the sleeping arrangements were quite chaste, she in the bed, he on the sofa—was something he had not done since Elena's sudden departure, years ago. The opportunities had presented themselves time and time again, but he had remained monastic, for some reason punishing himself for whatever he had done to send her away.

What *had* he done?

How much, he wondered, of their life together had been set up, stage-managed by Ted Waller?

And he thought back to the one time, the one important time, that he had lied to her. He had lied to protect her. He had concealed something from her. Waller was fond of quoting Blake: "We are led to believe a lie," he would orate, "when we see not through the eye."

But Bryson had not meant for Elena to see, to know, what he had done for her.

Now he searched his mind, recalling that evening in Bucharest that he had kept from her.

What was the truth? *Where* was the truth?

For all its paranoia and mayhem, the underworld of the black-operations specialist is a small one, and word travels fast. Bryson had received intelligence through several reliable contacts that a team of ex-Securitate "sweepers" was offering serious money for any leads that might unearth the location of one Dr. Andrei Petrescu, the mathematician and cryptologist who had betrayed the revolution by leaking the Ceauşescu government's ciphers. Among the disaffected former members of the notorious secret service there was great bitterness about the coup d'etat that had unseated their patron's government and removed them from power. They would never forgive or forget the traitors and were determined to hunt them down, whatever the cost, however much time it took. They had targeted several turncoats, Petrescu among them. Scores were to be settled, vengeance won.

Through a blind relay, Bryson arranged a meeting in Bucharest with the chief of the sweepers, the former number-two in the Securitate. Though Bryson's cover identity was not known to the Securitate man, his bona fides were established. The message was relayed that Bryson had urgent information that would undoubtedly be of great interest to the sweepers. He would come to the rendezvous site alone, verifiably so; the Securitate man was to do the same.

For Bryson, this was personal. He had made arrangements without the Directorate's knowledge. Such an off-the-books meeting would never have been approved; the potential ramifications were too serious. Yet Bryson could not risk having the contact vetoed; this was too important to Elena, and therefore to him. So he notified headquarters that upon the conclusion of an operation in Madrid he would be taking a much-needed, if altogether too brief, vacation, a long weekend in Barcelona. Permission was, of course, granted; he had long been owed vacation time. He was acting in direct contravention of Directorate policy, yes, but he had no choice. This had to be done. He purchased flight tickets in cash under an assumed name that appeared nowhere in Directorate databanks.

Neither did he tell Elena what he was doing, and here the deception was most important, for she would never have approved his meeting with the head of the team who sought to kill her father. Not only would she deem it far too dangerous to her husband, but she had made it abundantly clear on several occasions that under no circumstances was he to freelance in matters involving her parents. She was terrified of losing both her husband and her parents, of stirring up the hornet's nest of Securitate vengeance. Were it up to her, he would never have made such an appointment. And until now, he had respected her wishes. But this was an opportunity not to be passed up.

Bryson met the ex-Securitate man at a dark, subterranean bar. As promised, he had indeed come alone, although he had laid careful plans in advance. Favors had been called in, bribes paid.

"You have information on the Petrescus," said Major General Radu Dragan as Bryson joined him at a dimly lit booth.

Dragan knew nothing about Bryson, but Bryson, drawing upon his network of sources, had done his homework. Elena had first mentioned his name on the night of the exfiltration from Bucharest, to scare off the policeman who had been so interested in what was in the truck; as it turned out, she knew the man's name and phone number so well because Dragan had been the one who had enlisted her father's help; Andrei Petrescu's betrayal of the Securitate was therefore a very personal matter to Dragan.

"I certainly do," said Bryson. "But first we should discuss terms."

Dragan, a craggy, sallow-faced man of sixty, raised his brows. "I am happy to discuss 'terms,' as you put it, once I learn the nature of what you have to tell me."

Bryson smiled. "Absolutely. The 'information' I have to give you is quite simple." He slid a sheet of paper across the table; Dragan picked it up and scrutinized it in puzzlement.

"What—what is this?" asked Dragan. "But these names—"

"—are the names of every single member of your extended family, all relatives by blood or by marriages, along with their private addresses and telephone numbers. You, who have taken such security precautions to protect those near and dear to you, should recognize what immense resources I must have access to in order to have been able to unearth that information. Therefore you must know how easy it would be for me and my colleagues to track down each and every one of them, even if you were able to hide them all once again."

"Nu te mai piş a imprăş tiat!" barked Dragan. *Don't piss at me!* "Who the hell are you? How dare you talk to me like this!"

"I simply want your reassurance that all your sweepers will be called off immediately."

"You think that because one of my men sells information to you, you can make threats?"

"As you are well aware, none of your men has access to this information; even your most trusted aide knows but a few names and vague locations. Believe me, my information comes from sources far more reliable than any of your circle. Purge them all, execute them all; it will make no difference. Now, listen to me. If you, or anyone who works with or for you or is connected to you in any way whatsoever, harms a hair on the Petrescus' heads, my associates will personally maim and then murder every member of your family."

"Get out of here! Leave at once! Your threats are of no interest to me."

"I am giving you the opportunity to call off the sweepers right this very minute." Bryson glanced at his watch. "You have exactly seven minutes to issue the order."

"Or?"

"Or someone you care about very much will die."

Dragan laughed and poured himself more beer. "You are

wasting my time. My men are in this pub watching me, and all I have to do is signal and they will take you away before you have a chance to make a single phone call."

"Actually, it's you who are wasting time. The fact is, you want me to make a phone call. You see, my associate is in an apartment on Calea Victoriei at this very moment, with a gun to the head of a woman named Dumitra."

Dragan's already pale face went even paler.

"Yes, your mistress, who strips at the Sexy Club on Calea 13 Septembrie. Not your only mistress, but she has lasted several years already, so you must have at least some kindly feelings toward her. My associate is waiting for my telephone call to come in over his cell phone. If he does not receive it in"—Bryson glanced again at his watch—"six, no, five minutes, he has been instructed to put a bullet through her brain. All I can say is, you had better hope my phone is working, and his, too."

Dragan scoffed, but in his eyes Bryson could see the anxiety.

"You can save her life by rescinding the execution order on the Petrescus right now. Or you can do nothing, and she will die, and the blood will be on your hands. Here, you can use my cell phone if you don't have one with you. Just take care not to use up the battery—you really do want me to be able to reach my friend."

Dragan took a long sip of beer, feigning casualness.

But he did not speak, and four minutes passed by quickly. With barely one minute remaining before the execution deadline, Bryson called the Calea Victoriei.

"No," he said when the phone was answered. "Dragan refuses to rescind the order, so I'm afraid this call is just to ask you to go ahead. But do me a favor, and hand the phone to Dumitra so she can make a last-minute plea to her rather coldhearted lover." Bryson waited until he could hear the woman's desperate voice on the other end of the line, and then he handed the phone to Dragan.

Dragan took it, said a brusque hello, and even across the table Bryson could hear the mistress's shrieked pleas. Dragan's face began twitching, but he said nothing. Yet it was obvious that he recognized Dumitra's voice and knew this was no hoax.

"Time's up," said Bryson, glancing for a last time at his wristwatch.

Dragan shook his head. "You have bought the bitch off," he said. "I don't know how much you paid her to act out this little farce, but I'm sure it wasn't much."

The first shot exploded out of the earpiece; Bryson could hear it four feet away, followed instantly by the strangled scream. There was another shot, but this time there was no scream.

"Is she that good an actress? No?" Bryson stood up and took the phone back. "Your stubbornness and skepticism just cost the life of your woman. Your people will confirm for you what has just happened, or you can go to her apartment and see for yourself if you can stand to do it." He was sickened and horrified by what he'd had to do, but he knew there was no other way to prove that he was serious. "There are forty-six names on that piece of paper, and one of them will be murdered every day until your entire family is extinct. The only way you can stop it is by rescinding the orders on the Petrescus. And once again, let me remind you that if anything happens to them, anything at all—your family will be executed en masse at once."

He turned around and walked out of the pub and never saw Dragan again.

But within an hour the word went out that the Petrescus were not to be touched.

Bryson said nothing about it to either Elena or Ted Waller. When he returned home several days later, Elena asked him about his trip to Barcelona. Normally, they each respected the partitions between their lives and work, avoiding asking each other questions about what each other was doing; she had never before asked about his travels. But this time she studied his face as she asked him questions about Barcelona, far too many questions. He lied easily and persuasively. Was she jealous, was that it? Did she suspect him

*of meeting a lover on Las Ramblas? This was the first time
he had ever detected such a note of jealousy on her part and
it made him wish even more that he could tell her the truth.*

But did he even know the truth?

"I know almost nothing about you," he said, getting up from
the bed and sitting down on the sofa. "Except for the fact
that you've saved my life several times in the last twelve
hours."

"You need to get some rest," she said. She wore a pair
of gray sweatpants and a loose-fitting, oversized man's un-
dershirt that emphasized, rather than concealed, the swell of
her breasts. There were no clothes to pack, no busy work to
occupy her hands, so she sat on the edge of the bed, folding
her long, firm legs and crossing her arms across her breasts.
"We can talk in the morning."

He sensed she was evading his questions, so he persisted:

"You work for the Mossad, yet you come from the Bekaa
valley, speak with an Arabic accent. Are you Israeli? Lebanese?"

Looking down, she said quietly, "Neither. Either. My father was Israeli. My mother is Lebanese."

"Your father's dead."

She nodded. "He was an athlete, a superb athlete. He was
murdered by Palestine terrorists at the Olympic Games in
Munich."

Bryson nodded. "That was 1972. You must have been a
baby."

She continued looking down, her face flushed. "I was not
much more than two years old."

"You never knew him."

She looked up. Her brown eyes were fierce. "My mother
kept him alive for me. She never stopped telling stories about
him, showing us pictures."

"You must have grown up hating the Palestinians."

"No. The Palestinians are a good people. They are dis-
placed, homeless, stateless. I despise the fanatics who think
nothing of killing the innocent for the sake of lofty ideals.

Whether they're Black September or the Red Army Faction; whether they're Israeli or Arab. I hate zealots of any kind. When I was barely out of my teens, I married a fellow soldier in the Israeli Army. Yaron and I were deeply in love as only the very young can be. When he was killed in Lebanon, that was when I decided to work for Mossad. To fight the zealots."

"Yet you don't consider Mossad a band of zealots?"

"Many of them are. Yet some are not. Since I freelance for them, I can pick and choose my assignments. That way I can be sure that the work I'm doing is for a cause I believe in. Many jobs I turn down."

"They must think highly of you to give you such latitude."

She bowed her head modestly. "They know my deep-cover skills and my connections. Maybe I'm the only one foolish enough to accept certain assignments."

"Why *did* you accept the assignment on the *Spanish Armada*?"

She cocked her head at him, looking surprised. "Why else? Because that's where the fanatics buy the weapons without which they could not kill the innocent. Mossad had good information that agents of the Jihad National Front were stocking up there—feeding at the trough. Placing me there was a two-month operation."

"And if it weren't for me, you'd still be there."

"And what about you? You told me you're CIA, but you're not, are you?"

"What makes you say that?"

She touched her nose with the tip of her index finger. "Something smells wrong," she said with a knowing smile.

"Something about me?" Bryson said, amused.

"Well, actually, something about your enemies, your pursuers. The assassin squads—that violates standard accepted protocol. Either you're a freelancer like me, or you're with some other agency. But not CIA, I don't think."

"No," he admitted. "Not CIA, exactly. But I'm working for them."

"Freelance?"

"In a way."

"But you've been in the business a long time. The scars on your body give it away."

"It's true. I *was* in the business a long time. But I was forced out. Now they've brought me back in for one last assignment."

"Which is—"

He hesitated. How much to tell her? "It's a counterintelligence mission, in a sense."

" 'In a sense' . . . 'in a way' . . . If you don't want to tell me anything, fine, so be it." Her nostrils flared as she spoke with quiet intensity. "We'll each get on our separate aircrafts out of Spain first thing in the morning and never see each other again. When we get home and do the inevitable paperwork, we'll each file contact reports on each other, debrief as completely as we can what we know about the other's work, and that'll be the extent of it. Inquiries will be made, then dropped. A sealed file will be added to the Mossad's archives on CIA, another one added to CIA's Mossad files, mere drops of water in the ocean."

"Layla, I'm grateful to you for everything—"

"No," she interrupted. "I don't want your gratitude. You misunderstand me. You don't *know* me at all. I have my own reasons for interest—selfish reasons, if you wish. We're both following an arms trail—to different places, different endpoints. But the trails intersect, overlap. Now, it's obvious to me that whoever it is who wants you dead, they're not fringe actors. Their resources and access to information is too good. They're probably governmental."

Bryson nodded. She had a point.

"Now, I'm sorry, but I won't lie to you. The acoustics in the church were such that I could easily overhear your interrogation of the Italian, without even trying. If I wanted to double-deal you, I wouldn't have admitted that to you, but it's a fact."

He nodded again. Also true. "But you don't understand Friuliano, do you?"

"I understand names. You mentioned Anatoly Prishnikov,

a name that's well known to everyone in our line of work. And Jacques Arnaud—less well known, perhaps, but a provider of arms to many of Israel's enemies. He stokes the fires of the Middle East and gets enormously rich in the process. I know him, and I detest him. And I may have a way to get to him."

"What are you talking about?"

"I don't know where the trail leads you next. But I can confirm for you that one of Arnaud's agents was on the ship, selling weapons to Calacanis."

"The one with the long hair, double-breasted suit?"

"That's the one. He uses the name Jean-Marc Bertrand. He travels often to Chantilly."

"Chantilly?"

"The location of the château where Arnaud lives and entertains regularly, and quite lavishly." She stood, went briefly to the bathroom, and emerged a few minutes later, patting her face dry with a towel. Without her makeup her features were even more exquisite. Her nose was strong yet delicate, her lips full, and all dominated by wide brown eyes that were at once warm and intense, intelligent and playful.

"You know something about Jacques Arnaud?" Bryson asked.

She nodded. "I know a good deal about the man's world. The Mossad has had Arnaud in its sights for quite some time now, so I've been to Chantilly, as a guest at several of his parties."

"Under what sort of cover?"

She removed the coverlet from the bed. "As a commercial attaché at the Israeli embassy in Paris. Someone whose influence must be courted. Jacques Arnaud does not discriminate. He sells to the Israelis as readily as he sells to our enemies."

"Can you get me to him, do you think?"

She turned around slowly, her eyes wide. She shook her head. "I don't think that's a wise idea."

"Why not?"

"Because I can't risk compromising my operation any further."

"But you just said that we're on the same trail."

"That's *not* what I said. I said our trails intersected. That's a very different thing."

"And your trail doesn't lead to Jacques Arnaud?"

"It may," she acknowledged. "Or it may not."

"In any case it may be useful to you to go to Chantilly."

"In your company, I assume," she said teasingly.

"Obviously that's what I'm asking you. If you already have diplomatic contacts in Arnaud's social set, that would facilitate my entry."

"I prefer to work alone."

"A beautiful woman like you, on a social outing—wouldn't it be entirely plausible that you'd be accompanied by a male?"

She blushed again. "You flatter me."

"Only to twist your arm, Layla," Bryson said dryly.

"Whatever works, is that it?"

"Something like that."

She smiled, shook her head. "I'd never get clearance from Tel Aviv."

"Then don't request it."

She hesitated, dipped her head. "It would have to be a temporary alliance, which I may be forced to jettison at any moment."

"Just get me inside the château, and you can abandon me at the front door if you want. Now tell me something: Exactly *why* does Mossad have Jacques Arnaud in its sights?"

She gave him a look of surprise, as if the answer were so obvious it was scarcely worth saying. "Because in the last year or so, Jacques Arnaud has become one of the world's leading suppliers of arms to terrorists. This is why I found it interesting that the man who was summoned to see you—what was his name, Jenrette?—came aboard the ship in the company of Arnaud's agent, Jean-Marc Bertrand. I assumed this American named Jenrette was buying for terrorists. So I was quite intrigued to see that *you* were meeting with Jenrette. I must say, for much of the evening I wondered what you were doing."

Bryson fell silent, his mind working feverishly. Jenrette, the Directorate operative he knew as Vance Gifford, had come aboard with Jacques Arnaud's agent. Arnaud was selling weapons to terrorists; the Directorate was buying. Did that mean—by logical extension—that the Directorate was sponsoring terrorism around the globe?

"It's vital that I get to Jacques Arnaud," Bryson said very quietly.

She shook her head, smiling ruefully. "But we may get nothing out of it, either one of us. And that's really the least of our worries. These are very dangerous men who will stop at nothing."

"I'm willing to take that chance," Bryson said. "It's all I have right now."

The team of professional killers followed the screams. They had been assigned to mop up, which entailed searching the narrow, cobblestone streets that radiated off the Praza do Obradoiro in Santiago de Compostela. Now that it had been conclusively determined that their subject had eluded all location attempts, their next order of business was to locate all stray team members. The dead had been loaded into unmarked vehicles and brought to a cooperating local *mortuorio* where falsified papers would be drawn up, certificates of death stamped, the bodies buried in unmarked graves. Next of kin would be compensated handsomely and knew not to ask questions; this was standard operating procedure.

When the wounded and the dead had been rounded up and accounted for, there still remained two team members at large: the Friulian-speaking peasant brothers from the remote corner of northwestern Italy. A quick sweep of the streets turned up nothing; no emergency codes had been received. The brothers were not responding to repeated radio calls. They were presumed killed, but that was not a certainty, and black-operations procedures stipulated that the wounded were either to be extracted or finished off. So one way or another, the brothers had to be checked off on a list.

Finally it was a report of muffled screams emanating from a side street that drew the mop-up team's attention. They traced the sounds to an abandoned, boarded-up church. Once they burst in, they located first one brother, then the other. Both were manacled, tied up, and gagged, though one of the brother's gags was loose, which was fortunate: that had enabled his screams to be heard, and the brothers thereby located.

"Christ, what took you so long?" gasped the first brother in Spanish, through the loosened gag. "We could have died here! Paolo's lost a huge amount of blood."

"We couldn't permit that to happen," said one of the mop-up team. He took out his semiautomatic pistol and fired twice into the Italian's head, killing him instantly. "Weak links are unacceptable."

By the time he found the second brother, crouched in a fetus position, pale and shaking and surrounded by a large pool of blood, he could see that the brother knew what to expect. It was in Paolo's wide, unblinking eyes. Paolo did not even whimper before the two shots came.

CHAPTER TEN

CHANTILLY, FRANCE

The magnificent Château de Saint-Meurice was situated thirty-five kilometers from Paris, a vast seventeenth-century manse whose splendor was dramatically illuminated by scores of artfully placed spotlights. No less dramatic or magnificent were its surroundings, great sculpted gardens lit this evening like a stage set. This was most appropriate, for the Château de Saint-Meurice was indeed a stage on which the rich and powerful promenaded, making their skillfully timed entrances and exits, exchanging carefully scripted banter. The actors and the audience, however, were one and the same. All were there to impress each other; all knowingly played their roles within the artificial confines of an elaborate masque.

Although the evening's occasion was a gathering of European trade ministers, an offshoot of the annual G-7 Conference, the cast of characters did not change much from party to party at the Château de Saint-Meurice. The beautiful people of Paris and its environs were all there, *tout le beau monde,* or at least everyone who mattered. Clad in their finest evening wear, their tuxedoes or evening gowns, the women glittering with jewels normally sequestered in a safe or bank vault, they arrived in their sparkling, chauffeured Rolls Royces or Benzes. There were *comtes* and *comtesses*, *barons* and *baronnes*, *vicomtes* and *vicomtesses*; there were royalty from the corporate world and celebrities from the world of the broadcast media and the theater; they came from the highest levels of the Quai d'Orsay, from the most rarefied circles in which high society intersected with high finance.

Across the drawbridge and up the front steps of the château, the walkway lined with hundreds of candles whose flames danced in the gentle evening breezes, came elegant men with silver hair, but also inelegant men, squat and balding, whose coarse appearance belied the immense power and influence they wielded, some of whom wore on their arms their flashiest accoutrements, long-legged, glamorous mistresses to be displayed before one and all.

Bryson wore a tuxedo from Le Cor de Chasse, and Layla wore a spectacular strapless black gown obtained at Dior. Around her neck was a simple choker of pearls whose understated elegance did not detract from her extraordinary beauty. Bryson had been to many a function like this in his previous life, and had always felt like an observer rather than a participant, though he was meant to fit in as one of them—as he inevitably did. The semblance of poise came naturally to him, though not the sense of belonging.

Layla, however, seemed entirely at ease. A few traces of makeup, deftly and subtly applied—little more than eyeliner and lip gloss—accentuated her natural beauty, her olive skin, her large liquid brown eyes. Her wavy chestnut hair was pinned up, with just a few strands deliberately unrestrained, emphasizing her lovely swan neck; the risqué though tasteful décolletage of her gown highlighted her magnificent breasts. She could, and did, pass for either Israeli or Arab, being in fact both. She smiled easily, laughed merrily, her eyes inviting and withholding all at once.

She was greeted by several people, all of whom seemed to know her in her legend as an Israeli diplomatic functionary from the Foreign Ministry in Tel Aviv with mysterious clout and connections. Layla seemed to be known, yet not known, which was the perfect situation for a covert operative to be in. She had placed a call, earlier the day before, to a casual acquaintance at the Quai d'Orsay known to have close ties to Jacques Arnaud, the master of the Château de Saint-Meurice and a fixture at Arnaud's many parties. The acquaintance, who served as one of the arms manufacturer's social antennae, was *delighted* to hear that Layla was in Paris for a few days, *mortified* that she had not been directly invited to this fête, which was *surely* an oversight, and had insisted that Layla by all means *must* come; Monsieur Arnaud would be *most* offended, *appalled,* if she did not. And by all means, she must bring an escort, for the acquaintance knew that the lovely Layla was rarely without one.

Bryson and Layla had talked late into the night, strategizing their visit to Arnaud's château. For it was a supremely risky venture, after the destruction of the *Spanish Armada.* Obviously there were no survivors who might recognize either of them, but powerful men like Calacanis and any others aboard the ship, including the emissaries and agents sent by powerful men, simply did not perish in a fiery inferno without alarms going off in boardrooms and inner offices all around the world. Powerful men engaged in nefarious and hugely profitable enterprises would be on a heightened state of alert. Jacques Arnaud had lost one of his conduits, and therefore he had to be concerned for his own safety; who knew whether the obliteration of Calacanis's tanker had been merely the first shot fired in a campaign being waged against black-market arms dealers worldwide? As France's leading arms manufacturer, Jacques Arnaud would always be careful about possible threats to his life and livelihood; in the aftermath of the explosion off the Cabo Finisterre, he would be extra-cautious.

Layla had been a green-eyed blonde, so at least her appearance had been radically altered. Bryson, however, could not take the chance that he would not be recognized. If surveillance video had been uplinked from the ship via satellite at any time before the ship's destruction, then video stills of his likeness would have been circulated among private security forces with enormous resources.

So Bryson had purchased certain products at a stage-costume-supply shop near the Opera, and by the next day his appearance had been altered dramatically. His hair was now silver-gray, with the variegated tones of a blond man who had gone gray. The technical services wizards at the Directorate had tutored Bryson well in the black arts of disguise. Cheek inserts had turned his face jowelly; the application of spirit gum had put latex pouches under his eyes, as well as wrinkles and fine lines around the eyes and mouth. Subtlety was paramount, as Bryson had learned from years of disguise: minor changes could have major effects yet raise no suspicions. He now looked easily twenty years older, a distinguished older gentleman who fit right in with the other men of accomplishment and position who frequented the Château de Saint-Meurice. He had become James Collier, an investment banker and venture capitalist from Santa Fe, New Mexico. As was not uncommon among certain venture capitalists who preferred to work away from the glare of public scrutiny, he would say little about what he actually did, turning away polite inquiries with self-deprecating wit.

Bryson and Layla were staying at a small, moderately priced, anonymous hotel on rue Trousseau. Neither one of them had stayed there before; its chief distinction was its very mediocrity. Each of them had arrived in Paris by a different route from Labacolla Airport—Bryson via Frankfurt, and Layla via Madrid. There had been a certain awkwardness about the sleeping arrangements, no doubt unavoidable. They were traveling as a couple, which usually meant sharing a bed or at least a room. Yet Bryson had requested that the hotel put them in separate bedrooms in an adjoining suite. A bit out of the ordinary, perhaps, but it did bespeak a certain level of propriety on the part of the unmarried couple, an old-fashioned discretion. In truth, Bryson knew the temptations of the flesh threatened to overwhelm him. She was a beautiful, highly sexual woman, and he had been solitary for far too long. But he did not want to destabilize an already tenuous working relationship, he told himself. Or perhaps he feared losing a necessary wariness. Was that it? Was it that he *wanted* to keep his distance so long as Elena remained a question mark in his life?

Now, as Layla guided him across the crowded room, smiling and nodding to social acquaintances, she kept up a lilting patter. "The story is that the château was built in the seventeenth century by one of Louis the Fourteenth's ministers. It was so grand that the king became jealous, had the minister arrested, stole his architect and landscaper and all the furniture, and then, inspired by a fit of envy, started construction on Versailles, determined never to be outdone."

Bryson smiled and nodded, maintaining the appearance of a moneyed guest suitably impressed by his surroundings. As Layla spoke, his eyes roamed the crowd, ever alert for the familiar face, the quickly averted glance. He had done this sort of thing countless times before, but this time was different, nerve-racking: he had stepped into the unknown. Also, his plan was vague, a necessary improvisation based on his own finely honed instincts.

Exactly what *was* the connection, if any, between Jacques Arnaud and the Directorate? The team of assassins dispatched to kill him had been working with Arnaud's man on the *Spanish Armada*. The assassins—the Friulian brothers—were Directorate hires, which strongly indicated that Arnaud himself was at least affiliated with the Directorate in some mysterious, unspecified capacity. More than that, a man known by Bryson to be Directorate—Vance Gifford, or, as he'd styled himself, Jenrette—had been aboard the ship, having arrived in the company of Arnaud's emissary.

It was all highly circumstantial, but taken together, the pieces of circumstantial evidence created a mosaic that was highly suggestive. Jacques Arnaud was one of the shadowy powers who now controlled the Directorate.

What Bryson needed was *proof*. Hard, incontrovertible evidence.

It was here somewhere, but *where?*

According to Layla, the Israelis believed that Jacques Arnaud's firm was involved in laundering enormous sums of money for criminal elements that included the Russian *mafiya*. The Mossad's surveillance suggested that Arnaud often received and placed business-related calls here, at his château, and repeated attempts by the Mossad and other intelligence services to tap his phones had proven useless. His communications were undecipherable, protected by hard encryption. This strongly suggested to Bryson that somewhere in the château there had to be specialized telecommunications equipment, "black" telephones at least, capable of encrypting, and decrypting, telephonic signals—phone calls, faxes, and E-mails.

As they maneuvered through the crowds, from room to room, Bryson noticed the paintings that crowded the walls, and that gave him an idea.

In a small room upstairs, two men in business suits sat in semidarkness, their faces illuminated only by the eerie bluish flicker from the banks of video monitors. The stainless steel and brushed chrome, the fiber-optic cables and cathode-ray tubes, made up a peculiar modern-art installation mounted on the ancient stone walls. Each monitor displayed a different angle in a different room below. Miniaturized cameras concealed in the walls, in fixtures and fittings, unseen and unnoticed by the myriad guests, relayed high-resolution video images to the security men huddled before the monitors. The clarity was such that the watchers could zoom in on any face that was of interest or concern, pulling in tight for a closeup that took up an entire screen. Images could be digitized, electronically compared against other images stored in a vast off-site data bank known as the Network. Any questionable persons could be identified and discreetly invited to leave, if need be.

Buttons were pushed; a face was enlarged on one monitor, the features screened onto a grid and scrutinized by the two men. It was the silver-haired, slightly jowelly, sun-lined face of a man whose name, furnished in advance to Arnaud's security people, was James Collier of Santa Fe, New Mexico.

What drew the attention of the two men was not that they recognized the man's face. Instead, it was the fact that they did not recognize the face. The man was an unknown quantity. To Arnaud's ever-vigilant security force, the unknown was always a cause for concern.

Jacques Arnaud's wife, Giséle, was a tall, imperious woman of aristocratic bearing, with an aquiline nose and gray-streaked black hair. Her hairline was unnaturally high, her facial skin too taut, unmistakable evidence of regular visits to a "clinic" in Switzerland. Bryson spotted her holding court in a corner of the book-lined library, a small crowd hanging

on her every word. Bryson recognized her face from her
regular appearances in the society pages of *Paris Match,* several years of which he had pored over in the Bibliothèque
Nationale de France.

The hangers-on seemed dazzled by her cleverness, her
every aperçu received with uproarious merriment. Accepting
two flutes of champagne from a waiter and handing one to
Layla, Bryson pointed to a canvas that hung near where Madame Arnaud was holding forth. Striding up to it eagerly,
thereby positioning himself within earshot of the hostess,
Bryson remarked in a voice just loud enough to be overheard
by the adjacent gathering, "Fantastic, isn't it? Ever see his
portrait of Napoleon? Extraordinary—he turns Napoleon into
a Roman emperor, posing him frontally like a statue, a living
icon."

His gambit worked; the proud owner could not resist turning her head toward a conversation she found more intriguing, since it concerned one of her own works of art.
Bestowing upon Bryson a gracious smile, she said in fluent
English, "Ah, and have you ever seen a stare as hypnotic as
the one Ingres gives Napoleon?"

Bryson returned the smile, glowing as if he had found a
soul mate. He bowed his head and extended his hand. "You
must be Madame Arnaud. James Collier. A wonderful evening."

"Pardon me," she announced to her gathering, gently dis-
missing them. Moving closer, she said, "I see you're an admirer of Ingres, Mr. Collier."

"I would say I'm an admirer of *yours,* Madame Arnaud.
Your collection of pictures demonstrates a truly discriminat-
ing eye. Oh, may I introduce my friend, Layla Sharett, of the
Israeli embassy."

"We've met before," said the hostess. "So good to see
you again," she said, taking Layla's hand, though her attention remained riveted on Bryson. In her prime, Bryson saw,
she must have been a woman of striking beauty; even as a
woman in her early seventies, she was a coquette. She had
the courtesan's talent for making a man feel he was the most

fascinating man in the room, that no other man or woman existed. "My husband tells me he finds Ingres *boring*. He is not the connoisseur of art you seem to be."

Bryson, however, did not want to seize this potential opening to be introduced to Jacques Arnaud. On the contrary, he preferred not to be called to the arms tycoon's attention. "If only Ingres had been so fortunate as to have you as a subject for one of his portraits," he said, shaking his head wistfully.

She affected a scowl, though Bryson could see she was secretly pleased. "Please! I would *hate* to have my portrait done by Ingres!"

"He did take forever on some of his portraits, didn't he? Poor Madame Moitessier had to sit for twelve years."

"And he turned her into a Medusa, her fingers into *tentacles!*"

"But an extraordinary portrait."

"Claustrophobic, I think."

"They say he may have used a *camera lucida* to produce some of his compositions—in effect, spying on his subjects before he captured them, you might say."

"Is that right?"

"Still, as much as I admire his paintings, nothing compares to his drawings, don't you agree?" Bryson knew that the Arnauds' private collection included some of Ingres's drawings, displayed in less public rooms of the château.

"I couldn't agree more!" Giséle Arnaud exclaimed. "Though he himself considered his drawings to be potboilers."

"I know, I know—while he lived in poverty in Rome, he was forced to support himself by drawing pictures of visitors and tourists. Some of the greatest paintings were done by artists working just to keep food on the table. The fact is, Ingres's drawings are his best work by far. The use of white, of negative space, the way he captures light—they're truly masterpieces."

Madame Arnaud lowered her voice and said confidentially, "Actually, we have a few of his drawings hanging in the billiards room, you know."

The ruse had worked. Madame Arnaud had invited Bryson and his guest to stroll into parts of the house that were not open to the other guests. She had offered to show him the drawings herself, but Bryson had declined, refusing to steal her away; but if she really didn't mind, perhaps they could take a quick look by themselves?

As he and Layla wandered through halls and more intimate, less public rooms, whose walls were hung with less impressive works by lesser French artists, Bryson oriented himself. He had prepared well: he had located the collection of blueprints of historically important châteaux, maintained at the Bibliothèque Nationale de France, and had studied the layout of the Château de Saint-Meurice. He knew it was highly unlikely that the Arnauds would have done anything to alter Château de Saint-Meurice's floor plan; the only variable was the use they made of the rooms, the location of the bedrooms and offices, particularly Arnaud's private office.

Bryson walked idly arm-in-arm with Layla down one hallway, turning left into another. As they rounded a corner, they heard low, muffled, male voices.

They froze. The voices gradually became more audible and more distinct. The words were in French, but one speaker's French had a definite foreign accent, which Bryson quickly placed as Russian, probably from Odessa.

". . . to return to the party," the Frenchman was saying.

The Russian said something that Bryson couldn't quite make out. Then the Frenchman replied, "But once Lille happens, the outrage will be enormous. The way will be clear."

Signaling Layla to stay back, Bryson flattened himself against the wall and inched forward, his tread silent, all the while listening, concentrating. Neither the voices nor the footsteps seemed to be approaching. He took from the breast pocket of his tuxedo what looked like a silver ballpoint pen, then pulled from one end a long, thin, glasslike wire, tele-

scoping it to its maximum eighteen-inch length. He bent the
tip of the flexible fiber-optic periscope cable, then nudged it
along the wall until it jutted out no more than half an inch
beyond the wall's end. Looking into the small eyepiece, he
was able to see the two men clearly. One, a trim, compact
man with heavy black glasses, entirely bald, was clearly
Jacques Arnaud. He was conferring with a tall, florid-faced
man whom Bryson did not immediately recognize. A few
seconds later the man's identity came to him: Anatoly Prishnikov.

Prishnikov. The mogul widely believed to be the true
power behind the figurehead currently occupying the president's office in the Kremlin.

Shifting the fiber-optic periscope slightly, Bryson was
startled to discover another man, much closer, seated just
around the corner. A guard, clearly armed, stationed at the
beginning of the corridor. Shifting the scope yet again revealed another seated figure, another armed guard, stationed
halfway down the hall, where the men were standing, in front
of a large, steel-paneled door.

Arnaud's private office.

They were in a part of the château that had no windows;
ordinarily, it would be an unlikely location for an office. But
Arnaud's chief concern was security, not views.

The two men made the sort of final gestures that indicated
they were finished talking, and fortunately they headed down
the hall in the other direction. There was no need for Bryson
and Layla to disappear.

Withdrawing the fiber-optic periscope and collapsing it
back into its pen case, he turned toward Layla and nodded.
She understood without his saying anything. They had located their target, the locus of Jacques Arnaud's business
activities within the Château de Saint-Meurice.

Swiftly, his tread silent, he backtracked until he found the
open door to a room they had just passed. The sitting room
was, as he had previously noted, dark and sparsely furnished,
evidently rarely used. He consulted the luminous radium dial
of his Patek Philippe watch. After a full minute had elapsed,

he signaled to Layla, then ducked into the room, waiting in its dark recesses.

Layla began weaving down the hall toward the room that had to be Arnaud's private, secure office, staggering as if drunk. Suddenly she let out a whoop of laughter and said to herself, though loudly enough to be heard by at least the first guard, just around the corner, "There's *got* to be a bathroom around here *somewhere!*"

Turning the corner unstably, she came upon the armed guard, seated in a delicate antique chair. He straightened, stared at her with hostility. *"Puis-je vous aider?"* May I help you? he demanded stiffly in French, in a voice that commanded her to go no further. He was barely out of his twenties, with crew-cut black hair, heavy eyebrows, a pudgy, round face, and a five o'clock shadow. His small red mouth was turned down in a pugnacious frown.

She giggled and continued to stagger toward him. "I don't know," she replied provocatively, *"can* you help me? Why, what do we have here? *Un homme, un vrai*—a *real* man. Not like those *pédés,* those young fairies and old goats out there."

The guard's stern expression softened somewhat, his posture relaxed as he sized her up to be no threat to the security of Jacques Arnaud's sanctum. His cheeks reddened visibly. There was no doubt he was quite taken with Layla's voluptuous body, the swell of her breasts revealed by the low-cut black gown. "I'm sorry, mademoiselle," he said nervously, "please, stay right there—you must go no further."

Layla smiled coyly, bracing herself against the stone wall with one outstretched hand. "But why would I *want* to go any further?" she said huskily, suggestively, as she inched closer to him. "Looks like I've found what I've been looking for." She moved her hand along the wall, slinking ever closer to him, jutting her breasts forward.

The young guard's smile was uncomfortable. He cast a nervous glance down the hall at the other sentry, who seemed to be paying him no attention. *"Please,* mademoiselle—"

She lowered her voice. "Maybe you can help me . . . to find a bathroom."

"Back down the hall you came," he replied, attempting a businesslike tone, though without much success, "there is a restroom."

Her voice became even more breathy and suggestive. "But I keep losing my way around here, and if you wouldn't mind showing me . . ."

The guard again glanced uneasily at his compatriot, who was too far down the hall to take notice.

"Perhaps," she added, arching her brows, "a little guided tour. It needn't take long at all, hmm?"

Flush-faced and awkward, the guard rose from his chair. "Very well, mademoiselle," he said.

There were now, Layla calculated, several possible avenues the guard could pursue. If he happened to take her into the room in which Bryson was concealed, the guard would be taken down, the element of surprise a weapon as deadly as Nicholas Bryson's hands.

But the guard instead guided her into another room, this one a *chambre de fumeur,* comfortably furnished. He was, she noticed, quite unmistakably aroused. He gave a wolfish grin as he pulled the door closed.

It was time to put Plan B into effect. She turned to him, her face full of anticipation.

Silently, Bryson rushed into the hallway, turned the corner, and then slowed his pace, sauntering toward the sole remaining guard, who kept a solitary vigil before the closed steel-paneled door of Arnaud's presumably empty office.

Now it was Bryson's turn to feign drunkenness, though to a very different end. The guard looked up as Bryson approached with a loose-limbed, swaying walk.

"Monsieur," the guard said brusquely, part greeting and part warning.

As he sashayed closer to the guard, Bryson held up his gold Zippo lighter, shaking his head disgustedly. In English, he said, "The damnedest thing! Can you believe this? I remember my lighter, but it's the damned cigarettes I forget!"

"Sir?"

In French, Bryson said, *"Vous n'auriez pas une cigarette?"* He kept waving the Zippo and shaking his head. "You're a Frenchman—you *must* have one."

The guard obligingly reached into his jacket pocket at the same instant that Bryson flicked the Zippo's striker, which jetted forward not a tongue of flame but a quick spray of a powerful neural incapacitant. Before the guard even had a chance to reach for his gun, he was at once blinded and frozen in place; a few seconds later he slumped forward, unconscious.

Working quickly, Bryson propped the guard back on his chair like a mannequin, folding the man's hands in his lap. The guard's eyelids were closed, so Bryson, knowing from long experience that they could not be forced open, left him as he was. From a distance, one would assume the guard was on duty; a passerby who came near would assume the guard had fallen asleep.

The incapacitating spray was not the only item of security equipment Bryson had purchased in Paris; he also had with him an array of other small devices, including infrared- and RF-code scanners and grabbers and a security-gate scanner. But a quick inspection of the steel door confirmed that only one piece was necessary. No doubt Arnaud employed the usual alarms and intrusion detectors when he planned to be gone from his home for any lengthy period of time. This evening, however, having just stopped into his office and perhaps intending to return again within the next few hours, he had simply allowed the door to close behind him. Although the door locked automatically, it was by means of nothing more elaborate than a conventional pin-tumbler door lock. Bryson took out a small black device, a lock-pick gun that he had learned to use over the years and had found far speedier than a manual lock-pick set. He inserted it into the lock, then pulled the plunger back and forth a few times until the tumblers turned and the heavy door popped open.

Shining his small pen flashlight around the dark room, he was taken aback at how spare it was. There appeared to be no file cabinets, no locked credenza. In fact, the office had a barrackslike spareness. There was a small seating area with a couch, two chairs, and a coffee table, and a completely bare mahogany table used as a desk. On the desk were a Tensor lamp and two telephones. . . .

The phone.

The phone in question was there, a flat, charcoal-gray box about a foot square, apparently nothing more than a desk telephone with a lid. But Bryson recognized it at once. He had seen countless models, though few as sleek and compact: the latest generation of satellite encryption phone. The lid contained both the antenna and the RF. Built into the device was a chip containing the encryption algorithm, which used nonlinear-phase signal encryption, fixed-length convolver, unlimited 128-bit keys. Wiretapping the line would do no good, since the encryption key was never transmitted. An intercepted call would sound like garbled nonsense, the voices both highly encrypted and scrambled. The phone's satellite uplink capacity meant that it could work even from remote corners of the earth.

Bryson worked quickly, deftly dismantling the telephone. The door was locked behind him, and the guard would be out for at least half an hour, but there was a definite risk that Jacques Arnaud would return suddenly. If he did, and found one guard missing and the other passed out, he might simply attribute the wayward behavior to the party's carnival atmosphere, which had somehow infected his household staff. Of course, that was only if Layla had managed to keep the lustful young guard occupied. Somehow Bryson did not doubt her ability to do so.

There was nothing more he could do now than work as swiftly as he could.

Spread out before him on the burnished, bare surface of Arnaud's desk were the electronic guts of the telephone. Unseating the special read-only chip from the circuitry, he held it up, examining it in the strong light of the Tensor lamp.

It was precisely what he had hoped to find. The cryptochip was relatively bulky, as such proprietary chips typically were, having been produced in very small quantities to link a small cadre of conspirators while ensuring zero-knowledge encryption. The mere fact that Arnaud had such a piece of equipment sitting on his desk revealed that he was part of a tightly linked group, international in scope, that required absolute secrecy. Could he in fact be one of the hidden principals of the Directorate?

Bryson removed from his dinner jacket an object that looked like a miniature transistor radio. In the coin-size slot at one end he inserted the cryptochip, then switched the device on. An indicator light changed from green to red and then, some ten seconds later, back to green again. A signal had pulsed through the chip, capturing the data. He listened for any voices in the hallway or approaching footsteps; then, satisfied there were none, he ejected the cryptochip and replaced it in the satellite phone's circuitry. In a few minutes he had the phone reassembled. In the chip reader he now had stored all the specifications of the chip's "key," vast sequences of binary digits and algorithmic instructions. The encryption scheme changed each time the phone was used, never once repeating itself. It was a high-tech version of a self-replenishing one-time pad. Fortunately, he now had every single combination recorded. Making use of this information was a daunting task, but there were others who specialized in this highly specialized area.

Moments later Bryson was striding down the hall back toward the party. The guard in the corridor by the office door, he took note, was still out. When he came to, in ten minutes, he would quickly recall what had happened to him, but the odds were great he would do nothing, summon no help, for to reveal that he had been overpowered by one man was surely to ask for abrupt termination.

In the *chambre de fumeur,* the young guard stood with his trousers gathered around his feet, his shirt unbuttoned and hanging open, as he prepared for final gratification. Layla stroked his bare abdomen, kissing his neck. She had protracted things for just about as long as she plausibly could.

Glancing at the sweep second hand of her tiny gold wrist-watch, she took mental note of the time. According to their plan, it was just about time that . . .

A scuff on the stone floor outside.

Bryson's prearranged signal. He was precisely on schedule.

She stooped to grab her small black velvet evening bag, then gave the guard a quick, friendly peck on the check. *"Allons,"* she said crisply, rushing to the door. The guard gaped at her, his face flushed crimson, eyes half-maddened with desire. *"Les plus grands plaisirs sont ceux qui ne sont pas réalisés,"* she whispered as she glided out of the room. The highest pleasures are the unrealized ones. Just before she shut the door, she said, "But I will never forget you, my friend."

Layla's purse was heavier than it had been previously: it now contained his snub-nosed Beretta. She knew that the guard, however angry and frustrated he might be, would never say a word about her, for to do so would be to confess to an unforgivable security lapse. She checked her makeup in a compact mirror, reapplied her lip gloss, and then returned to the party, entering through the banquet room. Bryson, she saw, was himself just arriving.

A small string ensemble was playing chamber music in the banquet room, while coming quite audibly from the adjoining parlor were the thumping beat and blaring synthesizer sounds of rock music. The two sounds clashed bizarrely, the elegant strains of Mozart's eighteenth-century music easily overwhelmed by the jarring, earsplitting cacophony of the twenty-first.

Bryson placed an arm around Layla's slender waist and said to her quietly, "I hope you enjoyed yourself."

"Very funny," she murmured. "I'd much rather have traded places with you. Mission accomplished?"

As Bryson was about to reply, he noticed the balding head of Jacques Arnaud in a distant corner of the room. He seemed to be conferring with another man in a dinner jacket whose earpiece indicated that he was part of Arnaud's security team. Arnaud nodded, looking around the room. Then another man rushed up to the two, his gestures and facial expressions revealing great urgency. There was a brief, huddled consultation; then Bryson saw Arnaud's gaze flicker in his direction. Suspicions had been aroused, security breaches reported, a warning sounded. Bryson had little doubt that Arnaud was looking directly at him, and wondered whether the Frenchman had been tipped off by surveillance cameras in the vicinity of his office. Bryson knew there would be cameras. But everything at this point was calculated risk. In fact, to do nothing was the gravest risk of all.

The answer came a second or two later, when the two security men Arnaud had been huddling with suddenly broke away and began threading their way through the crowd, each taking a different path around the room toward Bryson and Layla. In their singleminded haste, the guards collided with several guests. Then a third raced into the room, and it became immediately evident what they were doing: all three exits from the room were now covered, and Bryson and Layla could not escape.

Closed-circuit surveillance cameras had indeed captured their movements through the halls of the château outside of the party. Bryson's surreptitious entry into Jacques Arnaud's office had been observed; or perhaps, given the delay in response time, only his exit from the office had been seen.

And now they were surrounded.

Layla squeezed his hand with almost painful pressure, a silent alert; she, too, saw the vise they were in. Their options were severely restricted. Guns would not be fired if it were at all avoidable; Arnaud's people would try to apprehend Bryson and Layla quietly without alarming the other guests. Appearances were to be preserved if possible. But Bryson had little doubt of the ruthlessness of the host and his security team. If shots had to be fired, they would be. Explanations could be offered later, lies furnished, the true circumstances covered up.

Bryson's head spun as he watched the security men race

toward him, slowed only by the obstacle presented by the other guests, in addition to Arnaud's preference to maintain some semblance of propriety. He felt Layla jabbing something into his hand and realized she was trying to hand him her black velvet handbag. But why? He had seen the bulge and had guessed that she had disarmed the guard in the *chambre de fumeur,* stolen his weapon. But surely she knew he had a weapon of his own.

The jabbing continued, and finally Bryson took the handbag from her, opening it, and realized at once what she had been so insistently trying to pass to him. He put the bag behind his back, slipped out the small canister, a leftover from the *Spanish Armada,* and yanked the lever before he dropped it to the floor. The grenade rolled a good distance along the ancient stone before it started spewing out dense gray smoke. Within seconds, a cloud of thick smoke began rising from the floor, along with an acrid, sulphuric odor.

Screams immediately erupted in the crowd, cries of *"Au feu!"* and "Run!" Arnaud's guards were a good six to eight feet away when the panic arose. Soon the separate cries were joined by others, male and female, the frenzy growing, hysteria overtaking the room as it filled with smoke. The proper, dignified party guests had become terrified lemmings, rushing toward the exits with shouts of fear. Alarms were clanging, presumably set off by smoke detectors. The music in both adjoining rooms had stopped; the chamber group and the rock group had joined the evacuation. The surging crowd was utter pandemonium, and Layla and Bryson disappeared into the stampede, unseen by Arnaud's security forces.

Guests screamed, clung to one another, elbowed others out of their way. As the two of them rushed through the main door, plunging through the flailing, panicked crowd, Bryson grabbed Layla and pulled her off in the direction of the elaborate topiary that surrounded the château. Within the thick hedges Bryson had concealed a motorcycle. He jumped astride the high-powered BMW and kick-started it, signaling for her to climb on.

Moments later they were roaring through the confusion

and madness, leaving behind guests spilling out of the château's front doors, limousines pulling up to the château, summoned to rescue their frantic passengers. Within three minutes they were speeding down the A-1 highway toward Paris, passing car after car.

But they were not alone.

As they left other cars far behind, Bryson soon became aware of a small, high-powered black sedan accelerating, closing in on them, coming closer and closer, leaving other vehicles far behind. One hundred feet, fifty feet, twenty . . . and then Bryson saw, in the motorcycle's rearview mirror, that the sedan was not just approaching, it was swerving madly, fishtailing back and forth. But it was not a car out of control; its bizarre movements were controlled, apparently deliberate.

It was trying to run Bryson off the road!

As Bryson opened the throttle fully, accelerating to the motorcycle's maximum capacity, he spotted an exit up ahead and abruptly changed lanes, veering toward the exit. The black sedan followed, cutting across several lanes of traffic, protesting horns blaring in its wake. Bryson could feel Layla's hands on his shoulders, her grip tightening. He winced; the pain was great, the shoulder wound exquisitely sensitive.

Bryson pulled on to the exit ramp, the car now less than ten or fifteen feet behind and gaining. "Hold on tight!" he shouted, and he felt Layla's hands squeeze even tighter in acknowledgment. He emitted an involuntary cry of agony.

Suddenly he spun off to the left, executing a one-hundred-and-eighty-degree "bootlegger's turn" in such a confined area that the motorcycle almost flipped over, but he somehow managed to regain balance, wheeling around until he was headed back down the ramp along the narrow shoulder, leaving the sedan still barreling up the exit.

Now, roaring down the highway the wrong way, he kept to the shoulder, which broadened somewhat. Headlights flashed furiously, horns blared. He glanced in the small rearview mirror. They had lost the black sedan; it had been forced by the cars behind it to continue up the ramp and off the highway.

Now the BMW's throttle was fully open; the engine straining, giving off a blatting noise. They were virtually flying along the side of the A-1, against traffic.

But they were still not in the clear, for rushing toward them was a single headlight of a motorcycle, speeding even faster than the other vehicles on the road, and Bryson knew it had to be another pursuer dispatched from the Château de Saint-Meurice.

There was a squealing of brakes, car horns honking, and suddenly the other motorcycle, too, had reversed direction and was just behind them. In the rearview, Bryson could see it gaining on them; though he could not see the make of the cycle, the engine roar told him that it was even more powerful than the BMW he had rented in Paris, capable of attaining even greater speeds.

Suddenly Bryson felt something slam into them. It was the other motorcycle, deliberately crashing into the rear wheel, almost knocking them over! Above the motorcycle's roar he could hear, very near his ear, Layla screaming in terror.

"Are you all right?" he shouted.

"Yes!" she screamed in reply. "But *move* it!"

He tried to put on another burst of speed, but the motorcycle was already traveling at its maximum.

Another impact sent the motorcycle veering off the side of the road. Just off the shoulder was a long flat meadow, cleared farmland interspersed with wooden boxes used to collect hay or other crops. Bryson righted the vehicle, then accelerated off the asphalt and onto the grass and dirt, the pursuing motorcycle right behind. No gunshots, which told him that the driver needed to use both hands for maneuvering and could not spare a hand to use a weapon.

Pursue your pursuer.

This had been one of Ted Waller's oft-repeated aperçus.

In the end, you *will decide who is predator and who is prey. The prey survives only by becoming the predator.*

Bryson now did the unexpected, circling around the

meadow, carving deep ruts in the soft earth, until he was charging straight at the other motorcycle.

The other motorcyclist, obviously taken aback by this change in strategy, tried to spin out of the way, but there was no time. Bryson crashed into him, and the driver was flung from his vehicle.

Slamming on his brakes, the cycle spewing dirt into the air, he came to a stop. Layla leaped off, then he did, flinging the bike to the ground.

The other driver was running away, and as he ran he was obviously reaching for a weapon, but Layla already had hers out, and she fired the Beretta three times in rapid succession.

With a scream, the pursuer tumbled to the ground, but he had managed to wrest his weapon from its holster, and he fired back. His aim was off; bullets spit into the ground near them. Layla fired again, then Bryson had his gun out and fired, hitting their enemy in the chest.

He flew backward, sprawled on the ground, dead.

Bryson raced toward him, flipping the prone body over, rummaging through the man's pockets for identification.

He pulled out a wallet. He was not surprised to find one; the pursuer had been given no notice, and thus no time to rid himself of identifying documents.

What he saw, however, he was not prepared for. It was beyond a surprise; the shock was deep, stunning, taking his breath away.

The detritus of bureaucracy, in this case, was straightforward. Documents could be forged, but Bryson was an expert at recognizing fake documents, and this was not one of them. There was no doubt. He examined it carefully in the bright moonlight, turning it over, locating the requisite fibers and irreproducible markings.

"What is it?" Layla asked. He handed it to her; she saw at once.

"Oh, my *God!*" she said, her voice hushed.

Their pursuer had been no mere rent-a-cop, nor even a French citizen on Arnaud's security payroll.

He was a U.S. citizen, employed at the Paris station of the CIA.

CHAPTER ELEVEN

The secretary had been with the Central Intelligence Agency for seventeen years, but she could count on the fingers of one hand the number of times anyone had tried to bypass her and barge into the office of her boss, Harry Dunne. Even on the few occasions when the Director of Central Intelligence dropped by his deputy's office unannounced (Harry almost always went to the director's office), and the matter was urgent, the director had at least waited for her to buzz Harry.

Yet this man had ignored her entreaties, her protestations and warnings, her firm insistence that Mr. Dunne was out of town, and had just done the unthinkable. He had stormed past her and had gone right into her boss's office. Marjorie knew the mandated security procedures; she pressed the emergency button mounted underneath her main desk drawer, thereby summoning Security, and only then had she frantically warned Harry Dunne over the intercom that, despite her best efforts, this lunatic was coming through.

Bryson knew there were only two choices now: retreat or confrontation, and he preferred confrontation, the only option that had a chance of eliciting spontaneous revelation, forcing unplanned truths. Layla had urged him to stay away from the Agency, counseling that survival was more important now than whatever information he could obtain. But to Bryson there was really no choice at all: to penetrate the lies, to finally learn the truth about Elena, about his entire life, he had to face Dunne.

Layla remained in France, trying to work her contacts, to learn what she could about Jacques Arnaud and his recent activities. He had not told her anything about the Directorate; it was still best to keep her in the dark. She said good-bye to him at Charles de Gaulle airport, surprising Bryson with the ardency of her hug, her kiss that was more than the fare-well kiss of a friend, immediately after which she turned away in flushed embarrassment.

Harry Dunne was standing at his plate-glass window, jacket off, smoking a cigarette on a very long ivory holder. Smoking in the headquarters building was, Bryson knew, against Agency regulations, but as deputy director, Dunne was unlikely to be called on it by anyone. He turned as Bryson entered, Marjorie right behind him.

"Mr. Dunne, I'm so *sorry,* I tried to *stop* this man!" Marjorie called frantically. "Security's on the way."

For an instant Dunne seemed to be examining him, his narrow, creased face compressed into a frown, the small bloodshot eyes glittering. Bryson had taken care to disguise himself, alter his appearance just enough to confound any video face-matching equipment. Then Dunne shook his head as he exhaled a plume of smoke with a loud, hacking cough. "Naw, it's all right, Margie, call off Security. I can deal with this fella myself."

Bewildered, the secretary looked from her boss to the intruder, then, straightening, she backed out of the room, closing the door behind her.

The white-haired Dunne took a step toward Bryson, visibly enraged. "All Security would do would be to restrain me from killing you with my bare hands," he snapped, "and I'm not sure I want that. What kind of game are you playing here, Bryson? You think we're fools, is that it? You think we don't get constant field reports, satellite feeds? I guess it's true what they say: once a traitor, always a traitor." Dunne snubbed out his cigarette in an overflowing glass ashtray on the edge of his desk. "I have no idea how the hell you got into the building, with all our vaunted security procedures. But I expect the surveillance video will tell the tale."

Bryson was jolted by the man's unbanked fury, and it caused him to hesitate. Fury was the last thing he expected on the part of Harry Dunne. Fear, defensiveness, bluster—but not anger. Through gritted teeth, Bryson said, "You sent out your henchmen to kill me. Low-level Paris-station flunkies."

Dunne snorted with derision as he pulled another cigarette from the jacket pocket of his rumpled gray suit. He inserted it in the ivory holder and lighted it, waving out the match and dropping it into the ashtray. "You can do better than that, Professor," Dunne said, shaking his head as he turned back to the picture window that looked over the verdant Virginia countryside. "Look, the facts are simple. We sent you out to worm your way back into the Directorate. Instead, all you seem to have done is blow up some of our most promising links to the Directorate. Then you disappeared, went to ground. Sort of like a mob hit man blowing away witnesses." He turned back to Bryson, exhaled a cloud of smoke into his face. "We thought you were *ex*-Directorate. I guess that's where we made our biggest mistake, huh?"

"What the hell are you trying to say to me?"

"I'd like to ask you to take a polygraph, but that's one of the first things they teach you boys, isn't it—how to beat the box?"

Disgusted, Bryson slapped a stiff blue plastic-laminate card onto the only bare spot of mahogany visible on Harry Dunne's desk. The Agency ID card he had pulled from the wallet of the dead motorcyclist outside of Paris, the pursuer dispatched from Jacques Arnaud's château. "You want to know how I got in here?"

Dunne picked it up, immediately examined the hologram: holding it up to the light, tipping it to bring out the three-dimensional CIA seal, finding the magnetic foil sandwiched between the plastic layers. It was an everyday object at the CIA, but only at the CIA—a high-tech, high-security identification card, virtually impossible to fake. Dunne slid it into a desktop card reader. On his large blue computer screen, a face popped up, along with an employee's basic personnel information. The face wasn't Bryson's, but at the moment, Bryson's altered and disguised face fairly closely resembled the one up on the monitor.

"Paris station. Where the *hell* did you get this?" Dunne demanded.

"You going to listen to me now?"

Dunne's face was wary. He exhaled twin plumes of smoke through his nostrils as he sank into his desk chair. He snubbed out the cigarette, prematurely. "At least let me call Finneran in here."

"Finneran?"

"You met him at Blue Ridge. My aide-de-camp."

"Forget it."

"He's my goddamned institutional memory—"

"Forget it! Just you and me and the listening devices."

Dunne shrugged. He pulled out another cigarette, but instead of placing it into the holder, he began toying with it between nicotine-stained fingers. Through the threadbare fabric of Dunne's blue button-down shirt, Bryson could see the outlines of an array of nicotine patches along his shoulders and biceps.

As Bryson recounted the events of the past few days, Dunne became grave. When he finally spoke, his voice was hushed. "A two-million-dollar bounty on your head, placed even *before* you showed up on Calacanis's ship. Somehow the word was out on the street that you were back in the game."

"You seem to forget they tried to dispatch me in Washington. They seemed to know I'd be coming back, looking for the old Directorate headquarters. That points to a leak in the pipes right here, in this building." Bryson inscribed a small circle in the air with an index finger.

"Christ!" shot back the deputy director, tearing the cigarette in half and flinging the pieces toward the ashtray. "The whole goddamned thing was off the books, the only record of your involvement your name in the Security data bank for purposes of clearing you in and out of the building."

"If the Directorate is wired into CIA, that's enough to do it."

"Come *on*, man, it wasn't even a true name! You were Jonas Barrett—a cover alias used in the Security logs being, incidentally, against every fucking rule in the playbook. You don't lie to Security. Never lie to Mother."

"Expense vouchers, equipment requisitions—"

"Buried, all messaging text in proprietary cipher, all need-to-know, all DDCI priority. Look, Bryson, I covered my ass, what the hell you think? You were a huge goddamned risk on my part, I gotta tell ya. I don't know what stress they put you under, how they might have burned you out. Put a guy's red-bordered folder under a fucking microscope, you still don't know shit about what's in his head. I mean, look, they put you out to pasture in your little cow-town college—"

"For God's sake," thundered Bryson, "do you think I *volunteered* for this? Your goons came and wrenched me out of retirement. I was just beginning to heal, and you came to tear open the scab! I'm not here to defend myself—I assume you boys did your homework on me. I want to know what the hell CIA was doing, following me outside Paris in order to kill me. I hope to hell you have a good explanation, or at least a convincing lie."

Dunne glowered. "I'm going to ignore that last dig, Bryson," he said quietly. "Think this through, wouldya? According to what you're telling me, you were recognized by this Directorate operative you worked with in Kowloon, Vance Gifford—"

"Yes, and according to the Sangiovanni brothers, I was also identified by Arnaud's man aboard the ship. That's obvious and beyond dispute. It's not hard to walk back the cat and see how Santiago de Compostela happened. I'm talking about Chantilly, about Paris! About one CIA operative I happened to flush out because he was sloppy enough to leave his ID papers on his person. And where there's one, there's always more, you know that as well as I. So what are you going to tell me—that the Agency is out of control? It's either that or you're double-dealing me, and I want to know which it is, *now!*"

"No!" Dunne shouted hoarsely, his voice then dissolving in a series of hacking coughs. "Those aren't the only possible explanations!"

"Then what are you trying to sell me?"

Dunne drew his own circle in the air with an index finger, mimicking Bryson's, signaling the room bugs. He scowled. "I'm saying I want to check some things out. I'm saying I think we ought to continue this discussion at another time and place." His face seemed even more lined, the hollows deeper, and for the first time his eyes looked haunted.

The Rosamund Cleary Extended Care Facility was, in plain English, a nursing home. It was a handsome, low-slung red-brick facility surrounded by a few acres of wooded land in Dutchess County, in upstate New York. Whatever it was called, it was an expensive, well-managed place, a last home for the financially privileged who needed medical attention that relatives and other loved ones could not give them. For the last twelve years it had been the home of Felicia Munroe, the woman who, with her husband, Peter, had taken the teen-aged Nicholas Bryson in after Bryson's parents had been killed in an automobile crash.

Bryson had loved the woman, had always had a close and loving relationship with her, but he had never thought of her as his mother. The accident had happened too late in his life for that. She was just Aunt Felicia, the doting wife of Uncle Pete, who'd been one of his father's best friends. They had taken loving care of him, welcomed him into their home, even paid his way through boarding school and then college, for which he was eternally grateful.

Peter Munroe had met George Bryson at the Officers Club in Bahrain. Colonel Bryson, as he was then, had been supervising construction of a major new barracks, and Munroe, a civil engineer for a multinational construction firm, had been a bidder on the project. Bryson and Munroe had become fast friends over too many beers—the specialty of the club in that nonalcoholic nation—and yet, when the bids were submitted, Colonel Bryson recommended *against* Pete Munroe's firm. He had no choice, really; another construction company had underbid them. Munroe took the bad news in good spirit, took Bryson out for a round of drinks on him,

and said he didn't really give a shit—he'd gotten more out
of this fucking country than he'd ever expected to—a friend.
Only later—too late, as it turned out—did the senior Bryson
learn why the winning bidder came in so low: dishonesty.
The firm tried to stick the army with millions of dollars in
cost overruns. When George Bryson tried to apologize, Munroe refused to accept his apology. "Corruption's a way of
life in this business," he said. "If I really wanted the job, I
would have lied, too. *I* was the naïve one." The friendship
between George Bryson and Pete Munroe, however, was
sealed.

But was that the truth? Was there really more to it? Was
Harry Dunne telling him the truth? Now that he had concrete
evidence that an active CIA operative on the Agency payroll
had attempted to kill him in France, everything was in question. For if Dunne had had anything to do with that, was
anything else he said to be trusted? In some ways Bryson
regretted not coming here first, before flying off to the *Spanish Armada*. He should have found old Aunt Felicia and
questioned her before agreeing to do Dunne's dirty work.
Bryson had visited Felicia twice before, once with Elena, but
not in several years.

Dunne's words to him that day in the Blue Ridge Mountains, the day that changed his life, still echoed in his head.
He would not soon forget them.

*"Let me ask you something, Bryson. Did you believe this
was an accident? You were fifteen, a brilliant student, terrific
athlete, prime of American youth, all that. Now both your
parents are suddenly killed. Your godparents take you in—"*

"Uncle Pete . . . Peter Munroe."

*"That was the name he took, sure. Not the name he was
born with. And he made sure you went to college where you
did, and made a lot of other decisions for you besides. All
of which pretty much guaranteed that you'd end up in their
hands. The Directorate's, I mean."*

Bryson found Aunt Felicia sitting in front of a television
set in a spacious public sitting room tastefully appointed with

Persian rugs and massive mahogany antiques. Several other elderly people were scattered about the room, a few reading or crocheting, several dozing. Felicia Munroe appeared to be watching golf with rapt fascination.

"Aunt Felicia," Bryson said heartily.

She turned to look at him, and for a fleeting instant recognition seemed to dawn on her face. But it immediately gave way to a foggy bewilderment. "Yes?" she said sharply.

"Aunt Felicia, I'm Nick. Remember me?"

She stared at him with incomprehension, squinting. He realized that the traces of senility he had seen in her years ago had grown into something far deeper and more serious. After staring for an uncomfortably long time, she gave a slow smile. "It *is* you," she breathed.

"Remember? I lived with you—you took care of me . . . ?"

"You've come back," she whispered, finally seeming to comprehend. Tears sprang to her eyes. "My heavens, how I've missed you."

Bryson's heart lifted.

"My darling George," she trilled. "My dearest darling George. How long it's been."

For a moment he was perplexed, and then he understood. Bryson was about the same age that his father, Gen. George Bryson, was when he died. In Aunt Felicia's confused mind—a mind that probably could recall clearly events of half a century ago, yet could not remember her own name—he *was* George Bryson. And indeed the resemblance was strong. He was often startled to see how much he was coming to look like his father, the older he got.

Then, as if she had suddenly grown bored with her visitor, she turned her gaze back to the television set. Bryson stood, shifting his weight from foot to foot, unsure what to do next. In a minute or so, Felicia seemed to become conscious of his presence, and she turned to look at him again.

"Why, hello there," she ventured tentatively. Her face looked worried, the expression rapidly turning frightened. "But you—but you're *dead!* I thought you were dead!"

Bryson simply looked at her neutrally, not wanting to disturb the illusion. *Let her believe what she wants to believe; perhaps she will say something. . . .*

"You died in that terrible accident," she said. Her face was racked with tension. "Yes, you did. That terrible, terrible accident. You and Nina both. What an awful thing. And you leaving poor young Nicky an orphan. Oh, I don't think I stopped crying for three days. Pete was always the strong one—he got me through it." The tears glistened in her eyes once again, and they began to course down her cheeks. "So much Pete didn't tell me about that night," she continued, her voice almost a singsong. "So much he couldn't tell me, *wouldn't* tell me. How the guilt must have eaten him up inside. For years he wouldn't talk to me about that night, about what he did."

A chill ran down Bryson's spine.

"And he'd *never* talk to your little Nicky about it, you know. What a thing to carry with you, what a terrible, terrible thing!" She shook her head, dabbing at her eyes with the frilly cuff of her white blouse. Then she turned back to the television.

Bryson strode to the TV, shut it off, and stood right in front of her. Though the poor woman's short-term memory had been destroyed by the effects of senility, or perhaps Alzheimer's disease, it appeared that many of her long-term memories might have been spared.

"Felicia," he said gently, "I want to talk to you about Pete. Pete Munroe, your husband."

The direct stare seemed to unnerve her; she studied the pattern on the carpet. "He used to make me a whiskey sling when I had a cold, you know," she said. She seemed lost in the memory, her manner now relaxed. "Honey and lemon juice and just a *wee* bit of bourbon. No, more than a wee bit. You'll be better in no time."

"Felicia, did he ever talk about something called the Directorate?"

She looked up at him blankly. "An untreated cold can linger for a week. But with treatment, it will pass in seven days!" She giggled, waggling her finger. "Peter always said an untreated cold can linger for a week . . ."

"Did he ever talk about my father?"

"Oh, he was a great talker. Told the funniest stories."

At the other end of the room, one of the patients had had an accident, and two janitors appeared with mops. The two custodians chattered to each other in Russian. A Russian phrase, spoken loudly, was audible. *Ya nye znayu*, one of them said brusquely: I don't know. The accent was Muscovite.

Felicia Munroe had heard it, too, and she perked up in response. *"Ya nye znayu,"* she repeated, then giggled. "Gibberish! Gibberish!"

"Not really gibberish, Aunt Felicia," Bryson put in.

"Gibberish!" she replied defiantly. "Just the sort of nonsense Pete would say in his sleep. *Ya nye znayu.* All that craziness. Whenever he talked in his sleep, he'd talk in that funny language, and he just *hated* when I teased him about it."

"He talked like that in his sleep?" Bryson said hollowly, his heart thudding in his rib cage.

"Oh, he was a terrible sleeper." For a moment she seemed lucid. "Always talked in his sleep."

Uncle Pete spoke Russian in his sleep, the one time when you can't control your utterances. Was Harry Dunne right: was Peter Munroe an associate of Gennady Rosovsky's, a.k.a. Ted Waller? Could it be true? Was any other explanation even *possible?* Bryson was dumbstruck.

But Felicia kept talking. "Particularly after you died, George. He was so sorry. He tossed and turned, he yelled and cried in his sleep, and always talking that *gibberish!*"

The area of Rock Creek Park in Washington, on the northern part of Beach Drive, was a good location for the rendezvous with Harry Dunne very early the next morning. Bryson had chosen it; Dunne had invited him to select the meeting point not out of deference to Bryson's field skills—after all, Dunne's experience as an operative with the Agency's clandestine division had been over twice as long as Bryson's with the Directorate—but more likely as a courtesy extended by a host to his honored guest.

The CIA deputy director's request to meet off site, outside Agency walls, was alarming to Bryson. It was hard to believe that Dunne, the number-two man in the Agency, feared his own office was bugged; that fact itself gave credence to the theory that the CIA had been penetrated by the Directorate—that Bryson's old handlers had somehow managed to extend their tentacles into the highest reaches of the CIA. Whatever information Dunne might have been able to collect, the mere fact that he insisted on continuing their discussion in a neutral, secure location was unnerving proof that something was very wrong.

Still, Bryson would take nothing at face value. *Trust no one,* Ted Waller used to say with a cackle, words now grotesquely appropriate: Waller himself had turned out to be the cardinal betrayer of trust. Bryson would not let down his guard; he would trust no one, Dunne included.

He arrived at the designated location a full hour early. It was barely four o'clock in the morning, the sky dark, the air cold and damp. Passing cars were few, spaced far apart in time: night-shift workers going home, their replacements arriving. The business of government was round-the-clock.

The silence was strange, unaccustomed. Bryson became aware of the sounds of twigs crackling underfoot as he paced the dense woods surrounding the clearing he had chosen, noises that would ordinarily be masked by the ambient roar of nearby traffic. He wore the crepe-soled shoes he favored for field work because they minimized such noise.

Bryson surveyed the location, searching for points of vulnerability. The wooded ridge overlooked a small patch of meadow, next to a small, asphalt-paved parking area, at the edge of which was a concrete, bunkerlike restroom facility, half sunken below ground, in which they had agreed to meet. Rain had been forecast, and though the forecast had turned out wrong, a sheltered location had seemed desirable. Too, the facility's thick concrete walls would provide protection in the event of ambush from without.

But Bryson was determined that there would be no ambush. He made a circuit around the wooded ridge, through the dense trees overlooking the meadow, checking for recently made footsteps or branches broken in a suspicious pattern, as well as for scopes, mounts, or other devices that might have been emplaced in advance. A second sweep revealed all possible avenues of approach; nothing would be left to chance. After two more sweeps, each from different directions and covering different vantage points, Bryson was satisfied that no ambush was already in place. That did not rule out any future arrivals, but at least he would be able to authoritatively detect subtle changes in background, divergences otherwise ignored.

At precisely five o'clock in the morning, a black government sedan pulled off Beach Drive and into the parking area. It was a Lincoln Continental, unmarked except for generic government license plates. Watching through small, high-powered binoculars from a blind he had chosen in a dense copse of trees, Bryson could make out Dunne's regular driver, a slender African American in a navy blue uniform. Dunne sat in the backseat clutching a file folder. There appeared to be no one else in the vehicle.

The limousine pulled up to the restroom and came to a stop. The driver got out and went to open the door for his boss, but Dunne, impatient as always, was already halfway out of the car. He was scowling, his habitual expression. Glancing briefly to either side, he descended the short flight of steps, his face illuminated garishly by the sulphurous fluorescent lights, and then disappeared into the small building.

Bryson waited. He watched the driver, waiting for any suspicious moves—furtive phone calls placed on a concealed cellular phone, quick signals to passing vehicles, even the loading of a gun. But the driver simply sat behind the wheel, waiting with the calm, still patience his boss lacked.

After a good ten minutes had elapsed, and Bryson was

sure that Dunne was probably fed up by now, he came down the hillside, following a path that kept him concealed from passersby, winding around to the back of the restroom, which was even with the ground level. Putting on a sudden burst of speed, he raced to the building, confident that he had not been observed. Now he leaped down into the moat that surrounded the bunker and circled around to the entrance, unseen.

The fluorescent lights flickered as he approached. The building reeked of urine and excrement, with an astringent overlay of cleaning solution, woefully insufficient. He listened at the door for a moment until he heard Dunne's signature hacking cough. He entered swiftly, closing the heavy steel door behind him and locking it with the strong padlock he had brought.

Dunne was standing at a urinal. He turned his head slowly when Bryson entered. "Nice of you to saunter in," he muttered. "Now I see why those Directorate fuckers fired your ass. Punctuality ain't your strong suit."

Bryson ignored the jabs. Dunne knew exactly why he was ten minutes late. Dunne zipped up, flushed, and went to the sink. They looked at each other in the mirror. "Bad news," Dunne said, his voice echoing, as he washed his hands. "The card's legit."

"The card?"

"The Agency ID card you took off the motorcyclist's body in Chantilly. It's not doctored paper. The guy was detailed to the Paris station for over a year as an operative *in extremis*—for when the real dirty stuff had to be done."

"Trace the personnel records, the name on the assignment authorization, even how he was recruited."

Dunne scowled again, radiating disgust. "Why didn't I think of that," he said with heavy irony. He shook his hands dry—there were no paper towels, and he refused to use the automatic hand-drying machine—then wiped them on his pants. He fished a crumpled Marlboro pack out of his breast pocket and fumbled out a partly crushed cigarette, which he placed in his mouth. Without lighting it, he went on, "I ordered a Code Sigma–priority search through all the computer banks, down to the last firewall. Nothing."

"What do you mean, nothing? You keep thick personnel files on everyone, from the director on down to the lady who cleans the washrooms in the imaging center."

Dunne grimaced. The unlit cigarette dangled from his lower lip.

"And you guys don't leave anything out. *Anything*. So don't tell me you turned up nothing in the guy's personnel file."

"No, I'm telling you the guy had no file. As far as Langley central is concerned, he didn't exist."

"Come on! There's health coverage, insurance, pay-checks—a bunch of administrative and bureaucratic horseshit that Personnel bombards every single employee with. You telling me he wasn't getting *paychecks?*"

"*Christ's* sake, you're not fucking *listening!* The guy didn't exist! It's not unheard of—the real serious wetwork-ers, we don't like to have a paper trail on them. Files are buried, requisitions deep-sixed after payments are authorized. So the precedent is there. Thing is, someone knew how to play the system, keep the guy's name off all the books. He was like a *ghost*—there but not there."

"So what does this mean?" Bryson asked quietly.

Dunne was silent for a moment. He coughed. "It means, buddy, that the CIA may not be the best agency to investigate the Directorate. Especially if the Directorate has its moles inside, which we have to assume."

Dunne's words, though not unexpected, came as a bolt of lightning because of the finality with which the CIA man uttered them. Bryson nodded. "Not easy for you to admit," he said.

Dunne tipped his head to one side in acknowledgment. "Not particularly," he conceded, an obvious understatement. The man was shaken, though obviously reluctant to admit it. "Look, I don't want to believe the goddamned Directorate might have reached out and touched my own people. But I didn't get where I did by indulging in wishful thinking. See,

I never went to one of your hoity-toity universities—I got into St. John's by the skin of my ass. I don't speak a dozen languages like you do, either—just English, and that none too good. But what I had, see—and still do, I like to think— was something that's a scarce commodity in the intelligence business, and that's horse sense. Or whatever the hell you want to call it. Look at what's happened to this goddamned country in the last forty years, from the Bay of Pigs to Vietnam to Panama to whatever's the latest fuckup in the *Washington Post* this morning. All brought to you by the so-called Wise Men, those 'best and the brightest' with their fancy Ivy League sheepskins and their trust funds, who keep getting us into all these scrapes. They got education, but no common sense. Me, I can *smell* when something's off, I got an instinct for it. And I don't go whistling past graveyards. So I can't dodge the possibility—and it's only a possibility, mind you— that someone on my team is involved. I'm not going to bullshit you. I don't want to have to play my last card, but I may have to."

"Which is?"

"What the fuck does the *Washington Post* call him, the 'last honest man in Washington'? Which isn't saying much in this corrupt city."

"Richard Lanchester," Bryson said, recalling the epithet often applied to the president's national security adviser and chairman of the White House National Security Council. He knew of Lanchester's unequalled reputation for probity. "Why is he your last card?"

"Because once I play it, it's out of my control. He may be the one man in government who can head this thing off, circumvent corrupted channels, but once I involve him, it's no longer contained in the intelligence community. It's all-out internecine war, and frankly, I don't know whether our government could survive it."

"Jesus," Bryson breathed. "You're saying the Directorate's reach is that high?"

"That's what it smells like to me."

"Well, I'm the one whose life is on the line out there.

From now on, I communicate only with you, *directly* with you. No intermediaries, no E-mail that can be cracked or faxes that can be intercepted. I want you to isolate a sterile line at Langley, routed through a lockbox, sequestered and segregated."

The CIA man nodded his acquiescence.

"I also want a code-word sequence so I can be certain you're not speaking under duress, or that your voice is being falsified. I want to know it's you, and that you're speaking freely. And one more thing: all communications go directly between you and me—not even through your secretary."

Bryson shrugged. "Point taken, but you're overreacting. I'd trust Marjorie with my life."

"Sorry. No exceptions. Elena once told me about something called Metcalf's Rule, which says that the porosity of a network increases as the square of the number of nodes. The nodes, in this case, refers to anyone who's knowledge-able about the operation."

"Elena," said the CIA man with heavy derision. "I guess she knows something about deception, huh, Bryson?"

The remark stung, despite everything that had happened, even despite his own bitterness over her unexplained disap-pearance. "Correct," Bryson returned. "Which is why you've got to help me get to her—"

"You think I sent you out there to save your marriage?" Dunne interrupted. "I sent you out there to save the goddam-ned world."

"Damn it, she *knows* something, she has to. Maybe quite a bit."

"Yeah, and if she's involved—"

"If she's involved, she's involved in a central way. If she's a dupe like I was—"

"Wishful thinking, Bryson, I *warned* you—"

"If she's a dupe like I was," Bryson thundered, "then her knowledge is *still* invaluable!"

"And of course she'll happily spill all the fucking beans to you out of, what, nostalgia? Remembrance of all the good times past?"

"If I can *get* to her," Bryson shouted, then he faltered. Quietly, he went on, "If I can get to her . . . damn it, I *know* her, I can tell when she's lying, when she tries to shade the truth, what she's trying to avoid discussing."

"You're dreaming," said Harry Dunne flatly. He coughed, a painful-sounding, rattling, liquid cough. "You think you know her. You pretend you know her, *knew* her. You're so sure, aren't you? Just like you were so sure you knew Ted Waller, a.k.a. Gennady Rosovsky. Or Pyotr Aksyonov—alias your 'uncle' Peter Munroe. Did your little visit to upstate New York enlighten you further?"

Bryson couldn't hide his astonishment. "God*damn* you to hell!" he shouted.

"Get real, Bryson. You think I haven't maintained a cordon of surveillance on that nursing home ever since I learned about the Directorate? Poor old biddy's so addled, our men could never get much out of her, so I could never be sure whether she knew the truth about her husband, or how *much* she knew. But there was a chance that she might be contacted by someone connected with her late husband."

"Bullshit!" Bryson shot back. "You don't have the resources to keep a team of watchers on her twenty-four hours a day, seven days a week, until she dies!"

"Christ," Dunne said impatiently. "Obviously not. One of the administrators there earns a nice chunk of change on the side from Felicia's 'dear old cousin Harry,' who's fiercely protective. Anyone calls for Felicia, arranges to come by, even drops by, an administrator named Shirley gives me a call first thing. She knows I like to protect sweet addle-brained Felicia from gold diggers or people who might upset her. I take care of my cousin. Shirley always has my phone number wherever I am. So I always know who Felicia's in touch with. No surprises. Point is, you work with what you've got; you cover what you can. Most of the others just seem to have disappeared without a fucking trace. Now we gotta stand here in this stinking shithole all day?"

"I don't like it much either, but it's remote, secluded, and safe."

"Aw, Christ. You care to tell me why you went to see Jacques Arnaud?"

"As I told you, his emissary, his agent on Calacanis's ship, was clearly working with both the Directorate and with Anatoly Prishnikov in Russia. Arnaud had to be a key node."

"But for what? You wanted to reach out to Arnaud directly?"

Bryson paused. Ted Waller's words—Gennady Rosovsky's—came back to him, as they did so often: *Tell no one anything they don't absolutely need to know. Even me.* He hadn't yet told Dunne about the cryptochip he had copied from Arnaud's secure satellite phone, and he would not. Not yet.

"I considered it," he lied. "At least to observe those around him."

"And?"

"Nothing. A waste of time." *Always hold back a card.*

Dunne took out from his battered leather portfolio a red-bordered manila envelope, from which he drew a batch of eight-by-ten photographs. "We've gone through the names you gave us in the debriefing, ran them through every available database, including every top-secret code-word proprietary. Wasn't easy, given how clever and thorough your friends at the Directorate seem to be—selecting and rotating aliases using computer algorithms, all that shit I don't really understand. Directorate operatives get reassigned, uprooted, their biographies rewritten, networks detached and reassembled. It was mind-numbing work, but we do have a few candidates for you to look at." He displayed the first black-and-white glossy.

Bryson shook his head. "Nope."

Dunne frowned, took out another.

"No recollection."

Dunne shook his head, showed him another.

"Doesn't register. You've got some dummies in here, don't you?—known fakes, hoping to trip me up."

A smile seemed to play at the corners of Dunne's lips. He coughed.

"Always testing, huh?"

Dunne didn't reply. He pulled out another photograph.

"Nope—hey, wait a minute." Bryson was looking at a photograph of an agent he recognized. "This one I know. That Dutchman, cover name Prospero."

Dunne nodded as if Bryson had finally answered the question right. "Jan Vansina, a senior official at the International Red Cross headquarters in Geneva. Director of management for international emergency relief coordination. Brilliant cover for traveling easily around the world, especially to crisis spots, and it gives him access even to places where foreigners are normally barred—North Korea, Iraq, Libya, and so on. You had a good relationship with him."

"I saved his life in Yemen. Warned him off an ambush, even though the standard operating procedure required me to contain what I knew, whether it meant his execution or not."

"Not big on following orders either, I see."

"Not when I think they're stupid. Prospero was quite impressive. We worked together once, jointly laying a snare for a NATO engineer and double agent. What's Vansina doing here? It looks like indoor surveillance cameras."

"Our people caught him in Geneva, at Banque Geneve Privée. Authorizing the rapid-sequence transfer of a total of five-point-five billion dollars through separate and commingled accounts."

"Laundering, in other words."

"But not for himself. He was apparently acting as a conduit for an immensely well-funded organization."

"You didn't get all this background from a hidden video camera."

"We have sources throughout the Swiss banking industry."

"Reliable?"

"Not all, to be sure. But in this case, it was somebody pretty damned plugged in. An ex–Directorate operative who traded confirmable information in exchange for the elimination of a long prison sentence." He glanced at his wristwatch. "Extortion usually works."

Bryson nodded. "You think Vansina's still active?"

"This photograph was taken two days ago," Dunne said quietly, taking a pager from his belt and pressing a button on it. "Sorry, I should have signaled Solomon, my driver, twenty minutes ago. Our agreement is that I'd send him a page when you showed up, if he wasn't able to establish visual confirmation. Which he didn't, since you made one of your Harry Houdini appearances."

"What's the point of signaling your driver? To let him know you're okay—that I didn't do you harm, is that the point?" Bryson's voice rose in annoyance. "You really don't trust me, do you?"

"Solomon just likes to keep close tabs on me."

"You can never be too cautious," Bryson said.

There was a sudden loud banging on the restroom door.

"You lock it or something?"

Bryson nodded.

"So who's the too-cautious one?" Dunne said derisively. "Christ, let me go assure my worrywart driver that everything's jake."

Dunne went to the restroom door, tugged at the padlock, and shook his head. "I'm alive," he called out hoarsely. "No guns to my head or anything."

A muffled voice from the other side of the door said, "You're needed out here, sir, please."

"Cool your jets, Solomon. I said I'm fine."

"That's not it, sir. It's something else."

"What is it?"

"A call just came in, immediately after you paged me. On the car phone, sir—the one that you said only's supposed to ring if it's National Security Maximum."

"Oh, Christ," said Dunne. "Bryson, would you mind . . . ?"

Bryson approached the side of the concrete doorjamb, reaching for his weapon at the same time that he inserted a key in the padlock, springing it open. He flattened himself against the wall, out of sight, gun drawn.

Dunne watched Bryson's preparations with undisguised

incredulity. The door came open, and Bryson was able to confirm that it was the same slender African-American man he'd seen behind the wheel of Dunne's government-issue car. Solomon seemed abashed, ill at ease. "I'm sorry to disturb you, sir," he said, "but it really does sound important." He was looking at his boss, his hands empty at his sides, no one else beside or behind him. The driver appeared not to have seen Bryson, who leaned against the wall, out of the intruder's line of sight.

Dunne nodded and, looking rankled, headed out toward the limousine, his driver following.

Suddenly the driver spun back around toward the open door, lunging with extraordinary, unexpected agility diagonally into the restroom toward Bryson, a large Magnum pistol in his right hand.

"What the hell—?" shouted Dunne, turning around with amazement.

The explosion thundered in the small interior, fragments of concrete flying everywhere, piercing Bryson's flesh as he dodged to his right, just missing the bullet. Several more came in rapid succession, shattering the walls, the floor inches from his head. The suddenness of the attack had caught Bryson off guard, forcing him to focus his energies on leaping out of the way, momentarily keeping him from leveling his own gun. The chauffeur was wild, firing madly, his face contorted with an animal-like fury. Bryson sprung forward, his gun extended, just as another explosion came, louder than any that had come before. A gaping red hole appeared at the center of the driver's chest, an explosion of blood, and the man tumbled forward, clearly dead.

Harry Dunne stood fifteen feet away, with his blue-steel Smith & Wesson .45 aloft, still pointed at his own chauffeur, a wisp of smoke curling from the barrel. He looked dazed, his expression almost crestfallen. Finally, the CIA man broke the silence. "Jesus Christ," he said, coughing so hard he almost doubled over. "Jesus Christ almighty."

CHAPTER TWELVE

The light in the Oval Office was eerie, silvery-gray, lending a somber cast to a gathering that did not need any more gloom. It was twilight, the end of a long, overcast day. President Malcolm Stephenson Davis sat in the small white sofa at the center of the seating area where he preferred to conduct his most serious meetings. In chairs on either side of him sat the directors of the CIA, the FBI, and the NSA; immediately next to him, at his right hand, was the special assistant to the president for national security affairs, Richard Lanchester. It was rare for such a senior collection of administration officials to gather outside the official confines of the Cabinet Room, the Situation Room, or the National Security Council. But the very unusual venue of the occasion underscored its gravity.

The reason for the meeting was abundantly clear. A little over nine hours earlier a powerful blast in the Dupont Circle station of the Washington Metro had killed twenty-three people and injured easily three times that; the fatality list grew longer as the day went on. The nation, though inured to tragedy, terrorist bombings, school shootings, was in a state of shock. This had happened in the very heart of the nation's capital—a mile from the White House, as CNN's commentators kept repeating.

A bomb left in what appeared to be a laptop computer case had gone off during the height of the morning rush hour. The sophisticated nature of the bomb, the details of which were being kept from the public, seemed to indicate the involvement of terrorists. In this age of all-news-all-the-time cable channels and radio stations, and the lightning-fast communications of the Internet, the terrible story seemed to reverberate, get worse by the minute.

Viewers seemed particularly fascinated by the most gruesome details—the pregnant woman and her three-year-old twin daughters, killed instantly; the elderly couple who had saved up for years to come to Washington from Iowa City; the group of nine-year-old elementary schoolchildren.

"It's more than a nightmare, it's a disgrace," the president said grimly. The other men shook their heads in silent assent. "I'm going to have to reassure the nation in an address either tonight, if we can coordinate it in time, or tomorrow. But I sure as hell don't know what I'm going to say."

"Mr. President," said FBI Director Chuck Faber, "I want to assure you that we have no fewer than seventy-five special agents on the case even as we speak, combing the city, co-ordinating the investigations as lead agency with the local police and ATF. Our materials analysis unit, the explosives unit—"

"I have no doubt," the president cut him off sharply, "that you folks are all over this like a cheap suit. I mean in no way to disparage the Bureau's capabilities, but you do seem to be quite good at handling terrorist events after the fact. I'm just curious why you never seem to be able to *prevent* them."

The FBI director's face flushed. Chuck Faber had won his reputation as the take-no-prisoners district attorney in Phil-adelphia, later becoming Pennsylvania's attorney general. He made no secret of the fact that he wanted to run Main Justice, wanted the attorney general's job, considered himself far more qualified than the current incumbent. Faber was prob-ably the most skilled bureaucratic games player in the room. He was famously confrontational, but he was also too polit-ically savvy ever to confront the president.

"Sir, respectfully, I think that's not quite fair to the men and women of the Bureau." The quiet, calm voice was that of Richard Lanchester, a tall, fit man with silver hair and aristocratic features whose understated suits were custom-tailored in London. Most White House correspondents, whose notion of high fashion tended to be the Euro-extremes of Giorgio Armani, mistakenly described Lanchester as an "unfashionable" or even "frumpy" dresser.

Lanchester, however, rarely paid much attention to such

personal descriptions in the newspapers or on television news. In fact, he preferred to steer clear of journalists altogether, since he strongly opposed leaking, which seemed to be a varsity sport in Washington. Somehow, though, he was admired by the Washington press corps anyway. Perhaps this was precisely because he refused to cultivate them, something most of them had never witnessed before. The label bestowed on him by *Time* magazine, "The Last Honest Man in Washington," was so often repeated in columns and on the Sunday-morning talking-head shows that it had become something of a Homeric epithet.

"It's just that their prevention efforts tend to go unheralded," Lanchester went on. "It's usually impossible to ascertain what *might* have happened were it not for any particular intervention."

The FBI director gave a grudging nod.

"There are news reports that we—that is, the U.S. government—could have prevented this tragedy," intoned the president. "Is there any truth to this?"

There was a moment of awkward silence. Finally, the director of the National Security Agency, Air Force Lt. Gen. John Corelli, replied. "Sir, the problem is that the target fell between the cracks. As you know, our charter forbids us from operating domestically, as does the CIA's, and this was a U.S.-based operation."

"And we're hamstrung by the legalities, sir," put in FBI Director Faber. "That is, we need probable cause to obtain a court-ordered wiretap, but unless we *know* to request such authorization, why in the world would we ask for it?"

"And as for the myth that the NSA is continuously sweeping for telephone calls, faxes, signals . . . ?"

"*Myth* is the word, sir," said NSA Director Corelli. "Even with the enormous capacity we've got at the Fort Meade campus, we can't possibly sweep every phone conversation in the world. Plus, we're not permitted to listen to conversations within the U.S."

"Hallelujah for that," said Dick Lanchester softly.

The FBI director turned to face Lanchester with an expression of purest contempt. "Really? And I suppose you applaud our inability to monitor encrypted conversations, whether over the phone or fax or over the Internet."

"You may not be aware of a little thing called the Fourth Amendment to the Constitution, Chuck," replied Lanchester dryly. "The right of the people to be protected against unreasonable searches and seizures—"

"And what about the right of the people to catch a subway train without being killed?" put in CIA Director James Exum. "I somehow doubt the framers contemplated digital telephony."

"The fact remains," said Lanchester, "that Americans don't want to sacrifice their privacy."

"Dick," the president said quietly, firmly. "The time for that discussion is over and done. The argument is moot. The treaty should pass the Senate any day now, creating an international surveillance agency that will protect us from such mayhem. And damn it, not a moment too soon, either."

Lanchester shook his head in sorrow. "This international agency is effectively going to expand the power of government a thousandfold," he said.

"No," the NSA director put in curtly. "It's going to level the playing field, that's all. For God's sake, the NSA isn't allowed to listen in on the conversations of Americans without a court order, and our British counterpart, the GCHQ, is similarly hamstrung by the legal restriction forbidding it to tap domestic calls in Britain. You seem to forget, Richard, that if the Allies didn't have the ability to read enemy messages during the Second World War, the Germans might well have won."

"We're not in a war."

"Oh, but we are," said the CIA director. "We're in the middle of a global war against terrorists, and the bad guys are winning. And if you're suggesting that we all just pack it in—"

A low tone sounded from the telephone on the small table next to where the president was sitting. The men in the room knew that the president's intercom went off only in the case of an urgent situation, as per Davis's explicit instructions. President Davis picked up the handset. "Yes?"

His face went ashen. He put the phone down, then looked around at the others. "That was the Situation Room," he said gravely. "An American jetliner just went down three miles from Kennedy Airport."

"What?" gasped several of the men at once.

"Blown out of the sky," President Davis murmured, eyes closed. "A minute or so after takeoff. A flight to Rome. One hundred and seventy-one passengers and crew members—all of them dead." He placed his hands over his eyes, massaging them with his fingers. When he removed his fingers, his eyes shone with tears, but the expression in them was fierce, even ferocious. His voice shook. "Jesus Christ, I will not go down in history as the Commander in Chief who sat by idly while terrorists seized control of our world. Goddamn it, we have *got* to *do* something!"

CHAPTER THIRTEEN

The glass office tower on rue de la Corraterie, just south of Place Bel-Air in the heart of Geneva's commercial and banking district, was the deep blue of the ocean, and it glistened in the afternoon sun. On the twenty-seventh floor were the offices of the Banque Geneve Privée, where Bryson and Layla waited in the small but luxuriously appointed waiting room. With its mahogany wainscoting, Oriental rugs, and delicate antiques, the bank was an island of nineteenth-century elegance perched twenty-seven floors above the ground within one of Geneva's most modernistic skyscrapers. The subliminal message it seemed to project was one of old-world civility in harmony with high technology. Its setting could not have been more apt.

Bryson had arrived at Geneva-Cointrin Airport, checked in to Le Richemond, and then met Layla's train, the Paris-Ventimiglia express, from Paris a few hours later at Gare Cornavin. There had been a warmth in their greeting, as if no time had elapsed since Bryson's Paris departure. She was excited, which she displayed in her quiet, vibrant way; she had dug quite a bit and uncovered only a few tiny nuggets, but they were, in her opinion, nuggets of gold. Still, there was no time for a debriefing; he took her to the hotel, where they checked into separate rooms; she changed into a suit, fixed her hair, and they immediately proceeded to rue de la Corraterie for the meeting Bryson had arranged with a Swiss banker.

They were not kept waiting long; this was Switzerland, where punctuality was holy writ. A matronly woman of middle age, with gray hair worn up in a bun, appeared in the waiting room at the exact time of their appointment.

She addressed him by his CIA-supplied cover name. "You must be Mr. Mason," she said haughtily. It was not the tone customarily used with favored clients; she knew he was from the U.S. government and therefore to be considered an annoyance. She then turned to Layla. "And you are—?"

"This is Anat Chafetz," Bryson said, using one of her Mossad-furnished aliases. "Mossad."

"Monsieur Bécot is expecting both of you? I had been told there would just be you, Mr. Mason." The assistant was perturbed.

"I assure you that Monsieur Bécot will want to see both of us," Bryson said, matching her hauteur.

She nodded brusquely. "Excuse me."

She returned a minute later. "Please come with me."

Jean-Luc Bécot was a compact, bespectacled man whose precise, economical movements revealed the precision of the man. He had short silver-gray hair, gold wire-rimmed glasses, and wore a tailored gray suit. He shook their hands politely but warily and asked them if they would like coffee.

Another assistant, this one a young man in a blue blazer, came in a moment later bearing three tiny cups of espresso on a gleaming silver tray. He silently set down two cups on the coffee table next to where Layla and Bryson sat, and then placed the third on the glass-topped desk behind which Jean-Luc Bécot was stationed.

Bécot's office was decorated in the same opulent style as the rest of the bank's offices, the same assemblage of delicate antiques and Persian carpets. One entire wall was a plate-glass window that looked over Geneva, the view breathtaking.

"Now then," Bécot said, "I am sure you both appreciate that I am a busy man, and so forgive me for asking you to come right to the point. You alluded to financial irregularities in the handling of one of our accounts. Let me assure you that Banque Geneve Privée permits no such irregularities. I am afraid you have come here in vain."

Bryson smiled tolerantly throughout the banker's opening remarks, tenting his fingers. When Bécot came to a halt, Bryson said, "Monsieur Bécot, the very fact that you are meeting with me indicates that you or one of your associates placed a call to Central Intelligence Agency headquarters in Langley, Virginia, to check on my bona fides." He paused, saw the unspoken acknowledgment in the banker's face. Bryson had no doubt that his phone call a few hours earlier had raised all sorts of alarm. The CIA had sent one of its operatives to Geneva to question a Swiss banker in connection with an account—all of Banque Geneve Privée was surely up in arms by now; there would have been frantic calls made, hurried consultations. There was a time when any self-respecting Swiss banker would simply have refused to see an officer of American intelligence: the secrecy of bank accounts was paramount. But times had changed, and although money laundering still continued in Switzerland on a massive scale, the Swiss had succumbed to international political pressure; they were much more cooperative these days. Or at least they were eager to give the appearance of cooperation.

Bryson resumed. "You know that I would not be here were it not a situation of some gravity—one that involves your bank directly, and that threatens to entangle your bank in a nasty legal mess, which I'm sure you wish to avoid."

Bécot gave an ugly, prim little smile. "Your threats will not work here, Mr.—Mr. Mason. And as for why you brought with you a Mossad officer, if this is your clumsy attempt to increase the pressure—"

"Monsieur Bécot, let us speak plainly," said Bryson, adopting the tone of an international law-enforcement agent who held all the cards. "Under the 1987 Convention of Diligence, neither you nor your bank can claim ignorance of an account holder or of any account holder's use of your bank to launder money for criminal purposes. The legal ramifications are quite serious, as you well know. Representatives of the intelligence agencies of two world powers have come before you to seek your assistance in a major international money-laundering investigation; you can either help us, as you are required to do by law, or you can turn us away, in which case we will be forced to report this suspected criminal activity to Lausanne."

The banker stared at Bryson impassively for a moment,

his coffee untouched. "What, precisely, is the nature of your investigation, Mr. Mason?"

Bryson sensed the man's vacillation; it was time to thrust. "We are examining the activities in Banque Geneve Privée account number 246322, held by one Jan Vansina."

Bécot hesitated for an instant. The name, if not the number, had registered immediately. "We never divulge the names of our clients—"

Bryson glanced at Layla, who took her cue. "Substantial monies have been wire-transferred into this account from a fictitious *Anstalt* in Liechtenstein, as you're well aware. From here the funds have been wired to an array of accounts: several different shell companies in the Isle of Man, and Jersey, in the Channel Islands; to the Caymans, Aguilla, the Netherlands Antilles. From there the funds have been split and routed to the Bahamas and San Marino—"

"There is nothing illegal about wire transfers!" snapped Bécot.

"Unless they are done to launder illicit monies," she said with equal vehemence. Bryson had filled her in with the few details Harry Dunne had provided on Vansina's bank account; the rest was sheer embellishment. Bryson was impressed. "In this case, these laundered funds have been used to fund the purchase of arms used in the activities of known terrorists around the world."

"This sounds suspiciously like a fishing expedition," said the Swiss.

"A fishing expedition?" repeated Layla. "More like an international criminal investigation undertaken by Washington and Tel Aviv simultaneously, which should be evidence enough of how seriously this is being taken at the highest levels. But I can see we are wasting Monsieur Bécot's time." She rose, and Bryson did the same. "Obviously we are not dealing on a high enough level here," she said to Bryson. "Monsieur Bécot either does not have the decision-making capability or is deliberately concealing his own criminal role. I am sure that the bank's director, Monsieur Etienne Broussard, will have a more enlightened view—"

"What is it that you want?" interrupted the banker, desperation now evident in his face, his voice.

Bryson, still standing, said, "Quite simply, we want you to telephone the account holder, Mr. Vansina, immediately, and request that he come into the bank at once."

"But Monsieur Vansina is never to be directly approached, that is the stipulation of his account! He contacts *us,* that is the way it is done. Besides, I have no contact number for him!"

"False. There are always contact numbers," said Bryson. "If you are doing business as you should, you have photocopies of his passport and other identification papers, addresses and telephone numbers of his home and place of work—"

"I cannot *do* that!" cried Bécot.

"Come, Mr. Mason, we are wasting time here. I'm sure Monsieur Bécot's superior will understand the gravity of the situation," said Layla. "Once the request is made through diplomatic liaison and the courts in Washington, Tel Aviv, and Lausanne, the Banque Geneve Privée will be publicly named as an accomplice in the funding of international terrorism and money laundering, and—"

"No! Sit down!" the banker said, all pretense at bankerly gravitas abandoned. "I will call Vansina."

Concealed in the small, stuffy, closet-size room, lined with video screens, where the bank's surveillance cameras were monitored, Bryson perspired heavily. The plan he had devised called for him to remain in hiding while Layla met with Vansina in Bécot's office, still in the guise of a Mossad officer investigating money laundering. She would interrogate Vansina, elicit whatever useful information she could, and then Bryson would appear suddenly, drawing upon the tactical value of surprise.

Layla remained in the dark about the Directorate and Bryson's relationship to it. As far as she was concerned, Bryson was simply uncovering a trail in the illicit arms trade. She knew a fragment of the whole; she did not yet need to know more. The time would come when Bryson would fill her in, but it was not yet.

Bryson had intended to secrete himself anywhere in the vicinity of Bécot's office—a neighboring office, a broom closet, whatever. He had not counted on the serendipity of discovering this surveillance station. From here he was able to observe the comings and goings in and out of the office building's lobby; several other feeds came from hidden cameras inside each elevator; two more covered the twenty-seventh-floor lobby area adjacent to the elevator bank and the bank's waiting room. Too, there were views of the main corridors on the twenty-seventh floor. There was no camera within Bécot's office, or any other office for that matter, but at least he would be able to view Vansina's arrival as well as the Dutchman's movements in the elevator. Vansina was a top-notch field operative and took nothing for granted. He would assume, for instance, that there were closed-circuit cameras concealed in the elevators, as there were in many modern office buildings. But he would likely also assume, as would Bryson, that such cameras were being watched by incurious, underpaid security staff looking only for obvious signs of violent crime. Vansina might use the semiprivate occasion to adjust a gun holster or a monitoring device taped to his chest. Then again, he might do nothing suspicious at all.

The call to Vansina had been placed in Bryson and Layla's presence, and then Layla had remained by the banker's side to ensure that he did not make any follow-up calls to Vansina, warning him off, or anything of the sort.

Bryson knew that Jan Vansina would respond quickly, and indeed, within twenty minutes the Directorate operative arrived in the main lobby. Vansina was a slight, hunch-shouldered man with a full but close-trimmed gray beard and tinted wire-rimmed spectacles. Between his unassuming physical presence and his benign cover as director of emergency medical assistance for the International Red Cross, he was not a man anyone would suspect of being the extremely clever killer that he was. Vansina's greatest attribute, in fact, was that he was constantly underestimated. A casual observer might in fact think Vansina kindly, even harmless. Bryson, however, knew well that Vansina was a powerful, ruthless man of great skill and wily intelligence. He knew better than to underestimate him.

Vansina shared an elevator with a young woman, who got off on the twenty-fifth floor, at which point he was alone for a few seconds. Yet Bryson found him impossible to read, neither apprehensive nor particularly tense. If the man's suspicions were at all aroused by this emergency summons from his private banker, his expression did not indicate it.

Bryson watched him emerge from the elevator and check in with the receptionist; Vansina was ushered in at once. Bryson saw him accompanied down the corridor by Bécot's matronly assistant, then into Bécot's office, at which point the surveillance ended.

No matter: Bryson knew the script that Layla was following, since he had designed it himself. He waited for the signal from Layla indicating that it was time for him to make his appearance. She would place a call to his cell phone, let it ring twice, then terminate the call.

Her interrogation of Vansina would last anywhere from five to ten minutes, depending on the degree of truculence Vansina presented. He looked at his watch, his eyes on the sweep–second hand, and waited.

Five minutes passed slowly, feeling like an eternity. There were two backup emergency signals, neither of which she had employed. The first would be to dial his cell phone, letting it ring. After the second ring, he would know the situation was urgent. In the alternative, she would open Bécot's office door, which he would be able to observe on the surveillance monitor.

Yet no emergency signals came.

As focused as he was on the matter at hand, he could not keep his mind from dwelling on the agent he knew as Prospero. What was it that Dunne had said? Vansina had been acting as a conduit, presumably for the Directorate, laundering over five billion dollars. Laundered funds were an everyday necessity for intelligence agencies, but almost always they were relatively small sums, untraceable payments to agents and contacts. *Five billion dollars,* however, was an order of magnitude beyond payments to assets. Such a quantity of money had to be funding something large. If Dunne's information was accurate—and it seemed less and less likely that the CIA man was deliberately misleading him, not when he had killed his own bodyguard to protect him—the Directorate was channeling money to, and in fact orchestrating, terrorist organizations. But which ones, why, and to what end? Perhaps the cryptochip that he had copied from Jacques Arnaud's secure phone would yield the answer, but whom could he trust with that crucial piece of evidence?

And if Jan Vansina was directly involved in the cycling of diverted funds, Bryson doubted the Dutchman was acting as a blind conduit. Vansina was far too skilled, and too senior, to act in such an innocent capacity. Vansina would *know.* For all Bryson knew, Vansina was one of the Directorate's principals by now.

Suddenly the door to the closet swung open, flooding the small room with light, and for an instant Bryson was blinded, unable to see who was there.

Within a few seconds Bryson could make out the shape, then the face. Jan Vansina, grim faced, eyes blazing. In his right hand a gun was pointed directly at Bryson; in his left hand he gripped a briefcase.

"Coleridge," Vansina said. "A flash from the past."

"Prospero," said Bryson, startled. Unprepared for the intrusion, he reached for the pistol holstered inside his suit jacket, then froze when he heard the click of the safety being released.

"*Don't* move," barked Vansina. "Hands at your side! I will not hesitate to use this. You know me, so you know I speak the truth."

Bryson stared, slowly lowered his hand. Vansina would indeed have no compunction about killing him in cold blood; why he had not done so already was a mystery.

"Thank you, *Bryson*," the Dutchman went on. "You wish to talk with me; we will talk."

"Where's the woman?"

"She is safe. Bound and locked in a storage closet. She is a strong and clever woman, but she must have expected this to be a, how do you say, cakewalk. I must say, her Mossad paper appears quite genuine. Your backstoppers are excellent."

"It *is* genuine, because she *is* Mossad."

"Even more intriguing, Bryson. I see you have established new alliances. New alliances for changing times. This is for you." He tossed the briefcase at Bryson, who made the split-second decision to catch it, not dodge it.

"Good catch," said Vansina jovially. "Now, please hold it out in front of you with both hands."

Bryson scowled. The Dutch operative was as quick-witted as ever.

"Come, let us talk," said Vansina. "Walk straight ahead, keeping the briefcase in front of you at all times. Any sudden moves, and I will shoot. Drop it, and I will shoot. You know me, my friend."

Bryson obeyed, silently berating himself. He had fallen into Vansina's trap by underestimating the wily old operative. How had he turned the tables on Layla? There had been no sound of gunfire, but perhaps he had used a silencer. Had he killed Layla? The thought tore at him, filled him with anguish. She had been serving as his accomplice; although Bryson had tried to dissuade her from working with him further, and she had insisted, he still felt responsible for whatever happened to her. Or had Vansina spoken the truth and bound and locked Layla up? He marched forward, urged along by the waving of Vansina's gun, crossing the narrow hall into an empty conference room. Although the lights in the room were off, there was still plenty of afternoon sun flooding in through the plate-glass window. The view of the city of Geneva from this high up was even more spectacular than that from Bécot's office window: the famous plume of the Jet d'eau and the Parc Mon Repos clearly visible from here, though not a sound from the city was audible.

Holding the briefcase, he was unable to retrieve his gun. Yet if he dropped the briefcase to go for his weapon, even that brief second would be time enough for Vansina to fire into the back of his head.

"Sit," commanded the Dutchman.

Bryson sat at the head of the table, placing the briefcase down on the table in front of him, still clutching it in both hands.

"Now place your left hand flat on top of the table, followed by your right. In that order, please. No sudden motions—you know the drill."

Bryson did so, his hands flat on the table on either side of the briefcase. Vansina sat at the other end of the table, his back to the plate-glass window, his weapon still aimed at Bryson.

"Move a hand to rub your nose, I shoot," said Vansina. "Move a hand to take a cigarette from your breast pocket, I shoot. Those are the ground rules, Mr. Bryson, and I know you understand them well. Now then, tell me this, please: Does Elena know?"

Stunned, Bryson tried to make sense of the question. *Does Elena know?* "What are you talking about?" he whispered.

"Does she know?"

"Does she know *what?* Where is she? Have you *spoken* with her?"

"Please don't affect to be concerned about the woman, Bryson—"

"Where *is* she?" Bryson interrupted.

The bearded man hesitated but a second before replying, "I am asking the questions here, Bryson. How long have you been with the Prometheans?"

Dully, Bryson repeated, "The Prometheans?"

"*Enough.* No more games! How long have you been in their employ, Bryson? Were you double-dealing while you were on active duty? Or perhaps you grew bored as a college professor, in search of adventure? You see, I'd really like to understand the inducement, the lure. An appeal to misbegotten idealism? Power? You see, we have so much to talk about, Bryson."

"Yet you insist on leveling a gun at me as if you've completely forgotten Yemen."

Vansina, looking amused, shook his head. "You are still a legend in the organization, Bryson. People still retell stories of your operational skill, your linguistic talent. You were a great asset—"

"Until I was shoved out the door by Ted Waller. Or should I say Gennady Rosovsky?"

Vansina paused a long while, unable to conceal the astonishment in his eyes. "We all have many names," he said at last. "Many identities. And sanity lies in the ability to distinguish among them, to keep them separate. Yet you seem to have lost that ability. You believe one thing, then another. You don't know where reality ends and fantasy begins. Ted Waller is a great man, Bryson. Greater than any of us."

"So he has you deceived still! You believe him, you believe his lies! You don't *know,* Prospero? We were puppets, drones—automatons, programmed by the overseers! We acted blindly, not understanding who our real masters were, what the *real* agenda was!"

"There are circles within circles," Vansina said solemnly. "There are things we know nothing about. The world has changed, and we must change with it, must adapt to the new realities. What have you been told, Bryson? What lies have *you* been fed?"

"The 'new realities,' " Bryson began hollowly, not understanding. He was stunned, baffled to the point of momentary speechlessness, when he saw the enormous shape suddenly looming in the plate-glass window, abruptly appearing from out of nowhere. He recognized it as a helicopter only at the instant that the fusillade of bullets riddled the glass, the automatic machine-gun fire shattering the glass into a crystalline hailstorm.

Bryson dove to the floor, tumbled beneath the long conference table, but Vansina, at the head of the table and therefore much closer to the window, had no such opportunity. His hands flew out to his side like a bird attempting flight, and then his entire body danced, animated grotesquely, almost prancing like some marionette. The bullets penetrated his face, his chest, blood erupted from his twitching body in scores of tiny geysers, and his bloodied face contorted in a horrible scream, a full-throated bellow that was entirely masked by the deafening racket of the hovering helicopter, the ear-splitting thunder of gunfire. As the wind howled through the conference room, the mahogany table was split, chewed up by a thousand bullets, the carpet crisscrossed, pitted. From his shelter under the thick tabletop, Bryson saw Vansina seem almost to rise into the air before crumpling against the gray carpet, red-spattered from his blood, limbs splayed unnaturally, his eyes hollow red cavities, his face and beard a horrifying bloodied pulp, the entire back of his head missing. Then, as suddenly as it had appeared, the helicopter lunged out of sight and was gone. The cacophony had abruptly ceased, the only sounds the faint traffic noises from the street hundreds of feet below, and the moaning of the wind as it whistled through stalactites of glass, whirling around the slaughterhouse of a room now gone eerily silent.

CHAPTER FOURTEEN

Racing from the conference room, from the nightmarish scene of blood and machine-gun rounds and broken glass, Bryson ran through a hall choked with horrified bystanders. There were screams, shouts in *Schweizerdeutsch* and French and English.

"Oh, *Jesus Christ!*"

"What happened, was it snipers? Terrorists?"

"Are they inside the building?"

"Call the police, an ambulance, *quickly!*"

"My God, the man's dead—he's, oh *God,* he's been *massacred!*"

As he ran, he thought of Layla. *Not her, too!* Could the helicopter have circled the building, locating targets in windows on the twenty-seventh floor?

And he thought: *Jan Vansina was the object of the freakish attack.* Not me. Vansina. It *had* to be. He ran through the kaleidoscopic images in his mind, sorting through them, recalling angles of fire. Yes. Whoever was manning the machine gun or guns from within the helicopter had been *deliberately aiming for Jan Vansina.* This was no random attack, nor a generalized attempt to kill whoever was present in the conference room. The gunfire had been aimed precisely, from at least three different and precise angles, at the Directorate operative.

But *why?*

And who? The Directorate could not have been killing its own, could it? Perhaps fearing that Vansina was meeting with an old friend, sharing information . . .

No, it stretched the imagination too far, made too little sense. The reasons, the logic behind the attack remained obscure. But the fact remained, Bryson was convinced, that the man who was supposed to be killed had in fact been killed.

These thoughts spun through his mind in a matter of seconds; he located Bécot's office, yanked open the closed door—and found it empty.

Neither Layla nor the banker was here. Turning to leave, he noticed a china espresso cup overturned on the floor beside the coffee table, a few papers scattered near the desk. Signs of either a hurried departure or a brief struggle.

Muffled sounds came from somewhere within the room or very nearby, thumping noises, cries. His eyes quickly searched the room, found the closet door. He ran to it, opened it. Layla and Jean-Luc Bécot were bound in ropes, gagged. Polyurethane "humane restraints," as strong as leather, secured their wrists and ankles. The banker's wire-rimmed glasses lay bent on the closet floor beside him, his tie askew, his shirt torn, hair wild. Through the wadded cloth gag stuffed in his mouth he tried to shout, his eyes bulging. Next to him, Layla was bound even more thoroughly, expertly, the gag tight in her mouth. Her gray Chanel suit was ripped; one of her matching gray high-heeled shoes had come off. She, too, had vinyl restraints around her wrists and ankles. Her face was bloodied and bruised; obviously she had struggled fiercely but had been overwhelmed by the superior strength of the man who had been Prospero.

The brute *animal* who had been Prospero, Jan Vansina. Bryson swelled with rage at the dead man. He pulled the gag from her mouth, then from the banker's; both captives took deep, gulping breaths, filling their lungs with much-needed air. Bécot gasped, cried out. Layla gasped, too: "Thank you. My God!"

"He didn't kill you, either of you," Bryson remarked as he worked quickly to untie the ropes. He searched for a knife or other blade to sever the strong plastic restraints; seeing nothing, he ran to the banker's desk and spied a silver letter opener, quickly rejecting it since it had a point but no blade. In a side desk drawer he found a small but sharp pair of scissors, ran back to the closet, and used it to release them both.

"Call Security!" the banker said through gulps of air.

Bryson, who could already hear the sirens of the approaching emergency vehicles growing steadily louder, said, "The police are on their way, I suspect." He took Layla by the arm, helped her to her feet, and the two of them ran from the room.

Passing the open conference room door, in front of which a crowd had gathered, she stopped.

"Come on," hissed Bryson. "There's no *time!*"

But she peered inside, saw the crumpled body of Jan Vansina surrounded by jagged shards of glass, the shattered window. "Oh, my God!" she breathed, horrified, quivering. "Oh, my *God!*"

Not until they reached the crowded Place Bel-Air did they come to a stop.

"We have to leave," Bryson said. "Travel separately—we can't be seen together, not any longer."

"Travel—but where?"

"*Out* of here—out of Geneva, out of Switzerland!"

"What are you saying—we can't just—" She stopped in midsentence when she realized that Bryson's attention was riveted on a newspaper displayed in a kiosk. It was a copy of *La Tribune de Genève.*

"My God," said Bryson, moving closer. He grabbed it from a tall stack, riveted by the large black banner headline above a photograph of some sort of terrible accident.

TERROR STRIKES FRANCE:
HIGH-SPEED PASSENGER TRAIN
DERAILED IN LILLE

LILLE—A powerful bomb blast derailed and tore apart the high-speed passenger train Eurostar abou* 'irty miles south of Lille early this morning, killing hundreds of French, British, American, Dutch, Belgian, and other business travelers. Although emergency workers and volunteers worked frantically throughout the day, searching the wreckage for survivors, French authorities fear that the death toll may exceed 700. An official at the crash site, who preferred to remain anonymous, speculated that the incident was the work of terrorists.

According to records made available by railroad officials, the train, Eurostar 9007-ERS, left the Gare du Nord in Paris, bound for London, at approximately 7:16 A.M., with nearly 770 passengers on board. At approximately 8:00 A.M., the 18-car train passed through France's Pas-de-Calais region, where a series of high-powered explosions, reportedly buried beneath the tracks, went off below the train's front and rear sections simultaneously. Although there was no immediate claim of responsibility, sources in the French security service, the Sûreté, have already compiled a list of possible suspects. Several anonymous sources in the Sûreté have confirmed rampant speculation that both the French and the British governments had received repeated warnings of an impending attack on the Eurostar in the last several days. A Eurostar spokesman would neither confirm nor deny a report provided to *La Tribune de Genève* that the intelligence services of both countries had leads pointing to suspected terrorists planning to blow up the train but were unable to intercept or monitor telephone conversations between the alleged terrorists because of legal constraints.

"This is an outrage," declared French National Assembly member Françoise Chouet. "We had the technical ability to prevent this sickening carnage, yet our police are hamstrung by our laws from doing anything about it." In London, Lord Miles Parmore renewed his call in Parliament for passage of the International Treaty on Surveillance and Security. "If the governments of France and England had the ability to keep this sabotage from happening, it is simply criminal that we sat there and did nothing about it. This is a national—no, an international—disgrace."

The United States national security adviser, Richard Lanchester, attending a NATO summit in Brussels, is-

sued a statement denouncing the "slaughter of innocents." He added, "In this period of mourning, we must
all ask ourselves how to make sure something like this
never happens again. With great reluctance and sad-
ness, the Davis administration joins its allies and good
friends England and France in calling for worldwide
passage of the International Treaty on Surveillance and
Security."

Lille.

Bryson's blood ran cold.

He remembered the low, conspiratorial voices of two men
emerging from Jacques Arnaud's private office in the Château de Saint-Meurice. One was the arms merchant himself,
the other Anatoly Prishnikov, the Russian tycoon.

"Once Lille happens," Arnaud had said, "the outrage will
be enormous. The way will be clear."

Once Lille happens.

Two of the world's most powerful businessmen, one an
arms dealer, the other a mogul who no doubt secretly owned
or controlled large segments of the Russian defense industry—Bryson would have to obtain a complete dossier—had
foreknowledge of the devastation at Lille, the attack that
killed seven hundred people.

Quite likely the men were among those who planned it.

Both of them principals of the Directorate. The Directorate was behind the nightmare at Lille; there was no question
about it.

But to what *end?* Senseless violence was not the Directorate's way; Waller and the other overseers had always
prided themselves on their strategic genius. Everything was
strategy, everything served an ultimate end. Even the murder
of Bryson's parents, even the massive deception that had
become his life. The murder of a few field operatives might
be justified by nothing more than the need to remove an
encumbrance, an obstacle, a threat. But the wholesale murder
of seven hundred innocent travelers was in another category
entirely, moved from low-level tactics to higher strategy.

The outrage will be enormous.

The public outcry over the derailing and destruction of the Eurostar train was indeed great, as it would inevitably be over such a preventable tragedy.

Preventable tragedy.

The key was preventable. Prophylaxis. The Directorate *wanted* this outrage, *wanted* to spur calls for prevention of any future terrorism. Yet *prevention* could mean any number of things. A treaty to fight terrorism was one thing, no doubt little more than window dressing. But surely any such treaty would lead to the bolstering of national defenses, the acquisition of weapons intended to protect public safety.

Arnaud and Prishnikov, merchants of death with a vested interest in world chaos, because chaos was a form of marketing—the marketing of their goods, their weapons, the increasing of demand. These two moguls were presumably behind Lille and . . .

And what else? Standing there on the street, he was oblivious to the bustle of passing pedestrians. Layla was reading the article over his shoulder, saying something to him, but he did not hear her. He was retrieving remembered news stories in the filing cabinet of his mind. Several recent incidents that he had read about, seen television coverage about, terrible things that at the time did not register as directly applicable to his own life, his mission.

Just a few days ago there had been a devastating explosion in a Washington, D.C., metro station during the morning rush hour that had killed dozens of people. And later that same day—he remembered because the timing was so unfortunate—an American jetliner had blown up just after taking off from Kennedy Airport, en route to Rome. One hundred fifty, one hundred seventy people had been killed.

The outcry in America had been anguished, clamorous. The president had issued a call for passage of the international security treaty, which had previously been stalled in the Senate. After Lille, the European nations would surely join the Americans in pushing for strong measures to restore sanity to a world spinning out of control.

Control.

Was this the "higher purpose," the underlying reason behind the Directorate's madness? A rogue intelligence agency, once a small but powerful behind-the-scenes player known to no one, making a bid to seize control where the rest of the world had failed?

Damn it, it was all vaporous speculation, theory upon theory, conclusions drawn from tentative suggestions. Unprovable, shadowy, insufficient. But an answer to Dunne's initial question, the reason why the CIA man had plucked Bryson from a contented retirement and all but forced him to investigate, was beginning to suggest itself. It was time to level with Harry Dunne, present him with a scenario, with hypotheses. To wait for firm, undeniable documentation of the Directorate's agenda would be to let another Lille happen, and that was morally repugnant. Did the CIA really need another seven hundred innocent people to die before it decided to do something?

And yet . . .

Yet the biggest piece of the puzzle remained missing.

"Does Elena know?" Vansina had asked. The implication being that the Directorate did not know where she was, or where her loyalties resided. It was more important than ever that she be located: the very question—*does Elena know?*— implied that she had to know something crucial. Something that would not only explain her disappearance from his life but also reveal the pattern, the key to the Directorate's true intentions.

"You know something about this." Layla's voice: a statement, not a question.

He realized that she had been speaking to him for a while. He turned to look at her. Had she not overheard Arnaud's remark about Lille at the château? Evidently not.

"I have a theory," he said.

"Which is?"

"I need to make a call." He handed her the newspaper. "I'll be right back."

"A call? To whom?"

"Give me a few minutes, Layla."

She raised her voice. "What are you *hiding* from me? What are you really up to?"

He saw in her beautiful brown eyes bewilderment, but something more: hurt, anger. She was justified in being angry. He had been using her as an accomplice while telling her almost nothing. It was more than hurtful, it was unacceptable, particularly to a field agent as skilled and knowledgeable as she was.

He hesitated, then spoke. "Let me make a phone call. When I return, I'll fill you in—but I warn you, I know a lot less than you must think I do."

She put a hand on his arm, a quick, affectionate gesture that said any number of things—thank you, I understand, I'm here for you. He was moved to kiss her, lightly and on the cheek: nothing sexual, but a moment of human contact, an expression of gratitude for her bravery and support.

He walked quickly to the end of the block, taking a side street off Place Bel-Air. There was a small *tabac* that sold, in addition to cigarettes and newspapers, prepaid telephone cards. He purchased one, located an international telephone in a booth on the street. He dialed 011, then 0, then a sequence of five numbers. There was a low electronic tone; then he dialed seven more digits.

It was a sterile line, a number that Harry Dunne had given him; it rang directly through to Dunne's CIA office and at Dunne's private study at home. Dunne had guaranteed that he, and only he, would answer it.

The phone rang once.

"Bryson."

Bryson, about to speak, caught his breath. The voice was unfamiliar; it did not sound like Dunne. "Who is this?" he said.

"It's Graham Finneran, Bryson. You—I think you know who I am."

Dunne had mentioned Finneran when they had last met in his CIA office. Dunne had identified Finneran as his aide-de-camp, one of the men who had accompanied Dunne to the CIA's Blue Ridge Mountains facility, one of Dunne's few trusted aides.

"What is this?" said Bryson guardedly.

"Bryson—I—Harry's in the hospital. He's quite ill."

"Ill?"

"You know he's got a terminal case of cancer—he won't talk about it, but it's obvious—and he collapsed yesterday and had to be taken to the hospital in an ambulance."

"You're saying he's dead, is that it?"

"No—thank God, no, but I don't know how long he's got, to be honest. But he's briefed me fully on your . . . your project. I know he was worried, frankly—"

"Which hospital?"

Finneran hesitated, barely a second or two, but it was too long. "I'm not sure I should say just yet—"

Bryson disconnected the call, his heart pounding, the blood rushing in his ears. His instincts commanded him to get off the line at once. Something was not right. Dunne had assured him that no one else would answer this telephone, and he would not violate protocol, even on his deathbed. Dunne knew Bryson, knew how Bryson would react.

No. Graham Finneran—if it *was* Graham Finneran; Bryson wouldn't recognize his voice in any case—would never have answered the phone. Dunne would never have permitted it.

Something was terribly wrong, and it was more than the health of the CIA man.

Had the Directorate finally reached its chief adversary within the Agency, finally neutralized the last institutional bulwark against their growing power?

He raced back through the Place Bel-Air, found Layla still standing by the news kiosk. "I have to go to Brussels," he said.

"What? Why Brussels? What are you *talking* about?"

"There's a man there—someone I need to reach."

She looked at him questioningly, beseechingly.

"Come on. I know of a pension in the Marolles. It's run-down and shabby, and it's not in a particularly pleasant part of town. But it's safe and anonymous, and it's not where anyone would think to look for us."

"But why *Brussels?*"

"It's a last resort, Layla. Someone who can help out, someone extremely highly placed. A person some people consider the last honest man in Washington."

CHAPTER FIFTEEN

The headquarters of the Systematix Corporation comprised seven large, gleaming glass-and-steel buildings on a sylvan, beautifully landscaped campus—twenty acres in all—outside Seattle, Washington. There were dining rooms and exercise rooms in each building; the corporation's employees, who were renowned for their loyalty and discretion, had little reason to leave while they labored away. They were a closely knit community, recruited from the best training programs around the world and compensated generously. They realized, too, that they had thousands of colleagues elsewhere whom they would never meet. Systematix, after all, had offices around the world, and owned controlling stakes in many more companies, though the extent of these holdings remained a matter of avid conjecture.

"I have a feeling we're not in Kansas anymore," Tony Gupta, the jovial chief technology officer of InfoMed, told his boss, Adam Parker, as the two were escorted to the meeting room. Parker smiled thinly. He was the CEO of a nine-hundred-million-dollar company, but even he had to feel some slight trepidation as he arrived at the fabled Systematix campus.

"Ever been here before?" Parker asked. He was a rangy man with salt-and-pepper hair who used to run marathons before a knee injury forced him to stop. Now he rowed and swam and, even with the bad knee, played tennis with a ferocity that made it hard for him to keep his partners for more than a few games. He was an intensely competitive man, a quality that enabled him to build his company, which specialized in medical "informatics" and data warehousing. But he knew when he was outmatched.

"Once," Gupta said. "Years ago. I was up for a job as a software engineer, but at the interview there was a brain-teaser that I flunked. And just to get that far, I had to sign three nondisclosure agreements. They were fanatical about secrecy." Gupta adjusted his tie, which he'd knotted too tightly. He wasn't accustomed to wearing one, but then this was no ordinary occasion; Systematix wasn't known to indulge the self-conscious informality that was de rigeur among so many New Economy corporations.

Parker didn't have a good feeling about the impending acquisition, and had made no secret about it to Gupta, who was the man he trusted most among his colleagues. "The board isn't going to let me stop the deal," Parker said softly. "You realize that, don't you?"

Gupta looked at their escort, a blond, lithe woman and shot his boss a warning glance. "Let's just listen to what the great man has to say," he replied.

Moments later, they took their seats along with twelve other men and women on the top floor of the largest building, with a breathtaking view of the surrounding hills. This was the centerpoint of the seemingly diffuse and decentralized company that was Systematix. For most of the assembled— the directors of InfoMed—it was their first time face-to-face with Systematix's legendary founder, chairman, and chief executive officer, the reclusive Gregson Manning. In the past year, as Adam Parker knew, Manning had acquired dozens of such companies in cash transactions.

"The great man," Gupta had called him, and though the words were arch, they were not ironic. Gregson Manning *was* a great man, almost everyone agreed. He was one of the richest men in the world, had created from nothing a vast corporation that manufactured much of the infrastructure of the Internet. Everyone knew his story—about how he dropped out of CalTech when he was eighteen, lived in a communal house with his techie friends, started Systematix out of a garage. Now it was hard to think of a single company anywhere that didn't rely upon Systematix technologies for some part of their operations. Systematix was, as *Forbes* once said, an industry unto itself.

Manning had also emerged as a major philanthropist, albeit a controversial one. He had given hundreds of millions of dollars to help bring inner-city schools on-line, to use modern technology to help further educational goals. Parker had heard rumors, too, that Manning had anonymously given billions to help underprivileged children in the form of scholarships to institutions of higher learning.

And, of course, the business press idolized him. For all his vast wealth, he always came across as unassuming and unpretentious; he was depicted not as reclusive so much as retiring. *Barron's* once dubbed him the "Daddy Warbucks" of the Information Age.

But Parker could not shake his feeling of unease. Yes, some of it had to do with the unpalatable prospect of relinquishing control—damn it, he'd nurtured InfoMed as if it were his own child, and it pained him to think of it being reduced to a tiny component of a giant conglomerate. But there was something more than that: it was almost a clash of cultures. At the end of the day, Parker was a businessman, plain and simple. His chief investors and advisers were businessmen. They talked the language of finance: of return on invested capital, market value added. Of cost centers and profit centers. Maybe it wasn't high-minded, but it was honest and Parker could understand it. Yet that wasn't how Manning's mind seemed to work. He thought and spoke in sweeping terms—about historical forces, global trends. The fact that Systematix was immense and exceedingly profitable seemed almost incidental to him. "Look, you've never cared for visionaries," Gupta once said to Parker, after one of their marathon strategy sessions, and no doubt he was on to something.

"I'm so pleased you could come, all of you," Gregson Manning told his visitors, shaking their hands firmly. Manning was tall, well built, and slender, his hair dark and glossy. He was ruggedly handsome, square-jawed and broad shouldered, with an unmistakably patrician air. His features were fine, his nose aquiline and strong, his skin unlined, nearly poreless. He radiated health, self-assurance, and, Parker had to admit to himself, charisma. He wore khakis, an open-necked white shirt, and a lightweight, cashmere blazer.

He gave a warm smile, revealing white, perfect teeth. "I wouldn't be here if I didn't respect what InfoMed has accomplished, and you wouldn't be here if . . ." Manning trailed off, his smile widening.

"If we didn't appreciate the forty percent premium you're offering for our shares," the rumpled, big-bellied chairman of the InfoMed board, Alex Garfield, interjected, laughing. Garfield was a venture capitalist of limited imagination who happened to have provided a much-needed infusion of cash during InfoMed's infancy. His interest in the company didn't go much beyond the terms for which he could swap his equity stake. Adam Parker didn't admire Garfield, but he always knew where he stood with him.

Manning's eyes sparkled. "Our interests converge."

"Mr. Manning," Parker said, "I do have some concerns— they may be moot in light of such financial considerations, but I may as well voice them."

"Please," said Manning with a tilt of his head.

"When you acquire InfoMed, you're not only acquiring a vast medical database, you're acquiring seven hundred dedicated employees. I'd like a sense of what's in store for them. Systematix is one of those companies that people know everything and nothing about. It's privately held, tightly controlled, and a lot of what it does is pretty damned mysterious. And the obsession with privacy can be a little unsettling, at least if you're outside it."

"Privacy?" Manning tilted his head, his smile fading. "I think you have things precisely backward. And I would very much regret if you found our larger aims here to be mysterious."

"I don't think anyone exactly understands your organization chart," Parker said testily. Looking around the room, sensing the awe with which the others regarded Gregson Manning, Parker realized that his remarks were less than welcome; he also realized that this was his last opportunity to voice them.

Manning fixed him with a stare, forthright yet not unfriendly. "My friend, I do not believe in the regalia of the traditional organization, the partitions and barriers and 'dotted-line reporting' relations. I think everyone here knows that. The key to our success at Systematix—our not inconsiderable success, I think I can say without immodesty—has been to jettison the old ways of doing things."

"But there's a logic to any corporate structure," Parker said, pressing the point, as the other men in the room looked at him with unfriendly stares. Even Tony Gupta reached over and put a cautioning hand on his arm. Still, Parker wasn't used to holding his tongue and he was damned if he was going to start now. "Subsidiary divisions and whatnot, there's a reason for flowcharts, I hate to say it. I just want to know how you intend to integrate the acquisition."

Manning spoke to him as if to a slow child. "Who invented the modern corporation? Men like John D. Rockefeller of Standard Oil, and Alfred Sloan of General Motors. In the postwar era of economic expansion, you had Robert McNamara at Ford and Harold Geneen at ITT, Reginald Jones at General Electric. It was the heyday of multiplex managerial strata, with chief executives assisted by staffs of planners and auditors and operations strategists. Rigid structures were necessary to conserve and manage the scarcest resource of all, the most *valuable* asset of all: information. Now, what happens if information becomes as free and copiously available as the air we breathe or the water we drink? All that becomes unnecessary. All that gives way."

Parker recalled a quote of Manning's that had once appeared in *Barron's*—something to the effect that the goal of Systematix was "to replace doors with windows." And he had to admit that the man was mesmerizing, as supernally articulate as his reputation had suggested. Still, Parker stirred in his seat uneasily. *All that gives way.* "Gives way to what?"

"If the old way was vertical hierarchy, the new way is the forging of horizontal networks, cutting across organizational boundaries. We're about building a network of companies that we can *collaborate* with, not direct from above. The boundaries are down. The logic of networking puts a premium on self-monitoring, information-driven systems. Continual monitoring means we eliminate risk factors within the organizational structure and outside of it, too." The setting sun behind Gregson Manning cast an aura around his head, adding to his unsettling intensity. "You're an entrepreneur. Look ahead of you, and what do you see? Atomized capital markets. Radically dispersed labor markets. Pyramidal organization yielding to fluid, self-organizing means of collaboration. All of which requires that we exploit connectivity, not just internally but externally as well, arriving at common strategies with our partners, extending control beyond the purview of ownership. Informational channels are recombinant. There must be transparency at all levels. I'm merely giving words to an inkling, an intuition I think we've all had about the future of capitalism."

Parker was baffled by Manning's words. "The way you're talking, it sounds as if Systematix isn't really a corporation at all."

"Call it what you like. When boundaries are truly permeable, there isn't anything so localizable as a traditional firm. But we've already lived through an era of managerialism answerable to no one. Ownership can only be fragmented, risk disaggregated only for so long. The poet Robert Frost said good fences make good neighbors. Well, I don't believe that. Porosity, walls you can see through, walls you can move whenever you need—that's what the world requires these days. To succeed, you've got to be able to walk through walls." Manning paused briefly. "Which is easier when there aren't any."

Alex Garfield turned toward his CEO. "I don't pretend to follow all this, but, Adam, the record speaks for itself. Gregson Manning doesn't have to defend himself to anyone. I think all he's saying is he doesn't believe in a collection of sealed-off business units. He's talking about integration in his own way."

"The walls have to fall," Manning said, sitting up very straight. "That's the reality behind the rhetoric of reengineering. You might say we're turning back the Industrial Revolution. The Industrial Revolution was about the division of work into tasks; we're trying to go from tasks to *process,* and to do so in a domain of absolute visibility."

Frustrated, Parker pursued his line of questioning. "Yet so many of the technologies you've been investing in—these networking technologies and the rest—well, I don't understand the thinking behind it," Parker said. "And then there's that FCC report that Systematix is about to launch another fleet of low-earth-orbit satellites. Why? There's already so much bandwidth available. Why *satellites?*"

Manning nodded as if pleased by the question. "Maybe it's time to raise our sights."

There were grunts of assent and laughter around the room.

"I've been talking about business," Manning went on. "But think about our own lives, too. You mentioned privacy earlier. The conventions of privacy treat the private sphere as a domain of personal freedom." Now Manning's expression became grave. "But for many, it may be the sphere of intimate violation and abuse, neither free nor personal. The housewife who is raped and robbed at knifepoint, the man whose home has been invaded by armed marauders—ask them about the value of privacy. Information in its full amplitude means *freedom from*—freedom from violation, freedom from abuse, freedom from harm. And if Systematix can move society toward that goal, then we are talking about something we've never had before in human history—something very near to *total security.* To some degree, surveillance has played a larger part in our lives, and I'm proud of the role we've had in that—the cameras in elevators and subways and parks, the Nannycams and all the rest of it. And yet truly sophisticated surveillance systems, what you might call panic buttons: these things currently remain the luxuries of the rich. Well, let's *democratize* them, I say. Bring everyone into view. Jane Jacobs wrote about 'eyes on the street,' and we can go even beyond that. The rhetoric about the global village has been just that, rhetoric, but it can be *real,* and technology can make it so."

"That's a lot of power for one organization to take on."

"Except that power, too, is no longer a discrete location,

but a *web* of sanctions throughout society. In any case, I think you're looking at it too narrowly. Once truly meaningful safety and security become pervasive, all of us end up finally having power over our own lives."

Manning was interrupted by a knock; his personal assistant stood at the door looking concerned.

"Yes, Daniel?" Manning asked, surprised by the intrusion.

"A phone call, sir."

"Not a good moment." Manning smiled.

The young assistant coughed quietly. "The Oval Office, sir. The president says it's urgent."

Manning turned to the assembled. "You'll forgive me, then. I'll be right back."

In his large, hexagonal office, sun-bathed yet cool, Manning settled into his chair and put the president on the speakerphone. "I'm here, Mr. President," he said.

"Listen, Greg, you know I wouldn't bother you if it weren't important. But we need a favor. There's a pattern to the terrorism, and we've got a missing link in the skies over Lille, in France. A dozen American businessmen were killed in that tragedy. Yet none of our satellites were overhead at the right time. The French government's been hammering us for years to stop the overflights, stop invading the privacy of their citizens, so the eyes are usually switched off over that segment of the continent. Or so my experts tell me, it's all Greek to me. But they're telling me that Systematix satellites were in position. They'd have the imagery we need."

"Mr. President, you recognize that our satellites haven't been approved for photo reconnaissance. They're strictly licensed for telecommunications, digital telephony."

"I know that's what your people told Corelli's guys."

"But it was your administration that decided to restrict nongovernmental surveillance instrumentation." As Manning spoke, his eyes drifted toward a photograph of his daughter on his desk: a sandy-haired girl with a dreamy, giddy smile, as if she were laughing at a private joke.

"If you want me to eat crow, Greg, I will. I'm not too

proud to beg. But goddamn it, this is serious. We need what you've got. For Chrissakes, cut me some slack. I haven't forgotten what you've done for me in the past, and I won't forget this."

Manning paused, allowing a few seconds of silence to elapse. "Have your NSA techies call Partovi at my office. We'll transmit whatever we've got."

"I appreciate it," President Davis said hoarsely.

"I'm just as concerned about the problem as you are," Manning said, his eyes lingering again on the sandy-haired little girl. He and his wife had named her Ariel, and she had indeed been a creature of magic. "We've all got to pull together."

"Understood," the president said, awkward in his importuning. "Understood. I knew you'd come through for me."

"We're all in this together, Mr. President."

Ariel's laugh had been like the tinkle of a music box, he remembered, and his mind, usually so tightly focused, began wandering.

"Good-bye, Gregson. And thank you."

It occurred to Manning, as he switched off the speakerphone, that he'd never heard President Malcolm Davis sound so strained. A taste of misfortune could do that to a man.

CHAPTER SIXTEEN

The pension was in a seedy area of Brussels, the Marolles, a refuge for the city's poor and disenfranchised. Many of the seventeenth-century buildings were crumbling, collapsing bit by bit. The impoverished residents of the tenements were mostly Mediterranean immigrants, many of them Maghrebis. A stout, suspicious Maghrebi woman was the proprietor of the pension La Samaritaine, perched glumly behind a desk in the dark, malodorous warren that served as the hotel's lobby. Her customary clientele were transients and petty criminals and destitute immigrants; she regarded the too-respectable-looking man who arrived in the middle of the night with minimal luggage, wearing good clothes, as peculiarly out of place here, and therefore suspect.

Bryson had arrived by rail, at the Gare du Nord, and had grabbed a quick late-night dinner of soggy *moules et frites* and watery pilsener at a snack bar on the way. He asked the dour proprietress for the room number of his female friend who had, he believed, checked in earlier. She raised her eyebrows insinuatingly and divulged the number with a smirk.

Layla had arrived a few hours earlier, via a Sabena flight into Zaventem Airport, having purchased a ticket at the last minute. Although it was after midnight, and he expected she was as bone-tired as he was, he noticed the light seeping through the crack between her door and the filthy carpet, and he knocked. Her room was as dismal, as dingy as his.

She poured them each a Scotch, neat, from a bottle she had picked up near the Vieux Marché. "So who is this 'honest man' from Washington you want to meet here?" She added impishly: "It can't be anyone from your CIA—unless you've actually found one honest man at Langley." The bruises on her face from the struggle with Jan Vansina were bluish-purple, nasty looking.

Bryson took a sip, took a seat in a rickety armchair. "No one from the Agency."

"Well?"

He shook his head. "Not yet."

"Not yet *what?*"

"I'll fill you in when the time is right. Just not yet."

Sitting in a mismatched, but equally rickety, chair on the other side of a small table whose wood-grain veneer was flaying off, she set down her drink. "You're withholding from me—you're *continuing* to withhold, really—and that's not the deal."

"There was no deal, Layla."

"Did you really think I would join you blindly, in a mission I don't understand?" She was angry, and it was more than the alcohol or the exhaustion.

"No, of course not," he said wearily. "Quite the opposite, Layla. Not only did I not ask your help, I've tried to discourage you, push you away. Not because I didn't think you'd be helpful—you've been remarkable, *invaluable*—but because I couldn't assume the responsibility of endangering your life the way I'm endangering my own. But this is *my* battle to fight, *my* mission. If there's a subsidiary benefit to you, if whatever we end up learning serves your purpose, too, so much the better."

"That's so coldhearted."

"Maybe I am coldhearted. Maybe I *have* to be."

"But there's a gentle, caring side to you as well. I can sense it."

He didn't reply.

"Also I think you've been married."

"Oh? What makes you say that?"

"You have, yes?"

"Yes," he admitted. "But why do you say it?"

"Something about the way you are with me, the way you are with women. You are wary, of course—you don't *know* me, after all—yet at the same time you're comfortable with me, yes?"

Bryson smiled, amused, but said nothing.

She continued, "I think that most men in our . . . our line of work are unsure how to treat women field operatives. Either we are neuters, sexless, or we are potential romantic conquests. You seem to understand that it is more complex than that—that a woman, like a man, can be both, or neither, or something else entirely."

"You speak in riddles."

"I don't mean to. I just think—well, I suppose I'm saying that we are man and woman . . ." She tipped her glass toward him, a strange sort of salute.

He understood what she was hinting at, yet he pretended not to. She was an extraordinary woman, and the truth was that he was strongly attracted to her, increasingly, the more time he spent with her. But to pursue the attraction was to be selfish, to raise expectations he did not intend to meet, *could* not meet, until he finally understood what had happened between himself and Elena. The physical pleasure might well be considerable, but it would be momentary, fleeting; and it would simply end up confusing them, altering their relationship, introducing a destabilizing element.

"You seem to speak from experience," he said. "About how some men don't understand women who do the sort of work you do. Your husband—you said you married an Israeli soldier—was he one of those men who didn't understand?"

"I was a different person then. Not even a young woman—I was a girl, half formed."

"Was it his death that changed you?" asked Bryson gently.

"And my father's death, even though I never knew him." She looked pensive, and took another sip.

He nodded.

Her head bowed, she said, "Yaron, that was my husband, he was stationed at Kiryat Shmona during the *intifada*, helping to defend the village. One day the Israeli Air Force launched a rocket attack on a Hezbollah terrorist base in the Bekaa Valley, not too far from where I lived as a child, and by accident they killed a mother and all five of her children. It was a nightmare. Hezbollah retaliated, of course, by launching their Katyusha rockets against Kiryat Shmona. Yaron was helping get villagers into bomb shelters. He was hit by one of the rockets, his body incinerated almost beyond recognition." She looked up, tears in her eyes. "So tell me, who was in the right? Hezbollah, whose sole mission seems to be to kill as many Israelis as they can? The Israeli Air Force, which was so determined to eliminate a Hezbollah camp that they didn't care if they killed the innocent?"

"You knew the mother who was killed with her five children, didn't you?" said Bryson quietly.

She nodded, finally losing her composure, biting her lip as the tears flowed. "She was my sister, my . . . my older sister. My little nieces and nephews." For a few moments she could not speak. Then she said, "You see, it is not always the men who fire the Katyushas who are the guilty ones. Sometimes it's the men who supply the Katyushas. Or the men who sit in their bunkers with their charts and plan the attack. A man like Jacques Arnaud, who owns half of the French National Assembly and grows rich selling to the terrorists, the madmen, the fanatics of the world. So I want you to know that when you finally decide you can trust me, when you finally tell me why you are risking your life, and what it is you hope to find . . . I want you to know who it is you'll be telling." She stood, kissed him on the cheek. "And now I need to go to sleep."

Bryson returned to his room, his mind working feverishly. It was vital that he reach Richard Lanchester as soon as possible; in the morning he would begin to make telephone calls to reach the national security adviser. He realized that he still had far too little information, and too little time. With Harry Dunne mysteriously vanished, for whatever reason, Lanchester was the one man in government with both the power and the independence of mind to do something about the Directorate's metastasizing power. Although Bryson had not met the man, he knew the rudimentary biography: Lanchester had made millions on Wall Street but gave up business in his mid-forties to pursue a life of public service. He had run his friend Malcolm Davis's successful presidential election campaign and in return had been named as Davis's national security adviser, where he rapidly distinguished himself. His probity and intelligence made him an anomaly among the grandstanding and corruption of the Beltway; he was notable for his fair-mindedness and an unassuming, amiable brilliance.

According to the newspaper account about the carnage at Lille, Lanchester was visiting Brussels on what was billed as a largely ceremonial visit to SHAPE, the Supreme Headquarters Allied Powers Europe; there, he was consulting with the secretary general of NATO.

It would not be easy to reach Lanchester, particularly in the environs of NATO's world headquarters.

But there might be a way.

Shortly after five in the morning, having passed a tense and restless night punctuated by the ceaseless cacophony of traffic and the shouts of all-night revelers, Bryson awoke, bathed in cold water since there seemed to be no hot, and drew up a plan.

He dressed quickly, went out to the street, located a news-stand that stayed open all night and sold a good selection of international newspapers and magazines, heavily favoring European. As he expected, many of the papers, from the *International Herald-Tribune* to the *Times* of London, from *Le Monde* and *Le Figaro* to *Die Welt*, published extensive coverage of the Lille attack. Many of them cited Richard Lanchester, often using the same quotation; a few of them ran longer, sidebar interviews with the White House adviser. Bryson bought an array of newspapers and took them to a café, ordered several strong cups of black coffee, and began reading through the articles, marking them up with a pen.

Several newspapers mentioned not only Lanchester but his spokesman, who was also the spokesman for the National Security Council, a man named Howard Lewin. Lewin was in Brussels as well, accompanying his boss and the White House delegation on their visit to NATO headquarters.

Press spokesmen like Howard Lewin had to be available

at all times to handle urgent inquiries from journalists. Returning to his hotel room, Bryson was able to reach the spokesman in just one phone call.

"Mr. Lewin, I don't believe we've ever spoken before," said Bryson in an urgent, hard-bitten voice. "I'm Jim Goddard, European bureau chief for the *Washington Post,* and I'm sorry to disturb you so early in the morning, but we've got a bombshell on our hands, and I'm going to need your help with it."

He had Lewin's attention at once. "Absolutely—uh, Jim?—what's up?"

"I wanted to give you a heads-up. We're about to go to press with a full-dress, above-the-fold, front-page story on Richard Lanchester. Banner headline, the works. I'm afraid you folks aren't going to be very happy with it. In fact, let me be blunt about it, it may well be the end of Lanchester's career. It's devastating stuff—the culmination of a three-month investigation."

"*Jesus!* What the hell are we talking about here?"

"Uh, Mr. Lewin, I ought to tell you, I've been getting major pressure from the top to just run with the damned thing, not let a word of it leak before it comes off the press, but personally, I see this series as hugely damaging not only to Lanchester but potentially to national security as well, and I . . ." Bryson let his voice trail off for a moment, to let his words sink in. Then he offered the lifeline, which the spokesman had no choice but to grab at. ". . . I wanted to give your boss an opportunity to at least respond to this—maybe even, hell, stall it for a while. I'm trying not to let my personal feelings, my admiration for the man, get in the way of my newsroom responsibilities here, and maybe I shouldn't have even made this call, but if I can get the great man himself on the horn, maybe I can finesse this thing—"

"Do you know what *time* it is in Brussels?" Lewin stammered. "This—this last-minute notice—this is a goddamned setup, it's *completely* irresponsible on the *Post*'s part—"

"Look, Mr. Lewin, I'm going to make this your judgment call, but I want us to be *absolutely* clear that I gave you the opportunity to put out this fire, that this is all going to be on your head—hold on a second"—he shouted across the room to an imaginary colleague, "No, *not* that photo, the *head shot* of Lanchester, you idiot!" and then resumed speaking into the phone—"but you tell your boss I need to hear from him on this cell number in the next ten minutes or we're running with this thing, including the line 'Mr. Lanchester declined to comment,' are we *clear?* Tell Lanchester—I'd advise you to use these exact words—that the brunt of the piece concerns his relationship with a Russian official named *Gennady Rosovsky,* got that?"

"Gennady . . . *what?*"

"Gennady Rosovsky," Bryson repeated, giving the Washington number of his cell phone, which would give no indication that he was in Brussels. "Ten minutes!"

Bryson's phone rang barely ninety seconds later.

Bryson recognized the cultured baritone, the mid-Atlantic accent, at once. "This is Richard Lanchester," the national security adviser said in a tone just short of frantic. "What the *hell's* going on here?"

"I assume your spokesman filled you in on the piece we're running with."

"He mentioned some Russian name I've never heard before—Gennady something-or-other. What's this all about, Mr. Goddard?"

"You know damned well Ted Waller's real name, Mr. Lanchester—"

"Who the hell is Ted Waller? What *is* this?"

"We need to talk, Mr. Lanchester. Immediately."

"Well, talk away! I'm here. What kind of hatchet job is the *Post* preparing? Goddard, I don't know you, but as I'm sure you're well aware, I do have your publisher's home number, I see her socially, and I won't hesitate for a second to call her!"

"We have to talk in person, not over the phone. I'm in Brussels; I can be at SHAPE headquarters in Mons in an hour. I want you to call ahead to the front-gate security post, so I can pass right through, and the two of us can have a heart-to-heart."

"You're in *Brussels?* But I thought you were in Washington! What the hell—?"

"One hour, Mr. Lanchester. And I suggest you make not a single phone call about this between now and the time I arrive."

He knocked softly at Layla's door. She opened it quickly; she was already dressed, freshly bathed, fragrant of shampoo and soap. "I passed by your room a few minutes ago," she said as he entered. "I overheard you talking on the phone. No, don't tell me—I won't ask; I know: 'when the time is right.' "

He sat down in the same rickety chair where he had sat last night. "Well, I think the time is right, Layla," he said, and he immediately felt a burden begin to lift, almost a physical sensation, of finally being able to breathe deeply after so long being deprived of oxygen. "I need to tell you this, because I'm going to need your help, and I'm certain they're going to try to take me out."

"*They* . . . ?" She touched his arm with her hand. "What are you telling me?"

Choosing his words carefully, he spoke, telling her of things he had not spoken of to anyone except the now-disappeared CIA deputy director Harry Dunne. He confided that he had just one mission, which was to infiltrate, and then destroy, a shadowy organization known, to the very few who knew about it, as the Directorate; and he told her of his desperate hope to involve Richard Lanchester in the effort.

She listened, wide-eyed, taking it all in; then she got to her feet and began pacing the room. "I don't think I completely understand. This is not an *American* agency—it's international, multilateral?"

"That's one way of putting it. When I worked for them, they were based in Washington, though their headquarters appear to have moved. Where, I don't know."

"What are you saying—they've just *disappeared?*"

"Something like that."

"Impossible! An intelligence agency is like any other bureaucracy—it has telephone numbers and faxes and computers, not to mention office staff. It's like—what's the expression in English, trying to hide an elephant in the middle of a room!"

"The Directorate, when I worked for it, was lean, barebones, agile. And skilled at various forms of camouflage. The way the CIA is able to disguise its proprietaries as benign-seeming private corporations, or the Soviets used to create so-called Potemkin villages, false fronts, turning biological-warfare facilities into laundry-soap factories or even colleges."

Pensive, she shook her head in disbelief. "And do you mean to say they *compete* with CIA and MI-6 and Mossad and the Sûreté? With the *knowledge* of the other agencies?"

"No, that's not it at all. Its members are given to understand that they do operations the more mainstream agencies are not permitted to do, whether by charter or by governmental policy."

She nodded, unsmiling. "Yet at the same time they are able to keep their own existence secret? How can this be? People gossip, secretaries have friends . . . there are congressional oversight committees . . ." She went to the dressing table and, visibly distraught, began fumbling with her small black leather handbag, rummaging through it, finally pulling out a lipstick. She applied a dab of color, blotted her lips with a tissue, put the lipstick back.

"But that's the ingenious thing! Through a combination of extremely tight compartmentalization and careful recruitment—members are chosen carefully, drawn from all around the world, their backgrounds especially conducive to this line of work, to maintaining a code of silence. The compartmentalization ensures that no one operative ever gets to know another more than fleetingly; no one ever works with more than one handler. My handler was a legend in the agency, one of the founders, a man named Ted Waller. A man I came to idolize," he added regretfully.

"But surely the president must know!"

"To be honest, I have no idea. I believe the existence of the Directorate has always been kept from whoever occupies the Oval Office. Partly to protect the president from knowing too much about wet work and other sordid business, to provide him with plausible deniability. That's standard operating procedure in intelligence outfits worldwide. And partly, I'm sure, because the president is considered by the permanent intelligence community to be a mere tenant of the White House. A renter. He moves in for four years, maybe eight if he's lucky, buys new china, redecorates, hires and fires, gives a bunch of speeches, and then he's gone. Whereas the spies remain. *They're* the permanent Washington, the true inheritors."

"And you think the one person in government most likely to know about its activities is the chairman of the president's Foreign Intelligence Advisory Board, yes? The group that meets in secret to oversee the NSA and the CIA and all the other American spy agencies?"

"Correct."

"And the chairman of this intelligence oversight is Richard Lanchester."

"Exactly."

Nodding, she said, "This is why you want to meet with him."

"Correct."

"But for *what?*" she cried. "To tell him *what?*"

"To tell him what I know about the Directorate, about what I think it's up to. This was the big question, the reason I was brought back from retirement: Who's controlling the Directorate now? What is it really doing?"

"And you think you have the answers?" She seemed belligerent, almost outright antagonistic.

"No, of course not. I have theories, backed up by evidence."

"What evidence? You have nothing!"

"Whose side are you on, Layla?"

"I'm on *yours!*" she shouted. "I want to protect *you,* and I think you're making a mistake."

"A mistake?"

"You go to see this man Lanchester with . . . with wisps of nothing, crackpot accusations—he'll dismiss you at once. He'll think you're crazy!"

"Quite possibly," conceded Bryson. "But it's my job to make him think otherwise, and I believe I can."

"And what makes you think you can trust him?"

"What choice do I have?"

"He could be one of the enemies, one of the liars! How can you be sure he's *not?*"

"I'm sure of *nothing* anymore, Layla. I feel like I'm in a maze, I'm lost. I don't know where I am, *who* I am anymore."

"What makes you so sure you can believe what this CIA man told you? What makes you so sure he's not one of them, one of the liars?"

"I'm not *sure,* I told you that! This is not a matter of certainty, it's a matter of calculation, of odds."

"Then you believed it when he told you your parents were killed?"

"My stepmother—the woman who was sort of my guardian after my parents were killed—pretty much confirmed it, though she's ill, I think she has Alzheimer's, her mind is going. The fact is, the only people who really know the truth are the people I'm desperate to find—Ted Waller, and Elena."

"Elena is your ex-wife."

"Officially not an ex-wife. We never divorced. She disappeared. I suppose you'd say we're separated."

"She *abandoned* you."

Bryson sighed. "I don't know what happened. I wish I knew; I badly *want* to know."

"She just disappeared, she never got in touch? One day there, next day gone?"

"Right."

She shook her head in disapproval. "Yet I think you love her still."

He nodded. "It's—it's just so hard for me to think straight about her, to know what to believe. Did she ever love me, or was she assigned to me? Did she run away from me in despair, or out of fear, or because she was forced to? What is the truth, *where* is the truth?" Had his secret mission to Bucharest somehow backfired? Had Elena been reached by the sweepers, frightened into hiding somehow? But if so, wouldn't she have left word for him to explain her actions? Another possibility: Had she somehow discovered that he had lied to her about his whereabouts that weekend? Had she found out that he hadn't been in Barcelona? She might feel violated, betrayed, but would that really drive her away without raising it with him first?

"And somehow you think you'll learn this truth by flying everywhere, looking for Directorate operatives? It's *insanity!*"

"Layla, once I track these wasps to their nest, they're over. They must know that I've got the goods on them. I have a detailed knowledge of operations going back twenty years, transgressions of just about every national and international law."

"And you will present all this to Richard Lanchester, and you hope he will expose them, put a stop to it?"

"If he's as good a man as people say he is, that's exactly what he'll do."

"And if he's not?"

Bryson was silent; she went on, "You'll bring a weapon."

"Of course."

"Where is yours? You don't have it on you."

He looked up, startled. She had a quick, discerning eye. "It's in my luggage, still disassembled so I could get it through airport security."

"Well, then," she said. She removed a .45 from her purse, the Heckler & Koch USP compact.

"Thanks, but I'll take the Beretta." He smiled. "Of course, if you still have that .50 caliber Desert Eagle . . ."

"No, Nick, I'm sorry."

"Nick?" He felt a hollow thudding in his chest; she knew his true name, though she had never before uttered it, and he had never told her. My God, what *else* did she know?

She was pointing it at him from halfway across the room. It took him a moment to realize what was going on. He was frozen in the chair, his normal split-second reactions dulled by disbelief.

Her eyes were doleful. "I can't let you meet with Lanchester, Nick. I'm truly sorry, but I can't."

"What the hell are you doing?" he demanded.

"My job. You've left us no choice. I never thought it would come to this."

He felt as if the air had gone out of the room. His body went cold; he registered the shock viscerally.

"No," he said hoarsely, the chair in which he sat spinning slowly a million miles away. "Not you. They've gotten to you, too. When did they—"

And he exploded from the chair with the force of a tightly coiled spring, lunging at her with a suddenness that startled her, causing her instinctively to draw back to brace herself, defensively repositioning herself, her fierce concentration broken for the barest instant. Thrown off-balance, she fired, the explosion filling the small room, percussive and deafening. Bryson felt the projectile whiz by his left cheek, the gunpowder searing his face and temple, heard the cartridge casing spit onto the floor, and at almost the same moment he vaulted into the air, knocking her body to the floor, sending the gun clattering across the floor.

But she was no longer the woman he'd thought he knew; she'd been transformed into a tigress, a wild-eyed jungle predator crazed by bloodlust. Layla reared up, her right hand a rigid claw jabbing into his throat, while she simultaneously slammed her left elbow into his solar plexus, knocking the wind out of him.

Still, he managed to rise, swinging a fist at her, but she suddenly ducked under and shot upward, wedging her right shoulder into his right armpit as she vised her right arm around his neck, and with a loud grunt she grabbed her own left biceps and pulled in toward herself, choking him.

He had fought hand-to-hand with some of the fiercest, most dangerous and highly trained assassins in the world, but she was in another league entirely. She was brutally strong, as untiring as a machine, and she fought with a ferocity he had never seen before. Somehow managing to free himself from the headlock, he reared up again, swinging at her, but she jumped backward, deflecting his blow with her left arm, then sank suddenly to the floor and slammed a fist into his stomach, guarding her face with her left hand.

Bryson gasped, grappled for the soft flesh at the base of her neck, but she was too quick: she delivered a hard kick to the back of his right knee, causing him to sag. Striking the back of his head with her elbow, she almost succeeded in knocking him to the ground, but Bryson forced himself to ignore the blinding pain, summoning all of his considerable strength along with combat techniques learned decades ago that now returned to him like ancient hindbrain reflexes.

He spun out of her way, then launched his body at her frontally, hurling all of his weight against hers while simultaneously throwing a left-handed punch into her right kidney. She screamed, a shrill, full-throated cry not of pain but of rage. Leaping into the air and pivoting, she thrust out her right leg, scissoring it into his abdomen with astonishing force. Bryson groaned; she landed with her right leg forward and threw her right hand back-knuckle against his face with the impact of steel; then, grabbing his shoulders, she drove her left knee into his groin. As he doubled over in agony, she raised her right elbow and drove it into his spine, the pain staggering, then reached for the left side of his face, wrenching his head clockwise as she took him down.

With one last surge of desperate energy, he thrust his hands out, blindly grasping for her legs, slamming the bony side of his hand hard against the nerve center just above her left knee, clutching at it, forcing her down as well, and as she stumbled backward, he thrust his knee into her midsection, cracking his elbow against the side of her neck. She screamed, loosening the grip of her right hand, reaching for something, and he saw what it was: the Heckler & Koch was just feet away; he could *not* let her regain control of it! He shifted slightly, then jammed his elbow into the cartilage of her throat. She gagged, instinctively reaching with her right hand to dislodge his elbow and protect the vulnerable area, and that was enough to allow him to grab the pistol with his left hand, spinning it around and crashing it against the top of her head, the blow carefully calculated neither to kill her nor seriously cripple her.

She crumpled to the floor, her eyes half open, only the whites visible. He felt her throat for a pulse and found it; she was alive, though she would be out for several hours. Whoever she was, *whatever* she was, she had had the chance to kill him at the outset, when she had the gun trained on him, but she hesitated; either she could not do it or she found it almost impossible to bear the thought of doing so. She, like he, was probably a pawn, lied to and manipulated, recruited to an assignment about which she was carefully kept in the dark. In a way she was a victim, too.

A victim of the Directorate?

It seemed likely, even probable.

And he needed to question her, find out everything she knew. But not now; there was no time.

He searched the tiny closet, where she had hung her few items of clothing and stowed a couple of pairs of shoes, for a rope or something similar to tie her up. Kneeling down, he felt along the floor, grabbing something that he realized was the spike heel that had somehow come loose from her gray shoes, the ones she had worn to the bank in Geneva. Something extremely sharp at one end of the heel lanced his finger. Wincing, he picked up the two-inch-long gray object and saw a small, razor-sharp blade protruding from the end that was intended to attach to the sole of the shoe. He inspected it more closely: the narrow blade, like an artist's X-Acto knife, fit into the base of the shoe, the heel threaded so that it screwed in.

He looked back at Layla. The whites of her eyes were

still exposed, her jaw slack; she was still unconscious.

Her spike-heeled shoes, he suddenly understood, had been ingeniously outfitted with a razor blade, which was accessible by twisting off the heel. He examined the other shoe, which had been adapted the same way. It was a brilliant little trick.

And then it struck him.

The image of her in the closet off the banker's office, bound with brightly colored polyurethane "humane restraints," the sort normally used by law-enforcement agents to transport dangerous prisoners. Jan Vansina, Directorate operative, had fettered her with strong plastic handcuffs—*which she could easily have cut her way out of.*

Geneva had been a setup.

Layla had been in cahoots with Vansina, both of them Directorate. Vansina had only pretended to attack her; she had cooperated. At any time she could have freed herself.

What did this mean?

There was a small, two-person elevator at the end of the dark hall, the kind that was operated by opening or closing an accordion inner gate. Fortunately, there seemed to be no one else on the floor. Bryson had seen no one else go in or out of rooms on the floor; likely, they were the only ones.

He hoisted her—though she was not big, she was now deadweight and quite heavy—and, putting her head on his shoulder, grasped her beneath the buttocks and carried her, as if she were a drunken spouse, to the elevator. Bryson had readied a rueful joke about his wife's perennial inebriation, but never had a chance to use it.

He took the elevator down to the hotel's basement, which stank of flooded sewage, and set her down on the gritty concrete floor. After searching for a few minutes, he found a storage closet, removed the buckets and mops, and placed her inside. With a length of old clothesline, he carefully bound her wrists and ankles with several tight knots, winding the rope around and around her legs and torso, looping it and tying it into slip knots, then tested the restraints to make sure she could not get out of them if she came to before he returned. The rope was secure—and she was barefoot, with no hidden blade anywhere.

Then, taking one more precaution—if she did become conscious unexpectedly soon, she might yell for help—he stuffed a gag in her mouth and tied it tight, checking to see that she could still breathe.

He turned the lock on the closet door, which would serve only to keep her in—he was convinced, however, that she would never have the opportunity to open the door herself—and not keep someone out.

Then Bryson returned to his hotel room to prepare to meet Richard Lanchester.

In a dark room halfway across the world, three men huddled around an electronic console, their tense faces bathed in the cool green light emitted by diodes.

"It's a digital relay feed direct from Mentor, one of our space-based satellites in the Intelsat fleet," intoned one of them.

The reply was urgent, the tone revealing long hours of stress. "But the voice-pattern ID—how reliable is Voice-cast?"

"Within a tolerance of between ninety-nine and ninety-nine-point-nine-seven degrees," the first man said. "Extremely reliable."

"The identification is affirmative," remarked the third man. "The communication was initiated by a GSM cellular phone on the ground whose coordinates indicate Brussels, Belgium, the recipient based in Mons." The third man adjusted a dial; the voice that emerged from the console was astonishingly clear.

"What is this?"

"We need to talk, Mr. Lanchester. Immediately."

"Well, talk away! I'm here. What kind of hatchet job is the Post *preparing? Goddard, I don't know you, but as I'm sure you're well aware, I do have your publisher's home number, I see her socially, and I won't hesitate for a second to call her!"*

"We have to talk in person, not over the phone. I'm in Brussels; I can be at SHAPE headquarters in Mons in an hour. I want you to call ahead to the front-gate security post, so I can pass right through, and the two of us can have a heart-to-heart."

"You're in Brussels? *But I thought you were in Washington! What the hell—?"*

"One hour, Mr. Lanchester. And I suggest you make not a single phone call about this between now and the time I arrive."

"Order an interception," one of the watchers said.

"The decision must be taken at a higher level," replied another, clearly his superior. "Prometheus may prefer to continue gathering information on the target's activities, on how much the target knows."

"But if the two meet in a secure facility—what kind of penetration can we expect?"

"Good *Christ*, McCabe! Is there *anywhere* we can't penetrate? Relay the sound file. Prometheus will decide the course of action."

PART THREE

CHAPTER SEVENTEEN

The president's national security adviser sat across the burnished mahogany conference table from Bryson, tension creasing his high forehead. For over twenty minutes Richard Lanchester had listened in rapt absorption to Bryson's account, nodding, taking notes, interrupting only for occasional clarifications. Every question he asked was not only pertinent but incisive, piercing through layers of ambiguity and confusion right to the crux of the issue. Bryson was impressed by the man, by his brilliance, his quick intelligence. He listened closely, concentrating deeply. Bryson spoke as he would debrief a handler or a case officer, just as he used to brief Waller after a field operation: calmly, objectively, coolly assessing probabilities while not injecting conjecture without basis. He tried to provide a context in which the revelations could be meaningfully placed. It was difficult.

The two men sat in a special secure facility located within the NATO secretary general's command-and-control center, an acoustically insulated room-within-a-room known informally as the "bubble." Its walls and floor were actually one module separated from the surrounding concrete walls by foot-thick rubber blocks that kept all sound vibrations from emanating outward. Technical surveillance countermeasures were employed daily to ensure that the bubble remained secure, free of any taps or listening devices. Security officers swept the room and its immediate environs daily. There were no windows, and thus no risk of laser or microwave bounces that could read the vibrations from human voices. Then there was an elaborate system of fallbacks: a spectral correlator was used at all times to detect surveillance using a spectrum analyzer, and an acoustic correlator used passive sound-pattern matching to automatically detect and classify any listening device. Finally, an acoustic noise generator was constantly on, generating an audio blanket of pink noise designed to defeat wired microphones inside walls, contact microphones, and any audio transmitters located in electrical outlets. Lanchester's insistence that they meet within the extraordinarily secure walls of the bubble was testimony to the seriousness with which he regarded Bryson's urgently imparted information.

Lanchester looked up, visibly shaken. "What you're telling me is preposterous, the sheerest madness, yet somehow it has the ring of truth. I say that because bits and pieces of what you say precisely confirm what little I know."

"But you *must* know about the existence of the Directorate. You're chairman of PFIAB; I'd have thought you'd know all about it."

Lanchester removed his rimless spectacles, polished them thoughtfully with a handkerchief. "The existence of the Directorate is one of the most closely held secrets in the government. Shortly after I was named to PFIAB I was briefed about it, and I must say at first I thought my briefer—one of those nameless, anonymous, behind-the-scenes intelligence officers who are part of the permanent establishment around Washington—had taken leave of his senses. It was one of the most fantastic, most implausible things I'd ever heard. A covert intel agency that operated entirely out of sight, without controls, without accountability or oversight—outlandish! If I'd dared to suggest the idea to the president, he'd have had me committed to St. Elizabeth's immediately, and quite justifiably so."

"Then what is it you find so implausible? You're referring to the true nature of the Directorate, the deception within the deception?"

"Actually, no. Harry Dunne did give me a briefing some months ago, when he'd apparently uncovered only part of the story. He told me of his belief that the Directorate's founders and principals were all Soviet GRU, that Ted Waller was a man named Gennady Rosovsky. What he told me was alarming, deeply astonishing, and by its very nature his findings had to be kept extremely protected: our government would be thrown into turmoil, security vulnerabilities exposed, shaken to its very foundations. That's why your mention of that name drew my immediate attention."

"Yet you must have been skeptical of what he told you."

"Oh yes, deeply so. I won't say I dismissed him, Dunne's credentials are too heavy to be ignored—but the notion of such a mammoth deception operation—it's difficult to accept, frankly. No, what I find most troubling is your assessment of the Directorate's present-day activities."

"Dunne must have kept you informed about all this."

He shook his head slowly, the barest movement. "I haven't spoken with him in weeks. If he was compiling this sort of dossier, by rights he should have kept me apprised. Perhaps he was waiting until he had more, until he'd amassed a substantive, incontrovertible file."

"You must have a way to reach him, locate him."

"I have no tricks up my sleeve. I'll make calls, see what I can do, but people don't just vanish from the seventh floor of the CIA. If he's been taken hostage, or if he's dead, I'll be able to find it out, Nick. I'm fairly confident I can track him down."

"When we spoke last, he was concerned about infiltration within the Agency—that the Directorate had extended its reach inside."

Lanchester nodded. "I'd say the identification you pulled off the would-be killer in Chantilly speaks volumes. It's always possible that the paper was simply stolen, or that the fellow was turned, hired locally. But I'd have to agree with both you and Dunne. We can't rule out the possibility that the CIA's been infiltrated pretty deeply. I'm flying back to Washington in a few hours, and I'll put in a call to Langley en route, speak with the Director myself. But let me be brutally frank with you, Nick. Look at the totality of what you're telling me. An overheard exchange at a French arms dealer's chateau, the implication that he and Anatoly Prishnikov were involved in planning the catastrophe at Lille. I don't doubt it's true, but what do we have, really?"

"The word of an intelligence operative of almost two decades," said Bryson quietly.

"An operative for this same, bizarre agency that we now know to be a hostile power operating on American soil against American interests. I'm sorry to be so brutal, but this is the way it reads. You're a defector, Nick. I don't doubt your honesty for a second, but you know how our government has always treated defectors—with the highest suspicion. For God's sake, look at what we did to the poor defector Nosenko, who broke from the KGB to warn that the Russians were behind the Kennedy assassination and that our own CIA had been penetrated by a high-level mole. We locked him up in solitary, in a prison cell, and interrogated him for years. James Jesus Angleton, the CIA counterintelligence chief back then, was certain this was a Soviet dangle, an attempt to manipulate us, mislead us, and he'd have none of it. Not only did he not believe the most significant KGB defector we'd ever had—even after Nosenko had passed polygraph after polygraph—but he brutalized the man, broke him. And Nosenko had specific names of agents, operations, controls. You're giving me rumors, overhears, suggestions."

"I'm giving you more than enough to act on," snapped Bryson.

"Nick, listen to me. Listen, and understand. Say I go to the president and tell him that there's some sort of *octopus*— a faceless, nebulous organization whose existence I can't definitively establish, can't substantiate, and whose aims I can only *guess* at. I'll be laughed out of the Oval Office, or worse."

"Not with your credibility."

"My credibility, as you put it, is based on my unwillingness to be alarmist, my insistence on having the goods before we act. Good Lord, if someone else spoke up at the National Security Council, or in the Oval Office, with such allegations without basis, I'd be furious."

"But you *know*—"

"I *know* nothing. Suspicions, inklings, those patterns we imagine we see. That isn't knowledge. In the jargon of international law, they don't constitute evidentiary warrant. It's insufficient—"

"You propose to do *nothing?*"

"I didn't say that. Listen, Nick, I believe in the rules. People chide me all the time for being a stickler. But that doesn't mean I'm going to sit back and let these *fanatics* take the world hostage. What I'm saying is that I need more. I need *proof.* I will mobilize every form of state authority we can muster, but to do that I need you to come back to me with something."

"Damn it, there's no *time.*"

"Bryson, *listen* to me!" Bryson saw the harrowed look in Lanchester's face. "I need more. I need specifics. I need to know *what they're planning!* I'm counting on you. We all are."

"I'm counting on you. We all are." Lanchester's voice came from the speaker console in the darkened room thousands of miles away. *"Now, how can I help? What resources can I place at your disposal?"*

The listener picked up a telephone handset and pressed a button. In a moment he spoke, his voice hushed. "So he's made contact. As we expected."

"It fits the profile, sir," came the voice at the other end of the line. "He goes straight to the top. I'm surprised only that he didn't attempt blackmail or other threats."

"I want to know exactly who he's working with, who he's working for."

"Yes, sir. Unfortunately, we don't know where he's going next."

"Don't worry. The world is a very small place today. He can't get away. There's no place to go."

Bryson left the rented car a few blocks from the Marolles and approached the pension on foot, alert for any disruptions in pattern, anyone who seemed not to belong. There was nothing out of the ordinary, but his mind was not set at ease. He had been manipulated, deceived too often. Richard Lanchester had not dismissed him out of hand, but neither had he been roused to immediate action. Did that mean he, too, was to be suspected? Paranoia bred upon itself; Bryson knew that that way lay madness. No, he would take Lanchester at face value, as a man who seemed genuinely concerned yet quite reasonably needed hard facts upon which to order action. It was a setback, but in another sense it was a step forward, because he had enlisted a powerful ally. Or if not an ally, at least a sympathetic ear.

Once past the glum woman at the front desk, Bryson took the stairs to the basement, to the storage closet. From the outside he could see it was still locked; that was a relief. But he put nothing past Layla anymore; he pulled his weapon out from his belt, concealed by his suit jacket, and stood to one side as he silently turned the lock, then suddenly whipped open the door.

She did not spring out; there was only silence.

From where he stood he could see that the closet was empty. The clothesline had been severed, pieces discarded on the floor.

She was gone.

She could not have escaped without outside assistance. There was no way she could have slipped the knots or severed them; she had no blade or other tool. He had made sure of that.

Now he was certain: *she had been working with others nearby.*

Her accomplices were likely in the vicinity now; they knew where he was staying, and if she had hesitated momentarily before firing her gun, they would not. Returning to his room was therefore out of the question, a risk he must not take.

He mentally ran through the contents of his suitcase upstairs. Over twenty years he had learned to travel with the minimum, to assume that his hotel room would be searched. Habitually, he arranged his things in such a way that he would inevitably be able to tell if someone had gone through them, information that often proved useful. Since he assumed his suitcase would be rifled, he had learned not to leave anything irreplaceable behind, unattended. He learned, too, to separate valuables into two broad categories: those with monetary value, and those of strategic value. It was items in the first category that were most likely to be stolen by casual thieves, larcenous maids and the like: money, jewelry, small electronics that looked expensive. Those in the second category—things like passports real and forged, identity papers and licenses and other documents, canisters of film, videotapes or computer disks—were least likely to be stolen by simple thieves, yet if pilfered often could not be replaced.

For that reason, Bryson was more likely to leave cash and such in his luggage, but take with him his false passports. True to habit, he had on his person all of his papers, his weapon, and the downloaded cryptographic key from Jacques Arnaud's secure phone, a tiny microchip he had been carrying with him for quite some time now. If he abandoned his hotel room and never returned, he would survive. He would need money, though that was fairly easily arranged. But he could continue.

But to where? Simple penetration of the Directorate was out of the question now. They knew of his hostile intent. The only remaining strategy was a frontal one: to try to locate Elena by using his standing as her former husband as a lure.

They didn't know what he knew, what he might have learned from her.

Whether she was assigned to him or not, whether tasked to manipulate him, keep him in the dark, she nevertheless might have told him things, inadvertently or intentionally. He had been her husband, however fraudulent the marriage was designed to be; there had been, of necessity, moments of intimacy, times when the two of them were entirely alone.

The deception could be doubled back, turned back on them as well. Why not? What if he let it be known that he had learned things from Elena, deliberately or not—facts they would not want him to know? Information that could be locked away, used as a bargaining chip, left with an attorney to be released in the event of death?

He had something here. A husband knew things about his

wife that no one else did. They didn't know what she might have passed on to him, intentionally or not. He would *use* the uncertainty, the ambiguity—use it as a bright, shining beacon, a lure.

Exactly how he would use it was still unclear, the plan inchoate. But there still remained agents he had had brief dealings with, operatives in Amsterdam and Copenhagen, Berlin and London, Sierra Leone and Pyongyang. He would begin the methodical, painstaking process of contacting them, or whichever ones of them whose names and contact information still functioned, using them as conduits to pass on the message to Ted Waller.

To do this he would need money, but that was fairly easily arranged. He had his hidden accounts in Luxembourg and Grand Cayman, as yet untouched; the necessity of hiding contingency funds was virtually a law of nature among Directorate operatives, a matter of survival. He would arrange wire transfers, secure the funds he needed to travel freely, now that he could no longer trust the CIA.

And then he would begin to contact former colleagues, using them to pass on the threat. And a demand: an insistence upon a meeting with Elena. A condition that, if not met, would result in the release of information he had until now held in reserve. Blackmail, pure and simple. Ted Waller would understand; it was mother's milk to him.

He closed the storage-closet door and searched for another way out of the hotel, an exit that didn't require going through the lobby. After circling the dark basement warrens for a few minutes, he found a little-used service exit, an iron door that was all but rusted shut. He struggled with it until he managed to loosen the handle; a little while later he wrenched it open. It gave on to a narrow, trash-strewn cobblestone alley, barely passable and evidently rarely used.

A side street, really little more than a parking area for residents of the neighboring tenements, led to the main thoroughfare, where he disappeared into the crowds of pedestrians. His first stop was a shabby department store, where he purchased an entirely new outfit of clothing, changing in the fitting room and discarding his old clothes there, to the bafflement of the clerk. He also picked up a knapsack, an assortment of other casual clothes, and a cheap airline carry-on bag.

Searching for a branch office of a large international bank, he passed the window of an electronics shop, dominated by a row of television sets all tuned to the same broadcast. The sight was immediately familiar: he recognized the landmarks of Geneva; it seemed to be a travel advertisement for Switzerland, then he realized it was actually news footage, and then he felt his legs go weak at what he saw next.

It was the Hôpital Cantonal in Geneva. The camera panned through its corridors, across its emergency room, jammed with people on stretchers, corpses in body bags. The camera panned across a hellish scene: bodies stacked up in preparation for carting away. The caption on the screen read: "Geneva, yesterday."

Yesterday? What catastrophe could possibly have just happened?

He turned back to the street, spotted a newsstand, saw the banner headlines: GENEVA. ANTHRAX. OUTBREAK. ATTACK.

He grabbed an *International Herald-Tribune,* noting the headline that ran across the top in thirty-six-point type: ANTHRAX VICTIMS CONTINUE TO FILL GENEVA HOSPITALS AS INTERNATIONAL AUTHORITIES SEARCH FOR ANSWERS; UP TO A THOUSAND DEATHS EXPECTED.

Reeling, he read with horror.

GENEVA—A sudden, widespread outbreak of anthrax has turned into an epidemic here, as the city's hospitals and clinics fill with stricken residents. An estimated 3,000 have been infected by the deadly disease, with some 650 persons already declared dead. Hospital administrators have instituted emergency procedures to prepare their facilities for what many fear will be an overwhelming influx of anthrax cases in the next 48 hours. City officials have ordered businesses, schools, and all governmental offices closed and have warned tourists and business visitors to stay away from Geneva until the source of the infection can be determined. The city's mayor, Alain Prisette, expressed his shock and grief, while warning residents and visitors alike to remain calm.

Patients began pouring into Geneva's hospitals and clinics yesterday in the predawn hours complaining of severe flulike symptoms. By five o'clock in the morning, over a dozen cases of anthrax had been diagnosed at the Hôpital Cantonal. By noon yesterday the victims numbered in the thousands.

City and health officials have been working around the clock to determine the source of the outbreak. Sources here refused to speculate on reports that the deadly disease may have been released by a truck driving through the city with a truck-mounted aerosolized dispenser emitting a cloud of spores.

Anthrax has a mortality rate as high as 90%. After exposure, the victim develops severe respiratory distress, followed by the rapid onset of shock and subsequent death within 36 hours.

Although inhalation anthrax can be treated with a repeated course of penicillin, authorities here point out that hospital staff must take protective measures or risk infection themselves. Anthrax spores can remain present for decades.

As Swiss authorities continue their investigation into the source of the infection, health officials estimate that by the end of the week victims will number in the tens of thousands.

The question many are asking here is, why? Why was Geneva targeted, and how? Speculation centers on the fact that Geneva serves as the headquarters of a number of powerful transnational organizations, including the World Health Organization. The mayor refused to comment on widespread speculation that the outbreak was the result of a biological weapon wielded by an unnamed terrorist organization that had been planning such an attack for weeks, if not months.

Bryson looked up from the newspaper, blood draining from his face. If this report was accurate, and there was no reason to suppose it was not, a biological-weapons attack had occurred in Geneva while he was still there, or immediately afterward.

An American jet blown out of the sky . . . the Eurostar train blown up in Lille . . . a bomb detonated in the Washington Metro during morning rush hour . . .

He was seeing a pattern of terrorism, increasing in frequency, the commonalities evident. Each was designed to incite chaos, wide-ranging public injury, and resulting fear. These were classically designed terrorist paradigms, except for one thing.

No one had claimed responsibility.

It was customary, though not inevitable, for terrorists to claim responsibility for their deeds, assert a justification. Otherwise, the incident had no purpose except random demoralization.

Since Bryson knew the Directorate had been behind Lille, it was by no means impossible that the Directorate had had a hand in the Geneva attack. In fact, it was likely.

But why?

What was the objective? What did the Directorate hope to accomplish? Why was a conspiracy of extremely powerful private citizens banding together to instigate a wave of terror in various sites around the world? To what end?

Bryson no longer accepted the theory that private arms dealers were trying to create an artificial demand for their goods. Uzis were useless against an outbreak of anthrax. There was more to it; there was another pattern, another logic. But *what?*

He had just come from Geneva, had been very close to Lille only days before. *In both cases, he had been there.* True, he had come to Geneva because of a report that Jan Vansina, a Directorate operative, was there. He had gone to

Chantilly—not Lille, but close to it—to track the activities of Jacques Arnaud.

Was it possible that he was being set up? Terrorist outbreaks in places he had just visited—would he somehow be tied in because he had been in the vicinity?

He thought about Harry Dunne and his insistence that he go to Geneva to confront Jan Vansina. In that case, Dunne had encouraged him to go there; Dunne could have had a hand in setting him up. But Chantilly? Dunne hadn't known in advance . . .

Layla had. In that case, Layla had let him know about Arnaud's château in Chantilly. She had been reluctant to take him there—or had *feigned* reluctance—but it was she who let him know about Chantilly. In effect, she had waved the red flag at the bull.

Harry Dunne had encouraged him to visit Geneva; Layla had induced him, subtly, to Chantilly. In both places, there had been terrorist strikes immediately afterward. Was it possible that Dunne and Layla had been working together, both on behalf of the Directorate, to manipulate him, set him up to take the fall for a series of devastating attacks?

Jesus, what was the *truth?*

He folded up the newspaper to take it with him, and that was when he noticed a small article, accompanied by an equally small photograph. It was the photograph that first caught his eye.

Bryson recognized the face at once: it was the florid-cheeked man he had seen emerging from Jacques Arnaud's private office at the château in Chantilly. Anatoly Prishnikov, chairman and CEO of the mammoth Russian conglomerate Nortek.

ARNAUD JOINT VENTURE ANNOUNCED, the headline read. Jacques Arnaud's far-flung corporate empire had just announced a joint business venture with the Russian conglomerate, which itself represented the consolidation of a number of industries that formerly belonged to the Soviet military.

The nature of the business venture was unspecified, but the article took note of Nortek's growing presence in the

European market, mentioning its role in a wave of mergers in the electronics industry. A pattern was beginning to emerge, but what was it exactly? A worldwide coalescence of major corporations, each of which was—*or could be*—a defense contractor.

Under the control of the Directorate, if his information was accurate. Did this mean that the Directorate was attempting to seize control of the defense establishments of the world's great powers? Could that have been what Harry Dunne was so fearful of?

Had Dunne been maneuvering to set him up as a dupe, a fall guy? Or was Dunne himself—if he was still alive—the dupe?

Now, at least, it was clear where he would have to go to look for answers.

There was a theatrical supply shop on rue d'Argent, two blocks north of the Theatre de la Monnaie, where Bryson made several purchases. Then he entered the branch office of an international bank, where he initiated a sequence of wire transfers from his Luxembourg account. By the end of the afternoon he had, discounting transaction fees, almost a hundred thousand dollars, mostly in American dollars, but also in a range of European currency as well.

He stopped into a travel agency and signed on as a last-minute member of a charter tour. Then he found a sporting-goods store and bought a few more items.

Departing from Zaventem Airport the next day was a leased, decrepit Aeroflot plane whose passengers were a motley, rowdy group of backpackers who had paid bargain-basement prices for the "Moscow Nights" package tour of Russia—three nights and four days in Moscow, followed by an overnight train to St. Petersburg, where they would spend two nights and three days. The accommodations would be inexpensive, which was a polite term for squalid, and all meals were included, which was not necessarily a plus.

One of the backpackers was a middle-aged man wearing

green fatigues, a baseball cap, and a bushy brown beard. He was traveling alone but he joined in the general hilarity. His new, instant friends knew him as Mitch Borowsky, a book-keeper from Quebec who had backpacked all around the world, and happened to be in Brussels when the urge to go to Moscow had struck him. He was lucky enough to get one of the last remaining empty seats on the charter flight. It was totally last-minute, he explained to his new comrades, but Mitch Borowsky liked to do things at the last minute.

CHAPTER EIGHTEEN

It was 10:00 A.M. in the Map Room, on the ground level of the White House, and an "impromptu" had been convened— an unscheduled meeting of agency heads and their deputies. It was at such irregular meetings that emergent situations were dealt with, fires extinguished and, at times, set. At such meetings, the incremental decisions that collectively produced the policies and doctrines of state were reached.

Rapid events required rapid responses: the needed consensus could only be reached in a free-form setting unencumbered by snail-paced bureaucracy, cabinet-level politicking, and endless second-guessing of timid analysts. Success in the executive branch meant mastery of one basic tenet. One did not present the commander in chief with problems; one presented him with solutions. It was at the impromptus—in the White House or the adjacent Old Executive Office Building—that solutions were crafted.

There were eight chairs around a long mahogany table, a white notepad in front of each seat. A rose damask sofa stood against one wall, a picture of orphaned gentility; above it, framed, was the last situation map used by President Roosevelt, who had overseen the American conduct of World War II from here. It was hand-labeled with a date: APRIL 3, 1945. Roosevelt had died a little more than a week later. In subsequent years, the once-top-secret command center had been converted to a storage area. Only in the current administration had the windowless room once more come into active use. Even so, the redolence of its history lent solemnity to the proceedings.

Richard Lanchester sat at one end of the table, looking around curiously at his colleagues. "I'm still not clear about the agenda this morning. Urgency was conveyed in the message I got, but very little content."

NSA Director John Corelli spoke first. "I would have

thought you were in the best position to appreciate the significance of what has happened," Corelli said, meeting Lanchester's level gaze. "He's made contact."

"*He?* Sorry?" Lanchester raised an eyebrow. He had taken a night flight from Brussels, had barely had a chance to shower and shave before the meeting was convened, and the wearing schedule told on his lined face.

Morton Culler, the senior intelligence officer at the NSA and a twenty-year veteran of the agency, exchanged glances with his boss. Culler's thinning hair was slicked back with gel, his slate eyes unblinking behind the thick lenses of his aviator-style glasses. "Nicholas Bryson, sir. We're talking about the visit he paid you in Brussels."

"Bryson," Lanchester repeated the name, his face impassive. "You know who he is?"

"Of course," Culler said. "It's all exactly as we'd expected. It fits his profile, you see. He goes straight to the top. Did he try to blackmail you? Use threats?"

"It wasn't like that," Lanchester protested.

"And yet you agreed to see him face-to-face."

"Anyone in public life accumulates a protective armamentarium, a Praetorian guard of receptionists and press officers and functionaries. He got past all that using deception. But he got my attention by revealing his knowledge of something very few of us know about."

"And did you find out what he wanted from us?"

Lanchester paused. "He talked of the Directorate."

"He admitted his allegiance, then," the CIA director, James Exum, said precisely.

"On the contrary. He described the Directorate as a global threat. He seemed impatient that we hadn't taken effective action against it. He alluded to patterns of deceptions, to a shadowy supranational organization. It sounded mad, much of it. And yet . . ." Lanchester fell silent for a moment.

"And yet?" Exum prompted.

"Frankly, a certain amount of what he said made sense. It scared me."

"He's a master at that, sir," Culler said. "A real spinner of tales. A genius at manipulation."

"You seem to know a great deal about this man," Lanchester said tartly. "Why don't you fill me in?"

"That's precisely what we intend to do," Corelli said. He nodded toward the two unfamiliar faces in the room. "Terence Martin and Gordon Wollenstein, from the joint intelligence task force we've assembled for the purpose. I've asked them here to brief everyone present."

Terence Martin was a tall man in his mid-thirties with a dry manner and a trace of Maine in his accent. His military background was evident from his ramrod posture. "Nicholas Bryson. Son of George Bryson, a one-star general in the United States Army before he died. Bryson was in the Forty-second Battalion, Mechanized, in North Korea, and later served in Vietnam, during the first phase of the engagement. A kit bag full of combat honors. Glowing fitness reports and officers' evaluations, all the way up. Nicholas, his only child, was born forty-two years ago. At that point, George Bryson was regularly on the move, with rotating posts around the world. Nina Bryson, his wife, was an accomplished pianist, taught music. Quiet, unassuming. Followed him from place to place. Young Nicholas spent his childhood in a dozen different countries. At one point, eight countries in the course of four years: Wiesbaden, Bangkok, Marrakech, Madrid, Riyadh, Taipei, Madrid, Okinawa."

"Sounds like a recipe for isolation," Lanchester said, nodding slowly. "It must have been easy to lose your bearings in that kaleidoscope of cultures. You pull into yourself, into a shell, withdraw from the people around you."

"Only here's where things get interesting," Gordon Wollenstein interjected politely. He was red-haired and ruddy, with a deeply creased face, and a tieless, slightly disheveled appearance. Only his quiet, observant manner suggested his disciplinary expertise in psychology. His Berkeley doctoral thesis on new-generation techniques of psychological profiling was what had first brought him to the attention of certain experts in the U.S. intelligence community. "You've got a child who, every time he gets settled, has to pull up stakes. Abruptly, and with little warning. And yet at every posting, he acquired perfect native command of the cultures, the customs, and the language of the locale. Not the army base, not the American cohort, but the *natives,* the people in whose land he was living. Presumably from contact with his parents' servants. Four months after he arrived at Bangkok, at the age of eight, he spoke fluent, accentless Thai. Shortly after arriving at Hanover, none of his German classmates would have guessed he was an American. Same with Italian. Chinese. Arabic. Even Basque, for God's sake. Not just the official languages, but the local dialectal variants—the language of the playground as well as of the radio broadcasts. It was as if he'd spent his whole life in the place. He was a sponge, a human chameleon, with a really astonishing capacity to, well, 'go native.' "

"We've confirmed that his test scores were remarkable, always at the top of his class," Terence Martin put in. He distributed a summary sheet to the others in the room. "Extraordinary intelligence, extraordinary athletic skills. Not a freak of nature, but close. Still, it's clear something happened to him during his adolescence." Martin nodded at Wollenstein, giving him the signal to proceed.

"Adaptability is a funny thing," Wollenstein said. "We talk about 'code switching,' when people grow up multilingual—effortlessly able to think and express themselves in many tongues. More troubling is the ability to adopt and discard different value systems. To exchange one code of honor for another. What if there's no bright line between being adaptable and being unmoored? We believe that Bryson changed after his parents were killed, when he was fifteen. Once the ties to those parental values were severed, violently, he became susceptible to other influences. Adolescent rebelliousness, steered and manipulated by interests hostile to ours, turned him into a very dangerous man indeed. We're talking about a man with a thousand faces. A man who may have cultivated grievances against the authorities that once governed his life. His father spent his life in the service of his nation. On some pre-rational level, he may blame the United States government for his father's death. This is not a man you want as an enemy."

Martin cleared his throat. "Unfortunately, we've never had the luxury of choosing our enemies."

"And in this case, he seems to have chosen us." Wollenstein paused. "A man whose powerful abilities to adapt to circumstance verge on something like multiple personality disorder. I'm frankly speculating here. But my team and I have grown convinced that multiplicity is the key to Nicholas Bryson. It isn't like dealing with one man with a stable set of habits and traits. Think of a one-man consortium, if you will."

"It's important that you understand what Gordon has been telling us," Martin said. "All the evidence suggests that he's been turned into a very dangerous man indeed. We know of his involvement in something called the Directorate. We know that 'Coleridge' is one of his field names. We know that he has been highly trained—"

Lanchester cut him off. "I told you, he spoke to me about the Directorate. Said he was trying to destroy it."

"Classic disinformation ploy," Corelli said. "He *is* the Directorate, for all intents and purposes."

Terence Martin opened a large manila envelope and withdrew a set of photographs, which he distributed to the assembled. "Some of these are grainy, some less so. You're seeing a lot of high-res satellite surveillance product. I'd direct your attention to the photograph labeled 34-12-A." The image showed Nicholas Bryson onboard a vast container vessel. "Spectroscopic analysis tells us he's holding a quartz container of 'red mercury,' so-called. An extremely efficient high explosive. The Russkies came up with it. Nasty stuff."

"Just ask the good citizens of Barcelona," Corelli said. "That's what was used in the recent explosion there."

"Photograph 34-12-B is grainy, but I think you can make it out," Martin went on. "We took it from a security camera in the Lille station. Bryson again." He held up another image, an aerial view of the landscape just ten miles east of Lille.

It was a scene of destruction, twisted rails and train cars in disarray, like the playthings of a bored child. "Again, we've got forensic trace-evidence confirmation that the explosive used was red mercury. Probably ten cc's would have done the trick."

Martin passed out another image: Bryson in Geneva. "You can just make him out from a cluttered street scene—outside the Temple de la Fusterie."

"We figured he kept a stash in one of the Geneva banks," Morton Culler said. "But he was up to something else there. We didn't know until a few hours ago."

"It wasn't until we learned about the release of weaponized anthrax there," Martin said. "Precisely in the sector of the Old Town where we'd photographed him. Presumably there were confederates, but they may have been unwitting. He's the one who orchestrated it, that much is clear."

Lanchester leaned back in his chair, his face drawn. "What are you telling me?"

"Call it what you like," Corelli said. "But I'd say your man is the Typhoid Mary of global terror."

"At whose behest?" Though Lanchester's gaze was fixed in the middle distance, his voice was insistent.

"That's the trillion-dollar question, isn't it?" Exum said, with his deceptive Southern languor. "John and I have some disagreements on this issue."

John Corelli glanced at Martin, prompting him. "I'm here because Lieutenant General Corelli asked me here in an advisory capacity," Martin said. "But there's no secret as to my own recommendation. However formidable Bryson is, he can't be acting alone. I say we follow him covertly, see where he leads us. Follow the hornet to the hive." He smiled, exposing small, off-white teeth. "Then apply a blowtorch."

"John's people are saying wait until we learn more," Exum said, in a tone of exquisite courtesy. He leaned across the table and picked up the photograph of the Eurostar disaster. "*This* is my answer." Abruptly, his voice grew hard. "It's too dangerous to delay any further. Forgive me, but this isn't a goddamn *science fair*. We cannot have another *mas-

sacre while the NSA boys wait until they've finished the crossword puzzle. And on this I think the president and I are on the same page."

"But suppose he's our one lead to a larger conspiracy . . ." Corelli began.

Exum snorted. "And if you can just get seven across, you'll figure out ten down. Five letters, starts with E . . ." He shook his head gravely. "John, Terence, I have the greatest respect for your gamesmanship. But you and your whiz kids forget one simple thing. *There's no time.*"

Lanchester turned to Morton Culler, the NSA ace. "Where do you come out?"

"Exum's right," Culler said heavily. "Let me be more precise. Bryson must be apprehended immediately. And if apprehension poses any difficulties, he must be terminated. We've got to dispatch the Alpha squad. And make their assignment very explicit. We're not talking about a guy who owes library fines for overdue books. We're talking about someone responsible for mass murder, and who seems to have an even bigger game afoot. So long as he's alive and out there, none of us can relax our vigilance."

Lanchester shifted uncomfortably. "The Alpha squad," he said quietly. "It isn't supposed to exist."

"It *doesn't* exist," Culler said. "Officially."

Lanchester placed his hands flat on the polished table. "Listen, I need to know how certain you are in this analysis," Lanchester said. "Because I'm the one man in this room who's met with Bryson, face-to-face. And—I just have to say it—that's just not the vibe I got from him. He struck me as a man of honor." Lanchester paused, and for a few moments, nobody spoke. "Still, I've been fooled before."

"Alpha will be dispatched immediately," Morton Culler said, and waited until his colleagues nodded in agreement. Disagreements having been aired, the consensus decision was joined. They all understood the significance of the order. The Alpha squad was composed of trained killers, equally skilled at sniper fire and hand-to-hand combat. To mobilize them against someone was to impose an almost certain death sentence.

"Good *Christ*. Wanted dead or alive," Lanchester said grimly. "It's uncomfortably like the Old West."

"We're all conscious of your *sensitivities,* sir," Culler said, his voice betraying a hint of sarcasm. "But this is the only way to handle it. Too many lives are at stake. He would have killed you in an instant if he judged that it suited his purposes, *sir.* For all we know, he may still try."

Lanchester nodded slowly, looking pensive. "This isn't a decision to be made lightly. It may be that my judgment has been impaired by my personal encounter. And I have to worry that—"

"You're doing the right thing, sir," Culler said quickly. "Let's just hope we're not too late."

CHAPTER NINETEEN

The nightclub was hidden on a tiny *pereulok*, an alley off Tversky Bul'var, near Moscow's Ring Road. It was truly concealed, like some speakeasy in 1920s America. Unlike an illicit liquor joint of Prohibition days, though, the Blackbird was secreted away not from the eyes of government liquor authorities but from the riffraff, the masses. For the Blackbird was meant to be a private oasis of wealth and vice for the elite, the select: the rich, the beautiful, and the heavily armed.

It was located in a shambling brick structure that looked like the abandoned factory it was: in pre-Revolutionary times, Singer sewing machines had been manufactured here. Its windows were blacked out, and there was a single door, of black-painted wood, though with steel-plate reinforcement, and on the door, in peeling, antique Cyrillic letters, were the Russian words *Shveiniye Mashini:* Sewing Machines. The only indication that anything was to be found within was the long line of black Mercedes limousines extending down the narrow alley, looking out of place, as if they had all somehow ended up in the wrong place, the whole lot of them.

Shortly after arriving at Sheremetyevo-2 Airport, and then, for appearance's sake, checking into the Intourist Hotel with the rest of his raggedy tour group, Bryson had placed a call to an old friend. Thirty minutes later a midnight-blue Mercedes sedan had pulled up in front of the Intourist, and a uniformed driver ushered him into the backseat of the car, where a single envelope had been placed.

It was twilight, but the traffic along Tverskaya Ulitsa was heavy, the drivers manic, changing lanes abruptly, ignoring any rules of the road, even driving up on the sidewalk in order to pass slower-moving vehicles. Russia had gone mad, chaotic and furious, since Bryson had last been there. Though much of the old architecture remained in place—the wedding-cake Stalinist Gothic skyscrapers and the mammoth Central Telegraph facility; a sprinkling of the old shops, like Yeliseyevsky's food emporium and the Aragvi, once the only decent restaurant in town—there were incredible changes. High-priced shops glittered along the once-somber avenue that had been, before the collapse of the Communist state, Gorky Street: Versace, Van Cleef & Arpels, Vacheron Constantin, Tiffany. Yet along with the visible signs of plutocratic wealth were evidence of far-reaching poverty, of a social system that had broken down. Soldiers openly begged for alms, *babushki* sold moonshine or fruits and vegetables, or else they pleaded with you to tell you your fortune for a few rubles. Peroxide hookers were more brazenly in evidence than ever before.

Bryson got out of the chauffeured sedan, took the small plastic card from the envelope that had been left for him, and inserted it in a slot like that of an automatic teller mounted on the splintering wooden door, the card's magnetized strip facing out. The door buzzed open, and he entered a completely dark area. Once the door had closed behind him, he felt around for the second door, which the driver had told him, in barely serviceable English, would be there. Grasping the cold steel knob, he pulled the next door open, revealing the bizarre, garish world within.

Purple and red and blue beams of light floated and rippled on clouds of white fog and bounced off alabaster Greek columns and plaster Roman statuaries, black marble counters and high stainless-steel stools. Spotlights spun from high above in the dark recesses of what had once been the factory floor. Rock music of a sort Bryson had never heard before, a kind of Russian techno-pop, thundered at earsplitting volume. The odor of marijuana mingled with strong, expensive French perfume and bad Russian aftershave.

He paid his admission fee, the equivalent of $250, and sidled through a dense, gyrating crowd of mobsters in gold chains and huge, gaudy Rolexes who were somehow talking on cell phones over the deafening music, accompanied by their molls and other women who were either hookers or trying to look like them, in low-cut tops and short-hemmed skirts that left nothing to the imagination. Burly, shaven-headed bodyguards glowered; the club's security guards skulked around the periphery, uniformed like ninjas in black fatigues with billy clubs. High above the pulsating, spastic throng was a glass-and-steel gallery, where spectators could watch, through a glass floor, the cavorting below, as if it were some exotic, otherworldly terrarium.

He climbed the steel spiral staircase to the gallery, which was revealed to be another world entirely. The chief attraction on this level were the strippers, mostly platinum blond, though a few of them were ebony-skinned, their outsized busts all obviously silicone-enhanced. They danced under bright spotlights, positioned throughout the gallery.

A hostess in a filmy, revealing outfit, wearing a telephone headset, stopped him; she spoke a few, quick words in Russian. Bryson replied wordlessly by slipping her a few twenty-dollar bills, and she escorted him to a steel-and-black-leather banquette.

As soon as he was seated, a waiter brought several trays of *zakuski,* Russian appetizers: pickled beef tongue with horseradish sauce, red and black caviar and blini, mushrooms in aspic, pickled vegetables, herring. Though Bryson was hungry, none of it looked particularly appetizing. A bottle of Dom Perignon appeared—"compliments of your host," the waiter explained. Bryson sat alone, watching the crowd, for a few more minutes until he spotted the elegant, slim figure of Yuri Tarnapolsky gliding toward the table, both hands extended in exuberant welcome. Tarnapolsky seemed to have materialized out of nowhere, though Bryson now realized that the wily ex-KGB man had in fact entered the gallery from the kitchen.

"Welcome to Russia, my dear Coleridge!" Yuri Tarnapolsky exulted. Bryson stood, and the two embraced.

Although Tarnapolsky had chosen an unlikely venue for their rendezvous, he was a man of exquisite and very expensive tastes. As usual, the ex–KGB agent was impeccably dressed in an English bespoke suit and foulard tie. It had been seven years since he and Bryson had worked together, and though Tarnapolsky was now well into his fifties, his tanned face was smooth and unlined. The Russian had always taken good care of himself, but he appeared to have been the beneficiary of some high-priced cosmetic surgery.

"You look younger than ever," said Bryson.

"Yes, well, money can buy anything," replied Tarnapolsky, sardonic and amused as ever. He gestured for the waiter to pour the Dom Perignon, along with small glasses of Georgian wine, a white Tsinandali and a red Khvanchkara. As Tarnapolsky raised his glass in a toast, a stripper approached the table; Yuri slid a few crisp, large-denomination ruble notes into her G-string and politely urged her in the direction of a table of dark-suited businessmen.

He and Bryson had worked a number of extremely sensitive jobs together, which Tarnapolsky had always found highly lucrative; the Vector operation had only been the most recent. International arms-inspections teams had been unable to find evidence to support the rumors that Moscow was illegally producing bioweapons. Whenever the inspectors made "surprise," unannounced visits to the Vector laboratory facilities, they turned up nothing. Their "surprise" visits were no surprise. So the Directorate controllers had instructed Bryson that in order to get hard evidence of Russian work in germ warfare, he would need to break into Vector's central laboratory in Novosibirsk. As resourceful as Bryson was, that was a daunting proposition. He needed assistance on the ground, and the name of Yuri Tarnapolsky had come up. Tarnapolsky had recently retired from the KGB and was in the private sector, meaning that he was for sale to the highest bidder.

Tarnapolsky had proved to be worth every kopek of his exorbitant fee. He had obtained for Bryson the blueprints of the laboratory facility, even arranged for the street sentry to be diverted to a "reported burglary" at the residence of the chairman of the city's governing council. Using his KGB identification to browbeat and intimidate the institute's internal security guards, Tarnapolsky had gotten Bryson into the third-containment-level refrigerated tanks, where Bryson was able to locate the ampules he needed. Then Tarnapolsky had arranged to have the ampules spirited out of the country by a circuitous route, concealed in a shipment of frozen lamb en route to Cuba. Bryson, and the Directorate, had thereby been able to prove what dozens of arms inspectors could not: that Vector, and therefore Russia, was involved in making biological weapons. They had the irrefutable proof in the form of seven ampules of weaponized anthrax, an extraordinarily rare strain.

At the time Bryson had been pleased with his success, with the ingenuity of the operation, and indeed, he had been highly lauded by Ted Waller. But the news from Geneva of the sudden outbreak of a rare strain of anthrax—precisely the same strain that he had pilfered from Novosibirsk—had now turned everything inside out. Now he felt sickened by the way he had been manipulated. There could be little question that the anthrax he had stolen years earlier had just been used in the Geneva attack.

Tarnapolsky smiled broadly at him. "You are enjoying our black-skinned beauties from Cameroon?" he inquired.

"I'm sure you understand the importance of telling no one about my visit," said Bryson, struggling to make himself heard over the cacophony.

Tarnapolsky shrugged, as if to say the question need not have been raised. "My friend, we all have our secrets. I have a few of my own, as you might imagine. But if you are in town, may I assume you are not here to take in the sights— unlike the rest of your group?"

Bryson explained the nature of the delicate operation for which he wished to hire Tarnapolsky. As soon as Bryson uttered the name Prishnikov, however, the KGB man's composure was quite clearly disturbed.

"Coleridge, my dear, I am not one to look a gift horse, as you say, in the mouth. As you know, I have always enjoyed our joint ventures." He gave Bryson a somber, even shaken, look. "The prime minister one fears less. You see, there are stories about this man. This is not an American-style businessman, this you must understand. When you are 'downsized' by Anatoly Prishnikov, you do not collect welfare checks. No, you are far more likely to end up as part of the cement that one of his companies manufactures. Perhaps you will end up as a component of the pigment in the lipstick another one of his companies sells. Do you know what you call a gangster who has, through graft and extortion, acquired ownership of large sectors of your country's industry?" Tarnapolsky gave a wan smile and answered his own question. "You call him CEO."

Bryson nodded. "A difficult target deserves handsome remuneration."

Tarnapolsky sidled close to Bryson in the banquette. "Coleridge, my friend, Anatoly Prishnikov is a dangerous and ruthless man. I am sure he has his confederates in this very club, if he doesn't own it outright."

"I understand, Yuri. But you are not a man to shy from a challenge, as I recall. Perhaps we can work something out to our mutual satisfaction."

Over the next several hours, at the Blackbird and then continuing at Tarnapolsky's immense apartment on Sadovo-Samotechnaya, the two men worked out both the financial terms and the highly complex arrangements. The assistance of two others would be required, and Tarnapolsky would supply them. "To get to Anatoly Prishnikov, blood will certainly be shed," Tarnapolsky warned. "And who's to say that some of it will not be our own, hmm?"

By the early hours of the morning, they had devised a plan.

They had given up on any direct approach to Prishnikov, who was far too well defended, far too dangerous a target. The point of vulnerability, Tarnapolsky concluded, after making a few highly discreet telephone calls to former KGB colleagues, was Prishnikov's senior deputy, a small, weedy man named Dmitri Labov. Prishnikov's longtime lieutenant, Dmitri Labov was known in certain circles as *chelovek kotory khranit sekrety*—the man who keeps the secrets.

But even Labov would hardly be a simple target. Tarna-polsky's research had determined that the deputy was driven every day between his heavily guarded residence and the heavily guarded Nortek office, in suburban Moscow near the old Exhibition of Economic Achievements of the USSR on Prospekt Mira.

Labov's chauffeured vehicle was a bullet- and bomb-resistant Bentley—there were, Bryson knew, no truly bullet-proof or bomb-proof vehicles—with almost two tons of armoring on the chassis. It was practically a tank, a Level IV armored vehicle, the highest level of protection that ex-ists, capable of withstanding super-powered military ammu-nition including 7.62 NATO rounds.

During stints in Mexico City and South America, he had acquired a familiarity with such fully armored vehicles. They were usually fabricated with a quarter-inch of 2024-T3 alu-minum as well as a high-performance synthetic composite, typically aramid and ultrahigh-molecular-weight poly-ethylene. Mounted inside the 19-gauge steel car doors would be a 24-ply sheet of high-strength fiberglass-reinforced plas-tic, half an inch thick, capable of stopping a .30-carbine slug fired from five feet away. The glass would be a polycarbon-ate/glass laminate; the fuel tank would be self-sealing, an-tiexplosive even when directly hit; a special dry-cell battery would keep the engine running after an attack. "Run-flat" tires would enable getaways at high speeds for up to fifty miles even when the tires were shot through by gunfire.

Labov's Bentley would have been modified specifically for Moscow, where gangs were likely to use AK-47 assault rifles. It would probably also be able to withstand grenades and small pipe bombs, probably even armor-piercing am-munition, high-velocity, full-metal-jacket rounds.

But there were always vulnerabilities.

For one, there was the driver, who was probably not pro-fessionally trained. For some reason, the Russian plutocrats tended to use their own personal assistants as drivers, not trusting professional ones and not bothering to have them trained in something they probably considered common sense, though it was not.

And there was one more vulnerability—around which Bryson had devised his plan.

Every morning at exactly seven o'clock in the morning Dmitri Labov left his apartment building just off the Arbat, a very exclusive, recently renovated nineteenth-century building that had once been reserved for ranking Central Committee officials and Politburo members. The apartment complex, now home to Russia's nouveaux riches, mostly *mafiya,* was sealed off and well guarded.

This consistency in schedule, the information obtained by Tarnapolsky, was an example of the slipshod security combined with flamboyantly showy protective measures that was peculiar to large-scale criminal enterprises, Bryson had learned. Security professionals knew the importance of varying their charges' schedules, ensuring that nothing was predictable.

Just as Tarnapolsky had been informed, Labov's Bentley pulled out of the newly built underground parking garage beneath Labov's apartment building and traveled a short distance before pulling onto Kalinin Prospekt. Bryson and Tarnapolsky, in a nondescript Volga, tailed the Bentley as it traveled the Ring Road all the way to Prospekt Mira. Shortly after the Bentley had passed the titanium-clad Sputnik obelisk, which soared majestically into the sky, it turned left onto Eizensteina Ulitsa, then proceeded three more blocks to the refurbished baronial palace that provided the headquarters for Nortek. There, Labov's car entered another underground parking garage.

It would remain there for the entire day.

The only somewhat unpredictable element to Labov's schedule concerned the time of his return home. He had a wife and three children and was known to be a family man who never missed dinner at home unless there was an emergency at work or Prishnikov summoned him back in. Most days, however, his limousine left the Nortek garage by seven or seven-fifteen in the evening.

This evening, Labov was clearly intent on getting home in time for dinner with the family. At five minutes after seven o'clock, his Bentley emerged from the Nortek garage. Tarnapolsky and Bryson were waiting, in a grimy white package-delivery panel truck across the street, and Tarnapolsky immediately radioed ahead to his confederate. The timing would be tight, but it should be manageable. Most important, it was still rush hour in this congested city.

Tarnapolsky, who had spent years in the early part of his career tailing dissidents and petty criminals around Moscow, knew the city intimately. He drove, following the Bentley at a discreet distance, only pulling up fairly close when the traffic was heavy enough to provide cover.

When the Bentley turned left onto Kalinin Prospekt, it ran into a serious traffic jam. A large truck was jackknifed and stalled across all lanes of traffic, halting all cars in either direction. Truck horns blared, car horns honked repeatedly; there were loud shouts as frustrated drivers stuck their heads out of their car windows to hurl epithets at the obstruction. But there was nothing to be done; the traffic was frozen.

The filthy white panel truck was stopped immediately ahead of Labov's Bentley, cars hemming them in on all sides. Tarnapolsky's confederate had abandoned his eighteen-wheeler truck, taking the keys with him, on the pretense of searching for help. Traffic would not move for a good long while.

Bryson, dressed in black jeans and a black turtleneck and wearing black leather gloves, crouched on the floor inside the truck and released the hinged trapdoor. There was enough clearance to the ground that he was able to drop to the pavement and belly under the panel truck and then under Labov's Bentley. In the extremely unlikely event that traffic somehow was able to move a few feet, the Bentley could not, since it was blocked by the delivery truck.

Moving quickly, his heart racing, Bryson slid under the Bentley's chassis until he located the precise spot he was looking for. Although the undercarriage was mostly one solid mass of molded steel, aluminum, and polyethylene, there was a small perforated area where the air-intake filter was located. This was the second vulnerability: after all, even passengers of armored vehicles had to breathe. Swiftly, he pressed an adhesive-backed aluminum-alloy filter panel over the vent, a specially designed, radio-controlled device Tarnapolsky had been able to acquire from contacts in the private-security industry in Moscow. Once he assured himself it was securely in place, he wriggled out from under the car and, still undetected, back under the panel truck, the hinged trapdoor still open. He lifted himself up and into the truck and shut the trapdoor behind him.

"*Nu, khorosho?*" asked Tarnapolsky. Everything okay?

"*Ladno,*" replied Bryson. It's fine.

Tarnapolsky called the driver of the jackknifed truck, ordering him to return to his abandoned truck and get it moving again, just as police sirens began to sound.

Traffic started moving a few minutes later, the blaring horns stopped, the cursing came to an end. The Bentley roared ahead, gunning its engine, passing the paneled delivery truck as it resumed its course down Kalinin Prospekt. Then it made its customary left turn, onto the quiet side street, essentially retracing its morning path.

It was then that Bryson pressed the switch on the transmitter he gripped in his hand. As Tarnapolsky maneuvered down the street after the Bentley, they could see an immediate reaction. The limousine cabin filled at once with thick, white tear gas. The Bentley veered crazily from one side to another before pulling over to the side of the deserted street; the driver had obviously been overcome. Both front and back doors of the limousine were flung open as both driver and Labov emerged, coughing and retching, hands pressed over their stinging eyes. The driver clutched a handgun uselessly at his side. Yuri Tarnapolsky veered the truck over to the side of the road as well, and the two men jumped out. Bryson fired a projectile at the driver, who toppled at once. The short-acting tranquilizer dart would knock him out for hours;

the amnesiac effect of the narcotic would ensure that he had little or no recollection of the evening's events. Then Bryson rushed over to Labov, who had collapsed on the sidewalk, coughing and temporarily blinded. Meanwhile, Tarnapolsky hoisted the driver back into the driver's seat of the Bentley. Taking out a bottle of cheap vodka he had bought on the street, he spilled a good quantity into the chauffeur's mouth and over his uniform, leaving the half-filled bottle on the seat beside him.

Bryson looked around to confirm that there was no one on the street who could see what they were doing; then he hustled Labov, half-dragging the small man, into the nondescript panel truck, a boxy vehicle like hundreds in the area, which would never be identified, particularly since its license plates, covered in mud, were illegible.

By just before eight o'clock in the evening, Dmitri Labov was bound, in a seated position, to a hard metal chair in a large deserted warehouse in the Cheryomushki district, not far from the wholesale fruit-and-vegetable market. The city government had confiscated it from a Tatar clan that had been caught selling produce on the black market to restaurants without paying the requisite tribute to city officials.

Labov was small and bespectacled, with receding, straw-colored hair and a round, pudgy face. Bryson stood before him and spoke in perfect Russian with a slight St. Petersburg accent, the legacy of his Directorate Russian-language tutor. "Your dinner is getting cold. We'd love to get you home before your wife gets frantic. In fact, if you play your cards right and cooperate fully, no one ever has to know you were abducted."

"What?" spat Labov. "You deceive yourself. Everyone already knows. My driver—"

"Your driver is passed out in the front seat of your limousine, parked by the side of the road. Any passing *militsiya* will simply assume he's dozing, drunk like half of Moscow."

"If you plan to drug me, go ahead," Labov said, at once frightened and defiant. "If you plan to torture me, go ahead.

Or just go ahead and kill me. If you dare. Do you have any *idea* who I am?"

"Of course," said Bryson. "That's why you're here."

"Do you have any idea what the consequences will be? Do you *know* whose wrath you are incurring?"

Bryson nodded slowly.

"Anatoly Prishnikov's anger knows no bounds! It is not impeded by national borders!"

"Mr. Labov, please understand, I wouldn't think of harming a hair on your head. Or that of your wife, Masha. Or little Irushka. I won't have to—there'll be nothing left of them after Prishnikov is through."

"What the fuck are you saying?" Labov shouted, red-faced.

"Let me explain," Bryson said patiently. "Tomorrow morning I will personally drive you to Nortek headquarters. You may still be a little woozy from the tranquilizers, but I will help you into the building. And then I will leave. But everything will be recorded on the security cameras. Then your boss will become extremely interested in who I am, and why you were in my company. You will tell him that you told me nothing." Bryson paused. "But do you think he will believe you?"

Outraged, Labov screamed, "I have been a loyal aide to him for twenty years! I have been nothing but loyal!"

"I don't doubt that. But can Anatoly Prishnikov afford to believe you? I ask you—you know him better than anyone. You know what kind of man he is, how deep-rooted is his suspicion."

Labov had begun to tremble.

"And if Prishnikov thought that there was even the slightest chance that you had betrayed him, how long do you think he would let you live?"

Labov shook his head, his eyes wide with terror.

"Let me answer my own question. He would let you live just long enough to know that your loved ones had died horribly. Long enough for you and everyone in the firm to be reminded of the price of betrayal—of *weakness*."

Yuri Tarnapolsky, who had been watching from the sidelines, stroking his chin idly, put in: "You remember poor Maksimov."

"Maksimov was a traitor!"

"Not according to Maksimov," Tarnapolsky said gently. He toyed with his service revolver, polishing its barrel with a soft white handkerchief. "Do you know he and Olga had an infant son? One would think that Prishnikov would spare the young and the innocent—"

"No! *Stop!*" gasped Labov, ashen-faced. He was having difficulty breathing. "I know much less—much less than you must think. There is a great deal I don't know."

"Please," said Bryson warningly. "Evasion will simply waste our time and will add to the length of time you are gone—the period of missing time you must somehow account for. I want to know about Prishnikov's alliance with Jacques Arnaud."

"There are so many deals, so many arrangements. They accelerate. There are more than ever now."

"Why?"

"I think he is preparing for something."

"For what?"

"Once, I heard him speaking on his secure phone to Arnaud and saying something about the 'Prometheus Group.'"

The name chimed in Bryson's head. He had heard it before. Yes! Jan Vansina had used the phrase in Geneva, wondering whether he was "with the Prometheans."

"What is the Prometheus Group?" Bryson demanded urgently.

"Prometheus—you have no idea. No one has any idea. I hardly know. They are powerful—immensely powerful. It is not clear to me whether Prishnikov follows their orders, or whether he gives them orders."

"Who are 'they'?"

"They are important, powerful people—"

"You've said that already. *Who are they?*"

"They are everywhere—and nowhere. Their names are not to be found on mastheads, on letterheads, on papers of incorporation. But Tolya—Prishnikov is among them, this I am sure of."

"Arnaud is one of them," prompted Bryson.

"Yes."

"Who else?"

Labov shook his head in defiance. "You know, if you kill me, Prishnikov will leave my family alone," he said reasonably. "Why don't you kill me?"

Tarnapolsky looked over, a wry smile on his face. "Do you know how they found Maksimov's child, Labov?" He approached Labov, still menacingly polishing his revolver with the handkerchief.

Labov jerked his head back and forth like a child unwilling to listen. Had his hands been free he would surely have clapped them over his ears. Quivering, he blurted out, "The Jade Master! He is making arrangements with . . . with the man they call the Jade Master."

Tarnapolsky gave Bryson a sharp look. They both knew whom the moniker referred to. The so-called Jade Master was a powerful general in the Chinese military, the People's Liberation Army. General Tsai, based in Shenzhen, was famously corrupt and had facilitated the efforts of certain international conglomerates to establish a foothold in the immense Chinese market—in exchange, of course, for certain considerations. General Tsai was also world-renowned as a collector of precious imperial Chinese jade and was known to sometimes accept blandishments in the form of valuable jade carvings.

Labov saw the look between the two men. "I don't know what you hope to accomplish," he said contemptuously. "Everything is about to change, and you cannot stop it."

Bryson turned back to Labov quizzically. "What do you mean, 'everything is about to change'?" he demanded.

"Days remain—only days," Labov said cryptically. "Only a few days I am given to prepare."

"To prepare *what*?"

"The machinery has already been put into place. Now

power is about to be transferred fully! Everything will come into view."

Tarnapolsky finished polishing his revolver, pocketed the handkerchief, and then pointed the gun a few inches away from Labov's face. "Are you referring to a coup d'etat?"

Bryson interrupted, "But Prishnikov is already the power behind the throne in Russia! Why the hell would he want something like that?"

Labov laughed dismissively. "Coup d'etat! How little you know! How narrow is your view! We Russians have always been happy to give up our freedom for safety and security. You will, too, all of you. Every last one. For now the forces are too great. The machinery is already in place. Everything is about to come into view!"

"What the hell are you talking about?" thundered Bryson. "Prishnikov and his colleagues—do they now aspire higher than the corporate world—do they aim to take over governments now, is that it? Have they become besotted with their own wealth and power?"

"We would appreciate some specifics, my friend," Tarnapolsky said, lowering his revolver, the threat no longer necessary.

"Governments? Governments are outdated! Look at Russia—what kind of power has the government? None! The government is powerless. It's the corporations that make the rules now! Maybe Lenin was right after all—it *is* the capitalists who control the world!"

Suddenly, with the speed of a cobra, Labov's right hand lunged out a few inches, the maximum play allowed by the constraints. It was just enough for him to grab Tarnapolsky's revolver, which was almost next to him. Tarnapolsky reacted swiftly, grabbing Labov's hand, twisting it hard to loosen Labov's grip on the revolver. For a moment, the gun was pointing upward and back, right at Labov's own face. Labov seemed to be staring at the muzzle, hypnotized by it, a strange, sweet smile on his face. Then, just before Tarnapolsky was able to wrench it away, Labov pointed it between his own eyes and squeezed the trigger.

CHAPTER TWENTY

The suicide of Anatoly Prishnikov's longtime aide-de-camp was a grim turn of events; Labov may have been a ruthless corporate functionary, the fax and the phone his deadly weapons, but he was no killer, and his death had meant the shedding of unnecessary blood. More than that, it was a complication, a deviation from their carefully laid-out plan.

Labov's driver would return to consciousness within the hour; whether or not he would have any specific recall of the Bentley filling with tear gas, his memory would be disjointed, hazy. He would awake to find his uniform reeking of cheap vodka, a bottle on the seat beside him, his passenger and charge gone; he would panic. No doubt he would place a call to Labov's home; that angle had to be covered as well.

Among the papers in Dmitri Labov's wallet, Yuri Tarnapolsky had turned up Labov's home phone number. From his cell phone—Moscow these days seemed to be overrun with mobile phones, Bryson had noticed—Tarnapolsky then placed a quick call to Masha, Labov's wife.

"*Gospozha* Labova," he said in the obsequious tones of a low-level office functionary, "this is Sasha from the office. Sorry for the interruption, but Dmitri wanted me to call to say he'll be somewhat delayed, he's on an urgent phone call to France that can't be interrupted, and he sends his apologies." Lowering his voice, he added confidentially, "It's just as well, since his regular driver seems to have hit the bottle again." He gave an aggrieved sigh. "Which means I'll have to make alternative arrangements. Ah, well. Good evening." And he hung up before the wife could ask any questions. It would do; such delays were unavoidable in Labov's line of work. When and if the chauffeur called in a state of agitation and disorientation, the wife would respond with anger or annoyance and would dismiss him at once.

All this was reasonably straightforward. Labov's suicide,

however, was a loose end that had to be tied up as best they could. Bryson and Tarnapolsky were limited in what they could do, because the ex-KGB man was absolutely unwilling to place any calls to the Nortek office; assuming that all calls incoming or outgoing were recorded, he did not want a tape of his voice to be found. A solution had to be quickly improvised, an explanation for the suicide that might be accepted without too much follow-up investigation. It was Tarnapolsky who came up with the idea of planting various suspect items on Labov's person and in his briefcase: a package of Vigor brand Russian-made condoms, a few soiled, dog-eared cards from less-than-reputable Moscow clubs known for the sexual hijinks that took place in private back rooms—Tarnapolsky had a small collection of such *cartes de visite*—and, the crowning touch, a half-used tube of ointment customarily used to treat the topical manifestation of certain more benign sexually communicable diseases. Quite likely such escapades were entirely alien to such a proper, work-oriented man as Labov; but it was precisely such a man who might react so violently to finding himself in the middle of a sordid embarrassment. Alcohol, tawdry sex: these were normal, everyday vices.

Now it was a race: against time, against the likelihood that, one way or another, Prishnikov would learn that Nortek had been penetrated. Far too much could go wrong, Bryson knew. Labov's limousine, with its semiconscious driver, could be identified by a vigilant *militsiyoner* and reported to Nortek headquarters. Labov's wife could call his office back, for one reason or another. The risks were enormous, and Prishnikov would be quick to react. Bryson had to get out of Russia as soon as possible.

Tarnapolsky drove his Audi at top speed to Vnukovo Airport, thirty kilometers southwest of Moscow. This was one of Russia's domestic airports, serving all regions of the country but particularly the south. He had arranged with one of the new private aviation firms for an emergency, late-night flight to Baku for one of his wealthy clients, a businessman

with extensive financial interests in Azerbaijan. Tarnapolsky
had not gone into detail, of course, except to mention a sudden eruption of labor unrest at a factory, the factory director
taken hostage. Given the suddenness of the booking, a substantial outlay of cash was required. Bryson had it, and was
glad to pay it. Customs Control had to be paid off, as well,
for expedited paperwork; this required another hefty sum.

"Yuri," said Bryson, "what's in it for Prishnikov?"

"You're talking about the Jade Master, I take it. Yes?"

"Yes. I know you're well versed in the Chinese military,
the PLA—you did your time in the KGB's China sector. So
what exactly would Prishnikov hope to gain from establish-
ing an alliance with General Tsai?"

"You heard what Labov said, my friend. Governments are
powerless now. It's the corporations that make the rules. If
you're an ambitious titan like Prishnikov and you want to
control half of the world's markets, there are few better partners than the Jade Master. He's a ranking member of the
PLA's General Staff, the one most responsible for turning
the People's Liberation Army into one of the world's largest
corporations, and the man in charge of all of its commercial
ventures."

"Such as?"

"The Chinese military controls an astonishingly complex
web of businesses, interlocking enterprises, vertically integrated. I mean, from automobile factories to airlines, from
pharmaceuticals to telecommunications. Their real-estate
holdings are vast—they own hotels all over Asia, including
Beijing's showpiece, the Palace Hotel. They own and operate
most of China's airports."

"But I thought the Chinese government had begun cracking down on the military—that the Chinese premier issued
an executive decree ordering the army to begin divesting
itself of all its businesses."

"Oh, Beijing tried, but the genie was already out of the
bottle. What do you Americans say, the toothpaste was out
of the tube? Perhaps it is better to talk of Pandora's box. The

fact is, it was too late. The PLA has become the most powerful force in China by far."

"But haven't the Chinese slashed their defense budget a number of times in recent years?"

Tarnapolsky snorted. "And then all the PLA has to do is go out and sell a few weapons of mass destruction to rogue nations. It's like having a bake sale, or do you call it a yard sale? My dear Coleridge, the PLA's economic might is simply beyond imagining. Now they've begun to recognize the strategic importance of telecom. They own and launch satellites; they own China's largest telecommunications company; they've been working with the giants of the West—Lucent, Motorola, Qualcomm, Systematix, Nortel—to develop immense mobile phone and paging networks, information systems. It is said that the PLA now owns the skies over China. And the one true owner, the man in charge, the man behind it all—is the Jade Master. General Tsai."

As Tarnapolsky's Audi pulled up to the airstrip, Bryson saw a small plane, a brand-new Yakovlev-112, waiting on the runway. He could see at once that it was a single-engine prop four-seater. It was tiny, surely the smallest craft in the company's fleet.

Tarnapolsky saw Bryson's surprise. "Believe me, my friend, this was the best I could do on such notice. There are far bigger, far nicer planes—they mentioned their YAK-40, their Antonov-26—but all were in use."

"It'll do, Yuri. Thanks. I owe you."

"Let's just call it a business gift. . . ."

Bryson cocked his head. He heard the squealing of brakes not far off; when he turned to look, he saw a massive, wide Humvee, black and glossy, roaring down the airstrip toward them.

"What the hell is this?" exclaimed Yuri. The Humvee's doors flew open, and three black-clad men jumped out, wearing black face masks and the black Kevlar-and-nylon garb of commandos.

"Get down!" shouted Bryson. "Shit! We have no *weapons!*"

Tarnapolsky, diving to the floor of the Audi, pulled out a
tray mounted under the front seat. It held several weapons
and piles of ammunition. Yuri handed Bryson a Makarov
9mm automatic pistol, then pulled out a large Kalashnikov
Bizon submachine gun, a Russian Spetsnaz weapon. There
was a sudden hail of bullets, and the Audi's windscreen
turned white with starburst cracks. The glass, Bryson realized, was at least partially bullet-resistant. He crouched
down. "This car isn't armored, is it?"

"Light," replied the KGB man as he shouldered the
weapon and took a deep, slow breath. "Level One. Use the
doors."

Bryson nodded; he understood. The doors were reinforced
with either high-strength fiberglass or a synthetic composite,
meaning he could use them as shields.

Another burst of ammunition, and the commandos, visible
through the side window, assumed firing stance. "Special delivery from Prishnikov," Tarnapolsky said, almost under his
breath.

"The wife called," Bryson said, the instant he realized it.
But how did Prishnikov know where to dispatch his commandos? Perhaps the answer was simple: the fastest way out
of Russia was by air, and anyone foolish enough to take
down Prishnikov's most valued assistant had better escape
the country without delay. Moreover, there were just a few
airports near Moscow, only two of them having the facilities
to handle private planes. A last-minute booking, made urgently . . . Prishnikov had made a calculated guess, and he
had guessed right.

Tarnapolsky sprang his door open, sprang to the ground,
crouching behind it, and fired off a burst of machine-gun
fire. *"Yob tvoyu mat!"* he growled: Fuck your mother.

One of the marksmen fell, taken out by Tarnapolsky.

"Good shot," Bryson said. A line of shots moved across
the opaque-white windshield, spraying tiny pebbles of tem-
pered glass at Bryson's face. He unlatched the car door on
his side, got directly behind it, and fired off a few rounds at
the two remaining commandos. At the same time, Tarnapol-

sky got off another burst of fire, and a second man sprawled to the paved landing strip.

One more remained—but where?

Bryson and Tarnapolsky scanned the dark field on either side, searching for movement. The landing lights illuminated the blacktop but not the surrounding fields, where the third man had to be concealed, lying in wait, weapon at the ready.

Tarnapolsky fired off a round at what appeared to be movement, but there was no response. He stood up, wheeled around, aiming the Bizon toward the dark area on the other side of the landing strip, nearest Bryson.

Where the hell was he?

Prishnikov's men were surely outfitted with rubber-soled boots, enabling them to move silently, stealthily. Gripping the Makarov in both hands, he moved it around in a slow circuit, starting from his far right and moving steadily counterclockwise.

By the time he saw the tiny, dancing red dot on the back of Tarnapolsky's head, it was too late for Bryson to do anything but cry out.

"Get down!" he shouted.

But an exploding bullet had entered Yuri Tarnapolsky's head, blowing his face off.

"Oh, *Christ!*" Bryson shouted in horror as he spun around. He caught a flicker of reflected light, saw a tiny movement on or near the plane, several hundred feet away. The third sniper had positioned himself against the aircraft, using it as protection. Bryson repositioned the Makarov, exhaled slowly, and squeezed off one precisely aimed shot.

There was a distant cry, the clatter of a weapon on the tarmac. The third commando, the one who had killed Yuri Ivanovich Tarnapolsky, was dead.

Casting a look back at the corpse of his friend, Bryson leaped out of the Audi and ran toward the plane. Others would be on the way, in greater numbers; his only chance of survival was to get on board the aircraft and pilot it himself.

He ran to the Yakovlev-112, jumped onto the wing, and

swung into the pilot's seat, closing the hatch behind him. He strapped himself in, sat back against the seat, closed his eyes. *Now what?* Flying the plane itself was not a problem; he had sufficient hours in the air and had performed numerous emergency departures in his Directorate years. The problem, instead, would be navigating in Russian air space without clearance, without support from the tower. But what choice was there? Returning to Tarnapolsky's car meant heading back into the jaws of Prishnikov's commandos, and that was not an acceptable option.

He inhaled, held his breath, then turned the ignition key. The engine caught right away. He checked the instruments and began slowly taxiing toward the end of the runway.

He couldn't ignore the tower, he knew. To take off without being in contact with the air-traffic controller was not only risky, even potentially fatal, but it would be viewed by the Russian Air Force as a deliberate provocation. Measures would be taken.

He keyed the microphone and spoke in English, the language spoken by international flight controllers. "Vnukovo Clearance, Yakovlev-112, RossTran three niner niner foxtrot. Number one for runway three, straight-out departure. Ready for clearance to Baku."

The reply came back after a few seconds, staticky yet brisk: "*Shto?* What? Did not copy, say again."

"RossTran three niner niner foxtrot," he repeated. "Ready for departure via Vnukovo three, ready to taxi."

"You have no flight plan, RossTran three nine nine!"

Undeterred, Bryson persisted. "Vnukovo Ground, Ross-Tran three niner niner foxtrot, ready for taxi. Climb and maintain ten thousand. Expect flight level two hundred fifty ten minutes after departure. Departure frequency one-one-eight point five five. Squawk four six three seven."

"RossTran, hold, I repeat, hold! You have no authorization!"

"Vnukovo Ground, I'm flying certain high-ranking Nortek executives on an emergency visit to Baku," he said, assuming the characteristic above-the-law arrogance of Prishnikov's minions. "The flight plans should have been filed. You have my serial number; you can call Dmitri Labov to verify."

"RossTran—"

"Anatoly Prishnikov would be *extremely* unhappy to learn that you are interfering with the administration of his businesses. Perhaps, Comrade Air Traffic controller, you could tell me *your* name and identification."

There was a pause, several seconds of radio silence. "Go ahead," the voice snapped. "Fly at your own risk."

Bryson applied the throttle, accelerated toward the end of the runway, and the plane lifted off.

CHAPTER TWENTY-ONE

Monsignor Lorenzo Battaglia, Ph.D.—senior curator at the Chiaramonti Museum, one of the many specialized collections within the Monumenti Musei e Gallerie Pontifice, the Vatican museums, in the Citta del Vaticano—had not seen Giles Hesketh-Haywood for many years, and he wasn't exactly overjoyed to see him again.

The two men were meeting in a magnificent, damask-walled reception room off the Galleria Lapidaria. Monsignor Battaglia had been a curator at the Vatican museums for twenty years, and his connoisseurship was respected around the world. Giles Hesketh-Haywood, his effete English visitor, had always struck him as a faintly absurd, even comical, creature, with those oversized round tortoise-shell spectacles, those bright silk neckties that swelled flamboyantly from a very tight knot, the checkered vests, those gold horseshoe cufflinks, the old briar bowl stuck jauntily in his breast pocket, the posh accent. He reeked of golden cavendish tobacco. His charm was boundless, if oily. Hesketh-Haywood was an upper-class twit, in some ways—so *teddibly* English—but his trade was an unsavory one. Ostensibly, he was a dealer in antiquities, but really he was nothing more than a high-end fence.

Hesketh-Haywood, part connoisseur, part out-and-out crook, was the sort of shady fellow who vanishes for years at a time before showing up on the yacht of some Middle Eastern oil sheik. Though he was steadfastly vague about his past, the Monsignor had heard all the rumors: that his family was once of the high-living English gentry but fell on hard times in the postwar Laborite era. That Hesketh-Haywood had been educated among the scions of great wealth, but by the time he got out of school, his family had nothing left but a mountain of debt. Giles was a scamp, a rogue, a delight-fully unscrupulous fellow who started out smuggling archaeological antiquities out of Italy, no doubt bribing the export licensing board. He was very gray-market, but some extraordinary artifacts had passed through his hands. If you didn't want to know how they came into his possession, you knew enough not to ask. Men like Hesketh-Haywood were tolerated in the art world only because of those rare occasions on which they could be useful—he had in fact once proved useful to the Monsignor, conducting a certain "transaction" that the Monsignor prayed the world would never learn about—but the cordiality displayed by the Monsignor was now paper-thin. For the favor that Hesketh-Haywood was now asking him was astonishing, appalling.

Monsignor Battaglia closed his eyes for a moment to summon the words he needed, and then he leaned forward and spoke gravely to his visitor. "What you propose is out of the question, Giles. It is far more than a 'prank.' It is an outright scandal."

The Monsignor had never seen Hesketh-Haywood's supreme self-satisfaction waver, and it wasn't wavering now. "A *scandal,* Monsignor?" Giles Hesketh-Haywood's eyes, magnified behind the thick lenses, looked both owlish and amused. "But there are so *many* kinds of scandal, are there not? For instance, the intelligence that a senior Vatican official, a world-renowned expert in the art and artifacts of the ancient world, an ordained *priest* to boot—that this gentleman maintains a mistress on Via Sebastiano Veniero—well, some people aren't quite so enlightened as *we* are about such things, isn't that so?"

The Englishman leaned back in his chair and waggled a long, slender finger in the air. "But it's the *money,* not the women, that may cause the greater dismay. And sweet young Alessandra continues to enjoy her comfortable *demaine,* I trust. Comfortable—some might say *lavish,* especially given the rather modest salary of the Vatican curator who supports her." He sighed, shook his head contentedly. "But I like to think that I've made my contribution to that worthy cause."

Monsignor Battaglia could feel his face turn red. A vein on his temple started to throb.

"Perhaps there is an accommodation that we might reach," Battaglia said at last.

Those thick-lensed round spectacles were starting to give Bryson a splitting headache, but at least he had achieved what he'd come to Rome to do. He was exhausted, having landed the small plane at an airfield outside of Kiev, safely outside of Russian airspace, and taken two connecting flights on a commercial airliner to Rome. The call he had placed to the Monsignor had been answered right away, as he knew it would be, for the curator was almost always interested in what Giles Hesketh-Haywood had to offer.

Giles Hesketh-Haywood, one of Bryson's many carefully manufactured legends, had often come in useful in his previous career.

As a connoisseur of, and dealer in, antiquities, he naturally had reason to travel to places like Sicily, Egypt, Sudan, Libya, and elsewhere. He deflected suspicion by *prompting* suspicion: an elementary exercise in misdirection. Since alert officials assumed he was a smuggler, it never crossed their minds that he might be a spy. And most of them, of course, were only too happy to accept his bribes: if they didn't, after all, others surely would.

The small item appeared the very next morning in *L'Osservatore Romano,* the official Vatican newspaper, with over five million copies sold worldwide. *OGGETTO SPARITO DAI MUSEI VATICANI?* ITEM STOLEN FROM VATICAN COLLECTION? the headline read.

According to the account, the Vatican museum had discovered, in their annual inventory, that it was missing a rare Sung Dynasty chess set made of carved jade. The exquisite jade set had been brought back from China by Marco Polo in the early fourteenth century and presented to the Doge of Venice. Cesare Borgia acquired the set in 1500, and after his death, it was presented to one of the Medici Popes, Leo X, who cherished it; it even appears in the background of one of his great portraits. In 1549, Pope Paul III used it to play a match against the legendary chess master Paulo Boi and was defeated.

The newspaper article quoted a spokesman for the Vatican museum emphatically denying the charge. At the same time, however, the museum refused to offer proof that it still possessed the rare chess set. There was a brief, indignant quote from senior curator Monsignor Lorenzo Battaglia to the effect that the Vatican museum had hundreds of thousands of distinct items in its catalogs, and that, given the vastness of its holdings, it was inevitable that some objects might be temporarily mislaid; there was no reason in the world to jump to the conclusion that an act of theft had taken place.

Over caffe latté in his suite at the Hassler, Nick Bryson read the piece with professional satisfaction. He hadn't asked that much of the Monsignor. The denials, after all, were true. The legendary Sung Dynasty jade chess set still safely reposed in one of the Vatican's hundreds of storage vaults; like most of the immense Vatican holdings, it was never displayed. It had not been displayed for over forty years, in fact. It had not been stolen—but anybody reading the paper would conclude otherwise.

And Bryson was certain that the right people would be reading this article.

He picked up the phone and called an old acquaintance in Beijing, a Chinese civil servant named Jiang Yingchao, now highly placed in the foreign ministry. Jiang had had dealings with Giles Hesketh-Haywood a decade ago; he recognized Giles's honking tones immediately.

"My English friend," exclaimed Jiang. "What a pleasure it is to hear from you, after so long a silence."

"You know I don't like to impose upon our friendship," Bryson replied. "But I trust our last transaction was . . . helpful to your career. Not that you needed it, of course: your ascent up the ranks of the diplomatic corps has been most impressive."

Giles did not need to remind his Chinese diplomat friend: Jiang had been a low-level cultural attaché in the Chinese embassy in Bonn when he had first been introduced to Giles

Hesketh-Haywood. It was not long after they had lunch together that Giles made good on his promise, obtaining for Jiang an extremely valuable ancient Chinese artifact at a cost that was far below what it would fetch if it ever hit the open market. The miniature, red-pottery walking horse from the Han Dynasty had made a very special gift from Jiang to the ambassador, no doubt greasing the wheels of his career. Over the years, Hesketh-Haywood had furnished a number of priceless objects to his diplomat friend, including ancient bronzes and a Qing Dynasty vase.

"And what have you been up to all these years?" asked the diplomat.

Bryson gave a long, aggrieved sigh. "I'm sure you saw that absolutely *scurrilous* article in *L'Osservatore Romano,*" he remarked.

"No, which article might that be?"

"Oh, dear, forget I even *mentioned* it. Anyway, an *extraordinary* object has just *happened* to fall into my possession, and I thought a *branché* chap such as yourself might know of someone who might be interested in it. I mean, there's a *terribly* long list of extremely interested potential buyers, but just for old times' sake I thought I'd call you first. . . ." He began to describe the jade chess set, but Jiang cut him off.

"I will call you back," Jiang said sharply. "Let me have your number."

There was a delay of half an hour before Jiang Yingchao called on a sterile line. No doubt he had located the Vatican newspaper and then made a few rapid, excited calls first.

"You do understand, my dear fellow, that this isn't the sort of thing that comes up very often," said Giles. "But it's positively frightful how careless some of these great institutions are about their treasures, isn't it? Positively *frightful.*"

"Yes, yes," Jiang interrupted impatiently. "There would be a great deal of interest, I'm sure. If we're talking about the same thing—the Sung Dynasty jade chess set—"

"I'm speaking *hypothetically,* my dear Jiang, of course. You do realize that. I'm saying that if such a *marvelous* set happened to become available, you might want to put out the word. *Discreetly,* of course. . . ."

The coded language was clear; it was like waving a red flag at a bull. "Yes, yes, I do know of someone, yes indeed. There is a general, you know, who is known to collect such things, these Sung Dynasty masterpieces of carved jade. It is the general's consuming passion. You may know his nickname, his moniker—the Jade Master."

"Hmm. Not sure I do, Jiang. But you think he might have any interest?"

"General Tsai is most interested in repatriating looted imperial treasures, bringing them back to the motherland. He is a fervent nationalist, you know."

"So I am given to understand. Well, I would need to know quite soon if the general has any interest, because I'm about to tell the hotel operator to *hold* all my *calls*—those *loathsome* oil sheiks from Oman and Kuwait simply won't stop *calling!*"

"No!" Jiang blurted out. "Give me two hours! This masterpiece *must* be returned to China!"

Bryson did not have to wait that long. The diplomat called back barely an hour later. The general was interested.

"Given the extraordinary nature of this property," Bryson said firmly, "I absolutely insist on meeting my customer face-to-face." At this point, Bryson knew he could pretty much set his own terms for the meeting with General Tsai.

"But—but of course," sputtered Jiang. "The . . . customer would require nothing less. He needs to have every assurance of the item's authenticity."

"Naturally. All certificates of provenance will be provided."

"Of course."

"The meeting must be immediate. I can accept no delay."

"That is not a problem. The Jade Master is in Shenzhen, and he looks forward to meeting with you as soon as possible."

"Good. I'll take the first flight to Shenzhen, and then the general and I will have an initial conversation."

"What do you mean, an *initial conversation* . . . ?"

"The general and I will pass a convivial hour or two, I'll show him photographs of the chess set, and if I feel we've established a comfort level, we'll proceed to the next step."

"Then you won't be taking the set with you to your meeting with the general?"

"Oh, good *Lord,* no. After all, such a customer would be in a position to expose me if he wanted to. Can't be too careful these days. You know my motto: I never deal with strangers." He chortled. "After I meet this chappy, of course, we won't be strangers anymore, now will we? If everything's in order—if everything *feels* right—we can discuss importation, filthy lucre, all those *boring* humdrum details."

"The general will insist on inspecting the jade chess set, Giles."

"Certainly, but not at first. Oh, no. China's terra incognita to me, I don't know the chappies in charge. I guess I feel a smidgen vulnerable there. Wouldn't want your General Whosit to *confiscate* the thing and bundle me off to one of those *cabbage* farms or what have you."

"The general is a man of his word," Jiang objected stiffly.

"My antennae have served me awfully well these last twenty years, old friend. Wouldn't want to ignore them at *this* late date. Fella can't be too careful with you inscrutable Orientals, you know." He chuckled; there was silence on the phone. "And you know me—a jigger of rice wine and I'm *anybody's!*"

Flamboyantly attired in a yellow kid-skin vest and a silk-and-cashmere checked suit, Giles Hesketh-Haywood arrived at Shenzhen's Huangtian Airport and was met by an emissary of General Tsai wearing the dark-green, rankless uniform of the Chinese People's Liberation Army, the standard red metal enamel star at the front of his standard-issue "Mao" cap. The emissary, a stony-faced middle-aged man who offered no name, whisked Bryson through customs and immigration. The way had been prepared; the airport personnel were deferential and inspected nothing.

That was left to General Tsai's men. Once they were clear of immigration, the emissary wordlessly hustled Bryson through an unmarked door where two other green-uniformed soldiers were waiting. One of them unceremoniously rifled through his luggage, leaving nothing unopened or unchecked. Meanwhile, the other began frisking him systematically, from head to foot, even slicing the insoles in the costly English leather shoes. Bryson was not surprised at the search, though he emitted squawks of indignation befitting his legend's prissy persona.

He had not arrived unarmed, though. Anticipating that he would be searched before being permitted to meet with the general, he had left behind any firearms, or in fact anything that would be out of character for Giles Hesketh-Haywood to carry. The risk of being caught, and therefore sabotaging the entire legend, was too great.

But concealed in Hesketh-Haywood's glove-soft leather belt was a weapon so well concealed that it was worth the risk. Sewn between two layers of the finest Italian cordovan leather was a long, flexible metal strip about an inch wide by twelve inches long, made of an aluminum-vanadium alloy, a razor-sharp blade down most of its length. The blade was easily and quickly removed from the belt by opening one snap and pulling hard. It was difficult to use without wounding oneself, but if employed properly, the blade would slash human skin down to the bone with virtually no pressure. And if that was insufficient, Bryson was confident that he could rely, as he often did, on his ability to improvise, to find weapons where others saw none. But he hoped weapons would not be needed. The uniformed soldier ordered Bryson to remove his belt; he ran it cursorily between his fingers and detected nothing.

A black, late-model Daimler limousine was idling in front of the terminal exit doors, a military chauffeur at the wheel, also in the green rankless uniform of the Chinese Army, with a bland, unreadable face, his chin tucked toward his chest in a gesture of humility.

The dour emissary opened the passenger's door for Bryson, placed the suitcase in the trunk, then got into the front seat. He did not speak a word; the driver steered the Daimler away from the curb and onto the airport access road toward Shenzhen.

Bryson had been to Shenzhen once, years before, but he scarcely recognized it. What was a tiny, sleepy fishing village and border town barely twenty years ago had exploded into a clamorous and chaotic metropolis of hastily paved roads, slapdash apartment complexes, and belching factories. From the rice paddies and virgin farmland of southern China's Pearl River Delta had sprouted the skyscrapers and power plants and industrialized sectors of the Special Economic Zone. The chaotic skyline bristled with construction cranes, the sky an ugly gray polluted haze. The bustling population of some four million people settled on the banks of the fetid Shenzhen River were mostly *mingong*, or peasant workers, lured from their rural provinces with the promise of jobs at subsistence wages.

Shenzhen was a megalopolis in a hurry, a boomtown city going at a furious pace twenty-four hours a day, running at full blast on the high-octane fuel that was the most profane of words in all of Communist China: capitalism. But it was capitalism at its brashest and cruelest, the dangerous hysteria of a frontier city, crime and prostitution rampant and evident. The glittering heights of consumer excess, the lurid bill-boards and flashing neon, the swanky shops of Louis Vuitton and Dior, were, Bryson knew, nothing more than a veneer. Behind it lay concealed the desperate poverty, the squalor of the *mingong*'s grim daily existence, the metal sheds housing dozens of migrant laborers with no plumbing, scrawny chickens running around tiny, filthy yards.

The traffic was thick, choked with late-model automobiles and bright red taxis. Every single building was new, tall, modernistic. The streets bustled with blinking signs, all of them in Chinese with the rare exception of an English letter here and there—an M for McDonald's, a KFC. Everywhere seemed to be lavish colors, gaudy restaurants, and stores selling consumer electronics—camcorders and digital cameras and computers and televisions and DVDs. Street merchants peddled roasted pigs and ducks and live crabs.

The crowds were dense, shoulder-to-shoulder, with almost everybody carrying a mobile phone. But unlike Hong Kong, twenty miles to the south, there were no elderly people practicing tai-chi in the parks; in fact, there were no old people here at all. The maximum length of stay in the Special Economic Zone was fifteen years, and only the able-bodied were welcome.

The emissary turned around in the front seat and began speaking. *"Ni laiguo Shenzhen ma?"*

"Pardon?" said Bryson.

"Ni budong Zhongguo hua ma?"

"Sorry, no speakee the lingo," Bryson drawled. The emissary had asked him if he understood Chinese, whether he had been here before; Bryson wondered whether he was being crudely tested.

"English?"

"I am, and I speak it, yes."

"This is your first time here?"

"Yes, it is. Charming place, though—wish I'd discovered it earlier."

"Why do you meet the general?" The emissary's expression had turned outright hostile.

"Business," Bryson said shortly. "That *is* what the general does, right?"

"The general is in charge of the Guandong Sector of the PLA," the emissary upbraided him.

"Well, there sure seems to be a lot of business going on here."

The driver grunted something, and the emissary fell silent, then turned around.

The Daimler crawled through the unbelievable congestion of the streets, the strange cacophony: the hysterical shrieks of high-pitched voices, the blaring of truck horns. In front of the Shangri-La Hotel the traffic finally came to a standstill. The chauffeur turned on his siren and flashing red light and veered up onto a crowded sidewalk, barking shrill orders through the car's loudspeakers, scattering the frightened pedestrians like so many pigeons. Then the Daimler zipped ahead of the knot of traffic.

Finally they came to a checkpoint, the entrance to a highly industrialized sector that appeared to be under the direct control of the military. Bryson assumed that it was here that General Tsai had his primary residence, perhaps maintained his headquarters. A soldier holding a clipboard leaned in and gestured rudely to the emissary, who quickly got out. The car continued down the street, past drab residential buildings into a more industrial-looking area, predominately warehouses.

Bryson was instantly wary. He was not being taken to the general's residence. But where was he being driven?

"Neng bu neng gaosong wo, ni song wo qu nar?" he demanded in a deliberately heavy British accent, the syntax that of a speaker ill at ease with the language. Care to tell me where you're driving me?

The driver did not reply.

Bryson raised his voice, now speaking with his customary fluency, that of a native speaker. "We're nowhere near the general's barracks, *siji!*"

"The general does not receive visitors at his residence. He keeps a very low profile." The driver spoke impertinently, even disrespectfully, not as a Chinese speaker of his station would address a superior, not using *shifu* for "master." It was disconcerting.

"General Tsai is famous for living extremely well. I advise you to turn this car around."

"The general believes that the truest power is exercised invisibly. He prefers to remain behind the scenes." They had pulled up before a large industrial warehouse, next to military-drab Jeeps and Humvees. Without turning around, the engine still running, the driver continued, "Do you know the story of the great eighteenth-century Emperor Qian Xing? He believed it was important for a ruler to have direct contact with those he ruled, without his subjects knowing. So he traveled throughout China disguised as a commoner."

Realizing what the driver was saying, Bryson jerked his head to the side, for the first time focusing on the driver's face. He cursed himself. The driver *was* General Tsai!

Suddenly the Daimler was surrounded by soldiers, and the general was barking out commands in Toishanese, his regional dialect. The car door opened, and Bryson was hustled out. He was grabbed by both arms, a soldier restraining him on either side.

"*Zhanzhu!* Stand still!" shouted one of the soldiers, training his sidearm at Bryson as he commanded him to keep his hands at his sides. "*Shou fang xia! Bie dong!*"

The general's window electrically rolled down; the general grinned. "It was very interesting speaking with you, Mr. Bryson. Your facility with our language grew stronger the longer we chatted. It makes me wonder what else you may be concealing. Now I suggest you meet your inevitable death with serenity."

Oh, Jesus! His true identity was known! How? And for how long?

His mind raced. Who could have revealed his true identity? More to the point, who *knew* about the Hesketh-Haywood ruse? Who knew he was coming to Shenzhen? Not Yuri Tarnapolsky. Then who?

Photographs of his face had been faxed, connections made. But it made no *sense!* There had to be someone close to the general who recognized his face, was able to penetrate the facade of the English high-end fence. Someone who knew him; no other explanation was logical.

As General Tsai drove off, the Daimler emitting a cloud of exhaust smoke in his face, Bryson was shoved and pulled toward the warehouse entrance. The handgun was still trained on him from behind. He calculated his odds, and they were not good. He would have to free a hand, preferably his right, and grab the vanadium blade from the sheathing of his belt in one rapid, smooth movement. In order to do that, though, he would need to arrange for a diversion, a distraction. For the instructions from the general were clear: he was to meet his "inevitable death." They would not hesitate to fire on him, he was sure, if he made any sudden attempt to break free. He did not want to test their orders.

Then why was he being brought into this warehouse? He looked around, seeing the immensity of the cavernous facility, clearly intended for the delivery and storage of motor freight. At one end was an enormous freight elevator large enough to accommodate a tank or a Humvee. The air was acrid with the smell of motor oil and diesel fuel. Trucks and tanks and other large military vehicles were stored in serried ranks, very close together, across the expanse of the warehouse floor. It looked like the storage area for a prosperous, high-volume car or truck dealership, though the concrete walls and floors were grimy with spilled motor oil and the residue of exhaust fumes.

What was going on? Why was he being brought here, when they could just as easily have executed him outside, where there were no nonmilitary witnesses?

And then he realized why.

His eyes were riveted on the man who stood in front of him. A man who was armed to the teeth. A man he knew.

A man named Ang Wu.

One of the few adversaries he'd ever encountered whom he'd have to describe as physically intimidating on every level. Ang Wu, a renegade officer in the Chinese Army, attached to Bomtec, the trading arm of the PLA. Ang Wu had been the local PLA representative in Sri Lanka; the Chinese had been shipping arms to both sides of the conflict, sowing dissent and suspicion, vending the highly flammable fuel for the region's smoldering resentments. Outside Colombo, Bryson and the ad hoc band of commandos he'd assembled for the task had headed off a lethal caravan of munitions under Ang Wu's direct control. In an exchange of gunfire, Bryson had shot Ang Wu in the gut, taking him down. His enemy was helicoptered out, reportedly back to Beijing.

But had there been more to the incident, an underlying meaning, an unexplained plan in which he had been merely a pawn? What *really* lay behind the exercise?

Now, Ang Wu stood before Bryson, a Chinese AK-47

machine gun hanging from his shoulders on a diagonal nylon sling. On each hip was holstered a handgun. Draped around his waist like a belt were bandoliers of machine-gun rounds, and sheathed at his side and ankles were gleaming knives.

The grip on each of Bryson's shoulders tightened. He could not free his hand to grab his belt, at least not without being shot down in the interim. *Oh, God!*

His old nemesis looked happy. "So many ways to die," Ang Wu said. "I always knew we would meet again. For a long time I am looking forward to our reunion." With a fluid motion he unholstered one of the handguns, a Chinese-made semiautomatic, hefting it, seemingly enjoying its solidity, its power to extinguish life. "This is General Tsai's gift to me, his generous reward for my years of service. A simple gift: that *I* get to kill you myself. It will be very—how do you say?—up close and personal."

There was a glacial smile, an array of very white teeth. "Ten years ago in Colombo, you took my spleen—did you know that? So we start with that first. Your spleen."

In his mind, the enormous warehouse had collapsed into a very small space, a narrow tunnel, with Bryson at one end and Ang Wu at the other. There was nothing else but his adversary. Bryson took a slow, deep breath. "It hardly seems a fair fight," he said with a forced, artificial calm.

The Chinese assassin smiled and, extending his arm, aimed the pistol at the lower left region of Bryson's torso. As his enemy thumbed the safety, Bryson suddenly lurched forward and twisted his body in an attempt to dislodge himself from his captors' grips, and then—

There was a small coughing noise, more like a spit, and a tiny red hole, like the beginning of a teardrop, appeared in the very center of Ang Wu's broad forehead. He slid to the floor very gently, like a drunk passing out.

"Aiya!" screamed one of the guards, whirling around, just in time to catch a second silenced round in his head as well. The second guard shrieked, reached for his weapon, then abruptly crumpled to the ground, the side of his head blown away.

Suddenly free, Bryson flung himself to the floor, at the same time spinning around and looking up. On a steel catwalk twenty feet above, a tall, portly man in a navy-blue business suit stepped from behind a concrete pillar. In his hand was a .357 Magnum, a long perforated cylinder attached to its barrel, a wisp of cordite curling from its end. The man's face was momentarily in shadow, but Bryson would know the heavy tread anywhere.

The portly man tossed the Magnum high into the air toward Bryson. "Catch," he said.

Bryson, thunderstruck, grabbed the weapon as it dropped.

"Glad to see your skills haven't gone completely rusty," said Ted Waller as he began descending a steep set of steps. He gave Bryson a look of what could be mistaken for amusement; he sounded out of breath. "The hard part's coming up."

CHAPTER TWENTY-TWO

Senator James Cassidy saw the headline in *The Washington Times*—saw the reference to his wife, her drug arrest, allegations of possible obstruction of justice—and read no more. So it was out, at last, all in the open—a source of profound personal anguish, something he had desperately sought to keep from the hard, raptor eyes of the media. A buried secret had been unearthed. But how?

Arriving at his office at six in the morning, hours before he usually appeared, he found his top staff already assembled, looking as ashen and enervated as he felt. Roger Fry spoke without preamble. "*The Washington Times* has been gunning for you for years. But we've already had more than a hundred phone calls from all the other media outlets. They're trying to track down your wife, too. This is out-and-out carpet bombing, Jim. I can't control this. None of us can."

"Is it *true?*" asked Mandy Greene, his press secretary. Mandy was forty, and had been with him for the last six years, but stress and anxiety made her seem older than she'd ever looked before. Cassidy couldn't remember her ever losing her composure. But this morning her eyes were red-rimmed.

The senator exchanged glances with his chief of staff; it was clear Roger had told the others nothing. "What exactly are they saying?"

Mandy picked up the newspaper, then tossed it angrily across the office. "That four years ago your wife was arrested for buying heroin. That you made phone calls, called in favors, and had the charges dropped, the arrest expunged. 'Obstruction of justice' is the phrase they're bandying about."

Senator Cassidy nodded, wordlessly. He sat down in his large leather office chair and turned away from his staffers for a moment, looking out the window into the gray light of

a cloudy Washington morning. There'd been phone calls
from the reporter yesterday, calls both for him and for his
wife, Claire, but they went unanswered. He'd had a bad feeling about it, had slept little.

Claire was at their family home in Wayland, Massachusetts. She had her problems; many politicians' wives did. But
he remembered how it started—the minor skiing accident
that led to back surgery, the fused vertebrae, the Percodans
she'd been given for the operative pain. Soon she started to
crave the narcotic for more than the cessation of pain. The
doctors wouldn't renew her prescription. They referred her
to a "pain management" group, which specialized in counseling. But the narcotics had introduced Claire to a kind of
sweet oblivion, a place protected from the stresses and strains
of public life, from a private life that didn't provide the comfort she required. He could blame himself for that—for not
having been there, by her side, when she needed him. He'd
come to understand how inimical his world was to her. It
was a world that, ultimately, relegated her to the sidelines,
and Claire, so beautiful, so accomplished, so loving, had not
been raised to sit out life on the bleachers. For Cassidy, there
were too many Beltway engagements, too many colleagues
to romance and inveigle and bully and cajole into doing the
right thing. And Claire was lonely; she experienced a pain
that was not merely physical. He never really knew which
was the real injury, the isolation or the accident, but he'd
come to suspect that the spiral of depression and dependency
to which she'd succumbed had merely been precipitated by
her hospitalization.

Desperate after she could no longer obtain her prescription
narcotics, desperate for a form of relief she knew was fleeting
yet somehow seemed to make things endurable, she went to
a corridor park near Eighth and H Streets in Washington and
tried to buy a quantity of street heroin. The man she met
there was encouraging, sympathetic, made it easy. He gave
her two small glassine bags of the stuff. She paid him with
crisp large bills freshly dispensed from an ATM.

And then he flashed a badge and took her down to the

station. When the precinct captain discovered who she was, he called the assistant D.A., Henry Kaminer, at home. And Henry Kaminer called his law-school classmate Jim Cassidy, who happened to be serving as the chairman of the Senate Judiciary Committee. That's how he found out. Cassidy remembered the phone call, the hesitance, the awkward small talk that preceded the shattering revelation. It was among the worst moments of his life.

Claire's delicate, drawn face filled his mind, and the words of a poem he'd once read echoed in his mind: *not waving but drowning.* How could he have been so blind to what was happening in his own household, his own marriage? Could a public life make a man so out of touch with his private one? Yet there was Claire: *not waving but drowning.*

Cassidy turned around to face his staff. "She wasn't a felon," he said stonily. "She needed *help,* damn it. She needed treatment. And she got it. Six months in rehab. Discreetly, quietly. Nobody needed to know. She didn't want the pitying glances, the knowing looks. The special scrutiny that comes with being a senator's wife."

"But your career . . ." Greene began.

"My goddamn *career* was what drove her to it in the *first* place! Claire had dreams, too, you know. Dreams of having a real family, with kids and a father who loved them and her, who made his wife and kids his first and last priority, the way a man should. Dreams of having a *normal life*—it probably didn't seem too much to ask. She wanted a *home,* that was all. She gave up her dreams so I could be—what did *The Wall Street Journal* call me last year?—the 'Polonius of the Potomac.' " Bitterness entered his voice.

"But how could she have jeopardized everything you'd worked for, everything you'd *both* worked for?" Mandy Greene could not conceal the flare of anger and frustration.

Cassidy shook his head slowly. "Claire was in agony, knowing that everyone would look at her as the woman who might have destroyed a senator's career. You'll never understand the sort of hell she went through. But she went *through* it; in a sense, we both did. And damn it, we came out the other side! Until now. Until this." He looked over at the receptionist's twelve-line telephone, all brightly lit and ringing nonstop in an electronic purr. "*How,* Roger? How did they find out?"

"I'm still not sure," Roger said. "But what they've got is incredibly detailed. An electronic record of the arrest record, somehow retrieved despite the fact that it was officially expunged. Claire's sizable cash withdrawal the evening in question. Municipal phone exchange records, itemizing a flurry of phone calls made between your home and Henry Kaminer's on the night of the arrest. More calls between Kaminer's private line and the precinct captain. Phone logs between the arresting officer and the station house. Even the electronic records of the payments you made to Silver Lakes for her rehabilitation."

Cassidy looked grim, but forced a wry grin. "No one person could have leaked all that. The most private, personal records have been breached. It's what I was warning about, I suppose. The surveillance society."

"Well, that's not how it's going to play," Mandy Greene said brusquely, regaining her air of professionalism at last. "It's going to look as if you were campaigning for privacy because of the skeletons in your *own* closet. You know that better than anyone."

Roger Fry started pacing around the office. "It's bad, Jim, I'm not going to minimize it. But I honestly think we can ride this thing out. It'll get worse before it gets better, but the people in Massachusetts know you're a good man, and your colleagues, whether they like you or not, know you're a good man. Time is the great healer, in politics as in everything else."

"I don't intend to find out, Rog," Cassidy said, gazing out the window again.

"I know it looks bad now," Fry said. "They'll try to crucify you. But you're strong. You'll show them."

"You don't understand, do you?" Cassidy spoke severely but not unkindly. "It isn't about me. It's about Claire. The first sentence of every news story refers to Claire Cassidy, the wife of Senator James Cassidy. That may continue for days, weeks, who the hell knows? I cannot subject her to this. I cannot put her *through* this. She will not survive it. And there's only one way to take this off the table. There's only one way to take this off the front pages and the talk shows and the news hours and the gossip columns." He shook his head, speaking in the mock-stentorian tones of a newsreel reader: "*Senator Cassidy braces for Senate investigation, Senator Cassidy fights to keep his seat, Senator Cassidy denies wrongdoing, Senator Cassidy's disgrace, did judiciary chair abuse office? Senator married to junkie.* Now, that's page-one news, and it can go on and on and on. *Senator Cassidy resigns in wake of damaging allegations* is a story, yes, but a two-day story. The travails of Jim and Claire Cassidy, private citizens, soon get buried somewhere after the wire reports from Somaliland. Five years ago, I made a solemn promise to my wife that we would put this behind us, whatever it took. Now that promise has come due."

"Jim," Fry said delicately, trying to keep his voice steady, "there's simply too much uncertainty now to make any binding decisions. I beg you to hold off."

"Uncertainty?" The senator laughed bitterly. "But I've never been more certain of anything in my life." He turned to Mandy Greene. "Mandy, it's time for you to earn your paycheck. You and I are going to draft the press release. *Now.*"

CHAPTER TWENTY-THREE

Bryson froze, barely able to breathe. He was in shock, his mind numb. It was as if a bolt of lightning had streaked down from the sky, searing his consciousness, tearing apart the filaments of reason. He gasped. Everything was madness, illogic; he could barely suppress a scream.

Ted Waller!

Gennady Rosovsky!

The great manipulator, the magician of the dark arts who had turned his life into a great and unthinkable deception.

Bryson grasped the semiautomatic pistol he'd just been thrown, felt it settle into his grip as if it were an appendage, a part of his body. He pointed it back at the man who had just given it to him, realizing that with one well-aimed shot he could kill Ted Waller, and *it would not be enough!*

It would not answer the questions that tormented him, nor would it satisfy his need for vengeance against the liars and manipulators who had made his life a lie. Still, he trained the weapon on Waller, aiming at his old mentor's face, overcome by fury yet roiled with questions, *so many questions!*

What came out, in a tight, strangled voice, was the first question that leaped into the forefront of his mind. "Who the hell *are* you?"

He thumbed back the safety, squeezed the trigger back until the gun clicked into automatic mode. A twitch of his index finger and he could discharge ten rounds into Ted Waller's head, and the liar would topple from his perch on the catwalk to the warehouse floor twenty feet below. Yet Waller, that finest of shots, aimed no weapon back at him. He simply stood there, an obese old man with a cryptic smile on his face.

Waller spoke, his voice echoing in the cavernous space. "Let's play True or False," he said, invoking his old pedagogical exercise.

"Fuck you," said Bryson in cold fury, his voice trembling with banked rage. "Your real name is Gennady Rosovsky."

"True," Waller replied, his face impassive.

"You attended the Moscow Institute of Foreign Languages."

"True." A smile flickered. *"Pravil'no. Otlichno."* That's correct. Excellent.

"You're GRU."

"True-ish. To be accurate, the verb tense is past. I *was*."

Bryson raised his voice until he was shouting. "And it was all *horseshit*, all that *shit* you told me about how we were saving the world! When all the time you were working for the other side!"

"False," said Waller, his voice clear and loud.

"Enough lies, you son of a bitch! *Enough lies!*"

"True."

"Goddamn you to hell, I don't know what the hell you're doing here—"

"At the risk of sounding like General Tsai: when the student is ready, the teacher appears."

"I don't have time for your Buddhist bullshit!" he thundered.

Bryson heard the footfalls, the clanking of weaponry, and he spun around. A pair of green-uniformed guards had entered the warehouse, carbines at the ready. Bryson squeezed off several shots, and at the same instant he heard the explosion of gunfire coming from above and behind, from the direction of Waller. The two guards were hit; they tumbled forward, sprawling to the ground. Bryson dove to the floor, atop Ang Wu's body, and he turned over the limp body, grabbed the dead assassin's submachine gun, yanking the sling from around his neck, gripping it in both hands and angling it upward as he dropped Waller's gun. He expected to see another set of guards, but there was none.

Then he tugged the handgun from Ang Wu's hand and shoved it into the front pocket of his ridiculous Hesketh-Haywood suit. Ang Wu had strapped hunting knives to each ankle; Bryson grabbed each, knife and scabbard together, and

carefully tucked each one under his belt. His belt! He suddenly remembered the aluminum-vanadium blade—but now
he had weaponry that was far more effective.

"This way!" called Waller, turning around and disappearing into the dim recesses of the concrete-walled balcony.
"Building's surrounded."

"Where the hell are you going?" shouted Bryson.

"Some of us have done our homework. Come *on*, Nick!"

What choice was there? Whoever, *whatever* Ted Waller
actually was, he was surely right: the warehouse was surrounded by PLA guards; if there was another exit at the
ground level, as there almost certainly was, it would simply
lead him into the ranks of his enemy. Of his *immediate* enemy. Bryson raced up the steel steps just in time to see the
fat man disappearing into a large open stairwell, just beyond
long rows of parked military vehicles. Weaving between the
serried ranks of Jeeps and Humvees and Chinese-
manufactured trucks, Bryson ran to the stairwell just in time
to see Waller climbing the stairs with speed and agility, the
almost balletic grace that had always surprised him. Still,
Bryson was fleeter of foot, and he caught up with Waller in
a matter of seconds. "To the roof," Waller muttered. "Only
way out."

"The *roof?*"

"No alternative. They'll be piling in momentarily, if they
aren't already." Waller was short of breath. "One stairwell.
One freight elevator, but it's frightfully slow."

By the time they had reached the third-floor landing, they
could already hear shouts from below, running footsteps.

"Shit," said Waller. "Now I wish I hadn't had the paté
last night. You go ahead."

Bryson shot ahead up the stairway, rounding the wide
bends until he reached what was obviously the top floor. He
emerged into the night air, the broad expanse of a parking
lot, row upon row of tanks and trucks. *What the hell now?*
What did Waller have in mind? To goddamned *jump* from
the top of the building? Leap across the ten- or twenty-foot
chasm to the next building?

"Burn the bridges," Waller panted as he came out of the stairwell, and Bryson understood what his ex-mentor was saying. Block the path of their pursuers—but *how?* With *what?* There were no doors to lock or barricade. . . .

There were *vehicles* galore, hundreds, *thousands* of them. He ran to the nearest row, tried the door handle, found it locked. *Shit!* He ran to the next; it was locked as well. There was no *time* for this!

Spying a row of soft-top Jeeps, he ran over to them. Pulling one of Ang Wu's hunting knives from its scabbard, he slashed at the canvas top, then poked his hand in and opened the locked door from inside. The key was in the ignition, which made sense in such a well-guarded warehouse, where separating each vehicle from its key would be a logistical nightmare. Waller was standing clear of the stairwell, a cell phone to his mouth, talking. Bryson keyed the ignition, revved the Jeep's engine, and drove it straight ahead, at top speed, toward the open stairs. As he approached, he saw that the Jeep was too wide to fit through the opening, but that would suit his purposes nicely. With a great crash, the Jeep smashed into the concrete wall, its front end jutting into the opening, then sank a few feet as the front tires dropped down to the second or third step before stopping. He could just manage to force open the driver-side door, and he squeezed out between the Jeep and the abutting concrete wall.

But it would be nothing more than a delay: several men pushing together could dislodge the vehicle. It wasn't enough! Searching the adjacent rows of vehicles, he spotted what he desperately hoped to find: a fifty-five-gallon heavy-gauge-steel fuel drum. Tipping it slowly to the ground, he rolled it toward the Jeep, now obstructing the exit onto the roof. He tugged at the plastic bung-hole seal, turned it, and popped it off. Gasoline began pouring out, forming a puddle on the concrete floor around the vehicle. He rolled it further, tipping the bottom up so that the fuel poured out even faster, a flood of it, torrents running around the Jeep's tires, rivers of gas advancing to the top of the stairwell, then seeping around the Jeep and down the steps. The gasoline odor was overpowering. In short order he had emptied the drum down the stairwell, just as he heard thundering footsteps, the guards running up the stairs to the roof.

No *time!*

Grabbing his tie, he yanked it free; dropping it into the puddle of fuel until it was soaked, he jammed it into the bung hole of the now-empty fuel drum. It was empty of liquid fuel, but full of gasoline vapor—or, more precisely, a mix of air and gasoline vapor. The proportions might not be ideal, but he knew from long experience that it would do. He took out Giles Hesketh-Haywood's brass lighter and touched the flame to the improvised fuse. The flame roared to life, and Bryson tossed the steel drum over the Jeep and down into the stairwell, then jumped backward and ran as fast as he could.

The explosion was immense, deafeningly loud. The entire stairwell had become a fireball, a roaring yellow inferno. Waller, seeing what he had done, raced across the rooftop as well. In a few seconds, there came another, fantastically loud explosion as the Jeep's fuel tank was ignited. The flames were dazzlingly bright, painful to look at: rolling, shimmering waves of fire, now billowing clouds of black smoke. Bryson came to a halt when he was halfway across the roof, and Waller loped up to him, flushed and sweat-soaked.

"Nicely done," Waller said, looking up at the sky. From the stairwell there came loud, agonized screams, but in a moment they were blotted out by a louder noise, a thundering racket from overhead: the sound of helicopter rotor blades. An armored helicopter, painted green with camouflage spots, roared directly above, hovering into place over a clearing free of vehicles, and slowly descended to the roof.

Bryson gasped. "What the *hell*—?"

The helicopter was an AH-64 Apache, clearly marked as U.S. Army, painted with an official army tail code.

Waller ran toward it, instinctively ducking his head though there was no need to do so. Bryson hesitated for just a moment before he, too, ran toward the mammoth helicopter. The pilot was clad in U.S. Army fatigues. How could it be? If the Directorate was GRU, how had Waller arranged for a U.S. Army combat helicopter?

As he clambered on, he saw Waller spin around, looking past Bryson with alarm. Waller cried out, said something that Bryson could not make out. Bryson turned, saw the dozens of PLA soldiers pouring out of the freight elevator no more than a hundred feet away, on the opposite side of the roof from the inferno that had been the stairwell. He clambered into the helicopter and suddenly felt an explosion of pain in his back, a crushing blow to the right side of his ribcage. He had been struck! The pain was immense, inconceivable. He screamed; his legs buckled, and Waller grabbed him by the arm and pulled him into the chopper as it lifted into the air. As they rose, he could see the massed troops below, the amber blaze, the billows of sooty black smoke.

Bryson had been shot before, a number of times, but this was worse than anything he had experienced earlier. The pain grew instead of subsiding; a nerve had been struck. He was losing volumes of blood, he was sure of it. As if from far away he could hear Waller saying, ". . . a U.S. Army chopper, they won't dare try to blast us out of the sky . . . international incident, and General Tsai isn't so foolish as to . . ."

Waller's voice was fading in and out, like a radio with poor reception. He felt ice-cold one moment, then feverishly hot the next.

He heard ". . . okay there, Nicky? . . ."

And: ". . . first-aid kit but there's an infirmary in the Hong Kong airport . . . long flight and I don't want to delay . . ."

And then: ". . . the eighteenth-century physicians might have been on to something, you know, Nicky. It's probably good to be bled from time to time. . . ."

He passed in and out of consciousness, through a kaleidoscope of images. There was a landing on a helipad somewhere; he was helped onto a stretcher.

He was brought into a modern building, hurried down a long hallway. A white-coated female nurse or doctor attended to him, stripping him to the waist, stitching the wound

. . . the flare-up of pain, astonishing and white-hot, followed by the steep and rapid descent into the darkness of a deep, drugged sleep.

"Truth? I just want to nail the guy." Adam Parker was steamed and didn't mind if Joel Tannenbaum, his longtime attorney, knew it. The two were meeting for lunch, as they did every month or so, at Patroon, an upscale, beef-and-claret restaurant on East Forty-seventh Street. The walls were paneled in dark wood and festooned with Kips engravings. Parker had reserved a private room where the two men could smoke Romeo y Juliets with their martinis. Parker prided himself on his physical condition, but whenever he was in Manhattan, he gravitated toward places like this one, redolent of a bygone Establishment and its venial excesses.

Tannenbaum tucked into his grilled veal chop. He'd been on the Law Review at Columbia, ran the corporate litigation department at Swarthmore & Barthelme, but beneath his high-powered credentials and high-toned affiliations, he was a street fighter, a scrappy kid who'd grown up in the Bronx and always gave as good as he got. "Guys like that don't like being nailed. They eat guys like you as an after-dinner mint. Sorry, Adam. I'm not going to start lying to you at this late date. You know the old joke about the mouse trying to screw an elephant? Trust me, you don't want to climb up Jumbo's back."

"Give me a break," Parker said. "We've made mischief before, you and me. I'm just asking you to file a few papers. An injunction."

"Saying what?"

"Enjoin them from commingling data from InfoMed with those other informational resources—we've got all these confidentiality agreements that have got to be honored. Charge that we've got prima facie evidence that they're conducting themselves in violation of these covenants as entered and agreed upon blah blah blah."

"Adam, you've got *bubkes.*"

"Sure, yeah, but I just want to tie them up. I don't want

to make it easy on them. They think they can swallow me in one easy gulp, and I want to give 'em a hairball they won't forget."

"Jumbo's not going to notice. They've got army battalions of lawyers on staff. They'll have it thrown out in two minutes."

"Nothing involving the law takes two minutes."

"Five."

"I'll take what I can get. Thing is, I'm not going to go quietly."

"Am I supposed to be moved by your poeticism?"

"Given the size of your retainer, yes." Parker laughed ruefully.

"Adam, I've known you for, what, fifteen years? You were my best man . . ."

"Marriage lasted eight months. I should have asked for my present back."

"Believe me, some people did." Tannenbaum took a careful sip of his martini.

"You were saying."

"Adam, you're an asshole, a prick, an arrogant, hyper-competitive, know-it-all son of a bitch without a trace of humility or any sense of your own limitations. That's probably why you've done so well for yourself. But this time? For once in your life, you're out of your league."

"Screw you."

"I'm a lawyer. I screw other people." Tannenbaum shrugged. "All I'm saying is, punch your own weight, Adam."

"That what they taught you at Columbia Law School?"

"If only they had. Look, you don't need me for this. You're here because you want my advice. So hear what I'm trying to tell you. Every law firm that's worth a damn has got some sort of relationship with Systematix or one of its affiliates. Look around you and what do you see? Expense-account lunches on every four-top. A sizable portion of which is ultimately defrayed by everybody's favorite client, vendor, or customer: Systematix."

"They think they're the goddamn Standard Oil of information."

"Don't even reach for historical analogies. Systematix makes Standard Oil look like the Little Pie Company. But does anybody make trouble for them? It's like you always say—life isn't fair. Fact is, the Department of Justice acts like their wholly owned subsidiary. That company's got its tentacles everywhere."

"You're shitting me."

"I swear on my mother's grave."

"Your mother lives in Flatbush."

"My point remains. They bought your company. You took their money. Now you're acting like a dog in the manger. Listen to yourself."

"No, you listen to *me*. They're going to be sorry they fucked with Adam Parker. If you won't do the papers, I'll find somebody who will. Sure, I took the money, but I didn't exactly have a choice. It was a hostile takeover."

"Adam. You really don't want to mess with these people. You know me. Not a lot scares me in this life. But this . . . well, trust me when I say it isn't business as usual. They follow their own rules."

Parker finished the martini and signaled for another. "I may be an asshole, and I may be an arrogant son of a bitch, but I am not a patsy," he said, undeterred. "Tell you one thing. Those Systematix drones are going to remember my name."

"We have your usual room ready for you, Mr. Parker," the concierge said as soon as Parker appeared at the St. Moritz that evening. The concierge knew Parker liked the assurance, liked knowing that they'd made a note of his usual preferences.

But on his infrequent visits to Manhattan, Adam Parker also liked to indulge in some unusual preferences indeed. That morning, he'd made a phone call to Madame Sevigny, as she styled herself, who'd promised "two *jeunes filles*, our very finest." Madame Sevigny advertised in no publication;

all her clients—they were mostly men of great wealth and power who lived in other parts of the country—had to have been properly introduced to her. For her part, she guaranteed absolute discretion. Her girls knew that a lapse of discretion was more than their lives were worth. They also knew that if they abided by Madame Sevigny's exacting rules, they could put away a sizable nest egg in just a couple of years. Madame Sevigny had a physician on retainer who conducted regular blood tests and pelvic examinations of the *jeunes filles,* ensuring that their health and hygiene were beyond reproach. All of them maintained exercise schedules and dietary regimens that would put a professional gymnast to shame, and before they kept their appointments, Madame Sevigny conducted her own private inspections. As she deemed necessary, eyebrows would be tweezed, skin exfoliated and moisturized, feet pumiced, eyelashes tinted, legs waxed, nails filed; every bodily crevice would be irrigated and perfumed. "It is so difficult to be a natural beauty," Madame Sevigny would sigh, as she gave her *jeunes filles* a final inspection.

At ten P.M. precisely, a phone call from the St. Moritz lobby announced the girls' arrival. Parker, lounging in his opulently appointed suite in a white terrycloth bathrobe, felt a sensation of warmth rise within him. All this stress he'd been under since the Systematix takeover—*God,* but he needed this. It had been too long. He was always quite precise in his instructions to Madame Sevigny—as the old semiconductor plutocrat who first sized him up and told him about Madame's special services had explained, there was no point in beating around the bush with Madame S. What he had in store this evening was the sort of thing that his wife—a horsey, *wholesome* woman—simply couldn't be expected to understand. It wouldn't have surprised him, though, if the semiconductor mogul understood something of his pleasures.

The knock on the door came minutes later.

"My name is Yvette," the striking, statuesque brunette said breathily.

"And my name is Eva," the lithesome blonde said. They closed the door behind themselves. "You like?"

Parker grinned widely. "Very much," he said. "But I thought Madame Sevigny said it would be Yvette and Erica."

"Erica took ill," Eva said. "She sent me instead and asked me to send her regrets. We are like sisters. I think maybe you will not be disappointed."

"I'm sure I won't," Parker said, eyeing with dry-mouthed anticipation the flat, gray briefcase Yvette carried. "Can I get you girls anything?"

The two girls exchanged glances and shook their heads. "We begin, *allons-y?*" Yvette said.

"Please," Parker said.

An hour later, Parker was bound to the brass bedposts with black silk scarves, moaning with pleasure as the two girls took turns spanking and stroking his reddened flesh. They were expert; every time he came too near to climaxing, they would move their attentions elsewhere, massaging his arms and chest with fingers that were as soft and as hard as anything he could image. Yvette now caressed his body with her soft breast and moist crotch as Eva readied the hot wax.

The fragrant beeswax dripped on his body with intensely erotic heat, in equal measure painful and pleasurable. "Yes," he panted, nearly delirious. *"Yes."* His torso was laced with sweat.

Finally, Yvette mounted him, taking his manhood into herself, enveloping him in her warmth. The silk bonds had been loosened enough to allow him to sit part of the way up, and now Eva clasped his chest from behind. Her fingers massaged his shoulders, and now his throat.

"And, I think, a final pleasure for you," Eva whispered in his ear. He barely saw a glint of the razor-sharp wire before she had looped it around his neck.

"Oh God," he groaned before the wire sliced through cartilage, fascia, and vessels, subtending his carotid arteries, trachea, and esophagus, and he spoke no more.

Yvette, her eyes closed, lost now in her own pleasure, noticed first the waning of turgor within her. Her eyes

opened, and she saw the gentleman's head slumped forward,
and the other girl, the girl who called herself Eva, holding a
shiny metal loop. Was this some new plaything?

"And now, I think, it is your turn," Eva said breathily,
and encircled Yvette's neck with the shiny wire. Only then
did Yvette notice the blood around the gentleman's neck, like
a bright red cravat, and just moments later she was conscious
of absolutely nothing at all.

CHAPTER TWENTY-FOUR

He awoke slowly, aching all over, his head throbbing. He was sitting in a recliner seat in a small, luxurious executive jet, a blanket over him, a fluffy pillow behind his head. The windows were black; the noise and vibration indicated that they were in flight. The cabin was empty except for two other passengers. A fortyish man in a navy-blue flight-attendant's uniform, blond crew cut, dozed in shadows at the rear of the cabin. And seated in a wide leather seat across the aisle from Bryson was Waller, reading a leather-bound volume under a small, bright circle of light.

"Nu, vot eti vot, tovarishch Rosovsky, dobri vecher," Bryson said in Russian. *"Shto vyi chitayete?"* His speech was slurred; he felt drugged.

Waller looked up, gave a slight smile. "I really haven't spoken that beastly language in decades, Nicky. I'm sure I'm quite rusty." He closed his book. "But in answer to your question, I'm rereading Dostoyevsky. The Brothers K. Just to confirm my recollection that he's really quite a bad writer. Lurid plotting, heavy-handed moralizing, and prose out of *The Police Gazette.*"

"Where are we?"

"Somewhere over France by now, I imagine."

"If you used chemicals on me, I hope you got whatever you wanted."

"Ah, Nick," Waller exhaled, "I'm sure you believe you have no reason to trust me, but the only chemical you received was a painkiller of some kind. Fortunately there's a half-decent, well-equipped emergency clinic for travelers at Chek Lap Kok. But that's a nasty little bullet wound you sustained. Apparently your second in a matter of weeks, the last being a superficial graze wound in the left shoulder. You always were a quick healer, but you're starting to get a little long in the tooth, you know. It's really a young man's game, like American football. I told you that when I pulled you out five years ago."

"How'd you find me?"

Waller shrugged, settled back in his seat. "We have our sources, both electronic and human. As you well know."

"Pretty audacious to use a U.S. military chopper in foreign airspace."

"Not especially. Unless you really believe Harry Dunne's fabrications about our being some sort of rogue elephant."

"You're claiming it's not true?"

"I'm not claiming anything, Nick."

"You've already admitted you're Russian-born. Gennady Rosovsky, born in Vladivostok. Trained as a GRU sleeper penetration agent, a *paminyatchik,* by the Soviet Union's top spymasters, specialists in the English language, American culture and way of life, right? And a chess prodigy. Yuri Tarnapolsky confirmed all this for me. Even in your youth you had a reputation—some called you the Sorcerer."

"You flatter me."

Bryson gazed at his old mentor, who was now stretching his legs, his hands interlaced behind his neck. Waller—that was how he knew him, inasmuch as he *did* know him— looked supremely comfortable.

"Somewhere in the back of my mind," Waller went on, "I always knew there was the remote, theoretical chance that my GRU file might somehow, someday, make its way out of a safe in cold storage to U.S. intelligence. The way a long-buried corpse might wash up from its grave in a flood. But who'd ever have predicted it, really? Not even us. Everyone mocks the CIA for not anticipating the sudden collapse of the Soviet Union, and I'm hardly a defender of theirs, but I always thought that unfair—even *Gorbachev* didn't see it coming, for God's sake."

"Aren't you dodging the great unasked question here?"

"Why not ask it?"

"Are you a *paminyatchik,* a GRU sleeper, or not?"

" 'Am I now or have I ever been,' to paraphrase the buffoon Senator McCarthy? I *was*; I am *not*. Is that unambiguous enough?"

"Unambiguous, but vague."

"I defected in place."

"To our side."

"Naturally. I was an illegal here seeking to make it legal."

"When?"

"Nineteen fifty-six. I had arrived in 1949 as a boy of fourteen, when legends were plentiful and not thoroughly vetted. By the mid-fifties I saw the light and terminated my ties to Moscow. By then I'd seen, and heard, enough of Comrade Stalin to shatter whatever youthful illusions I'd once had about the radiant future of a communist world. After the Cuban Missile Crisis, I wasn't alone in realizing the idiocies, the follies, the essential flabbiness of the CIA. That was when I and Jim Angleton and a few others founded the Directorate."

Bryson shook his head, mulling. "A GRU sleeper defects in place, there are consequences. His handlers in Moscow will be greatly displeased, retaliation threatened and inevitably carried out. Yet you're maintaining that your true identity remained cloaked for *decades*. I find it hard to believe."

"Completely understandable. But do you imagine I simply sent them a Dear Ivan letter—'Oh, and you can stop sending those paychecks, because I'm switching sides'? Not bloody likely. I took some care with it, as you can imagine. My controller was a greedy bastard and not a little careless. He liked to live well and supported his habit by double-dipping and feeding from the expense-account trough a little too often."

"Translation: he embezzled."

"Indeed. In those days, that was grounds for either the gulag or a bullet in the neck in the Lubyanka courtyard. And with what I knew, and could pretend to know, I forced him to write me off the books. I disappear, he stays alive, everyone goes home happy."

"Then Harry Dunne's story *wasn't* a fabrication, was it?"

"Not one hundred percent, no. An ingenious pastiche of

truths and half-truths and outright falsehoods. Like the very best lies."

"What part of it isn't true?"

"What did he tell you?"

Bryson's heart began to pound slowly. His adrenaline surged, combating whatever narcotic was in his bloodstream. "That the Directorate was founded in the early 1960s by a small cell of fanatics at the GRU, or maybe VKR, brilliant strategists known as the *Shakhmatisti,* the chess players. Inspired by the classic Russian deception operation, the Trust, from the twenties. A penetration operation on American soil, the most brazen intelligence ruse of the twentieth century, far eclipsing the ambitions of the Trust. Controlled by a tight inner circle of directors, the Consortium, with all officers and staff outside that circle deluded into the belief that they were working for a maximum-security American intelligence unit—and constrained by zealous compartmentalization and gradated code-word secrecy from revealing anything, to anyone, about their work."

Waller smiled, his eyes closed.

"And according to Dunne, the true origins of the Directorate in Moscow would never have been discovered were it not for the collapse of the Soviet Union. Which resulted in the dissemination of a few stray documents inadvertently revealing code-name operations that didn't fit into known KGB or GRU structures; a contact name here and there; then the entirety confirmed by midlevel defectors."

Waller's grin broadened. He opened his eyes. "You almost have *me* convinced, Nick. Alas, Harry Dunne is in the wrong line of work. He should have written fiction; he has a wild imagination. His tale is at once outlandish and quite persuasive."

"What part of it is fiction?"

"Where do I begin?" Waller sighed petulantly.

"How about with the goddamned *truth?*" exploded Bryson, unable to tolerate his coyness any longer. "If you even *know* it anymore! How about starting with my *parents?*"

"What about them?"

"*I spoke with Felicia Munroe, Ted!* My parents were *murdered* by you goddamned fanatics! To put me under the direct control of Pete Munroe, to bring me into the Directorate."

"By murdering your parents? Come *on,* Nicky!"

"You're denying that Pete Munroe was secretly Russian-born, like you? Felicia as good as confirmed for me Harry Dunne's version of the 'accident' that ended their lives."

"Which was *what,* precisely?"

"That my 'Uncle Pete' did it—that he was wracked with guilt afterward."

"The poor old woman is senile, Nicky. Who's to say what the hell she meant?"

"You're not going to dismiss it that easily, Ted. She said that Pete talked Russian in his sleep. Dunne said that Pete Munroe's actual name was Pyotr Aksyonov."

"He's right."

"Oh *Jesus!*"

"He *was* Russian-born, Nick. I recruited him. Fanatically anticommunist. His family disappeared in the purges of the nineteen-thirties. *But he didn't kill your parents.*"

"Then who did?"

"They weren't killed, for God's sake. *Listen* to me." Waller studied the circular pool of light on his tray-table. "There are things I never told you, for reasons of compartmentalization—things I thought it better for you not to know—but I'm sure you already know the basic contours. The Directorate is, and was, a supranational agency established by a small cadre of enlightened members of U.S. and British intelligence, as well as a few high-level Soviet defectors whose bona fides were beyond reproach, yours truly included."

"When?"

"In nineteen-sixty-two, shortly after the Bay of Pigs debacle. We were determined to see that such a disgrace never happened again. It was my idea initially, if you'll allow me a brief immodesty, but my dear friend James Jesus Angleton of the CIA was my earliest and most vociferous supporter. He felt, as did I, that American intelligence was being eviscerated by amateurs and bumblers—the so-called Old Boys, really a bunch of overprivileged Ivy League frat boys—patriotic perhaps, but laughably arrogant, convinced they knew what they were doing. A Wall Street clique who basically ceded Eastern Europe to Stalin out of a simple failure of nerve. A bunch of elitist corporate lawyers who lacked the *cojones* to do things the way they had to be done, who lacked the necessary ruthlessness. Who didn't *understand* Moscow as I did.

"Remember, not long after the Bay of Pigs, a KGB officer named Anatoly Golitsyn defected and laid it all out for Angleton in a series of debriefings—how the CIA was riddled with moles—penetrated, corrupted, to its very core. And the less said about the British, with Kim Philby and his ilk, the better. Well, that about did it for Angleton. He not only provided the Directorate's initial black-box funding and set up the covert funding channels, but he also approved the basic, cellular organizational structure. He helped me devise the box-within-a-box strategy, the decentralization and internal segmentation, as a way of maintaining maximum secrecy. He emphasized the necessity of keeping our very *existence* unknown from all but the heads of the governments we served. Only by cloaking its very existence could this new organization hope to escape the mire of penetration, disinformation, and politics to which spy agencies on both sides of the Cold War had been held hostage."

"You don't expect me to believe that Harry Dunne was so far off base, so *misinformed* about the Directorate's true origins."

"Absolutely not. He wasn't misinformed. Harry Dunne was a man on a mission. He constructed a straw man. An *argumentum ad logicam,* a brilliant caricature, plausible-sounding and laced with shards of the truth. An imaginary garden filled with real toads, as it were."

"To what end?"

"To point you toward us, urge you to go after us and, if possible, destroy us."

"*To what end?*"

Waller sighed in exasperation, but before he could speak, Bryson went on: "Are you going to sit there and *deny* that you tried to have me terminated?"

Waller shook his head slowly, almost sadly. "There are others I might try to deceive, Nicky. You are far too clever."

"In the parking garage in Washington, after I went to K Street and found headquarters gone. *You* were behind that."

"Yes, that was our hire. It's not easy to find top-notch talent these days. Why did it not surprise me that you bested the fellow?"

But Bryson, not so easily mollified, stared at him furiously. "You ordered a sanction on me because you were afraid I'd expose the *truth!*"

"Actually, no. We were alarmed by your behavior. All external signs seemed to indicate that you'd gone bad, that you'd joined forces with Harry Dunne and had turned against your old employers. Who can fathom the human heart? Were you embittered by your early termination? Did Dunne turn your head with his lies? We couldn't know, and so we had to take protective measures. You knew far too much about us. Even despite all the compartmentalization, you knew *far* too much. Yes, a beyond-salvage order went out."

"Christ!"

"Yet all the while I remained skeptical. I know you better than perhaps anyone, and I was unwilling to accept the dossier, the analysts' assessments, at least without further corroboration. So I deployed one of our finest new recruits to cover you on Calacanis's ship, monitor your activities until I could be sure one way or the other. I handpicked her to watch you, check up on you, report back."

"Layla."

Waller nodded once.

"She was assigned as a limpet?"

"Correct."

"That's *horseshit!*" Bryson shouted. "She was far more than a goddamned limpet. She tried to *kill* me in Brussels!"

Bryson watched Waller's face for telltale signs of deception, but of course it was unreadable. "She acted on her own, in contravention to my orders. I'm not denying that, Nick. But you have to consider the chronology."

"This is *pathetic*. You're weaving back and forth, backing and filling, desperately trying to cover the holes in your story!"

"*Listen* to me, please. At least give that much to the man who saved your life. Part of her charge was to watch out for you too, Nick. To presume innocence on your part unless and until we learned otherwise. When she saw that you were about to be ambushed on Calacanis's ship, she warned you off."

"Then how do you explain *Brussels?*"

"A regrettable impulse on her part. Her intention was essentially a protective one. To protect the Directorate and our mission. When she learned you were about to meet with Richard Lanchester in order to blow apart the Directorate, she tried to talk you out of it. And when you persisted, she panicked; she took matters into her own hands. She assumed there simply wasn't time to contact me for instructions; she had to move at once. It was a bad decision, a miscalculation. It was unfortunate, and impulsive, and she tends to be impulsive. No one is perfect. She's a fine operative, one of the best to come out of Tel Aviv, and she's beautiful. A rare combination. One tends to overlook the faults. She's doing fine, incidentally. Thank you for asking."

Bryson ignored the sarcasm. "Let me get this straight: you're saying she *wasn't* tasked with killing me?"

"As I said, her mission was observation and reporting, protection where needed, not termination. But at Santiago de Compostela it became evident that termination orders had been taken out against you by others. Calacanis had been killed, his security forces decimated; it seemed unlikely to have originated with him, given the rapid sequence of events. I deduced that you were being exploited as a cat's paw; the question was, by whom?"

"Ted, I *saw* some of the agents arrayed against me—I *recognized* them! A blond operative, a dispatch agent from Khartoum. The peasant brothers from Cividale I used in the

Vector operation. These were *Directorate hires!*"

"*No,* Nick. The killers at Santiago de Compostela were freelancers who sell their talent to the highest bidders, not exclusively for us—and they'd been hired to do the job at Santiago precisely *because* they knew your face. Presumably they were told you were a sellout, that you might give up their names. Self-survival is a powerful incentive."

"That and a two-million-dollar bounty on my head."

"Indeed. I mean, for heaven's sakes, you were traveling around the world using an old Directorate legend. I could have rolled you up in a second. Did you seriously assume we didn't have 'John T. Coleridge' in our database?"

"Then who hired them?"

"The possibilities are numerous. You had put out so many feelers by then; you spoke to old KGB sources to verify my true identity. You think they don't talk? Or *sell* information, to be exact, the mercenary bastards?"

"You're not going to argue it was CIA, I hope. Harry Dunne obviously wasn't sending me out to do his dirty work while at the same time ordering me killed."

"Granted. But presumably a team was monitoring the situation on the *Spanish Armada,* and when the vessel was destroyed, a decision was made that you were a hostile."

"A decision made by *whom?* Dunne kept the whole operation off the books, no records maintained, only my 'Jonas Barrett' alias recorded in the Security data banks."

"Expenses, perhaps."

"Buried, encrypted. All requisitions DDCI-need-to-know Priority."

"The place leaks like a sieve, you know that. Always has. That's why we exist."

"Richard Lanchester agreed to see me as soon as I mentioned your true name. He made it clear he knew about the Directorate's origins—as outlined by Harry Dunne. Are you saying Lanchester was lying too?"

"He's a brilliant man, but he's vain, and vain men are easily gulled. Dunne might have debriefed him as artfully as he did you."

"He wanted me to probe further."

"Naturally. As would you, if you were in his position. He must have been a frightened man."

Bryson's head was spinning; he was overcome by vertigo. Too many pieces didn't *fit!* Too much remained unexplained, inconsistent. "Prospero—Jan Vansina—kept asking me whether Elena 'knew' something. What was he talking about?"

"I'm afraid some suspicion fell on Elena at the same time we were wondering about your defection to the enemy. Vansina needed to determine whether she was complicit. I maintained that you'd been false-flagged, and of course I was proven correct."

"And what about the roster of operations you devised or controlled—Sri Lanka, Peru, Libya, Iraq? Dunne said that they were all secretly designed to defeat American interests abroad—but under such a deep cloak of secrecy that even the participants didn't see the chess moves because we were too close to the board."

"Poppycock."

"What about Tunisia? Was Abu not a CIA asset?"

"I don't know everything, Nicky."

"It looks as if your whole elaborate penetration operation, ostensibly to defeat a coup, was engineered to unmask and neutralize a key CIA asset. To eliminate an Agency direct feed into a network of Islamic terrorist cells throughout the region—one hand undoing the work of the other!"

"Twaddle."

"And the Comoros, in 1982—you sent us to foil an attempt by mercenaries from Executive Outcome to take over. But according to Dunne, they were CIA hires attempting to free British and American hostages. *What's the truth?*"

"Check the records. The hostages were only freed later, after our operation. Check the employment records if you can locate them. Unwind the sequence. These weren't CIA hires, they were underwritten by nationalist elements. Do your homework, my boy."

"*Goddamn you!* I was *there*, you know. And I was on

board the *Spanish Armada,* ostensibly carrying a blueprint of a new-generation Javelin antitank missile as a bargaining chip. Calacanis knew immediately who the interested buyer would be, and it was *your man!* It was Directorate—Vance Gifford or whatever his real name is. Calacanis himself confirmed the pattern of increased acquisition out of Washington."

"We're not Washington-based anymore, Nicky, you know that. We had to relocate; we were penetrated."

"And why the hell was your operative so interested in acquiring the blueprint? For your personal *collection,* was that it?"

"Nicky—"

"And why did he arrive on the ship in the company of Jacques Arnaud's man, Jean-Marc Bertrand? Are you pretending you weren't acquiring weapons?"

"Gifford was doing his *job,* Nick."

"His job being *what,* exactly? According to Calacanis, the man was on a spending spree."

"In this world, as you know better than most, you don't just inspect the goods without buying. Browsers are quickly detected and dispatched."

"The same way Prospero—Jan Vansina—laundered five billion dollars in Geneva? A penetration ruse?"

"Who told you that—Dunne?"

Bryson didn't reply, but simply stared at his old mentor, his heart pounding. He felt his right ribcage begin to throb; the painkiller had obviously begun to wear off.

Ted Waller went on in a voice rich with sarcasm, "Did he tell you this off-site? Wouldn't talk in his office? Told you he feared wiretaps?"

When Bryson didn't reply, Waller continued. "The deputy director of Central Intelligence doesn't have the power to have his own office swept, Nick?"

"Bugs come in plastic, too. Sweeping won't detect them— nothing will, short of tearing apart the plaster."

Waller snorted softly. "It was a show, Nicky. A goddam- ned piece of *theater.* An attempt, successful as it turned out, to persuade you that he was the good guy, the forces of darkness arrayed against him—the forces, in this case, being the entire CIA. In which he's the number two." Waller shook his head sadly. "Really."

"I gave him an Agency ID card I took off the body of one of the black-operatives who tried to terminate me outside Chantilly."

"And let me guess. He had the card tested and found it to be fake."

"Wrong."

"Maybe he was unable to turn up any records. He did a Code Sigma, found that it had been assigned to an operator in extremis, and there the trail went cold. He couldn't trace the name."

"That's not exactly far-fetched. Agency extremis operators don't leave tracks, you know that. Dunne admitted to me the CIA wasn't the best agency to investigate the Directorate."

"Ah, and it made you trust him all the more, didn't it? I mean, trust him *personally.*"

"You're saying he was trying to have me terminated while at the same time he was directing me to investigate the Directorate's activities? That's not just illogical, that's *insane!*"

"Directing complex field operations is always a shifting calculation. My guess? Once he saw you had survived the attack, he realized you could be reprogrammed, redeployed against another lead. But it's time to return your seat to an upright and locked position, as they say. We're there."

Waller seemed to be speaking from a great distance, and Bryson didn't understand what he meant; he could feel everything receding, and the next thing he knew he was aware of a bright white light. He opened his eyes and saw that he was in a room that was all white and steel. He was lying down in a tightly made bed between heavy linens; his eyes ached from the brightness of the light; his throat was parched and his lips were dry, cracked.

Before him were figures silhouetted against the light, one of them unmistakably Waller, the other much thinner and

smaller, presumably a nurse. He heard Waller's rich baritone:
". . . he's coming to even as we speak. Hello there, Nicky."

Bryson grunted, tried to swallow.

"He must be thirsty," came a female voice that was quite
familiar. "Can someone get him some water?"

It couldn't be. Bryson blinked, squinted, tried to get the
room into focus. He could see Waller's face, then hers.

His heart began hammering. He squinted again; he was
sure he was imagining things. He looked again, and then he
was sure.

He said, "Is that you, Elena?"

PART
FOUR

CHAPTER TWENTY-FIVE

"Nicholas," she said, coming closer. She came into focus. It was Elena, still ravishingly beautiful, though she had changed: her face had gotten thinner, more angular, which made her eyes seem even larger. She looked wary, even frightened, but her voice was matter-of-fact. "It's been so long. You've aged so."

Bryson nodded, managed to rasp, "Thanks."

Someone handed him a plastic cup of water: a nurse. He took it, gulped it down, handed back the cup. The nurse refilled it and gave it to him again. He drank greedily, gratefully. Elena sat beside the bed, close to him. "We must talk," she said, suddenly urgent.

"Yes," he said. His throat was raw; it hurt to speak. "There's—there's so much to talk about, Elena—I don't know where to begin."

"But there's so little time," she said. Her voice was brusque and businesslike.

There's no time, her voice echoed in his head. There's no time? For five years I've had nothing *but* time, time to ponder, to agonize.

She went on, "We need to know everything you've learned, everything you have. Any way in to Prometheus. Any way we can break the cryptographic perimeter."

He looked at her in astonishment. Was he hearing her right? She was questioning him about cryptography, about something called "Prometheus" . . . She had disappeared from his life for five years and she wanted to talk about *cryptography?*

"I want to know where you went," Bryson said hoarsely. "*Why* you vanished."

"Nicholas," she said briskly, "you told Ted that you took the key from Jacques Arnaud's encrypted phone. Where is it?"

"I . . . I did? When did I . . . ?"

"On the plane," said Waller. "Have you forgotten? You said you had a disk or a chip, some such thing. You took it, or copied it, from Arnaud's private office—you weren't entirely clear about it. And no, you weren't under the influence of chemicals. Though you were somewhat delirious, I must say."

"Where am I?"

"In a Directorate facility in the Dordogne. France. That IV in your arm is just for rehydration and antibiotics to ward off sepsis from your wounds."

"A Directorate . . ."

"Our headquarters. We've had to move here in order to maintain operational security. Washington was breached; we had to take evasive action, we had to leave the country in order to do our work."

"What do you want with me?"

"We need whatever you have, and we need it immediately," said Elena. "If our calculations are right, we have just a few days, perhaps only *hours.*"

"Before *what?*"

"Before Prometheus takes over," said Waller.

"Who is Prometheus?"

"The question is, *what* is Prometheus, and we don't have the answer. That's why we need the cryptochip."

"And I want to know what happened!" thundered Bryson. He gasped; he felt as if his throat would split. "With *you,* Elena! Where you went—*why* you went!"

He could see by the set of her jaw that she was determined not to be diverted from her line of questioning. "Nick, let us please talk about these personal matters another time. The time is very short—"

"What *was* I to you?" Bryson said. "Our marriage, our life together—what was that to you? If that's ancient history, if that's the past, you at least owe me an explanation—what happened, why you had to leave!"

"No, Nick—"

"I know it had something to do with Bucharest!"

Her lower lip seemed to be trembling, her eyes brimmed with tears.

"It did, didn't it?" he said in a softer voice. "If you know *anything,* you must know that what I did, I did for you!"

"Nick," she said desperately. "Please. I'm trying to hold myself together here, and you're not helping things."

"What do you think happened in Bucharest? What lies were you told?"

"Lies?" she suddenly exploded. "Don't talk to me about lies! You lied to me, you lied straight to my *face!"*

"Excuse me," said Waller. "You two want privacy." He turned and left the room, and then the nurse did too, and they were alone.

Bryson's head ached, his throat was so raw it felt as if it were bleeding inside. But he talked through the pain, desperate to communicate, to arrive at the truth. "Yes, I lied to you," he said. "It was the biggest mistake I ever made. You asked me about my weekend in Barcelona, and I lied. And you know that—you *knew* that. At the *time* you knew that, didn't you?"

She nodded, tears spilling down her cheeks.

"But if you knew I was lying, you must have known *why* I lied! You must have known I went to Bucharest because I loved you."

"I didn't know *what* you did, Nick!" she cried, looking up at him.

He ached for her, for the intimacy they had once shared. He wanted to throw his arms around her, but at the same time he wanted to grab her by the collar, shake the truth out of her. "But you know *now,* don't you?"

"I—I don't know *what* I know, Nick! I was terrified, and I felt so hurt, so horribly betrayed by you—so frightened for my life, for my parents—that I had to disappear. I know how good you are at finding people, so I had to leave without a trace."

"Waller knew where you were all along."

She looked up at the ceiling, and he followed her eyes to a tiny red dot: a video surveillance camera; there was no doubt that if this were a Directorate facility there were cameras throughout. What did that mean, that Waller was likely watching, listening? If he was, then he was; so what?

She was clenching and unclenching her hands. "It was just a few days after you said you were going to Barcelona for the weekend. In the normal course of my work—processing the 'harvest,' the signals-intercept product—that I came across a report that a Directorate operative had made an unscheduled appearance in Romania, in Bucharest."

"Oh, *Jesus.*"

"You know, I was just doing my job, and so of course I followed up the lead and found that it was you. I was—I was devastated, because I knew you were supposed to be in Barcelona. I knew this wasn't any cover story: it was such a rare thing for you to have a weekend off, and you had coordinated all your plans in an entirely overt way. And well—you know me, I'm very emotional, I feel things so strongly—I went to see Ted and told him what I had found. *Demanded,* really, that he level with me. He could see at once he was dealing with a distraught wife, a *jealous* wife, and yet he didn't attempt to cover for you. It was a relief yet not a relief. If he had tried to cover for you, I would have been angry, *terribly* angry. Yet the fact that he wasn't trying to do so told me that this was news to him—this information had taken him by surprise. And that was even more of a worry for me. Even Ted didn't know you were in Bucharest."

Bryson covered his eyes with a hand, shaking his head. Good God, he had been under surveillance the entire time! He had been so thorough in his "dry-cleaning," so careful to shake any tails. How could this have happened? What did this mean?

"Did he investigate?" Bryson asked. "Or have you investigate?"

"Both, I'm sure. I downlinked the photo-reconnaissance, so now I had a photo of you in Bucharest, which somehow made it more concrete, more awfully true. Then a separate and independent source, an agent code-named Titan, corroborated the information and added more. This was the intelligence that nearly did me in. Titan reported that you had had a secret meeting with Radu Dragan, the head of the ex-Securitate's vengeance squad."

"God, *no!*" Bryson cried out. "You must have thought—since I was being so secretive, you must have thought I was doing something underhanded, something I had to keep hidden from you!"

"Because I knew through Ted that you were meeting with Dragan without Directorate knowledge! You had to be making a deal, one you weren't proud of, one you had to conceal. But I gave you a chance. I asked you one day—asked you point-blank."

"You had never asked me before about anything I did when I wasn't home."

"You could tell how important the answer was to me, I'm sure. Yet you continued to lie! Baldly!"

"Elena, darling, I was protecting you! I didn't want to alarm you, I knew you would object if I'd given you advance notice. If I'd told you after the fact you'd have worried endlessly, you couldn't have *taken* it!"

She shook her head. "I know this now. But then Titan reported that you had cut a deal with Dragan, that you had given up my parents' location in exchange for some larger concession—"

"That was a *lie!*"

"But I didn't *know* that at the time!"

"How could you have thought I was capable of selling them out? How could you have accepted that?"

"Because you had *lied* to me, Nicholas!" she screamed. "You gave me no reason to think otherwise! You *lied!*"

"Dear God, what you must have thought of me."

"I went to Ted and demanded that he get me out of the country. Hide me somewhere, somewhere *safe!* Somewhere you could never track me down. And I wanted my parents moved as well—at once—which was an enormous expense because of the security cordon that was in place. Ted agreed this was for the best. I was wounded to—to the marrow by your betrayal, and most of all I was desperate to protect my parents. Waller moved me here, to the Dordogne facility, and settled Mama and Papa an hour or so from here."

"Waller believed that I'd done this?"

"Waller knew only that you'd lied to him as well, that you were doing something off the books."

"But he never raised it with me, never once mentioned it!"

"Does that surprise you? You know how he keeps things close to the vest. And I begged him not to say a thing to you, not to alert you."

"But don't you know what I *did?*" Bryson shouted. "Don't you *know?* Yes, I *did* make a deal with the sweepers—a deal to protect your parents! I threatened them, I made it clear that if ever anyone so much as laid a finger on your parents, Dragan's entire extended family would be wiped out. That this was personal for me! I knew that only the threat of a Sicilian-style revenge would get his attention."

Now Elena was sobbing. "In the years—the years since—I've wondered. Papa died two years ago, and Mama last year. Without him she had no will to live. Oh, God, Nicholas. I thought you were a monster!"

His arms went up to embrace her, though he could barely sit up. Weeping, she fell forward, collapsing into his arms. She touched the bandaged wound, hit a nerve; the pain almost took off the top of his head. But his arms closed around her, patting her gently, reassuring her. She seemed fragile, her beautiful eyes liquid, bloodshot. "What I did," she moaned. "What I assumed of you, what I assumed you did . . . !"

"Compounded by my failure to trust you, be honest with you. But Elena, this was not just a simple misunderstanding—you were deliberately and systematically misled by this agent code-named Titan. Why? To what *end?*"

"It must be Prometheus. They know we're on to them, closing in on them. And they must have seized upon the circumstance to poison the well, to spread a fog of uncertainty and dissension within our ranks. To set one against another, husband against wife in this case. False reports were filed in order to exploit the vulnerability—to hobble us where they could."

" 'Prometheus' . . . you and Waller both keep mentioning it. But you must know *something,* have some notion as to what it is, its objectives . . ."

Elena caressed his face, looked into his eyes. "How I've missed you, my darling." She sat up, took his hand in hers and squeezed, then slowly she got up off the bed. She began pacing as she spoke, just as she had always done whenever puzzling out a particularly complex problem. It was as if the physical activity, the repetitive motion catalyzed something in her thought processes.

"Prometheus is a name we first encountered only some twenty months ago," she said slowly, distantly. "It appears to refer to some sort of international syndicate, perhaps a cartel, and as best we can make out the Prometheus Group involves a consortium of technology companies and defense contractors, and their agents highly placed in governments around the world."

Bryson nodded. "Jacques Arnaud's vertically integrated defense corporations, General Tsai's PLA-owned defense contractors, Anatoly Prishnikov's extensive holdings throughout the old Soviet Union, the new Russia. Corporate alliances being established on a global scale."

She looked at him sharply, stopped pacing for a moment. "Yes. Those three cardinal among them. But there seem to be many participants, acting in concert."

"Acting *how?* Doing *what?*"

"Corporate acquisitions, mergers, consolidation—all seem to be accelerating."

"Mergers, consolidations in the defense sector?"

"Yes. But with an emphasis on telecommunications and satellites and computers. And it's more, *much* more than the amassing of a corporate empire. Because in the last five months there has been an epidemic of terrorist incidents, from Washington and New York to Geneva and Lille . . ."

"Prishnikov and Arnaud both knew about Lille in advance," Bryson said suddenly. "I overheard this, saw them discussing Lille a few days before. 'The way will be clear,' they said. 'The outrage will be enormous.' "

" 'The way will be clear,' " she mused aloud. "Defense industry insiders, owners fomenting chaos in order to boost the value of their stock . . ." She shook her head. "No, that doesn't track. The most direct way to increase demand for armaments is to foment *war,* not isolated, individual terrorist attacks. It's one of the theories behind the massive arming that led to World War Two, that international cartels of arms dealers built up the young Nazi Germany knowing that not too far down the line there would be a global war."

"But this is a different era—"

"Nicholas, think this through. Key players in Russia, China, and France—at least, and surely there are others—in a position to pit their nations against one another, sound the drumbeats of coming war, the need to strengthen national defenses . . . *That's* how it *should* be done."

"There's more than one way to spur calls for 'defense readiness.' "

"But if you hold the levers of power, there must be a good reason why you don't pull them. No, we're not seeing a global arms race. That's not the pattern at all. Separate incidents, that's what we're seeing. Individual acts of terrorism, unclaimed, unattributed. All happening on an accelerating schedule. But *why?*"

"Terrorism is another form of war," Bryson said slowly. "War by other means. A *psychological* war whose intent is to demoralize."

"But a war requires at least two sides."

"The terrorists and those who fight them."

She shook her head. "It still doesn't track. 'Those who fight them'—that's too nebulous."

"Terrorism is a form of theater. It's committed by an actor for an audience."

"So the desired end result is not the destruction itself, but the publicity caused by the destruction."

"Exactly."

"The publicity almost always helps attract attention to some cause, some group. But this recent wave of terrorism had no known authors, no cause or group. So we have to examine the publicity, the news, to see what links them all. What do these terrorist incidents all have in common?"

"That they could have been prevented," said Bryson abruptly.

Elena stopped and turned toward him with a curious smile. "What makes you say that?"

"Go back over the newspaper accounts, the transcripts of the television and radio coverage. Every time, after each incident, a comment appeared in the stories—usually attributed to some unnamed government official—to the effect that had adequate surveillance measures been in place, the tragedy would certainly have been prevented."

"Surveillance measures," she repeated.

"The treaty. The International Treaty on Surveillance and Security, which has just been agreed to by most of the countries of the world."

"The treaty creates a sort of international watchdog agency, right? A sort of super-FBI?"

"Right."

"Which would require the investment of billions and billions of dollars in new satellite equipment, police equipment, and the like. Potentially very lucrative for the companies . . . like Arnaud's, Prishnikov's, Tsai's . . . maybe that's it. An international treaty that serves as a mask, a cover for massive buildups in defense. So that we're all armed, protected against terrorists—terrorism being the new, post–Cold War threat to peace. And all the members of the U.N. Security Council have signed it and ratified it by now, isn't that right?"

"All but one. Great Britain. That's supposed to happen any day now. The main agitator there is Lord Miles Parmore."

"Yes, yes. He's a—how do you say—he's a blowhard, but he's been quite effective at organizing support for the treaty. Never underestimate the man who's willing to put himself out there. Remember the Reichstag in 1933."

Bryson shook his head. "That's not how the Prometheans operate. Lord Parmore has been brilliantly effective, but I suspect he's not a brilliant man. I'll bet the controlling intellect is elsewhere. It's what our fearless leader likes to say—'follow the brawn, look for the brains.' "

"You're saying there are puppetmasters in London directing the Parliamentary debate?"

"Count on it."

"But who? If we could find out . . ."

"I'm going to have to go there, meet with Parmore, question him, dig as deeply as I can."

"But can you go? Are you well enough?"

"If you get these damned tubes out of my arm, I'm fine."

She fell silent for a moment. "Nicholas, normally I'd be the overprotective wife, insisting you stay in bed and get better. But if you honestly feel well enough—time is of the essence—"

"I can go to London. I *want* to go. As soon as we can get a flight there."

"I'll make a call, arrange for them to get the private jet ready for a departure in six hours or so, assuming Ted doesn't need it."

"Good. The airstrip is close."

"A very short drive." She nodded, stopped in mid-pace. "So now Cassidy makes sense."

"Cassidy? Senator Cassidy?"

"Right."

"What about him? He was forced out of office because of revelations having to do with—what was it, his wife was caught dealing drugs or something?"

"Well, it's a little more complicated than that, but those are the basic outlines of the story. Years ago his wife was addicted to painkillers, and she bought drugs from an undercover police officer. Senator James Cassidy was able to get her police record expunged, then he got her into a treatment program."

"What does that have to do with the treaty?"

"First of all, he was the Senate's leading opponent of the treaty. He saw it as marking the end of individual privacy. In fact, he was the loudest voice in Washington warning of the steady erosion of privacy in the age of the computer. Many commentators saw irony in the fact that a senator so obsessed with privacy would be brought down because of something hidden in his past—they sniggered that he obviously had something to hide, that's why he was so obsessed with privacy."

"There may be something to that."

"That's not the point. The thing is, he's the ninth member of Congress in the last few months to either resign or announce he wasn't going to run again."

"It's a difficult time to be a politician, that's all."

"No question. But you know me—I'm trained to look for patterns where others don't necessarily see them. I noticed that among those nine were five who resigned under a cloud, you might say. In disgrace. And those five had been outspoken opponents of the international treaty on surveillance. Surely that was no coincidence—and it doesn't take an expert in elliptic curve cryptography or asymmetric key cryptosystems to see that. Private information had been leaked. Information that somehow became public—mental-health treatment in one case, extensive use of antidepressant medication, renting pornographic videos, a check written to an abortion clinic . . ."

"So supporters of the treaty are playing rough."

"More than that. Supporters of the treaty with access to the most private records."

"Some renegade elements within the FBI?"

"But the FBI generally doesn't *have* such information on people, you know that! Certainly not since the days of J. Edgar Hoover. Maybe when they do an in-depth investigation of a criminal suspect, but otherwise they don't."

"Then who, or what?"

"I began to look for the deeper pattern to see whether there might be a controlling intelligence behind this pattern of exposure. What did these congressmen all have in common? I inputted extensive biographies on them, whatever I could get, whatever financial information I could gather on the Internet—and, as you know, there's quite a bit out there as long as you can get a Social Security number, which is simple to get. And a curious fact turned up. Two of the disgraced congressmen had mortgages from a Washington, D.C., bank, First Washington Mutual Bancorp. And then I found the link: *all five of them* were clients of First Washington."

"So either the bank is somehow complicit in the blackmail, or somehow someone managed to access the bank's records."

"Right. Bank records, checks, money transfers . . . which can lead to health-insurance records, then medical records."

"Harry Dunne," Bryson said.

"Another Prometheus member. The CIA's deputy director of central intelligence."

"*Dunne* is?"

"Yes, yes, or so we speculate," she said hastily. "Go on, what about him?"

"Dunne was the one who plucked me out of retirement, yanked me from my quiet life and all but forced me to investigate the Directorate. By then you were already on the track of Prometheus, and Dunne wanted to find out what you knew, presumably to neutralize you. Because the CIA is behind this treaty—they want to see increased surveillance around the world."

"It may be, yes. For a variety of reasons, not least being the CIA's need for a mission, a reason to survive now that the Cold War's over. And yes, I have been on the track of Prometheus, but I still haven't been able to get a clear sense of its outlines. I've been using the Directorate's computers here, hacking away at Prometheus signals. We've identified certain members, like Arnaud, Prishnikov, Tsai, and Dunne; we're also able to record communications between and among them. But everything is encrypted, of course. We can see the *pattern* of transmissions, but we can't see the *content*.

It's sort of like a hologram—you need two 'data spaces' to be able to read the signals in the clear. I've been struggling with that long and hard, and so far without success. But if you have code information, *anything* . . ."

Bryson sat up in the hospital bed. He was feeling stronger; his legs felt crampy and needed to be exercised. "Hand me my phone, could you? It's right there, on the table."

"Nicholas, it's not likely to work well here—we're underground, and the signal—"

"Just hand it to me." She gave him his small silver GSM mobile phone. He turned it over and pulled something out of its battery compartment. It was a tiny black oblong. "This may help you."

She took it. "It's—a chip, a silicon chip . . . ?"

"An encryption chip, to be precise," he said. "Copied from Jacques Arnaud's office phone."

CHAPTER TWENTY-SIX

She took him down a long subterranean passage that led from the clinic to another wing of the facility. The floors were highly polished stone, the walls white, the low ceilings acoustically insulated. There was no sunlight, no window; they could have been anywhere in the world.

"This facility was built a decade ago or so as the Directorate's European base of operations," she explained. "And I've been working here since—well, since I left the States." She left unspoken: *since I left you.* "But when it became clear that our U.S. operations had been breached—likely a result of our investigation into Prometheus—Waller ordered the entire Washington office transferred here, which necessitated additional construction. As you'll see, very little is visible from the outside; it appears to be nothing more than a posh little research facility built into the side of a mountain."

"I'll take your word for it that we're in the Dordogne," Bryson said. His legs were fine; the only discomfort came from the wound in his side, which shot daggers of pain up and down his back as he walked.

"Well, you'll see soon enough when I take you for a walk outside. We'll probably have a little downtime waiting for the chip to process."

They came to a brushed-steel double-door where Elena entered a code on a small pad and then placed her thumb on a sensor. The doors slid open. The air inside was cool and dry.

The walls of the low-ceilinged room were lined with racks of supercomputers, workstations, television monitors. "We believe this is the most powerful supercomputer center in the world," Elena said. "We have Crays with petaflops of processing power, capable of *quadrillions* of operations per second. There are linked IBM-SP nodes, multithreaded-architecture computers, an SGI Onyx Reality Engine system.

There's a mass-storage system with a hundred and twenty gig-abytes of on-line capacity, a twenty-terabyte robotic tape server."

"You're losing me, darling."

But her excitement was palpable; she could barely contain it. She was in her element here, the Romanian graduate student who'd learned advanced mathematics on blackboards and rudimentary 1970s-era computers and now suddenly found herself in wonderland. She had always been like this, as long as he'd known her—transported by her work, be-witched by the technology that made it all possible.

"Don't forget the seventy-five miles of fiber-optic cable that's here, Elena." It was Chris Edgecomb, the tall, slender, green-eyed Guyanan with mocha skin. "Man, every time I see you, you look rougher and rougher!" Chris threw his arms around Bryson, hugged him hard. "They brought you back."

Bryson winced but smiled, happy to see the computer spe-cialist again after so long a time. "I guess I can't stay away."

"Well, I know your wife must be glad to see you again too."

"I don't think 'glad' is a strong enough word," said Elena.

"Saint Christopher seems to take good care of you, though," said Chris. "No matter what you go through. I'm not going to ask where you've been or what you've been doing, of course. But it's good to see you. I've been helping Elena on the software side of things, trying to crack the Pro-metheus message traffic. But it's a bear. *Strong* crypto. And we've got *toys* here, man—a serious, high-speed connection to the Internet backbone for distributed computing. An all-digital, gigabit-capacity communication satellite operating in the K- and Ka-frequency bands, in geosynchronous orbit, with the ability to carry digital communications at fiber-optic data rates."

Elena inserted the cryptochip in a port in one of the Dig-ital Alpha machines. "You see, stored on tape here are five months of encrypted communications among the Promethe-ans," she explained. "We've been able to pick it up by means of simple phone taps and satellite sweeps, but we haven't been able to crack them—we haven't been able to read them, listen to them, to *understand!* The encryption is too strong. If this is really a bug-free copy of the Prometheus algorithmic 'key,' we may have a breakthrough."

"How quickly will you know?" asked Bryson.

"It might be an hour, maybe several hours. Or maybe less, depending on a number of factors, including what level the key is from. Think of it as a key to an apartment building: the key may be a master, the kind that opens every door in the whole building. Or maybe it just opens the door to an individual unit. We'll see. Either way, it's exactly what we've needed to break Prometheus."

"Why don't I give you a page or a call when I have a hit?" Chris said. "In the meantime I think Ted Waller wants to see you two."

Waller's spacious, though windowless, office was furnished identically to his old one on K Street—the same seventeenth-century Kurdish rugs on the floor, the same British oil paintings of dogs grasping fowl in their mouths.

Waller was sitting behind his same massive French oak desk. "Nicky, Elena, I have a morsel of information that might be of interest to you. Elena, I don't believe you've met one of our most talented and redoubtable field operatives, who's honoring us with an all-too-infrequent visit home." A large, high-backed chair that had been facing Waller's desk swiveled around slowly. It was Layla.

"Ah, yes," Elena said, taking Layla's hand icily. "I've heard quite a bit about you."

"And I of you," Layla replied, her tone no warmer. She did not get up. "Hello, Nick."

Bryson nodded. "I believe last time we saw each other you were trying to kill me."

"Oh, that," Layla said, blushing. "Nothing personal, you understand."

"Of course."

"In any case, I thought you might want to know that it

seems as if our friend Jacques Arnaud may be taking himself out of the picture," Layla said, regarding them both with a clear, confident gaze.

"How do you mean?" Bryson asked.

"He's taking steps to liquidate all his holdings. The actions, I'd have to say, of a frightened man. This isn't an orderly retreat, or the migration of assets from one sector to another. Not business as usual, so to say. The merchant of death is putting himself out to pasture."

"But that makes no sense!" Bryson said. "I don't see the logic—do you?"

"Well," Layla said, almost smiling, "that's why we have analysts like Elena. To make sense of what operatives like you and I work so hard to collect."

Elena had been silent, her lips forming a thoughtful moue. Now her eyes focused. "Your source, Layla?"

"One of Arnaud's great rivals. A man nearly as estimable, and every bit as amoral, as Arnaud himself—a brother in malevolence—and yet he despises him with the enmity Cain felt for Abel. His name is Alain Poirier. It will not be new to you, I am sure."

"So you've just learned from Arnaud's great rival about the incipient dissolution of Arnaud's enterprises," Elena said.

"That's pretty much the shape of it," Layla said. "In English, anyway. You'd no doubt find it more memorable couched in the language of algorithms. I'm sure your methods are unfathomably obscure."

Waller watched the jousting between the two women as if at Wimbledon.

"Actually," Elena replied, "they begin with a pretty commonplace axiom: consider the source. For instance, you believe that Poirier is an enemy of Arnaud's. This is a natural assumption. They have depicted themselves in that light. In fact, they have done so all too assiduously."

"What are you trying to say?" Layla said coolly.

"I think if you investigate further, you'll discover that Poirier and Arnaud are actually business partners. Principals in a series of interconnected, widely dispersed holding companies. The rivalry is a ruse, pure and simple."

Layla narrowed her eyes. "You're saying the information I have is worthless?"

"Not at all," Elena said. "The fact that you've been 'rumbled'—identified and fed a line—is very useful intelligence indeed. Obviously Arnaud wishes us to believe this about him. We must attend not to the falsehood so much as the attempt to propagate the falsehood."

Layla fell silent for a moment. "You may have a point," she conceded sullenly.

"If Arnaud is trying to discourage our scrutiny," Bryson said, "the natural conclusion is that he's part of an enterprise that must elude scrutiny to succeed. They want us off our guard, to sow confusion. Something is happening, and soon. We can't let anything escape us now. Christ, we're dealing with forces that have marshaled an unprecedented degree of power and knowledge. Our best hope is that they underestimate us."

"My fear," Layla said ruefully, "is that they'll be right to."

Waller had left Directorate headquarters for an urgent meeting in Paris, and in the meantime Bryson and Elena had to wait. They passed the time by going for a long hike outside, down the mountainside, through hedges of rosemary, along the banks of the Dordogne. They were indeed in France, as Bryson realized once they'd emerged from the subterranean tunnels of the Directorate facility. The main entrance and exit seemed to be through an ancient stone villa built into the mountain face. Observers and passersby would see only the villa, which was large enough to plausibly contain offices and research facilities for an American think tank, presumably an off-site boondoggle for American scientists. It would explain the traffic in and out of the facility, the flights arriving and departing from the local airstrip. No one would have any idea of how large and far-ranging the facility really was, how deeply carved into the mountain.

Bryson walked more carefully than he otherwise might

have, favoring his wounded right side, from time to time grimacing at the pain. They descended the craggy cliffs, walking along an old pilgrim path through a valley of walnut farms that hugged the Dordogne River, that ancient watercourse that wound its way past Souillac and down to Bordeaux. These were the farms of solid peasants, the salt of the earth and the dour custodians of the French countryside, though some of the simple stone cottages had over the years become the homes of Englishmen who couldn't afford to vacation in Provence or Tuscany. Higher on the cliffs were the local wine châteaux that made good *vin du pays*. In the distance, the verdant landscape north of Cahors was dotted with medieval hill towns where the small restaurants served up humble but serious *cuisine du terroir* to the large peasant families on Sundays. Bryson and Elena wended their way through the woods, with their famous truffles hidden away beneath the roots of ancient trees, whose secret locations are passed down in families from generation to generation, kept secret even from the very owners of the land.

"It was Ted's idea to relocate here," Elena explained as they walked, hand in hand. "You can see why a man who so loves to eat would fall in love with the countryside, with the chevres and the walnut oil and the truffles. But it's quite practical as well. We're quite well hidden here, the cover is plausible, the airstrip convenient. And there are fast, efficient highways in every direction—north to Paris, east to Switzerland and Italy, south to the Mediterranean, west to Bordeaux and the Atlantic. My parents loved it here." Her voice became soft, pensive. "They missed the homeland, of course, but it was such a wonderful place to spend their last years." She pointed to a cluster of stone cottages far off in the distance. "We lived in one of those little houses there."

" 'We'?"

"I lived with them, took care of them."

"I'm happy for you. My loss was their gain."

She smiled, squeezed his hand. "You know, the old saying is true. *Mai rǔrut, mai drǎgut.*"

"Absence makes the heart grow fonder," he translated.

"And what did you always used to say—*celor ce duc mai mult dorul, le pare mai dulce odorul?* Absence sharpens love, but presence strengthens it, right?"

"Nicholas, it's been hard for me, you know. Very hard."

"And for me. More so."

"I've had to rebuild my life without you. But the ache, the sense of loss, never went away. Was it the same for you?"

"I suspect it was much harder for me, because of the uncertainty. Because of never knowing *why*—why you disappeared, where you went, what you *thought*."

"Oh, *iubito! Te ador!* We were both victims—victims, hostages to a world of distrust and suspicion."

"I was told you were 'assigned' to me as a watcher."

"*Assigned?* We fell in love, and that quite by accident. How can I ever prove to you I was *not*? I was in *love* with you, Nicholas. I still am."

He took her through Harry Dunne's lies, the tale of a young man selected for his athletic and linguistic abilities, then recruited blind, manipulated, his parents killed.

"They are very clever, the Prometheans," she said. "With an organization that is so cloaked in layers of secrecy like ours, it is not difficult to construct a plausible lie. Then they made it seem that you were a hostile, that you were trying to destroy us—so you could not check on the accuracy of what they told you."

"But did you know about Waller?"

"About—"

"About his . . ." Bryson spoke tentatively. "His background."

She nodded. "About Russia. Yes, he briefed me. But not long ago, just recently. I think only because he was planning to bring you in, and he knew we would talk."

Her phone rang. "Yes?" Her face brightened. "Thank you, Chris."

Hanging up, she said to Bryson, "We have something."

Chris Edgecomb handed Elena a pile of red-bordered folders, each thick with printouts. "Man, when this code cracked, it *cracked.* We had five high-speed laser printers smoking, printing out all this stuff. The main thing that slowed us down was the artificial-intelligence transcript agent—converting the spoken word to the printed one requires huge computing power and a lot of time, even at the speed of our processors. And we're still nowhere close to done. I tried to winnow out anything extraneous, but I decided to err on the side of being inclusive, and leave the main decisions to you as to what's important and what's not."

"Thanks, Chris," she said, taking the folders and laying them out on the long table in the conference room adjacent to the supercomputer center.

"I'll have coffee brought in for you two. I have a feeling you're going to need it."

They divided up the pile of printouts and began poring over them. By far the most valuable product was the decrypts of telephone conversations among the principals, of which there were many, some extensive, some conference calls. Since the exchanges were encrypted, the participants tended to speak freely. Some of them—the more canny ones, including Arnaud and Prishnikov—remained circumspect. They used coded language, references that the other would understand without having to resort to explicitness. Here, Elena's knowledge of speech patterns, her ability to discern deliberate concealment even in plain speech, was crucial. She flagged quite a few transcripts with sticky pads. And since Bryson was more familiar with the players and their backgrounds, as well as with the specifics of certain operations, he was able to pick up on different references, other meanings.

Barely had they started reading through the papers than Bryson said, "I'd say we've got the goods on them. It's no longer a matter of hearsay. Here, Prishnikov is actually planning the Geneva anthrax attack, fully three weeks in advance."

"But they're clearly not running the show," Elena said. "They're deferring to another—really, to two others, possibly Americans."

"Who?"

"So far they don't use the names. There's a reference to West Coast time, so one of them may be either in California or somewhere on the Pacific Coast of the U.S."

"What about London? Any idea who the puppetmaster might be there?"

"No. . . ."

Chris Edgecomb suddenly came into the room, holding aloft a few sheets of paper. "This just broke," he said, excitement evident in his face. "It's a pattern of funds-transfer traffic into and out of the First Washington Mutual Bancorp—I think you might find it interesting." He handed Elena several sheets of paper, each covered with columns of figures.

"That's the bank in Washington used by a majority of members of Congress, isn't that right?" said Bryson. "The one you suspect was involved in blackmailing—leaking personal information on opponents of the treaty?"

"Yes," said Elena. "These are proprietary transfers."

Edgecomb nodded.

"The cycles, the periodicity—it's unmistakable."

"What is it?" asked Bryson.

"This is a sequence of authorization codes characteristic of a wholly owned entity. A trail, as it were."

"Meaning what?" Bryson demanded.

"This Washington bank appears to be owned and controlled by another, larger financial institution."

"That's not uncommon," Bryson said.

"The point is, there's a pattern of deliberate obfuscation going on here—that is, the ownership is elaborately concealed, carefully hidden."

"Is there a way to find out who the secret owner is?" Bryson asked.

Elena nodded, distracted, as she studied the figures. "Chris, the recurring number here has to be the ABA routing code. Do you think you can run it down, identify which—"

"I'm one step ahead of you, Elena," he said. "It's a New York–based firm called Meredith Waterman . . . ?"

"My *God*," she said. "That's one of the oldest, most respected investment banks on Wall Street. It makes Morgan Stanley or Brown Brothers Harriman look like upstarts. I don't understand—why would Meredith Waterman be involved in blackmailing senators and congressmen into supporting the International Treaty on Surveillance and Security . . . ?"

"Meredith Waterman is probably privately held," said Bryson.

"So?"

"So it may itself be a holding company, in a sense—a front. In other words, maybe it's being used by another institution or an individual or a group of individuals—say, the Prometheus Group—to mask their true holdings. So if there's a way to get a list of all past and present partners in Meredith Waterman, maybe also majority owners . . ."

"That shouldn't be hard at all," said Edgecomb. "Even privately held firms are strictly regulated by the SEC and the FDIC, and they're required to file all sorts of documents which we should be able to access."

"One or more of those names may indicate Prometheus ownership," said Bryson.

Edgecomb nodded and left the room.

Bryson suddenly thought of something. "Richard Lanchester was a partner at Meredith Waterman."

"What?"

"Before he left Wall Street and went into public service, he was a big star in investment banking. Meredith Waterman's golden boy. That's how he made his fortune."

"Lanchester? But he—you said he was sympathetic, he was helpful to you."

"He lent a sympathetic ear, yes. He seemed genuinely alarmed. He listened, but in reality he did nothing."

"He said he wanted you to come back to him with more evidence."

"Which is just a variant of what Harry Dunne wanted—to use me as a cat's paw."

"You think Richard Lanchester could be part of Prometheus?"

"I wouldn't rule him out."

Elena returned to the transcript she'd been scrutinizing, and then she looked up suddenly. "Listen to this," she said. " 'The transfer of power will be complete forty-eight hours after the British ratify the treaty.' "

"Who's speaking?" asked Bryson.

"I—I don't know. The call originates in Washington, routed through a sterile pipeline. The unnamed caller is speaking to Prishnikov."

"Can you get a voice ID?"

"Possibly. I'd have to listen to the actual recording, determine whether the voice was altered, and if so, how well it was altered."

"Forty-eight hours ... the 'transfer of power' ... *to* whom, *from* whom? Or to *what, from* what? Jesus, I've got to get to London right away. When is the jet scheduled to leave?"

She looked at her watch. "Three hours and twenty minutes from now."

"Not soon enough. If we drove ..."

"No, it would take far too long. I suggest we just go out to the airstrip and invoke Ted Waller's name, pull all the strings we've got, ask them to fly out as soon as absolutely possible."

"It's just as Dmitri Labov said."

"Who?"

"Prishnikov's deputy. He said, 'The machinery has just about fallen into place. *Power is to be transferred fully!* Everything will come into view.' He said that only days remained."

"This must be the deadline he was talking about. My God, Nick, you're right, there's no time to waste."

As she stood up, the lights in the room seemed to flicker briefly, the interruption a fraction of a second at most.

"What was that?" she asked.

"Is there an emergency generator in the facility somewhere?"

"Yes, of course, there must be."

"It just went on."

"But it would only go on in case of a true emergency," she said, puzzled. "Nothing has happened, as far as I can tell—"

"*Move!*" shouted Bryson suddenly. "*Out of here!*"

"What?"

"*Run!* Elena, *move* it—*now!* Something's been patched into the power grid. . . . Where's the nearest exit to outside?"

Elena turned, pointed to the left.

"*Jesus,* Elena, let's *go!* I'll bet the doors lock automatically, sealing intruders in as well as out. I know that's what's going on!"

He raced down the hallway; Elena scooped up several computer diskettes from the table and then ran after him.

"Which *way?*" he screamed.

"Straight through those doors!"

She led the way, and he followed. In a matter of seconds they had come to a set of steel doors marked EMERGENCY EXIT; a red crash-bar at the middle of the doors was used to force the doors open, probably setting off an alarm at the same time. Bryson slammed himself against the crash-bar; the double-doors opened outward into the dark night as an alarm rang. A rush of cold air came at them. No more than two feet in front of them was a floor-to-ceiling gate constructed of steel bars. The gate was slowly closing, automatically, from left to right.

"Jump!" shouted Bryson, diving through the steadily narrowing space. He spun around and grabbed Elena, dragging her through the gap between the gate and the stone wall, her body just barely clearing it. They were on the steep hillside next to the old stone villa, the electric gate concealed by tall hedges.

Bryson and Elena ran directly ahead, away from the villa and down the hill. "Is there a car around here somewhere?" asked Bryson.

"There's an all-terrain vehicle parked right in front of the villa," she replied. "It's—there it is!"

A small, boxy, four-wheel-drive Land Rover Defender 90 glinted in the moonlight twenty yards ahead. Bryson ran toward it, jumped into the front seat, and felt for the key. It wasn't in the ignition. Jesus, where the hell was it? In a remote setting like this, wouldn't it be left in the car? Elena leaped into the car. "Under the mat," she said.

He reached down, felt the key under the rubber floor mat. Inserting the key in the ignition, he started it; the Land Rover roared to life.

"Nick, what's happening?" Elena cried out as the car lurched forward and down the steep path away from the compound.

But before Bryson had a chance to speak, there was an immense, dazzlingly bright flash of white light, and a rumbling explosion that seemed to come from deep in the mountain. In a second or two the blast surfaced, the sound terrifyingly loud, deafening, all-enveloping. As Bryson steered the Land Rover around a sharp twist, crashing into and then through vegetation, he could feel the heat sear his back, exactly as hot as if he'd leaned right back into the fire.

Elena turned back, gripping the handrails to steady herself. "Oh, my God, Nick!" she screamed. "The facility—the compound—it's been completely destroyed! Oh, *God*, Nick, look at that!"

But Bryson would not turn around; he did not dare. They had to keep moving. There was not a second to lose. The wheels spun through the underbrush as he accelerated, faster and faster, and he thought just one thing: *My love—you're safe.*

You're safe, you're alive, you're with me.

For now.

Dear God, for now.

CHAPTER TWENTY-SEVEN

They arrived in London, both of them, by ten o'clock in the evening, by which point it was too late to accomplish what they had to do. They spent the night together in a hotel in Russell Square, in the same bed for the first time in five years. They were strangers to each other, in a sense, but each found the other's body immediately familiar—reassuringly yet excitingly so. For the first time in five years they made love, the passion urgent, almost desperate. They fell asleep entangled in each other, exhausted both from the lovemaking and from the enormous strains that had impelled them there.

In the morning they spoke of the nightmare they had both witnessed, sifting details, trying to make some sense of the penetration.

"When you called the airstrip to reserve the jet," asked Bryson, "you probably didn't use a sterile line, did you?"

She shook her head slowly, her face taut with anxiety. "The airstrip wasn't equipped with a scrambler on its end, so there was no point. But calls originating in the Directorate facility were generally considered safe, since our internal communications center was beyond the reach of outside interference. If we phoned London or Paris or Munich, say, we usually used the sterile channels—but only to protect the other end."

"But calls made across such a distance—a hundred miles or more, for instance—generally are routed from landlines to microwave towers, and it's the microwave transmission that's penetrable by satellite surveillance, right?"

"That's right—landlines can be tapped into, but not by satellite. It has to be by conventional means—phone taps placed on the wires and such. And that requires knowing exactly where the calls originated."

"Prometheus obviously knew the details of the Dordogne center," Bryson said quietly. "For all Waller's precautions, the comings and goings, into and out of the airfield, must have been observed, noted. And the airstrip was an easy target for a conventional phone tap."

"Waller—thank God, he was gone! But we have to reach him."

"Jesus. I'm sure he knows. But Chris Edgecomb—"

She covered her eyes with her hand. "Oh, dear God, Chris! And Layla!"

"And dozens of others. Most of them I didn't know any longer, but you must have had quite a few friends among them."

She nodded silently, removed her hand from her eyes, which were flooded with tears.

After a moment's silence, Bryson resumed. "They must have patched into the power grid and planted explosives—plastique—throughout and *beneath* the facility. Without inside resources—without human beings who'd been turned—they could never have done it. The Directorate was on the verge of unraveling the Prometheus Group's plans, and so it had to be neutralized. They sent me—and others, I'm sure—and when those efforts didn't pan out, they went for the direct approach." He closed his eyes. "Whatever secrets, plans they're protecting, we have to assume they're of monumental importance to the men behind Prometheus."

A direct, frontal approach to the treaty's most vocal proponent, Lord Miles Parmore, was therefore doomed to fail: it would only alert their enemies without yielding information; such men were well guarded, well prepared for deception, misdirection. Moreover, Bryson's instinct told him that Lord Parmore was not their man. He was a figurehead, a very public figure, closely watched, incapable of maneuvering behind the scenes. He could not be a Prometheus control. The true control would have to be someone affiliated with Parmore, connected to him in a tangential way. But connected *how?*

The Prometheus conspirators were too clever, too thorough, to allow connections to remain visible. Records would be altered, erased. Even close scrutiny would not reveal the hidden controls, the puppetmasters. The only giveaway would be what was *not* there, records missing, obviously deleted. Yet the search for such gaps would be the proverbial search for a needle in a haystack.

Finally, it was Bryson's idea that they dig more deeply, dig into the past. It had been his experience that the truth could often be discerned there, in old files and books—records rarely accessed, too dispersed, too difficult to alter convincingly.

It was a theory, but only a theory, and it took them that morning to the British Library at St. Pancras, which lay sprawled across a landscaped square off Euston Road, its orange, hand-molded Leicester brick shimmering in the bright morning sun. Bryson and Elena made their way through the plaza, past the large bronze of Newton by Sir Eduardo Paolozzi, and into the spacious entrance hall. Bryson scanned the faces of the people he passed, attuned to the slightest sign of recognition. He had to assume that the Promethean networks had been alerted to him, perhaps even to their presence in London, though so far there was no sign of it. Inside the library, a broad flight of travertine steps took them to the main reading room—an expanse of oak desks with individual desk lamps—and they walked through the discreet paneled doors that led to the carrels. The double carrel they had reserved was private but not cramped, its round-backed oak chairs and green leather-topped desks creating a slightly clubby feeling.

Within an hour, they had gathered most of the necessary volumes, starting with selections from the official proceedings of Parliament—heavy, large volumes with rugged, black library bindings. Many had been unopened for years, and gave off a musty smell of decay when the pages were turned. Nick and Elena went through them with intense and single-minded focus. Had there been earlier debates about civil threats and civil liberties—other decisions with implications for civilian surveillance? On a pad, they each jotted down errant facts—unexplained references, names, sites. These were areas where the marks of the sculptor's chisel might be in evidence.

It was Elena who first spoke the name aloud. *Rupert Vere.* A low-key, soft-spoken, and highly expert maneuverer, the embodiment of political moderation but also—the chronicles made this clear over the years—a master of procedural cunning. Was it possible? Was the intuition worth checking out?

Rupert Vere, Member of Parliament from Chelsea, was Britain's foreign secretary.

Bryson followed the intricate tracery of the Chelsea MP's career through the smaller regional papers, which were more attuned to incidental details, less preoccupied with the official significance of events. It was painstaking, even stupefying work, the matter of collating a hundred tiny articles in dozens of local gazettes and circulars, the paper often yellowed and brittle. At times, Bryson was seized with exasperation—it seemed like madness to think that they'd find clues to the most concealed of conspiracies right out there in the open, in the public record.

But he persevered. They both did. Elena made the analogy to her signals-intercept work: within the cascade of noise, the abundance of useless information, might be a signal somewhere—if only they could make it out. Rupert Vere had graduated with a first from Brasenose College, Oxford; he had a reputation for laziness, which was quite likely a cunning subterfuge. He also had a distinct gift for cultivating friendships, a *Guardian* columnist noted: ". . . and so his influence goes beyond the formal ambit of his authority." A picture was coming gradually into focus: for years, Foreign Secretary Rupert Vere had been working behind the scenes to prepare the way for passage of the treaty, calling in political debts, inveigling friends and allies. And yet his own pronouncements were temperate, his ties to the firebrands nowhere in evidence.

Finally, it was a seemingly trivial piece of data that caught Bryson's attention. In the yellowing pages of the *Evening Standard,* there was an account of the 1965 rowing races in Pangbourne, on the Thames, where nationally ranked teams from secondary schools around the country competed. In small agate type, the paper reported on the teams. Vere, it appeared, rowed for Marlborough, where he was a sixth-former. The language was stilted, the account seemingly innocuous.

At the Pangbourne Junior Sculls, a number of the quads and doubles distinguished themselves. In particular, the J18 quad from Sir William Borlase School recorded the fastest time of the day (10m 28s), but were pressed quite close by the crews in the strong J16 class where St George's College Crew (10m 35s), with the GBv France double scullers Matthews and Loake aboard, were chased hard by Westminster. In both the J14 classes the Hereford Cathedral School doubles proved outstanding (12m 11s, and 13m 22s). There were also some high-class performers among the J16 singles. At the front Rupert Vere (11m 50s) had 13 seconds on his Marlborough team mate Miles Parmore, while David Houghton (13m 5s) finished almost half a minute clear of his pursuers. Showing real promise, Parrish of St George's (12m 6s) and Kellman of Dragon School (12m 10s) headed the MJ16 class, finishing fourth and fifth overall. The younger age groups race over a 1500m distance at Pangbourne. The WJ13 winner, Dawson of Marlborough (8m 51s), had finished a creditable second-equal in the morning's WJ14 race and now finished fifth overall, behind MJ13 winner Goodey.

He reread the item and soon found a couple of similar ones. Vere had rowed for Marlborough, in the same eight as Miles Parmore.

Yes. The British Foreign Secretary and MP from Chelsea, an early champion of the treaty, had been a teammate and longtime friend of Lord Miles Parmore.

Had they found their man?

The New Palace of Westminster—better known as the Houses of Parliament—was, in its very blend of antiquity and modernity, a quintessentially British institution. As far back as the Viking King Canute, a royal palace existed on these grounds. But it was Edward the Confessor and William the Conqueror in the eleventh century who enlarged the ancient dream of royal munificence and splendor. The historical continuities were as real as the Magna Carta; the discontinuities were greater still. And when the structure was rebuilt in the mid-nineteenth century, it represented the height of the Gothic Revival style, an enduring legacy to the ingenuity of its architects—a vision of an artificial, invented antiquity, which would be reinvented once more when a World War II blitzkrieg destroyed the Commons Chamber. Carefully restored, albeit in a more subdued interpretation of late Gothic, it was a replica of a replica.

Even as it opened onto one of London's busiest centers of traffic, Parliament Square, the Houses of Parliament themselves remained aloof and protected by their eight-acre arcadian redoubt. The "new palace" itself was a whirlpool of human traffic. It had almost twelve hundred rooms, and fully two miles of passages. The areas of the buildings that members routinely used, that tourists routinely saw, were impressive indeed, but there was much more, the plans for which were, for reasons of security, not readily accessible. But they, too, could be found in the historical archives. Bryson had given himself two hours to learn and master their details. A series of shifting orthogonal forms arranged themselves in his mind into a layout that had a visceral immediacy to him. He knew precisely how the Peers' Library related to the Prince's Chamber; he knew the distance between the Speaker's Residence and the Sergeant-at-Arms residence, knew how long it would take to go from the Commons Lobby to the first of the Minister's rooms. In an era without central heating, it was essential to have some special chambers that were protected from the exterior wall by unused, insulating spaces. Moreover, any vast public work would, it was understood, be in constant need of repair and refurbishment, and there had to be passageways for workmen to go about their tasks without disturbing the grandeur of the public spaces. Like government itself, its functioning required complex spaces and relays that were invisible to the citizenry.

Elena, meanwhile, scoured every recorded detail of Rupert Vere's life. Another tiny detail had caught her attention: when Vere was sixteen, he'd won a *Sunday Times* crossword puzzle competition. He was a gamesman, which seemed somehow apt: yet the game he was playing was anything but trivial.

At five o'clock in the morning, a backpacker in a leather flight jacket and black plastic glasses walked around the perimeter of the Houses of Parliament, like a sleepless tourist trying to walk off a hangover. Or at least Bryson hoped he would be taken for one. He stopped before the black statue of Cromwell, near St. Stephen's Entrance, and read the carefully lettered sign: PACKAGES LARGER THAN A4, OTHER THAN FLOWERS, MUST BE DELIVERED VIA THE BLACK ROD'S GARDEN ENTRANCE. He walked past the Peer's Entrance, noting its precise location vis-à-vis the others; then made his way through the small stand of horse-chestnut trees and noted the location of each security camera, invariably posted high in white enameled hoods. The Metropolitan Police of London, Bryson had learned, maintains a network of traffic cameras, three hundred of them fixed on posts and high buildings across the city. Each has a number, and if an authorized person types in the number, he or she can call up a clear, color image of London. It is possible to rotate the camera and zoom it in. It is possible to follow police chases, moving from camera to camera, and to follow a motorist or pedestrian without being detected. It would not be wise to spend much time on surveillance here, he decided; this would have to be brief.

He took in the four-tiered structure of the main gallery, mapping the physical structure itself with the mental representations he had formed, turning the abstract metrics into concrete perceptions. It was essential to transmute data into intuition, which could be accessed instantly and unreflectively, without calculation and consideration. That was one

of Waller's early lessons to him, and among the most valuable. *In the field, the only maps that matter are in your head.*

St. Stephen's Tower, the clock tower at the north end of
the Parliament building, was three hundred and twenty feet
tall. The Victoria Tower, on the opposite end of the complex,
was wider but nearly as high. Between the towers, the roof-
ing was garlanded with scaffolding; the process of exterior
repair work was almost unceasing. External stairs sur-
mounted the roof twenty feet from the Victoria Tower. And
then he ambled toward the Thames and scanned the far side
of the complex, which abutted directly onto the Thames. By
the galleries, there was a fifteen-foot terrace, but at the towers
to either end, the drop was sheer, a plumb line. Across the
river, he saw a few anchored boats. Some were designated
for sightseeing trips, others for maintenance purposes. One
was stenciled FUEL AND LUBRICATION SERVICE. He took note
of it.

The plan was set, the schedule determined. Bryson made
his way back to their hotel and changed, and then he and
Elena went over the plan twice more. Yet his concerns were
not allayed. The plan had too many moving parts; he knew
the probability of a mishap grew geometrically as the sequence of constituent events lengthened. But there was no
choice now.

Smartly attired in a double-breasted, pin-striped suit and
round horn-rimmed glasses, Bryson—or rather, as his pass
attested, Nigel Hilbreth—ascended the stairs from the lower
waiting hall to the upper waiting hall of the Chamber of
Commons and took his seat in the gallery. His face was composed into a mask of bland disinterest, his sandy hair neatly
parted, mustache tidy. He was every inch a midlevel civil
servant, including even the fragrance—Penhaligon's Blen-
heim, purchased on Wellington Street. A simple expedient
perhaps, but in some ways equally as effective as the dye,
glasses, and adhesive-backed facial hair. It was originally
Waller, too, who first alerted him to the rarely discussed
olfactory aspects of camouflage. When Bryson had an as-

signment in East Asia, he would abstain from meat and dairy products for several weeks: Asians, with their diets of fish and soy, found Westerners to have a characteristically "meaty" smell, their skin proteins affected by their beef-rich diet. He made similar dietary accommodations preceding assignments in the various Arabic regions. An adjustment in fragrance was a trivial change, but Bryson knew that it was often through such subliminal clues that we detect the strangers among us.

"Nigel Hilbreth" sat quietly observing the tense parliamentary deliberations, a small black briefcase by his feet. Below, on the long, green leather-upholstered benches, the MPs sat with an unusual measure of attentiveness, their documents lit by the small capsule lamps that dangled just above their heads, suspended on long wires from a vaulted ceiling. It was an ungainly solution to a problem that admitted no elegant one. The ministers of the current government sat on the front bench to the right side; the opposition faced them to the left. The gallery benches, paneled with precisely incised dark-brown woodwork, rose steeply above them, in balcony formation.

Bryson had arrived in the middle of the emergency session, but he knew precisely what was being bruited about: it was the issue that was at the forefront of every organ of governmental deliberation in the world right now, or had been only recently: the Treaty on Surveillance and Security. In this instance, however, the precipitating incident was the horrendous damage wrought by a recidivist splinter faction of Sinn Fein, which had detonated a shrapnel bomb in the middle of Harrods during one of its busiest hours, wounding hundreds. *Was that, too, secretly funded and instigated by the Prometheus Group?*

For the first time, he was able to see Rupert Vere in the flesh. Foreign Secretary Vere was a deceptively wizened-looking man, seemingly older than his fifty-six years, but one could tell that his small, darting eyes missed little. Bryson glanced at his watch—another subtle prop, an old tank watch from McCallister & Son.

Half an hour earlier, Bryson had, adopting the blasé manner of a Whitehall civil servant, asked a messenger to deliver a note, presumably official and semiurgent Whitehall business, to the foreign secretary. Any minute now it would be brought to Vere by one of his assistants. Bryson wanted to study his reaction when he opened the note and read its contents. The note—a simple, almost childish contrivance that Elena, a lover of puzzles, had devised—was framed like an English crossword-puzzle clue:

> *Put yourself between support and a definite article, then add a couple. Puzzled? See you at your alcove suite during the intersession.*

It had been Elena's inspiration to put, in the form of a clue, the one watchword that he could not ignore.

As a member of the Opposition held forth on the threats to civil liberties posed by the prospective treaty, Rupert Vere was handed an envelope. He opened it, scanned the note, and then looked up into the gallery directly at Bryson. He had an intent yet nearly unreadable expression. It was all Bryson could do not to flinch; long seconds passed before he realized the foreign secretary was merely gazing up into the middle distance, that his eyes weren't focusing on anyone at all. Bryson struggled to maintain his placid, bored expression, but it was not easy. If he attracted notice, he was done for: that had to be the operating assumption. The sentries controlled by the Prometheus Group undoubtedly knew exactly what he looked like. But there was a good chance that they hadn't been notified about Elena, or that if they knew about her, they would assume she had been killed in the destruction of the Directorate's Dordogne headquarters.

It was Elena, therefore, who would have to make the direct approach. The session would adjourn in ten minutes. What happened next would determine everything.

Members of the British cabinet typically have offices on Whitehall and other nearby streets; the foreign secretary is the titular head of the Foreign and Commonwealth Office, and his official quarters are on King Charles Street. But Bryson knew that because of his hours negotiating with members of parliament, Rupert Vere also maintained quarters beneath the sloping roof of the Palace of Westminster. The suite was a mere five-minute walk from the Commons chambers, and provided a discreet meeting area for matters that required sensitivity and immediacy.

Would Vere do what the note had suggested, or would he surprise them with another response altogether? Bryson believed that Vere's primary reaction would be curiosity, that he would indeed return directly to his office under the eaves. But in case Vere panicked, or decided for some reason to go elsewhere, Bryson had to tail him. Having identified the foreign secretary, he was able to follow him out of the Commons Chambers by picking him out of the crowd of Parliament members. He shadowed Vere as he made his way up the stone committee staircase, past busts of prime ministers past, to his Parliamentary office, until he could follow him no longer without attracting attention.

Rupert Vere's personal secretary was Belinda Headlam, a thickset woman in her early sixties who wore her gray hair in a tight bun. "This lady says you're expecting her," she murmured to the foreign secretary as he entered the antechamber. "She says she's left you a note?"

"Yes, well," Vere replied, and then he saw Elena sitting on the tufted leather sofa outside his office. She had taken care to project the right image: her navy suit revealed décolletage, though not inappropriately so; her glossy brown hair was pulled back; her lips were painted in eggplant gloss. She looked stunning, yet at the same time professional.

Vere raised his eyebrows and smiled rapaciously. "I don't believe we've met," he said. "But you've certainly got my attention. Your note, that is." He beckoned her to follow him into his small, dim, but exquisitely appointed office built in the eaves beneath the Parliament building's vast slate roof. He sat behind his desk and indicated that she should sit in a leather chair a few feet away.

For a moment, he shuffled his correspondence. Elena was conscious of Vere sizing her up—less, it almost seemed to her, as an adversary than as a potential conquest.

"You must be a puzzler, too," he said at last. "The answer is 'Prometheus,' is that right? A rather crude clue, though. *Me* between *pro* and *the,* plus *us.*" He paused, his eyes boring into hers. "To what do I owe the pleasure of your company, Miss . . . ?"

"Goldoni," she replied. She had not lost her accent, so it would have to be a foreign name. She watched him closely but could not read him. Rather than pretending he didn't understand what she was hinting at, he had immediately acknowledged the word Prometheus—yet his bland reaction revealed no alarm, no fear, not even any defensiveness. If he was acting, he was skilled, though that would not have surprised her: he had not gotten as far as he had without some talent at dissembling.

"I assume your office is sterile?" Elena said. He gave her a look of puzzled incomprehension, but she persisted. "You know who sent me. You'll have to excuse the irregularity of this means of making contact, but then that's the reason for my visit. The matter is urgent. The existing channels of communication may have been compromised."

"I beg your pardon," he said haughtily.

"You must not use the existing codes," Elena said, watching his face closely. "This is of utmost importance, particularly with so little time remaining before the Prometheus plan goes into force. I will be in touch with you soon to indicate when the channels have been normalized."

Vere's tolerant smile faded. He cleared his throat and got to his feet. "You're bonkers," he said. "Now, if you'll please excuse me—"

"No!" Elena interrupted in an urgent whisper. "All cryptosystems have been compromised. Their integrity *cannot* be relied upon! We are changing all the codes. You must await further instructions."

All of Vere's professional charm had vanished; his face grew hard. "Get out of here at once!" he demanded in a loud, clipped voice. Was that panic in his voice? Was he using indignation to cover his fear? "I'll be reporting you to the constabulary, and you'll be making a grave mistake if you ever try to enter these halls again."

Vere reached over to press his intercom button, but before he could do so, the door to his chambers swung open. A slim, tweedy man entered, shutting the door behind him. Elena recognized the face from her recent researches: it was Rupert Vere's longtime deputy, Simon Dawson, the senior-most member of Vere's staff, who was charged with formulating policy.

"Rupes," Simon Dawson said in an almost languorous drawl. "I couldn't help overhearing. Is this woman being tiresome?" Dawson's pale brown hair, apple cheeks, and lanky figure gave him the unsettling look of a middle-aged schoolboy.

Vere was visibly relieved. "As a matter of fact, Simon, yes," Vere said. "She's nattering at me all kinds of hog-wash—about something called Prometheus, about crypto-something-or-other, 'Prometheus plans being in force'—utter madness! The lady must be reported to MI-5 at once—she's a public danger."

Elena took a few steps away from Vere's desk, her gaze shifting from one man to the other. Something was very wrong. Dawson had closed the heavy oak door behind him, she noticed. That made no sense.

Unless . . .

Dawson withdrew a flat, silenced Browning from his Harris tweed jacket.

"Crikey, Simon, what are you doing with a pistol?" Vere asked. "That really shouldn't be necessary. I'm sure this woman has the sense to leave at once, don't you?" She studied the shifting expressions of Vere's face, a rapid sequence of puzzlement, dismay, and fear.

The civil servant's long, tapered fingers rested by the trig-ger with practiced ease. Elena's heart was pounding, her eyes darting wildly around the room hoping to find an opportunity for disruption or escape.

Dawson looked into her eyes, and she returned the stare, boldly, brazenly, almost daring him to fire. Suddenly Dawson squeezed the trigger. Frozen with terror, she watched as the pistol bucked slightly in his hand. There was a spitting sound of a silenced bullet, and then a splotch of crimson spread across Foreign Secretary Rupert Vere's heavily starched white shirt, and he collapsed onto the oriental carpet.

Dawson turned to Elena with a faint, glacial smile. "Now, that was unfortunate, wasn't it? Having to cut short such a distinguished career. But then you really left me no choice. You told him far too much. He's a clever man, and he'd easily put things together, and that wouldn't do at all. That's something you can understand, can't you?" He moved closer to her, then closer still, until she could feel the clammy moisture of his breath. "Rupes may have been an indolent fellow, but he wasn't dim. What did you think you were up to, chatting to him about Prometheus? This really isn't on. But let's talk about *you*, shall we?"

My God! Simon Dawson! It was another name she'd come across in the old Pangbourne news clips, the name of a younger classmate she'd assumed had later become Vere's protégé.

Wrong.

Dawson was the control.

The same logic that had ruled out Miles Parmore should have ruled out Rupert Vere: he was too visible. The real puppetmaster was the faceless deputy, working through his oblivious superior.

"So you kept him in the dark all along," Elena said, half to herself.

"Rupes? There was no need for him to know. He's always trusted my advice implicitly. But nobody had his charm. One needed the charming stooge. *Needed*, past tense. He's not exactly necessary any longer, is he?"

She took a step back. "You mean because Britain's now a signatory to the treaty."

"Exactly. As of ten minutes ago. But who are you? I fancy

we haven't been introduced properly." The Browning still rested comfortably in Dawson's right hand. He pulled a flat metallic case from his breast pocket, evidently some sort of wireless personal digital assistant. "Let's see what the Network has to say," Dawson murmured. He held the device up in the air and pointed it toward her. An image of her face immediately appeared on the square LCD screen. Then the screen began to flicker as hundreds of faces flashed by almost in a blur, until a match was found.

"Elena Petrescu," he said. He read from an electronic file. "Born in 1969, Bucharest, Romania. Only daughter of Andrei and Simona Petrescu, Andrei having been Romania's leading specialist in cryptography. Ah, *most* intriguing. Exfiltrated from Bucharest just before the 1989 coup d'etat by . . . Nicholas Bryson." He looked up. "You're *married* to Nicholas Bryson. Now it comes together. Directorate employees, both of you. Separated for five years . . . in the year before you left, you bought, let's see, three ovulation kits—obviously trying to get pregnant. Hmm . . . didn't happen, I take it. Regular weekly sessions with a psychotherapist—I wonder, were you dealing with the difficulty of being a political defector in a strange country, or working at an agency as secret as the Directorate, or was it the crumbling marriage?"

There was something about the disjunction between what he was saying and his casual tone that made Elena shudder. She noticed that although he was still holding his Browning, he was paying it little attention.

"Your plans have leaked, you should know that," Elena said.

"It really doesn't concern me," Dawson replied airily.

"I doubt that. You were concerned enough about Rupert Vere knowing and informing MI-5 that you killed him."

"The CIA and MI-6 and MI-5 and all the other three-letter spy agencies have all been neutralized. The Directorate took us longer—perhaps by virtue of your paranoid structure—though the very secrecy that insulated you from penetration also made it that much easier for us to paralyze you, funnily enough. It's strange how long it's taken you people to realize that time has passed you by, that there's simply no need for you any longer! The NSA is overwhelmed with the sheer volume of traffic—the E-mails and cell-phone calls it struggles to vacuum up, all the Internet traffic. Good God, it's a Cold War relic—it thinks the Soviet Union never went away! And to think that there was once a time when the NSA was the crown jewel of American intelligence, the biggest, the best! Well, encryption has pretty much ended that reign. And the CIA—the folks who accidentally had us bomb the Chinese embassy in Belgrade, who had no *idea* India had nuclear weapons! The ineptitude! The less said of them, the better. Intelligence agencies are a thing of the past. No wonder you all try so hard to block the rise of Prometheus—you're like dinosaurs impotently raging against the inevitability of evolution! But by this weekend, your demise will be evident to the entire world. On the shores of the lake, a new global order will be assured, and the welfare of the human race will be secure as it's never been before." He turned his attention to the Browning once again, pointing it at her. "Sometimes the few must be sacrificed at the altar of the many. I can already see the headlines in the *Telegraph*—FOREIGN SECRETARY VERE SLAIN BY SUICIDAL STALKER. And in the *Sun*, something like SLAYS CAB MIN, THEN SELF. They'll probably intimate some sordid sexual angle. And the gun and the powder spray will positively identify you as the killer."

As Dawson spoke, he was unscrewing the silencer from the Browning; then, as tightly coiled as a mountain cat, he took two long, rapid steps toward Elena. With a grip of iron, he placed the gun in her hand, crushing her fingers around it, then bent her arm so that the barrel pressed hard against her temple. Elena started thrashing violently, convulsively: if nothing else, she would spoil the tableau he had planned. She screamed at the top of her lungs. She felt as if another force altogether had taken possession of her body, the concentrated will to survive transmuting into a primal muscular response. She writhed and flailed, and when she heard another voice it seemed to come from a great distance.

Nick Bryson's voice.

"Dawson, what on earth are you doing? She's one of *ours!*" Bryson shouted. The door to the closet opened, and Bryson stepped out, disguised as a Whitehall civil servant with hairpiece, mustache, and glasses; only upon close examination did he bear any resemblance to Nicholas Bryson. The shoulders of his suit were flecked with wood splinters and dust, evidence that he had made his way into the office through a crawl space. "She was dispatched personally by Jacques Arnaud!" Bryson warned.

"What—who the hell are you?" gasped Dawson, spinning around to look at the intruder with mingled astonishment and uncertainty; in so doing, he momentarily loosened his grip on Elena, who suddenly lunged to one side. In one violent motion she was able to wrench the pistol, which Dawson had been forcing into her hand, away from him. Elena hurled it toward Bryson, who dove into the air and retrieved it.

Bryson gripped it in both hands, aiming it at Vere's deputy. "*Don't* move," he said sharply. "Or there'll be two bodies on the floor."

Dawson froze, staring malevolently at Bryson, then shifting his eyes toward Elena.

"Now, we have a few questions for you," Bryson said, advancing toward Dawson, the gun still pointed. "And you'd be wise to answer them as completely and truthfully as you can."

Dawson shook his head in disgust, backing up slowly. "You're sadly mistaken to think that you can threaten me. Prometheus has been in the planning for over a decade. It's larger than any one person, any one *nation* for that matter."

"Freeze!" Bryson shouted.

"You can kill me," said Dawson, still backing up, edging closer and closer to Elena, "but it's not going to change a thing, or even slow anything down. The gun in your hands was used to kill my dear friend there; if you're so foolish as to kill me too, you'll have two homicides on your head. And it's only fair to warn you that this office is equipped with electronic eavesdropping devices; the moment your friend here entered the foreign secretary's office and I saw what she was really up to, I placed a call to the Alpha squad, Grosvenor Square detachment. I'm sure you know about the Alpha squad."

Bryson only stared.

"They'll be here any moment now. They're probably entering the building already, you goddamned son of a *bitch!*" And as he raised his voice, he leaped toward Elena, grabbing her by the throat, his thumbs squeezing the cartilage in a death grip. Elena's screams quickly became gagging, strangulated sounds.

There was a thunderous explosion as the bullet was fired from the unsilenced Browning in Bryson's hands. At the top of his forehead, near the hairline, a tiny oval wept blood. Dawson, his face oddly immobile, slumped face forward onto the floor.

"Quick!" Bryson said. "Grab his pocket computer, his wallet, whatever else is in his pockets."

Her face wrinkled with distaste, she searched the dead man's pockets, taking keys, wallet, Palm Pilot, and assorted scraps of paper. Then she followed him through the open closet door and saw where Bryson had removed the plywood backing.

Belinda Headlam's experience in Foreign Secretary Rupert Vere's employ had taught her the supreme importance of discretion. She knew that he conducted negotiations of exquisite sensitivity in his alcove suite, and she had her suspicions that it might also be his lair for the occasional assignation, as well. Last year, the young woman from the agricultural ministry had seemed ever so slightly flushed and dishabille when she'd had to interrupt their conversation with the urgent summons from the prime minister. Foreign Secretary Vere had been just a little short with her for a few days afterward, as if he had been embarrassed by the interruption and displeased at her. But all that passed and she tried to put the episode out of her head. Men had their weaknesses, she knew; they all did.

Yet the foreign secretary was a most eminent man, one of the most capable members of the government, as the leader page of the *Express* often repeated, and she was honored that he had handpicked her as his personal assistant. But *surely* something was wrong. She wrung her hands, agonized about what to do, and finally decided she couldn't dither any longer. The foreign secretary's office was well soundproofed—he had insisted on that—but that noise, muffled though it was, sounded terribly like a gunshot. Could that be? And if it *were* a gunshot and she'd done nothing—why, then what? What if the foreign secretary were wounded and in dire need of help? Then there was the fact that Simon Dawson, his deputy, had joined them, and it wasn't like him to stay for so long. There was, furthermore, something *peculiar* about the tarted-up woman who'd passed him a note. Mrs. Headlam had an inkling of what Foreign Secretary Vere's appraising look might mean, but the woman didn't seem as if she were there on such . . . *business.*

Something was dodgy.

Belinda Headlam stood up and rapped sharply on the secretary's door. She waited five seconds and rapped again. Then, saying, "I'm so terribly sorry," she pushed open the door. And then she screamed.

The sight was so shattering it took her almost half a minute before she had enough sense to notify security.

Sergeant Robby Sullivan of the Palace of Westminster Division of the Metropolitan Police kept himself lean and taut with an hour of hard jogging each morning, and he looked askance at his colleagues who, as the years wore on, allowed themselves to—well, get a little podgy. You might have thought they didn't take the beat seriously. Robby had been assigned to Westminster Division for seven years, charged with policing the halls of Parliament, ousting intruders, and generally keeping the peace. Though the time had passed with relatively few incidents, years of IRA threats had given him much practice at responding to alarms.

Still, nothing had prepared him for the scene in the foreign secretary's suite. He and Police Constable Eric Belson, his young redheaded deputy, radioed New Scotland Yard for immediate backup, but in the interim they sealed off Vere's chambers and used the existing detail to station an officer by every major stairwell. From Mrs. Headlam's account, there was likely a killer on the loose in the building—a woman, at that. Though how she'd managed to get out of the office without going past Mrs. Headlam was a puzzlement. She would not be permitted to escape from the building, he was determined—not on his watch. He'd gone through regular drills, knew all the requisite moves and maneuvers. Of course, this time it was the real thing. The adrenaline reminded him of that.

The air in the long, dark passageway was musty, dead, and stifling, evidently having been undisturbed for years. Bryson and Elena moved quickly yet silently through the gloom, crawling on hands and knees in some places, walking erect with an awkward, stoop-shouldered gait where space allowed. Bryson carried with him the briefcase he had brought into the Parliament building, an encumbrance but perhaps a vital asset. The only light came from the daylight that filtered in through cracks in the mortise work or ceiling molding. The ancient wood flooring creaked alarmingly as they passed between offices and public spaces and supply rooms. Voices on the other side of the wall were muffled, louder in some places than in others. At one point Bryson noticed something, a peculiar noise pattern, and he stopped. Their eyes were beginning to get used to the dark; he could see Elena turn to him quizzically, and he put a finger to his lips as he peered through a crack.

He saw the boots, then the fatigues, of U.S. Marines. The secret Alpha squad had arrived and had dispersed to search the building. The welcoming committee. He guessed that the Marines were ordinarily assigned to the American embassy in Grosvenor Square, interspersed among the regular contingent whose job it was to guard the building and the ambassador. Their lethal presence was alarming in the extreme: the highly trained hit squad would be mobilized only upon top-secret-code-word orders dispatched at the highest levels of the U.S. government. Oval Office authority was required. Whatever the terrifying agenda of Prometheus—he had overheard part of Dawson's rant, which seemed in some way to concern a new generation of governmental espionage—it was being put into place with the cooperation of the White House, knowingly or not.

Madness! This was no mere bureaucratic transformation, no simple governmental shift. The Prometheus killers seemed instead to be front men of some kind of officially sanctioned power struggle, an epochal transfer of power. But what could it be?

Immediately ahead of them, the crawlspace was interrupted by a metal enclosure: an air duct. Feeling with his fingertips, he located a hinged access door for maintenance purposes. Panels of air filters were tightly lodged in place. Bryson pulled out a long, flat screwdriver from the briefcase and worked the filters loose from their frames until the passageway was unblocked. Now he and Elena entered the square-sided steel enclosure, shimmying and sliding down a steep decline through a narrow space of ribbed steel, which vibrated with regular bursts of cold air. "This leads to a space over the Chancellor's Gate," Bryson said, his voice echoing and metallic, "and then to Victoria Tower. But we're going to have to play this by ear."

However large the Alpha squad detachment, it would not be numerous enough to search the immense Palace of Westminster, which contained, in seven acres, the two houses of Parliament—twelve hundred rooms, more than a hundred staircases, over three kilometers of passages. There would undoubtedly be others in plainclothes searching for them who would be no less lethal: field operatives in the employ of the Prometheus Group. They could be anywhere. Bryson's mind was a whirl of memorized maps and plans; he needed to simplify, to find the order in the chaos. If he and Elena were to survive, he'd have to trust his instincts, and the training that shaped them. It was all they had.

Their pursuers would, he was sure, examine all possible means of egress, of escape, from Rupert Vere's office; that would determine the avenues of their search. Calculations would be made, search routes decided, based upon a fixed set of variables. The window was one obvious way out, but that was high above the ground, and no evidence would be found of any ropes or climbing apparatus. Vere's personal secretary, who guarded the entrance to the office suite, would assert that no one had run past here, though it was possible that she had been absent, away from her desk, for some period of time, in which case that route could not be ruled out.

That left one more avenue that had to be searched by their pursuers, and it would not take the killers long to realize that the plywood panel at the back of the closet was loose, though propped back into place. This meant that several killers from the Alpha squad or Prometheus were likely to be already finding their way through the crawlspace. Bryson and Elena's only hope was that the searchers might be confounded by the maze of hidden passages.

But a few seconds after they emerged from the steel air duct, Bryson could hear footsteps whose proximity seemed to indicate that they were coming from within the crawlspace, and not from outside. There was a certain echoing tonality, accompanied by a wooden creak. *Yes.* Bryson was now sure of it. Someone was following them through the concealed passage.

He felt Elena grab his shoulder, put her mouth to his ear, and whisper, "Listen!"

He nodded: *I hear.*

His mind raced. He had Dawson's Browning, with whatever ammunition was loaded in the chamber and magazine, and he had several implements in the briefcase that would be less effective in hand-to-hand combat. But the dismal fact was, there would be no hand-to-hand, close-range struggle. If they were spotted, guns would be fired, whether silenced or not.

Bryson stopped suddenly at another crack of light that seeped through the mortise work, and he peered through. He was looking into a fluorescent-lit utility room, its floors covered with old green linoleum. Looking more closely, he could make out shelving on one end stacked with what appeared to be cleaning supplies. Though the room was lit, it also appeared to be empty. He felt along the walls of the crawlspace until he found the detachable plywood panel that likely covered an egress into a closet that gave onto the utility room. With a small Phillips-head screwdriver he took from his briefcase, he unscrewed the panel and then pulled it loose. The wood squeaked and groaned as it came off. Indirect light shone through the opening; they could make out the outlines of the small closet, illuminated by a narrow slit of light that came in where the closet door met the linoleum floor.

Quietly, they squatted down and squeezed through the low, small opening. Bryson went first into the cluttered closet, and Elena followed. There was a sudden, jarring sound: Elena had knocked against a bucket, sending the wooden handle of a mop or broom clattering against the wall. They froze. Bryson held a hand in the air, signifying a command to halt. They listened, waited. Bryson's heart thundered.

After an endless minute, Bryson was satisfied that the noise had not attracted attention, and they resumed. Slowly, carefully, he opened the closet door. The utility room was indeed empty, though the lights were on; it was likely that someone had been here only recently, a cleaning person, who would therefore be returning at any time.

They raced silently across the room to the door that had to lead to a hallway. It was open a crack. Bryson pushed it open just enough to get his head through; he looked to either side down the dim hall. He saw no one. He whispered to Elena, "Stay here until I signal that it's safe to come out."

Bryson passed a vending machine and an old brown bucket in which stood a wet-mop, and then a figure appeared. He stopped short, reached for the Browning, which he had jammed into his waistband.

But it was only an old lady, a slow-moving cleaning

woman pushing a metal cart. Relieved, Bryson continued down the hall toward her, mentally preparing a response in case he was asked questions. He was a civil servant, as his clothing—though dust-covered—indicated. Yet he was mindful that the old woman could become a resource as well, and they could afford to bypass no resources.

"Excuse me," Bryson said as he approached, dusting off his shoulders with a flick of his hand.

"Lost, are you?" the cleaning woman said. "Can I help you, dearie?" She had a kindly, wrinkled face, her white hair thin and wispy. She seemed old to be doing such manual labor, and she moved with such apparent physical exhaustion that she stirred Bryson's sympathy. Yet her eyes regarded him shrewdly.

Lost? But wasn't it a natural question: dressed as he was, Bryson appeared to be out of place in this service corridor. Had the word been circulated so quickly that one—or more—fugitives were roaming the building? He thought rapidly.

"I'm with Scotland Yard," Bryson replied in a flawless English lower-middle-class accent. "Some security breaches in the area. Maybe you've heard . . . ?"

"Aye," the old lady said wearily. "I don't ask questions. Be more than my job's worf, it would." She wheeled the cart down the hall toward them and parked it against the wall. "Lot of rumors flying around." She mopped her careworn brow with an old faded-red kerchief as she waddled up to him. "But you mind answerin' me just one question?"

Guardedly, Bryson said, "What's that?"

The ancient cleaning lady gave a perplexed look as she sidled up to Bryson and continued in a low, confiding voice, "What the hell are you doing *still alive?*" She whipped out a large blue-steel gun from the folds of her smock, pointed it at Bryson, and squeezed the trigger. Lightning-fast, Bryson swung his Kevlar-lined briefcase upward in a sharp arc, crashing it *hard* into her forearm. The gun clattered to the floor, skidding across the linoleum down the hall, away from him.

With a shrill scream, the harridan crouched and then sprang forward, her face contorted, her hands extended like claws, like deadly instruments. She slammed into him, knocking him to the floor just as he was reaching for the concealed gun. The wound in his side ached. *She's a god-damned old lady!* Bryson thought, then realizing—as she clawed at his eyes—that she was no old lady, she was far younger, far stronger, something more akin to a wild beast than a woman. She jabbed one thumb directly into his eye socket, the pain immense, blinding him, while she slammed her knee into his crotch, connecting at once with his genitals. Bryson roared with agony and determination, summoning his considerable strength, and slammed her to the floor. His right eye was bloodied, but he could still see through it, and what he saw made an eel of fear wriggle in his belly. She had pulled out a flashing blade, a long, thin stiletto. It gleamed wetly, as if coated with a viscous fluid. He knew at once that the blade must be coated with the alkaloid toxiferene, which made it an extremely dangerous weapon. The slightest nick or scrape would lead to immediate paralysis and a suffocating death.

Bryson could smell the blade and its acrid poison as it whisked millimeters from his face: he had jerked his head back just in time to save his life. Now the crazed woman reared up and lunged, and again Bryson's evasive action was only just sufficient; a button from his shirt was sliced off and went flying into the air. He went at her with both hands, with all of his strength, unable to risk reaching for the gun. The stiletto flashed in a blur near Bryson's face, but now Bryson lashed out with his left arm, like a cobra, directly *toward* the blade—a counterintuitive move, because it meant rising up and greeting the instrument of death, or the appendage that held it, rather than retreating from it—and as he seized the wrist of the hand holding the stiletto, the harridan was clearly taken by surprise.

But only for an instant. Bryson's strength would normally be far superior, but he was no longer in peak physical condition, nowhere close to it. He was, he was now realizing,

badly weakened by the gunshot wound in Shenzhen; he had
not given himself time to recover. And she had a mastery of
moves he had never seen before. As her arm struggled
against Bryson's grip, the long blade trembling, her left foot,
clad in a steel-toed leather shoe, swung around, striking him
again in the genitals. He groaned as he felt the pain radiating
coldly through his testicles; he felt sick to his stomach. He
shoved her again, slamming her back to the floor and knocking her white wig off her head, revealing close-cropped black
hair and the lines of a latex face mask.

They were locked in struggle. She screamed again, her
eyes wild. She was powerful and extraordinarily coordinated,
and she lashed back and forth like a rabid beast. She tried
to kick at him again, using her other foot, but Bryson had
anticipated the move and rolled onto her, locking her legs in
place, using his greater body mass, still holding her wrist,
the stiletto blade still pointed at him. He had to move carefully around it, keeping all skin, all appendages clear of its
lethal point. She was bucking violently, but he concentrated
his strength, his energy, on angling her wrist back at her,
directing the slickly gleaming stiletto toward her neck. Her
arm shook with all the muscular resistance she could summon, but it was not enough: Bryson commanded more brute
strength. Inch by inch, he pushed the tremulous blade back
toward the soft exposed skin of the rabid woman's neck. Her
eyes, hooded with latex skin folds, widened in terror as the
blade gently creased her skin.

The effect was immediate. Her lips spread into a contorted
rictus, spittle coming from her mouth, and she suddenly went
limp against the floor and began to thrash wildly, her mouth
opening again and again like a fish out of water, in soundless
gasps. Then, as the deadening paralysis spread through her
body, all respiration ceased; only a few muscles continued
to twitch spasmodically.

Bryson pulled the blade from the dead woman's slackened
grip, located the leather scabbard in the folds of her smock,
and replaced the stiletto inside, then slid the scabbard into
the breast pocket of his suit jacket. He gasped for breath,

touched the sticky blood that covered his right eye. He heard a cry: Elena rushed forward from the utility room, placing her hands on either side of his face, her panicked eyes searching his face. "Oh, God, my darling!" she whispered. "I think your eye looks worse than it actually is. Was that a poison of some sort?"

"Toxiferene."

"She could have killed you, so easily!"

"She was strong, and very, very good."

"Alpha, do you think?"

"Almost certainly Prometheus. Alpha units are marines or navy SEALs. She was some sort of an exotic, probably hired from Bulgaria or the old East Germany—one of the defunct Eastern-bloc services."

"I hated staying back there, doing nothing!"

"You would have just gotten hurt, and she might have used you against me. No, I'm glad you did."

"Oh, Nicholas, I'm *useless*. I know *nothing* about combat, about fighting! *Draga mea,* we have to get out of here. They want to kill you and me both!"

Bryson nodded, gulped. "I think we should separate—"

"No!"

"Elena, by now they know there are two of us, a man and a woman. Their surveillance is too good, too complete. The foreign secretary of England has been assassinated, and all forces are going to be on alert, not just Prometheus and Alpha."

"There must be a thousand people in this building. Surely there's safety in numbers."

"Crowds are better for killers than their targets, especially when the killers know what the marks look like. These are people who will *not* be deterred by normal considerations of prudence."

"I can't! I'm sorry—on my own I can't fight, you know that! I can help you in many ways, but . . . please!"

Bryson nodded; she was terrified, and he couldn't send her off on her own in such a state. "All right. But we're going to have to take back hallways wherever we can find them, service corridors, that sort of thing. The crawlspaces and air ducts are no longer safe—they're probably crawling with agents by now. Somehow we have to get to the east side of the building if our escape plan's going to have any chance of succeeding."

Standing to one side of the utility room window so that he could not be seen from outside, Bryson saw at once that it was worse than he'd imagined. He counted six men in fatigues—members of the Alpha squad. Two of them were patrolling the state officer's courtyard; two others were checking building exits, and two were walking along the roof, surveying the area with binoculars.

He turned back to Elena. "Well, that's just modified the plan. We're going to have to go out to the hallway and look for a freight elevator."

"To the ground floor?"

He shook his head. "That's going to be crawling with police—and others. First or second floor, and then we'll look for an alternative way out." He walked quickly to the door and listened for a few seconds. He heard nothing; no one had come by even during his struggle with the crone. Obviously this was a little-used area. But the fact was, the Prometheus decoy had been circulating here, obviously expecting one or both of them to come by. That told him two things: that this was probably near a convergence point, where various routes came together and led to an exit from the building; and that there would be others not too far away. The sooner they were out of this section, the better.

He opened the door a crack, peered out, then looked to either side; it was clear. He signaled to Elena. They raced down the empty service corridor to the left, and when they reached a turning, Bryson stopped, looked right, spotted an elevator. He ran toward it, Elena close behind. It was an old-fashioned type of elevator with a tiny diamond-shaped glass window and a folding accordion gate inside. This was good: it meant that it was not likely to require a key to operate, since it predated such security precautions. He pressed the call button, and the cab whined slowly up, its compartment dimly illuminated. It was empty. He pulled the gate open, and they got in. He pressed the button marked 2.

For a moment he closed his eyes, visualizing the map. Obviously this would open on to a back service hall, used for cleaning and maintenance, but exactly where it led he wasn't certain. The layout of the Parliament building was exceedingly ornate; he had managed to memorize the main routes, though not all of them.

The elevator stopped on the second floor. Bryson looked out, surveying as much as he could of the area, which also looked clear. He pushed the door open, and they got out. Turning to the right, he saw an old green-painted door, with a scuffed crash-bar mounted at hip-height. He approached it and pushed it open easily. Now they were in an ornate, marble-tiled hallway lined with mahogany doors labeled with gilt numerals. This was not a public, ceremonial area, nor was it grand enough for Parliament members, and there were no names or titles on the doors. Apparently these were offices belonging to committee staff—office clerks, executive officers, audit officers, secretaries, and other support staff. It was long and dimly lit; several people, presumably civil servants, walked unhurriedly into and out of offices. None of them seemed to glance at Bryson or Elena, nor did anything about their body language suggest that they were watchers or undercover operatives. *Instinct,* again: Bryson had nothing else to go on.

He stopped for a moment, trying to orient himself. The eastern end of the building was to the right; that was therefore the direction in which they should head. A well-dressed woman strode down the hall toward them, her heels clicking against the marble and echoing in the long hallway. Instinctively he looked at her, sizing her up; she approached them and passed with a curious stare. He suddenly remembered that, though he was still nominally attired as a respectable clerk, he had to be a frightful sight: one eye was bloodied, perhaps blackened, and his clothes were torn and disheveled from doing battle with the decoy cleaning lady. Elena's clothes were disheveled as well. Both of them looked decidedly out of place, their physical appearance drawing attention, which was exactly what he did not want. There was no time to look for a restroom in which to clean themselves up; now they would have to rely on a combination of speed and good luck. But luck was something he never liked to count on; luck inevitably ran out just when you took it for granted.

He continued down the hall, his head down as if deep in thought, walking quickly, holding Elena's hand, pulling her along. Here and there an office door was open and clusters of people stood talking quietly. If they glanced at the two of them, at least they might not see his bloodied face.

But something was not right here; he was overcome by anxiety. He felt the hairs on the back of his neck become prickly. The noises were *wrong*. The normal pattern of ringing telephones was absent; instead, the phones seemed to be ringing in sequence, at different offices and on different sides of the hallway. He could not rationally articulate why this bothered him, and he knew it was possible that he was beginning to imagine things. Too, he noticed that people engaged in conversation seemed to fall silent as he passed. Was he being *paranoid?*

He'd spent fifteen years in the field, and he had learned above all that one's instinct was the most valuable weapon one had. He did not ignore feelings that others might dismiss as delusional or paranoid.

They were being watched.

But if they were really being watched, why was nothing happening?

Pulling Elena's hand, he quickened his stride. He no longer cared whether his actions stood out or attracted attention; the situation was beyond that now.

About seventy-five yards ahead of them was a small leaded stained-glass window of the sort usually seen in a medieval cathedral. He knew that the windows here overlooked the Thames. "Straight ahead and to the left," he said to Elena under his breath.

She squeezed his hand in silent response. In a few seconds

the corridor ended, and they turned left. Elena whispered, "Look—a committee room—it's probably empty. Do you think we should duck into there?"

"Excellent idea." He did not want to turn around to see whether they were being followed, but he heard no footsteps close behind. On their right was a massive, arched, oak double-door labeled, on a frosted-glass pane, COMMITTEE TWELVE. If they were able to enter it quickly, they might be able to lose any followers, or at the very least confuse them for a while. The doorknob turned freely; the door was unlocked, but the lights—two massive crystal chandeliers—were switched off and the immense room was vacant. It was an amphitheater, with several raised seating areas of leather-backed, brass-studded wooden chairs above a depressed center floor, which was of highly decorated, brightly colored encaustic tile. At the center of the room was a long wooden conference table, topped with green leather, and behind it two long, tall wooden pews—the benches for the committee members. Light came in through two large, tall leaded windows on the opposite side of the room facing the doors, a long rectangular shade running down the middle of each to block the direct sunlight that reflected off the Thames. Even in repose the room was at once solemn and grand. The vaulted ceiling was at least thirty feet high; the walls were wainscoted in dark wood more than halfway up, and above the wainscoting was elaborate burgundy wallpaper of a Gothic pattern. Several large, dreary nineteenth-century oil paintings hung on each wall: battle scenes, portraits of early kings commanding troops at sea, swords poised, Westminster Abbey crowded with nineteenth-century subjects mourning a casket draped with the Union Jack. The only touches of modernity were jarring: several microphones that dangled on long wires from the ceiling, and a television monitor mounted on one wall and labeled HOUSE OF COMMONS ANNUNCIATOR.

"Nicholas, we're not going to be able to hide in here," Elena said quietly. "At least not for long. Are you thinking of—the windows?"

He nodded, setting down his briefcase. "We're three flights above ground level."

"Such a drop!"

"It's not without risks," he agreed. "But it could be worse."

"Nick, I'll do it if you insist, if you really think we have no choice. But if there's any way—"

There was a noise in the hallway immediately outside. The doors flung open, and Bryson dropped to the ground, pulling her down after him. Two men entered, dark silhouettes, then two more. Bryson saw at once that they were *policemen,* wearing the blue uniforms of the Metropolitan Police!

And Bryson knew he and Elena had been spotted. "Freeze!" one of the policemen shouted. "Police!"

The men, unusual for British police, were carrying sidearms, aimed at them.

"Hold it right there!" another man shouted.

Elena screamed.

Bryson whipped out his Browning but did not draw. He calculated: four policemen, four handguns. It was far from impossible to take them on, using the wooden chairs as shields, as obstacles.

But *were* they in fact policemen? He could not be certain. They looked resolute, their expressions fierce. *But they did not fire.* Prometheus killers would probably not have hesitated. Would they?

"That's the buggers!" one of the policemen shouted. "The assassins!"

"Drop the weapon," called the one who appeared to be in charge. "Drop it at once. You got nowhere to go now." Bryson turned around, saw that they were indeed trapped; they were fish in a barrel. The four police constables continued to advance into the room, closer and closer, spreading out so that they had Bryson and Elena surrounded.

"Drop it!" the same one repeated, now shouting. "Drop it, you scum. Get to your feet, hands in the air. *Move it!"*

Elena looked at Bryson, desperate, unsure what to do.

Bryson considered his option. To surrender was to give themselves up to a questionable authority, to police who might in fact *not* be police, might be Prometheus killers in disguise.

And if they were legitimate members of the Metropolitan Police? If so, he could not kill them. Yet if they were true police constables, they believed they were on the verge of apprehending a couple of assassins, a man and a woman who had just killed the foreign secretary. They would be taken into custody and questioned for hours—hours they could not spare. With no certainty that they would be released.

No, they could not surrender to them! Yet to do anything else was *madness,* was *suicide!*

He inhaled deeply, closed his eyes for a moment, and when he opened them again, he got to his feet. "All right," he said. "All right. You've got us."

CHAPTER TWENTY-EIGHT

One of the men seemed clearly to be in charge: a tall, fit man whose name tag said SULLIVAN.

"All right, drop the gun and put your hands in the air, and you won't get hurt," Sullivan said steadily. "There's four of us and only two of you, but I guess you've already figured that out."

Bryson held his pistol up, though not directly pointed at anyone. *Were they really who they said they were?* That was his greatest concern right now.

"Agreed," Bryson answered with forced calm. "But I first want to see some identification."

"Shutcher gob!" bellowed one of the policemen. "Here's *my* identification right *here,* you sod." He indicated his pistol. "Try me."

But Sullivan replied, "Fine. As soon as you're cuffed you'll have all the time in the world to study our warrant cards."

"No," Bryson said. He raised the Browning ever so slightly, still pointed at no one in particular. "I'll be happy to cooperate once I'm confident you are who you say you are. But there are teams of mercenaries and assassins roaming the halls of Parliament, operating in violation of about a dozen British laws. Once I'm satisfied you're not one of them, I'll drop the gun."

"Take the arsehole down," growled one of the men.

"We fire when I give the order, Constable," Sullivan said. Then, addressing Bryson: "I'll show you my warrant card, but be warned—you've killed the foreign secretary, you bastard, so you're probably fool enough to try for one of us blokes. If you're lucky enough to squeeze off a shot, it'll be the last thing you ever do, so don't fuck with us, you hear me?"

"Understood. Take it out with your left hand, *slowly,* and display it for me, palm open. Got it?"

"Got it," Sullivan said, following Bryson's instructions. The leather folding wallet lay open in his left hand.

"Good. Now slide it across the floor to me—toss it slowly, *gently.* No quick moves—don't startle me or I'm likely to fire in self-defense."

Sullivan flicked his left wrist, sending the wallet across the floor. It stopped right at Bryson's feet. As Bryson leaned to pick it up, he became aware of one of the men—the one who was obviously itching to fire—advancing on him from the left side. Bryson whirled around, gun pointed directly at the constable's face. "Don't move, you *idiot.* I meant what I said. If you believe I really murdered the foreign secretary in cold blood, then you surely don't think I'd hesitate to blow you away, do you?" The trigger-happy man froze, backed up a few steps, but kept his gun still leveled at Bryson.

"That's it," said Bryson. He sank slowly to his knees to retrieve the wallet, all the while keeping the gun level, shifting it back and forth from man to man. He quickly snatched the leather wallet from the floor, opened it, and glanced at the silver badge on the right flap in the form of the Metropolitan Police crest. Inside the plastic sleeve on the left side was a white laminated card with Sergeant Robert Sullivan's photograph, in uniform, along with his warrant number, rank, serial number, and signature. It certainly looked legitimate, though it was easily within the Prometheus team's capabilities to obtain genuine or cleverly forged police identification. The name, Sullivan, matched the leader's name tag, and the collar number on the epaulet of his navy blue sweater matched the number on the warrant card. Sullivan was identified as a member of the Special Operations Unit, meaning that he, and presumably the others, were allowed to carry weapons. It was possible, of course, that they had simply been thorough about these details. In truth, very little could be determined conclusively from the badge, in fact, except for the fact that there *was* one and, upon quick examination, it checked out. An undercover team of assassins assembled on such short notice was not likely to have every detail of their disguises straight, yet so far he had not spotted a gaffe.

His instincts told him the policemen were legitimate. He based this assessment on a whole range of minor details, behavioral cues, attitudes, and, most important, the fact that they had held their fire. They could easily have killed him, but they had not done so. In the end it was that simple fact that led Bryson to drop his gun and raise his hands in the air, and Elena did the same.

"All right, nice and easy now, move toward that wall, the both of you, and put your hands flat against it," said Sullivan.

They walked slowly to the closest wall and placed their hands against it. Bryson kept alert for any departure from expected behavior patterns. Weapons were now lowered; that was good. Two members of the team approached, quickly locked handcuffs on their wrists, then patted both of them down for concealed weapons. Another scooped up Bryson's gun.

"My name is Police Sergeant Sullivan. You're both under arrest in connection with the murder of Foreign Secretary Rupert Vere and Undersecretary Simon Dawson." Sullivan flipped a switch on his two-way pocket radio and detailed his location, calling for backup.

"I understand the necessity for going through established procedures," said Bryson, "but a careful ballistic examination will reveal that it was Dawson who murdered the foreign secretary."

"Murdered by his own deputy? Bloody likely."

"Dawson was a control, an agent of an international syndicate with a significant interest in passing the surveillance treaty. He was far too careful, I'm sure, to leave any evidence in plain sight linking him to this group, but there *will* be evidence—altered phone logs, visitors admitted to the Parliament building to see him yet not recorded in his own records—"

Suddenly the great arched doors banged open again, and two large, heavily muscled, uniformed men carrying automatic submachine guns came rushing into the room. "Ministry of Defense, Special Forces!" called the taller of the two men in a husky baritone.

Officer Sullivan turned in surprise. "We weren't notified of your participation, sir."

"Nor we of yours. We'll take over from here," the tall man said. He had steel-gray brush-cut hair and cold blue eyes.

"That won't be necessary," Sullivan said. His tone was calm, but there was no mistaking his resolve. "We've got everything under control."

Bryson turned with alarm, his hands cuffed. The machine guns were Czech, nothing that would have been issued by the British Ministry of Defense. *"No!"* he shouted. "Mother of *Christ,* they're not who they say!"

Baffled, Sullivan looked from Bryson to the crew-cut man. "You're Ministry of Defense, you say?"

"Right," the man replied brusquely. "We've got the situation under control."

"Get down!" Bryson screamed. "They're *killers*!"

Elena dove to the floor, screaming, and Bryson dove next to her, a row of wooden chairs the only barrier between them and the intruders.

But it was too late. Even before he finished speaking, the hall echoed with the deafening thunder of automatic fire as the gray-haired killer and his cohort sprayed bullets into the four police constables, *riddled* their bodies with bullets. Stray rounds pinged against the stone floor and chewed into the mahogany wainscoting. Caught off guard, their sidearms holstered, the genuine policemen were easy targets. A few of them reached, seconds too late, for their weapons. They staggered, their bodies twisting from side to side, almost dancing in a pathetic but vain attempt to dodge the bullets before they crumpled to the floor.

Elena shrieked, "Oh, my *God! Oh, my God!*"

Horrified and sickened, Bryson watched, powerless to do anything.

The air was acrid with cordite, with the coppery smell of

blood. The brush-cut Promethean killer consulted his wrist-watch.

Bryson understood what had just happened and why. The Prometheus Group would never countenance the risk of letting the two of them be taken into official custody: the dangers posed by what they might divulge could not be gauged with precision. Rather, the Promethean hirelings would themselves want to interrogate them, and only then kill them. That was the only possible explanation for why they were still alive.

Now the tall killer spoke in a deep voice. His accent, which on first hearing had sounded British, now seemed to be Dutch, Bryson decided. "We're going to have a few hours of fun together," the Prometheus killer said. "Chemical interrogation has become quite advanced in recent years, as you'll see."

On the floor, Bryson struggled, quietly and discreetly, with the handcuffs, but without a key, or something he could use as a key, it was no use. He looked around; the policemen who lay dead, their bodies riddled with bullets, were no closer than six to eight feet away. He would not be able to take a handcuff key off one of their bodies without being seen doing so; he would never get away with it. But to stay here meant to face chemicals, probably administered inexpertly and in such quantities that they would sustain serious and irreversible damage.

No, he corrected himself. *After the chemicals will be death.*

Robby Sullivan had felt the impact across his midriff like the kick of a horse, and the next thing he knew he was slumped to the floor. His shirtfront was soaked with blood; he couldn't get his breath. A bullet must have punctured a lung, because he felt as if he were slowly drowning. His breathing was shallow, labored. And all the while, his mind fought for some semblance of comprehension. What was going on? The couple who had surrendered appeared to be unharmed, even while his loyal and devoted men, good men all of them with girlfriends or wives and families, had been brutally mowed down. They had all been trained to expect such a possibility, but in reality their jobs in the Westminster Division could not have been more peaceful. What had happened to his men was ghastly, *unthinkable! And me too,* he thought ruefully. *I'm not long for this world either.* But he didn't understand: had the armed men come to *rescue* the assassins? Then why had the handcuffed man tried to warn him? He stared at the ceiling, his gaze moving in and out of focus, steadily weakening, wondering how much longer he would remain conscious.

He had been unable to get his gun out in time, but who on God's green earth would have expected soldiers from the Ministry of Defense to suddenly turn on them with machine guns? They weren't, of course, from the Ministry. The uniforms—their uniforms weren't Ministry of Defense . . . something was definitely off. The handcuffed man was right, which might well mean that the protestations of innocence were justified. Things were happening beyond his ability to understand, but this much seemed clear: the handcuffed man had surrendered peacefully, his protests plausible; and the intruders with machine guns were unquestionably cold-blooded killers. Robby Sullivan felt reasonably certain that he was dying, that he was just minutes from death, and he prayed to the Lord Jesus Christ that He would allow him just one more chance to set things right. Slowly, through a haze, he felt around for his gun.

"You are wanted internationally, as I'm sure you know," said the Dutchman matter-of-factly.

Elena was weeping, her cuffed hands up to her face. "No, please," she moaned softly. "Please."

He noticed that the second man, who had the slightly thickened features of a pugilist, had shifted position and was moving in closer, his machine gun clutched in one hand and what looked like a hypodermic needle in the other.

"The assassination of a British cabinet member is a most serious crime. But we simply want to talk to you—we want to know why you are so determined to interfere, to instigate such trouble."

Bryson's keen ears heard a faint sound from a few feet away. He allowed himself to glance quickly and saw that the constable named Sullivan was moving his hand, reaching . . .

Bryson moved his eyes back to the brush-cut killer, staring at him fiercely. *Don't let him see what I just saw.*

"The Directorate is no longer, I'm sure you know that," continued the gray-haired man. "You have no support, no backup—no resources. You are alone, and you are tilting at windmills, as the saying goes."

Keep him occupied! Don't let his attention stray, don't let him hear . . . "We're far from alone," Bryson said intensely, his eyes flashing. "Long before you destroyed the Directorate, we had put out the word. You and your co-conspirators have already been found out, and whatever the hell you're attempting to pull off is already finished."

The police constable's fingertips were brushing the barrel of the handgun, clawing at it, flailing at it; it was mere inches beyond his reach!

The crew-cut man continued as if he hadn't heard a word Bryson said. "There's really no reason for any more blood to be shed," he said reasonably. "We simply want to have an honest, heart-to-heart conversation with you. That's all."

Bryson did not dare look again, but he heard the tiniest scrape of metal against the stone floor. *Distract him! Engage his attention elsewhere—he must not hear, must not notice!* Bryson abruptly raised his voice. "What is it that's worth all the destruction, the terrorism?" he shouted. "The *bombs?* What is it that justifies blowing an airliner out of the sky that's packed with hundreds of people—with innocent men and women and children?"

"But you see, we believe that the few must be sacrificed at the altar of the many. The lives of a few hundred mean *nothing* compared to the safety and security of millions—of *billions*—the protection of untold generations of . . ." The Prometheus killer's words trailed off as his face creased with suspicion. He cocked his head to one side, listening. "To-mas!" he called.

The two gunshots were nearly deafening, twin explosions, one immediately following the other. The policeman had done it! He had lifted his pistol and, summoning a strength and resolve that momentarily banished the shock and leth-argy of extreme blood loss, had fired two very well-aimed shots. There was a spray of blood as the large-caliber bullet drilled through the Promethean's head and exited at the back, the round freezing him in mid-turn, his expression a com-bination of fury and surprise. His shorter cohort twitched spasmodically before sinking to his knees: the bullet had passed through his neck, obviously having intersected with both his spinal cord and a major artery.

Elena had rolled out of the way, frightened by the sudden gunfire and not understanding where it had come from. When the explosions stopped, she waited a few seconds and then raised her head, and this time she did not scream; the shock was too great, and she was probably numbed by now to all the violence. Eyes wide and liquid with tears, she murmured a low prayer, clasping her cuffed hands.

The police constable who had done it, Sergeant Sullivan, was breathing noisily, a death rattle. He'd been wounded badly in the torso, a sucking wound. Bryson looked over and saw that the sergeant had probably a few minutes left.

"I don't know . . . who you are . . ." the policeman said weakly. "Not who we thought . . ."

"We're not killers!" Elena called. "You know that, I *know* you do!" In a trembling voice she added, quietly, "You've just saved our lives."

Bryson heard the jangle of metal on the floor right by his head: Sullivan had tossed him his key ring.

Must hurry, he thought. *How much time remained before others would arrive, attracted by the explosions? Two minutes? One? Seconds?*

Bryson reached over with his manacled hands and grabbed the key ring, quickly locating a handcuff key. With a little maneuvering, Bryson worked the small key into

Elena's cuffs, springing them open; she then took the key and swiftly unlocked his. One of the policeman's two-way radios crackled to life: "Jesus, what's going on?" a tinny, staticky voice demanded.

"Go," the sergeant told the two in a faint whisper.

Elena saw Bryson racing toward the right-hand arched window. "We can't leave this man here—not after what he's done for us!" she protested.

"He's not answering his radio," Bryson replied quickly as he unhooked the long shade and threw it, clatteringly, to the floor, then began working loose a bolt on the window frame. "They'll locate him quickly, and they'll be able to do more for him than we could do." *But there's nothing they can do for him,* he thought but didn't say. "Come *on!*" he shouted.

Elena rushed to the window, tugged at a sliding bolt until it came free. Bryson turned, saw Sullivan slump back on to the floor, now silent and still. *The man turned out to be a hero,* Bryson thought. *There aren't many of them.* He yanked at the window, hard. It seemed not to have been opened in years, perhaps decades. But after another hard tug it yielded, admitting a rush of cold air into the room.

This side of the Palace of Westminster, the east side, fronted directly onto the Thames, the length of the building running nearly nine hundred feet. Most of it, about seven hundred feet, was taken up by a terrace, furnished with chairs and tables, where members of Parliament had tea or entertained; but on either side of the terrace two narrow, somewhat taller sections of the building jutted out, with just a short stone embankment and a low steel fence, and then water. They were in one of the two protruding ends, as Bryson had planned; the river was directly below them, almost a straight plumb line down.

Elena looked out, turned to Bryson with a frightened expression, but then, to Bryson's astonishment, she said, "I'll go first. I'll—I'll pretend I'm diving off the highest diving board in Bucharest."

Bryson smiled. "Protect your head and neck from the impact. Better to cannonball it, tuck your head and neck into your arms as you drop. And jump out as far as you can so you're sure to hit the water."

She nodded, bit her lower lip.

"I see it—the boat," he said.

She looked, nodded again. "At least that much I did right," she said with a wan smile. "Thames River Cruises was happy to rent a speedboat to my boss, a rich and eccentric unnamed Member of Parliament who wanted to impress his latest lady friend by taking her directly from the Parliament embankment to the Millennium Dome in the fastest boat they had. That was the easy part. But their boats are moored at the Westminster pier—to get one of them to rope it up right in front of the palace required a rather sizable bribe. In case you wonder where all the cash went."

Bryson smiled. "You did great." He could see the boat bobbing in the water about twenty feet to the left, tied to the steel fence in front of the terrace. Elena took a short step from the floor to the bottom of the window, Bryson assisting her. He looked around, saw no sharpshooters on this section of the roof, nor any patrolling the terrace, this hardly being a logical or expected escape route. Valuable resources had to be expended carefully, priorities assessed, men assigned where they were deemed to be most needed.

She stood on the ledge of the open window, took a deep breath. Her left hand squeezed his shoulder. Then she leaped straight out into the air, tucking herself into a ball, and dropped the fifty feet into the water with a loud splash. He waited for her to give him the thumbs-up signaling that she was fine, and then Bryson climbed onto the window ledge and jumped.

The water was cold and murky, the current powerful; when he surfaced, he saw that Elena, a strong swimmer, had almost reached the boat. By the time he had swum to it, she had started the motor. He climbed up and jumped into the cockpit and within seconds they were speeding across the water, away from Parliament, from the teams of killers.

Within a few hours they were in their hotel room on Russell Square. Bryson had gone shopping, with a highly specific list Elena had provided, and returned with the equipment she needed: the fastest and most powerful laptop computer he could buy, equipped with an infrared port; a fast modem; a variety of computer cables.

She looked up from the laptop, which was connected by telephone wire to the phone jack, and from there to the Internet. "I think I need a drink, darling."

Bryson poured her a Scotch, neat, from the room's bar, then poured one for himself. "You're downloading something?" he asked.

She nodded and took a grateful sip. "Password-recovery software—shareware. Dawson took precautions—his hand-held device was password-protected. Until and unless I can crack that, we're not going to get a thing. But once we get past the password, I'll bet we're in."

He picked up Dawson's billfold. "Anything here?"

"Just credit cards, some cash, a bunch of papers. Nothing useful—I've checked." She turned back to the laptop. "This may be it." She entered a password into Dawson's personal digital assistant. A moment later her face lit up. "We're in."

Bryson took a celebratory drink. "You're a remarkable woman."

She shook her head. "I am a woman who loves her work. You, Nicholas, are the remarkable one. I've never known a man like you."

"You must not know many men."

She smiled. "I've known my share. Maybe more than my share. But no one like you—no one as brave and as . . . *stubborn,* I would say. You never gave up on me."

"I don't know if that's quite true. Maybe for a while—in my deepest, darkest depression, when I was drinking far too much of this stuff"—he held up his glass, toasted her—"maybe then I did. I was angry—hurt and confused and angry. But I was never sure, I was never certain—"

"About what?"

"About the reasons why you left. I had to know. I knew

I'd never be satisfied until I knew the truth, even if it tore the heart out of me."

"You never asked Ted Waller?"

"I knew better than to ask him. I knew that if he knew anything—or if he wanted to tell me anything—he would."

She looked distant, vaguely troubled, and she began tapping at the device with a small black stylus. "I've often wondered," she said, her voice trailing off. "Oh, my."

"What?"

"There's an entry here in his date book. 'Call H. Dunne.' "

Bryson looked up suddenly. "Harry Dunne. *Jesus.* Is there a phone number?"

"No. Just 'Call H. Dunne.' "

"When is the entry?"

"It's—it's three days ago!"

"*What?* My God, of course—of course he's still around—still reachable by those who he's willing to talk to. Does that thing have phone numbers or an address book?"

"It seems to have everything—an enormous amount of data." She tapped again at the screen. "Shit."

"Now what?"

"It's encrypted. Both the telephone and address-book database, and something else that's labeled 'transfers.' "

"Shit."

"Well, that's good and bad."

"How is that good?"

"You only encrypt something valuable, so there must be something interesting here. The locked room is the one you want to go into."

"That's one way of looking at it."

"The problem here is limited resources. This is a top-of-the-line notebook computer, but it doesn't have a fraction of the computing power of the supercomputers we had in the Dordogne. Now, this is a 56-bit DES encryption algorithm, fortunately—it doesn't use 128-bit keys, thank God—but it's still strong."

"Can you crack it?"

"Eventually."

"Eventually meaning . . . hours?"

"Days or weeks with this computer, and that's only be- cause I know these utilities, these systems, inside out."

"We don't even have *days*."

She was silent for a long time. "I know," she said at last. "I suppose I can try to improvise—basically, parcel out the work to different hacker sites on the Internet, distribute the chore of crunching billions of number combinations. And see if we get anything that way. It's sort of like that old saying about how an infinite number of monkeys with typewriters will eventually come up with Shakespeare."

"Sounds dubious."

"Well, I'll be frank—I'm not very hopeful."

Three hours later, when Bryson returned with carry-out Indian food, Elena looked careworn and gloomy.

"No luck, huh?" Bryson said.

She shook her head. She was smoking, something Bryson had not seen her do since first escaping Romania. Popping out from the computer's floppy drive one of the diskettes she had rescued from the Dordogne facility, containing decrypted Prometheus information, she put out her cigarette and went to the bathroom. She returned with a wet washcloth plastered on her forehead, then sank into an armchair. "My head hurts," she said. "From thinking too much."

"Take a break," Bryson said. He set down the paper bags of food and came around to the back of her chair, then began massaging her neck.

"Oh, that feels great," she murmured. After a moment, she said, "We have to reach Waller."

"I can try one of the emergency relay channels, but I have no idea how deeply the Directorate has been penetrated. I can't even be sure he'll get it."

"It's worth a try."

"Yes, but only if it doesn't compromise our own security. Waller would understand that, approve of it."

"Our security," she mumbled. "Yes."

"What are you saying?"

" 'Security' made me think of passwords and encryption."

"Naturally."

"And that made me think of Dawson, and how an obviously busy and careful man like that keeps track of all his passwords. Because someone like that never uses just one password—it's not secure."

"How would he keep track?"

"There would be a list somewhere."

"It's always been my experience that the weakest link in computer security in an office is always the secretary who keeps the password taped in her desk drawer because she can never remember it."

"I'm sure Dawson was more cunning than that. Yet the cryptographic 'key' is a long series of numbers—truly impossible to memorize. So he has to keep it . . . can you hand me his Palm Pilot?"

Bryson retrieved it from her work station and gave it to her. She turned it on and tapped at the screen with the stylus. For the first time in hours she smiled. "There's a list here, all right. With the mysterious label '*Tesserae.*' "

"If I remember my high school Latin, that's plural for *tessera,* meaning 'password.' Is the list in the clear?"

"No, it's encrypted, but it's a light encryption utility—it's called 'secure information management software.' A password protector. This is not difficult at all. It's sort of like locking the front door but leaving the garage door open. I can use the same password-recovery software I downloaded earlier. Child's play."

Her usual energy and enthusiasm having been restored, she returned to the work table. Ten minutes later, she announced that she had broken the code. She was able to read through all of the data Dawson had so carefully locked away.

"Dear *God,* Nick. The file marked 'Transfers' is a record of wire-transfer payments made into a long list of London bank accounts. Amounts ranging from fifty thousand to a hundred thousand pounds, in some cases triple that!"

"Who are the recipients?"

"These names! This is like a Who's Who of Parliament—members of the House of Commons across the whole political spectrum—Labor, Liberal Democrat, Conservative, even Ulster Unionists. He's got names, dates of receipt, amounts, even times and locations of his meetings with them. A complete documentary record."

Bryson's pulse was racing. "Bribery *and* blackmail. The two cardinal elements of illicit political influence-peddling. It's an old Soviet technique for blackmailing Westerners— they'd pay you some token amount for your services as a consultant, perfectly legitimate-seeming, and then they'd have you—they had proof of Soviet payments into your bank account. So Dawson not only paid off members of Parliament, but he kept the proof of it, as potential blackmail, in case anyone wavered. *That's* how Simon Dawson exerted power. That's how he became the secret control behind Rupert Vere, his boss, the foreign secretary. And probably behind Lord Parmore, and no doubt behind dozens of other influential voices in Parliament. Simon Dawson was the secret *paymaster*. If you want to influence a political debate as charged and as crucial as the debate over the surveillance treaty in Parliament, money certainly helps grease the wheels. Payoffs. Bribes to unscrupulous politicians, to those whose votes are for sale."

"Apparently most of the most influential politicians in Parliament were selling their votes."

"I'm willing to wager there was more to some of those cases than simple bribery. If we were to go through the British press in the last year or so, I'll bet we'd find a pattern similar to what happened in the Congress in the U.S.—leaks of sensitive, private information, embarrassing and damaging secrets, human weakness revealed to the world. I'll bet the most diehard opponents of the treaty were forced out of office, just as Senator Cassidy was forced out in America. And the others were warned, compromised—and then given the carrot, a nice, fat 'campaign contribution.' "

"In laundered funds," Elena said. "Untraceable."

"Is there any way to determine the source of the funds?"

She popped one of the diskettes from the Dordogne facility into the computer. "Dawson's record is so complete it even has the bank codes for the originating bank. He doesn't list the bank name, just the code."

"You're comparing it against the data Chris Edgecomb downloaded?"

Her face seemed to cloud at the mention of Edgecomb's name; it had obviously recalled the nightmare. She didn't answer, but instead peered at the screen, at the long columns of numbers flashing by. "We have a match."

"Let me guess," Bryson said. "Meredith Waterman."

"That's right. The same firm that secretly owns the, uh, First Washington Mutual Bancorp. The place where you say Richard Lanchester made his fortune."

He inhaled sharply. "An old-line investment banking house has somehow become the conduit of illicit funds into Washington and London."

"And maybe other world-power centers as well—Paris, Moscow, Berlin . . ."

"No doubt. Meredith Waterman in effect owns Congress and Parliament."

"You said Richard Lanchester got very rich there."

"Right, but the story is that he left all that behind to go to Washington. That he severed all formal ties, all financial connections."

"I learned as a child never to believe what I read in the Bucharest papers. I was taught always to distrust the official story."

"A useful lesson, I'm sorry to say. You're speculating that Lanchester still has influence there, and that's how he's able to use his old bank to channel massive amounts of bribes?"

"Meredith Waterman is a privately held bank—a limited partnership, from what I've learned. It's basically owned by ten or twelve general partners. Do you think it's possible that he's still a partner there?"

"No. Can't be. Once he started working in the government, he would have had to give all that up—resign his partnership and put any assets there into a blind trust. To work at the White House requires full financial disclosure."

"No, Nick. Financial disclosure to the FBI, not *public* disclosure. He's never had to go through a Senate confirmation, has he? *Think* about it—maybe this is the reason why he refuses to accept the president's nomination to become secretary of state! Maybe it's *not* some kind of modesty—maybe he just doesn't want to go through the additional public attention, the scrutiny, that would come with it. Maybe he has things to hide—skeletons in his closet."

"Well, you're right that a national security adviser doesn't have to go through the same baptism by fire that the secretary of state does," Bryson conceded. "But White House officials are still under the microscope no matter who they are, their every move scrutinized, everyone always looking for financial improprieties."

Elena seemed impatient; she was a mathematician comfortable with abstract principles most of all, and she was developing a theory that he insisted on poking holes in. "I want you to consider this about Lanchester. In the last few months I've been watching closely what's happening with this International Treaty on Surveillance and Security. In our line of work, we're naturally very interested, right?"

He nodded.

"And, well, once this treaty is ratified, it will create an international executive, a new, global law-enforcement body with sweeping powers. And *who's going to head this new agency?* In the last few weeks, if you've been reading the newspaper reports very closely, you'd always find the same few names mentioned—always deep into the article, always couched as speculation—as possible directors. The term they always use is 'czar'—a word that always makes me nervous. You know how we Romanians felt about the Russian czar."

"The czar being Lanchester."

"His name is being floated—what do they call that, a 'trial balloon'?"

"But that makes no sense—he's known to be opposed to the treaty! He's supposed to be one of the voices in the White House who lobbied hardest *against* it, believing that such a worldwide law-enforcement agency could be abused, could infringe upon fundamental personal freedoms . . ."

"And how do we *know* he's opposed to it? Leaks, right? Isn't that how it works? But leaks to the press always have a hidden motive—people have reasons for making things known, for influencing public perceptions. Maybe Richard Lanchester wanted to sort of cloak his ambitions because he actually *wants* to be named to this position—which he would then reluctantly accept!"

"*Jesus.* I suppose it's possible he's been engaged in some sort of diversion for some reason."

"That 'some reason' being that at the same time he's behind the Prometheus conspiracy, and it's important to him that he not seem to be connected to any such maneuverings. Think of that game that is played with the shells and little ball, where you move the shells around and people try to guess which shell the ball is under. A shell game, yes? So this is a diversion, as you put it—a deflection. We all watch the public battle over legislation, over laws—while behind the scenes the *real* battle is being waged. The one involving immense amounts of money and power! A battle waged by wealthy and powerful private citizens who stand to become ten *times* as wealthy and powerful."

Bryson shook his head. Much of what she was saying was logical, made sense. Yet a national security adviser to the president, a White House official—a man in such a goldfish bowl simply could not orchestrate such a massive conspiracy. The risks were too great, the danger of exposure too grave. That did *not* make sense. And then there was the question of motive. The drive for money and power was as old as human civilization itself—older, perhaps. But . . . all of this simply to ensure that Lanchester was named to another bureaucratic position? *Ludicrous.* It couldn't be.

Yet he was now convinced that Richard Lanchester was the key to Prometheus—a vital link in the chain that *led* to Prometheus. "We have to get inside," he whispered urgently.

"Inside Meredith Waterman?"

Bryson nodded, deep in thought.

"In New York?"

"Right."

"But to do what?"

"To find out the truth. To find out what the exact connection is between this Richard Lanchester and Meredith Waterman and the Prometheus conspiracy."

"But if you're right—if Meredith Waterman is really the node, the locus of massive payments around the world—then it's going to be locked as tight as a drum. It's going to be well guarded, every file cabinet triple-locked, every computer code word protected, the files encrypted."

"That's why I want to get you inside."

"Nicholas, that's *crazy!*"

He chewed at his lower lip. "Let's think this through fully. To adapt one of your metaphors, if the door is locked, go in through the window."

"What's the window?"

"If we want to find out how a reputable old merchant bank got into the money-laundering business, I guarantee we're not going to dig up records in the expected places. Because, as you say, it'll be locked tight as a drum. All contemporary records will be sealed, locked away, unreachable. So we have to look at *yesterday*—at the *old* Meredith Waterman, the prestigious investment bank, back in its glory days. At the *past.*"

"What are you saying?"

"Look, Meredith Waterman used to be one of those old-shoe Wall Street partnerships—a bunch of doddering old in-bred geezers who made all the decisions around a coffin-shaped conference table under oil paintings of their ancestors. So when—*how*—did they start channeling money for bribes? And who did it? How did it happen, and when?"

She shrugged. "But where do you look for such records?"

"The archives. Every old-line bank with a sense of history stores its old files, archives, saving every damned scrap of paper, filing them away, labeling them for posterity. They had a true sense of history, these old guys, a sense—no doubt inflated—of their own immortality. The new owners would be unlikely to discard the old records, considering them essentially benign, since they came from the days before all the secret funds transactions. And *that's* our window, the soft underbelly. The place where security is most likely to be lax. Now, can you book us a couple of plane tickets on that thing?"

"Of course. To New York, right?"

"Right."

"Tomorrow?"

"*Tonight.* If you can find two seats tonight, grab them, on any airline, together or not, it makes no difference. We have to get to New York as soon as possible."

To the Wall Street headquarters of a venerable old investment bank, he thought. *A once-reputable bank that is now a vital link to the Prometheus deception.*

CHAPTER TWENTY-NINE

The headquarters of the eminent investment bank Meredith Waterman was located on Maiden Lane in southernmost Manhattan, just a few blocks from Wall Street, in the shadow of the World Trade Center. Unlike the mock-Renaissance palazzo of the Federal Reserve Bank of New York nearby, where much of the nation's gold reserve was stored in five underground floors, the Meredith Waterman building was unassuming yet proud, quietly elegant. It was a graceful, four-story neoclassical building with a mansard roof and brick-and-limestone façade, constructed a century earlier in the style of the French Second Empire; it seemed to belong to a different place, a different era—to Paris in the time of Napoleon, when the French dared to dream of a world empire.

Surrounded by the new skyscrapers of the financial district as it was, the landmark Meredith Waterman building radiated a serene confidence born of its aristocratic pedigree, for Meredith Waterman was the oldest private bank in America. It was famous for its genteel reputation, for managing the fortunes of generations of America's wealthiest families, its clients the oldest of old money. The name Meredith Waterman called to mind its legendary mahogany-paneled partners' room, yet at the same time it had a global reach. Articles and profiles in financial publications from *Fortune* to *Forbes* to *The Wall Street Journal* talked of the privately held bank's clubbiness, of the fact that it was owned by fourteen general partners whose families traced their roots back to the very founding of Manhattan, that it was the last remaining private partnership among America's large investment banks.

Bryson and Elena had spent a few hours in preparation. She had done considerable on-line research on Meredith Waterman, using the Internet facilities of the New York Public Library. Very little financial information about the bank was available: since it was not a publicly held corporation, it was required to divulge relatively little about its operations. About the general partners she was able to pull up considerably more, though largely in the realm of straightforward biography. Richard Lanchester was not among the listed partners; he had resigned shortly after being named the president's national security adviser. Since then he seemed to have no ties at all to his old employer.

And what about *social* ties, personal ones, friendships dating back to school days, family connections? Elena searched and searched, and found nothing. Lanchester's social circles seemed not to overlap with those of his old partners; neither had he gone to the same schools. If there was a Lanchester connection, it was not overt.

In the meantime, Bryson gathered information in the way in which he was most comfortable: by foot, by eye, by telephone call. He spent several hours walking around the neighborhood, posing as a telephone repairman, as a software salesman, as an entrepreneur in search of office space to rent, chatting up computer specialists who worked out of neighboring buildings. By the late afternoon he had amassed a decent amount of information about Meredith Waterman's physical plant, its computer systems, even its old corporate records.

Then in a final sweep of the area before his rendezvous with Elena, he walked past the building, directly in front of it, with the casual curiosity of a tourist from out of town. The main entrance was at the top of a broad, steep granite staircase. Inside, the oval marble lobby was illuminated dramatically, the centerpiece a large bronze statue on a pedestal. It appeared, at first glance, to be a Greek mythological figure; it looked familiar. Bryson had seen it somewhere before. Then he remembered: the skating rink at Rockefeller Center.

Yes. It appeared to be modeled after the famous gilded bronze statue in Rockefeller Center.

The statue of Prometheus.

————

It was five o'clock in the afternoon; they had completed their preparations, yet Bryson's surveillance indicated that they should not attempt a covert entry until after midnight. At least seven hours from now.

So long a wait, yet so short a time. Time was a scarce commodity, not to be wasted. Others had to be reached, chief among them Harry Dunne. Yet he was not to be found, no information offered as to his whereabouts beyond a vague statement that the deputy director of Central Intelligence was "on leave" for unspecified "family reasons"; rumors circulated that "family" was coded language for "medical," that the senior intelligence official was seriously ill.

Elena had done searches, made inquiries, yet turned up nothing.

"I tried the front-door approach," she said. "I called his home number, but the person who answered, a housekeeper, said he was very ill, and no, she had no information as to where he was."

"I don't believe she doesn't know."

"I don't either. But she was obviously very well briefed, and she was very quick to get off the phone. So that's a dead end."

"But obviously he *is* reachable—if we're correctly interpreting that note in Simon Dawson's Palm Pilot from a few days ago."

"I went through Dawson's PDA, and there's no phone number for Harry Dunne. Not even encrypted. Nothing."

"What about on-line records searches—medical records?"

"Easier said than done. I tried all the conventional medical-records searches using his name and social-security number, but nothing came up. I even tried a little outright deception, which I was fairly sure would work. I called the CIA personnel office pretending to be a White House secretary—I said the president wants to send flowers to his old friend Harry Dunne, and I needed an address to send them."

"That's nice. Didn't work?"

"Unfortunately, no. Dunne obviously doesn't want to be found. They insisted they had no information. Whatever his reasons, he's got a pretty effective cordon of privacy."

Cordon of privacy. A realization dawned on Bryson. What was the term Dunne had used once, in connection with Aunt Felicia? A 'security cordon'? "There may be another way," he said softly.

"Oh? How so?"

"There's an administrator at the nursing home where my Aunt Felicia lives—a woman named Shirley, as I recall—who always knows how to reach Harry Dunne. Always has his phone number so she can call him whenever anyone calls or visits Felicia."

"What? Why would Harry Dunne care who sees Felicia Munroe? The last time we saw Felicia together, wasn't she in very bad shape, mentally?"

"Sadly, yes. But Dunne obviously thinks it's important to keep a careful watch on her—*a security cordon,* he called it. Dunne wouldn't have placed a security cordon on her unless he feared she had something to reveal. Presumably whatever she knows—whether she's aware of its importance or not—had to do with the fact that Pete Munroe was in the Directorate."

"He *was?*"

"There's so much to tell you—more than we have time for now. We'll talk on the way."

"On the way where?"

"To the Rosamund Cleary Extended Care Facility. We're going to take a little drive upstate, to Dutchess County. To pay an unannounced, unscheduled visit to my Aunt Felicia."

"When?"

"*Now.*"

They arrived at the well manicured, beautifully landscaped grounds of the Rosamund Cleary Extended Care Facility shortly after six-thirty. The air was cool, fragrant of flowers and newly mown lawn and the end of a long, hot day.

Elena entered first and asked to speak to an administrator. She was driving by—she was staying with friends in town—and she had heard such wonderful things about the facility.

It sounded like the perfect environment for her ailing father. Of course, it was late in the day, but was there maybe someone who worked there named Shirley? One of her friends had mentioned a Shirley. . . .

A short while later, Bryson entered and asked for Felicia Munroe. Since Elena was monopolizing Shirley's time, and Shirley was Dunne's contact, it was possible that a call might *not* be placed to Dunne. That would make things easier, but Bryson was not counting on that. For there was nothing wrong, really, with misleading Dunne into thinking that Bryson remained preoccupied with his own past. Perhaps it would falsely reassure the Prometheans that Bryson was on the wrong path, that he was therefore not that immediate a threat.

Let them think that I am dwelling on the past, on my own history. Let them think I'm obsessed.

But I am.

I am obsessed with unearthing the truth.

He prayed that Felicia would be in a lucid state.

She was eating dinner when Bryson was shown in, sitting by herself at a small, round mahogany table in the handsome dining room, where other residents sat by themselves or with one another at similar round tables. She looked up as he approached, and it was as if she were seeing someone she had just been speaking to five minutes earlier. Her eyes displayed no surprise. Bryson's heart sank.

"George!" she trilled, delighted. She smiled, her pearly dentures smeared with lipstick. "Oh, but this is so very confusing. You're dead!" Her tone became scolding, as if lecturing a naughty child. "You really shouldn't *be* here, George."

Bryson smiled, gave her a peck on the cheek, and sat across the table from her. She still mistook him for his father. "You caught me, Felicia," Bryson said sheepishly, his tone lighthearted. "But tell me again—how *did* I die?"

Felicia's eyes narrowed shrewdly. "George, none of that! You know very well how it happened. Let's not rehash all that. Pete feels bad enough, you know." She took a forkful of mashed potatoes.

"Why does he feel bad, Felicia?"

"He wishes it were him instead. Not you and Nina. He just berates himself over and over again. Why did George and Nina have to die?"

"Why *did* we have to die?"

"You know very well. I don't need to tell you."

"But *I* don't know why. Perhaps you can tell *me*."

Bryson looked up and was surprised to see Elena. She put her arms around Felicia, then sat down next to her, clasping in her two hands Felicia's bony, liver-spotted hand.

Did Felicia recognize Elena? It was impossible, of course; they had seen each other on only one occasion, years earlier. But there was something about Elena's manner that Felicia found comforting. Bryson wanted to catch Elena's eye, to find out what had happened, but Elena was devoting all her attention to Felicia.

"He really shouldn't be here," Felicia said, giving Bryson a sidelong glance. "He's dead, you know."

"Yes, I know that," said Elena gently. "But tell me what happened. Wouldn't it make you feel a little better to talk about what happened?"

Felicia looked troubled. "I always blame myself. Pete always says he wishes they didn't have to die—he wishes it were him. George was his best friend, you know."

"I know. Is it too painful for you to talk about? What happened, I mean? How they were killed?"

"Well, it's my birthday, you know."

"Is it? Happy birthday, Felicia!"

"Happy? No, it's not happy at all. It's so very, very sad. It's such a terrible night."

"Tell me about that night."

"Such a beautiful, snowy night! I made dinner for us all, but I didn't care if dinner got cold! I *told* Pete that. But no, he didn't want to spoil my birthday dinner. He kept telling George to hurry, *hurry!* Drive faster! And George didn't want to, he said the old Chrysler couldn't handle the icy roads, the brakes were bad. Nina was upset—she wanted them all to pull over and wait out the storm. But Pete kept *pushing* them, urging them on! *Hurry, hurry!*" Her eyes grew wide and filled with tears; she looked at Elena desperately. "When the car went out of control and George and Nina were killed . . . oh, my Pete was in the hospital for over a month, and the whole time he kept saying, over and over and over again, 'It should have been me who was killed! Not them! It should have been *me!*'" The tears were spilling down her cheeks as the painful memory emerged from deep in the confused mind of a woman for whom the past and the present were a mingled palimpsest. "They were best friends, you know."

Elena put a comforting arm around the old woman's fragile shoulders. "But it was an accident," she said. "It was an accident. Everyone knows that."

Bryson reached over and hugged Felicia, blinking back tears himself. She was tiny, birdlike in his embrace.

"It's all right," he said soothingly. "It's all right."

"It must be such a relief for you," said Elena, sitting beside Bryson in the rented green Buick.

Bryson nodded as he drove. "I think I needed to hear it— even given the circumstances, even given the confused state of her mind."

"There's a certain observable consistency to her thoughts, even given the confusion, the thought disorder. Her long-term memory is sharp: that usually remains intact. She might not remember where she is at any given moment, but she'll clearly remember her wedding night."

"Yes. I suspect Dunne was counting on her advanced senility in the event that I contacted her for confirmation of his carefully constructed lies. As the sole surviving witness to the events, she's as unreliable as they come; Dunne knew that, knew she wouldn't be able to effectively contradict his fraudulent version."

"Though she just did," Elena pointed out.

"She did. But it took a degree of trust, of patience and

persistence, of *gentleness* that I doubt Dunne's CIA men possess. Well, thank God for you, is all I can say. You're the one with the gentleness, and I think she picked up on it. Who'd ever have thought that such a gentle creature could have the makings of a deep-cover operative?"

She smiled. "You mean the phone number?"

"How'd you get it, and so quickly?"

"For one thing, I simply thought about where I'd put it if I were her, a place where I could get it quickly. I also figured that if Harry Dunne wanted the administrator to think he was a concerned relative, he wasn't at the same time going to insist on security precautions."

"Where was it, in her Rolodex, right on her desk?"

"Close. A list of 'emergency' contact numbers taped to the top lefthand corner of her desk blotter. I spotted it as soon as I sat down, so I 'accidentally' left my purse on the chair next to her desk, and as we were leaving for a tour, I suddenly remembered. I went to pick it up, spilled out its contents all over her desk and the floor. As I picked things up I took a glance and memorized it."

"And if it hadn't been right there?"

"Plan B would have required me to leave the purse there longer and retrieve it during her cigarette break. She's a heavy smoker."

"Was there a Plan C?"

"Yes. You."

He laughed, a rare moment of much-needed levity relieving the prevailing tension. "You give me too much credit."

"I don't think so. Now it's my turn, though. The reverse-number lookup has gotten easy these days, thanks to the Internet. I won't even have to do it myself—I can E-mail it to one of a hundred search services that'll get me the address in half an hour or less. Even call it in."

"The area code is eight-one-four—where is that? There are so many area codes these days."

"The note she scrawled beside it said 'PA'—Pennsylvania, I assume, right?"

"*Pennsylvania?* Why would Harry Dunne be there?"

"Maybe he's originally from there? A childhood home?"

"His accent is purest New Jersey."

"Relatives, then? I'll do a reverse-number lookup; that much should be easy to find out."

At one o'clock in the morning there was only a skeleton staff on duty at the Meredith Waterman building: a handful of security guards and one information technology staffer.

The tough-looking female security guard stationed at the employees' entrance at the side of the building was in the middle of reading a Harlequin romance, and she did not look happy about being disturbed.

"You're not on the admit list," she said dourly, her long-nailed index finger holding her place in the book.

The short-haired man in the aviator glasses and the shirt with MCCAFFREY INFORMATION STORAGE SERVICES stitched on it just shrugged. "Hey, fine. I'll just head back to New Jersey and tell 'em you wouldn't let me in. Makes my job easier, and I still get paid."

Bryson turned around, readying his next riposte, when the guard relented somewhat. "What's the purpose of your—"

"Like I told you. Meredith is one of our clients. We do the off-site backup—it's an after-hours download. But we're getting digital collation errors. Doesn't happen a lot, but it happens. And it means I gotta check the routers on site here."

She sighed in irritation and picked up the phone, punching a number. "Charlie, do we have a contract with a Mc-Caffrey"—she examined the stitching on Bryson's shirt—"Information Storage Services?"

She listened in silence. "The guy says he has to check on something here because of errors or something."

She listened again. "All right, thanks." She hung up, a superior smirk on her face. "You're supposed to call ahead," she said with a reproving scowl. "The service elevator's on the right down the hall. Take it down to B."

As soon as he reached the basement level, he raced to the freight-delivery entrance, which he had located during his earlier surveillance. Elena was waiting there, wearing the identical uniform and carrying an aluminum clipboard. The corporate records center was one large below-ground room, with a low acoustic-tiled ceiling, buzzing fluorescent lights, and row upon row of open steel warehouse shelves that held endless-seeming lines of identical, tall gray archive boxes. The boxes were arranged chronologically, with just a few entries for 1860, the year it was founded by Elias Meredith, an erstwhile trader in Irish linen. Each succeeding year took up more linear shelf space, until 1989—the last year whose paper files were stored here—which occupied an entire row. Each year was broken down into various categories—client records, personnel records, minutes of partners' and committee meetings, consent resolutions, amendments to bylaws, and so on. Folders were color-coded, with end tabs and bar codes.

Time was extremely limited: they knew they could not stay down here for much more than an hour before Security would begin to wonder what was taking so long. They divided up responsibilities, with Bryson surveying the paper files and Elena sitting at the computer terminal and examining the records-management database. This was an electronic records-tracking and inventory-management system, up-to-date though not password-protected. There would be no reason for it to be protected, since it was set up for ease of use by the bank's record clerks.

It was laborious work, made even more difficult by the fact that they had no idea exactly what they were looking for. Client records? But which clients? Records of large money transfers to offshore accounts? But how could they distinguish between a wire transfer that was nothing more shady than the semilegitimate parking of clients' assets offshore to avoid scrutiny by the IRS, or by a divorcing wife— and one that might be the beginning of a long sequence of transfers from one offshore bank to another, eventually ending up in the pocket of a senator? Elena came up with the idea of using the computer to search for them—by feeding in key words and pulling up file references. Yet after an hour they still had nothing.

In fact, they began to find documents missing, whole sections of them. After 1985, there were no partners' income records or earning statements to be found. It was not as if the documents had been removed. Elena was able to confirm, by poring over the electronic database manager, that not a single document pertaining to monies brought in by the partners was to be found after 1985.

Frustrated, increasingly tense as the minutes ticked by, Bryson finally decided to narrow his focus to just one partner: Richard Lanchester. He proceeded to examine all the Lanchester files—personnel, compensation, clients. The story they told was, just as the Lanchester myth had it, one of the genesis of a Wall Street whiz. He started at Meredith Waterman immediately after graduation from Harvard, and did not do grunt work for long. Within a very few years he emerged as an aggressive bond trader, generating huge income for the firm. He soon headed the department. Then he added another specialty—currency speculation and investment. The money he made there made what he was doing before look like begging for pocket change. Richard Lanchester had become, in ten years, the biggest earner in the bank's history.

The Wall Street whiz kid had become a financial powerhouse, making himself and the other general partners extremely rich through his deals, and most of all through a complex series of financial trades. He had apparently mastered the delicate art of trading in financial instruments called derivatives, placing immense, multibillion-dollar wagers on stock-index futures and interest-rate futures. Essentially he was gambling on a massive scale, the casino being the global capital markets. He kept winning and winning and winning; no doubt, like a true gambler, he believed his luck would never run out.

It was late in 1985 when his luck ran out.

In 1985, everything changed. With rapt fascination, sitting on the cold concrete floor of the records room, Bryson came upon a thin folder of internal auditors' reports that described a reversal of fortune so abrupt, so devastating, that it was almost impossible to believe.

One of his immense bets, on Eurodollar futures, went bad. Overnight, Lanchester had lost the bank three *billion* dollars. This exceeded the bank's assets many times over.

Meredith Waterman was insolvent. It had survived a century and a half of financial crises, even the Great Depression; and then Richard Lanchester lost a bet, and America's oldest private bank was broke.

"My *God*," Elena breathed as she looked through the auditors' reports. "But . . . none of this was ever made known to the public!"

Bryson, as astonished as she, shook his head slowly. "Nothing. Never. Not an article, not a mention in the press— *nothing*."

"How can this be?"

Bryson glanced at his watch. They had been down here for almost two hours; they were pressing their luck.

Suddenly he looked at her, eyes wide. "I think I understand now why we couldn't find any partners' income records after 1985."

"Why?"

"Because they found a benefactor. Someone to bail them out."

"What do you mean?"

He got up, found the gray file box that was marked, blandly, PARTNERSHIP INTEREST ASSIGNMENTS. He had seen it but hadn't bothered to open it; there was far too much to look through and that seemed unlikely to yield anything interesting. He opened the box and found only one thin manila file folder inside. The folder contained fourteen thin, stapled legal documents of no more than three pages each.

Each was headed PARTNERSHIP INTEREST ASSIGNMENT. He read the first one with a racing heart. Although he knew what it would say, it was nevertheless stunning, even terrifying, to see on the page.

"Nicholas, *what?* What is it?"

He read phrases aloud as he skimmed. "The undersigned

agrees to sell all rights, title, and interest in my interest as a partner in the partnership . . . In consideration thereof . . . succeed to all rights and liabilities associated with that interest."

"What are you reading? Nicholas, what *are* these documents?"

"In November of 1985, each of the fourteen general partners in Meredith Waterman signed a legal document selling their stake in the partnership," Bryson said. His mouth was dry. "Each of the partners was directly and personally responsible for the more than three billion dollars of debt that Lanchester had run up. Obviously they had no choice; they were all backed into a corner. They had to sell out."

"But . . . I don't understand—what was there left to sell?"

"Just the name. An empty shell of a bank."

"And the buyer got—what?"

"The buyer paid fourteen million dollars—one million to each partner. And they were extraordinarily lucky to get that. Because the buyer was now saddled with billions of dollars of debt. Fortunately for him, he could afford it. Part of the condition of the sale was that each partner was required to sign a side confidentiality agreement—a nondisclosure agreement. A vow of secrecy. Enforceable by the threat of having their payment—the money disbursed over five years— revoked."

"This is . . . it's so *bizarre,*" she said, shaking her head. "Am I understanding this right? Are you saying that in 1985 Meredith Waterman was *secretly* sold to one person? And no one knew it?"

"Exactly."

"But who was the buyer? Who'd be crazy enough to make such a deal?"

"Someone who wanted to become the secret owner of a prestigious, highly regarded investment bank—which he could then use as a vehicle. A front for illicit payments around the world."

"But who?"

Bryson gave a small, wan smile, and he too shook his

head in puzzlement. "A billionaire named Gregson Manning."

"Gregson Manning—Systematix . . . ?"

Bryson paused. "The man behind the Prometheus conspiracy."

There was a quiet scuffing noise, which jolted Bryson— the sound of a leather shoe scraping against the concrete floor. He looked up from the files, which were spread out on a small table before them, and saw the tall, stout man in a blue security-officer's uniform. The man was staring at them with undisguised hostility. "You—hey, what the goddamned hell . . . ? You're—you're supposed to be from the computer company. *What the hell are you doing here?*"

CHAPTER THIRTY

They were nowhere near the main bank of computers, the server on the other side of the large room. A file box, clearly labeled, stood in front of them; the fourteen legal documents spread out like a fan on the table.

"What the hell took you so long?" said Bryson in disgust. "I've been calling up to security for the last half hour!"

Gimlet-eyed, the security man regarded them with suspicion. His two-way radio crackled. "What the hell you talking about? I didn't get any calls."

Elena got up, waving her clipboard. "Look, without the service contract, we're just wasting our time! It's supposed to be left for us in the same place each time! We're not supposed to dig around for it—do you have any *idea* how much data's going to be lost?" She gesticulated wildly, thrusting an index finger toward his chest.

Bryson watched her, impressed; he followed her lead. "Security must have shut down the system," he said with a petulant shake of the head, getting up slowly.

"Hey lady," the guard protested, facing her, "I don't know what the hell you're talking—"

Bryson's hands shot out like the strike of a cobra, grabbing the security man's throat from behind with his left hand, and striking, with the hard edge of his rigid right hand, the brachial plexus nerve bundle at the base of the neck. The man went suddenly limp, slumping into Bryson's arms. He set the unconscious guard down on the floor gently, dragging him the short distance to the warehouse shelving, propping him up in the aisle between two rows of shelves. He would be out for at least an hour, possibly more.

As soon as they exited the bank through the freight entrance, they ran to the rented car, parked down the block and across the street. Not until they were several blocks away did either of them say anything. They were each in a state of shock. Exhaustion would be tolerated; there was nothing to do about that now except to grab sleep when they could; otherwise, they were surviving on caffeine and adrenaline.

It was three-twenty in the morning, the streets dark and deserted. Bryson drove through the empty streets of lower Manhattan, and when he reached the area of the South Street Seaport he found a narrow side street and pulled over to the curb.

"It's amazing," Bryson said quietly. "One of the richest men in the country—in the *world*—and America's most respected political figure. 'The last honest man in Washington,' or whatever the hell they call him. A partnership sealed years ago, in conditions of absolute secrecy. Manning and Lanchester never appear in public together, they're never mentioned in the same sentence; they seem to have no connection."

"Appearances are important."

"Crucial. For all kinds of reasons. I'm sure Manning wanted to preserve Meredith Waterman's impeccable reputation—it was far more valuable to him that way, as a paragon of old-line Wall Street that he could secretly use to control political leaders the world over. Now he had the perfect cover, the camouflage of unimpeachable respectability, concealing his conduit for bribes and other illegal funds channeled to Parliament and Congress, probably to the Russian Duma and Parliament, the French General Assembly— you name it. And he had a front that could in turn buy stakes in other banks, other companies, without his name ever being associated. Like the Washington bank where most Congressmen do their banking. It's all there—bribery, the potential for blackmail by using the most sensitive personal information . . ."

"And of course the White House," she put in. "Through Lanchester."

"Certainly Manning has major influence on U.S. foreign policy through him. That's why it was equally important to both men that not a word of how Manning bailed out Meredith Waterman ever leak. Richard Lanchester's reputation had to remain intact. If the word got out that he had single-handedly brought down America's oldest private bank with reckless speculation, he'd have been ruined. Instead, he was able to preserve the mystique of his financial genius. The brilliant but ethical man who made a fortune on Wall Street, who became so rich he was incorruptible, was willing to give it all up to work on behalf of his country. In 'public service.' How could America *not* be honored to have such a man in the White House assisting the president?"

A moment of silence passed. "I wonder whether Gregson Manning actually *sent* Lanchester to the White House? That maybe was one of the conditions of his saving Meredith Waterman."

"Interesting. But don't forget, Lanchester already knew Malcolm Davis before Davis announced his run for the presidency."

"Lanchester was one of his key supporters on the street, right? In politics, money buys friendship rather easily. And then he volunteered to run Davis's campaign."

"No doubt Manning secretly helped out there too—shoving a lot of money Davis's way, from Systematix, from his employees and friends and associates, and who knows how else. Thereby making Lanchester look good, look damned *invaluable,* in fact. So Richard Lanchester, who stared ruin in the face, who saw his illustrious career crash and burn, was suddenly a major player on the world stage. His career went supernova."

"And he owed it all to Manning. We have no way in to Manning, do we?"

Bryson shook his head.

"But you know Lanchester—you met in Geneva. He'll see you."

"Not now, he won't. By now he knows everything he needs to know about me—enough to know that I'm a threat to him. He'll never agree to see me."

"Unless you make that threat explicit. And demand a meeting."

"For what? Meet with him for what, to accomplish *what*? No, a direct, unmediated approach to him is just too blunt an instrument. As I see it, the best way in is Harry Dunne."

"Dunne?"

"I know the guy's temperament. He won't be able to resist an approach from me; he knows what I know. He'll *have* to see me."

"Well, I don't know about that, Nicholas. He may not be in any shape to meet with anyone."

"What are you talking about?"

"That telephone number we got at the nursing home—it's a town called Franklin, Pennsylvania. The phone number is listed as belonging to a small, private, very exclusive medical facility. A hospice. Harry Dunne may be in hiding—but he's also dying."

There were no direct flights to Franklin, Pennsylvania; the fastest way was to drive. But they desperately needed rest, even if only for a few hours. It was vital that they remained alert: there was still much to do, Bryson was sure of it.

Three or four hours of sleep, however, turned out to be worse than none at all. Bryson awoke groggy—they had found a motel about half an hour outside of Manhattan that looked suitably anonymous—to the sound of the tapping of computer keys.

Elena looked rested, apparently having showered, and she sat in front of her notebook computer, which was plugged into the phone jack in the wall.

She spoke without turning around, obviously having heard him stir. "Systematix," she said, "is either the most impressive evidence of unrestrained global capitalism, or the most frightening corporation that ever existed. It depends on how you look at it."

Bryson sat up. "I need coffee before I can look at it."

Elena pointed to a carry-out cardboard cup next to his side of the bed. "I went out about an hour ago. It might be cold by now; I'm sorry."

"Thank you. Cold is just fine. Did you sleep at all?"

She shook her head. "I got up after half an hour or so. Too much on my mind."

"Tell me what you found."

She turned around to face him. "Well, if knowledge is power, then Systematix is the most powerful corporate entity on the face of the earth. Their corporate motto is 'The Knowledge Business,' and that seems to be the only organizing principle—the only element that unites its immense holdings."

Bryson took a sip of coffee. It was indeed cold. "But I thought Systematix was a software company—one of Microsoft's chief rivals."

"Software and computers—that turns out to be a fraction of its real business. But it's extraordinarily diversified. We already know it owns Meredith Waterman, and through them the First Washington Mutual Bancorp. I can't *prove* it controls the banks in Great Britain where most members of Parliament have their accounts, but I strongly suspect it."

"Based on what? Given the elaborate precautions Manning took to conceal his ownership of Meredith, it can't be any easier to connect him to British banks."

"It's the *law* firms—the foreign law firms it has on retainer—that tell the story. And those firms, whether in London or Buenos Aires or Rome, are known to have close relationships to certain banks. That's how I can connect the dots."

"That's an impressive line of reasoning."

"Now, through Systematix, Manning has major stakes in the military-industrial giants. And recently it's launched a fleet of low-earth-orbit satellites. But listen to this: Systematix also owns two of America's three major credit-reporting agencies."

"Credit . . . ?"

"Think of how much information a credit company has on you. It's staggering. An incredible amount of highly personal information. And there's more. Systematix owns several of the largest health-insurance firms—and it also owns data-management firms that maintain the *records* for those insurance companies. It owns the medical data companies that manage the medical records for virtually all of the country's HMOs."

"My *God*."

"As I said, the one element that unites all these entities, or at least many of them, is information. What they know. The information they have access to. Just step back and look at it—life insurance and health insurance records, medical records, credit and banking records. Through its web of corporate holdings, Systematix has access to the most intimate, most private records on what I estimate to be ninety percent of the citizens of the United States."

"And that's just Manning."

"Hmm?"

"Manning is just one member of the Prometheus Group. Don't forget about Anatoly Prishnikov, who probably has similar holdings in Russia. And Jacques Arnaud in France. And General Tsai in China. Who knows what personal information this group has control over?"

"This is really frightening, Nicholas, you know that? For a girl who grew up in a totalitarian state, with the Securitate, with every other person informing on you—the possibilities are terrifying."

Bryson stood up, folded his arms. He could feel his body tense; he had the eerie and uncomfortable sensation of headlong *movement,* of plunging through an endless tunnel. "What Prometheus has managed to do in Washington—obtaining personal information that no one should ever have, then releasing it or threatening its release—it has the ability to do around the world. Systematix may be about information, but *Prometheus*—Prometheus is about *control*."

"Yes," Elena said, her voice seeming to come from very far away. "But for *what?* To *what end?*"

Control is about to be transferred . . . We see clearly now . . .

"I don't know," Bryson replied. "And by the time we learn the answer, it may well be too late."

————

Shortly after noon they pulled their rented car into the semicircular drive of a Georgian red-brick building that appeared to have once been a grand private home. It was marked with discreet brass letters on a low brick wall: FRANKLIN HOUSE. Elena waited in the car.

Bryson wore a white doctor's coat, purchased at a medical supply house on the way, and identified himself as a pain-management specialist from the University of Pittsburgh Medical Center, called in for a consult by the family of a hospice patient. Bryson relied on the generally unsuspicious environment of hospitals and other medical establishments, and he was not disappointed. No one asked to see identification. He struck an attitude of professional detachment, though with the appropriate air of concern: the family had contacted him through a colleague and asked them for any help he might suggest to ease the dying man's last days. With amused chagrin, Bryson showed them a pink "While You Were Out" message slip with the phone number on it.

"My secretary didn't write down the patient's name," he said, "and I'm embarrassed to say I left my office without the fax. . . . Do you have any idea who this might be?"

The receptionist glanced at the number and looked it up on her list of extensions. "Certainly, Doctor. That'd be a Mr. John McDonald in 322."

Harry Dunne looked like a cadaver on life support. His narrow face was now sunken; most of his white hair was gone; his skin looked unnaturally bronzed, though blotchy. His eyes bulged. An oxygen tube was in his nose; he was hooked up to an intravenous drip as well as an array of monitors that recorded his respiration and heart rate, tracing irregular green squiggles on the screen behind him, beeping audibly.

There was a direct phone line, even a fax machine, but both were silent.

He looked up when Bryson entered the room. He seemed woozy but alert, and after a few seconds he grinned, a cadaver's horrific smile. "You come to kill me, Bryson?" Dunne said with a mordant laugh. "That'd be a laugh. They got me on fucking life support. Keep the corpse breathing. Just like the goddamned CIA. No more of that shit."

"You're not an easy man to find," Bryson said.

"That's 'cause I don't want to be found, Bryson. I got no relatives to visit me on my deathbed, and I know what happens over at Langley when they hear you're sick—they're already breaking the seal on your safe, pawing through your files, moving you out of your office. Like the good old Soviet Union—the premier goes on vacation to Yalta, comes back to find his stuff in banker boxes on the street outside the Kremlin." He gave a guttural, rattling cough. "Got to cover your flanks."

"For how much longer?" Bryson's question was pointed and ruthless, meant to provoke. Dunne stared for a long time before he replied.

"Six weeks ago I was diagnosed with metastatic lung cancer. Did a last-ditch course of chemo, even radiation. The shit's in my stomach, in my bones—my goddamned hands and feet even. You know they're ordering me to stop fucking *smoking?* That's a hoot. I said, shit, maybe I should just go on a high-fiber diet, for all the good it's gonna do me."

"You really set me up well," Bryson said, not bothering to hide his anger. "Spun a whole elaborate lie about my past, about the Directorate, about how it began and what it was up to. . . . Was the point just to use me like your own personal cat's paw? Do your dirty work, get me back inside the Directorate to find out what we . . ." He paused, wondering about his use of the pronoun 'we.' *Is that how I think of me, of them? I'm part of 'we,' once more part of an agency that doesn't exist?* ". . . what we knew about the Prometheus group? Because we were the only intelligence agency in the world who'd managed to find out what was going on?"

"And what did you find out, after all that? Chicken shit." He smiled grimly, lapsed into another coughing spell. "I'm like goddamned Moses. Never gonna live to see the Promised Land. Just point the way, that's all."

"The Promised Land? *Whose* 'promised land'? *Gregson Manning's?*"

"Forget about it, Bryson," Dunne said, closing his eyes, a contorted smile on his face.

Bryson looked over at the pouch of clear liquid hanging on Dunne's IV stand. It said Ketamine. A painkiller, but it also had other uses. In the right quantities it could induce euphoria and delirium; it had even been used, upon occasion, as a crude truth serum by both Directorate and CIA. He strode quickly over to it, found the stopcock, and turned it to increase the flow.

"The hell are you doing?" Dunne said. "Don't shut me off. Morphine stopped working for me, they had to move me to harder stuff."

The increased flow of the opioid had an immediate effect. Dunne flushed, began perspiring heavily. "You don't get it, do you?"

"Get *what*?"

"You ever hear what happened to his kid?"

"Whose kid?"

"Manning's."

Elena had downloaded Manning's biography. "He had a daughter who was kidnapped, didn't he?"

"Kidnapped? That's not the half of it, Bryson. Guy was divorced, had an eight-year-old daughter who was the whole fucking world to him." His words began to slur. "He's visiting Manhattan, being honored . . . some big charity thing, daughter Ariel's in his apartment at the Plaza with the au pair . . . returns home that night, finds the au pair murdered, daughter's gone . . ."

"Jesus."

"Some wiseguys . . . make a little cash . . ." His words trailed off. "Paid the ransom . . . nothing . . . they took her to some remote cabin . . . Pennsylvania." Dunne broke out into another coughing fit. "Manning . . . not fuck around . . ." His eyes fell shut.

Bryson waited a moment. Had he overdone the dose? He stood up, readjusted the IV valve just as Manning's eyes were opening again. "The guy owns a whole fuggin' electronics empire . . . offered to help out the FBI . . . crack it . . .

We got satellites, only we can't use 'em—they're shuttered . . . fuggin' Executive Order 1233—whatever the hell . . ."

Dunne's eyes were becoming more focused again. "Assholes over at Justice won't approve wiretap . . . cell phones of the kidnappers . . . Whole thing fucked up by bureau—bureaucratic bullshit. Protecting the privacy of criminals. Meanwhile, this pretty little eight-year-old girl . . . buried alive in a coffin three feet underground . . . asphyxiating slowly."

"Dear God . . . What a nightmare."

"Manning never the same after that. Saw the light."

"What—what was 'the light'?"

Dunne shook his head, smiled strangely.

Bryson stood up. "Where's *Lanchester?*" he demanded. "They say he's on vacation in the Pacific Northwest. It's a bunch of crap—not at this time he's not. Where *is* he?"

"Where they all are. The whole Prometheus gang, except yours truly. The hell you think? Lakeside."

"Lakeside . . . ?"

"Manning's house. On that lake outside Seattle." His voice was getting progressively weaker. His eyes closed. "Now go away, Bryson. I don't feel so good."

"What's the objective?" demanded Bryson. "What's the *point?*"

"It's a fucking freight train bearing down on you, brother," said Dunne. He stopped and hacked for almost a full minute. "Can't be stopped. You're too late. So you might as well get out of the fucking way."

Bryson noticed someone approaching from down the corridor: a slim black man, a male nurse, somehow familiar. *But from where?*

Abruptly he rose and left the room; his instincts warned him of impending trouble. He strode quickly, an over-scheduled doctor perennially late for his next appointment.

As he reached the end of the corridor, he glanced back and saw the black man entering Dunne's room. The man was definitely familiar. All too familiar. *But who was he?*

Bryson ducked into a lounge filled with vending machines

and Formica-topped tables, and he wracked his brain. From where, from what operation, from what country? Or was it from his civilian life, his teaching days?

A few minutes later he stuck his head into the hall and looked down toward Dunne's room. Seeing nobody in the area, he walked toward it, intending to glance into the room as he passed, try to catch a glimpse of the male nurse.

He approached Dunne's room. The door was open. He glanced inside; no one was there except Dunne, sleeping.

No.

The single unbroken tone from the heart-rate monitor caused him to look over. The EKG, normally jagged, was a flat line. Dunne's heart was no longer beating. He was dead.

He rushed into the room. Dunne's face was chalky white; he was unquestionably dead. Turning to the IV stand, he saw that the valve on the ketamine had been turned all the way, and the pouch of liquid was just about empty.

The nurse had turned the spigot. *He had killed Dunne.*

They had been under surveillance the entire time. The 'nurse'—whoever it was, he was not a nurse—had killed Dunne.

For talking?

Bryson raced from the hospice.

"Sir, we have a sighting."

The atrium was filled with banks of flat monitors, displaying constantly shifting, high-resolution images relayed from geosynchronous satellites. It was located in an upper level of a strip mall in Sunnyvale, California, above a diet center, the immense electronic capabilities well concealed as a result.

The young communications specialist pointed toward monitor 23A, striding quickly toward it. His middle-aged supervisor, wearing a lightweight telephone headset, approached the screen, squinting.

"Right there—a green Buick," said the younger man. "License plates match. Driver is the male, passenger the female."

"Facial recognition software?"

"Positive, sir. A confirmation. It's them."

"What's the direction?"

"South."

The supervisor nodded. "Dispatch Team 27," he ordered.

Bryson drove.

They had to get to Seattle immediately, had to find the closest airport, and from there find a commercial flight—or charter one. Lakeside. Gregson Manning's house on the lake. Outside Seattle.

The Prometheus Group was assembling there, all of them. Meeting—to do what?

Whatever they were doing, they were all in one place. He had to get there at once.

"The male nurse," Bryson began. He had recalled to Elena this oddly familiar person. He stopped short.

Suddenly Bryson's head was reeling. Vividly recalled images flashed by. A concrete bunker at Rock Creek Park. Dunne's driver bursting in, demanding to see his boss. *A slender, lithe, well-muscled black man.* Solomon. Firing at him, his eyes cruel, almost sadistic; the same man lying dead, crumpled on the cement floor, blood erupting from bullet wounds in his chest after being shot down by his boss.

The realization dawned, sickeningly.

"That was Dunne's chauffeur. Obviously a Prometheus control."

"But—but I thought you said he was *dead,* that Dunne *killed* him!"

"Christ, what was I thinking! We all have special-effects wizards on staff—blood packs, those little explosive charges triggered by battery—squibs, I think they're called. The rigged wardrobe. The whole bag of tricks! I was straying, and Dunne had to do something dramatic to get me back into the fold. . . . Wait . . . *listen.*"

She cocked her head. "What do you hear?"

It was definitely there, the distant whump-whump of a

helicopter. They were not near any helicopter facilities; there was no airstrip nearby.

"It's a chopper, but one of those extremely quiet models. It's got to be directly overhead. Do you have a makeup mirror, a compact, in your purse?"

"Of course."

"I want you to lower your window and hold it up, catch a reflection of the sky above. Look without letting anyone see that you're looking."

"You think it's following us?"

"For the last few minutes the sound has been fairly constant, neither louder nor softer. It's been right above us for miles now."

She opened her compact and thrust it out the open window. "There *is* something, Nicholas. Yes. A helicopter."

"Son of a bitch," Bryson muttered. A sign they had just passed indicated a rest stop a mile ahead. He accelerated, got into the right lane, following a beat-up, rust-bucket El Dorado into the rest area parking lot. The car's body was perforated by rust, part of the tail pipe dragged almost touching the ground, and the hood was secured with twine. He watched the car's driver get out, a scruffy-looking, bleary-eyed, longhaired man in grungy jeans, a black beret, and a black Grateful Dead T-shirt under a green canvas army jacket. A stoner, Bryson thought. A pothead.

"What are you doing?" Elena asked.

"Countermeasures." Bryson grabbed some papers from the glove compartment of the rented car. "Follow me. Take your purse and whatever else you've got with you."

Bewildered, she got out.

"You see that guy who just got out of that wreck of a car?"

"What about him?"

"Remember his face."

"How can I forget it?"

"I want you to wait right here until he comes out."

Bryson walked through the fast-food restaurant and saw that the driver of the El Dorado was neither in line nor seated at a table. *Either the vending machines, buying cigarettes or candy or soda, or else the restroom,* Bryson thought. The stoner wasn't at the vending machines, but he was in the men's room. Bryson recognized the man's ratty black sneakers under the door of one of the toilet stalls. He relieved himself, then stood by the sink, washing his hands. Finally, the man came out of the stall and went up to the sink. That in itself was a surprise; Bryson hadn't figured him for being much on cleanliness.

Bryson caught the stoner's eye in the mirror. "Hey," he said, "lemme ask you a favor."

The stoner glanced over at him suspiciously, didn't answer for a few seconds as he soaped his hands. Without catching Bryson's eye, he said with hostility, "What?"

"I know this might seem bizarre, but I need you to check outside for me, see if my wife's out there. I think she followed me."

"Sorry, man, I'm kinda in a hurry here." He shook off his hands and looked around for the paper-towel dispenser.

"Look, I'm desperate," Bryson said. "I wouldn't ask you if I wasn't. I'm willing to compensate you for your time." He pulled out a wad of bills and peeled off a couple of twenties. *Not too much money or it'll seem suspicious.* "Just look out there, that's all. Tell me if you see her."

"Aw, man. No fuckin' paper towels. I hate those fuckin' hot-air things." He shook the water off his hands, then he took the proffered bills. "This better not be no setup, man— I'll fuck you up but good."

"On the level, man. Totally on the level."

"What does she look like?"

"Brunette, early thirties, red blouse, tan skirt. Real pretty. You can't miss her."

"I get to keep this even if she's not there?"

"Oh, yeah, of course. Man, I *hope* she's gone." Bryson thought for a moment. "Come back and tell me and then I'll double it."

"Jeez, I don't know what the hell you're up to, man," the stoner said, shaking his head as he left the men's room.

He walked through the vending-machine area to the outside and looked around. Elena was stationed nearby, acting the part they had worked out, her arms folded, head swiveling from side to side, a furious expression on her face.

In a minute he returned to the men's room. "Yeah, I see her. That's one pissed-off chick."

"Shit," Bryson said, handing the man another couple of twenties. "I gotta shake that bitch. I'm a desperate man." He pulled out the roll of bills, this time removing hundred-dollar bills. When he had counted out twenty banknotes, he fanned them. "She's like a fucking stalker now, really making my life a total nightmare."

The stoner eyed the hundreds greedily. Distrustfully, he said, "What now? I'm not doin' anything illegal or anything—nothin' that gets me in trouble."

"No, no, of course not. Don't misunderstand me. Nothing like that."

Another man came into the rest room and glanced at the two of them warily before using the urinal. Bryson fell silent until the man left.

Then he said, "Your car that old El Dorado?"

"Yeah, it's a piece of shit—what about it?"

"Let me buy it from you. I'll give you two thousand bucks."

"No way, man, I got twenty five hundred bucks into it, with the new shocks."

"Make it three thousand." Bryson held up the keys to the Buick. "You can take mine."

"That better not be hot."

"Don't worry about it."

"Hey, that's a rental," he said suspiciously, seeing the Hertz key fob.

"Right. I'm not a *total* idiot. It's just a set of wheels to get you wherever you need to go. It's all paid for, and you can drop it wherever you want, I'll take care of it."

The stoner thought for a minute. "I don't want you coming back to me and complaining about the car being a piece of shit and all. I already told you that. She's got a hundred seventy-five thousand miles on her."

"Not to worry. I don't know you, I don't even know your name. You'll never see me again. All I care is, your car gets me away from my wife. It's worth it to me."

"Is it worth thirty-five hundred to you?"

"Yeah, yeah," Bryson said with feigned irritation.

"I got stuff in there."

"So go get it and come back with your stuff."

The stoner went to the parking lot, took a green army duffel bag from the trunk and filled it with old clothes, bottles, newspapers and books, a Walkman, a broken set of headphones. He came back to the men's room.

"I'll throw in another hundred for your beret and jacket." Bryson took off his expensive blue blazer and handed it to the man. "Take my jacket. You definitely got the better end of this deal. Plus you sold your car for three times what it's worth."

"It's a good car, man," he said sullenly.

Bryson handed him the hundred-dollar bill, then one more. "Wait for me to drive out of here before you take off, okay?"

The stoner shrugged. "Whatever."

Bryson took the keys to the El Dorado and shook the man's hand.

The stoner stood by the plate-glass windows of the vending-machine area until he saw his crappy old El Dorado drive slowly by. The car stopped, and then the man saw, to his astonishment, the pretty brunette wife in the red blouse run up to the car and jump in, and then the car drove away.

No freaks like suburban freaks, he thought, shaking his head in disbelief. *Shit.*

The Bell 300 helicopter hovered directly above the rest stop.

"We have a positive visual ID," said the observer in the front passenger's seat, peering through binoculars and speaking into his headset. He watched the man in the blue blazer get into the late-model Buick.

"Roger that," the voice replied. "We're going to satellite feed now, so give me the Buick's license plate again."

The observer dialed up the binoculars until he could read the license plate, then he read off the numbers. "Christ, will you look at the way that guy's driving? Guy must have stopped off for a couple of drinks—no wonder it took him so long."

The staticky voice came over the headset again. "You got a positive on the woman?"

"Uh, that's a negative," the observer replied. "There wasn't any woman with him. Think he might have left her there?"

The stoner in the black Grateful Dead T-shirt and elegant French blue blazer couldn't believe his luck. First he unloads the piece-of-shit El Dorado he hadn't been able to sell for five hundred bucks last summer for thirty-five hundred. Then he gets a free rental, with what looked like no time limit. And between selling his foul army jacket and beret, and poking his head outside to ogle some fucked-up guy's chick, he'd made more in half an hour than he'd made all month. Whatever the hell that idiot's trip was, paying all that money to get away from his wife and then letting the bitch back in the car, who cared?

He had the radio blasting and was cruising at almost ninety when all of a sudden he saw the huge tractor-trailer bearing down on him from the left, pulling up even with him . . .

And then forcing him to the side of the road!

What the hell was this? The pothead swung the wheel hard to the right as the eighteen-wheeler forced him off the road and onto the shoulder.

"The fuck—!" he bellowed as he leapt out of the car, waving his fist at the truck driver. "What the *fuck* you think you're doin', you *fuck?*"

A man got out of the passenger's side of the truck's cab, a well-muscled man of around forty with a crew cut. He walked around the car, looking in the windows, then rapped his knuckles on the trunk lid. "Open it," he commanded.

"Who the *fuck* you think you are, you gas-guzzling fascist son—" the stoner screamed, stopping short when he saw the flat silver pistol pointed at his eyes. "Oh, shit."

"Open the trunk."

Trembling, the stoner went right to the car, opened the door, and fumbled around looking for the lever on the floor. "Shoulda known I'd get fucked," he muttered.

The crew-cut man inspected the trunk, then looked again in the backseat. He opened the back door and prodded the large green duffel bag. Just to be safe, he fired two shots into it, then another couple of shots into the front and rear seat cushions just for good measure.

The stoner just looked, still shaking, terrified.

The crew-cut man asked a few quick questions and then he put away his gun. "Get a haircut—and get a job," he grunted as he returned to the truck.

"What the hell happened?" barked the supervisor in the surveillance control center in Sunnyvale, California.

"I—I'm not sure," faltered the technician.

"What's that in the rear seat? Zoom it in."

"That there. It's a big bundle—a bag, a sort of duffel bag. Where'd that come from?"

"I didn't see it before, sir."

"Replay the feed from sector S23-994, time fourteen-eleven." He turned to the adjacent monitor. In a few seconds, he saw the strange man in the black T-shirt carrying the big green duffel bag out of the rest area and over to the late-model Buick.

"Same object," the supervisor said. "Switcheroo."

"Rewind it. Where'd that bag come out of?"

In a few seconds they could see the longhaired man gathering what looked like trash from the trunk and front and backseats of the rusty El Dorado.

"Shit. All right, do a capture of that vehicle—quick, now, just cut and paste the image and run a search on the visual signature."

"Got it."

Within thirty seconds there was a chime, and the El Dorado came into focus on the live satellite feed. "Zoom it," the supervisor said.

"Driver is a male, passenger female," said the technician. "We've got a confirmation. Subject in view again, sir."

The El Dorado belched clouds of oil smoke as Elena and Bryson roared down the highway.

It's still there. We didn't lose them.

A large, square wooden sign on the lefthand side of the road about fifty feet ahead announced, in letters crudely formed out of twigs, CAMP CHIPPEWAH. The entrance was little more than a gap in the trees, a rutted dirt road leading somewhere off into the woods.

Bryson looked more closely and saw a smaller sign hanging from the larger one on which was painted CLOSED.

The racket from above gradually became louder: the helicopter was changing altitude, descending.

Why?

He knew why. The road was sufficiently deserted; the helicopter was shifting into position.

He suddenly veered off the highway and onto the dirt road. It would likely lead to a wooded area.

"Nicholas, what are you doing?" Elena cried.

"The leaf canopy should help us evade detection," Bryson explained. "Maybe give us the opportunity to lose the chopper."

"We didn't lose it back at the rest stop, then . . . ?"

"Only for a while."

"It's not just following us, is it?"

"No, honey. I think they've got other plans for us."

The steady drone told him that the helicopter had easily spotted the turn-off and was moving accordingly. The rutted dirt road led to a clearing, and then to a dirt path, apparently not meant for cars. He drove at top speed. The car was not suited to the terrain; the low-hanging undercarriage scraped continuously against the rocks. Tree branches on either side of the narrow lane scraped against the body of the car.

Then, just up ahead, he could see the helicopter hovering, slowly dropping into view. There was a clearing about a hundred feet ahead, the car speeding through the woods directly toward it. He slammed on the brakes; the car fishtailed, crashing into trees on either side. Elena screamed involuntarily and grabbed hold of the dashboard to brace herself.

Can't turn around—no room here to maneuver!

Just as the El Dorado entered the grassy clearing, with several small wooden cabins scattered around, the helicopter dropped down until it hovered not more than twenty feet above the ground, its front end tipped down.

"Use your gun!" Elena shouted.

"Won't do any good—it's bulletproof, and too far off, anyway."

He stole a lightning-fast glance at the chopper, searching for the gun turret, and instead saw a rocket launcher. He just narrowly missed plowing into a cabin, veered suddenly around it.

Suddenly there was an immense explosion: the cabin had turned into a fireball. They were firing incendiary devices, some kind of missiles!

Elena screamed again. "They're aiming at us! They're trying to kill us!"

With steely concentration, Bryson caught a peripheral glance at the helicopter, saw it shift again. He spun the wheel crazily to the right, sending the car careering, its wheels spinning noisily in the dirt.

Another blast! Just feet from the car, another cabin erupted in flames an instant after a missile streaked into it.

Focus! Don't be distracted, don't look—focus!

Need an escape, but what—where? Must get out of this clearing, out of the path of the missiles!

Bryson's thoughts were frantic. *Nowhere to go, nowhere out of range, nowhere a missile can't reach us!*

Jesus Christ! A missile streaked by so closely he could see it almost brush against the hood of the car, then hit a large oak tree, where it exploded. Fire was raging all around them now, the grassy meadow ablaze. The two destroyed cabins roared with pluming flames, pillars of fire.

"*My God!*" he heard himself shouting. He was nearly crazed with terror, overwhelmed by the sense of futility, the *madness* of the situation!

Then he spotted a bridge. Just across the burning field, a short path led down to a wide, muddy river, a rickety-looking, old wooden beam bridge across it. Flooring the accelerator, he drove straight ahead at top speed. Elena screamed, "What are you *doing?* You can't—the bridge won't hold us—it's not for cars!"

The trees just ahead exploded into orange flames, as another missile narrowly missed its mark. They plunged ahead straight into the inferno. For a second or two everything was orange-white as flames licked the glass, blackening it, and then they emerged on the other side of the conflagration, propelled forward onto the wooden bridge. It swayed perilously ten feet above the slow-moving river of mud.

"No!" Elena screamed. "*It won't hold us!*"

"Quick, roll down your window," Bryson shouted as he did the same. "And take a deep breath."

"What . . . ?"

The helicopter's blades thundered ever closer, a sound Bryson could feel more than hear.

He floored the accelerator once more, and the car lurched forward, crashing through the wooden parapets.

"No! *Nicholas!*"

The sensation was one of slow motion, as if time had almost come to a stop. The car teetered forward, then plunged into the river. Bryson roared, clutching the wheel and the dashboard; Elena clung to him, screaming as well.

The splash was enormous. The El Dorado plunged bumper first into the water, hurtling down. In the seconds before they were submerged in the opaque waters, Bryson heard a blast just behind them; he turned to see the bridge collapse in a starburst of flame.

Their world was dark, murky; the car sank; the brown water rushed into the windows, rapidly filling the interior.

Bryson could see just a short distance ahead underwater. Holding his breath, he unbuckled the seat belt and helped Elena out of her seat belt, then out of the car, moving slowly, balletically, through the shadows, the billowy murk. Pulling her with all of his strength, they moved along just beneath the surface of the brackish water, carried along by the current, until he could no longer hold his breath and they came to the surface, surrounded by reeds and marsh grass.

They each gasped for air, gulping it in. "Stay down," he panted. They were surrounded by tall reeds, shielded from view. He could hear, but not see, the helicopter; he pointed toward the water, and Elena nodded, then they filled their lungs with air and went under again.

The instinct for survival is a potent source of energy: it urged them along, allowed them to stay under for a longer time than they might otherwise have done, made them swim with greater endurance. When they came up for air again, still camouflaged by reeds and grass, the helicopter roar seemed to have diminished; it seemed to be farther away. Keeping his head down, Bryson looked skyward and saw that the chopper had gained altitude, likely to survey a broader area.

Good; they're not sure where we've gone, whether we were trapped in the car to drown slowly . . .

"Again," Bryson said. They took deep breaths, filling their lungs to the bottom, then plunged. There was a rhythm now, a pattern to their flight; they swam, let the current carry them downstream, and when they couldn't hold their breath any longer they came up, sheltered by the wild aquatic vegetation.

They went down again, and up, then down again, and soon half an hour had gone by, and Bryson looked at the sky and saw that the helicopter had left. There were no signs of life to be observed; the watchers had lost their targets, no doubt hoping that the targets were dead.

Finally they reached a place where the river got shallow and they could stand and rest. Elena shook the muddy water from her hair, coughing a few times before she was able to catch her breath. Their faces were mud-covered; Bryson could not help laughing, though more from relief than from amusement.

"So this is what your life was like," she said, the analyst speaking to the field operative. She coughed again. "You're welcome to it."

Half smiling, he said, "This is nothing. You haven't lived until you've had to take a dive into the canals of Amsterdam. Three meters deep. A third of that's muck and filth. Another third's a layer of abandoned bicycles—they're sharp and rusty, and when they scrape you it hurts like hell. Then you stink for about a week. As far as I'm concerned, this is a refreshing dip in a nature preserve."

They climbed up onto the riverbank, the water draining from their soaked clothing. A cold breeze was blowing, rippling the reeds and chilling them both. Elena had begun shivering, and Bryson held her close, warming her as best he could.

About three-quarters of a mile from Camp Chippewah was a bar and restaurant. Sodden and cold, mud-encrusted, they sat at the bar, sipping hot coffee, talking quietly and ignoring the looks from the bartender and the other patrons.

A television mounted on the wall was blaring a soap opera, which had just begun; the bartender pointed a remote at it, changing the channel to CNN.

Richard Lanchester's patrician face occupied the entire screen, file footage from one of his numerous appearances before Congress. An announcer's voice came on in midsentence: ". . . sources say will be named to head the new international security agency. The reaction in Washington has been overwhelmingly favorable. Lanchester, who is reportedly enjoying a rare working vacation in the Pacific Northwest, was unavailable for comment . . ."

Elena went rigid. "It's happening," she breathed. "They're not even bothering to hide anything any longer. Dear God, what is it, what are they doing—what is it *really?*"

Two hours later they had chartered a private plane to Seattle.

Neither one slept; they spoke quietly, urgently. They planned, strategized; they held each other, neither able to vocalize what they both feared, what the dying Harry Dunne had taunted Bryson with: *they were too late.*

CHAPTER THIRTY-ONE

Their suite at the Four Seasons Olympic Hotel in Seattle—the busy hotel, situated conveniently near the Interstate 5 Expressway, seemed their best bet for escaping notice—was converted into a command center: it was strewn with maps, computer equipment, cables, modems, and printouts.

The tension was almost palpable. They had found the nerve center of a shadowy organization known as Prometheus, the site of a meeting this evening of enormous consequence. Harry Dunne's ravings had been confirmed by a variety of means. The city's limousine services all reported they had nothing available; there was a "function" tonight requiring quite a few cars. Most were discreet, though one owner could not resist dropping the name of the host: Gregson Manning. Flights were arriving throughout the day at Seattle-Tacoma Airport, pickups of VIPs arranged, many with security escorts. Yet not a single name of an arriving guest was revealed. The cordon of secrecy was extraordinarily tight.

So too was the secrecy that seemed to surround the life and career of Gregson Manning. It was as if two or three sanitized accounts of his personal life had been doled out to fatuous journalists, published prominently, and then recycled endlessly. The result was that although much was written about Manning, little was known.

They had more success in obtaining information about Manning's famous mansion on the shores of a lake outside of Seattle. The building of this digital fortress, this so-called "smart house," had taken years and was accompanied by much press coverage, a great deal of voyeuristic speculation. Apparently, after a period of trying to suppress reporting on his house, Manning had shifted to trying to control the reporting. That he had managed well. The mansion was described in tones of breathless astonishment, in "tours" published in such magazines as *Architectural Digest* and *House & Garden*, as well as in various wire-service reports and in *The New York Times Magazine* and *The Wall Street Journal*.

Many of the articles were accompanied by photographs; a few even included rudimentary plans which, though no doubt incomplete, allowed Elena and Bryson to note the approximate layout and the purpose of many of the rooms. The futuristic, hundred-million-dollar estate was cut so deep into the steep hillside that much of it was underground. There was an indoor pool; a tennis court; an art deco, state-of-the-art theater. There were conference rooms, exercise facilities with a trampoline room, bowling alley, shooting range, basketball court, a putting green. The mansion's front lawn, Bryson was careful to note, was directly on the shores of the lake, with two boat docks. Deep under the front lawn was a giant concrete-and-steel parking garage.

But what Bryson found most intriguing about Manning's house was that it was a fully digital house: all its electronic devices, all its appliances, were networked and controlled both locally and remotely, from the Seattle campus of Systematix. The house was programmed to serve the every want of its residents and guests. Every visitor was given an electronic badge programmed with their likes and dislikes, their tastes and preferences, from art to music, from lighting to temperature. Signals were relayed from the badge to hundreds of sensors. Wherever they moved throughout the house, the lights would dim or brighten according to their wishes, temperatures would adjust, their favorite music would come on the concealed sound system. Video screens were embedded in the walls, disguised as picture frames; they displayed a constantly changing selection of artwork from some twenty million images and pieces of art to which Manning had quietly acquired the rights. Visitors to the house would therefore see the walls hung with only the art they loved, whether it was great Russian icons or Van Gogh, Picasso or Monet, Kandinsky or Vermeer. Apparently the resolution of the video monitors was so fine that guests were astonished to realize they were not viewing actual canvases.

But very little existed in the public record about the security of Gregson Manning's high-tech Xanadu. All Bryson could turn up was that the security system was, of course, redundant; that there were hidden cameras everywhere, even secreted within the interior stone walls; and that the electronic badges that all visitors and staff wore did more than change the music and the lighting: they also kept track of every visitor's whereabouts to within six inches. The system was said to be monitored at the Systematix campus. The place was said to be more heavily guarded than the White House. *No surprise*, thought Bryson grimly. *Manning has more power than the president.*

"It would be a big help if we could get the building plans," Bryson said after he and Elena had gone through the piles of articles photocopied from the public library and downloaded from the Internet.

"But how?"

"They're supposedly on file at city hall, blueprints occupying seven drawers. Under lock and key. But I have a strong impression that they've been 'lost.' Men like Manning frequently arrange to have municipal copies of sensitive documents 'misplaced.' And the architect, unfortunately, lives and works in Scottsdale, Arizona. Presumably he has the stamped originals, but there's no time to fly to Arizona. So we'll just have to wing it."

"Nicholas," she said, turning to him with anxiety in her face, "what do you intend to do?"

"I need to get inside. It's the seat of the conspiracy, and the only way to blow it, and them, out of the water is to confront and *witness*."

"Witness?"

"Witness, observe the members. See who they are, the ones whose names we don't know. Take photographs, record video evidence. Shine daylight into the darkness. It's the only way."

"But Nicholas, it's like trying to infiltrate Fort Knox, isn't it?"

"In some ways easier, in some ways harder."

"But even more dangerous."

"Yes. Even more dangerous. Especially without the Directorate as backup. We're on our own."

"We need Ted Waller."

"I don't know how to raise him, how to locate him."

"If he's still alive, he'll want to contact us."

"He knows how to. The telephone numbers are still answered by answering services, coded messages taken and given to the right caller. I keep checking, but he still hasn't surfaced. He's a man who's skilled at disappearing without a trace if circumstances require it."

"But to try to enter the Manning estate on your own—"

"Will be difficult. But with your help—your expertise at computer systems—we may have a chance. One of the articles mentioned that the security at Manning's house is monitored both locally and at Systematix headquarters."

"That doesn't really help us—Systematix is probably even more secure than Manning's residence."

Bryson nodded. "No doubt. But the point of vulnerability may be the link. How would the house be connected to the company?"

"I'm sure they'd use the most secure method possible."

"What's that?"

"Fiber-optic line. Buried in the ground and physically connecting the two locations."

"Can fiber-optic lines be tapped?"

She looked up suddenly, startled, and then a slow smile started across her face. "Just about everyone believes it's impossible."

"And you?"

"I *know* it's possible."

"How do you know?"

"We've done it. A few years ago the Directorate devised several clever techniques."

"You know how to do it?"

"Of course. It takes some equipment, though nothing you can't get at a decent computer store."

Bryson kissed her. "Terrific. I have a lot of equipment to buy, and I need to conduct some surveillance on Manning's house and property. But first I need to make a phone call to California."

"Who's in California?"

"A company in Palo Alto I've dealt with before, in one of my Directorate aliases. Founded by a Russian émigré, Victor Shevchenko, an optics genius. He's got a Pentagon contract and yet he used to sell a fair amount of obscure, classified equipment on the black market, which is how I got to know him, during an international sting operation. I left him in place, didn't report his activities to Justice, because I figured he'd be more useful as a lead to much bigger fish. He was deeply grateful for my forbearance—and now it's time to collect. Victor is one of the very few sources for the instrument I need, and if I get to him now he may just have the time to air-freight it to us by this evening."

Bryson spent the next hour conducting discreet surveillance of Manning's estate, using small but high-powered binoculars, from the national forest land that adjoined it. The lakeside property occupied five acres. On the other side was a far more modest house on about an acre and a half.

The security, or at least as much as Bryson could observe, was extremely sophisticated. The chain-link perimeter fence was eight feet high, with fiber-optic stress-sensor line enmeshed throughout it. This ruled out climbing over the fence or attempting to cut through it. The bottom of the fence was buried in concrete, which made digging underneath difficult. Buried under the topsoil in front of the fence was a distributed pressure–sensor system, also fiber-optic lines, which detected the footsteps of intruders above a certain pre-set weight: pressure on the sensors disturbed the light flow and set off an alarm. In addition, the entire area was watched by surveillance cameras mounted on poles along the fence. Getting in this way had to be ruled out.

But every security system had its vulnerabilities.

For one thing, there was the forest that adjoined the Manning property, where he now stood. Then there was the lake, which seemed to Bryson to present the best opportunity to infiltrate undetected. He returned to the rented Jeep, hidden among the trees and far from the nearest road. As he drove down the access road he passed a small white van that was turning into the gated Manning estate. It was painted with the words Fabulous Food. Caterers, no doubt preparing for the evening's festivities. He caught a glance of the van's passengers.

Another possibility had just suggested itself.

There were errands to run, purchases to make, and far too little time remaining. Bryson had no difficulty locating a sporting-goods store specializing in mountain climbing, not in this capital of the Pacific Northwest. It was a large and well-stocked shop that also catered to the diverse need of hunters, which eliminated the need to make two other stops. But scuba-diving equipment had to be obtained at a separate dive shop. The yellow pages identified for him the location of an industrial safety products supply house, which serviced construction companies, telephone linemen, window washers, and the like; there, he found precisely what he needed: a portable electric winch, battery operated and quiet, in lightweight aluminum housing with a self-retracting lifeline—two hundred and twenty-five feet of galvanized steel cable, a controlled descent device, and a centrifugal braking mechanism.

An elevator parts supply company had exactly what he needed, as did a military surplus warehouse, where an employee recommended a decent shooting range close by. There he bought a .45 semiautomatic pistol for cash from a young, grubby-looking man practicing with it, who shared Bryson's vocal disgust with the goddamned gun-control laws and the goddamned waiting period, especially when a guy just wanted to pick up a piece for recreational purposes on the way out of town for a camping trip.

Batteries and bell wire were easily found at an ordinary hardware store, but he expected it to be far more difficult to find a decent theatrical supply house than it turned out to be.

Hollywood Theatrical Supply, on North Fairview Avenue, sold and rented a complete range of equipment for stage and motion-picture industry use; Hollywood studios and production companies often went on location in the northwest and needed a local supplier.

All that remained was the single exotic piece of classified military equipment. Victor Shevchenko, the inventor of the virtual cathode oscillator, had been reluctant to part with one of them, but relented when Bryson let him know that there was no statute of limitations on violations of U.S. national security law. That, and fifty thousand dollars wired into the scientist-entrepreneur's Grand Caymans account, was enough to twist his arm.

By the time Bryson returned to the Four Seasons, Elena had purchased what she needed. She had even downloaded a U.S. geological-survey topographical map of the national forestland abutting Manning's estate.

After he explained what he had observed on his visit to the area surrounding the Manning estate, she asked, "Wouldn't it be much simpler for you to get in as a caterer, or maybe a florist?"

"I don't think so. I've thought it over, and my calculation is that the florists are probably accompanied in, they do their work, and they're accompanied out. Even assuming I could somehow enter with them, which I wouldn't count on, it would be next to impossible for me to disappear into the house—to not leave with the others—without putting the whole place on alert."

"But the caterers—they come in, they stay throughout the festivities . . ."

"The caterers may well turn out to be useful to me. But from what little I've read about Manning's security paranoia, we can assume that all of the caterer's employees are going to be background-investigated, photographed and finger-printed, and issued electronic security passes only upon arrival. Getting into the house as a caterer will be next to impossible. I've rented a boat; it's the only way to get up on shore."

"But . . . but then what? I'm sure he has the front lawn protected!"

"No question about it. But from everything I can tell, it's the least secure entry point. Now, what have you learned about the security system link between Manning's house and Systematix?"

"I'm going to need a van," she said.

Outside of Seattle the U.S. Department of Agriculture maintains a garage facility where the Seattle-area employees of the U.S. Forest Service kept their government vehicles. In the adjacent open-air parking lot were several small green trucks marked with the forest service pine-tree shield. The security was virtually nonexistent.

Bryson drove Elena into the woods adjoining the Manning property. She was attired in green pants and shirt purchased at an army-navy surplus store, the closest thing they could get to a U.S. Forest Service uniform on such short notice.

Four hours remained before their strike time of nine o'clock P.M.

They walked through the forest near the high-security chain-link fence that marked the boundary of Manning's estate, careful to keep back far enough from the cameras and the pressure-detection alarm system next to the fence. Elena was looking for a buried fiber-optic cable that ran from the Manning mansion through a small area of the national forest.

She knew it was there. Manning's house was approximately three miles from Systematix headquarters, the communications linked by fiber-optic cable. During the construction of the house, Manning's contractor had filed an official request with the U.S. Department of Agriculture for an easement to run just twenty feet of fiber-optic line between his house and the public road. The form, which was a matter of public record and easily obtained on-line, mentioned one detail that especially intrigued Elena: the need to put down a device called an optical repeater. This was a box that served in effect as an amplifier, to boost the signal along the way, since there was always some leakage over long distances.

A repeater could easily be tapped into, if you knew what you were doing. Most did not; Elena most certainly did.

The only question was: where was the line?

A few minutes later she punched out a Seattle telephone number for the contractor listed in the easement request, the one who had installed the miles of cable.

"Mr. Manzanelli? My name is Nadya; I'm calling from the U.S. Geological Survey. We're taking soil samples to test for acidification, and we want to make sure we don't accidentally cut any fiber-optic cable out here. . . ."

When she explained what section of the national forest she was digging in, the contractor replied, "Jesus Christ, come on! Doesn't anyone there remember the hassle you folks gave us over digging the trench through government land?"

"I'm sorry, sir, I'm not familiar—"

"Goddamned Forest Service wouldn't permit it, and Mr. Manning was willing to kick in half a million bucks for new plantings and everything! But no—we had to run an aboveground conduit right along the fence!"

"Sir, I'm terribly sorry to hear that—I'm sure our new administrator would happily have granted Mr. Manning's request."

"You have any idea what kind of money Manning pays in property taxes alone?"

"At least there's no chance of our severing one of Mr. Manning's lines. Next time you speak with him, you tell him that all of us here at the U.S. Geological Survey appreciate what he's done for the country."

She disconnected the call and turned to Bryson. "Good news. We've just saved ourselves more than three hours."

At shortly after four o'clock P.M., Bryson was notified by Pacific Air Freight that a delivery had been received at the Seattle-Tacoma Airport. There was a problem, however: it could not be trucked into Seattle until the next morning.

"You gotta be kiddin' me," Bryson roared into the phone. "I need it at the quality-control lab *tonight,* and I got a fifty-thousand-dollar contract ridin' on it!"

"I'm sorry, sir, but if there's anything we can do to help you out in the meantime . . ."

At a few minutes before six o'clock, Bryson pulled the rented U-Haul van into the Pacific Air Freight terminal at the airport, where the thousand-pound machine was loaded onto the van by means of a hoist and the assistance of three apologetic employees.

Within an hour he drove the van deep into the thickly forested area next to the Manning property, a hundred yards from the green forest-service truck. He backed the van up so that its tail end faced the chain-link perimeter fence, though far enough away that it would not be detected by the security cameras. He slid the van door up and then positioned the machinery so that it had a direct line-of-sight to the Manning compound. The numerous trees and dense foliage that blanketed Manning's property and concealed his estate were no problem at all. Quite the opposite: they helped camouflage the Russian scientist's device.

Then he took a knapsack full of small round disks, each one connected to a firing pod that would detonate when it received a signal from a wireless transmitter. He hiked almost a quarter of a mile through the woods, back toward the main road. Then, strolling along the property line, out of sight of the cameras and removed from the pressure-triggered intrusion-detection system, he began tossing the disks over the fence, one by one, each separated from the other by approximately two hundred feet. The cartridges were small enough that they would attract no notice. If anyone happened to be monitoring the cameras—which was unlikely; the cameras were mostly there to provide a set of eyes in case one of the perimeter alarms went off—he would see nothing more than a blur, something presumably dropped by a bird, perhaps an insect. Nothing worth a second look.

———

Inside the cargo bay of the green forest-service truck, Elena quickly assembled her tools. Her laptop was now connected to the optical repeater by means of a twenty-foot cable that ran undetectably under the truck, concealed by dirt and leaves, and right to the junction box. She had a tap in place, at first just listening and watching, not transmitting anything. She had come prepared with loads of software, both commercial and specially written for the occasion. She did what was called a "stealth scan" to fingerprint the system, see what sort of intrusion-detection software was present; and she inserted a pre-written script designed to overload the system with an unexpectedly large quantity of data—create a buffer overflow. Then she ran a network packet sniffer to map out the systems on the security network, to find out what kind of network traffic was being sent and received, what the basic organization looked like.

Within the space of a few seconds she "owned the box," as the hackers liked to say. Though she was no hacker, she had long ago made it a point to learn the hacker's trade, just as a good field operative would learn the burglar's methods, the safecracker's techniques.

The training had paid off. She was in.

The fourteen-foot aluminum fishing boat was powered by a quiet, forty-horsepower Evinrude outboard motor. Bryson moved quickly across the lake, buffeted gently by the swells. The sound was minimal, carried away from the Manning property by a prevailing wind. As soon as he saw the string of bright orange barrier floats that demarcated the protected waters before Manning's dock and front lawn, he reduced speed and then cut the engine, which coughed and died. Theoretically he could have charged the line of floats, but he had to assume, even if he didn't know for sure, that Manning had some sort of security in place to detect the approach of intruder craft.

Even from here he could see the mansion, illuminated by floodlights, low-slung and hugging the hillside. Most of it was underground, making the structure appear more modest than it actually was. He dropped anchor, mindful of keeping the skiff in place as an escape option, if he was so fortunate as to be able to escape. He had told Elena, *assured* her, that his plan provided for a way out, but it was not true; he wondered if she secretly suspected it. He would win and survive, or he would lose and be killed. There was nothing in between.

Quickly, he began to assemble his equipment. Although he needed to travel as light as possible, he also had to provide for dozens of different obstacles that he simply could not foresee, which meant a range of equipment. It would be unfortunate to blow the entire operation for want of the right lockpick set. His tactical vest was heavy with various weapons, neatly folded clothing, and other objects, all sealed in plastic.

He radioed Elena on the secure two-way communicator.

"How's it going?"

"Good." Her voice was strong and clear, sounding upbeat. "The eyes are open."

She had succeeded in penetrating the video surveillance feed through the fiber-optic line. "How far can the eyes see?" Bryson asked.

"Uh, there are clear areas and areas that are not so clear."

"What's not so clear?"

"Private, residential areas and the like. They seem to be monitored locally." She meant that the cameras in the non-public parts of the house were watched not at Systematix headquarters but within Manning's house itself. Manning obviously wanted at least *some* semblance of privacy.

"That's unfortunate."

"True. But there is some good news. There are some good reruns on TV." She had located yesterday's video feed and had figured out how to pipe it back to the video monitoring system so that it appeared to be today's!

"That's excellent news. But wait until after stage one is completed. All right, now I'll be back in touch after I've gone for a swim."

The lightweight black Nomex bodysuit he preferred for

infiltrating the residence was water absorbent, so he wore a scuba wetsuit over it. He felt overheated, but the cold lake water would soon cool him down. Over the tac vest he now fastened his inflatable BC, or buoyancy compensator, which was already strapped to the tank, adjusted the quick-release buckles, adjusted the weight belt, donned his silicone dive mask, put the second-stage regulator into his mouth. After a quick double-check of his equipment, he knelt on the side of the boat and plunged in, headfirst.

There was a splash, and he was floating on the surface of the lake. He looked around, oriented himself, and started deflating his vest. He sank slowly beneath the surface of the water, which was cold and crystalline. As he descended, he noticed that the water became steadily muddier and more opaque. He stopped to equalize the air pressure, felt his ears pop. When he had reached a depth of about sixty feet, it was hard to see much farther than ten or twenty feet ahead. This was not good; he would have to proceed carefully, slowly. Feeling weightless, he began swimming in the direction of the shore.

He listened for the distinctive, bass-toned moan of sonar, but he heard only silence—which was reassuring in one sense, nerve-racking in another: there *had* to be some sort of security system in place.

And then he saw it.

There, floating no more than ten feet ahead of him, swaying in the water like some marine predator. Netting.

But no mere netting. An underwater alarmed security barrier. Webbing with fiber-optic mesh woven into the structure, linked fiber-optic panels that formed alarm zones, sensors connected to electronic control units via optical fiber–communications cables. This was an intrusion-detection system of unusual sophistication, used to protect military marine installations.

The Aquamesh was rigged to a series of buoys and anchored to the lakebed by means of weights. He could not swim through it, of course; nor could he cut or tear it without setting off the alarm. He deflated his BC until he was standing on the lakebed, then approached it, examined it. He had in fact set something like this up in Sri Lanka, and he knew that false alarms were not uncommon. It was prone to chafing and breaking, since water is constantly moving, and underwater creatures, whether fish or crabs, might wriggle through, get caught, even nip into the cables. It was not a perfect system by any means.

But he could not take the chance of setting it off. Manning's security personnel would be on heightened alert tonight, of all nights. They were likely to respond to any alarms.

He found that he was breathing shallowly, a reaction to fear, and this was causing him to feel unpleasantly short of breath, as if he could not fill his lungs; he felt a momentary panic. He closed his eyes for a moment, forced himself to be calm until his breathing became steady.

This is designed for boats, for underwater craft, he remembered. Not for divers, not swimmers.

He settled to his knees, inspected the sinkers that held the netting down. The lake floor was silt, a soft muddy sediment that yielded as soon as he touched it. He pushed at the silt, then began digging with his fingers, his hands cupped like spades. A cloud arose all around him, turning the water opaque. Swiftly, and with remarkable ease, he had dug an elongated trench beneath the bottom of the mesh, through which he was able to half wriggle, half slither. As he passed by, the movement of the water rippled the sensor net. But that could not possibly be enough to set it off: the water in the lake was always moving.

He was on the other side now: in Manning's water. He listened again for the lowing of an active sonar system, but he still heard nothing.

And if I'm wrong?

If I'm wrong, he thought, *I'll know soon enough.* Speculation would do no good now. He swam onward with single-minded determination until he approached the pilings beneath the dock, mossy with algae. Maneuvering around to the far side of the dock, where he knew the boathouse was situated, he came closer and closer, the water increasingly shallow; now his feet touched bottom, the surface of the lake just two feet above. He deflated his vest completely, walking across the lake floor until his head emerged from the water and he was directly beneath the dock. He removed his mask, listened, peered around as far as he could see, and was satisfied that there was no one in sight; then he unbuckled the BC vest and attached tank of air and hoses, placing the scuba gear securely on a broad support beam. There he hoped it would remain in case he needed it again.

If I'm so lucky.

Then he grabbed the side of the dock and lifted himself up.

The boathouse blocked his view of the house; it also served to conceal him from anyone who happened to be looking out the front windows. The lawn was dark, the only illumination spilling onto the grass nearest the house from the tall arched windows. Sitting on the edge of the dock, he took off the tac vest, peeled off the wetsuit, and put the vest back on over the black Nomex bodysuit. One by one he removed the weapons and other instruments from the vest, pulled them out of their plastic bags, and replaced them. He crawled the length of the dock and got to his feet in front of the boathouse. It was dark, seemingly empty. If he had miscalculated, he had the snub-nosed .45 handy in one of the front pockets of his vest. He pulled it out and gripped it as he walked toward the main expanse of lawn.

So far, so good. But there was more to come, much more, and the security precautions would no doubt intensify as he approached the residence itself. He could not allow himself to relax his vigilance. He took out a black knit balaclava and pulled it down over his face. From another pocket of the utility vest he took the Metascope, the night-vision monocular that detected infrared light, and put it to his right eye.

He saw the beams at once.

The lawn was crisscrossed with them, motion-detector beam sensors, probably connected to infrared cameras. Anyone walking across the front lawn would break a beam and trigger the alarm.

But they went no lower than approximately three feet, in order to keep from being set off by small animals.

Dogs?

It was possible. It was, in fact, likely that there were guard dogs as well, though he had not heard or seen any.

The Metascope came with a head-mount assembly, allowing hands-free operation. He would need his hands free. He strapped the monocular on, the eyecup securely in place. Now he would be able to traverse the lawn while evading the infrared beams.

But as he dropped to his hands and knees, crawling under the level of the lowest beam, he heard something that made him freeze.

A low whine, a canine growl. He looked up, saw several dogs trotting across the lawn, their pace quickening. Not house pets: Dobermans. Bullet-headed, trained, vicious.

He felt his stomach tighten. Good Christ.

They galloped, stiff-legged, like horses, barking wildly, throatily, sharp teeth bared. Twenty yards off, he estimated, but gaining rapidly. From his tac vest he whipped out the tranquilizer dart gun, which looked like a pistol; he aimed, heart thudding, and fired. Four short coughs, and the carbon-dioxide-powered short-range projector shot four four-inch tranquilizer darts, the first one wide of the mark, the remaining three hitting their targets. It was a silent business: two of the dogs sagged to the ground almost instantly, the largest one continuing on unsteadily for another few yards before wobbling and then crashing. Each syringe injected 10 cc's of a fentanyl-based neuromuscular incapacitant, which worked immediately.

He was perspiring heavily, trembling involuntarily. Although he had prepared for the contingency, he had almost been caught unawares with neither dart gun nor .45 at the ready; a matter of seconds, and he would have been surrounded, powerful jaws at his throat, his groin. He lay flat on the dewy lawn, waiting. There might be other dogs, a second wave. The barking might have attracted the attention of the security guards. That was likely. But even highly trained dogs could have false alarms; if their barking stopped, attention would be turned elsewhere.

Thirty, forty-five seconds of silence. The black Nomex suit and black balaclava over his face enabled him to blend into the dark night. There were no other dogs in the vicinity; in any case, he could not afford to wait any longer. Built into the front lawn, as required by state building code, would be several grates, ventilation for the underground parking garage immediately below. One of the accounts he had read of the travails of constructing the mansion had alluded to a minor battle with the building inspector over the placement of the garage, invariably and inevitably called the Bat Cave because Manning and his guests entered it via an access ramp carved deep into the hillside on the other side of the house. Under the heat of public scrutiny, Manning had made concessions, adding ventilation shafts that opened unobtrusively into the front lawn.

Bryson resumed crawling across the lawn, moving to the left, careful to stay below the lower shaft of focused infrared light. He saw nothing. He crawled straight ahead another ten feet or so up the gradual slope toward the house, and then he felt it: the steel grille of a ventilation grate. He grabbed at the grating, prepared to unbolt it if need be, but it loosened after a few tugs.

The opening was not large, maybe eighteen by twenty-four inches, but it was enough for him to enter. The only question was, how far down? The inner walls of the ventilation shaft were smooth concrete: nothing to grip on to, no handholds. He had hoped for an easier descent, though he had prepared for the situation he now found. He had learned over twenty years of field operations to prepare for the worst; it was the only guarantor of success. The collar of the shaft, into which the grate was seated, was steel; at least that was something of a relief.

Peering through the night-vision monocular into the shaft, he satisfied himself that there were no infrared beams here.

He finally removed the head-mounting apparatus of the night-vision monocular, which had begun to chafe uncomfortably, and pocketed it.

Taking out the two-way radio, he radioed Elena. "I'm going in," he said. "Cue the effects. Ignition stage one."

CHAPTER THIRTY-TWO

The security guard stared at the image, dumbstruck. "John, will you take a look at this?" The room in which they sat was round, the smooth walls a mosaic of views, yet unbroken by individual monitors. Each rectangle represented the feed from a different camera.

The second guard in the control room swiveled around in his chair and did a double-take. There was no mistaking it. A fire was raging on the border of the property. Cameras 16 and 17, stationed on the western perimeter fence, showed flames shooting up from the woods, thick smoke.

"Shit," said the second man. "That's a goddamned brush-fire! Some damned fool camper must have left a cigarette burning in the forest, and it's spreading!"

"What's the protocol? I've never had one of these before."

"What the hell do you think, asshole? First things first. Call the fire department. Then notify Mr. Manning."

As soon as Bryson gave her the word, Elena had pressed the button on the small wireless transmitter, which emitted a signal that instantly detonated the firing pods Bryson had wired to each of the twelve theatrical flash cartridges and the four flame-projector tubes. The flash cartridges, which nestled among the leaves and low foliage just over the perimeter fence on Manning's property, immediately generated thick plumes of dense brushfire smoke, mushroom clouds of gray-ish and black smoke; the flame-projector tubes produced flames that shot eight feet into the air, lasting only a few seconds. Bryson had timed them to go off in sequence, sim-ulating the effect of a wildly spreading brushfire. These were props, special effects used in theatrical and film productions to imitate forest fires convincingly yet safely, without actu-ally causing one. He had no interest in burning down national forestland; there was no need to do so.

"Seattle Fire Department Dispatch, go ahead."

"This is Security at Gregson Manning's estate. Get over here right away—we've got a huge fire that seems to have started in the national forest—"

"Thank you, but we're already on the way."

"What?"

"We've already been notified."

"You *have?*"

"Yes, sir. By one of your neighbors. The situation appears to be quite serious. We advise complete evacuation of the residence immediately."

"That's out of the *question!* Mr. Manning is in the middle of an *extremely important* function, with guests invited from all around the world, *important* guests—"

"Then it's all the more *crucial*, sir, that you evacuate your *important* guests to safety," snapped the dispatcher. *"Now!"*

Working at top speed, Bryson hooked the compact mechanical winch on to the steel collar at the head of the ventilation shaft. The double-locking snaphook at the end of the galvanized steel cable he connected to a carabiner, which hooked on the full body harness sewn into the tactical vest.

Built into the portable winch was a controlled descent device, user-controlled, with an auto-lock cam that gripped the rope as it was pulled through the spring-loaded reel, regulating the speed of the descent. It allowed him to lower himself down the shaft at a steady, metered rate.

As he lowered himself, he reached over and replaced the grate, shoving it up against the sturdy black thermoplastic casing of the winch, which would not be obtrusive at a distance. Then he resumed his descent down the dark, seemingly endless duct. In the distance he thought he could hear the warbling sirens of fire engines; they had responded even more speedily than he had anticipated. As the line continued its metered payout, he reflected that he was about to enter the zone of heaviest surveillance. The mock brushfire would raise all sorts of alarms, diverting the precious resources of

Manning's security complement. Attention would be riveted on the threat of an enveloping forest fire, a far more immediate concern than any theoretical intrusion. Any alarms Bryson inadvertently set off would be attributed to the arrival of firefighters on the property. Confusion would reign, controlled panic: the ideal cover for his infiltration. Bryson had been careful to plant the smoke-generating cartridges sufficiently distant from Elena's truck that her presence would not create suspicion; still, she had to remain alert for questions. Bryson was confident she could handle them.

As the cable continued to spool out from the specially designed pulley far above, Bryson marveled at the distance, the astonishing *depth!* When he saw the red end-of-travel indicator near the cable's end, he knew that he had descended almost 225 feet, the maximum length of the line. Finally the line jerked to a stop. He looked down; another five or six feet remained. He dropped down to the polished concrete floor, his crouch absorbing the impact of the fall. He left the line dangling, in place in case it was needed.

Capt. Matthew Kimball of the Seattle Fire Department, an African-American man of imposing height and girth, planted both feet before Gregson Manning's chief of security, a stocky man in a blue blazer named Charles Ramsey who was only a few inches shorter.

"There's no evidence whatsoever of any brushfire," the firefighter said.

"Well, two of my men saw it on the cameras," Ramsey replied defiantly.

"Did you see it with your own eyes?"

"No, but—"

"Did *any* of your men see the fire with their own eyes?"

"That I don't know. But the cameras don't lie."

"Well, someone was in error," Captain Kimball grumbled, turning back to his crew.

Charles Ramsey glanced at the security man next to him, his eyes narrowing. "I want a head count of every single firefighter who entered the property," he snapped. "Something's definitely suspicious here."

Bryson found himself in a spacious parking garage whose floors were of concrete polished to the sheen of marble. There had to have been more than fifty vehicles here: antiques, collectors' cars—Duesenbergs, Rolls-Royces, Bentleys, classic Porsches. All Manning's, he was sure. At the far end was an elevator, which went to the main house directly above.

Depressing the talk button on the two-way communicator, Bryson said quietly, "Everything okay?"

Elena's voice was faint but audible. "Fine. The last of the fire trucks has left. The flames and the smoke dissipated long before they arrived, leaving no trace."

"As planned. Now, as soon as all exterior activity returns to normal, I want you to . . . go to reruns." It was far too risky to feed in yesterday's surveillance video as long as there was activity outdoors, movement whose absence would be noticed by anyone watching the monitors. "And as soon as I'm in the house, I'm going to need you in close radio contact to guide me through the minefields."

Bryson became conscious of a movement in the shadows to his left, a shifting between the rows of automobiles. He turned, saw a blue-jacketed guard with a gun pointed.

"Hey!" shouted the guard.

Bryson spun out of the guard's line of sight, then dropped to the floor. The gun fired, the explosion reverberant in the chasmlike bunker. A round hit the concrete inches from his head, ricocheting, the spent cartridge clattering to the floor. Bryson whipped out the .45, aimed with split-second timing, then fired. The guard attempted to dodge the bullet, but caught it in his chest. He bellowed, his body twisting; Bryson fired again, and the man was down.

Bryson raced to the fallen man. The guard's eyes were wide, staring, his face contorted and frozen in pain. Clipped to the lapel of his blazer was a security pass. Bryson took it, examined it carefully. The house's security system was struc-

tured into zones, Bryson concluded, and controlled by means
of a conditional-access system. The entrance to each separate
zone would be equipped with a proximal scanner, much like
the electric eyes of supermarket doors that opened automatically as you approached. The security pass, worn on the
breast pocket of a shirt or blazer, was scanned, the unseen
computer noting the wearer's ID as well as his location and
the time and date, and checking which level of access the
individual was allowed. For unauthorized persons, doors
would not open, and alarms would sound. The system kept
track of where everyone was at all times.

But Bryson also knew that penetrating the house's security had to be more complex than simply stealing a guard's
security pass. Either there was a backup, biometric system—
fingerprints or handprints, retinal scans and the like—or
codes would have to be entered by the person seeking entrance.

The guard's security pass might in fact do nothing to help
him get into the house. He would soon know for sure.

The elevator was his way into the house, the *only* way.
He raced toward it. He would have to move quickly now,
for where there was one guard there would be others; the
slain guard's failure to answer a routine, radioed question
would raise alarms—alarms that could not be masked by
diversionary measures.

The elevator doors were brushed steel, with a call button
and keypad mounted on the wall beside them. He pressed
the button, but it did not light up. He pressed again, and
again no response: a code had to be entered on the key pad
in order to summon the elevator—probably a series of four
numbers. Unless the sequence was entered, the call button
did not function. The security badge he had taken from the
guard and clipped to the front of his tactical vest would do
no good here.

He inspected the walls nearest the elevator, looking for
concealed cameras. It was almost certain that there were in
fact security cameras here, but Elena had spoofed them by
substituting yesterday's surveillance footage in the system. If

for some reason she had been unable to do that, or she had reason to believe that her ruse was not working, she would have radioed him already. She was his eyes and ears; he had to rely on her thoroughness, her skill. And he did; he always had.

The elevator doors could, of course, be forced open by brute force and a crowbar, but that would be a mistake. Modern elevators, even those of rudimentary technology, ran on electronic circuitry, like so much else these days. Prying the doors open by ax or crowbar would break the elevator interlocks and stop the elevator from running; as long as any door on the shaft was open, the elevator would not run. That was a safety feature common to almost all elevators built in the last quarter century. And if the elevator did not run, Bryson ran the risk of drawing the attention of security personnel. Though by then he might already be inside, he did not want to alert security to his intrusion, raise an alarm. An effective covert entry required that tracks be covered.

For that reason he had brought a special tool called an interlock key, used by licensed elevator repairmen for emergency entry. It was a six-inch length of stainless steel about half an inch wide, flat and hinged at the top. He inserted it at the top of the brushed-steel doors, just inside the head door jamb, the flat steel frame around the doors, and moved it to the right. Between three and six inches in, just inside the frame and atop the right door panel, was the mechanical interlock. The hinged interlock key moved easily until it hit an obstruction: the protruding oblong of the interlock. The hinged flap of the key slid to the right, knocking the interlock to the right as well, and the doors slid smoothly open.

Cold air emerged from the dark, empty shaft. The elevator cab had been parked somewhere on an upper floor. Bryson took out a halogen penlight and shone it into the shaft, moving the small, bright circle of light from side to side, up and down. What he found was not encouraging. This was not a conventional residential elevator with a drum-and-winch system, nor was it traction-operated, with cables and counterweights. That meant he could not hope to use the cables to grab on to and pull himself up, using mountain-climbing techniques—there *were* no cables to grab! All there was inside the steel-enclosed shaft was one large rail on the right side, along which the elevator was raised and lowered by hydraulic pressure. And that rail was slippery, highly lubricated; he could not grab it and pull himself up.

He had expected the worst, and he had gotten it.

Elena had already located the archive for past surveillance feeds. They were stored in flash memory in the database back at Systematix, easily reachable on this system. Ten days' worth of digitized video was stored, each by date, then further broken down by sector. It was a simple matter to retrieve a copy of yesterday's video and rename it with today's date. Then she inserted it into the video monitoring system. Now, instead of viewing live footage, Security was watching yesterday's archived footage, at the exact same time of day, just twenty-four hours earlier. Of course, this would work only for cameras one through eighteen, the outside and certain interior areas where foot traffic was light or nonexistent.

In the rear pockets of Bryson's tac vest were small, lightweight magnetic gripper devices that were customarily used for bridge and tank inspections, as well as underwater examinations of ships' hulls and offshore oil rigs. He strapped one onto each boot, then onto both hands, and he began to climb, scaling the smooth steel wall slowly: releasing and repositioning hands, feet, moving upward pace by pace, release and reposition. It was arduous work and slow going. As he mounted the wall, he remembered the distance he had dropped to enter the garage: over 225 feet, and that was from ground level, down the hill from the mansion. There would be at least one or two underground levels at which the elevator would stop, but he needed to go to the main level of the residence.

At last he saw, by the halogen beam of the penlight, the first of the basement elevator landings. He was conscious at all times that the elevator might be called to the parking level, that it would descend quickly toward him; in such an event, if he did not release the magnetic grippers quickly and flatten himself into the eighteen-inch clearance space between shaft and elevator car, he would be killed instantly. So he had to remain constantly alert for the sound of the machinery starting up.

Now only ten feet or so remained before he reached the level marked ONE where, inconveniently, the elevator car was stopped. Inconvenient, but not unexpected. Bryson sidled over, shifting hands and feet one by one, until he was directly underneath the cab. Then, turning around methodically, he placed the hand grippers one by one, with a metallic clang, onto the lower edge of the steel-sided car. Now he hung from the car itself, his feet dangling into the empty expanse of the seemingly bottomless shaft. He looked down for a moment, which was a mistake: the drop was some two hundred and fifty feet to a concrete floor. If anything went wrong, if the magnetic grippers somehow malfunctioned, that was it. He was not acrophobic, but neither was he immune to the fleeting sensation of terror. This was not a time to slow down, not when the elevator might be summoned at any moment. Moving as swiftly as he could manage, he began climbing up the side of the cab, sandwiched between the cab and the steel wall of the shaft with mere inches of wiggle room.

Don't let it move, he thought. *Don't let it move, don't let anyone call it. Not now, not at this moment.*

Reaching the top of the cab, he rested there for a moment, unfastening the grippers, jamming them back into the pockets of his vest. Then he swung over, grabbed the interlock at the top inside of the doors, and slid it to the left.

The doors opened.

And if someone's on the other side?

He hoped not. But he was prepared for that, too.

He was looking down at a dimly lit, elegantly furnished lobby in what seemed to be the main part of the house. He looked down, saw no one in the vicinity, then grabbed hold of the steel beam inside the doorframe and swung himself down, landing on a burnished marble floor.

The lights went on, subdued lighting from several sconces along the wall, probably activated by the security guard's badge.

He was in.

The two men in the Security Control room went through the tedious laundry list, the regular security check they performed countless times throughout the day.

"Camera one?"

"Clear."

"Camera two?"

"Clear."

"Camera three?"

"Cl—wait, yeah, it's clear."

"What's the problem?"

"I thought I saw some movement through the big picture windows, but it was just rain."

"Camera four?"

"Charlie, hold on a second. Jesus, it's really coming down out there—just like yesterday. And it was beautiful, really sunny, when my shift started. Fucking Seattle weather. You mind if I take a quick break?"

"A *break?*"

"Yeah, I brought the Mustang convertible and I left it open."

"You didn't park in the underground lot?"

"Got here sort of late," the guard admitted sheepishly. "So I used the front outside lot. I just want to run out there and put up the top before the leather gets ruined."

Charles Ramsey, head of security, sighed with irritation. "Christ, Bain, if you'd get here on time . . . all right, take a break, but make it fast."

Heart pounding from the exertion and from the tension, he sprang to his feet and turned back to the gaping elevator shaft. He approached, reaching carefully up for the interlock to close the doors, aware of the depth of the dark shaft. A fall would be fatal. Strangely, only now that he was out of the shaft did he fully appreciate that.

The movement was almost imperceptible, a quick flickering of lights in his peripheral vision. Bryson pivoted, saw the guard almost on top of him, about to tackle Bryson to the floor. When Bryson slammed the guard with all his weight, the guard threw a lunging punch, which Bryson blocked, grabbing the guard's right forearm while, at the same time, kicking the back of his knee with a steel-toed boot. The guard groaned, sagged for only an instant, then immediately regained his balance as he reached for his gun, struggling with the waist holster.

A mistake not to have the gun at the ready, Bryson thought. A mistake we both made. He took advantage of the man's momentary lapse and delivered a hard kick to the guard's groin. The guard bellowed, knocked backward maybe a foot or two from the open elevator shaft. Still, he somehow managed to get his pistol out, aimed, and prepared to fire. Bryson lunged to the left, confusing the guard's aim, and then spun back toward his enemy, kicking at the gun and sending it flying out of his hand.

"Goddamned bastard," the guard shouted as he leaped backward, arms extended, in an attempt to retrieve the gun; there was a look of almost indignant surprise on his face as he realized that there was no floor beneath him, nothing to break his fall as he threw himself backward, his feet up in the air, higher than his head. The expression of surprise immediately became terror: arms flailing in the air in a vain attempt to clutch on to something, anything, his feet scrambling; he let out an enormous scream of horror, which echoed metallically in the air shaft as he plunged quickly out of sight. The scream was long and sustained, gradually diminishing in volume as he fell away, ever more distant, then stopping abruptly as the body hit bottom.

The security guard, a sandy-haired young man, exited the house through the service entrance, emerging outside not far from the outdoor parking lot. He looked around, bewildered.

Just minutes ago it was pouring rain—torrential rain, same as yesterday—and now it was a totally clear night, warm, with not a trace of precipitation anywhere.

Not a trace of rain.

No puddles on the ground, not even wet leaves on the trees.

Ten minutes ago he had seen rain coming down like some biblical flood; now it was a dry, warm night with no evidence that it had ever rained today.

"What the holy hell . . . ?" he exclaimed, taking out his handheld radio and calling Ramsey back in Control.

Ramsey exploded, as he knew the guy would. A string of profanities ensued, but when Ramsey finally got a grip on himself, he began issuing orders all around. "We got a perimeter breach," he said. "They're checking back at corporate, so now we got to follow the fiber-optic line from right outside the gates, see if there's a break."

Sweat poured down Bryson's face; his black Nomex suit itched. He took several deep breaths, then stepped forward toward the shaft, reached up to the interlock, flicked it closed. The steel doors closed silently.

Now he needed to orient himself, to determine which direction to move in order to find the security control room. That was the first order of business. It would tell him what he needed to know, where everything was. It was also the eyes of the enemy, and therefore it needed to be shut down.

He pressed the talk button on the communicator. "I'm at the main level," he said softly.

"Thank God," came Elena's voice. Bryson smiled: she was unlike any field backup he had ever worked with. Instead of being briskly, coldly professional, she was emotional, caring, concerned.

"Now which way to Control?"

"If you're facing the elevator, it's left. There's a long corridor running to either side . . . ?"

"Check." She was working off an array of video surveillance images, going by sight rather than by blueprint.

"Take the one to your left. When it ends, left again. There it widens out into a sort of long portrait gallery. That looks like the most direct route."

"Okay, roger. How are the eyes?"

"Shuttered."

"Great. Thanks."

He turned to the left and ran down the hall. Fiber-optic cables were threaded through the walls and foundations of this house, Bryson was certain. Miles and miles of the stuff, connected to miniature lenses whose pinhole apertures probably dotted the walls and ceilings. Unlike visible security cameras of old, these could not be detected, so they could not be spray-painted or duct-taped over. Were it not for Elena's ability to replace the actual feeds with yesterday's, Bryson would have been observed everywhere he went, with nothing to do about it. Now at least he could move freely, unseen. The security pass he had taken from the guard in the underground garage had so far done him no good at all. It hadn't admitted him to the elevator, though it had switched on the lights once he entered the house. It seemed to be more for keeping track of its wearer than for penetrating security; it had to go. He unclipped it and placed it on the floor of the corridor, against the wall, as if it had been lost by the person to whom it had been issued.

Elena put down the two-way communicator when she heard the crunch of footsteps right outside the truck. It was going too smoothly, she thought. The forest patrol is going to ask questions, and she would have to be persuasive in her answers.

She slid open the back of the van and let out a scream when she saw the muzzle of the pistol pointed at her eyes.

"Let's go!" shouted the man in the blue blazer.

"I'm with the U.S. Geological Survey!" she protested.

"Tapping into our security line? I don't think so. Hands down at your side, and no fucking around! We've got some questions to ask you."

Bryson had reached the long, rectangular room that Elena had called the portrait gallery. It was a peculiar-looking chamber, lined with ornate gilded frames like a room in the Louvre, except that each frame was empty. Or, rather, each frame held a flat grayish monitor, which probably turned into a high-resolution reproduction of a classic oil portrait, the picture changing according to the tastes of the person passing through, as broadcast by the electronic badge.

Bryson was about to step into the gallery when he noticed a line of tiny black beads running up the wall in a vertical line between frames. Every four feet or so another line of these minuscule black dots ran up one wall of the gallery. It almost looked ornamental, like part of the décor, except that it was ever so slightly discordant with the flocked wallpaper, the French Renaissance style. Bryson stood at the entrance of the gallery without entering. The black dots began about eighteen inches from the floor and ended about six feet up. He was fairly sure he knew what they were, but in order to make certain, he took out the night-vision monocular and put it to one eye.

Now he could see row upon row of thin filaments strung across the width of the long room every few feet, starting a few feet from the floor. What looked like glowing green strings were, he knew, laser beams in the infrared frequency: point-to-point sensors with columnated beams of light, invisible to the naked eye. But when the beams were broken by someone passing through—someone unauthorized—an alarm would be set off. They started eighteen inches off the floor, Bryson figured, so that they would not be triggered by any house pets.

The only way to traverse the room was by moving along the floor, staying below eighteen inches at all times so as not to break the lowest infrared-laser beam. And there was no clean and easy way to do it, either. He fastened the monocular on to the head-mounting apparatus; then, when it was securely in place, he dropped to the floor and began sliding on his back, pushing off with his boots. The whole while he was looking up, making sure he did not cross the beam. The

Nomex suit was slick enough to allow rapid, smooth movement. Although the cameras had been digitally blinded, the rest of the systems were live; the slightest misstep would trigger an alarm. Yet the greatest threat came not from technology at all but from human beings: the possibility of a guard coming upon him during rounds, as had already happened twice.

He slid under a third, a fourth, a fifth infrared-laser beam. No beam was broken, no alarms triggered, not here.

Finally he slipped under the last light beam. He paused, still on his back, and peered closely around to make sure there were no others. Satisfied, he sat up, then got carefully to his feet. Now he was not far from the security control room; Elena would guide him in the right direction.

He depressed the talk button. "Passage successful," he whispered. "Where to now?"

No answer, so he spoke again, a bit louder.

Again, no response, just staticky dead air.

"Elena, come in."

Nothing.

"Elena, come in. I need guidance."

Silence.

"Which way, damn it?"

Christ, no! Were the communicators malfunctioning? He spoke again and received no response. Was there some jamming technology in place here, keeping her from receiving his signal, him from receiving hers?

But his people had to communicate! There was no way to jam all possible radio frequencies but the one you wanted to use yourself. That was an impossibility.

Then where was she?

He radioed her again, and again. No answer, no answer, nothing.

She was gone.

Had something happened to her? That was a possibility he had not seriously considered.

He felt a cold dread come over him.

But he could not stop, he could not expend any time figuring out where she was or what had happened to their communications. He had to move.

Bryson didn't need radioed instructions to tell him where the caterer's kitchen was. He could smell it down the hall, the enticing aroma of the hot hors d'oeuvres. A door slid open at the far end of the hall and a caterer came through, dressed in black pants and a long-sleeved white shirt, with a large, empty silver tray at his side. Bryson ducked back into the gallery, though not so far as to set off an alarm. There was enough room here, sufficiently removed from infrared beams, for him to change clothes. He quickly removed the tactical vest, then stripped off the black body suit. Taking a neatly folded set of black dress pants and a white shirt from a plastic-sealed package in the tac vest, he got into them at once, then changed his combat boots for rubber-soled black dress shoes.

Sticking his head into the hall that led to the kitchen, he heard laughter, bantering conversation, the metallic clink of pans and utensils. He stepped back into the gallery, waited until he heard the sound of the kitchen's double-doors swing open, then emerged stealthily. The same waiter who had come in five or so minutes earlier was now holding aloft a large tray loaded with appetizers.

Treading silently along the hallway, Bryson stole up behind the waiter. He knew the man would be an easy mark, yet he could not afford noise, could not afford to attract attention. When he was just a few feet behind the caterer Bryson lunged, clapping one hand over his mouth, crooking his elbow around the neck, forcing the man to the floor while, at the same time, grabbing the tray of food. The waiter tried to scream, his cry muffled behind Bryson's hand. Bryson set the tray down carefully and, with his free hand, squeezed hard at the nerve bundle under the man's jaw. The waiter slumped to the floor, unconscious.

Quickly dragging the body back into the gallery, he pushed the waiter into a seated position, hands folded, head down, as if grabbing a quick catnap. Then he ran back down the hall and grabbed the tray of food.

Move it, he told himself. At any moment another waiter could enter the hall and see his face, not recognize him. He knew the security control room was nearby, but where?

He turned into another hall, the door sliding automatically, initiated by electric eye. No: this led directly to the formal dining room, which tonight was unused. He turned around, heading back in the direction of the kitchen, then retraced the path the waiter had taken when first approaching the kitchen. Another set of electronically operated doors slid open to a corridor that he could see led to the main reception hall, but another hall intersected long before then, branching off to the right. Perhaps. He took the right, walked about fifty yards, saw a door marked:

SECURITY
AUTHORIZED PERSONNEL ONLY!

He stopped before it, took a deep breath to calm himself, then knocked on the door.

No answer. He noticed a small inset button on the doorjamb, which he pushed once.

In ten seconds, just when he was about to push the button again, a voice came over a speaker mounted on the wall outside the room. "Yes?"

"Hi, it's catering—I've got your dinner," Bryson said in a singsong voice.

A pause. "We didn't order anything," the voice said suspiciously.

"Okay, fine, you don't want any, no problem. Mr. Manning said to make sure his security people got fed tonight, but I'll just tell him you didn't want any."

The door flew open. The man who stood there in the blue blazer was stocky, his hair dyed brown with an unfortunate orange tint. The name badge on his lapel said *Ramsey.* "I'll take that," the man said, reaching for the tray.

"Sorry, I'm going to need the tray back—it's a big crowd out there! I'll set it up for you." Bryson stepped forward into the security room; Ramsey relaxed somewhat and let him through.

Bryson looked around, saw that there was just one other guard there monitoring. The room was round, high-tech to the point of being futuristic, its walls smooth and unbroken by individual monitor screens, yet dozens of individual panels showed different views in and around the property.

"We've got smoked duck breast, caviar, *gougere*, smoked salmon, tenderloin . . . Do you have a surface where I can set this up for you? This room seems awfully crowded."

"Put it anywhere," the man named Ramsey said, turning his attention back to the images on the wall. Bryson set down the tray gingerly on a bare area of console, then reached over to his left ankle as if to scratch. He quickly pulled out the tranquilizer gun and fired off two quick shots. Two sharp coughing sounds, and each of the security guards was struck, one in the throat, one in the chest. Both would be out for hours.

Now he rushed to the computer keyboards that controlled the images. Pictures could be enlarged, moved around, brought to the center. He located the set of images that represented the views of the main reception hall.

The reception hall, where a banquet was taking place. A meeting of the Prometheus Group on the eve of its takeover.

But a takeover of what?

And by whom?

He tapped at the keyboard, quickly figuring out how to manipulate the images. By moving a computer mouse, he realized, he was able to move a security camera, basically pan it from side to side, up or down, even move in for a close-up.

The reception hall was immense, several stories high, ringed with several balconies overlooking the atrium. Around dozens of elaborately set tables, covered in white tablecloths, with flowers, crystal, bottles of wine, were dozens of people—no, over a hundred people. Faces, familiar faces.

At one end of the room was a great, dazzling, gilded-bronze sculpture, twice life-size, of Joan of Arc astride her horse, sword drawn and pointing straight up, leading her countrymen into the battle of Orléans. Strange but somehow fitting for the crusader who was Gregson Manning.

And at the other end of the room, standing at a sleek, minimalistic podium, was Gregson Manning himself, wearing an elegant black suit, hair brushed back. He clutched the sides of the podium, his fervor evident even without any sound. Most remarkable was the wall behind him, which was lined with twenty-four giant video screens, each broadcasting a live image of Manning speaking. It was the sort of egomaniacal display one expected of a Hitler, a Mussolini.

Bryson moved the mouse to zoom in on the audience, the seated guests, and what he saw stunned him, paralyzed him.

He did not recognize all the faces by far, but many of those whom he did recognize would be known anywhere in the world.

There was the head of the FBI.

The Speaker of the House.

The chairman of the Joint Chiefs of Staff.

Several leading United States senators.

The secretary general of the United Nations, a soft-spoken Ghanaian admired for his civility and statesmanship.

The head of Britain's MI-6.

The head of the International Monetary Fund.

The democratically elected head of Nigeria. The chiefs of the militaries and security services in another half-dozen third-world nations, from Argentina to Turkey.

Bryson stared, jaw agape, gasping.

The CEOs of quite a few multinational technology corporations, some of whom he recognized quickly, some vaguely familiar. All of them, dressed in black tie, the women in formal evening gowns, were listening to Manning with riveted attention.

Jacques Arnaud.

Anatoly Prishnikov.

And . . . Richard Lanchester.

"My God . . . !" he breathed.

He found the volume knob and dialed it up.

Manning's voice came over the speakers, velvety smooth.

". . . a revolution in global surveillance. I'm also pleased to announce that Systematix facial-recognition software will also be ready for use in all public places. With the CCTV capabilities already in place, we will now have the ability to scan crowds and match faces against a stored, *international* database. And this is only possible because of the cooperation of all of us, representatives of forty-seven nations and growing daily—all of us *working together*."

Manning raised his hands as if delivering a benediction to the crowd.

"What about vehicles?" The accent was African; the speaker a dark-skinned man in a dashiki.

"Thank you, Mr. Obutu," Manning replied. "Our neural network technology allows us to not only recognize vehicles instantly but track them around the cities, around countries. And we can record and store that information for future use. You see, I like to think that we are not only widening the net, we're narrowing the *mesh*."

Another question, which Bryson couldn't make out.

Manning smiled. "I know my good friend Rupert Smith-Davies of MI-6 will heartily agree with me when I say that it's long past time that both the NSA and GCHQ must struggle with legal handcuffs. How ridiculous that, until now, the British could monitor the Americans but not themselves, and vice versa! Were Harry Dunne, our CIA coordinator, well enough to be here, I know he would stand up and tell us all a tale or two in his inimitably profane way."

There was general laughter.

Another question: a woman, her accent Russian. "When will the International Security Agency's powers become effective?"

Manning glanced at his watch. "The same moment that the treaty takes effect—which is in approximately thirteen hours. The esteemed Richard Lanchester will be its director—global security czar, you might say. Then, my friends, we will all bear witness to a true New World Order, one in which we can take pride in having created. No longer will the citizens of the world be hostage to drug cartels and drug smugglers, terrorists and violent criminals. No longer will public safety be forced to take a backseat to the *privacy 'rights'* of child pornographers, pedophiles, and kidnappers."

A deafening round of applause.

"No longer will we all live in fear of another Oklahoma City bombing, another World Trade Center, another downed airliner. No longer will the U.S. government have to *beg* courts for *permission* to place wiretaps on the phones of kidnappers and terrorists and drug lords. To those who will complain—and there will always be complainers—that their individual liberties are being abridged, we will simply tell them this: those who do not break the law will have nothing to fear!"

Bryson did not hear the door to the control room open until he heard the familiar voice.

"Nicky."

He whirled around. "Ted! What the hell are you doing here?"

"The same question might be asked of you, Nicky. It's always what you don't see that gets you, hmm?"

Bryson took in Waller's attire, his tuxedo and black tie.

Ted Waller was a guest.

CHAPTER THIRTY-THREE

"You're—you're one of them!" Bryson whispered.

"Oh, Nicky, good Lord—what's all this talk of *sides?* This isn't some schoolyard game—shirts and skins, Jets and Sharks!"

"You *bastard!*"

"What did I tell you about the need for a continual re-appraisal and reassessment of strategic alliances? Adversaries? Allies? Such terms are, finally, meaningless. If I've taught you nothing else, at least I taught you that."

"What are you *doing?* This was your battle, you enlisted all of us, for *years* . . ."

"The Directorate has been destroyed. You know that— you saw it happen."

"Has this been some sort of deception all along?" Bryson said, raising his voice to a shout.

"Nicky, Nicky. Prometheus is now our best chance, really—"

"Our best *chance?*"

"And besides, are our goals really all that different? The Directorate was a dream—a fond dream, which we actually had the good fortune to realize for a few years, against all odds. Ensuring global stability, protecting it from the crazies, the terrorists, the madmen. As I always say, the prey survives only by becoming the predator."

"This—this is no last-minute conversion," Bryson said, his voice hushed. "You've been behind this for years."

"I've been a supporter of the possibility."

"A supporter . . . wait. Wait a second! Those assets I once found missing from that offshore bank . . . a billion dollars— but you were never interested in amassing personal wealth. It *was* you! You helped *create* Prometheus, didn't you?"

"Seed money, I believe they call it. Sixteen years ago Greg Manning was a bit overextended, and the Prometheus project needed an immediate infusion of cash. You might say I became a principal stakeholder."

Bryson felt as if he had been kicked in the stomach. "But it makes no sense—if Prometheus were the enemy . . ."

"Survival of the fittest, my dear. Have you never entered two competitors in the same race? It's backup contingency planning—redundancy that assures victory. Communism had fallen, and the Directorate had lost its sense of purpose. I looked around and examined the options, and I knew that conventional spycraft was doomed. Either we were the way of the future or Prometheus was. One horse had to win."

"And so you went with whichever horse won, morality be damned. It made no difference to you what the different objectives were, did it?"

"Manning was one of the most brilliant men I ever met. It occurred to me that his idea was worth incubating, worth nurturing as a contingency."

"You *hedged* your goddamned *bets!*"

"Think of it as political arbitrage. It was the only prudent course. I've always told you, Nick, spycraft isn't a team sport. And I know you have the talent ultimately to recognize the good sense in my reasoning."

"Where's Elena?" Bryson shot back.

"She's a smart woman, Nick, but she didn't plan on being discovered, apparently."

"Where *is* she?"

"Manning's people have her here somewhere in the residence; I'm assured she's being treated with the respect you and I both know she deserves. Nick, do I really have to ask you outright? Is it that important to you that I put the question so bluntly? Will you join us—can you recognize the way of the future?"

Bryson raised his pistol, pointing it at Waller, his heart racing. *Why did you make me do this?* he pleaded inwardly. *Why, damn it?*

Waller saw the gun but did not flinch. "Ah, I see. I have my answer. I didn't think so. Alas."

The door flew open again, and a small army of Manning's

security guards entered, guns pointed, outnumbering him some twelve to one. Bryson spun, saw others pouring in through another, concealed door in the round wall, and as his back was turned, he was grabbed from behind. He felt the cold steel of the muzzle against the back of his head, another gun to his right temple. He turned back, much more slowly this time, and Ted Waller was gone.

"Hands in the air," a voice commanded. "And don't even think about making any sudden movements. Don't try to grab the gun out of anyone's hands. You're a smart guy—you know about smart guns."

Electronic pistols, Bryson realized. Developed by Colt, by Sandia, by several European weapons firms . . . Capable of firing three shots with a single pull of the trigger.

"Hands up! Move it!"

Bryson nodded, thrust his hands in the air. There was nothing more to do, probably no hope of saving Elena either. The technology had been developed at the request of law enforcement, to keep police officers from being killed with their own firearms, when the gun is grabbed from them in a confrontation. There were fingerprint sensors on the trigger, each gun personally programmed so that only the authorized user could fire it.

He was marched, half-pushed, down the hallway outside the control room, down another short corridor. Guns at his temple, at the back of his head, he was frisked, the .45 caliber discovered and taken from him. One of the guards pocketed his snub-nosed pistol with ill-disguised triumph. He was disarmed totally, they had missed nothing. He had his hands, his instincts, his training, but it was all useless in the face of such an overwhelming artillery.

But why had they not killed him? What were they waiting for?

A door was opened, and he was shoved through it. He was in another oblong room, its dimensions similar to the portrait gallery. The lighting was dim, but he was able to make out the books lining the walls: russet leather-bound volumes in mahogany shelves that went from floor to a twenty-foot ceiling. A beautiful, grand library such as might be found in an English manor. The floor was parquet, perfectly worn.

Bryson stood, alone, inspecting the bookshelves, filled with a sense of foreboding, a sense that something was about to happen.

And suddenly the library disappeared: the book-lined walls glimmered, went silvery gray. It was an illusion! Like the portraits in the gallery, the books were a digital phantasm. He stepped forward to touch the smooth, yet slightly sandpapery gray walls, and then they lit up, this time bright, filled with *hundreds* of different images!

He stared in horror. The images were of himself! Film, video footage.

Of himself strolling on the beach with Elena. In bed with Elena, making love. Showering, shaving, urinating.

Arguing with Elena. Kissing her. Sitting in Ted Waller's office, shouting.

Elena and him riding horseback.

Bryson and Layla running through the passages of the *Spanish Armada,* evading Calacanis's gunmen. Hiding in the abandoned cathedral in Santiago de Campostela. Furtively searching Jacques Arnaud's private office. Meeting with Lanchester. Meeting with Tarnapolsky in Moscow. Running.

Meeting with Harry Dunne.

Scene after scene—surveillance video, taken from a distance, from close up, Bryson the star of each one. Scenes from his life, from the most intimate moments of his life. The most secret field operations. Nothing, not a single moment of the last ten years had gone unfilmed. The images were kaleidoscopic, flickering, horrifying.

Even footage of him lowering himself into the garage and climbing the elevator shaft. *They had seen him infiltrating the house, just moments ago.*

They had seen everything.

Bryson was dazed. His head spun; he felt overcome by vertigo; he felt violated, raped, sick to his stomach. He dropped to his knees and was sick, retching and retching until there was nothing more in his stomach, yet the dry heaves did not stop.

The whole thing was a setup. They knew he was coming; they wanted to observe; he had been under surveillance the entire time.

"Prometheus, you may recall, stole the gift of fire from the gods and gave this great gift to downtrodden mankind," said a calm voice, a soothing voice, amplified by hidden speakers throughout the room.

Bryson looked up. At the far end of the room, standing in a marble alcove, was Gregson Manning.

"They say you're a formidable linguist. You must know, then, the etymological derivation of the name Prometheus. It means fore-seeing, or fore-thinking. It seemed an apt name for us. Prometheus, according to the classical tradition, gave man civilization—language, philosophy, mathematics—and brought us from savagery to civility. This was the meaning of the gift of fire—light, illumination, knowledge. Making visible what had been concealed in the shadows. Prometheus, that Titan, willfully and knowingly committed a crime when he brought fire down from the heavens and taught the mortals how to use it. It was treason! He was threatening to put humans on an equal footing with the gods themselves! But in so doing he created civilization. And it is our task to make its continued existence secure."

Bryson walked a few steps closer to Manning. "So what do you have in mind?" he said. "Stasi on a global scale?"

"Stasi?" Manning replied scornfully. "Organize half the populace to spy on the other half, no one trusting anyone? I hardly think so."

"No," Bryson said, taking another few steps closer to the marble alcove. "The East Germans' technology was strictly Iron Age, wasn't it? No, you have supercomputers and miniaturized fiber-optic lenses. You have the ability to put *everybody* under the microscope. You and everyone in that hall out there—they've all bought into your nightmare vision. The Treaty on Surveillance and Security is merely a cover for a system of global surveillance that will make Big Brother seem benign—isn't that right?"

"Come now, Mr. Bryson. We teach our children when they're toddlers about Santa Claus—'he knows if you've been bad or good, so be good for goodness' sake.' Whether you acknowledge it or not, the ethical principle has always been linked to what is *known* about us. The all-seeing eye. Good conduct tracks with transparency. When everything is visible, crime disappears. Terrorism becomes a thing of the past. Rape, murder, child abuse—all gone. Mass murders— wars—gone. As will be the fear that grips every man, woman, and child, our inability to leave our houses, to walk through our cities, to simply live our lives *as we want to live them,* free from *fear!*"

"And who will be watching?"

"The computer. Massively parallel computational systems around the globe, girded with evolutionary algorithms and neural networks. There's never been anything like it."

"And at the center of it all is the despot-voyeur, Gregson Manning, orchestrating your computers into a billion virtual Peeping Toms."

Manning smiled. "Do you know about the Igbo people, in eastern Nigeria? They live surrounded by the tumult and corruption of Nigeria, but they are free of it. Do you know why? Because their culture prizes what they call the transparent life. They believe that there is nothing about an upright person that his fellow villagers should not be allowed to know. Any sort of exchange is conducted in front of witnesses. They abhor any form of secrecy or concealment, even solitude. The ideal of total transparency is so highly developed that if a scintilla of distrust develops between two people, they may resort to a curious ritual known as *igbandu,* wherein each drinks the blood of the other. An idealistic but rather cumbersome regime, in the logistics of it, you'll concede. The Promethean networks produce the same results with an altogether bloodless technique."

"Irrelevant tales!" Bryson shouted, taking a few steps closer. "That has nothing to do with us!"

"You must be aware that, over the last decade, the crime rate in the United States, particularly in the major cities, dropped to a fraction of what it once was. Now, why do you think that was?"

"What the hell do I know?" Bryson snapped. "I suppose you have a theory."

"No theory. I *know*. Our social scientists come up with theory after theory, but they fail to explain it."

"You're not implying . . ." Bryson said slowly.

Manning nodded. "It was a pilot study of our outdoor surveillance capabilities. Years before we had our current capacities and resources, but you have to start small, don't you?" A ten-foot-square section of the wall to his left went blank for a moment, and then a map of midtown Manhattan snapped into view. Small blue dots peppered the street grid. "Those are the hidden rotational cameras that we installed," Manning went on, pointing toward the dots. "It starts with anonymous tips to the police. Suddenly, the arrest record begins to improve, mysteriously. And, for the first time in decades, crime doesn't seem to pay anymore. The police crow about their new methods, criminologists talk about the ebbs and flows of the crack wars, yet *nobody* talks about the cameras that record everything. The safety blanket of surveillance we've unfolded over the city. Nobody talks about the fact that the crime-ridden alleys are now a panopticon. Nobody talks about the Systematix pilot project, because *nobody wants to know*. Are you beginning to understand what we're capable of doing for humanity? Poor *homo sapiens*. First they have to live through millennia of marauding tribalisms, and when the Enlightenment arrives, the Industrial Revolution hunkers down. Industrialization and urbanization bring a whole new wave of social disruptions, unleashing ordinary crime on a scale never before seen in human history. Two world wars, more atrocities on and off the battlefield. And when there are no wars, hand-to-hand combat breaks out in urban war zones. Is that any way to live? Is that any way to *die?* The members of the Prometheus Group come from every rank in every country of the world, but they all understand the paramount importance of security."

Bryson took another few steps closer to Manning.

"And this is your idea of freedom." *Must keep him talking*.

"Real freedom is freedom *from*. We seek to create a world in which its citizens can live their lives free from the fear of the sadistic wife-beater, the drug-addicted car-jacker, or any of a thousand other threats to life and limb. That, Mr. Bryson, is *true* freedom. Where people are free to be at their best behavior—the way they are when they *know* somebody is watching."

Another two, three steps closer. Casual. Keep talking.
"And so goes our privacy," Bryson said. He was now no more than ten or fifteen feet from where Manning stood talking. He glanced at his watch.

"The real problem with privacy is that we have too much of it. It's a luxury we can no longer afford. Now, thanks to Systematix, we have a powerful worldwide surveillance system in place—satellites orbiting the globe, millions of video cameras. Even, soon, implantable microchips."

"None of this will bring your daughter back," said Bryson softly.

Manning's face colored briefly. The walls went dark, plunging the room into a sepulchral gloom. "You know nothing about it," he hissed.

"No," Bryson admitted. Suddenly he leaped toward Manning, his hands extended to clutch Manning's throat in a powerful vise, *crush* his throat. At once he found himself falling through thin air, through nothingness! He slammed against the marble floor of the alcove, stunned, his jaw cracking hard against the stone, the pain immense. He spun around, looked for Manning—and then he saw the array of laser diodes lining the interior of the alcove. He had been witnessing a three-dimensional laser holographic projection— a high-resolution, lifelike image, the volumetric 3-D illusion created by lasers projecting video images onto microscopic particles in the air.

It was a hoax, an illusion. A *phantom*.

Bryson heard slow clapping, the clapping of one pair of

hands, from the far side of the room, the side through which he had entered moments ago. It was Manning, walking toward him as he clapped, a phalanx of guards surrounding him.

"Well, if that's the way you feel," Manning said, a half-smile on his face. "Guards?"

The security guards rushed toward him, smart guns extended, and once again he was enclosed by them. He struggled, but they had his arms, his legs.

Manning paused on his way out the door. "Most men in your line of work die ignominious deaths. A bullet in the back of the head, the assailant unseen, unknown. Or one of a thousand possible accidents in the field. Nobody will be surprised to learn of the deaths of two more operatives, a man and a woman, killed in a foolhardy attempt to assassinate an assemblage of world leaders. An unexplainable attempt that will never be explained, because men and women like you, who live lives of secrecy and darkness, always die in secret, in the dark. Now, if you'll excuse me, I must rejoin my guests." And Manning was gone from the room.

As he struggled with the guards, Bryson sneaked a glance at his watch. Now! It should have happened by now! Or did they move the U-Haul van as well?

Smart guns were pressed against his forehead, his temple, the back of his head. He saw his confiscated snub-nosed .45 in the holster of a guard just a few feet away.

Suddenly the dim lights in the room were extinguished, and they were plunged into absolute darkness. At the same instant came a series of clicks, and he could hear the locked doors to the library slide halfway open.

It had happened.

Bryson lurched forward and grabbed his .45 from the guard's holster. A clutch of security guards pummeled him to the floor. "One more move and you're dead!" shouted one of them.

"Go ahead," Bryson screamed. He saw them point their guns at him, saw the triggers being squeezed—

And nothing.

Nothing happened. The guns were dead. The electronic brains had been incapacitated, fried, along with all of the electronics in Manning's house.

There were bewildered shouts, screams, as Bryson fired a few shots into the air with his mechanically operated pistol, warning them to back off. They did back away from him, all twelve of them, realizing that somehow they were powerless, impotent, their guns dead in their hands.

Bryson ran to the half-open door, his gun still blazing, and slipped out into the hallway.

He had to get out, had to get to Elena—but where was she?

And how long would his ammunition last?

Some of the guards pursued him; he fired at them, now aware of the need to conserve ammunition, and they backed away. He was fairly sure he had another round in the chamber, maybe one in the magazine as well, but rather than stop for a second to check, he had to run, it was vital to *run*. He ran through the house, through corridors once lined with great oil paintings and covered in the finest wallpaper, now gone silvery-gray, like the dusty wings of dead moths. Everywhere doors were half-open.

The Russian scientist's device had worked, just as Bryson had heard it did. The virtual cathode oscillator was invented by Soviet scientists in the 1980s as a means of targeting the electronic circuitry of American nuclear weapons. Soviet nuclear bombs were far more primitive; this was a way of turning an advantage into a disadvantage. The Soviets were, as a result, far ahead of the Americans when it came to what was called radio-frequency weapons. When activated, the device emitted a high-powered electromagnetic pulse no longer than a microsecond—long enough, however, to burn out all electronic circuitry, heat up the microscopic junctions inside computers, and burn them up. All computers, everything with circuit boards and microchips within a quarter mile, would be affected. There were rumors that such a weapon had been used by terrorists to bring down several international plane flights.

Cars and trucks with electronic circuitry would not start, smart guns were struck dumb, and Manning's entire digital mansion had become inert.

And there was more.

The tiny fires in thousands of circuits throughout the house had caught on. Fires were burning in hundreds of places around Manning's house, smoke accumulating, wafting everywhere. Bryson remembered that the KGB had used this weapon to start a fire inside the U.S. Embassy in Moscow in the 1980s.

Bryson could hear screams from the reception hall. *Could she be there?* he wondered.

He flung open the doors to the banquet facility, found himself on a balcony overlooking the great hall. Fire had begun to rage below, flames licking the walls. Smoke was everywhere; panicked guests were running to the exits, tugging at doors that would not open, shouting, screaming. For some reason, whether it was a malfunction in the electronic equipment or some sort of security precaution, all the doors to the hall seemed to have locked automatically.

Was Waller down there? Was Manning?

Was Elena?

"Elena!" he shouted into the din.

No response.

She was not down there, or she had not heard him.

"Elena!" he shouted again, hoarsely.

Nothing.

He felt the cold steel of the blade at the exact same moment as the hot breath in his ear, the whispered Arabic words. The seven-inch combat knife pressed against the soft skin and delicate cartilage of his throat, the high-carbon-steel blade sharper than a brand-new razor. It slid slowly, the silky pain at once cold and hot, the sensation delayed for a second; but when it came his entire body screamed in agony.

And the whisper: "The rope of lies is always too short, Bryson."

Abu.

"I should have finished the job in Tunisia, traitor," the

Arab terrorist hissed. "Now I will not waste the opportunity I am given."

Bryson went rigid, flooded with fear, with adrenaline. "If you'll *listen* . . ." Bryson replied, almost under his breath, the remark intended to distract for a second or two. At the same time he gripped the .45 at his side, placed his finger on the trigger, and then in one swift arc lifted the weapon and fired backward at his enemy.

There was only a muted click. *The gun was empty.*

Abu batted the gun away with a flick of his left hand; it went flying off to one side, clattering to the floor, useless.

Bryson had lost valuable seconds in reaction time. The blade sliced across the skin of his neck just as Bryson jammed the fingers of his right hand upward and under the handle. He grabbed the knife handle, twisting it violently to loosen Abu's grip; at the same time, he slammed the heel of his left foot into the back of Abu's right knee to knock him off balance. Abu grunted, and Bryson suddenly sank to the ground, lowering his center of gravity while still twisting the knife blade and Abu's wrist with it.

The knife clanged against the floor.

Bryson reached for it, but Abu, quicker, scooped it up. Clutching the knife in his fist like a dagger, Abu plunged it downward, sinking it into the soft meat of Bryson's left shoulder.

Bryson gasped; the pain was shattering, forcing him to his knees. He swung his right arm toward Abu's head; Abu sidestepped the punch easily, moving around him effortlessly, almost dancing. He didn't seem to break a sweat. He shifted his weight from foot to foot, his knees slightly bent, his stance soft and comfortable, the blood-slicked knife blade glittering in his right hand. Bryson staggered to his feet, kicked his right foot toward the inside of Abu's knee. But Abu sidestepped the kick, backing off just enough to cause Bryson to lose his balance, then catching the kicking leg and yanking it hard, forcing Bryson down again.

Abu seemed to know Bryson's moves before they happened. Bryson shot his arms forward to grab Abu's legs, but

Abu simply slammed an elbow into Bryson's neck, trapping
Bryson's head between his knees, and slammed him into the
ground. Bryson's teeth cracked against his lips; he could taste
blood, and he thought he might have lost a couple of teeth.
Weakened by the knife wound in his shoulder, Bryson's reactions were slowed, delayed. He groaned, thrust out his
right arm, and grabbed his enemy's ankle; then, locking it in
his crooked elbow, he turned it until Abu bellowed in pain.

Suddenly Abu's arm shot out, the knife aimed directly at
Bryson's heart. Bryson dodged, but not quite in time: the
knife plunged into his side, between his ribs; the pain was
searing, white-hot.

Bryson looked down, saw what had happened, and
grabbed the knife handle. He yanked at it; it tugged horribly
at his viscera, but it came out. Bryson hurled it over the
balcony, groaning in pain: it was much better to be rid of a
weapon that Abu was so skilled with. The knife dropped
down into the inferno, clanking a second later against the
floor far below.

Now they were both disarmed. But Bryson, down on the
floor and badly weakened, was at a disadvantage. Moreover,
Abu was immensely strong, all muscle, a coiled python. His
movements were relaxed, fluid, flowing one into another.
Bryson rolled back away from Abu; Abu kicked him, hard,
in the abdomen. Bryson felt the wind come out of him; he
almost passed out, but he struggled to his feet, swinging
wildly.

Abu's face was blank, unreadable. When Bryson threw a
punch at Abu's head, Abu's hands shot out, lightning-fast,
and grabbed his wrists, twisting hard. Bryson tried to force
Abu to relieve the hold by thrusting his knees into Abu's
abdomen, but Abu jammed him with his own knees first,
sending Bryson crashing to the floor, while at the same time
twisting his wrists.

Bryson attempted to get up, but Abu threw his weight on
top of him, flattening him against the floor; then, jumping
into the air, he stomped up and down on Bryson's chest,
putting all of his considerable weight into it. Bryson moaned;

he could feel, actually *hear,* several ribs crack.

Abu went at him again, flipping him over so that his face cracked to the floor again. Now Abu wrapped one arm around his throat, pushing down on the back of his neck with his elbow in a rear choke-hold. At the same time Abu went down on his right knee and folded his left leg so that he was in a one-legged kneeling position, extremely stable. He began pulling Bryson back toward his left leg. Bryson tried to rise, but each time he did, Abu pushed him back with his elbow. He had no leverage! He was losing consciousness, his strength was fading. The airflow to his brain was cut off; he began to see black-and-purple spots.

Part of him wanted to succumb to unconsciousness, a comfortable defeat, but he knew that any defeat would mean death. He screamed, summoned his last reserves of strength, flung his hands into Abu's face, and jabbed his fingers into his enemy's eye sockets.

Abu involuntarily released some of the pressure on Bryson's throat—not much, but just enough to allow Bryson to swing his fists around in an arc, one of them connecting hard with the brachial plexus nerve bundle in Abu's right underarm area. Bryson felt Abu's right arm go slack, momentarily paralyzed. He took advantage of the brief pause to grab a handful of Abu's groin, yanking hard. The choke-hold was broken.

Bryson tilted his right shoulder down and body-slammed Abu up against the balustrade overlooking the inferno. Bryson was now moving almost by instinct; his oxygen-starved brain felt distant from his hands, which seemed to move of their own volition. But fueled by rage and revenge, Bryson managed to force Abu's head and shoulders over the edge of the balcony. The two men were entwined, pushing and pulling at each other on the ledge, their muscles trembling. Abu's right arm was dead, the paralysis lasting longer even than Bryson had hoped. Bryson pushed, shoved as hard as he could, forcing Abu's shoulders out over the balcony, while Abu scissored both legs around Bryson's, locking the two men together. Bryson was feeble but determined; Abu had lost the use of one arm. They seemed evenly matched. Bryson straight-armed Abu's neck downward, but Abu came back up; Bryson straight-armed him again, this time keeping him down with all of his strength, the muscles in his right arm straining, trembling. Abu's eyes were fierce. He began hammering his good fist into Bryson's abdomen. For a few seconds Bryson held him down, clutching Abu's throat and squeezing with all his strength, trying to cut off the air, trying to compress the nerves and induce paralysis, but he was fading; he could no longer summon the strength; the pain from the stab wound radiated, depleting his power further. His hands trembled. Bryson summoned one last, superhuman surge of energy, his entire body an instrument of anger and revenge, but it was not enough; he didn't have the strength.

Abu roared, his crimson face contorted in pain and rage, spittle flying from his purpled lips, and he began to rise—

The explosion seemed to come out of nowhere, the bullet lodging itself in his enemy's right upper arm. Abu's legs loosened their viselike grip on Bryson's as he lost his balance and plummeted over the balcony.

Bryson stared as his enemy fell, wriggling in space, landing with a crash on top of the massive bronze equestrian sculpture, impaling himself on the sharpened point of the sword. As the bronze blade came out of his abdomen, Abu's scream was shrill, almost inhuman, and then it came to an abrupt, gargling stop.

Dazed, sickened, Bryson turned and saw the source of the gunshot. Elena was holding the pistol he had given her; staring at it as if it were some alien object, she lowered it slowly. Her eyes were wide.

Bryson staggered to his feet, made it a few steps, and collapsed into her arms. "You escaped," he panted.

"The room they locked me in was no longer locked."

"The gun . . ."

"The smart guns don't work, but their bullets are still good, aren't they?"

"We need to get out of here," he said, out of breath. "*Must* get out of here."

"I know," she said. She shifted her arms, putting one arm around his shoulders tenderly, supporting him as they walked out of the balcony and through the smoke-filled corridor toward the exit.

EPILOGUE

The New York Times, page 1.

SCORES OF WORLD LEADERS KILLED IN
FREAK HOUSE FIRE IN WASHINGTON STATE
Blame Laid to Faulty Wiring in
'Digital San Simeon'

SEATTLE, Wash.—A glittering conference on the New
Global Economy at the high-tech lakeside mansion
belonging to Systematix founder and CEO Gregson
Manning ended in tragedy today as dozens of prominent officials from around the world were trapped in a
blaze that burned the $100-million estate to the ground.

A Seattle Fire Department spokesman, speaking to
reporters early this morning, speculated that the fire
may have begun within the delicate electronic circuitry
hidden in the walls of this entirely computerized home,
the residence of the computer pioneer and host of the
conference. According to the spokesman, malfunctioning computer chips may have caused exit doors in the
banquet hall where a gala dinner was taking place to
seal automatically.

The body count is believed to number over one
hundred. Among them is reportedly the Speaker of the
House of Representatives . . .

MANNING TAKEN IN FOR QUESTIONING

Washington (AP)—Systematix chairman Gregson
Manning, whose Seattle mansion burned to the ground
overnight, trapping over one hundred government officials from around the world, was taken into custody
at noon today at the Justice Department. Sources in the

Attorney General's office insist that Mr. Manning's arraignment, on unspecified charges of national security violations, was unrelated to this morning's tragedy. Mr. Manning is said to have been under suspicion for several weeks.

Although a sealed courtroom is highly unusual, it is not unheard of. In cases involving matters of government secrecy, the Attorney General has the legal right to convene a special national security court, not open to the public. . . .

The Wall Street Journal, page 1.

PRESIDENT'S NATIONAL SECURITY ADVISER, RICHARD LANCHESTER, A SUICIDE AT 61

Richard Lanchester, the widely respected White House adviser and director of the National Security Council, took his own life yesterday afternoon, according to White House sources.

Said to be inconsolable over the loss of several close friends who perished in the recent fire that destroyed the residence of Systematix chief Gregson Manning and 102 prominent officials attending a conference there, and suffering as well from clinical depression and a failing marriage, Mr. Lanchester . . .

ONE YEAR LATER

Getting the morning paper was a ritual, her ritual. Not because she liked to read the news; she didn't. That was Nicholas's habit, his need to stay in touch with the developments in the world they had left behind. It was a habit she disapproved of, precisely *because* they had left the world behind, at least the world of violence and weapons and lies.

But getting the paper from town was the way she liked to start the day. She would arise early and go for a swim—their bungalow was just up the bluff from one of the most beautiful, bluest, and most isolated beaches they had ever seen—and then she would ride her horse into the tiny collection of ramshackle huts that passed for a village here. Along with the groceries flown in from a nearby, larger island, the proprietor of the general store always received a small stack of newspapers from the U.S.; she always set aside one for the lovely woman with the lilting foreign accent who came riding in each morning.

Then Elena would gallop back along the deserted beach, the mile and a half to their bungalow. By that time, Nicholas was usually sitting on the stone patio he had laid himself, drinking coffee and reading. After breakfast they would go for another swim. So passed their days. It was paradise.

Even when the blood test administered by the island's sole doctor confirmed what she'd been feeling for several days, that she was pregnant, Elena continued to ride, though more carefully. They were overjoyed, planning for the arrival of a son or a daughter, discussing for hours how their lives would change and yet not change, their love deepening by the day.

Money was not a concern. The government had provided them a generous lump-sum settlement which, invested carefully, yielded more than enough to live on. Rarely did they discuss what had brought them here, why it was so important for them to escape, why they had to live here under new identities. It was understood between them: that was the past, a terribly painful episode, and the less said about it the better.

The mini-DVD she had recorded from Manning's surveillance system that night had provided them with all the protection they needed. Not because it afforded them the opportunity to blackmail, strictly speaking—but because the explosive secrets it contained were secrets everyone preferred to remain buried. It could only be destabilizing for the world to know how close it had come to a bloodless coup, a nonviolent takeover by a group of individuals who believed that governments were obsolete—yet were on the verge of creating a supranational security administration that would have made Stalin's U.S.S.R. or Hitler's *Bundesrepublik* seem lax.

Most of those individuals had perished in the fire at Manning's San Simeon, burned alive in a terrible end. Yet there were others who had aided and abetted those men and women; and so arrests were made. Quietly and discreetly, the reasons understood without being made explicit, deals were struck. Gregson Manning was believed to be in a special federal facility in North Carolina, serving time for unspecified violations of section 1435 of the National Security Act, said to involve economic espionage; he was rumored to be isolated from all contacts or means of communication. Powerful voices in the Senate called for a recall vote on the treaty, renouncing votes made in haste. Some blamed Richard Lanchester for manipulating the process. Without American backing, the treaty agreement fell apart. The truth never had to come out.

So sixteen copies of the DVD were made; one was couriered to the White House, using a code that Bryson knew marked it for the president's eyes only; a second went to the Attorney General of the United States. Others went to London, Moscow, Beijing, Berlin, Paris, and other world capitals. Heads of state had to know what had almost transpired, or else the virus would endure.

Of the three copies that remained, one was deposited with a lawyer Bryson knew to be trustworthy above and beyond, another was sealed in a safe-deposit box, and a third went with them, hidden somewhere on the island, insulated and protected. They were insurance policies. Bryson and Elena hoped they'd never have to collect on them.

This morning, about an hour after bringing the morning paper, Elena emerged from the perfect water to find Bryson absorbed in the newspaper, which rippled and crinkled in the wind.

"Only when you finally give up that nasty habit will you finally be free," she scolded him.

"You make it sound like smoking."

"It's almost as bad."

"And probably almost as hard to give up. But if I do, what excuse will you have for your morning ride?"

She chuckled. "Milk? Eggs? I'll think of something."

"Jesus." He was leaning close over the paper.

"What is it?"

"Buried on page D-16. The business section."

"What does it say?"

"It's a tiny item—reads like nothing more than a rewritten press release from the Systematix Corporation in Seattle."

"But . . . but Manning's in prison!"

"He is. His company's being run by certain of his deputies in the interim. This dispatch says that the National Security Agency has just acquired a fleet of low-orbit surveillance satellites manufactured by Systematix."

"They try to bury the news, but it's really not very subtle, is it? Where are you going?"

Bryson had gotten up from his beach chair and was bounding up the dune to their bungalow. She followed him up. The wind carried the sound to her, so that she knew he had the television on. Another terrible habit she wanted to break him of: he had rigged up a satellite dish so that he could watch the news, though he had promised to keep that to a minimum.

Bryson was watching CNN, but was frustrated that there was no news, just some fashion segment. He turned toward her. "Ted Waller didn't die in that fire, you know. I saw the forensic reports, everything out of the Seattle Medical Examiner's office, and all the bodies were identified. Waller wasn't among them."

"I *know* that. We've known that for a year. What are you saying?"

"I'm saying that I see Waller's hand in this. Wherever he went, wherever he disappeared to, he has to be involved in this. I'm certain of it."

"Trust your instincts, I always say," came the voice from the television.

Elena screamed, pointed at the television. Bryson whirled around. His heart was thudding rapidly. Ted Waller's face filled the screen.

"What is this?" Elena gasped. "Is this a *show* . . . ?"

"Call it reality TV," said Waller.

"*We were assured we'd be left alone!*" Bryson thundered.

"However you managed this satellite-feed interruption, it's a *violation!*" Bryson started pressing buttons on the remote, changing channels frantically. Waller's face was on each one, staring out at them phlegmatically.

"I still regret that we weren't able to say good-bye properly," Waller said from the TV screen. "I really do hope there's no bad blood."

Speechless, Bryson scanned the small living room frantically. Microscopic surveillance devices could be planted absolutely anywhere and everywhere, undetectable . . .

"I'll be in touch when the time is right, Nicky. Now may be premature." Waller looked off into the distance as if about to add something, and a hint of a smile came to his lips. "Well, I'll be seeing you."

"Not if I see you first, Ted," Bryson said acidly, and now he settled back in his chair. "We have a great deal of evidence in safekeeping, evidence we won't hesitate to release."

On the screen, Waller's gaze turned wary.

"Remember, Ted—it's what you don't see that always gets you."

Abruptly, Waller's image disappeared, replaced by a game show.

A move had been made. And countered. Bryson felt fury, outrage at the violation—and yet, after so many years in the service of the great game, oddly stirred as well. If Elena caught a glimpse of this, she kept it to herself. She still went for her early-morning rides, and they still spent much of the day outdoors, either on the shimmering white beach or on their wooden deck, surrounded by bougainvillea and shaded by young palm trees that undulated gently in the breeze.

Bryson had made a complete break from his past life, while he and Elena prepared to nurture the new life that was on its way. In the sun, his scars faded, and there were days when—the air fragrant with frangipani and lime and salt water—the dull ache from his old wounds grew imperceptible, like memories just out of reach. At moments, he almost thought he had left the world behind.

Almost.

CHAPTER ONE

The caretaker stirred when he heard the crunch of tires on gravel. There was barely any light left in the sky, and he had just made coffee and was reluctant to get up. But his curiosity got the better of him. Visitors to Alexandria seldom ventured into the cemetery at Ivy Hill; the historic town on the Potomac had a brace of other, more colorful attractions and amusements to offer the living. As for the locals, not many came out on a weekday; fewer still on a late afternoon when the April rains lashed the sky.

Peering through his gatehouse window, the caretaker saw a man get out of an ordinary-looking sedan. *Government?* He guessed that his visitor was in his early forties, tall and very fit. Dressed for the weather, he had on a waterproof jacket, dark pants, and workman's boots.

The caretaker watched the way the man stepped away from the car and looked around, taking in his surroundings. *Not government—military.* He opened the door and came out under the overhang, observing how his visitor stood there, gazing through the gates of the cemetery, oblivious to the rain matting his dark hair.

Maybe this is his first trip back here, the caretaker thought. They were all hesitant their first time, loath to enter a place associated with pain, grief, and loss. He looked at the man's left hand and saw no ring. *A widower?* He tried to remember if a young woman had been interred recently.

"Hello."

The voice startled the caretaker. It was gentle for such a big man, and soft, as if he'd thrown the salutation like a ventriloquist.

"Howdy. If you're fixin' to visit, I got an umbrella I can let you have."

"I'd appreciate that, thank you," the man said, but he didn't move.

The caretaker reached around the corner into a stand made from an old watering can. He gripped the handle of the umbrella and stepped toward the man, taking in his visitor's high-planed face and startling navy-blue eyes.

"Name's Barnes. I'm the caretaker. If you tell me who you're visiting, I can save you wandering around in this mess."

"Sophia Russell."

"Russell, you say? Doesn't ring a bell. Let me look it up. Won't take but a minute."

"Don't bother. I can find my way."

"I still gotta have you sign the visitors' book."

The man unfurled the umbrella. "Jon Smith. Dr. Jon Smith. I know where to find her. Thank you."

The caretaker thought he detected a break in the man's voice. He raised his arm, about to call after him, but the man was already walking away, his strides long and smooth, like a soldier's, until he disappeared into the gray sheets of rain.

The caretaker stared after him. Something cold and sharp danced along his spine, made him shudder. Stepping back into the gatehouse, he closed the door and bolted it firmly.

From his desk, he removed the visitors' ledger, opened it to today's date, and carefully entered both the man's name and the time he had arrived. Then, on impulse, he turned to the back of the ledger, where the interred were listed in alphabetical order.

Russell . . . Sophia Russell. Here she is: row 17, plot 12. Put into the ground . . . exactly one year ago!

Among the three mourners who'd signed the register was Jon Smith, M.D.

So why didn't you bring flowers?

Smith was grateful for the rain as he walked along the road that wended its way through Ivy Hill. It was like a shroud, strung across memories that still had the power to cut and burn, memories that had been his omnipresent companions this past year, whispering to him in the night, mocking his tears, forcing him to relive that terrible moment over and over again.

He sees the cold white room in the hospital at the United

States Army Medical Research Institute for Infectious Diseases in Frederick, Maryland. He is watching Sophia, his love, his wife-to-be, writhing under the oxygen tent, gasping for breath. He stands, only inches away, yet powerless to help her. His screams at the medical staff echo off the walls and return to mock him. They don't know what's wrong with her. They, too, are powerless.

Suddenly she cries out—a sound Smith still hears in his nightmares, and prays never to hear again. Her spine, bent like a bow, arches to an impossible angle; sweat pours off her as if to rid her body of the toxin. Her face is bright with fever. For an instant she is frozen like that. Then she collapses. Blood pours out of her nose and throat. From deep within comes the death rattle, followed by a gentle sigh, as her soul, free at last, escapes its tortured confines. . . .

Smith shivered and looked around quickly. He didn't realize that he had stopped walking. The rain continued to drum on the umbrella, but it seemed to fall in slow motion. He thought he could hear every drop as it spattered off the nylon.

He wasn't sure how long he stood there, like an abandoned, forgotten statue, or what finally made him take a step. He didn't know how he came to be on the path that led to her grave or how he found himself standing in front of it.

SOPHIA RUSSELL
NOW IN THE SHELTER OF THE LORD

Smith leaned forward and ran his fingertips across the smooth top of the pink-and-white granite headstone.

"I should have come more often, I know," he whispered. "But I couldn't bring myself to do it. I thought that if I came here, I would have to admit that I've lost you forever. I couldn't do that . . . until now.

" 'The Hades Project.' That's what they called it, Sophia, the terror that took you away from me. You never saw the faces of the men who were involved; God spared you that. But I want you to know that they have paid for their crimes.

"I had my taste of revenge, my darling, and I believed that it would bring me peace. But it did not. For months I have been asking myself how I might earn that serenity; in the end, the answer was always the same."

From his jacket pocket, Smith took out a small jeweler's box. Opening the lid, he stared at a six-carat, marquis-cut diamond in a platinum setting that he had picked out at Van Cleef & Arpel in London. It was the wedding ring he had intended to slip on the finger of the woman who would have become his wife.

Smith crouched and pushed the ring into the soft earth at the base of the headstone.

"I love you, Sophia. I will always love you. Your heart is still the light of my life. But it is time for me to move on. I don't know where I'll go or how I'll get there. But I must go."

Smith brought his fingertips to his lips, then touched the cold stone.

"May God bless you and look after you always."

He picked up the umbrella and took a step back, staring at the headstone as though imprinting its image in his mind for all time. Then he heard the soft footfall behind him and turned around fast.

The woman holding the black umbrella was in her mid-thirties, tall, with brilliant red hair pulled back in a ponytail. A spray of freckles dotted her nose and high cheekbones. Her eyes, green like reef waters, widened when she saw Smith.

"Jon? Jon Smith?"

"Megan . . . ?"

Megan Olson walked up quickly, took Smith's arm and squeezed it.

"Is it really you? My God, it's been . . ."

"A long time."

Megan looked past him at Sophia's grave. "I'm so sorry, Jon. I didn't know that anyone would be here. I didn't mean to intrude."

"It's all right. I did what I came to do."

"I guess we're both here for the same reason," she said softly.

She drew him under the shelter of a massive oak and looked at him keenly. The lines and creases on his face were deeper than she remembered, and there was a host of new ones. She could only imagine the kind of year Jon Smith had endured.

"I'm sorry for your loss, Jon," she said. "I wish I could have told you that sooner." She hesitated. "I wish I had been here when you needed someone."

"I tried calling but you were away," he replied. "The job . . ."

Megan nodded ruefully. "I was away," she said vaguely.

Sophia Russell and Megan Olson had both grown up in Santa Barbara, had gone to school there, then on to UCLA. After college, their paths had diverged. Sophia had gone to complete her Ph.D. in cell and molecular biology and had joined USAMRIID. After receiving her master's in biochemistry, Megan had accepted a position at the National Institutes of Health. But after only a three-year tenure she had switched to the medical research division of the World Health Organization. Sophia had received postcards from all over the world and had pasted them in a scrapbook as a way to keep track of her globe-trotting friend. Now, without warning, Megan was back.

"NASA," Megan said, answering Smith's unspoken question. "I got tired of the Gypsy life, applied to the space-shuttle candidate school, and was accepted. Now I'm first alternate on the next space mission."

Smith couldn't hide his amazement. "Sophia always said she never knew what to expect from you. Congratulations."

Megan smiled wanly. "Thanks. I guess none of us knows what we can expect. Are you still with the army, at USAMRIID?"

"I'm at loose ends," Smith replied. It wasn't the whole truth but close enough. He changed the subject. "Are you going to be in Washington for a while? Might give us a chance to catch up."

Megan shook her head. "I'd love to. But I have to go back to Houston tonight. But I *don't* want to lose touch with you, Jon. Are you still living out in Thurmont?"

"No, I sold the place. Too many memories."

On the back of a card he jotted down his address in Bethesda, along with a phone number that he was actually listed under.

Handing her the card, he said, "Don't be a stranger."

"I won't," Megan replied. "Look after yourself, Jon."

"You too. It was good to see you, Megan. Good luck on the mission."

She watched him walk out of the overhang and disappear into the drizzle.

"I'm at loose ends. . . ."

Megan had never thought of Smith as a man without purpose or direction. She was still wondering about his cryptic comment as she walked over to Sophia's grave, the rain drumming on her umbrella.

CHAPTER TWO

The Pentagon employs over twenty-three thousand workers—military and civilian—housing them in a unique structure that covers almost four million square feet. Anyone looking for security, anonymity, and access to both the world's most sophisticated communications plus the power centers of Washington could not ask for a more perfect venue.

The Leased Facilities Division occupies a tiny portion of the offices in the Pentagon's E block. As its name implies, Leased Facilities oversees the procurement, management, and security of buildings and land for the military, everything from storage warehouses in St. Louis to vast tracts of Nevada desert for an air force testing ground. Given the decidedly unglamorous nature of its work, the men and women in the division are more civilian than military in character. They arrive at the offices at nine o'clock in the morning, put in a dutiful day's work, and leave at five. World events that might keep their colleagues at their desks for days on end have no impact on them. Most of them like it that way.

Nathaniel Fredrick Klein liked it too—but for altogether different reasons. Klein's office was at the very end of a hall, tucked between doors that were marked ELECTRICAL ROOM and MAINTENANCE. Except there were no such service rooms behind those doors and their locks could not be opened even with the most sophisticated key card. That space was part of Klein's secret suite.

There was no nameplate on Klein's door, only an internal Pentagon designation: 2E377. If asked, the few coworkers who'd actually seen him would describe a man in his early sixties, medium height, unprepossessing except for his rather long nose and wire-framed glasses. They might recall his conservative and somewhat rumpled suits, perhaps the way he would smile briefly when passed in the hall. They might have heard that Klein was sometimes called before the joint chiefs or a congressional committee. But that would be in keeping with his seniority. They might also know that he was vested with the responsibility of checking the properties the Pentagon leased or had an interest in throughout the world. That would account for the fact that one seldom saw him at all. In fact it was sometimes difficult to say who or what Nathaniel Klein really was.

At eight o'clock in the evening, Klein was still behind his desk in the modest office that was identical to all the others in the wing. He had added a few personal touches: framed prints depicting the world as imagined by sixteenth-century cartographers; an old-fashioned pedestal-mounted globe; and a large, framed photograph of the earth taken from the space shuttle.

Although very few people were aware of it, Klein's affinity for things global was a direct reflection of his real mandate: to serve as the eyes and ears of the president. From this nondescript office Klein ran a loosely knit organization known as Covert-One. Conceived by the president after the horror known as the Hades Project, Covert-One was designed to be the chief executive's early warning system and secret response option.

Because Covert-One worked outside the usual military-intelligence bureaucracy and well away from the scrutiny of Congress, it had no formal organization or headquarters. Instead of accredited operatives, Klein recruited men and women whom he called "mobile ciphers"—individuals who were acknowledged experts in their fields yet who, through circumstances or dispositions, found themselves outside the mainstream of society. Most—but certainly not all—had some military background, were holders of numerous citations and awards, but had chafed under structured command, and so had elected to leave their respective services. Others came from the civilian world: former investigators—state and federal; linguists who were fluent in a dozen languages; doctors who had traveled the world and were accustomed to the harshest conditions. The very best, like Colonel Jon Smith, bridged the two worlds.

They also possessed one factor that disqualified so many Klein looked at: their lives were strictly their own. They had little or no family, few encumbrances, and a professional reputation that would stand up to the closest scrutiny. These were invaluable assets for an individual sent in harm's way thousands of miles from home.

Klein closed the folder on the report he had been reading, removed his glasses, and rubbed his weary eyes. He was looking forward to going home, being greeted by his cocker spaniel, Buck, and enjoying a finger of single-malt scotch followed by whatever dinner his housekeeper had left in the oven. He was about to get up when the connecting door to the next room opened.

"Nathaniel?"

The speaker was a trim woman a few years younger than Klein, with bright robin's eyes and graying blond hair done in a French twist. She wore a conservative blue business suit accented by a string of pearls and a filigree gold bracelet.

"I thought you'd gone home, Maggie."

Maggie Templeton, who'd been Klein's assistant for the ten years he had worked at the National Security Agency, arched her neatly sculptured brows.

"When was the last time I left before you did? Good thing I didn't, too. You'd better have a look at this."

Klein followed Maggie into the next room, which was really one large computer station. Three monitors were lined up side by side, along with a host of servers and storage units, all driven by the government's most advanced software. Klein stood back and admired the dexterity and proficiency with which Maggie worked her keyboard. It was like watching a virtuoso performance by a concert pianist.

Besides the president, Maggie Templeton was the only person familiar with the entire workings of Covert-One. Knowing he would need a skilled and trusted right hand, Klein had insisted on Maggie's being involved from the get-go. Besides having worked for him at the NSA, she had better than twenty years experience as a senior CIA administrator. But most important to Klein, she was family. Maggie's sister, Judith, had been Klein's wife, taken by cancer years ago. Maggie too had had her share of tragedy: her husband, a CIA covert operative, had never returned from a mission abroad. As fate would have it, Maggie and Klein were the only family each had.

Finished on the keyboard, Maggie tapped on the screen with an elegantly manicured fingernail.

VECTOR SIX.

The two words pulsed in the center of the screen like a blinking traffic light at an empty intersection in a country town. Klein felt the hairs on his forearms push against his shirtsleeves. He knew exactly who Vector Six was; he could see his face as clearly as if the man were standing next to him. Vector Six: the code name, if it ever appeared, was to be construed by Klein as a panic signal.

"Shall I pull up the message?" Maggie asked quietly.

"Please. . . ."

She touched a series of keys and the encrypted message of letters, symbols, and numbers shot up on the screen. She then repeated the process with different keys to activate the decryption software. Seconds later, the message appeared in clear text:

> *Dîner—prix fixe—8 euro*
> *Spécialité: Fruits de mer*
> *Spécialité du bar: Bellini*
> *Fermé entre 14–16 heures*

Even if a third party somehow managed to decode the message, this menu of a nameless French restaurant was both innocuous and misleading. Klein had set up the simple code the last time he had met Vector Six face to face. Its meaning had nothing to do with Gallic cuisine. It was the call of last resort, a plea for immediate extraction.

Klein didn't hesitate. "Please reply as follows: *Reservations pour deux.*"

Maggie's fingers flew over the keys, tapping out the secure response. The single sentence bounced off two military satellites before being sent back to earth. Klein didn't know where Vector Six was at that moment, but as long as he had access to the laptop Klein had given him, he could download and decrypt the reply.

Come on! Talk to me!

Klein checked the time stamp on the message: The message was less than two minutes old.

A reply flashed across the screen: *Reservations confirmées*.

Klein exhaled as the screen faded to black. Vector Six would not stay on-line any longer than was absolutely necessary. Contact had been established, an itinerary proposed, accepted, and verified. Vector Six would not use this channel of communications again.

As Maggie shut down the link, Klein sat down in the only other chair in the room, wondering what extraordinary circumstances had prompted Vector Six to contact him.

Unlike the CIA and other intelligence agencies, Covert-One did not run a string of foreign agents. Nonetheless, Klein had a handful of contacts abroad. Some had been cultivated during his days at the NSA; others were the results of chance meetings that had blossomed into a relationship based on both trust and mutual self-interest.

They were a diverse group: a doctor in Egypt whose patients included most of the country's ruling elite; a computer entrepreneur in New Delhi who provided his skills and equipment to his government; a banker in Malaysia adept at moving, hiding, or ferreting out offshore funds anywhere in the world. None of these people knew each other. They had nothing in common beyond their friendship with Klein and the computer notebook he had given each one of them. They accepted Klein as a midlevel bureaucrat but knew that secretly he was much more than that. And they agreed to serve as his eyes and ears not only out of friendship and belief in what he represented, but because they trusted him to help them if, for any reason, their respective homelands suddenly became a dangerous place for them.

Vector Six was one of the handful.

"Nate?"

Klein glanced at Maggie.

"Who gets the call?" she asked.

Good question. . . .

Klein always used his Pentagon ID when traveling abroad.

If he was going to meet a contact, he made sure it would be in a public place, at a secure location. Official functions at a U.S. embassy were the best choices. But Vector Six was nowhere near an embassy. He was on the run.

"Smith," Klein said at last. "Get him on the line, please, Maggie."

Smith was dreaming of Sophia when the insistent beep of the telephone intruded. He was watching the two of them sitting on a riverbank, in the shadows of immense triangular structures. In the distance was a great city. The air was hot, filled with the attar of roses and of Sophia. *Cairo* . . . They were at the pyramids of Giza, outside Cairo.

The secure line . . .

Smith sat up fast on the couch where he had fallen asleep, fully dressed, after coming home from the cemetery. Beyond the windows streaked with rain, the wind moaned as it drove heavy clouds across the sky. A former combat internist and battlefield surgeon, Smith had developed the gift of waking up fully alert. That ability had served him well during his time at USAMRIID, where sleep was often snatched between long, grueling hours of work. It served him well now.

Smith checked the time at the bottom right-hand corner of the monitor: almost nine o'clock. He had been asleep for two hours. Emotionally spent, his mind still filled with images of Sophia, he had driven himself home, heated up some soup, then stretched out on the couch and listened to the rain churn overhead. He had not intended to fall asleep, but was grateful that he had done so. Only one man could call him on that particular line. Whatever message he had could signal the beginning of a day of infinite hours.

"Good evening, Mr. Klein."

"Good evening to you too, Jon. I hope I'm not disturbing your dinner."

"No, sir. I ate earlier on."

"In that case, how soon can you get out to Andrews Air Force base?"

Smith took a deep breath. Klein usually had a calm, businesslike demeanor. Smith had seldom found him curt or abrupt.

Which means there's trouble—and it's closing fast.

"About forty-five minutes, sir."

"Good. And Jon? Pack for a few days."

Smith stared at the dead phone in his hand. "Yes, sir."

Smith's drill was so ingrained that he was hardly aware of going through the motions. Three minutes for a shower and shave; two minutes to dress; two more to double-check and add a few things to the ready bag in the walk-in closet. On his way out, he set the security system for the house; once he had the sedan out in the driveway, he armed the garage using the remote.

The rain made the ride to Andrews Air Force base longer than usual. Smith avoided the main entry and turned in at the supply gate. A poncho-covered guard examined his laminated ID, checked his name against those on the list of approved personnel, and waved him through.

Smith had flown out of Andrews often enough to know his way around. He had no trouble finding the hangar housing the fleet of executive jets that, most times, ferried around the brass. He parked in a designated area well away from the aircraft taxi lanes, grabbed his ready bag from the trunk, and splashed his way into the immense hangar.

"Good evening, Jon," Klein said. "Crappy night. It'll probably get worse."

Smith set down his bag. "Yes, sir. But only for the navy."

The age-old joke didn't get a grin out of Klein this time.

"I'm sorry to have dragged you out on a night like this. Something's come up. Walk with me."

Smith looked around as he followed Klein to the coffee station. There were four Gulfstream jets in the hangar, but no maintenance personnel. Smith guessed that Klein had ordered them out to ensure privacy.

"They're fueling a bird with long-range tanks," Klein said, glancing at his watch. "Should be ready in ten minutes."

He handed Smith a Styrofoam cup filled with steaming black coffee, then looked at him carefully.

"Jon, this is an extraction. That's the reason for the rush."

And the need for a mobile cipher.

Given his army background, Smith was familiar with the terms "extraction," as Klein had used it. It meant getting someone or something out of a place or a situation as quickly and quietly as possible—usually under duress and on a tight schedule.

But Smith also knew that there were specialists—military and civilian—who handled this kind of work.

When he said as much, Klein replied, "There are certain considerations in this case. I don't want to involve any other agencies—at least not yet. Also, I know this individual—and so do you."

Smith started. "Excuse me, sir?"

"The man you are going to meet and bring out is Yuri Danko."

"Danko . . ."

In his mind's eye Smith saw a bearlike man, a few years older than he, with a gentle moon face pockmarked by childhood acne. Yuri Danko, the son of a Dobnets coal miner, born with a defective leg, had gone on to become a full colonel in the Russian army's Medical Intelligence Division.

Smith couldn't shake his surprise. Smith knew that before signing the security agreement that had made him part of Covert-One, Klein had put his entire life under a microscope. That meant Klein was aware that Smith knew Danko. But never in all the briefings had Klein ever hinted that *he* had a relationship with the Russian.

"Is Danko part of—?"

"Covert-One? No. And you are not to mention the fact that you are. As far as Danko is concerned, I'm sending a friendly face to bring him out. That's all."

Smith doubted that. There was always more to Klein than met the eye. But one thing he was sure of: Klein would never place an operative in harm's way by not telling him everything he needed to know.

"The last time Danko and I met," Klein was saying, "we established a simple code that would be used only in an emergency scenario. The code was a menu. The price—8 euros—indicates the date, April 8, two days from now. One, if we're working on European time.

"The specialty is seafood, which stands for the way Danko will be coming: by sea. The Bellini is a cocktail that was first made in Harry's Bar in Venice. The hours that the restaurant is closed, between two and four in the afternoon, is the time the contact is supposed to be at the rendezvous point." Klein paused. "It's a simple but very effective code. Even if the encryption was compromised and the message intercepted, it would be impossible to make sense of the menu."

"If Danko isn't due in for another twenty-four hours at least, why hit the panic button?" Smith asked.

"Because Danko hit it first," Klein replied, his concern obvious. "He might get to Venice ahead of schedule; he might run late. If it's the former, I don't want him twisting in the wind."

Smith nodded as he sipped his coffee. "Understood. Now, for the sixty-four-thousand-dollar question: What made Danko jackrabbit?"

"Only he'll be able to tell us his reasons. And believe me, I want to know them. Danko is in a unique position. He would never have compromised it . . ."

Smith raised an eyebrow. "Unless?"

"Unless *he* was on the verge of being compromised." Klein put down his coffee. "I can't say for sure, Jon, but I think Danko is carrying information. If so, it means he thinks I need to have it."

Klein glanced over Smith's shoulder at an air police sergeant who entered the hangar.

"The aircraft's ready for takeoff, sir," the sergeant announced smartly.

Klein touched Smith's elbow and they walked to the doors.

"Go to Venice," he said softly. "Pick up Danko and find out what he has. Find out fast."

"I will. Sir, there's something I'll need in Venice."

Smith needn't have lowered his voice as they stepped outside. The drumbeat of the rain drowned out his words. Only Klein's nod indicated that Smith was talking at all.